DEMNS

ENCOUNTERS WITH THE DEVIL AND HIS MINIONS, FALLEN ANGELS, AND THE POSSESSED

EDITED WITH COMMENTARY BY

JOHN SKIPP

NEW YORK TIMES BESTSELLING AUTHOR

BLACK DOG
& LEVENTHAL
PUBLISHERS
NEW YORK

Library of Congress Cataloging-in-Publication Data available upon request.

Published by Black Dog & Leventhal Publishers, Inc.
151 West 19th Street, New York, NY 10011

Distributed by Workman Publishing Company
225 Varick Street, New York, NY 10014

Design by Red Herring Design
Printed in the United States
ISBN: 978-1-57912-879-1
h g f e d c b a

TABLE OF CONTENTS

1   **INTRODUCTION:**
The Terrible Things That Make Us Do
All of the Terrible Things We Do **JOHN SKIPP**

7   Cherub **ADAM-TROY CASTRO**

37   The Devil **GUY DE MAUPASSANT**

47   The Book **MARGARET IRWIN**

63   The Monkey's Paw **W. W. JACOBS**

77   The Hound **H. P. LOVECRAFT**

87   The Black Cat **EDGAR ALLEN POE**

99   The Devil and Daniel Webster **STEPHEN VINCENT BENET**

115 Nellthu **ANTHONY BOUCHER**

119 The Howling Man **CHARLES BEAUMONT**

137 The Exorcist (excerpt) **WILLIAM PETER BLATTY**

163 Hell **RICHARD CHRISTIAN MATHESON**

169 Empathy **JOHN SKIPP**

179 Visitation **DAVID J. SCHOW**

199 Best Friends **ROBERT R. McCAMMON**

243 Into Whose Hands **KARL EDWARD WAGNER**

265 Pilgrims to the Cathedral **MARK ARNOLD**

307 The Bespelled **KIM HARRISON**

323 *Non Quis, Sed Quid* **MAGGIE STIEFVATER**

327 Demon Girl **ATHENA VILLAVERDE**

339 He Waits **K. H. KOEHLER**

359 Happy Hour **LAURA LEE BAHR**

375 Staying the Night **AMELIA BEAMER**

381 Daisies and Demons **MERCEDES M. YARDLEY**

389 And Love Shall Have No Dominion **LIVIA LLEWELLYN**

401 Mom **BENTLEY LITTLE**

415 20th-Level Chaotic Evil Rogue
Seeks Whole Wide World To Conquer **WESTON OCHSE**

435   Consuela Hates a Vacuum **CODY GOODFELLOW**

453   Our Blood in Its Blind Circuit **J. DAVID OSBORNE**

469   Empty Church **JAMES STEELE**

489   Angelology (excerpt) **DANIELLE TRUSSONI**

499   The Coda of Solomon **NICK MAMATAS**

507   The Law of Resonance **ZAK JARVIS**

527   Stupid Fucking Reason
to Sell Your Soul **CARLTON MELLICK III**

535   Halt and Catch Fire **VIOLET LeVOIT**

543   Scars in Progress **BRIAN HODGE**

571   The Unicorn Hunter **ALETHEA KONTIS**

587   Other People **NEIL GAIMAN**

593   **APPENDIX A:**
Demonic Roots: On the History of the Devil
CHRISTOPHER KAMPE AND ANTHONY GAMBOL

601   **APPENDIX B:**
You Must Be Certain of the Devil: Demons in Popular
Culture **JOHN SKIPP AND CODY GOODFELLOW**

THE TERRIBLE THINGS THAT MAKE US DO ALL THE TERRIBLE THINGS WE DO

AN INSPIRATIONAL INTRODUCTION BY *John Skipp*

This world, as I'm sure you already know, is a scorching hot potato of temptation and sin. We may not want to catch it, but if someone chucks it at us, odds are good that we'll automatically reach right out, even though we know it's gonna burn like crazy.

It's as if we were perversely programmed to do the wrong thing, even though doing the right thing is often just as easy and makes a lot more sense.

Such is the comedy and horror of life.

And, of course, I blame the demons.

Don't you?

They're *everywhere*: in everything we touch, taste, smell, hear, or see. They're in our hearts. They're in our minds. They're in our souls.

It's as if we can't imagine the world without them.

How else can one explain everything from the most expansive global warfare to the most intimate acts of domestic violence, all of which are actively going on right this very second? Is *original sin* really enough to cover the full range of human atrocity? Can science, alone, come up with the answers to these seemingly intrinsic design flaws in not just our nature, but all of Nature itself?

Or do fallen angels and their odious hellspawn have a hand in all this?

WHAT IS THE MATTER WITH US, ANYWAY?

Questions, questions, questions. Many as old as the species, if not older than good ol' Time itself.

Questions that are constantly being refined, in the hope of maybe finding better answers at last.

That's why I happily hot-potato you the enormous book you now hold in your hands. It's a playfully scathing treasure trove of inspired speculations both old and new: some tragic, some hysterical, some ennobling, some despairing. Many of them running the full gamut at once.

And—believe me—all of them utterly crawling with demons, of every conceivable type.

Of all the monsters that regularly prey upon mankind—in our religions and mythologies (and depending on whom you talk to, in our everyday lives as well)—demons are by far the sneakiest, connivingest, most wicked and insidious of the batch.

This is because they are specifically designed to corrupt and torment us every chance they get. To trick, seduce, cajole, or force us to horribly, irrevocably lose our way. To subvert our finest impulses by homing in on all our inherent weaknesses, using every rotten, time-dishonored gambit at their disposal.

As such, they're pretty much the poster boys for evil. (Which, for the purposes of this conversation, I'll define simply as *willful malign intent.*)

The Seven Deadly Sins—greed, lust, sloth, gluttony, wrath, envy, and pride—aren't actually listed in the Bible as such; but whether you subscribe to the Good Book or not, the same principles still apply to each and every one of us, shot through and through as we are with wicked thoughts and even worse potentialities.

Given half a chance in Hell or Earth, we will doubtlessly ruin everything.

And as if our own sinful nature weren't enough by itself, we've got demons to tempt us every step of the way.

Or do we?

Which is to say: Is this whole thing just our own little way of letting ourselves off the hook?

The biggest difference between demons and the rest of the go-to monsters is that just about NOBODY believes in vampires, werewolves, zombies, and such. They're story-spinning myths aimed at giving us the fictional willies, while attempting to make sense of their particular concerns. And in that, they do just fine.

Demons, on the other hand, remain an active part of many contemporary belief systems. Modern evangelicals, for example, still engage in spiritual warfare, even though many of them believe the war has already been won in Heaven. As such, their writings on the subject rarely appear in the "Fiction" section of anybody's bookstore; insofar as they're concerned, those stories are true.

And good God-fearing Christians ain't but the half of it. If you believe in *any* gods—by whatever name or names—the odds are fairly good that you also believe in some form of the Devil/Tempter/Trickster/Deceiver. Or, at the very least, in terrible forces—supernatural, extradimensional, karmic, or otherwise metaphysical—that actively campaign to bring us down. And that are far larger than our tiny selves.

(Far more on this in Appendix A, which concerns itself with the verrrry long history and dare-I-say *evolution* of our experience with the agencies of darkness.)

On the flip side of faith is the scientific notion of dysfunction: of systems gone awry, in any of the trillion ways that systems *always* go awry when the wiring goes wrong, or the chemicals are imbalanced, or Mommy or Daddy or Not-So-Funny Uncle Bob do monstrous things that utterly fuck somebody up for the rest of their miserable life.

There's a lot to be said for this model as well. That this poor damaged soul would have been just fine if x and y didn't happen: that if the chemical x and the behavioral y hadn't come together in just the wrong way, they could have been a respectable pillar of society, instead of the blood-drinking, baby-raping, scalp-taking sociopath they actually turned out to be.

But there's a lot of widely charted wiggle room in between, with more than enough evidence on either side to honestly make me wonder which came first—the synapse or the sin?

To which my answer is always:

Why dicker when you can have both?

The war between science and religion has always struck me as one of the silliest debates in the long jabbering history of the human race. Science tries to explain *how* things happen. Religion tries to explain *why* things happen. They both seem like reasonable inquiries to me, albeit with wildly differing criteria, and varying burdens of proof versus faith.

Which brings us to art—my personal favorite because it allows us to bridge these seemingly polar opposites in ways that both expand and dissolve the rigid boundaries between them.

Exploring what it all means and how it plays out, from the micro to the macro, in distinctly human terms.

That's where the artists and storytellers come in, as they have for as long as we've been around. Forever trying to puzzle it out. Asking questions. Supposing what-ifs. Laying out the possibilities in poignantly recognizable ways that make us wonder how *we* might respond if faced with such evil.

And reflect on how we already have.

Or hope to, next time around.

(Substantially more on this in Appendix B, which traces the equally long and colorful history of demons in popular culture.)

So here, I guess, is the point, if I have one:

The horrible truth is, WE REALLY DON'T KNOW which came first in this chicken-or-the-egg scenario of evil. We can debate it till the mad cows come home, and doubtlessly will.

But I'm sorry. *We just really don't know.*

We want to, and we're trying, in every single way we can, from the secular to the sacred to everything in between. And I give us lots of credit for trying so hard. Using every kind of evidence. Seeking every sort of pattern. Both trusting and fearing our intuitions, because when push comes to shove, we're not 100 percent sure about them, either.

Which is, frankly, probably all for the best.

So just to be clear: This book is not a theological text. Nor is it an atheistic refutation of faith. Instead of swinging one way or the other, I have cheerfully opted for both, and more: letting some of the finest writers I've ever read weave their own inspired assessments of this tangled web we're in.

From horror to romance to far-flung fantasia to even-further-flung Bizarro frontiers, every stratum of literature from highbrow to low has explored this terrain, and will continue to do so.

Because these are the central issues of our lives.

And that's what great storytelling is all about.

Whoever you are, however you see things—and whatever it is that you do or don't believe—it is my hope that you will find a staggering abundance of profound, provocative, exciting, enlightening, horrific, hilarious, charming, and alarming stories herein, many of which will hit you right where you live.

As always, your mind is your own, whether by existential autonomy or God-given free will.

Or is it?

(Insert sinister laughter and rising organ music here.)

And with that, I toss this astonishing hot potato directly into your lap. Catch it or drop it or pass it along, as is your wont.

That's entirely up to you. Your God, or gods.

And your personal demons. ✦

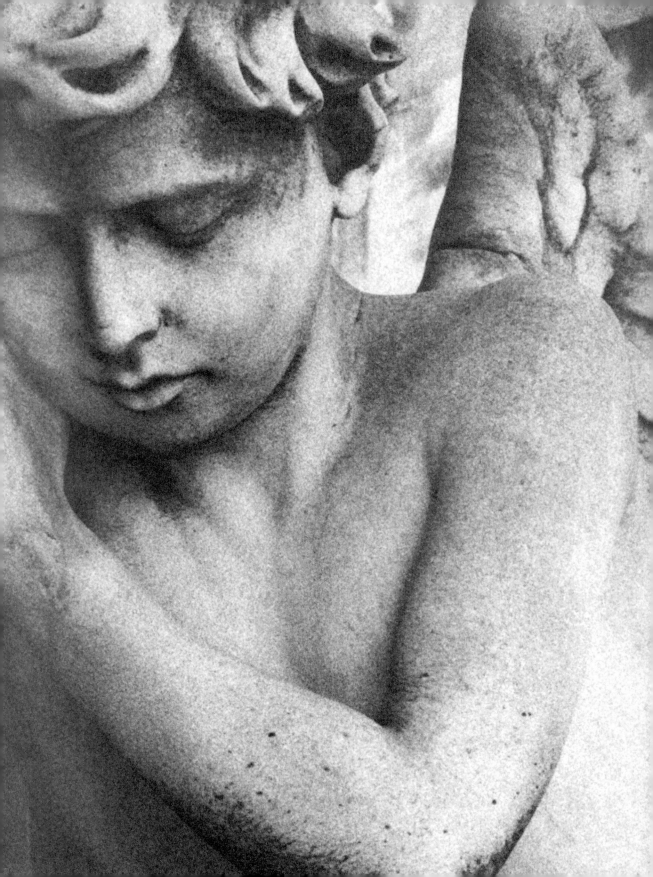

CHERUB

BY *Adam-Troy Castro*

It's always tempting to yearn for the fabled olden days, when confirming the veracity of so-called "eternal verities" seemed a whole lot simpler and clearer.

After all, if the gods actually trod the earth before you—or if the One True God visibly filled the sky, every once in a while, just to remind you He was there—my guess is that it would make disbelief a much trickier proposition.

And if we do enter this life with our souls already scarred by our future transgressions, then how great and horrible would it be to have that all laid out from the beginning?

And so we open with this remarkable tale by Adam-Troy Castro: a modern writer with an uncanny knack for nailing the quintessence of whatever weird topic he's thrown.

Which is to say: a master of the defining moment.

"Cherub" is a fresh-off-the-press original that feels authentically torn from some terrible, unknown past.

Let it propel you into shocking gnosis, and pave the way for all that is to come.

Childbirth always means pain, and not just for the mother who must strain to expel both the squalling infant and its parasitic demon rider from her womb. It also torments those of us who must stand around the outer wall of the birthing shed and watch, both eager for our first look at the baby and dreading our first glimpse of the hateful attached thing bearing the face of the corruption in that child's heart.

It is midday. A peremptory daylight enters the shed in stripes, illuminating the dust in the air, but not the bleakness of these last moments before we discern the nature of the monster who will accompany the child into the land of the living. My beloved wife Faith squats in the center of the room, slick with sweat and tears. Her straw hair clings to her cheeks, and her toes sink into the diarrheic puddle she expelled as the ordeal entered its final stage. She has uttered curses since dawn that prove the common wisdom that women turn savage during birth: oaths of terrible hatred directed against the child inside her and me, the man who planted the seed. I believe she would kill me—and it—right now, just to be rid of the pain.

I know I'm right about the rage because of her own personal rider, a hideous idiot monkey-thing riding piggyback on her soft shoulders, whose spindly leprous arms lead to scaled claws buried knuckle-deep in her temples, and whose bug eyes peer at me over the top of her head. It is the embodiment of everything that is bad about this mostly good woman I married, and it mocks me with the deep pleasure it takes in her suffering. Its tiny piggish eyes and moronic leer, all sharp teeth and pointed tongue, manifest the vindictive cruelty my darling wife is prone to whenever the world requires more of her than she can freely give. Despite the genuine affection she has always shown for me, Faith has also always been capable in heated moments of flinging words that flay all my self-respect away in a single lashing sentence. Even as she strains with the effort of expelling our son, her rider's face betrays the few secrets Faith bothers to keep, her unspoken resentment of every passing disappointment I've ever caused her rippling across its noxious features like pus flowing from a septic wound.

Nor am I any better. My own demon rider, whose petty features betray my cowardice, my pettiness, and my secret selfishness, tightens its grip on my skull and tickles the part of me that cares nothing for Faith's pain and wants only for this long, stinking, noisome day to end. I'm certain that Faith can see that and I can only hope that she sees the best of me as easily as my rider obliges her to see the worst.

The men of the village form a circle around the wall of the shed, their arms linked in the traditional last gesture of defiance against whatever evil thing comes to join us atop the child about to burst from Faith's slit. They are silent. Their riders keep up an animated conversation among themselves: not one we can hear, thank the Lord, for if riders spoke aloud, their voices would drown out our own. It is not a nice conversation. The riders make faces, they make obscene gestures, they laugh long and hard, they pull their talons from the bore holes in our skulls and nail them in again, in cruel emphasis of their dominion over us. I think they are arguing among themselves. I think they are wagering on the new arrival. I think they are as tired of the wait as we are.

On either side of me, my brothers Noah and Eben hold my arms, counseling strength. They have always been good men, but Noah's gibbering imp of arrogance and Eben's stone-faced golem of coldness peer over their respective faces. I am entitled to hate my brothers a little for this. No doubt my own rider—that loathsome many-eyed insectile thing that whispers obscene things to me in the night, that assures my wife of the vile rape fantasies I must sometimes employ to keep me hard during the act of love—now shares that secret with them, over whatever pretense of a grateful look I can place on my own merely human features.

Then Faith screams, her voice hoarse and breathless. "They're coming!" The word becomes a bellow as she puts all she has into the final push, expelling a gout of blood and the head of a baby, which for a moment dangles between her spread legs, glistening scarlet. She gasps, takes a sideways crab-step to relieve the horrendous cramps in her knees, and squeezes again. My newborn son lands in the dirt we're all heir to—the dirt that greets us as we enter the world and embraces us again as we leave. There is, of course, something on the back of his neck, something as soft and as rounded and as new to the world as he is: the passenger that will define much of what he is, even now grasping him by the neck, cementing its grip on who he will be.

This is the most terrifying moment for any parent. In my life I have attended births where the first sight of the rider was enough to prove that no joy would ever come from the child, where the rider's distinct features branded its human mount as thief or rapist or murderer, and the babe for all its apparent innocence was revealed as naught but a seed from which nothing but evil would ever grow. True, even those were usually permitted to live, for even a future murderer might be able to live a worthy life blessed to his kin until the moment he commits his terrible sin. And it remains possible to value such a person, even if it will always be impossible to look at him without some inner voice raising that dread question, *when?* But that is still a shattering thing to see for the first time, on what should be a day of celebration.

And even that would not be the worst. I still have nightmares about that foul morning some five years gone when my neighbor Jeremiah's son was born and the thing on his back bore the face of something so savage that we could scarcely bear to look at it: an awfulness that we could only compare to riders of legend whose human hosts had not just killed once or twice out of greed or rage, but slaughtered freely, sometimes entire families and sometimes entire populations, in sprees driven only by their sheer love of killing. When Jeremiah took the child from his shrieking wife and headed for the village well, we all knew what he intended to do and none saw the point in stirring a muscle to stop him. After all, he'd borne his own murderer imp since birth, and the time had now come for him to live up to it.

Now I have to behold my own child, and see whether the sins on his back bring more heartbreak than joy. My brothers release me, and I join my darling Faith, who still strains with the afterbirth. I tell her I love her and I take a deep breath and lifetimes later raise my son from the filthy puddle that is his first introduction to a debased and sinful world.

He is a tiny thing, bearing the correct number of arms and legs and a scrunched-up face indignant about the ordeal just forced on him. He coughs out a mouthful of liquid and then starts to cry, a high-pitched, angry wail that assails me with his fury at me for inviting him into a place filled with such pain and fear. I sense that he is strong, and, before I allow myself to feel the first stirrings of love for him, turn my attention to the creature on his back, which is, of course, even smaller than he is, and so covered with slime and blood that it is at first impossible to determine its true nature. Somebody hands me a wet cloth so I can clean it enough to see; and as I wipe away the blood and the piss and all the other shiny effluvia of life, I first feel fear and then puzzlement and then relief and then the dawning amazement of a man faced with the kind of miracle no man dares hope for.

From the shadows, Eben asks me what it is.

The tiny creature clinging to the back of my son's neck is beautiful. It is pure and it is innocent. Its face is as smooth and as unmarked by any of the possible cruelties or follies as the mirrored surface of a lake can be when undisturbed by wind or current. Its eyes are closed, its expression sweet. Its hands are not the sharp, raking claws we all know from our own riders, but hands that could belong to any other baby's, and they cling to my son's neck without breaking the skin, their touch more gentle caress than possessive grasp. It is absolute innocence personified—something that exists only in legend, something that no man I know has ever worn, something no parent I've ever heard of has ever dared hope for.

"It's a cherub," I say.

Fifteen years later, I am at home, tending to my infant daughter, when Eben rushes in with the bad news. My son Job has been beaten and robbed again.

I wish I could say this was a shock. It is not the first time, or the tenth, that others have seen my son's innocence as weakness, and done whatever they wanted to him, whether robbery, bullying, or—on one terrible occasion—rape. His back is a relief map of scars, his face a history of all the brutal things other boys have done to the one perfect boy who will not defend himself for any reason. Many of these are also visible on the back of his rider; not just because our riders tend to take on the same ravages time inflicts on us, but because more than one boy ridden by something foul and angry has attempted to peel my son's harmless rider away, with fingernails and sticks and even knives, in the apparent belief that the boy envied and despised by all should not even be left that which marks him as what he is.

I know it is my duty to go with Eben, to tend to the son cursed by a birth that failed to sufficiently damn him. I should, but I feel a great weariness, the kind that only comes after years and years of watching someone you care for live through one torment after another. I am tired of hearing that the other boys have beaten him. I am tired of hearing that strangers have robbed him. I am tired of hearing him lashed with the kind of horrible words that leave barbs in the skin and continue to fester even after the surface wounds have healed.

It is not that I don't know of other children who have been almost as brutally treated; there is a man in my village, Jared, who is ridden by a thing of perverted carnality, and whose fifteen-year-old daughter Ruth avoids all eyes as she carries his latest rape-spawn to term. Everyone knows what Jared does to her at night. But she at least bears the imp of a future patricide on her back. She deserves what she gets and he deserves what she will do. A case can be made that Jared is only doing what he has to do, to punish her in advance for the inevitable moment when she will destroy him. But what of Job, who has never sinned and never will sin? Who, it seems, may even be incapable of sin? How does he deserve what they do to him? How will his scales ever be righted?

I glance down at my new infant daughter Miriam, who is round-faced and beautiful and (I know from the hateful second face grinning at me over the smooth curve of her head) a brat, a user, a castrating bitch who will someday brandish her sex like a weapon to manipulate men who will give up their dignity and their principles for a mere moment of her favor. When she is old enough to know what her eldest brother is, she will doubtless manipulate him as well, showing him moments of kindness in between vivid demonstrations that she feels nothing for him but contempt. I feel no fear about her ability to make her way in the world. If anything, I take comfort in fearing for the world's capacity to survive her attentions.

Faith enters from the other room leading our other son, the dull-eyed seven-year-old Paul, who is not feeble-minded as he would like us to believe but (we know from the features of the creature on his back) has an utter contempt for anyone but himself and a low and animal cunning that leads him to pretend dependence on others in order to get them to do things for him. It was difficult to be patient with him when he resisted toilet training as a means of remaining a coddled, indulged infant; it will be even more difficult to endure the selfish, spoiled, half-formed being he will be as an adult. I know that my rider's face clarifies the depth of my growing disgust for him, so I turn to Faith, who has aged thirty years in the past fifteen, and tell her that I need to go to Job.

Even as she takes Miriam from me and coos to her, the rider on her back flashes the mien of any mother who sometimes hates her own children, for making her worry about them, for making her spend time on them, for making her subsume everything she is to them. Paul, jealous of any attention spent on any human being other than himself, starts to tug at her sleeve. Faith reassures him, her sweetness never wavering even as her rider underlines how much she'd like to kill him.

I tell Eben to take me to my eldest son.

The two of us trudge through the streets of our village, which are cold and ankle-deep in slush from recent snowfalls. I do not look at the familiar faces of my neighbors, or at the faces of those who ride them. I do not look at the liars or the thieves or the bullies or the connivers or the bigots or the hypocrites or the self-satisfied stupid ones. I do not look at the adulterous or the violent or the ones who show compassion but exult when others feel pain. I do not look at the boy who kicks dogs or the girl who twists her little sister's hair when their parents aren't looking. I do not look at the other boy, the surprisingly gentle one who everybody knows will kill somebody someday, and who once tearfully confessed within my earshot that he wishes he didn't know this, because the knowledge leaves him unable to look at any other person, even the girl he likes, without wondering if that's his future victim. And when I pass the glass window of Judah's bakery, I do not look at my reflection in the glass. I almost never look at my reflection in glass.

It is not that long a walk, overall. It is only an eternity.

In less than ten minutes we arrive at the crossroads on the edge of the village, where a small crowd has gathered around my bleeding son. There are wagons, some drawn by oxen and some by horses, left untethered in the grass, as their owners hopped down to bear witness. Two local girls, who have always been kind and even loving to Job—despite what I know about their true natures from the savage crones clinging to their respective backs—tend to his wounds, cleaning the gash in his forehead and stanching the copious flow of blood from his nose. He whispers something to one of them and she blushes. Then he sees me and his wounded but still beautiful features brighten at the sight.

As always, it takes my breath away, to see nothing hiding behind that love but more love; it is not something I'm used to.

This is the beautiful and the terrible thing about my boy Job. He is always as he seems. When he smiles, there is nothing behind that smile but warmth. When he offers to lend a hand, there is nothing behind that generosity but an eagerness to help. When he is hurt by others and later professes forgiveness, it is true forgiveness and not the kind of grumbling, suppressed resentment that amounts to vengeance biding its time, but the absolute inability to pollute himself with grudges of any kind, even when he has been wronged so grievously that he could be forgiven for seething with hatred. He puts me, puts all of us, to shame. Maybe that's why he's so hated. People may think they despise those not as virtuous as themselves, but there's no end to the reservoirs of wrath we bear for those we know to be better.

He tells me what happened. There was a gang of them. They came upon him as he returned from the next town with the goods I sent him to get, and swarmed him like rats, ripping his clothes, kicking his ribs, stealing his money, and taking his goods. In the end, they took turns pissing on him.

I am livid. "Who?"

"You know I can't tell you. I won't subject them to your anger."

"If you won't give names, it'll only happen again. You'll never know a moment's peace."

I know it's the wrong argument as soon as the words leave my mouth.

He says, "I already know peace." And there is no denying that, in the same way that there is no denying that the sun rises, or that rain falls from the sky.

There is no denying that because, even now, even after Job was savaged by savages, his cherub sleeps. Riders never sleep, not even when they ride those marked by indolence and sloth. A man's sins always cling to him, even when he slumbers. Like all married men, I sometimes spend time on sleepless nights studying the features of the woman who shares my life, and even when her own face is a peaceful mask buried by the false death of sleep, her rider is always peering over the tousled curve of her hair, miming its endless caricatures of all the waking woman's sins. But in all these years Job's cherub has never once opened its eyes. It has always hugged his back in gentle acceptance of all that befell him, its dozing features testifying to a soul as placid, and yet as possessed, as great depths as a vast becalmed sea.

This is not a state of being I understand, as I would track down those responsible for this outrage and carve their punishment from their own flesh, with even less mercy than they showed my son . . . but then my passenger has always borne the features that mark me as vengeful at heart, and Job's has always borne features marking him as a boy who refuses to hate.

"Tell me their names. I won't hurt them. I'll just make sure they never hurt you again."

He tells me, "I'm sorry, father. I forgive them."

From deep in the surrounding crowd there's a rumble of derisive laughter, the kind a bully makes when he dismisses a weaker soul's right to conduct his life without fear. I recognize the laugh before I turn, and find myself cursed by the awareness that it comes from a man who either knows who beat my son or happily participated. He is a man known to me, whose own boys bore bruises and furtive looks before they grew old enough and large enough to become, like their father, blights on the lives of any with the misfortune to know them. He says, "It is like they all say. Your son is useless."

The man's name is Kenneth. He owns a pig farm outside of town, but lives better than his income from that enterprise could explain were, it not supplemented by extortion and theft. He has burly arms and a weather-beaten face marked by too many scowls and not enough smiles; his shoulder-length red hair and beard frame his harsh features, always unruly, always catching the wind in a manner like a corona of fire.

These are the things I know about Kenneth. I know that he is stupid—in the way that the worst cruel and bullying men are stupid. He is incapable of considering any concerns but his own, and sees any objections to his conduct as a personal affront, demanding of punishment. I also know that he is crafty, in the way that the worst cruel and bullying men are crafty; that he knows how to hurt people, and when, and has an infinite imagination when it comes to breaking them. I know that his wife is little more than a despised slave, who rarely opens her mouth for fear that he'll shut it for her. I know that he lives with four other women, each of whom joined his extended family while barely more than children, at least two of whom he simply took from their families and rendered utterly devoted to him by the simple method of alternating brutality with unexpected kindness until they were willing to do anything he asked of them if it guaranteed the latter. I know that he has punished their prior families for trying to interfere, that homes have been burned, and livestock killed. And I know that, even without his rider's terrible visage, a mask of cruel self-satisfaction not all that much more offensive than Kenneth's own, it would be just as easy to see it in the set of his tiny black eyes.

A couple of his younger sons, who are still not coarsened to the degree he wants, refuse to meet my eyes. The three eldest meet them with defiance, enjoying my hatred. All five of their riders grin at me, their demented faces as exultant in their evil as Kenneth has always been in his.

Whether they witnessed the beating or not, everyone in the crowd knows at once that Kenneth directed his sons to beat and rob mine: and that he doesn't care that we know.

The old man sneers. "Your son's a woman. If you took his trousers off, you would find a hole where a boy should have a good strong rope. A true man would have dirtied his knuckles with the blood of at least one of the scoundrels who attacked him, or at least now had the stones to name them. This one's less a boy and more a mushroom, planted in shit, born without backbone, and doomed to wither as soon as the sun strikes him."

Even as I stand, my hands curl into fists. But I know it's no good. I cannot stand against Kenneth alone, let alone his sons. Nor will any of my neighbors or family stand with me; certainly not Job, whose gentle right hand even now reaches up to touch my wrist, to assure me as always that this is nothing, that he can bear it, that no wound can be inflicted on him that his infinitely forgiving soul will not heal.

I have never wanted to kill a man so much, and I have never been as shackled to the cowardice that is the least of my sins. I burn from the awareness that my rider shows Kenneth both.

His look of answering recognition is the worst thing I've ever seen.

"Leave him alone," I say, "or I'll kill you."

He chuckles and gathers his sons for the journey back home. I have no doubt that were I to wade into them with angry fists, and by some miracle reduce them to as battered a state as they left Job, I would find in their pockets the money they took from him, and in their cart the goods they stole. And I know that were I to raise my voice and demand that the other onlookers aid me in finding justice for my boy, there would be no takers. Even those who hate Kenneth agree with him on this: innocence has made Job worthless, as far as defending himself is concerned.

Even so, the moment would not pain me quite so much if one of the two pretty girls tending Job did not stand up and leave him behind, to hop aboard Kenneth's wagon and sit pressed up against one of his sons.

Three years later, Leah enters our life for the first time.

She has been brought to us by her father, a man whose rider marks him as a cheat and occasional petty thief, but there is nothing in its manner or in his that marks him as anything but a parent who loves and cares for his daughter. I might keep an eye on my coin purse, but I believe him when he says that his only concern now is for her.

Leah is a fragile wisp of a thing, with skin so pale it is almost translucent and hair so blonde that it is almost white. I would mistake her for albino if not for the tracing of freckles that form a constellation across both cheeks and the tip of her nose. She has weak eyes, by which I mean that she refuses to meet mine, not even when I speak kindly to her, and not when I tell her, in all honesty, that she is a pretty girl and that I am charmed by her face. In truth I am even charmed by her rider—it is no cherub, like my son's, but it is so unmarked by anything terrible that it might as well be, resembling an innocent babe in all ways but for a powerful stormy affront about its eyes. It is not a happy thing, but neither is she. I have seen riders like hers on the shoulders of other souls too sensitive for this world, souls so helpless at fending off the cruelty of others that they don't even grew inured to the sharp and cutting places inside themselves. It is the look of self-hatred, which can be as great a sin as any other, a look that anyone would recognize as the mark of a possible future suicide.

Leah and her father, who are strangers to us, come from a village farther down the coast and have spent weeks on the road traveling here. The reason is obvious. It is often said that a marriage can only be happy if the rider of the man and the rider of the woman betray sins of equal weight. A man whose rider marks him as an epic monster will bring nothing but misery to the life of a woman whose rider marks her as one whose sins amount to little more than weakness. And certainly a woman of cutting tongue and demeaning temperament will always drain the life from a man whose rider embodies nothing worse that a shiftless soul. No man or woman seeking some semblance of happiness should ever join with anyone much worse than themselves, else they risk bearing the weight of their partner's rider as well as their own.

Leah's father has always despaired of finding her a man capable of treating her with the kindness she will need to survive. And our greatest fear for Job's future has always been the impossibility of finding him a wife who would not take advantage of his unassuming nature and enslave him in ways beyond the chains that should be forged by love. It is indeed part of why we have ordered him to remain close to home these past few years; not just because of the danger he faces from rapacious people like Kenneth's family, but because too many of the local girls have divined at a glance just how much power they would have over him if ever they ensnared him into marriage. I have seen what rides the shoulders of those with the kindest eyes and sweetest faces and shuddered at the thought of my poor son, subjected to their version of love without any rider of his own to give him the strength he would need to have any will of his own.

So, yes, I understand why Leah's father thinks his daughter and my son might be the greatest hope for one another. But as we all sit together in our home's largest room, the unshuttered windows admitting a hot, dry wind from the west, the conversation erupts only in fits and starts. Three-year-old Miriam cries nonstop and tugs at her mother's leg, upset beyond reason that the gathering isn't about her. Ten-year-old Paul, who always resents the attention she gets, tugs at her ear and makes her cry. Leah averts her eyes to avoid meeting Job's, he struggles to find words that won't be embarrassing or shameful, and the air itself thickens like amber, trapping us all in an afternoon in which time seems to have stopped.

A few minutes after Faith goes into the other room to stir the stewpot—Paul following so closely behind her that he might as well be a second rider, clinging to her with the insistent intimacy of a mistake—I mutter that I'd better go check on her and find my beloved wife weeping in utter despair that anything will ever turn out all right. Nothing I say to her, no reminder of how shy I was the day we met, will stanch the tears. I ask her what's wrong. She draws close and beats at my chest with her fists, while Paul continues to tug at her apron. She asks me, "What did God think he was doing, when he gave us one son too good for this world?"

This prompts a tantrum from Paul, who hates the special regard his mother has for Job. The screeching begins.

Dinner is grim.

It is not until much later, when the smaller children have been banished to bed and the adults have wandered to a different part of the house to talk about something, anything, but the fiasco we believe we're experiencing, that I look out the window and spot something in the gathering twilight that takes my breath away.

Unnoticed by any of us, Job and Leah have stolen off together to the edge of the meadow, well within the distance we have declared safe for him but farther than he has ventured since the last time he was rendered bloody from a neighbor child's hurled stones. It is late in the year, and the sun is just starting to set. They stand facing one another, but not eye-to-eye the way they would be if about to kiss. She's looking down at his feet, her long hair hanging like a curtain over any emotions that might be betrayed by her features. He's doing something that most people would consider obscene even in marriage, and downright scandalous when seen in two young people who have only met a few hours ago—reaching past her face to stroke her unhappy, self-loathing rider on the back of its head.

From the window, I can see the face of Leah's rider far more clearly than I can see her own. I can see that stormy scowl so redolent of misery resist his touch and even grimace from resenting it. And then I see that scowl falter, come back as angry as ever as the rider realizes it's losing, and then disappear completely. The rider's features smooth over, becoming placid. Its eyes close. It adopts the expression of a baby lost in sleep. It becomes a cherub, as unpolluted by darkness as his own.

As Leah looks up to face my son, the curtain of blonde hair falls away from her delicate profile, revealing cheeks slick with tears that are just beginning to curl into an unaccustomed smile.

Job and Leah don't kiss, yet, but instead just stand there looking at one another, their lips moving in words I would almost kill to hear. She looks down again, but this is just a flicker, a moment of vestigial reflex no longer relevant after a lifetime. Her rider continues to doze. His never stirs. The setting sun makes the meadow glow red, cradling boy, girl, and riders in what might as well be a wreath of flame.

The news that a boy and girl ridden by cherubim—his that way from birth, hers created by a moment of kindness from him—have betrothed spreads from village to village, bringing not just curiosity-seekers but monsters, seeking to spread the hurt as a matter of principle. Our neighbors close ranks. Many of those who abused Job in the past take to watching the roads in and out for strangers whose riders signal their intent to do him more harm.

Even that human viper Kenneth takes part, driving his boys against a caravan of ragged and unshaven men whose riders all bear faces marking them as the worst kind of vindictive destroyers, the kind of men who spread misery not out of greed or hatred but for the sheer joy of shattering the lives of those more fortunate than themselves. Kenneth and his sons confront this wolf pack, determine that they have come from many miles away to entertain themselves by committing malicious mischief against this couple they have heard about, this man and woman who consider themselves so special, and with remarkable efficiency send them on their way, missing coin purses, wagon, clothing, a number of teeth, and in one case a right eye. I do not forgive Kenneth and his family for what they have done to mine in the past, but I now give him a nod when we make eye contact upon encountering each other in public. Maybe he's decided that his family has tormented Job enough.

My brothers, alas, are less sanguine about our newfound hope for a better future. They buy me ales at the inn and congratulate me on the upcoming new addition to the family, but turn dark as the brew poisons their blood and hint at bad times to come.

Noah says, "I fear for the children of such sinless people. Whether ridden by cherubim or demons themselves, they'll have the misfortune of growing up with parents unable to summon enough anger or hatred to protect them from anyone not quite so pure."

Eben has other worries. "They will have trouble if they become parents. A mother and father without so much as a dark thought in their heads will never be able to tend to children prone to lies, cruelty, or worse." He goes on to tell us the story of a mother and father he knew during the five years he lived farther down the coast, whose riders were, though not quite cherubim, also not quite formidable enough to arm them against their son, who was a little monster. By the time that boy reached adolescence, he ruled their home like a despot, reducing mother and father to beasts of burden too terrified to do anything but indulge his slightest whim. Nor did it ever end for them, for why would such a little monster ever seek a life away from his parents, when his parents were so incapable of denying him?

Eben tosses back another drink and tells me that I should take special care that Paul does not end up like that. "You need to take him in hand now or know the nightmare he will become later."

It is all true, every word of it, but from the way my other brother Noah peers with sudden alarm over my shoulder I know that my rider reflects the extent of my growing anger. He mutters some words about how I should take all this as well-meaning advice and not as mockery.

I allow myself to be mollified, and return to my drink. But when I walk home, later that night, more than one of my neighbors, passing me on the way, walks a little faster when they see me, or the terrible aspect of my rider. For I know that my brothers are right.

I sleep that night in a downstairs bed to avoid frightening Faith with the rage of my rider. She will never miss me, not when Paul still insists on sleeping between us, a living barrier erected to exclude his invasive father from the territory on his mother's side of the bed. My dreams are terrible, though when I wake I don't remember how terrible. With dawn still hours away, I trudge to the outhouse and return, taking a protective detour past Job's door, which is always ajar, an invitation to a world that he insists on treating with trust. He is sleeping. I stand there for long minutes and listen to him breathing, marveling as any father would at the miracle of a boy now on the threshold of becoming a man, and reeling from the terrible vertigo that can only be known by the parent of a child in danger.

Job and Leah become husband and wife seven months later, in the tradition of our village. We stand them in the public square, carve a tight circle in the dirt around both, and bid them to spend four hours back to back, their riders pressed together in mutual acceptance of the respective sins borne by both man and woman. This has always been, by our teachings, the most intimate covenant by which the betrothed can demonstrate not just their love for each other, but their acceptance of the very worst to come.

Tradition among us holds that if either the bride or groom can be driven from the circle before the time is up, their sins will always stand between them and that they must therefore not be wed. Friends, family, and strangers are encouraged to surround them, shouting whatever they can to drive the pair apart . . . sometimes bribes, sometimes declarations of love, sometimes just mocking recitations of all the reasons why they're bound to make one another miserable. In my day I have seen many a wedding end with the bride breaking down in tears and fleeing, face in hands, minutes before the end of that four hours, and have never doubted the ceremony's efficiency at preventing marriages doomed to misery.

Other villages do it differently, I hear. Eben says that some far from here, which he visited during the years he spent as a wanderer, have a specific series of prayers recited by a designated holy man. This makes no sense to me at all, as I have never seen a man anywhere who could be called holy. Even Job isn't holy, the more appropriate word for him being *innocent*. All I know is that if I ever did meet a self-professed holy man who claimed the power to preside over the most intimate moments of my life, I wouldn't let him speak prayers about anything having to do with my family unless I first spent long minutes examining whatever rode on his back. I personally suspect that the riders of these holy men may be even worse than those carried by those of us who don't claim freedom from sin.

For hours Job and Leah stand back to back inside the small circle, the spine of his sleeping rider pressed tight against the spine of hers, both demonstrating a level of divine peace well beyond the reach of those of us whose riders snarled and spat and brandished our worst secrets on this special day. Both Job and Leah are calm, smiling, confident of their ability to outlast the ordeal.

Outside the circle, the required ritual abuse by our neighbors is mostly restrained, limited to little more than good-natured teasing. The unmarried girls cavort and waggle their tongues at Job, promising him endless nights of wanton abandon should he give up his foolish devotion to this girl with no idea how to set a fire in a wedding bed. The unmarried men advise Leah that they understand her ignorance in these matters, but feel obligated to tell her that Job has a root doomed to remain soft for life and that she'd be better off spreading her legs for a man who can make his stand at attention. There is a bad moment when Kenneth strides from the crowd and circles the pair, looking over both of them as if appraising pigs that have come to market, but after two orbits he nods his head and ambles away, with a nod at me that I can almost consider friendly. It is never possible to tell for certain, but there is nothing in his eyes or in the eyes of his rider that betrays simmering malice against my son and his bride. He doesn't seem to be letting the day pass without incident only so that he can indulge his cruel appetites later. There is reason for hope.

The afternoon is, of course, not completely without trouble. Paul, who we gave the honor of drawing the circle, grows upset that his contribution is over with and that he is no longer the focus of all eyes. He starts whining that he's bored and then wailing that he wants to go home, and is unstirred by appeals that this is his brother's day and that he should be as happy for him as we all are. Miriam gets sick from something she's eaten and is soon as cranky and as inconsolable as her middle brother. The tension Faith has felt up until this day, combined with the poor behavior of our younger children, makes her blame me for being so useless a father.

But all this pales next to something else I see, something that I have never heard tell of happening before, and that as far as I can tell only I can see, because I will afterward question my wife and friends and neighbors and find not a one who confesses to beholding what my eyes are blessed to behold now. As I watch, amazed, Job's sleeping rider turns its little head and, without ever opening its eyes, brushes its lips against the cheeks of Leah's rider. Her rider, without opening its eyes, turns its head and kisses his on the lips. Both riders then turn their attentions back to those they ride. I look up at the faces of my son and his bride and see from both blinding smiles that both are fully aware of what just happened, and both know what it means. This is not just the only possible union for a boy born without sin and a girl who lived too long without hope; nor is it just the loving union we all hoped for. It is the kind of union they write about in the stories, the kind that is not supposed to happen in the real world. Maybe it is why even Kenneth would not wield his evil against them. I can only dare to hope, my knees turning weak at the thought.

As the ceremony ends, a great weight lifts from me as a cheer erupts from my friends and family and neighbors and the couple is mobbed by well-wishers who hoist them aloft and carry them about like trophies for long minutes before once again allowing their feet to touch the ground. Another cheer splits the sky as the couple kiss a second time. Job embraces his mother and then me and tells me that it does his heart good to know that I was watching on this glorious day. Leah kisses me on the cheeks and tells me that she will take joy, from this day forward, in being able to call me father. Even Paul senses the tug of family and congratulates his older brother. The songs and dancing begin, and then the feasts. It should be the happiest day of my life.

I can only wish I knew why I remain afraid.

Another two years later, something big happens. I do not know how to classify it in my heart. There must be a special word for an event of staggering, undiluted evil that can only stun you with its depravity, that you are bound by all standards of human decency to regard and that you cannot help face with any emotion darker than relief. But I do not know it. I can only report what's happened and try to measure my feelings later.

Kenneth has been murdered.

It should be no surprise. His family has, if anything, gotten worse over the past few years, robbing homes and stealing livestock and growing their little colony of corruption by taking girls by force and making them too frightened to leave. In the last three years, three men who decided to stand against him had their homes burned, and one disappeared on his way home from an errand, leaving no signs of the nature of the misfortune that befell him. Kenneth was always in a public place, making himself visible, whenever these things happened, though he never showed any surprise whenever somebody came running from a distance to report the news. Nor were his sons anywhere to be seen. There was always a terrible, mocking knowledge in his eyes, showing us how much he relished our awareness that the responsibility remained his even when his hands were empty and displayed in plain sight. He loved our impotence.

I have always known that it was just a matter of time before somebody did what so many have wanted to do.

Noah, who witnessed the event, brings the news while I am at Job's house helping to add a room for the baby now only two months away. We have been working all afternoon, enjoying the heat of the day and the slick sheen of sweat our labor summons to our skin, and when Noah rides up, his horse shining from a hard gallop, we wave at him, thinking at first that he's only come to help us. But then he gasps out the news and we put down our hammers and we step away from the skeletal frame of the nursery under construction and join my brother on the front porch so he can tell us what happened while we were here preparing for the miracle of new life. After a few seconds, Leah comes out, preceded by her belly, to hand him a cup of water, then stays to listen.

This is what he tells us.

It happened a little more than an hour ago.

Kenneth rode his open wagon into the village to pick up some supplies he'd sent for, accompanied by his eldest son and the youngest of the young girls to join his extended family. She is Amelia and she is fourteen and she has been with him for three years, a relationship that began when she reported being raped by him at eleven, changed when she recanted two days later, and became whatever it is now when she left her parents and two younger sisters and moved in with Kenneth, calling him her "husband." Following the usual pattern, her parents expressed outrage and appealed to her neighbors to help them rescue their darling girl, receiving little help, before inevitably showing up bearing cuts and bruises and frightened expressions to go along with their insistence that it was all a misunderstanding and that Amelia's new marriage had their blessing. The girl was rarely seen in public, since then. Today, the first time in months, her little belly was as swollen with new life as Leah's.

Kenneth pulled his wagon up to the community store, tied up the horses, then took his boy and went inside to get and carry out his goods. It took several trips. Amelia remained silent where she sat, not answering anybody who tried to speak to her. A crowd started to form. By the time Kenneth and his son finished the loading, half the village was there, many surrounding the wagon in a crowd five bodies thick.

Shaking his head, Noah tells us that Kenneth was not afraid, even then. He had always been untouchable and he thought he was untouchable still. When he took the reins and told the crowd that they'd better move, because they were hemming him in, he had the eyes of a man who was memorizing faces. His rider's burning visage declared a dozen separate vendettas. Then somebody—it could have been anybody—shouted a call to action. Somebody—it could have been anybody—dragged Kenneth's son from his seat. Somebody—it could have been anybody—grabbed Kenneth as well and forced him to the ground, where he was engulfed by a wave of shouting people.

He would have survived the beating.

But somebody—it could have been anybody—stabbed him in the heart.

So far, nobody had confessed to seeing who drove the blade between his ribs, though a number of the people there had long borne riders bearing the face of murder and a number bore riders bearing the face of complicity. No one will testify against a killer. In a sense, they may all be killers.

I do not know how to feel about this. Kenneth's family hurt someone I loved as much as anyone I loved has ever been hurt. There was once a time when I might have snuffed out his life myself, had I believed there was a chance that I might get away with it. But either I've grown soft with the years or the long time he's left my loved ones alone has diluted any hatred I feel. No weight has been lifted from my heart.

Leah, looking sad, asks, "Is his son all right?"

Noah tells her, "As all right as any boy can be when his father is murdered mere steps away from him."

"And the girl?" Job asks.

Noah tells him, "She is unharmed as well. She has been brought to the home of her mother and father, neither of whom she has seen in more than a year. There is no telling whether she will stay there, rather than return to Kenneth's family, but for the moment she is where she should be."

Job says, "Good."

It is his only immediate reaction.

After a little while, Noah takes his leave of us and gets back on his horse, to bring the news to some of our more distant neighbors. We return to working on the new room. More than an hour passes, by my estimation, before I ask Job to stop.

He puts his hammer down and waits.

"If you were not the man I know you to be, and if I were not with you all day today, I would have wondered all my life whether you'd been the one to put that knife through that bastard's ribs."

Unhurt and unsurprised, he says, "But I am, and you were."

"True. But with the man dead, there's no reason not to tell me the truth. Was Kenneth the one who beat and robbed you, that last time?"

"Yes. Him and one of his sons. I won't say which son, but it was one of them."

"God. Are you all right?"

He considers his answer a long time before answering. "If you're asking me whether I feel any pleasure at Kenneth's death, the answer is no. It solves nothing. The world is still awash with brutality, and becoming part of it, even taking distant pleasure in it, interests me not at all. All I feel is sadness for a man whose rider so bubbled with hatred and pain that he could only achieve release by sharing it."

"But don't you feel safer?"

"Of course not." He takes up his hammer again and strikes a protruding nail just once before looking ill and putting the tool down. "One day I was born. Someday I will die. What takes place between the beginning and the end is too short to fill with fear. The bad days happen from time to time, and more must be coming, but I've had far too many good ones in between to give the bad more weight than they're worth."

My vision blurs. "You're a far better man than I'll ever be."

"No, I'm not. I will not lie to you, father. I fear that I'm not the man you and so many others believe me to be. I'm capable of hating people who hurt me, and wishing for bad things to happen to them. But I don't want to hurt anyone back. While I'm alive I just want to live the best life I can, and this is the only way I know how."

I know him well enough to recognize the closest he ever comes to annoyance. It hurts him, hurts everything he is, to be pressed for some form of celebration at his old tormentor's death. It is the chief disadvantage of having a paragon for a son. Sometimes, many times, I cannot live up to him.

It is only late that night, as I lie beside Faith, that I wake and realize that it must not have been Kenneth I've feared all these years, for in asking Job whether he felt any safer, I neglected to notice that I do not.

The wheel of time continues to turn. Life in the village becomes much more peaceful without Kenneth around to prey on us. His sons heed the warning that there is only so much their neighbors will take from them, and scale back their criminality, without ever ceasing it. Leah strains a day in the birthing shed and presents Job with a son they name Isaac, whose gentle rider betrays no sin worse than mischief. I put the baby in twelve-year-old Paul's hands and he looks down at his new nephew with harmless bafflement, almost dropping him when the baby's lips burble over with cheese. Miriam toddles about, stealing hearts with sideways glances. Leah brings me a jacket she has made for me and kisses me sweetly on the forehead, telling me that I am her second father, blessed for raising a man who could tame her rider and teach her that life can be an occasion filled with joy.

While playing with my grandchild, I catch a glimpse of my face in a mirror and am stunned to see that my own rider has been tamed as well. All my adult life I have tried to be a good husband to Faith and a loving father to the children, but I have also always been aware, as much from the way it felt in my heart as from the terrible aspect of the second face peering over my own, that it has always been more the act of a man pretending to be good than a man who could just be. I have always told myself that this is true for everybody, because we all feel the weight of our riders and we all know the evils we bear. It does not mean that the good among us are frauds. But I have always felt that way anyway . . . until this moment when I see the reflection in the glass and realize for the first time that happiness, years of fighting the worst in myself, and the example of a man better than any I ever hoped to be can calm the greatest beast. My rider's gnarled features have smoothed, its aspect turned more human than ever before. It is not the peace Job and Leah know. But it is still more than any man could ever hope for. I turn to Faith, beaming, and see her beaming back, her own rider as soft and innocent as it has ever been. This may be the most loving moment of all our years together.

We make love that night: the kind of love that only long-marrieds can make, when they are reminded of how hot their flames burned in youth.

I don't know why, but I remain awake long after Faith has surrendered to sleep, all the strangeness of the world large in my thoughts. After a long time I kiss the back of my dozing wife's hand and go to the common room, lighting a candle so I can look at myself in the mirror again. My face is lined with the kind of furrows that come with years and hard work and broad smiles, and—it stuns me to see—wisdom.

My rider, wide-awake and curious, blinks at me, wondering what I'm up to. I find myself, wondering, idly, if its current strange purity would be at all affected by deliberate and conscious evil on my part. It is the kind of game played at least once by all children who ever picked up a mirror, tired of making silly faces at themselves, and wondered if their rider could be induced to do the same.

It could be done. The philosophers say that our riders don't define us. We would not be perfect people, if we were lucky enough to be born without them. We would instead be people whose sins were hidden, who could conceal their most vile natures behind the most angelic countenances. We would never know if a man was fated to become a rapist, or a woman a murderess; we would not find out until the sins were committed, and the evidence of their crimes lay bleeding on cold earth. There would even be those of monstrous aspect but innocent hearts condemned for deeds committed by others—a terrible thought that speaks to alien possibilities, and worlds even worse off than our own. What would the world be like if the prisons could fill with innocent men?

I have not indulged in this kind of experiment since I was young. But a strange whim drives me to make the attempt now. I concentrate on the very worst atrocities I can think of, trying to see them as more than ridiculous abstractions. *I will go back to our bed and take Faith by force. I will go to Miriam's bed, take her by the ankles, and smash her skull open against the wall. I will do what some monstrous parents do and take Paul as a man takes a woman. I will go out in the night and knock on Job's door, pretending an emergency just so I can strangle him with my bare hands once we are alone. I will hold Isaac below water and . . .*

I cannot go on. I am too sickened by even thinking these things, and feel ashamed for allowing them to take root, for even a moment, in the imperfect soil of my mind. Maybe I am an evil man, after all. But my rider just blinks at me, its expression as placid as before, marked only by the confusion of a child who has just seen his father spouting inane gibberish.

Our riders are part of us. They know our pretenses. They know what we are and what we only pretend to be. I cannot summon enough pretend evil to fool my own, any more than I could have summoned enough pretend good.

Maybe that's what prevents true evil from overrunning the earth.

I put down the mirror, blow out the candle, and return to my wife's side, imagining myself at peace.

And then one day two years afterward Job shows up at my front door carrying Isaac's shattered body.

If a man's life is like a ribbon of time, stretched out upon the earth and extending from the moment his parents conceive him to the moment some bedridden old man releases his last breath into a world that has long since robbed him of all his reasons for living, then there are during those years moments that cut like daggers, that can plunge from the sky and snap that ribbon in two. They can even be poisoned, these moments, carrying toxins so foul they shrivel everything to come and everything that came before. Any happiness that ever existed becomes a lie, any hope that ever beckoned toward the future a fraud.

I don't refer to my grandson's death. It has only been one day since he toddled away from his mother and some damned drunken wagon master crushed him in the road. It has only been one day since I saw his chest staved in, his little body opened by a scarlet groove where his ribs should have been. It is only one day since I heard Faith scream when she saw him, one day since I had to look into the eyes that had been laughing, just earlier that morning, now burst cherries in a darling face.

All of that was terrible and all of that was like having all the joy torn from the world, but that is not what tears the ribbon of my life in twain and poisons everything that came after and came before. It cannot be. I have lived a long time. I have had people I love die before; parents, friends, and once before all that, the baby sister I had to go along with my brothers, who drowned at seven and left a hole I still feel after a life of never mentioning her name. I know that life is what you live in between watching the people you care about die, and though it breaks my heart it is not the dagger that cuts my life in half and makes all our lives a lie.

That happens later in the evening, when we are all gathered at Job's home, offering what shallow comfort we can. Leah sits on the floor, her eyes staring, her hands shaking, her rider once again assuming the self-hating aspect it possessed when first we met. Faith sits by her side, whispering one empty reassurance after another. Miriam stays close to me, stunned by her first encounter with death in all its fullness. Noah and Eben stand silently by the wall, their hands folded before them, their shaggy heads turned toward a floor that fails to offer any clues as to what they can do to make the tragedy bearable, if not better. Job answers the many knocks at the door and accepts the condolences of neighbors who have heard about the tragedy and want us to know how sorry they are, kindly ushering away those who want to come in long after a lesser bereaved father might have gone mad.

At one point I recognize the visitor at the door as one of Kenneth's sons, a brute who I've always believed to have participated in Job's beating, and though he comes hat in hand and delivers his condolences in the tone of a man who dearly wishes he could be anywhere else, I feel the fury rise in me and almost race to the door to lash him with all the hatred of a father and grandfather, irate that this pig still breathes while Isaac waits at the gravedigger's house for his new home beneath dirt. But Job takes his old tormentor by the hand and thanks him, with a sincerity that shames me, as so many of the examples he's set have shamed me.

The worst begins not long after that, as Leah starts talking about her fallen baby boy, the way he ran and played, the golden way he laughed. The memories wound her so much she starts to sob again. Job rushes to embrace her, to tell her that Isaac is not truly gone and all that nonsense. Faith holds her hand and murmurs sweet lies of her own, and all this might help, but I cannot tell, because we're entering the worst of it, that horrid point in the shattering grief of the bereaved mother that only comes after the immediate shock of the tragedy passes and she finds herself seeing for the very first time that this is now her world, the only world she'll have.

And there's no way to get past this moment except by living it, and in another few seconds we might be able to, but my other son Paul, who at twelve is more than old enough to know better but who has been simmering throughout all of this with the impatience known only to those who need every moment to be about themselves, incredibly chooses *this* of all possible moments, *this* one, to start tugging Faith's sleeve and start whining that he's bored, that he's hungry, that he wants to go home . . .

Job curses him and shoves him away.

It's a light shove, even if it does leave Paul sitting on his rear end with a comical look on his face. It would be forgiven from any bereaved father, seeking a moment's respite from a brother half his age who has never been anything but an entitled brat. But from Job, who has never in his entire life lost his patience, it hits with the impact of a thunderclap.

All sound in the room ceases.

Job's lips move without making sound. He peers down at Paul and then at Faith and then at me, and each time he bears the look of any man caught in a monstrous lie. For the very first time I am able to see beyond his placid and compassionate eyes to an infinite and stormy place beneath. His face contorts with what might be shame and might be rage, though it's impossible to tell because he has never betrayed either.

The shock is so great that it cuts through even Leah's bottomless grief. She blinks up at him and says, "*Job?*"

He flees past my gaping brothers and barrels out into the night. Noah and Eben make to go after him, but their hesitation allows me to beat them to the door, where I assert my responsibility as his father. Eben relents, muttering about this being the first time he could be sure the boy was even human. I glare at him and he looks away before I depart.

It is not long before I find my son, kneeling in the meadow with his forehead pressed against a bare patch of dirt. He shakes and sobs as he pounds his fists against the ground. I can only approach and kneel beside him, allowing him to wail, thinking of how I might have acted if a catastrophe just as stupid had taken him or Faith or Paul or Miriam. After a few seconds I say, "Come on, son. You need to be better than this."

Without looking up at me he murmurs, "Why?"

"Because this isn't you. Because your wife and your mother expect you to be strong . . . and when you're not, it scares them." I hesitate. "And me."

The sound that bubbles up from the ground strikes me first as chuckle and then as sob, and then as some terrible mixture of the two, celebrating and mourning all at the same time. He claws furrows in the ground with his fingers and mutters something I cannot hear, something followed by the long seconds of weeping and then by the same words, repeated in a voice as empty as the shell he must feel he's become. "This is me, father. This has always been me. You just never really knew who I was."

I pull him upright and face him. "Yes, I did."

This, again, seems to strike him as hilarious. He giggles and weeps, the tears pouring from him in waves. "I thought I could be a good man. I thought I could live the life of a good son, a good husband, a good father. I thought I could do it and that nobody I loved would ever be hurt."

"It's not your fault. These things happen."

"You think so?"

"I know it, Job. You're the best man I've ever known."

"Oh, Father." He bows his head and lays his fists against my chest, pounding me with a frustration that, even now, he keeps in check. "I keep telling you. I'm no man at all."

"Don't be ridiculous, son. That's just the likes of Kenneth talking—"

He chokes on his snot and tears. "No, it's true. I'm no man. I've sinned more than any true man could, every second of every day you've known me. I sinned by being liar and murderer and thief all at the same time, taking everything that belonged and ever would belong to another. Isaac's death is just one of my punishments . . . and I'm afraid, so afraid, that the way you'll look at me from now on is another."

I have no idea what he's going on about, not right away, but my incomprehension shatters him further, and he falls back to hands and knees, clawing at the ground as if hoping to dig himself a home there. Knowing only that whatever's bothering him, however foolish, is as real to him as Isaac's death, I draw closer and wrap my arms around his back, lending him the strength that is all I have to offer.

It is while I am doing this that the little creature on his back turns its little infant head to face me. Though it has made its own soul known once or twice in its many years among us, it has up until now always been the placid embodiment of innocence, the one quality we all remember from childhood that we all lose as we make the foul compromises required by life. But now, in the instant before it opens its eyes, it occurs to me that innocence is not always a measurement of virtue. It can also be the domain of fetuses or infants, those who have not yet known life, or ever been permitted it.

The thing clinging to Job's back opens its eyes and looks at me. I see through those eyes into a soul that should not be rider, but man: a soul trapped there by another, that now wakens after a lifetime of sleep.

For the very first time in my own life, I know the true face of my eldest son . . . and recognize his rider for what he is. ✦

THE DEVIL

BY *Guy de Mauppasant*

On the flip side of faith lie the faithless, bless their poor peasant souls, often forced to lie their asses off when the godly come around. If your life gets hard enough, you might wind up a little flinty yourself.

Waggish, haunted bohemian Guy de Maupassant's most famous short story, "The Horla," is much renowned for its psychological first-person expression of demonic possession.

But I much prefer this caustic little gem, fresh-cut in the mid-1800s, which knows the price of everything.

And which suggests that sometimes the Devil's a good guy to have around, whether he truly exists or not.

The peasant was standing opposite the doctor, by the bedside of the dying old woman, and she, calmly resigned and quite lucid, looked at them and listened to their talking. She was going to die, and she did not rebel at it, for her life was over —she was ninety-two.

The July sun streamed in at the window and through the open door and cast its hot flames on to the uneven brown clay floor, which had been stamped down by four generations of clodhoppers. The smell of the fields came in also, driven by the brisk wind, and parched by the noontide heat. The grasshoppers chirped themselves hoarse, filling the air with their shrill noise, like that of the wooden crickets which are sold to children at fair time.

The doctor raised his voice and said: "Honore, you cannot leave your mother in this state; she may die at any moment." And the peasant, in great distress, replied: "But I must get in my wheat, for it has been lying on the ground a long time, and the weather is just right for it; what do you say about it, mother?" And the dying woman, still possessed by her Norman avariciousness, replied *yes* with her eyes and her forehead, and so urged her son to get in his wheat, and to leave her to die alone. But the doctor got angry, and stamping his foot he said: "You are no better than a brute, do you hear, and I will not allow you to do it. Do you understand? And if you must get in your wheat to-day, go and fetch Rapet's wife and make her look after your mother. I *will* have it. And if you do not obey me, I will let you die like a dog, when you are ill in your turn; do you hear me?"

The peasant, a tall, thin fellow with slow movements, who was tormented by indecision, by his fear of the doctor and his keen love of saving, hesitated, calculated, and stammered out: "How much does La Rapet charge for attending sick people?"

"How should I know?" the doctor cried. "That depends upon how long she is wanted for. Settle it with her, by Jove! But I want her to be here within an hour, do you hear."

So the man made up his mind. "I will go for her," he replied; "don't get angry, doctor." And the latter left, calling out as he went: "Take care, you know, for I do not joke when I am angry!" And as soon as they were alone, the peasant turned to his mother, and said in a resigned voice: "I will go and fetch La Rapet, as the man will have it. Don't go off while I am away."

And he went out in his turn.

La Rapet, who was an old washerwoman, watched the dead and the dying of the neighborhood, and then, as soon as she had sewn her customers into that linen cloth from which they would emerge no more, she went and took up her irons to smooth the linen of the living. Wrinkled like a last year's apple, spiteful, envious, avaricious with a phenomenal avarice, bent double, as if she had been broken in half across the loins, by the constant movement of the iron over the linen, one might have said that she had a kind of monstrous and cynical affection for a death struggle. She never spoke of anything but of the people she had seen die, of the various kinds of deaths at which she had been present, and she related, with the greatest minuteness, details which were always the same, just like a sportsman talks of his shots.

When Honore Bontemps entered her cottage, he found her preparing the starch for the collars of the village women, and he said: "Good evening; I hope you are pretty well, Mother Rapet."

She turned her head round to look at him and said: "Fairly well, fairly well, and you?"

"Oh! as for me, I am as well as I could wish, but my mother is very sick."

"Your mother?"

"Yes, my mother!"

"What's the matter with her?"

"She is going to turn up her toes, that's what's the matter with her!"

The old woman took her hands out of the water and asked with sudden sympathy: "Is she as bad as all that?"

"The doctor says she will not last till morning."

"Then she certainly is very bad!"

Honore hesitated, for he wanted to make a few preliminary remarks before coming to his proposal, but as he could hit upon nothing, he made up his mind suddenly.

"How much are you going to ask to stop with her till the end? You know that I am not rich, and I cannot even afford to keep a servant-girl. It is just that which has brought my poor mother to this state, too much work and fatigue! She used to work for ten, in spite of her ninety-two years. You don't find any made of that stuff nowadays!"

La Rapet answered gravely: "There are two prices. Forty sous by day and three francs by night for the rich, and twenty sous by day, and forty by night for the others. You shall pay me the twenty and forty." But the peasant reflected, for he knew his mother well. He knew how tenacious of life, how vigorous and unyielding she was. He knew, too, that she might last another week, in spite of the doctor's opinion, and so he said resolutely: "No, I would rather you would fix a price until the end. I will take my chance, one way or the other. The doctor says she will die very soon. If that happens, so much the better for you, and so much the worse for me, but if she holds out till tomorrow or longer, so much the better for me and so much the worse for you!"

The nurse looked at the man in astonishment, for she had never treated a death as a speculative job, and she hesitated, tempted by the idea of the possible gain. But almost immediately she suspected that he wanted to juggle her. "I can say nothing until I have seen your mother," she replied.

"Then come with me and see her."

She washed her hands, and went with him immediately. They did not speak on the road; she walked with short, hasty steps, while he strode on with his long legs, as if he were crossing a brook at every step. The cows lying down in the fields, overcome by the heat, raised their heads heavily and lowed feebly at the two passers-by, as if to ask them for some green grass.

When they got near the house, Honore Bontemps murmured: "Suppose it is all over?" And the unconscious wish that it might be so showed itself in the sound of his voice.

But the old woman was not dead. She was lying on her back, on her wretched bed, her hands covered with a pink cotton counterpane, horribly thin, knotty paws, like some strange animal's, or like crabs' claws, hands closed by rheumatism, fatigue, and the work of nearly a century which she had accomplished.

La Rapet went up to the bed and looked at the dying woman, felt her pulse, tapped her on the chest, listened to her breathing, and asked her questions, so as to hear her speak: then, having looked at her for some time longer, she went out of the room, followed by Honore. His decided opinion was that the old woman would not last out the night, and he asked: "Well?" And the sick-nurse replied: "Well, she may last two days, perhaps three. You will have to give me six francs, everything included."

"Six francs! six francs!" he shouted. "Are you out of your mind? I tell you that she cannot last more than five or six hours!" And they disputed angrily for some time, but as the nurse said she would go home, as the time was slipping away, and as his wheat would not come to the farmyard of its own accord, he agreed to her terms at last:

"Very well, then, that is settled; six francs including everything, until the corpse is taken out."

"That is settled, six francs."

And he went away, with long strides, to his wheat, which was lying on the ground under the hot sun which ripens the grain, while the sick-nurse returned to the house.

She had brought some work with her, for she worked without stopping by the side of the dead and dying, sometimes for herself, sometimes for the family, who employed her as seamstress also, paying her rather more in that capacity. Suddenly she asked:

"Have you received the last sacrament, Mother Bontemps?"

The old peasant woman said "No" with her head, and La Rapet, who was very devout, got up quickly: "Good heavens, is it possible? I will go and fetch the priest"; and she rushed off to the parsonage so quickly, that the urchins in the street thought some accident had happened, when they saw her trotting off like that.

The priest came immediately in his surplice, preceded by a choir-boy, who rang a bell to announce the passage of the Host through the parched and quiet country. Some men, working at a distance, took off their large hats and remained motionless until the white vestment had disappeared behind some farm buildings; the women who were making up the sheaves stood up to make the sign of the cross; the frightened black hens ran away along the ditch until they reached a well-known hole through which they suddenly disappeared, while a foal, which was tied up in a meadow, took fright at the sight of the surplice and began to gallop round at the length of its rope, kicking violently. The choir-boy, in his red cassock, walked quickly, and the priest, the square biretta on his bowed head, followed him, muttering some prayers. Last of all came La Rapet, bent almost double, as if she wished to prostrate herself; she walked with folded hands, as if she were in church.

Honore saw them pass in the distance, and he asked: "Where is our priest going to?" And his man, who was more acute, replied: "He is taking the sacrament to your mother, of course!"

The peasant was not surprised and said: "That is quite possible," and went on with his work.

Mother Bontemps confessed, received absolution and extreme unction, and the priest took his departure, leaving the two women alone in the suffocating cottage. La Rapet began to look at the dying woman, and to ask herself whether it could last much longer.

The day was on the wane, and a cooler air came in stronger puffs, making a view of Epinal, which was fastened to the wall by two pins, flap up and down. The scanty window curtains, which had formerly been white, but were now yellow and covered with fly-specks, looked as if they were going to fly off, and seemed to struggle to get away, like the old woman's soul.

Lying motionless, with her eyes open, the old mother seemed to await the death which was so near, and which yet delayed its coming, with perfect indifference. Her short breath whistled in her throat. It would stop altogether soon, and there would be one woman less in the world, one whom nobody would regret.

At nightfall Honore returned, and when he went up to the bed and saw that his mother was still alive, he asked: "How is she?" just as he had done formerly, when she had been sick. Then he sent La Rapet away, saying to her: "To-morrow morning at five o'clock, without fail." And she replied: "To-morrow at five o'clock."

She came at daybreak, and found Honore eating his soup, which he had made himself, before going to work.

"Well, is your mother dead?" asked the nurse.

"She is rather better, on the contrary," he replied, with a malignant look out of the corner of his eyes. Then he went out.

La Rapet was seized with anxiety, and went up to the dying woman, who was in the same state, lethargic and impassive, her eyes open and her hands clutching the counterpane. The nurse perceived that this might go on thus for two days, four days, eight days, even, and her avaricious mind was seized with fear. She was excited to fury against the cunning fellow who had tricked her, and against the woman who would not die.

Nevertheless, she began to sew and waited with her eyes fixed on the wrinkled face of Mother Bontemps. When Honore returned to breakfast he seemed quite satisfied, and even in a bantering humor, for he was carrying in his wheat under very favorable circumstances.

La Rapet was getting exasperated; every passing minute now seemed to her so much time and money stolen from her. She felt a mad inclination to choke this old ass, this headstrong old fool, this obstinate old wretch—to stop that short, rapid breath, which was robbing her of her time and money, by squeezing her throat a little. But then she reflected on the danger of doing so, and other thoughts came into her head, so she went up to the bed and said to her: "Have you ever seen the Devil?"

Mother Bontemps whispered: "No."

Then the sick-nurse began to talk and to tell her tales likely to terrify her weak and dying mind. "Some minutes before one dies the Devil appears," she said, "to all. He has a broom in his hand, a saucepan on his head and he utters loud cries. When anybody had seen him, all was over, and that person had only a few moments longer to live", and she enumerated all those to whom the Devil had appeared that year: Josephine Loisel, Eulalie Ratier, Sophie Padagnau, Seraphine Grospied.

Mother Bontemps, who was at last most disturbed in mind, moved about, wrung her hands, and tried to turn her head to look at the other end of the room. Suddenly La Rapet disappeared at the foot of the bed. She took a sheet out of the cupboard and wrapped herself up in it; then she put the iron pot on to her head, so that its three short bent feet rose up like horns, took a broom in her right hand and a tin pail in her left, which she threw up suddenly, so that it might fall to the ground noisily.

Certainly when it came down, it made a terrible noise. Then, climbing on to a chair, the nurse showed herself, gesticulating and uttering shrill cries into the pot which covered her face, while she menaced the old peasant woman, who was nearly dead, with her broom. Terrified, with a mad look on her face, the dying woman made a superhuman effort to get up and escape; she even got her shoulders and chest out of bed; then she fell back with a deep sigh. All was over, and La Rapet calmly put everything back into its place; the broom into the corner by the cupboard, the sheet inside it, the pot on to the hearth, the pail on to the floor, and the chair against the wall. Then with a professional air, she closed the dead woman's enormous eyes, put a plate on the bed and poured some holy water into it, dipped the twig of boxwood into it, and kneeling down, she fervently repeated the prayers for the dead, which she knew by heart, as a matter of business.

When Honore returned in the evening, he found her praying. He calculated immediately that she had made twenty sous out of him, for she had only spent three days and one night there, which made five francs altogether, instead of the six which he owed her. ✦

вотъ однажды

THE BOOK

BY *Margaret Irwin*

I first encountered this underappreciated gem in The Second Fontana Book of Great Horror Stories, *as a wee little lad in the early 60s whose U.S. government father had stationed us all in Argentina. For some reason, the military commissary in Buenos Aires had a better line on British titles than it did for its American counterparts; and Fontana and Pan were pedigreed publishers whose editors carried with them a clear sense of what was classic, or clearly ought to be.*

I knew nothing, at the time, of Margaret Irwin's renowned historical novels. Am embarrassed to admit I've never read another thing she's written.

But I remember being sucked in, and subsequently floored, by how meticulously this genteel chamber piece of demonic seduction played its hand.

In full agreement with Fontana, I rank this one amongst the greats.

On a foggy night in November, Mr. Corbett, having guessed the murderer by the third chapter of his detective story, arose in disappointment from his bed and went downstairs in search of something more satisfactory to send him to sleep.

The fog had crept through the closed and curtained windows of the dining-room and hung thick on the air, in a silence that seemed as heavy and breathless as the fog.

The dining-room bookcase was the only considerable one in the house and held a careless unselected collection to suit all the tastes of the household, together with a few dull and obscure old theological books that had been left over from the sale of a learned uncle's library. Cheap red novels bought on railway stalls by Mrs. Corbett, who thought a journey the only time to read, were thrust in like pert undersized intruders among the respectable nineteenth-century works of culture, chastely bound in dark blue or green, which Mr. Corbett had considered the right thing to buy during his Oxford days; beside these there swaggered the children's large, gaily bound story-books and collections of fairy tales in every colour.

From among this neat new cloth-bound crowd, there towered here and there a musty sepulchre of learning, brown with the colour of dust rather than leather, with no trace of gilded letters, however faded, on its crumbling back to tell what lay inside. A few of these moribund survivors from the Dean's library were inhospitably fastened with rusty clasps; all remained closed, and appeared impenetrable, their blank forbidding backs uplifted above their frivolous surroundings, with the air of scorn that belongs to a private and concealed knowledge.

It was an unusual flight of fancy for Mr. Corbett to imagine that the vaporous and fog-ridden air that seemed to hang more thickly about the bookcase was like a dank and poisonous breath exhaled by one or other of these slowly rotting volumes.

He hurriedly chose a Dickens from the second shelf as appropriate to a London fog, and had returned to the foot of the stairs when he decided that his reading to-night should by contrast be of blue Italian skies and white statues, in beautiful rhythmic sentences. He went back for a Walter Pater.

He found *Marius the Epicurean* tipped sideways across the gap left by his withdrawal of *The Old Curiosity Shop*.

It was a very wide gap to have been left by a single volume for the books on that shelf had been closely wedged together. He put the Dickens back into it and saw that there was still space for a large book. He said to himself in careful and precise words: "This is nonsense. No one can possibly have gone into the dining-room and removed a book while I was crossing the hall. There must have been a gap before in the second shelf." But another part of his mind kept saying, in a hurried, tumbled torrent: "There was no gap in the second shelf."

He snatched at both the *Marius* and *The Old Curiosity Shop* and went to his room in a haste that was unnecessary and absurd.

To-night, Dickens struck him in a different light. Beneath the author's sentimental pity for the weak and helpless he could discern a revolting pleasure in cruelty and suffering, while the grotesque figures of the people in Cruikshank's illustrations revealed too clearly the hideous distortions of their souls. What had seemed humorous now appeared diabolic, and in disgust at these two old favourites he turned to Walter Pater for the repose and dignity of a classic spirit.

But presently he wondered if this spirit were not in itself of a marble quality, frigid and lifeless, contrary to the purpose of nature. "I have often thought," he said to himself, "that there is something evil in the austere worship of beauty for its own sake." He had never thought so before but he liked to think that this impulse of fancy was the result of mature consideration, and with this satisfaction he composed himself for sleep.

He woke two or three times in the night, an unusual occurrence, but he was glad of it, for each time he had been dreaming horribly of these blameless Victorian works. Sprightly devils in whiskers and peg-top trousers tortured a lovely maiden and leered in delight at her anguish; the gods and heroes of classic fable acted deeds whose naked crime and shame Mr. Corbett had never appreciated in Latin and Greek Unseens.

When he had wakened in a cold sweat from the spectacle of the ravished Philomel's torn and bleeding tongue, he decided there was nothing for it but to go down and get another book that would turn his thoughts in some more pleasant direction. But his increasing reluctance to do this found a hundred excuses. The recollection of the gap in the shelf now recurred to him with a sense of unnatural importance; in the troubled dozes that followed, this gap between two books seemed the most hideous deformity, like a gap between the front teeth of some grinning monster.

But in the clear daylight of the morning Mr. Corbett came down to the pleasant dining-room, its sunny windows and smell of coffee and toast, and ate an undiminished breakfast with a mind chiefly occupied in self-congratulation that the wind had blown the fog away in time for his Saturday game of golf. Whistling happily, he was pouring out his final cup of coffee when his hand remained arrested in the act, as his glance, roving across the bookcase, noticed that there was now no gap at all in the second shelf.

He asked who had been at the bookcase already but neither of the girls had, nor Dicky, and Mrs. Corbett was not yet down. The maid never touched the books. They wanted to know what book he missed in it, which made him look foolish, as he could not say.

"I thought there was a gap in the second shelf," he said, "but it doesn't matter."

"There never is a gap in the second shelf," said little Jean brightly. "You can take out lots of books from it, and when you go back the gap's always filled up. Haven't you noticed that? I have."

Nora, the middle one in age, said Jean was always being silly; she had been found crying over the funny pictures in the *Rose and the Ring*, because she said all the people in them had such wicked faces.

Mr. Corbett did not like to think of such fancies for his Jeannie. She retaliated briskly by saying Dicky was just as bad, and he was a big boy. He had kicked a book across the room and said, "Filthy stuff," just like that.

Jean was a good mimic; her tone expressed a venom of disgust, and she made the gesture of dropping a book as though the very touch of it were loathsome. Dicky, who had been making violent signs at her, now told her she was a beastly little sneak, and he would never again take her for rides on the step of his bicycle. Mr. Corbett was disturbed as he gravely asked his son how he had got hold of this book.

"Took it out of that bookcase, of course," said Dick furiously.

It turned out to be the *Boy's Gulliver's Travels* that Granny had given him, and

Dicky had at last to explain his rage with the devil who wrote it to show that men were worse than beasts and the human race a wash-out.

Mr. Corbett, with some annoyance, advised his son to take out a nice bright modern boy's adventure story that could not depress anybody. It appeared, however, that Dicky was "off reading just now," and the girls echoed this.

Mr. Corbett soon found that he, too, was "off reading." Every new book seemed to him weak, tasteless, and insipid, while his old and familiar books were depressing or even, in some obscure way, disgusting. Authors must all be filthy-minded; they probably wrote what they dared not express in their lives.

His taste for reading revived as he explored with relish the hidden infirmities of minds that had been valued by fools as great and noble. He saw Jane Austen and Charlotte Brontë as two unpleasant examples of spinsterhood: the one as a prying, sub-acid busybody in everyone else's flirtations, the other as a raving, craving maenad seeking self-immolation on the altar of her frustrated passions.

These powers of penetration astonished him. With a mind so acute and original he should have achieved greatness yet he was a mere solicitor and not prosperous at that. If he had but the money he might do something with those ivory shares, but it would be a pure gamble, and he had no luck. His natural envy of his wealthier acquaintances now mingled with a contempt for their stupidity that approached loathing. The digestion of his lunch in the City was ruined by meeting sentimental yet successful dotards, whom he had once regarded as pleasant fellows. The very sight of them spoiled his game of golf, so that he came to prefer reading alone in the dining-room even on sunny afternoons.

He discovered also, and with a slight shock, that Mrs. Corbett had always bored him. Dicky he began actively to dislike as an impudent blockhead, and the two girls were as insipidly alike as white mice; it was a relief when he abolished their tiresome habit of coming in to say good night.

In the now unbroken silence and seclusion of the dining-room he read with feverish haste, as though he were seeking for some clue to knowledge, some secret key to existence which would quicken and inflame it.

He even explored the few decaying remains of his uncle's theological library. One of these books had diagrams and symbols in the margin, which he took to be mathematical formulae of a kind he did not know. He presently discovered that they were drawn, not printed, and that the book was in manuscript, in a very neat, crabbed black writing that resembled black letter printing. It was, moreover, in Latin, a fact that gave Mr. Corbett a shock of unreasoning disappointment. For while examining the signs on the margin he had been filled with an extraordinary exultation, as though he knew himself to be on the edge of a discovery that should alter his whole life. But he had forgotten his Latin.

With a secret and guilty air, which would have looked absurd to anyone who knew his harmless purpose, he stole to the schoolroom for Dicky's Latin dictionary and grammar, and hurried back to the dining-room, where he tried to discover what the book was about with an anxious industry that surprised himself. There was no name to it, nor of the author. Several blank pages had been left at the end, and the writing ended at the bottom of a page, with no flourish nor superscription, as though the book had been left unfinished. From what sentences he could translate it seemed to be a work on theology.

There were constant references to the Master, to his wishes and injunctions, which appeared to be of a complicated kind. Mr. Corbett began by skipping these as mere accounts of ceremonial, but a word caught his eye as one unlikely to occur in such an account. He read this passage attentively looking up each word in the dictionary, and could hardly believe the result of his translation. "Clearly," he decided, "this book must be by some early missionary, and the passage I have just read the account of some horrible rite practised by a savage tribe of devil-worshippers. Though he called it "horrible," he reflected on it, committing each detail to memory. He then amused himself by copying the signs in the margin near it and trying to discover their significance. But a sensation of sickly cold came over him, his head swam, and he could hardly see the figures before his eyes. He suspected a sudden attack of influenza and went to ask his wife for medicine.

They were all in the drawing-room, Mrs. Corbett helping Nora and Jean with a new game, Dicky playing the pianola, and Mike, the Irish terrier, who had lately deserted his accustomed place on the dining-room hearth-rug, stretched by the fire. He thought how like sheep they looked and sounded. Nothing in his appearance in the mirror struck him as odd: it was their gaping faces that were unfamiliar. He then noticed the extraordinary behaviour of Mike, who had sprung from the hearth-rug and was crouched in the farthest corner uttering no sound, but with his eyes distended and foam round his bared teeth. Under Mr. Corbett's glance he slunk towards the door, whimpering in a faint and abject manner, and then as his master called him he snarled horribly, and the hair bristled on the scruff of his neck.

"What can be the matter with Mike?" asked Mrs. Corbett. Her question broke a silence that seemed to have lasted a long time. Jean began to cry. Mr. Corbett said irritably that he did not know what was the matter with any of them.

Then Nora asked: "What is that red mark on your face?"

He looked again in the glass and could see nothing.

"It's quite clear from here," said Dicky. "I can see the lines in the fingerprint."

"Yes, that's what it is," said Mrs. Corbett in her brisk staccato voice: "the print of a finger on your forehead. Have you been writing in red ink?"

Mr. Corbett precipitately left the room for his own, where he sent down a message that he was suffering from headache and would have his dinner in bed. He wanted no one fussing round him. By next morning he was amazed at his fancies of influenza, for he had never felt so well in his life.

No one commented on his looks at breakfast, so that he concluded the mark had disappeared. The old Latin book he had been translating on the previous night had been moved from the writing bureau, although Dick's grammar and dictionary were still there. The second shelf was, as always in the daytime, closely packed; the book had, he remembered, been in the second shelf. But this time he did not ask who put it back.

That day he had an unexpected stroke of luck in a new client of the name of Crab, who entrusted him with large sums of money; nor was he irritated by the sight of his more prosperous acquaintances; but with difficulty restrained from grinning in their faces, so confident was he that his remarkable ability must soon place him higher than any of them. At dinner he chaffed his family with what he felt to be the gaiety of a schoolboy.

In spite of this new alertness, he could not attend to the letters he should have written that evening, and drifted to the bookcase for a little light distraction, but found that for the first time there was nothing he wished to read. He pulled out a book from above his head at random, and saw that it was the old Latin book in manuscript.

As he turned over its stiff and yellow pages, he noticed with pleasure the smell of corruption that had first repelled him in these decaying volumes, a smell, he now thought, of ancient and secret knowledge.

This idea of secrecy seemed to affect him personally, for on hearing a step in the hall he hastily closed the book and put it back in its place. He went to the schoolroom where Dicky was doing his homework and told him he required his Latin grammar and dictionary again for an old law report. To his annoyance he stammered and put his words awkwardly; he thought that the boy looked oddly at him and he cursed him in his heart for a suspicious young devil, though of what he should be suspicious he could not say. Nevertheless, when back in the dining-room, he listened at the door and then softly turned the lock before he opened the books on the writing bureau.

The script and Latin seemed much clearer than on the previous evening and he was able to read at random a passage relating to a trial of a German midwife in 1620 for the murder and dissection of 783 children.

It appeared to be an account of some secret society whose activities and ritual were of a nature so obscure, and when not, so vile and terrible, that Mr. Corbett would not at first believe that this could be a record of any human mind.

He read until far later than his usual hour for bed, and when at last he rose, it was with the book in his hands. To defer his parting with it, he stood turning over the pages until he reached the end of the writing, and was struck by a new peculiarity.

The ink was much fresher and of a far poorer quality than the thick rusted ink in the bulk of the book; on close inspection he would have said that it was of modern manufacture and written quite recently, were it not for the fact that it was in the same crabbed late-seventeenth century handwriting.

This, however, did not explain the perplexity, even dismay and fear he now felt as he started at the last sentence. It ran: *Continue te in perennibus studiis*, and he had at once recognized it as a Ciceronian tag that had been dinned into him at school. He could not understand how he had failed to notice it yesterday.

Then he remembered that the book had ended at the bottom of a page. But now, the last two sentences were written at the very top of a page. However long he looked at them, he could come to no other conclusion than that they had been added since the previous evening.

He now read the sentence before the last: *Re imperfecta mortuus sum*, and translated the whole as "I died with my purposes unachieved. Continue, thou, the never-ending studies."

With his eyes still fixed upon it, Mr. Corbett replaced the book on the writing bureau and stepped back from it to the door, his hand outstretched behind him, groping and then tugging at the door handle. As the door failed to open, his breath came in a faint, hardly articulate scream. Then he remembered that he had himself locked it, and he fumbled with the key in frantic ineffectual movements until at last he opened it and banged it after him as he plunged backwards into the hall.

For a moment he stood there looking at the door handle; then with a stealthy, sneaking movement, his hand crept out towards it, touched it, began to turn it, when suddenly he pulled his hand away and went up to his bedroom, three steps at a time.

There he hid his face in the pillow, cried and raved in meaningless words, repeating: "Never, never, never. I will never do it again. Help me never to do it again." With the words "Help me," he noticed what he was saying—they reminded him of other words, and he began to pray aloud.

But the words sounded jumbled, they persisted in coming into his head in a reverse order so that he found he was saying his prayers backwards, and at this final absurdity he suddenly began to laugh very loud. He sat up on the bed, delighted at this return to sanity, common sense and humour, when the door leading into Mrs. Corbett's room opened, and he saw his wife staring at him with a strange, grey, drawn face that made her seem like the terror-stricken ghost of her usually smug and placid self.

"It's not burglars," he said irritably. "I've come to bed late, that is all, and must have wakened you."

"Henry," said Mrs. Corbett, and he noticed that she had not heard him: "Henry, didn't you hear it?"

"What?"

"That laugh."

He was silent, an instinctive caution warning him to wait until she spoke again. And this she did, imploring him with her eyes to reassure her.

"It was not a human laugh. It was like the laugh of a devil."

He checked his violent inclination to laugh again. It was wiser not to let her know that it was only his laughter she had heard. He told her to stop being fanciful, and Mrs. Corbett gradually recovered her docility. The next morning, Mr. Corbett rose before any of the servants and crept down to the dining-room. As before the dictionary and grammar alone remained on the writing bureau; the book was back on the second shelf. He opened it at the end. Two more lines had been added, carrying the writing down to the middle of the page. They ran:

Ex auro canceris
In dentem elephantis.

Which translated as:

Out of the money of the crab
Into the tooth of the elephant.

From this time on, his acquaintances in the City noticed a change in the mediocre, rather flabby and unenterprising "old Corbett." His recent sour depression dropped from him; he seemed to have grown twenty years younger, strong, brisk, and cheerful, and with a self-confidence in business that struck them as lunacy. They waited with a not unpleasant excitement for the inevitable crash, but his every speculation, however wild and hare-brained, turned out successful.

He never stayed in town for dinners or theatres, for he was always now in a hurry to get home, where, as soon as he was sure of being undisturbed, he would take down the manuscript book from the second shelf of the dining-room and turn to the last pages.

Every morning he found that a few words had been added since the evening before, and always they formed, as he considered, injunctions to himself. These were at first only with regard to his money transactions, giving assurance to his boldest fancies, and since the brilliant and unforeseen success that had attended his gamble with Mr. Crab's money in African ivory, he followed all such advice unhesitatingly.

But presently, interspersed with these commands, were others of a meaningless, childish, yet revolting character, such as might be invented by a decadent imbecile.

He at first paid no attention to these directions, but found that his new speculations declined so rapidly that he became terrified not merely for his fortune but for his reputation and even safety, since the money of various of his clients was involved. It was made clear to him that he must follow the commands in the book altogether or not at all, and he began to carry out their puerile and grotesque blasphemies with a contemptuous amusement, which, however, gradually changed to a sense of their monstrous significance. They became more capricious and difficult of execution, but he now never hesitated to obey blindly, urged by a fear that he could not understand.

By now he understood the effect of this book on the others near it and the reason that had impelled its mysterious agent to move the books into the second shelf, so that all in turn should come under the influence of that ancient and secret knowledge.

In respect to it, he encouraged his children, with jeers at their stupidity, to read more, but he could not observe that they ever now took a book from the dining-room bookcase. He himself no longer needed to read, but went to bed early and slept soundly. The things that all his life he had longed to do when he should have enough money now seemed to him insipid. His most exciting pleasure was the smell and touch of these mouldering pages, as he turned them to find the last message inscribed to him.

One evening it was in two words only: *Canem occide.*

He laughed at this simple and pleasant request to kill the dog, for he bore Mike a grudge for his change from devotion to slinking aversion, Moreover, it could not have come more opportunely, since in turning out an old desk he had just discovered some packets of rat poison bought years ago and forgotten. He whistled light-heartedly as he ran upstairs to rummage for the packets, and returned to empty one in the dog's dish of water in the hall.

That night the household was awakened by terrified screams proceeding from the stairs. Mr. Corbett was the first to hasten there, prompted by the instinctive caution that was always with him these days. He saw Jean, in her nightdress, scrambling up on to the landing on her hands and knees, clutching at anything that afforded support and screaming in a choking, tearless, unnatural manner. He carried her to the room she shared with Nora, where they were quickly followed by Mrs. Corbett.

Nothing coherent could be got from Jean. Nora said that she must have been having her old dream again: when her father demanded what this was, she said that Jean sometimes woke in the night, crying, because she had dreamed of a hand passing backwards and forwards over the dining-room bookcase, until it found a certain book and took it out of the shelf. At this point she was always so frightened that she woke up.

On hearing this, Jean broke into fresh screams, and Mrs. Corbett would have no more explanations. Mr. Corbett went out on to the stairs to find what had brought the child there from her bed. On looking down into the lighted hall he saw Mike's dish overturned. He went down to examine it and saw that the water he had poisoned must have been upset and absorbed by the rough doormat, which was quite wet.

He went back to the little girls' room, told his wife that she was tired and must go to bed, and he would now take his turn at comforting Jean. She was now much quieter. He took her on his knee, where at first she shrank from him. Mr. Corbett remembered with an awed sense of injury that she never now sat on his knee, and would have liked to pay her out for it by mocking and frightening her. But he had to coax her into telling him what he wanted, and with this object he soothed her, calling her by pet names that he thought he had forgotten, telling her that nothing could hurt her now he was with her. He listened to what he had at last induced her to tell him.

She and Nora had kept Mike with them all the evening and taken him to sleep in their room for a treat. He had lain at the foot of Jean's bed and they had all gone to sleep. Then Jean began her old dream of the hand moving over the books in the dining-room bookcase; but instead of taking out a book it came across the dining-room and out on to the stairs. It came up over the banisters and to the door of their room and turned their door handle very softly and opened it. At this point she jumped up, wide awake, and turned on the light, calling to Nora. The door, which had been shut when they went to sleep, was wide open, and Mike was gone.

She told Nora that she was sure something dreadful would happen to him if she did not go and bring him back, and ran down into the hall, where she saw him just about to drink from his dish. She called to him and he looked up, but did not come, so she ran to him and began to pull him along with her when her nightdress was clutched from behind and then she felt a hand seize her arm.

She fell down and then clambered upstairs as fast as she could, screaming all the way.

It was now clear to Mr. Corbett that Mike's dish must have been upset in the scuffle. She was again crying, but this time he felt himself unable to comfort her. He retired to his room, where he walked up and down in an agitation he could not understand.

"I am not a bad man," he kept saying to himself. "I have never done anything actually wrong. My clients are none the worse for my speculations, only the better."

Presently he added: "It is not wrong to try and kill a dog, an ill-tempered brute. It turned against me. It might have bitten Jeannie."

He noticed that he had thought of her as Jeannie which he had not done for some time; it must have been because he had called her that to-night. He must forbid her ever to leave her room at night; he could not have her meddling. It would be safer for him if she were not there at all.

Again that sick and cold sensation of fear swept over him; he seized the bedpost as though he were falling, and held on to it for some minutes. "I was thinking of a boarding school," he told himself, and then, "I must go down and find out— find out—" He would not think what it was he must find out.

He opened his door and listened. The house was quiet. He crept on to the landing and along to Nora's and Jean's door, where again he stood, listening. There was no sound, and at that he was again overcome with unreasonable terror. He imagined Jean lying very still in her bed, too still. He hastened away from the door, shuffling in his bedroom slippers along the passage and down the stairs.

A bright fire still burned in the dining-room grate. A glance at the clock told him it was not yet twelve. He stared at the bookcase. On the second shelf was a gap which had not been there when he had left. On the writing bureau lay a large open book. He knew that he must cross the room and see what was written in it. Then, as before, words that he did not intend came sobbing and crying to his lips, muttering "No, no, not that. Never, never, never." But he crossed the room and looked down at the book. As last time, the message was in only two words: "*Infantem occide.*"

He slipped and fell forwards against the bureau. His hands clutched at the book, lifted it as he recovered himself, and with his finger he traced out the words that had been written. The smell of corruption crept into his nostrils. He told himself that he was not a snivelling dotard but a man stronger and wiser than his fellows, superior to the common emotions of humanity, who held in his hands the sources of ancient and secret power.

He had known what the message would be. It was after all the only safe and logical thing to do. Jean had acquired dangerous knowledge. She was a spy, an antagonist. That she was so unconsciously, that she was eight years old, his youngest and favourite child, were sentimental appeals that could make no difference to a man of sane reasoning power such as his own.

Jean had sided with Mike against him. "All that are not for me are against me," he repeated softly. He would kill both dog and child with the white powder that no one knew to be in his possession.

He laid down the book and went to the door. What he had to do he would do quickly, for again that sensation of deadly cold was sweeping over him. He wished he had not to do it to-night; last night it would have been easier, but to-night she had sat on his knee and made him afraid. He imagined her lying very still in her bed, too still.

He held on to the door-handle but his fingers seemed to have grown numb, for he could not turn it. He clung to it, crouched and shivering, bending over it until he knelt on the ground, his head beneath the handle which he still clutched with upraised hands. Suddenly the hands were loosened and flung outwards with the frantic gesture of a man falling from a great height, and he stumbled to his feet.

He seized the book and threw it on the fire. A violent sensation of choking overcame him, he felt he was being strangled, as in a nightmare he tried again and again to shriek aloud, but his breath would make no sound. His breath would not come at all. He fell backwards heavily down on the floor, where he lay very still.

In the morning the maid who came to open the dining-room windows found her master dead. The sensation caused by this was scarcely so great in the City as that given by the simultaneous collapse of all Mr. Corbett's recent speculations. It was instantly assumed that he must have had previous knowledge of this and so committed suicide.

The stumbling-block of this theory was that the medical report defined the cause of Mr. Corbett's death as strangulation of the windpipe by the pressure of a hand which had left the marks of its fingers on his throat. ◆

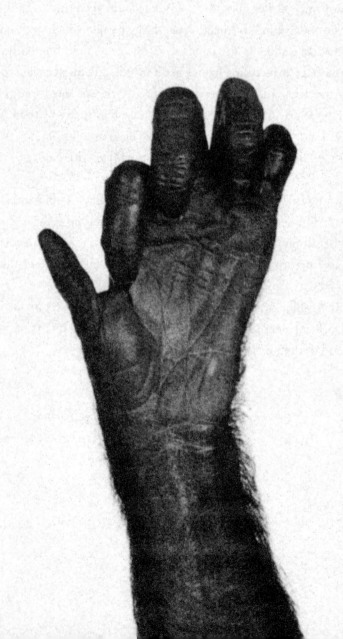

THE MONKEY'S PAW

BY *W. W. Jacobs*

One way to distinguish a bona fide classic from the rest of the pack is to chart its influence on future generations. And by that standard, "The Monkey's Paw" is certainly one of the most classic horror stories every written.

Since its first appearance in 1902, this variation on "I'll grant you three wishes" is probably tied with the genie in Aladdin's lamp for the coveted "Most Referenced Deal-With-The Devil-That-Didn't-Actually-Call-Itself-The-Devil Story".

If you only know it from watching The Simpsons, *or one of the trillion other riffs done upon it, then I am thrilled to take you back to the source.*

William Wymark Jacobs was a one-hit wonder in the horror field, though his many humorous writings kept him solvent till his death.

Be he looking down from Heaven or up from Hell, I hope he finds that as amusing as I do.

One

Without, the night was cold and wet, but in the small parlour of Laburnam Villa the blinds were drawn and the fire burned brightly. Father and son were at chess, the former, who possessed ideas about the game involving radical changes, putting his king into such sharp and unnecessary perils that it even provoked comment from the white-haired old lady knitting placidly by the fire.

"Hark at the wind," said Mr. White, who, having seen a fatal mistake after it was too late, was amiably desirous of preventing his son from seeing it.

"I'm listening," said the latter, grimly surveying the board as he stretched out his hand. "Check."

"I should hardly think that he'd come to-night," said his father, with his hand poised over the board.

"Mate," replied the son.

"That's the worst of living so far out," bawled Mr. White, with sudden and unlooked-for violence; "of all the beastly, slushy, out-of-the-way places to live in, this is the worst. Pathway's a bog, and the road's a torrent. I don't know what people are thinking about. I suppose because only two houses on the road are let, they think it doesn't matter."

"Never mind, dear," said his wife soothingly; "perhaps you'll win the next one."

Mr. White looked up sharply, just in time to intercept a knowing glance between mother and son. The words died away on his lips, and he hid a guilty grin in his thin grey beard.

"There he is," said Herbert White, as the gate banged to loudly and heavy footsteps came toward the door.

The old man rose with hospitable haste, and opening the door, was heard condoling with the new arrival. The new arrival also condoled with himself, so that Mrs. White said, "Tut, tut!" and coughed gently as her husband entered the room, followed by a tall burly man, beady of eye and rubicund of visage.

"Sergeant-Major Morris," he said, introducing him.

The sergeant-major shook hands, and taking the proffered seat by the fire, watched contentedly while his host got out whisky and tumblers and stood a small copper kettle on the fire.

At the third glass his eyes got brighter, and he began to talk, the little family circle regarding with eager interest this visitor from distant parts, as he squared his broad shoulders in the chair and spoke of strange scenes and doughty deeds; of wars and plagues and strange peoples.

"Twenty-one years of it," said Mr. White, nodding at his wife and son. "When he went away he was a slip of a youth in the warehouse. Now look at him."

"He don't look to have taken much harm," said Mrs. White, politely.

"I'd like to go to India myself," said the old man, "just to look round a bit, you know."

"Better where you are," said the sergeant-major, shaking his head. He put down the empty glass, and sighing softly, shook it again.

"I should like to see those old temples and fakirs and jugglers," said the old man. "What was that you started telling me the other day about a monkey's paw or something, Morris?"

"Nothing," said the soldier hastily. "Leastways, nothing worth hearing."

"Monkey's paw?" said Mrs. White curiously.

"Well, it's just a bit of what you might call magic, perhaps," said the sergeant-major off-handedly.

His three listeners leaned forward eagerly. The visitor absentmindedly put his empty glass to his lips and then set it down again. His host filled it for him.

"To look at," said the sergeant-major, fumbling in his pocket, "it's just an ordinary little paw, dried to a mummy."

He took something out of his pocket and proffered it. Mrs. White drew back with a grimace, but her son, taking it, examined it curiously.

"And what is there special about it?" inquired Mr. White, as he took it from his son and, having examined it, placed it upon the table.

"It had a spell put on it by an old fakir," said the sergeant-major, "a very holy man. He wanted to show that fate ruled people's lives, and that those who interfered with it did so to their sorrow. He put a spell on it so that three separate men could each have three wishes from it."

His manner was so impressive that his hearers were conscious that their light laughter jarred somewhat.

"Well, why don't you have three, sir?" said Herbert White cleverly.

The soldier regarded him in the way that middle age is wont to regard presumptuous youth. "I have," he said quietly, and his blotchy face whitened.

"And did you really have the three wishes granted?" asked Mrs. White.

"I did," said the sergeant-major, and his glass tapped against his strong teeth.

"And has anybody else wished?" inquired the old lady.

"The first man had his three wishes, yes," was the reply. "I don't know what the first two were, but the third was for death. That's how I got the paw."

His tones were so grave that a hush fell upon the group.

"If you've had your three wishes, it's no good to you now, then, Morris," said the old man at last. "What do you keep it for?"

The soldier shook his head. "Fancy, I suppose," he said slowly.

"If you could have another three wishes," said the old man, eyeing him keenly, "would you have them?"

"I don't know," said the other. "I don't know."

He took the paw, and dangling it between his front finger and thumb, suddenly threw it upon the fire. White, with a slight cry, stooped down and snatched it off.

"Better let it burn," said the soldier solemnly.

"If you don't want it, Morris," said the old man, "give it to me."

"I won't," said his friend doggedly. "I threw it on the fire. If you keep it, don't blame me for what happens. Pitch it on the fire again, like a sensible man."

The other shook his head and examined his new possession closely. "How do you do it?" he inquired.

"Hold it up in your right hand and wish aloud,' said the sergeant-major, "but I warn you of the consequences."

"Sounds like the *Arabian Nights*," said Mrs. White, as she rose and began to set the supper. "Don't you think you might wish for four pairs of hands for me?"

Her husband drew the talisman from his pocket and then all three burst into laughter as the sergeant-major, with a look of alarm on his face, caught him by the arm.

"If you must wish," he said gruffly, "wish for something sensible."

Mr. White dropped it back into his pocket, and placing chairs, motioned his friend to the table. In the business of supper the talisman was partly forgotten, and afterward the three sat listening in an enthralled fashion to a second instalment of the soldier's adventures in India.

"If the tale about the monkey paw is not more truthful than those he has been telling us," said Herbert, as the door closed behind their guest, just in time for him to catch the last train, "we shan't make much out of it."

"Did you give him anything for it, father?" inquired Mrs. White, regarding her husband closely.

"A trifle," said he, colouring slightly. "He didn't want it, but I made him take it. And he pressed me again to throw it away."

"Likely," said Herbert, with pretended horror. "Why, we're going to be rich, and famous, and happy. Wish to be an emperor, father, to begin with; then you can't be henpecked."

He darted round the table, pursued by the maligned Mrs. White armed with an antimacassar.

Mr. White took the paw from his pocket and eyed it dubiously. "I don't know what to wish for, and that's a fact," he said slowly. "It seems to me I've got all I want."

"If you only cleared the house, you'd be quite happy, wouldn't you?" said Herbert, with his hand on his shoulder. "Well, wish for two hundred pounds, then; that'll just do it."

His father, smiling shamefacedly at his own credulity, held up the talisman, as his son, with a solemn face somewhat marred by a wink at his mother, sat down at the piano and struck a few impressive chords.

"I wish for two hundred pounds," said the old man distinctly.

A fine crash from the piano greeted the words, interrupted by a shuddering cry from the old man. His wife and son ran toward him.

"It moved," he cried, with a glance of disgust at the object as it lay on the floor. "As I wished it twisted in my hands like a snake."

"Well, I don't see the money," said his son, as he picked it up and placed it on the table, "and I bet I never shall."

"It must have been your fancy, father," said his wife, regarding him anxiously.

He shook his head. "Never mind, though; there's no harm done, but it gave me a shock all the same."

They sat down by the fire again while the two men finished their pipes. Outside, the wind was higher than ever, and the old man started nervously at the sound of a door banging upstairs. A silence unusual and depressing settled upon all three, which lasted until the old couple rose to retire for the night.

"I expect you'll find the cash tied up in a big bag in the middle of your bed," said Herbert, as he bade them good-night, "and something horrible squatting up on top of the wardrobe watching you as you pocket your ill-gotten gains."

He sat alone in the darkness, gazing at the dying fire, and seeing faces in it. The last face was so horrible and so simian that he gazed at it in amazement. It got so vivid that, with a little uneasy laugh, he felt on the table for a glass containing a little water to throw over it. His hand grasped the monkey's paw, and with a little shiver he wiped his hand on his coat and went up to bed.

Two

In the brightness of the wintry sun next morning as it streamed over the breakfast table Herbert laughed at his fears. There was an air of prosaic wholesomeness about the room which it had lacked on the previous night, and the dirty, shrivelled little paw was pitched on the sideboard with a carelessness which betokened no great belief in its virtues.

"I suppose all old soldiers are the same," said Mrs. White. "The idea of our listening to such nonsense! How could wishes be granted in these days? And if they could, how could two hundred pounds hurt you, father?"

"Might drop on his head from the sky," said the frivolous Herbert.

"Morris said the things happened so naturally," said his father, "that you might if you so wished attribute it to coincidence."

"Well, don't break into the money before I come back," said Herbert, as he rose from the table. "I'm afraid it'll turn you into a mean, avaricious man, and we shall have to disown you."

His mother laughed, and following him to the door, watched him down the road, and returning to the breakfast table, was very happy at the expense of her husband's credulity. All of which did not prevent her from scurrying to the door at the postman's knock, nor prevent her from referring somewhat shortly to retired sergeant-majors of bibulous habits when she found that the post brought a tailor's bill.

"Herbert will have some more of his funny remarks, I expect, when he comes home," she said, as they sat at dinner.

"I dare say," said Mr. White, pouring himself out some beer; "but for all that, the thing moved in my hand; that I'll swear to."

"You thought it did," said the old lady soothingly.

"I say it did," replied the other. "There was no thought about it; I had just— What's the matter?"

His wife made no reply. She was watching the mysterious movements of a man outside, who, peering in an undecided fashion at the house, appeared to be trying to make up his mind to enter. In mental connection with the two hundred pounds, she noticed that the stranger was well dressed and wore a silk hat of glossy newness. Three times he paused at the gate, and then walked on again. The fourth time he stood with his hand upon it, and then with sudden resolution flung it open and walked up the path. Mrs. White at the same moment placed her hands behind her, and hurriedly unfastening the strings of her apron, put that useful article of apparel beneath the cushion of her chair.

She brought the stranger, who seemed ill at ease, into the room. He gazed at her furtively, and listened in a preoccupied fashion as the old lady apologized for the appearance of the room, and her husband's coat, a garment which he usually reserved for the garden. She then waited as patiently as her sex would permit, for him to broach his business, but he was at first strangely silent.

"I--was asked to call," he said at last, and stooped and picked a piece of cotton from his trousers. "I come from Maw and Meggins."

The old lady started. "Is anything the matter?" she asked breathlessly. "Has anything happened to Herbert? What is it? What is it?"

Her husband interposed. "There, there, mother," he said hastily. "Sit down, and don't jump to conclusions. You've not brought bad news, I'm sure, sir" and he eyed the other wistfully.

"I'm sorry—" began the visitor.

"Is he hurt?" demanded the mother.

The visitor bowed in assent. "Badly hurt," he said quietly, "but he is not in any pain."

"Oh, thank God!" said the old woman, clasping her hands. "Thank God for that! Thank—"

She broke off suddenly as the sinister meaning of the assurance dawned upon her and she saw the awful confirmation of her fears in the other's averted face. She caught her breath, and turning to her slower-witted husband, laid her trembling old hand upon his. There was a long silence.

"He was caught in the machinery," said the visitor at length, in a low voice. "Caught in the machinery," repeated Mr. White, in a dazed fashion, "yes."

He sat staring blankly out at the window, and taking his wife's hand between his own, pressed it as he had been wont to do in their old courting days nearly forty years before.

"He was the only one left to us," he said, turning gently to the visitor. "It is hard."

The other coughed, and rising, walked slowly to the window. "The firm wished me to convey their sincere sympathy with you in your great loss," he said, without looking round. "I beg that you will understand I am only their servant and merely obeying orders."

There was no reply; the old woman's face was white, her eyes staring, and her breath inaudible; on the husband's face was a look such as his friend the sergeant might have carried into his first action.

"I was to say that Maw and Meggins disclaim all responsibility," continued the other. "They admit no liability at all, but in consideration of your son's services they wish to present you with a certain sum as compensation."

Mr. White dropped his wife's hand, and rising to his feet, gazed with a look of horror at his visitor. His dry lips shaped the words, "How much?"

"Two hundred pounds," was the answer.

Unconscious of his wife's shriek, the old man smiled faintly, put out his hands like a sightless man, and dropped, a senseless heap, to the floor.

Three

In the huge new cemetery, some two miles distant, the old people buried their dead, and came back to a house steeped in shadow and silence. It was all over so quickly that at first they could hardly realize it, and remained in a state of expectation as though of something else to happen—something else which was to lighten this load, too heavy for old hearts to bear.

But the days passed, and expectation gave place to resignation--the hopeless resignation of the old, sometimes miscalled, apathy. Sometimes they hardly exchanged a word, for now they had nothing to talk about, and their days were long to weariness.

It was about a week after that that the old man, waking suddenly in the night, stretched out his hand and found himself alone. The room was in darkness, and the sound of subdued weeping came from the window. He raised himself in bed and listened.

"Come back," he said tenderly. "You will be cold."

"It is colder for my son," said the old woman, and wept afresh.

The sound of her sobs died away on his ears. The bed was warm, and his eyes heavy with sleep. He dozed fitfully, and then slept until a sudden wild cry from his wife awoke him with a start.

"*The paw!*" she cried wildly. "The monkey's paw!"

He started up in alarm. "Where? Where is it? What's the matter?"

She came stumbling across the room toward him. "I want it," she said quietly. "You've not destroyed it?"

"It's in the parlour, on the bracket," he replied, marvelling. "Why?"

She cried and laughed together, and bending over, kissed his cheek.

"I only just thought of it," she said hysterically. "Why didn't I think of it before? Why didn't *you* think of it?"

"Think of what?" he questioned.

"The other two wishes," she replied rapidly. "We've only had one."

"Was not that enough?" he demanded fiercely.

"No," she cried, triumphantly; "we'll have one more. Go down and get it quickly, and wish our boy alive again."

The man sat up in bed and flung the bedclothes from his quaking limbs. "Good God, you are mad!" he cried aghast.

"Get it," she panted; "get it quickly, and wish— Oh, my boy, my boy!"

Her husband struck a match and lit the candle. "Get back to bed," he said, unsteadily. "You don't know what you are saying."

"We had the first wish granted," said the old woman, feverishly; "why not the second."

"A coincidence," stammered the old man.

"Go and get it and wish," cried the old woman, quivering with excitement.

The old man turned and regarded her, and his voice shook. "He has been dead ten days, and besides he—I would not tell you else, but--I could only recognize him by his clothing. If he was too terrible for you to see then, how now?"

"Bring him back," cried the old woman, and dragged him toward the door. "Do you think I fear the child I have nursed?"

He went down in the darkness, and felt his way to the parlour, and then to the mantelpiece. The talisman was in its place, and a horrible fear that the unspoken wish might bring his mutilated son before him ere he could escape from the room seized upon him, and he caught his breath as he found that he had lost the direction of the door. His brow cold with sweat, he felt his way round the table, and groped along the wall until he found himself in the small passage with the unwholesome thing in his hand.

Even his wife's face seemed changed as he entered the room. It was white and expectant, and to his fears seemed to have an unnatural look upon it. He was afraid of her.

"*Wish!*" she cried, in a strong voice.

"It is foolish and wicked," he faltered.

"*Wish!*" repeated his wife.

He raised his hand. "I wish my son alive again."

The talisman fell to the floor, and he regarded it fearfully. Then he sank trembling into a chair as the old woman, with burning eyes, walked to the window and raised the blind.

He sat until he was chilled with the cold, glancing occasionally at the figure of the old woman peering through the window. The candle end, which had burnt below the rim of the china candlestick, was throwing pulsating shadows on the ceiling and walls, until, with a flicker larger than the rest, it expired. The old man, with an unspeakable sense of relief at the failure of the talisman, crept back to his bed, and a minute or two afterward the old woman came silently and apathetically beside him.

Neither spoke, but both lay silently listening to the ticking of the clock. A stair creaked, and a squeaky mouse scurried noisily through the wall. The darkness was oppressive, and after lying for some time screwing up his courage, the husband took the box of matches, and striking one, went downstairs for a candle.

At the foot of the stairs the match went out, and he paused to strike another, and at the same moment a knock, so quiet and stealthy as to be scarcely audible, sounded on the front door.

The matches fell from his hand. He stood motionless, his breath suspended until the knock was repeated. Then he turned and fled swiftly back to his room, and closed the door behind him. A third knock sounded through the house.

"*What's that?*" cried the old woman, starting up.

"A rat," said the old man, in shaking tones—"a rat. It passed me on the stairs."

His wife sat up in bed listening. A loud knock resounded through the house.

"It's Herbert!" she screamed. "It's Herbert!"

She ran to the door, but her husband was before her, and catching her by the arm, held her tightly.

"What are you going to do?" he whispered hoarsely.

"It's my boy; it's Herbert!" she cried, struggling mechanically. "I forgot it was two miles away. What are you holding me for? Let go. I must open the door."

"For God's sake, don't let it in," cried the old man trembling.

"You're afraid of your own son," she cried, struggling. "Let me go. I'm coming, Herbert; I'm coming."

There was another knock, and another. The old woman with a sudden wrench broke free and ran from the room. Her husband followed to the landing, and called after her appealingly as she hurried downstairs. He heard the chain rattle back and the bottom bolt drawn slowly and stiffly from the socket. Then the old woman's voice, strained and panting.

"The bolt," she cried loudly. "Come down. I can't reach it."

But her husband was on his hands and knees groping wildly on the floor in search of the paw. If he could only find it before the thing outside got in. A perfect fusillade of knocks reverberated through the house, and he heard the scraping of a chair as his wife put it down in the passage against the door. He heard the creaking of the bolt as it came slowly back, and at the same moment he found the monkey's paw, and frantically breathed his third and last wish.

The knocking ceased suddenly, although the echoes of it were still in the house. He heard the chair drawn back and the door opened. A cold wind rushed up the staircase, and a long loud wail of disappointment and misery from his wife gave him courage to run down to her side, and then to the gate beyond. The street lamp flickering opposite shone on a quiet and deserted road. ✦

THE HOUND

BY *H.P. Lovecraft*

If there's one thing we can safely say about H.P. Lovecraft, it's that he opened far more unfortunate doors than we will ever be able to close. Like Pandora, only minus the hope.

What's singular about "The Hound", in his body of work—aside from its unusually brisk pace and clear desire to entertain—is its groundbreaking introduction of the unholy Necronomicon: surely the most evil book ever not actually written, but merely made up and then whispered about as the ultimate one-stop shopping guide for making the bad things come.

It's an early work, but a signature one.

Which I suspect you will greatly enjoy.

In my tortured ears there sounds unceasingly a nightmare whirring and flapping, and a faint distant baying as of some gigantic hound. It is not dream—it is not, I fear, even madness—for too much has already happened to give me these merciful doubts.

St John is a mangled corpse; I alone know why, and such is my knowledge that I am about to blow out my brains for fear I shall be mangled in the same way. Down unlit and illimitable corridors of eldrith phantasy sweeps the black, shapeless Nemesis that drives me to self-annihilation.

May heaven forgive the folly and morbidity which led us both to so monstrous a fate! Wearied with the commonplaces of a prosaic world, where even the joys of romance and adventure soon grow stale, St John and I had followed enthusiastically every aesthetic and intellectual movement which promised respite from our devastating ennui. The enigmas of the symbolists and the ecstasies of the pre-Raphaelites all were ours in their time, but each new mood was drained too soon, of its diverting novelty and appeal.

Only the somber philosophy of the decadents could help us, and this we found potent only by increasing gradually the depth and diabolism of our penetrations. Baudelaire and Huysmans were soon exhausted of thrills, till finally there remained for us only the more direct stimuli of unnatural personal experiences and adventures. It was this frightful emotional need which led us eventually to that detestable course which even in my present fear I mention with shame and timidity—that hideous extremity of human outrage, the abhorred practice of grave-robbing.

I cannot reveal the details of our shocking expeditions, or catalogue even partly the worst of the trophies adorning the nameless museum we prepared in the great stone house where we jointly dwelt, alone and servantless. Our museum was a blasphemous, unthinkable place, where with the satanic taste of neurotic virtuosi we had assembled a universe of terror and decay to excite our jaded sensibilities. It was a secret room, far, far, underground; where huge winged daemons carven of basalt and onyx vomited from wide grinning mouths weird green and orange light, and hidden pneumatic pipes ruffled into kaleidoscopic dances of death the lines of red charnel things hand in hand woven in voluminous black hangings. Through these pipes came at will the odors our moods most craved; sometimes the scent of pale funeral lilies; sometimes the narcotic incense of imagined Eastern shrines of the kingly dead, and sometimes—how I shudder to recall it!—the frightful, soul-upheaving stenches of the uncovered-grave.

Around the walls of this repellent chamber were cases of antique mummies alternating with comely, lifelike bodies perfectly stuffed and cured by the taxidermist's art, and with headstones snatched from the oldest churchyards of the world. Niches here and there contained skulls of all shapes, and heads preserved in various stages of dissolution. There one might find the rotting, bald pates of famous noblemen, and the fresh and radiantly golden heads of new-buried children.

Statues and paintings there were, all of fiendish subjects and some executed by St John and myself. A locked portfolio, bound in tanned human skin, held certain unknown and unnameable drawings which it was rumored Goya had perpetrated but dared not acknowledge. There were nauseous musical instruments, stringed, brass, and wood-wind, on which St John and I sometimes produced dissonances of exquisite morbidity and cacodaemoniacal ghastliness; whilst in a multitude of inlaid ebony cabinets reposed the most incredible and unimaginable variety of tomb-loot ever assembled by human madness and perversity. It is of this loot in particular that I must not speak—thank God I had the courage to destroy it long before I thought of destroying myself!

The predatory excursions on which we collected our unmentionable treasures were always artistically memorable events. We were no vulgar ghouls, but worked only under certain conditions of mood, landscape, environment, weather, season, and moonlight. These pastimes were to us the most exquisite form of aesthetic expression, and we gave their details a fastidious technical care. An inappropriate hour, a jarring lighting effect, or a clumsy manipulation of the damp sod, would almost totally destroy for us that ecstatic titillation which followed the exhumation of some ominous, grinning secret of the earth. Our quest for novel scenes and piquant conditions was feverish and insatiate—St John was always the leader, and he it was who led the way at last to that mocking, accursed spot which brought us our hideous and inevitable doom.

By what malign fatality were we lured to that terrible Holland churchyard? I think it was the dark rumor and legendry, the tales of one buried for five centuries, who had himself been a ghoul in his time and had stolen a potent thing from a mighty sepulchre. I can recall the scene in these final moments—the pale autumnal moon over the graves, casting long horrible shadows; the grotesque trees, drooping sullenly to meet the neglected grass and the crumbling slabs; the vast legions of strangely colossal bats that flew against the moon; the antique ivied church pointing a huge spectral finger at the livid sky; the phosphorescent insects that danced like death-fires under the yews in a distant corner; the odors of mould, vegetation, and less explicable things that mingled feebly with the night-wind from over far swamps and seas; and, worst of all, the faint deep-toned baying of some gigantic hound which we could neither see nor definitely place. As we heard this suggestion of baying we shuddered, remembering the tales of the peasantry; for he whom we sought had centuries before been found in this self same spot, torn and mangled by the claws and teeth of some unspeakable beast.

I remember how we delved in the ghoul's grave with our spades, and how we thrilled at the picture of ourselves, the grave, the pale watching moon, the horrible shadows, the grotesque trees, the titanic bats, the antique church, the dancing death-fires, the sickening odors, the gently moaning night-wind, and the strange, half-heard directionless baying of whose objective existence we could scarcely be sure.

Then we struck a substance harder than the damp mould, and beheld a rotting oblong box crusted with mineral deposits from the long undisturbed ground. It was incredibly tough and thick, but so old that we finally pried it open and feasted our eyes on what it held.

Much—amazingly much—was left of the object despite the lapse of five hundred years. The skeleton, though crushed in places by the jaws of the thing that had killed it, held together with surprising firmness, and we gloated over the clean white skull and its long, firm teeth and its eyeless sockets that once had glowed with a charnel fever like our own. In the coffin lay an amulet of curious and exotic design, which had apparently been worn around the sleeper's neck. It was the oddly conventionalised figure of a crouching winged hound, or sphinx with a semi-canine face, and was exquisitely carved in antique Oriental fashion from a small piece of green jade. The expression of its features was repellent in the extreme, savoring at once of death, bestiality and malevolence. Around the base was an inscription in characters which neither St John nor I could identify; and on the bottom, like a maker's seal, was graven a grotesque and formidable skull.

Immediately upon beholding this amulet we knew that we must possess it; that this treasure alone was our logical pelf from the centuried grave. Even had its outlines been unfamiliar we would have desired it, but as we looked more closely we saw that it was not wholly unfamiliar. Alien it indeed was to all art and literature which sane and balanced readers know, but we recognized it as the thing hinted of in the forbidden *Necronomicon* of the mad Arab Abdul Alhazred; the ghastly soul-symbol of the corpse-eating cult of inaccessible Leng, in Central Asia. All too well did we trace the sinister lineaments described by the old Arab daemonologist; lineaments, he wrote, drawn from some obscure supernatural manifestation of the souls of those who vexed and gnawed at the dead.

Seizing the green jade object, we gave a last glance at the bleached and cavern-eyed face of its owner and closed up the grave as we found it. As we hastened from the abhorrent spot, the stolen amulet in St John's pocket, we thought we saw the bats descend in a body to the earth we had so lately rifled, as if seeking for some cursed and unholy nourishment. But the autumn moon shone weak and pale, and we could not be sure.

So, too, as we sailed the next day away from Holland to our home, we thought we heard the faint distant baying of some gigantic hound in the background. But the autumn wind moaned sad and wan, and we could not be sure.

Less than a week after our return to England, strange things began to happen. We lived as recluses; devoid of friends, alone, and without servants in a few rooms of an ancient manor-house on a bleak and unfrequented moor; so that our doors were seldom disturbed by the knock of the visitor.

Now, however, we were troubled by what seemed to be a frequent fumbling in the night, not only around the doors but around the windows also, upper as well as lower. Once we fancied that a large, opaque body darkened the library window when the moon was shining against it, and another time we thought we heard a whirring or flapping sound not far off. On each occasion investigation revealed nothing, and we began to ascribe the occurrences to imagination which still prolonged in our ears the faint far baying we thought we had heard in the Holland churchyard. The jade amulet now reposed in a niche in our museum, and sometimes we burned a strangely scented candle before it. We read much in Alhazred's *Necronomicon* about its properties, and about the relation of ghosts' souls to the objects it symbolized; and were disturbed by what we read.

Then terror came.

On the night of September 24, 19--, I heard a knock at my chamber door. Fancying it St John's, I bade the knocker enter, but was answered only by a shrill laugh. There was no one in the corridor. When I aroused St John from his sleep, he professed entire ignorance of the event, and became as worried as I. It was the night that the faint, distant baying over the moor became to us a certain and dreaded reality.

Four days later, whilst we were both in the hidden museum, there came a low, cautious scratching at the single door which led to the secret library staircase. Our alarm was now divided, for, besides our fear of the unknown, we had always entertained a dread that our grisly collection might be discovered. Extinguishing all lights, we proceeded to the door and threw it suddenly open; whereupon we felt an unaccountable rush of air, and heard, as if receding far away, a queer combination of rustling, tittering, and articulate chatter. Whether we were mad, dreaming, or in our senses, we did not try to determine. We only realized, with the blackest of apprehensions, that the apparently disembodied chatter was beyond a doubt *in the Dutch language*.

After that we lived in growing horror and fascination. Mostly we held to the theory that we were jointly going mad from our life of unnatural excitements, but sometimes it pleased us more to dramatize ourselves as the victims of some creeping and appalling doom. Bizarre manifestations were now too frequent to count. Our lonely house was seemingly alive with the presence of some malign being whose nature we could not guess, and every night that daemoniac baying rolled over the wind-swept moor, always louder and louder. On October 29 we found in the soft earth underneath the library window a series of footprints utterly impossible to describe. They were as baffling as the hordes of great bats which haunted the old manor-house in unprecedented and increasing numbers.

The horror reached a culmination on November 18, when St John, walking home after dark from the dismal railway station, was seized by some frightful carnivorous thing and torn to ribbons. His screams had reached the house, and I had hastened to the terrible scene in time to hear a whir of wings and see a vague black cloudy thing silhouetted against the rising moon.

My friend was dying when I spoke to him, and he could not answer coherently. All he could do was to whisper, "The amulet—that damned thing -"

Then he collapsed, an inert mass of mangled flesh.

I buried him the next midnight in one of our neglected gardens, and mumbled over his body one of the devilish rituals he had loved in life. And as I pronounced the last daemoniac sentence I heard afar on the moor the faint baying of some gigantic hound. The moon was up, but I dared not look at it. And when I saw on the dim-lighted moor a wide-nebulous shadow sweeping from mound to mound, I shut my eyes and threw myself face down upon the ground. When I arose, trembling, I know not how much later, I staggered into the house and made shocking obeisances before the enshrined amulet of green jade.

Being now afraid to live alone in the ancient house on the moor, I departed on the following day for London, taking with me the amulet after destroying by fire and burial the rest of the impious collection in the museum. But after three nights I heard the baying again, and before a week was over felt strange eyes upon me whenever it was dark. One evening as I strolled on Victoria Embankment for some needed air, I saw a black shape obscure one of the reflections of the lamps in the water. A wind, stronger than the night-wind, rushed by, and I knew that what had befallen St John must soon befall me.

The next day I carefully wrapped the green jade amulet and sailed for Holland. What mercy I might gain by returning the thing to its silent, sleeping owner I knew not; but I felt that I must try any step conceivably logical. What the hound was, and why it had pursued me, were questions still vague; but I had first heard the baying in that ancient churchyard, and every subsequent event including St

John's dying whisper had served to connect the curse with the stealing of the amulet. Accordingly I sank into the nethermost abysses of despair when, at an inn in Rotterdam, I discovered that thieves had despoiled me of this sole means of salvation.

The baying was loud that evening, and in the morning I read of a nameless deed in the vilest quarter of the city. The rabble were in terror, for upon an evil tenement had fallen a red death beyond the foulest previous crime of the neighborhood. In a squalid thieves' den an entire family had been torn to shreds by an unknown thing which left no trace, and those around had heard all night a faint, deep, insistent note as of a gigantic hound.

So at last I stood again in the unwholesome churchyard where a pale winter moon cast hideous shadows and leafless trees drooped sullenly to meet the withered, frosty grass and cracking slabs, and the ivied church pointed a jeering finger at the unfriendly sky, and the night-wind howled maniacally from over frozen swamps and frigid seas. The baying was very faint now, and it ceased altogether as I approached the ancient grave I had once violated, and frightened away an abnormally large horde of bats which had been hovering curiously around it.

I know not why I went thither unless to pray, or gibber out insane pleas and apologies to the calm white thing that lay within; but, whatever my reason, I attacked the half frozen sod with a desperation partly mine and partly that of a dominating will outside myself. Excavation was much easier than I expected, though at one point I encountered a queer interruption; when a lean vulture darted down out of the cold sky and pecked frantically at the grave-earth until I killed him with a blow of my spade. Finally I reached the rotting oblong box and removed the damp nitrous cover. This is the last rational act I ever performed.

For crouched within that centuried coffin, embraced by a closepacked nightmare retinue of huge, sinewy, sleeping bats, was the bony thing my friend and I had robbed; not clean and placid as we had seen it then, but covered with caked blood and shreds of alien flesh and hair, and leering sentiently at me with phosphorescent sockets and sharp ensanguined fangs yawning twistedly in mockery of my inevitable doom. And when it gave from those grinning jaws a deep, sardonic bay as of some gigantic hound, and I saw that it held in its gory filthy claw the lost and fateful amulet of green jade, I merely screamed and ran away idiotically, my screams soon dissolving into peals of hysterical laughter.

Madness rides the star-wind . . . claws and teeth sharpened on centuries of corpses . . . dripping death astride a bacchanale of bats from nigh-black ruins of buried temples of Belial . . . Now, as the baying of that dead fleshless monstrosity grows louder and louder, and the stealthy whirring and flapping of those accursed web-wings closer and closer, I shall seek with my revolver the oblivion which is my only refuge from the unnamed and unnameable. ✦

THE BLACK CAT

BY *Edgar Allan Poe*

Edgar Allen Poe was my first horror writer; and after Dr. Seuss, my first literary hero. He was verbally extravagant, imaginatively wild, fiercely intelligent, painfully honest, soulfully poetic, and utterly haunted. Plus, he understood crazy like nobody's business. And he lived and died for his art.

Last year, I saw Jeffrey Combs play Poe, in a stunning one-man show called Nevermore; *and the playwrite, Dennis Paoli, drew 90% of his text from Poe's essays, reviews, personal correspondence, poems, and stories.*

It was a revelation. Having read him so young, I'd never realized how scathingly funny, deeply Southern, and truly enraged he was. Nor had I imagined him going from sober and lucid to roaring drunk and lucid, in the course of an hour.

Which brings us to this masterpiece.

If ever the phrase "that demon liquor" could be readily applied to a short horror tale…

And the weirdest, saddest, funniest thing is, he was probably hammered when he wrote it.

For the most wild, yet most homely narrative which I am about to pen, I neither expect nor solicit belief. Mad indeed would I be to expect it, in a case where my very senses reject their own evidence. Yet, mad am I not—and very surely do I not dream. But to-morrow I die, and to-day I would unburthen my soul. My immediate purpose is to place before the world, plainly, succinctly, and without comment, a series of mere household events. In their consequences, these events have terrified—have tortured—have destroyed me. Yet I will not attempt to expound them. To me, they have presented little but Horror—to many they will seem less terrible than barroques. Hereafter, perhaps, some intellect may be found which will reduce my phantasm to the common-place—some intellect more calm, more logical, and far less excitable than my own, which will perceive, in the circumstances I detail with awe, nothing more than an ordinary succession of very natural causes and effects.

From my infancy I was noted for the docility and humanity of my disposition. My tenderness of heart was even so conspicuous as to make me the jest of my companions. I was especially fond of animals, and was indulged by my parents with a great variety of pets. With these I spent most of my time, and never was so happy as when feeding and caressing them. This peculiarity of character grew with my growth, and in my manhood, I derived from it one of my principal sources of pleasure. To those who have cherished an affection for a faithful and sagacious dog, I need hardly be at the trouble of explaining the nature or the intensity of the gratification thus derivable. There is something in the unselfish and self-sacrificing love of a brute, which goes directly to the heart of him who has had frequent occasion to test the paltry friendship and gossamer fidelity of mere Man.

I married early, and was happy to find in my wife a disposition not uncongenial with my own. Observing my partiality for domestic pets, she lost no opportunity of procuring those of the most agreeable kind. We had birds, gold-fish, a fine dog, rabbits, a small monkey, and a cat.

This latter was a remarkably large and beautiful animal, entirely black, and sagacious to an astonishing degree. In speaking of his intelligence, my wife, who at heart was not a little tinctured with superstition, made frequent allusion to the ancient popular notion, which regarded all black cats as witches in disguise. Not that she was ever serious upon this point—and I mention the matter at all for no better reason than that it happens, just now, to be remembered.

Pluto—this was the cat's name—was my favorite pet and playmate. I alone fed him, and he attended me wherever I went about the house. It was even with difficulty that I could prevent him from following me through the streets.

Our friendship lasted, in this manner, for several years, during which my general temperament and character—through the instrumentality of the Fiend Intemperance—had (I blush to confess it) experienced a radical alteration for the worse. I grew, day by day, more moody, more irritable, more regardless of the feelings of others. I suffered myself to use intemperate language to my wife. At length, I even offered her personal violence. My pets, of course, were made to feel the change in my disposition. I not only neglected, but ill-used them. For Pluto, however, I still retained sufficient regard to restrain me from maltreating him, as I made no scruple of maltreating the rabbits, the monkey, or even the dog, when by accident, or through affection, they came in my way. But my disease grew upon me—for what disease is like Alcohol!—and at length even Pluto, who was now becoming old, and consequently somewhat peevish—even Pluto began to experience the effects of my ill temper.

One night, returning home, much intoxicated, from one of my haunts about town, I fancied that the cat avoided my presence. I seized him; when, in his fright at my violence, he inflicted a slight wound upon my hand with his teeth. The fury of a demon instantly possessed me. I knew myself no longer. My original soul seemed, at once, to take its flight from my body and a more than fiendish malevolence, gin-nurtured, thrilled every fibre of my frame. I took from my waistcoat-pocket a pen-knife, opened it, grasped the poor beast by the throat, and deliberately cut one of its eyes from the socket! I blush, I burn, I shudder, while I pen the damnable atrocity.

When reason returned with the morning—when I had slept off the fumes of the night's debauch—I experienced a sentiment half of horror, half of remorse, for the crime of which I had been guilty; but it was, at best, a feeble and equivocal feeling, and the soul remained untouched. I again plunged into excess, and soon drowned in wine all memory of the deed.

In the meantime the cat slowly recovered. The socket of the lost eye presented, it is true, a frightful appearance, but he no longer appeared to suffer any pain. He went about the house as usual, but, as might be expected, fled in extreme terror at my approach. I had so much of my old heart left, as to be at first grieved by this evident dislike on the part of a creature which had once so loved me. But this feeling soon gave place to irritation. And then came, as if to my final and irrevocable overthrow, the spirit of PERVERSENESS. Of this spirit philosophy takes no account. Yet I am not more sure that my soul lives, than I am that perverseness is one of the primitive impulses of the human heart—one of the indivisible primary faculties, or sentiments, which give direction to the character of Man. Who has not, a hundred times, found himself committing a vile or a silly action, for no other reason than because he knows he should not? Have we not a perpetual inclination, in the teeth of our best judgment, to violate that which is Law merely because we understand it to be such? This spirit of perverseness, I say, came to my final overthrow. It was this unfathomable longing of the soul to vex itself—to offer violence to its own nature—to do wrong for the wrong's sake only—that urged me to continue and finally to consummate the injury I had inflicted upon the unoffending brute. One morning, in cool blood, I slipped a noose about its neck and hung it to the limb of a tree;— hung it with the tears streaming from my eyes, and with the bitterest remorse at my heart;—hung it because I knew that it had loved me, and because I felt it had given me no reason of offence;—hung it because I knew that in so doing I was committing a sin—a deadly sin that would so jeopardize my immortal soul as to place it—if such a thing wore possible—even beyond the reach of the infinite mercy of the Most Merciful and Most Terrible God.

On the night of the day on which this cruel deed was done, I was aroused from sleep by the cry of fire. The curtains of my bed were in flames. The whole house was blazing. It was with great difficulty that my wife, a servant, and myself, made our escape from the conflagration. The destruction was complete. My entire worldly wealth was swallowed up, and I resigned myself thenceforward to despair.

I am above the weakness of seeking to establish a sequence of cause and effect, between the disaster and the atrocity. But I am detailing a chain of facts—and wish not to leave even a possible link imperfect. On the day succeeding the fire, I visited the ruins. The walls, with one exception, had fallen in. This exception was found in a compartment wall, not very thick, which stood about the middle of the house, and against which had rested the head of my bed. The plastering had here, in great measure, resisted the action of the fire—a fact which I attributed to its having been recently spread. About this wall a dense crowd were collected, and many persons seemed to be examining a particular portion of it with very minute and eager attention. The words "strange!" "singular!" and other similar expressions, excited my curiosity. I approached and saw, as if graven in bas relief upon the white surface, the figure of a gigantic cat. The impression was given with an accuracy truly marvellous. There was a rope about the animal's neck.

When I first beheld this apparition—for I could scarcely regard it as less—my wonder and my terror were extreme. But at length reflection came to my aid. The cat, I remembered, had been hung in a garden adjacent to the house. Upon the alarm of fire, this garden had been immediately filled by the crowd—by some one of whom the animal must have been cut from the tree and thrown, through an open window, into my chamber. This had probably been done with the view of arousing me from sleep. The falling of other walls had compressed the victim of my cruelty into the substance of the freshly-spread plaster; the lime of which, with the flames, and the ammonia from the carcass, had then accomplished the portraiture as I saw it.

Although I thus readily accounted to my reason, if not altogether to my conscience, for the startling fact just detailed, it did not the less fail to make a deep impression upon my fancy. For months I could not rid myself of the phantasm of the cat; and, during this period, there came back into my spirit a half-sentiment that seemed, but was not, remorse. I went so far as to regret the loss of the animal, and to look about me, among the vile haunts which I now habitually frequented, for another pet of the same species, and of somewhat similar appearance, with which to supply its place.

One night as I sat, half stupified, in a den of more than infamy, my attention was suddenly drawn to some black object, reposing upon the head of one of the immense hogsheads of Gin, or of Rum, which constituted the chief furniture of the apartment. I had been looking steadily at the top of this hogshead for some minutes, and what now caused me surprise was the fact that I had not sooner perceived the object thereupon. I approached it, and touched it with my hand. It was a black cat—a very large one—fully as large as Pluto, and closely resembling him in every respect but one. Pluto had not a white hair upon any portion of his body; but this cat had a large, although indefinite splotch of white, covering nearly the whole region of the breast. Upon my touching him, he immediately arose, purred loudly, rubbed against my hand, and appeared delighted with my notice. This, then, was the very creature of which I was in search. I at once offered to purchase it of the landlord; but this person made no claim to it—knew nothing of it—had never seen it before.

I continued my caresses, and, when I prepared to go home, the animal evinced a disposition to accompany me. I permitted it to do so; occasionally stooping and patting it as I proceeded. When it reached the house it domesticated itself at once, and became immediately a great favorite with my wife.

For my own part, I soon found a dislike to it arising within me. This was just the reverse of what I had anticipated; but—I know not how or why it was—its evident fondness for myself rather disgusted and annoyed. By slow degrees, these feelings of disgust and annoyance rose into the bitterness of hatred. I avoided the creature; a certain sense of shame, and the remembrance of my former deed of cruelty, preventing me from physically abusing it. I did not, for some weeks, strike, or otherwise violently ill use it; but gradually—very gradually—I came to look upon it with unutterable loathing, and to flee silently from its odious presence, as from the breath of a pestilence.

What added, no doubt, to my hatred of the beast, was the discovery, on the morning after I brought it home, that, like Pluto, it also had been deprived of one of its eyes. This circumstance, however, only endeared it to my wife, who, as I have already said, possessed, in a high degree, that humanity of feeling which had once been my distinguishing trait, and the source of many of my simplest and purest pleasures.

With my aversion to this cat, however, its partiality for myself seemed to increase. It followed my footsteps with a pertinacity which it would be difficult to make the reader comprehend. Whenever I sat, it would crouch beneath my chair, or spring upon my knees, covering me with its loathsome caresses. If I arose to walk it would get between my feet and thus nearly throw me down, or, fastening its long and sharp claws in my dress, clamber, in this manner, to my breast. At such times, although I longed to destroy it with a blow, I was yet withheld from so doing, partly by a memory of my former crime, but chiefly—let me confess it at once—by absolute dread of the beast.

This dread was not exactly a dread of physical evil—and yet I should be at a loss how otherwise to define it. I am almost ashamed to own—yes, even in this felon's cell, I am almost ashamed to own—that the terror and horror with which the animal inspired me, had been heightened by one of the merest chimaeras it would be possible to conceive. My wife had called my attention, more than once, to the character of the mark of white hair, of which I have spoken, and which constituted the sole visible difference between the strange beast and the one I had destroyed. The reader will remember that this mark, although large, had been originally very indefinite; but, by slow degrees—degrees nearly imperceptible, and which for a long time my Reason struggled to reject as fanciful—it had, at length, assumed a rigorous distinctness of outline. It was now the representation of an object that I shudder to name—and for this, above all, I loathed, and dreaded, and would have rid myself of the monster had I dared—it was now, I say, the image of a hideous—of a ghastly thing—of the GALLOWS!—oh, mournful and terrible engine of Horror and of Crime—of Agony and of Death!

And now was I indeed wretched beyond the wretchedness of mere Humanity. And a brute beast—whose fellow I had contemptuously destroyed—a brute beast to work out for me—for me a man, fashioned in the image of the High God—so much of insufferable woe! Alas! neither by day nor by night knew I the blessing of Rest any more! During the former the creature left me no moment alone; and, in the latter, I started, hourly, from dreams of unutterable fear, to find the hot breath of the thing upon my face, and its vast weight—an incarnate Night-Mare that I had no power to shake off—incumbent eternally upon my heart !

Beneath the pressure of torments such as these, the feeble remnant of the good within me succumbed. Evil thoughts became my sole intimates—the darkest and most evil of thoughts. The moodiness of my usual temper increased to hatred of all things and of all mankind; while, from the sudden, frequent, and ungovernable outbursts of a fury to which I now blindly abandoned myself, my uncomplaining wife, alas! was the most usual and the most patient of sufferers.

One day she accompanied me, upon some household errand, into the cellar of the old building which our poverty compelled us to inhabit. The cat followed me down the steep stairs, and, nearly throwing me headlong, exasperated me to madness. Uplifting an axe, and forgetting, in my wrath, the childish dread which had hitherto stayed my hand, I aimed a blow at the animal which, of course, would have proved instantly fatal had it descended as I wished. But this blow was arrested by the hand of my wife. Goaded, by the interference, into a rage more than demoniacal, I withdrew my arm from her grasp and buried the axe in her brain. She fell dead upon the spot, without a groan.

This hideous murder accomplished, I set myself forthwith, and with entire deliberation, to the task of concealing the body. I knew that I could not remove it from the house, either by day or by night, without the risk of being observed by the neighbors. Many projects entered my mind. At one period I thought of cutting the corpse into minute fragments, and destroying them by fire. At another, I resolved to dig a grave for it in the floor of the cellar. Again, I deliberated about casting it in the well in the yard—about packing it in a box, as if merchandize, with the usual arrangements, and so getting a porter to take it from the house. Finally I hit upon what I considered a far better expedient than either of these. I determined to wall it up in the cellar—as the monks of the middle ages are recorded to have walled up their victims.

For a purpose such as this the cellar was well adapted. Its walls were loosely constructed, and had lately been plastered throughout with a rough plaster, which the dampness of the atmosphere had prevented from hardening. Moreover, in one of the walls was a projection, caused by a false chimney, or fireplace, that had been filled up, and made to resemble the red of the cellar. I made no doubt that I could readily displace the bricks at this point, insert the corpse, and wall the whole up as before, so that no eye could detect any thing suspicious. And in this calculation I was not deceived. By means of a crow-bar I easily dislodged the bricks, and, having carefully deposited the body against the inner wall, I propped it in that position, while, with little trouble, I re-laid the whole structure as it originally stood. Having procured mortar, sand, and hair, with every possible precaution, I prepared a plaster which could not be distinguished from the old, and with this I very carefully went over the new brickwork. When I had finished, I felt satisfied that all was right. The wall did not present the slightest appearance of having been disturbed. The rubbish on the floor was picked up with the minutest care. I looked around triumphantly, and said to myself—"Here at least, then, my labor has not been in vain."

My next step was to look for the beast which had been the cause of so much wretchedness; for I had, at length, firmly resolved to put it to death. Had I been able to meet with it, at the moment, there could have been no doubt of its fate; but it appeared that the crafty animal had been alarmed at the violence of my previous anger, and forebore to present itself in my present mood. It is impossible to describe, or to imagine, the deep, the blissful sense of relief which the absence of the detested creature occasioned in my bosom. It did not make its appearance during the night—and thus for one night at least, since its introduction into the house, I soundly and tranquilly slept; aye, slept even with the burden of murder upon my soul!

The second and the third day passed, and still my tormentor came not. Once again I breathed as a freeman. The monster, in terror, had fled the premises forever! I should behold it no more! My happiness was supreme! The guilt of my dark deed disturbed me but little. Some few inquiries had been made, but these had been readily answered. Even a search had been instituted—but of course nothing was to be discovered. I looked upon my future felicity as secured.

Upon the fourth day of the assassination, a party of the police came, very unexpectedly, into the house, and proceeded again to make rigorous investigation of the premises. Secure, however, in the inscrutability of my place of concealment,

I felt no embarrassment whatever. The officers bade me accompany them in their search. They left no nook or corner unexplored. At length, for the third or fourth time, they descended into the cellar. I quivered not in a muscle. My heart beat calmly as that of one who slumbers in innocence. I walked the cellar from end to end. I folded my arms upon my bosom, and roamed easily to and fro. The police were thoroughly satisfied and prepared to depart. The glee at my heart was too strong to be restrained. I burned to say if but one word, by way of triumph, and to render doubly sure their assurance of my guiltlessness.

"Gentlemen," I said at last, as the party ascended the steps, "I delight to have allayed your suspicions. I wish you all health, and a little more courtesy. By the bye, gentlemen, this—this is a very well constructed house." [In the rabid desire to say something easily, I scarcely knew what I uttered at all.]—"I may say an excellently well constructed house. These walls—are you going, gentlemen?— these walls are solidly put together;" and here, through the mere phrenzy of bravado, I rapped heavily, with a cane which I held in my hand, upon that very portion of the brick-work behind which stood the corpse of the wife of my bosom.

But may God shield and deliver me from the fangs of the Arch-Fiend! No sooner had the reverberation of my blows sunk into silence, than I was answered by a voice from within the tomb!—by a cry, at first muffled and broken, like the sobbing of a child, and then quickly swelling into one long, loud, and continuous scream, utterly anomalous and inhuman—a howl—a wailing shriek, half of horror and half of triumph, such as might have arisen only out of hell, conjointly from the throats of the damned in their agony and of the demons that exult in the damnation.

Of my own thoughts it is folly to speak. Swooning, I staggered to the opposite wall. For one instant the party upon the stairs remained motionless, through extremity of terror and of awe. In the next, a dozen stout arms were toiling at the wall. It fell bodily. The corpse, already greatly decayed and clotted with gore, stood erect before the eyes of the spectators. Upon its head, with red extended mouth and solitary eye of fire, sat the hideous beast whose craft had seduced me into murder, and whose informing voice had consigned me to the hangman. I had walled the monster up within the tomb! ✦

THE DEVIL AND DANIEL WEBSTER

BY *Stephen Vincent Benet*

If there's one guy you wanna go into business with, it's Old Nick, the Prince of Darkness. Not only is he a very sharply-dressed fellow, but he's already got the contracts drawn up! And you'd be amazed by how little blood it actually takes to sign on the dotted line.

While we're at it… Faust, Shmaust! All the best deals with the Devil are conducted right here in the U.S. of A.

Case in point: this piece of priceless Americana, which feels so much older than it actually is. In fact, I was stunned to discover it was really first published in 1937, with the film following closely in '41. It just seems like it's been a part of our national folklore forever.

I don't know if this one's still being taught in public schools. If not, I'm more than happy to share this absolute classic, and one of the other most parodied tales in publishing history.

It's a story they tell in the border country, where Massachusetts joins Vermont and New Hampshire.

Yes, Dan'l Webster's dead—or, at least, they buried him. But every time there's a thunderstorm around Marshfield, they say you can hear his rolling voice in the hollows of the sky. And they say that if you go to his grave and speak loud and clear, "Dan'l Webster—Dan'l Webster!" the ground'll begin to shiver and the trees begin to shake. And after a while you'll hear a deep voice saying, "Neighbor, how stands the Union?" Then you better answer the Union stands as she stood, rock bottomed and copper sheathed, one and indivisible, or he's liable to rear right out of the ground. At least, that's what I was told when I was a youngster.

You see, for a while, he was the biggest man in the country. He never got to be President, but he was the biggest man. There were thousands that trusted in him right next to God Almighty, and they told stories about him and all the things that belonged to him that were like the stories of patriarchs and such. They said, when he stood up to speak, stars and stripes came right out in the sky, and once he spoke against a river and made it sink into the ground. They said, when he walked the woods with his fishing rod, Killall, the trout would jump out of the streams right into his pockets, for they knew it was no use putting up a fight against him; and, when he argued a case, he could turn on the harps of the blessed and the shaking of the earth underground. That was the kind of man he was, and his big farm up at Marshfield was suitable to him. The chickens he raised were all white meat down through the drumsticks, the cows were tended like children, and the big ram he called Goliath had horns with a curl like a morning-glory vine and could butt through an iron door. But Dan'l wasn't one of your gentleman farmers; he knew all the ways of the land, and he'd be up by candlelight to see that the chores got done. A man with a mouth like a mastiff, a brow like a mountain and eyes with burning anthracite—that was Dan'l Webster in his prime. And the biggest case he argued never got written down in the books, for he argued it against the devil, nip and tuck and no holds barred. And this is the way I used to hear it told.

There was a man named Jabez Stone, lived at Cross Corners, New Hampshire. He wasn't a bad man to start with, but he was an unlucky man. If he planted corn, he got borers; if he planted potatoes, he got blight. He had good-enough land, but it didn't prosper him; he had a decent wife and children, but the more children he had, the less there was to feed them. If stones cropped up in his neighbor's fields, boulders boiled up in his; if he had a horse with the spavins, he'd trade it for one with the staggers and give something extra. There's some folks bound to be like that, apparently. But one day Jabez Stone got sick of the whole business.

He'd been plowing that morning and he'd just broke the plowshare on a rock that he could have sworn hadn't been there yesterday. And, as he stood looking at the plowshare, the off horse began to cough—that ropy kind of cough that means sickness and horse doctors. There were two children down with the measles, his wife was ailing, and he had a whitlow on his thumb. It was about the last straw for Jabez Stone. "I vow," he said, and he looked around him kind of desperate, "I vow it's enough to make a man want to sell his soul to the devil. And I would, too, for two cents!"

Then he felt a kind of queerness come over him at having said what he'd said; though, naturally, being a New Hampshireman, he wouldn't take it back. But, all the same, when it got to be evening and, as far as he could see, no notice had been taken, he felt relieved in his mind, for he was a religious man. But notice is always taken, sooner or later, just like the Good Book says. And, sure enough, next day, about suppertime, a soft-spoken, dark-dressed stranger drove up in a handsome buggy and asked for Jabez Stone.

Well, Jabez told his family it was a lawyer, come to see him about a legacy. But he knew who it was. He didn't like the looks of the stranger, nor the way he smiled with his teeth. They were white teeth, and plentiful—some say they didn't like it when the dog took one look at the stranger and ran away howling, with his tail between his legs. But having passed the word, more or less, he stuck to it, and they went out behind the barn and made their bargain. Jabez Stone had to prick his finger to sign, and the stranger lent him a silver pin. The wound healed clean, but it left a little white scar.

After that, all of a sudden, things began to pick up and prosper for Jabez Stone. His cows got fat and his horses sleek, his crops were the envy of the neighborhood, and lightning might strike all over the valley, but it wouldn't strike his barn. Pretty soon he was one of the prosperous people of the county; they asked him to stand for selectman, and he stood for it; there began to be talk of running him for state senate. All in all, you might say the Stone family was as happy and contented as cats in a dairy. And so they were, except for Jabez Stone.

He'd been contented enough for the first few years. It's a great thing when bad luck turns; it drives most other things out of your head. True, every now and then, especially in rainy weather, the little white scar on his finger would give him a twinge. And once a year, punctual as clockwork, the stranger with the handsome buggy would come driving by. But the sixth year the stranger lighted, and, after that, his peace was over for Jabez Stone.

The stranger came up through the lower field, switching his boots with a cane—they were handsome black boots, but Jabez Stone never liked the look of them, particularly the toes. And, after he'd passed the time of day, he said, "Well, Mr. Stone, you're a hummer! It's a very pretty property you've got here, Mr. Stone."

"Well, some might favor it and others might not," said Jabez Stone, for he was a New Hampshireman.

"Oh, no need to decry your industry!" said the stranger, very easy, showing his teeth in a smile. "After all, we know what's been done, and it's been according to contract and specifications. So when—ahem—the mortgage falls due next year, you shouldn't have any regrets."

"Speaking of that mortgage, mister," said Jabez Stone, and he looked around for help to the earth and the sky, "I'm beginning to have one or two doubts about it."

"Doubts?" said the stranger not quite so pleasantly.

"Why, yes," said Jabez Stone. "This being the U.S.A. and me always having been a religious man." He cleared his throat and got bolder. "Yes, sir," he said, "I'm beginning to have considerable doubts as to that mortgage holding in court."

"There's courts and courts," said the stranger, clicking his teeth. "Still, we might as well have a look at the original document." And he hauled out a big black pocketbook, full of papers. "Sherwin, Slater, Stevens, Stone," he muttered.

"'I, Jabez Stone, for a term of seven years—' Oh, it's quite in order, I think."

But Jabez Stone wasn't listening, for he saw something else flutter out of the black pocketbook. It was something that looked like a moth, but it wasn't a moth. And as Jabez Stone stared at it, it seemed to speak to him in a small sort of piping voice, terrible small and thin, but terrible human. "Neighbor Stone!" it squeaked, "Neighbor Stone! Help me! For God's sake, help me!"

But before Jabez Stone could stir hand or foot, the stranger whipped out a big bandanna handkerchief, caught the creature in it, just like a butterfly, and started tying up the ends of the bandanna.

"Sorry for the interruption," he said. "As I was saying—"

But Jabez Stone was shaking all over like a scared horse.

"That's Miser Stevens' voice!" he said in a croak. "And you've got him in your handkerchief!"

The stranger looked a little embarrassed.

"Yes, I really should have transferred him to the collecting box," he said with a simper, "but there were some rather unusual specimens there and I don't want them crowded. Well, well, these little contretemps will occur."

"I don't know what you mean by contertan," said Jabez Stone, "but that was Miser Stevens' voice! And he ain't dead! You can't tell me he is! He was just as spry and mean as a woodchuck Tuesday!"

"In the midst of life..." said the stranger, kind of pious. "Listen!" Then a bell began to toll in the valley and Jabez Stone listened, with the sweat running down his face. For he knew it was tolled for Miser Stevens and that he was dead.

"These long-standing accounts," said the stranger with a sigh; "one really hates to close them. But business is business."

He still had the bandanna in his hand, and Jabez Stone felt sick as he saw the cloth struggle and flutter.

"Are they all as small as that?" he asked hoarsely.

"Small?" said the stranger. "Oh, I see what you mean. Why, they vary." He measured Jabez Stone with his eyes, and his teeth showed. "Don't worry, Mr. Stone," he said. "You'll go with a very good grade. I wouldn't trust you outside the collecting box. Now, a man like Dan'l Webster, of course—well, we'd have to build a special box for him, and even at that, I imagine the wing spread would astonish you. He'd certainly be a prize. I wish we could see our way clear to him. But, in your case, as I was saying—"

"Put that handkerchief away!" said Jabez Stone, and he began to beg and to pray. But the best he could get at the end was a three years' extension, with conditions.

But till you make a bargain like that, you've got no idea of how fast four years can run. By the last months of those years Jabez Stone's known all over the state and there's talk of running him for governor—and it's dust and ashes in his mouth. For every day, when he gets up, he thinks, "There's one more night gone," and every night, when he lies down, he thinks of the black pocketbook and the soul of Miser Stevens, and it makes him sick at heart. Till, finally, he can't bear it any longer, and, in the last days of the last year, he hitches up his horse and drives off to seek Dan'l Webster. For Dan'l was born in New Hampshire, only a few miles from Cross Corners, and it's well known that he has a particular soft spot for old neighbors.

It was early in the morning when he got to Marshfield, but Dan'l was up already, talking Latin to the farm hands and wrestling with the ram, Goliath, and trying out a new trotter and working up speeches to make against John C. Calhoun. But when he heard a New Hampshireman had come to see him, he dropped everything else he was doing, for that was Dan'l's way. He gave Jabez Stone a breakfast that five men couldn't eat, went into the living history of every man and woman in Cross Corners, and finally asked him how he could serve him.

Jabez Stone allowed that it was a kind of mortgage case.

"Well, I haven't pleaded a mortgage case in a long time, and I don't generally plead now, except before the Supreme Court," said Dan'l, "but if I can, I'll help you."

"Then I've got hope for the first time in ten years," said Jabez Stone and told him the details.

Dan'l walked up and down as he listened, hands behind his back, now and then asking a question, now and then plunging his eyes at the floor, as if they'd bore through it like gimlets. When Jabez Stone had finished, Dan'l puffed out his cheeks and blew. Then he turned to Jabez Stone and a smile broke over his face like the sunrise over Monadnock.

"You've certainly given yourself the devil's own row to hoe, Neighbor Stone," he said, "but I'll take your case."

"You'll take it?" said Jabez Stone, hardly daring to believe.

"Yes," said Dan'l Webster. "I've got about seventy-five other things to do and the Missouri Compromise to straighten out, but I'll take your case. For if two New Hampshiremen aren't a match for the devil, we might as well give the country back to the Indians."

Then he shook Jabez Stone by the hand and said, "Did you come down here in a hurry?"

"Well, I admit I made time," said Jabez Stone.

"You'll go back faster," said Dan'l Webster, and he told 'em to hitch up Constitution and Constellation to the carriage. They were matched grays with one white forefoot, and they stepped like greased lightning.

Well, I won't describe how excited and pleased the whole Stone family was to have the great Dan'l Webster for a guest, when they finally got there. Jabez Stone had lost his hat on the way, blown off when they overtook a wind, but he didn't take much account of that. But after supper he sent the family off to bed, for he had most particular business with Mr. Webster. Mrs. Stone wanted him to sit in the front parlor, but Dan'l Webster knew front parlors and said he preferred the kitchen. So it was there they sat, waiting for the stranger, with a jug on the table between them and a bright fire on the hearth—the stranger being scheduled to show up on the stroke of midnight, according to specification.

Well, most men wouldn't have asked for better company than Dan'l Webster and a jug. But with every tick of the clock, Jabez Stone got sadder and sadder. His eyes roved round, and though he sampled the jug you could see he couldn't taste it. Finally, on the stroke of 11:30 he reached over and grabbed Dan'l Webster by the arm.

"Mr. Webster, Mr. Webster!" he said, and his voice was shaking with fear and a desperate courage. "For God's sake, Mr. Webster, harness your horses and get away from this place while you can!"

"You've brought me a long way, neighbor, to tell me you don't like my company," said Dan'l Webster, quite peaceable, pulling at the jug.

"Miserable wretch that I am!" groaned Jabez Stone. "I've brought you a devilish way, and now I see my folly. Let him take me if he wills. I don't hanker after it, I must say, but I can stand it. But you're the Union's stay and New

Hampshire's pride! He mustn't get you, Mr. Webster! He mustn't get you!"

Dan'l Webster looked at the distracted man, all gray and shaking in the firelight, and laid a hand on his shoulder.

"I'm obliged to you, Neighbor Stone," he said gently. "It's kindly thought of. But there's a jug on the table and a case in hand. And I never left a jug or a case half finished in my life."

And just at that moment there was a sharp rap on the door.

"Ah," said Dan'l Webster very coolly, "I thought your clock was a trifle slow, Neighbor Stone." He stepped to the door and opened it. "Come in!" he said.

The stranger came in—very dark and tall he looked in the firelight. He was carrying a box under his arm—a black japanned box with little air holes in the lid. At the sight of the box Jabez Stone gave a low cry and shrank into a corner of the room.

"Mr. Webster, I presume," said the stranger, very polite, but with his eyes glowing like a fox's deep in the woods.

"Attorney of record for Jabez Stone," said Dan'l Webster, but his eyes were glowing too. "Might I ask your name?"

"I've gone by a good many," said the stranger carelessly. "Perhaps Scratch will do for the evening. I'm often called that in these regions."

Then he sat down at the table and poured himself a drink from the jug. The liquor was cold in the jug, but it came steaming into the glass.

"And now," said the stranger, smiling and showing his teeth, "I shall call upon you, as a law-abiding citizen, to assist me in taking possession of my property."

Well, with that the argument began—and it went hot and heavy. At first Jabez Stone had a flicker of hope, but when he saw Dan'l Webster being forced back at point after point, he just sat scrunched in his corner, with his eyes on that japanned box. For there wasn't any doubt as to the deed or the signature—that was the worst of it. Dan'l Webster twisted and turned and thumped his fist on the table, but he couldn't get away from that. He offered to compromise the case; the stranger wouldn't hear of it. He pointed out the property had increased in value, and state senators ought to be worth more; the stranger stuck to the letter of the law. He was a great lawyer, Dan'l Webster, but we know who's the King of Lawyers, as the Good Book tells us, and it seemed as if, for the first time, Dan'l Webster had met his match.

Finally, the stranger yawned a little. "Your spirited efforts on behalf of your client do you credit, Mr. Webster," he said, "but if you have no more arguments to adduce, I'm rather pressed for time…" and Jabez Stone shuddered.

Dan'l Webster's brow looked dark as a thundercloud.

"Pressed or not, you shall not have this man!" he thundered. "Mr. Stone is an American citizen, and no American citizen may be forced into the service of a foreign prince. We fought England for that in '12 and we'll fight all hell for it again!"

"Foreign?" said the stranger. "And who calls me a foreigner?"

"Well, I never yet heard of the dev—of your claiming American citizenship," said Dan'l Webster with surprise.

"And who with better right?" said the stranger with one of his terrible smiles. "When the first wrong was done to the first Indian, I was there. When the first slaver put out for the Congo, I stood on her deck. Am I not in your books and stories and beliefs, from the first settlements on? Am I not spoken of still in every church in New England? 'Tis true the North claims me for a Southerner and the South for a Northerner, but I am neither. I am merely an honest American like yourself—and of the best descent—for, to tell the truth, Mr. Webster, though I don't like to boast of it, my name is older in this country than yours."

"Aha!" said Dan'l Webster with the veins standing out in his forehead. "Then I stand on the Constitution! I demand a trial for my client!"

"The case is hardly one for an ordinary court," said the stranger, his eyes flickering. "And, indeed, the lateness of the hour—"

"Let it be any court you choose, so it is an American judge and an American jury!" said Dan'l Webster in his pride. "Let it be the quick or the dead; I'll abide the issue!"

"You have said it," said the stranger, and pointed his finger at the door. And with that, and all of a sudden, there was a rushing of wind outside and a noise of footsteps. They came, clear and distinct, through the night. And yet they were not like the footsteps of living men.

"In God's name, who comes by so late?" cried Jabez Stone in an ague of fear.

"The jury Mr. Webster demands," said the stranger, sipping at his boiling glass. "You must pardon the rough appearances of one or two; they will have come a long way."

And with that the fire burned blue and the door blew open and twelve men entered, one by one.

If Jabez Stone had been sick with terror before, he was blind with terror now. For there was Walter Butler, the loyalist, who spread fire and horror through the Mohawk Valley in the times of the Revolution; and there was Simon Girty, the renegade, who saw white men burned at the stake and whooped with the Indians to see them burn. His eyes were green, like a catamount's, and the stains on his hunting shirt did not come from the blood of the deer. King Philip was there, wild and proud as he had been in life, with the great gash in his head that gave him his death wound, and cruel Governor Dale, who broke men on the wheel. There was Morton of Merry Mount, who so vexed the Plymouth Colony, with his flushed, loose, handsome face and his hate of the godly. There was Teach, the bloody pirate, with his black beard curling on his breast. The Reverend John Smeet, with his strangler's hands and his Geneva gown, walked as daintily as he had to the gallows. The red print of the rope was still around his neck, but he carried a perfumed handkerchief in one hand. One and all, they came into the room with the fires of hell still upon them, and the stranger named their names and their deeds as they came, till the tale of twelve was told. Yet the stranger had told the truth—they had all played a part in America.

"Are you satisfied with the jury, Mr. Webster?" said the stranger mockingly, when they had taken their places.

The sweat stood upon Dan'l Webster's brow, but his voice was clear.

"Quite satisfied," he said. "Though I miss General Arnold from the company."

"Benedict Arnold is engaged upon other business," said the stranger with a glower. "Ah, you asked for a justice, I believe."

He pointed his finger once more, and a tall man, soberly clad in Puritan garb, with the burning gaze of the fanatic, stalked into the room and took his judge's place.

"Justice Hathorne is a jurist of experience," said the stranger. "He presided at certain witch trials once held in Salem. There were others who repented of the business later, but not he."

"Repent of such notable wonders and undertakings?" said the stern old justice. "Nay, hang them—hang them all!" And he muttered to himself in a way that struck ice into the soul of Jabez Stone.

THE DEVIL AND DANIEL WEBSTER

Then the trial began, and, as you might expect, it didn't look anyways good for the defense. And Jabez Stone didn't make much of a witness in his own behalf. He took one look at Simon Girty and screeched, and they had to put him back in his corner in a kind of swoon.

It didn't halt the trial though; the trial went on, as trials do. Dan'l Webster had faced some hard juries and hanging judges in his time, but this was the hardest he'd ever faced, and he knew it. They sat there with a kind of glitter in their eyes, and the stranger's smooth voice went on and on. Every time he'd raise an objection, it'd be "Objection sustained," but whenever Dan'l objected, it'd be "Objection denied." Well, you couldn't expect fair play from a fellow like this Mr. Scratch.

It got to Dan'l in the end, and he began to heat, like iron in the forge. When he got up to speak he was going to flay that stranger with every trick known to the law, and the judge and jury too. He didn't care if it was contempt of court or what would happen to him for it. He didn't care any more what happened to Jabez Stone. He just got madder and madder, thinking of what he'd say. And yet, curiously enough, the more he thought about it, the less he was able to arrange his speech in his mind.

Till, finally, it was time for him to get up on his feet, and he did so, all ready to bust out with lightnings and denunciations. But before he started he looked over the judge and jury for a moment, such being his custom. And he noticed the glitter in their eyes was twice as strong as before, and they all leaned forward. Like hounds just before they get the fox, they looked, and the blue mist of evil in the room thickened as he watched them. Then he saw what he'd been about to do, and he wiped his forehead, as a man might who's just escaped falling into a pit in the dark.

For it was him they'd come for, not only Jabez Stone. He read it in the glitter of their eyes and in the way the stranger hid his mouth with one hand. And if he fought them with their own weapons, he'd fall into their power; he knew that, though he couldn't have told you how. It was his own anger and horror that burned in their eyes; and he'd have to wipe that out or the case was lost. He stood there for a moment, his black eyes burning like anthracite. And then he began to speak.

He started off in a low voice, though you could hear every word. They say he could call on the harps of the blessed when he chose. And this was just as simple and easy as a man could talk. But he didn't start out by condemning or reviling. He was talking about the things that make a country a country and a man a man.

And he began with the simple things that everybody's known and felt—the freshness of a fine morning when you're young, and the taste of food when you're hungry, and the new day that's every day when you're a child. He took them up and he turned them in his hands. They were good things for any man. But without freedom they sickened. And when he talked of those enslaved, and the sorrows of slavery, his voice got like a big bell. He talked of the early days of America and the men who had made those days. It wasn't a spread-eagle speech, but he made you see it. He admitted all the wrong that had ever been done. But he showed how, out of the wrong and the right, the suffering and the starvations, something new had come. And everybody had played a part in it, even the traitors.

Then he turned to Jabez Stone and showed him as he was—an ordinary man who'd had hard luck and wanted to change it. And, because he'd wanted to change it, now he was going to be punished for all eternity. And yet there was good in Jabez Stone, and he showed that good. He was hard and mean, in some ways, but he was a man. There was sadness in being a man, but it was a proud thing too. And he showed what the pride of it was till you couldn't help feeling it. Yes, even in hell, if a man was a man, you'd know it. And he wasn't pleading for any one person any more, though his voice rang like an organ. He was telling the story and the failures and the endless journey of mankind. They got tricked and trapped and bamboozled, but it was a great journey. And no demon that was ever foaled could know the inwardness of it—it took a man to do that.

The fire began to die on the hearth and the wind before morning to blow. The light was getting gray in the room when Dan'l Webster finished. And his words came back at the end to New Hampshire ground, and the one spot of land that each man loves and clings to. He painted a picture of that, and to each one of that jury he spoke of things long forgotten. For his voice could search the heart, and that was his gift and his strength. And to one his voice was like the forest and its secrecy, and to another like the sea and the storms of the sea; and one heard the cry of his lost nation in it, and another saw a little harmless scene he hadn't remembered for years. But each saw something. And when Dan'l Webster finished he didn't know whether or not he'd saved Jabez Stone. But he knew he'd done a miracle. For the glitter was gone from the eyes of judge and jury, and, for the moment, they were men again, and knew they were men.

"The defense rests," said Dan'l Webster and stood there like a mountain. His ears were still ringing with his speech, and he didn't hear anything else till he heard Judge Hathorne say, "The jury will retire to consider its verdict."

Walter Butler rose in his place and his face had a dark, gay pride on it. "The jury has considered its verdict," he said and looked the stranger full in the eye. "We find for the defendant, Jabez Stone."

With that, the smile left the stranger's face, but Walter Butler did not flinch. "Perhaps 'tis not strictly in accordance with the evidence," he said, "but even the damned may salute the eloquence of Mr. Webster."

With that, the long crow of a rooster split the gray morning sky, and judge and jury were gone from the room like a puff of smoke, as if they had never been there. The stranger returned to Dan'l Webster, smiling wryly.

"Major Butler was always a bold man," he said. "I had not thought him quite so bold. Nevertheless, my congratulations, as between two gentlemen."

"I'll have that paper first, if you please," said Dan'l Webster, and he took it and tore it into four pieces. It was queerly warm to the touch. "And now," he said, "I'll have you!" and his hand came down like a bear trap on the stranger's arm. For he knew that once you bested anybody like Mr. Scratch in fair fight, his power on you was gone. And he could see that Mr. Scratch knew it too.

The stranger twisted and wriggled, but he couldn't get out of that grip. "Come, come, Mr. Webster," he said, smiling palely. "This sort of thing is ridic—ouch!—is ridiculous. If you're worried about the costs of the case, naturally, I'd be glad to pay—"

"And so you shall!" said Dan'l Webster, shaking him till his teeth rattled. "For you'll sit right down at that table and draw up a document, promising never to bother Jabez Stone nor his heirs or assigns nor any other New Hampshireman till doomsday! For any hades we want to raise in this state, we can raise ourselves, without assistance from strangers."

"Ouch!" said the stranger. "Ouch! Well, they never did run very big to the barrel, but—ouch!—I agree!"

So he sat down and drew up the document. But Dan'l Webster kept his hand on his coat collar all the time.

"And now may I go?" said the stranger, quite humble, when Dan'l'd seen the documents in proper and legal form.

"Go?" said Dan'l, giving him another shake. "I'm still trying to figure out what I'll do with you. For you've settled the costs of the case, but you haven't settled with me. I think I'll take you back to Marshfield," he said, kind of reflective. "I've got a ram there named Goliath that can butt through an iron door. I'd kind of like to turn you loose in his field and see what he'd do."

Well, with that the stranger began to beg and to plead. And he begged and he pled so humble that finally Dan'l, who was naturally kindhearted, agreed to let him go. The stranger seemed terrible grateful for that and said, just to show they were friends, he'd tell Dan'l's fortune before leaving. So Dan'l agreed to that, though he didn't take much stock in fortune-tellers ordinarily. But, naturally, the stranger was a little different.

Well, he pried and he peered at the lines in Dan'l's hands. And he told him one thing and another that was quite remarkable. But they were all in the past.

"Yes, all that's true, and it happened," said Dan'l Webster. "But what's to come in the future?"

The stranger grinned, kind of happily, and shook his head.

"The future's not as you think it," he said. "It's dark. You have a great ambition, Mr. Webster."

"I have," said Dan'l firmly, for everybody knew he wanted to be President.

"It seems almost within your grasp," said the stranger, "but you will not attain it. Lesser men will be made President and you will be passed over."

"And, if I am, I'll still be Daniel Webster," said Dan'l. "Say on."

"You have two strong sons," said the stranger, shaking his head. "You look to found a line. But each will die in war and neither reach greatness."

"Live or die, they are still my sons," said Dan'l Webster. "Say on."

"You have made great speeches," said the stranger. "You will make more."

"Ah," said Dan'l Webster.

"But the last great speech you make will turn many of your own against you," said the stranger. "They will call you Ichabod; they will call you by other names. Even in New England some will say you have turned your coat and sold your country, and their voices will be loud against you till you die."

"So it is an honest speech, it does not matter what men say," said Dan'l Webster. Then he looked at the stranger and their glances locked.

"One question," he said. "I have fought for the Union all my life. Will I see that fight won against those who would tear it apart?"

"Not while you live," said the stranger grimly, "but it will be won. And after you are dead, there are thousands who will fight for your cause, because of words that you spoke."

"Why, then, you long-barreled, slab-sided, lantern-jawed, fortune-telling note shaver," said Dan'l Webster with a great roar of laughter, "be off with you to your own place before I put my mark on you! For, by the thirteen original colonies, I'd go to the Pit itself to save the Union!"

And with that he drew back his foot for a kick that would have stunned a horse. It was only the tip of his shoe that caught the stranger, but he went flying out of the door with his collecting box under his arm.

"And now," said Dan'l Webster, seeing Jabez Stone beginning to rouse from his swoon, "let's see what's left in the jug, for it's dry work talking all night. I hope there's pie for breakfast, Neighbor Stone."

But they say that whenever the devil comes near Marshfield, even now, he gives it a wide berth. And he hasn't been seen in the state of New Hampshire from that day to this.

I'm not talking about Massachusetts or Vermont. ✦

NELLTHU

BY *Anthony Boucher*

In the 1950s and 60s, there was a boom in urbane, smart-alecky "deal with the Devil" stories, mostly from crime writers, mostly involving sleazy lowlife schemers roughly half as clever as they thought they were, making foolproof bargains that always blew up in their faces with a cunning, snappy last-minute twist.

Anthony Boucher was one of those guys—a hugely influential writer and editor of mystery and science fiction, who gave as good as he brought—but "Nellthu" stands out from the pack in several intriguing ways.

None of which I'm going to tell you.

Enjoy.

Ailsa had been easily the homeliest and the least talented girl in the University, if also the most logical and level-headed. Now, almost twenty-five years later, she was the most attractive woman Martin had ever seen and, to judge from their surroundings, by some lengths the richest.

"...so lucky running into you again after all these years," she was saying, in that indescribably aphrodisiac voice. "You know about publishers, and you can advise me on this novel. I was getting so tired of the piano...."

Martin had heard her piano recordings and knew they were superb—as the vocal recordings had been before them and the non-representational paintings before them and the fashion signs and that astonishing paper on prime numbers. He also knew that the income from all these together could hardly have furnished the Silver Room in which they dined or the Gold Room in which he later read the novel (which was of course superb) or the room whose color he never noticed because he did not sleep alone (and the word superb is inadequate).

There was only one answer, and Martin was gratified to observe that the coffee-bringing servant cast no shadow in the morning sun. While Ailsa still slept (superbly), Martin said, "So you're a demon."

"Naturally, sir," the unshadowed servant said, his eyes adoringly upon the sleeper. "Nellthu, at your service."

"But such service! I can imagine Ailsa-that-was working out a good spell and even wishing logically. But I thought you fellows were limited in what you could grant."

"We are, sir. Three wishes."

"But she has wealth, beauty, youth, fame, a remarkable variety of talents—all on three wishes?"

"On one, sir. Oh, I foxed her prettily on the first two." Nellthu smiled reminiscently. 'Beauty'—but she didn't specify, and I made her the most beautiful centenarian in the world. 'Wealth beyond the dreams of avarice'—and of course nothing is beyond such dreams, and nothing she got. Ah, I was in form that day, sir! But the third wish..."

"Don't tell me she tried the old 'For my third wish I want three more wishes!' I thought that was illegal."

"It is, sir. The paradoxes involved go beyond even our powers.

"No, sir," said Nellthu, with a sort of rueful admiration, "her third wish was stronger than that. She said: 'I wish that you fall permanently and unselfishly in love with me.'"

"She was always logical," Martin admitted. "So for your own sake you had to make her beautiful and…adept, and since then you have been compelled to gratify her every—" He broke off and looked from the bed to the demon. "How lucky for me that she included unselfishly!"

"Yes, sir," said Nellthu. ◆

THE HOWLING MAN

BY *Charles Beaumont*

Charles Beaumont is another guy, like Poe, who died tragically young, but has gone on to be worshiped by those in the know. If anything, poor Poe wished he had a cadre of close friends so supportive and inspired by his presence and his gifts.

Odds are good that you first experienced this tale as a legendary Twilight Zone episode. Frankly, one of the best. And it would be sad, if not uncommon, for you to know him primarily for that, and his work on Rod Serling's seminal show.

But it's in the quality and character of his prose that you can see how seriously goddam talented he was.

Ladies and gentlemen, "The Howling Man."

The Germany of that time was a land of valleys and mountains and swift dark rivers, a green and fertile land where everything grew tall and straight out of the earth. There was no other country like it. Stepping across the border from Belgium, where the rain-caped, mustached guards saluted, grinning, like operetta soldiers, you entered a different world entirely. Here the grass became as rich and smooth as velvet; deep, thick woods appeared; the air itself, which had been heavy with the French perfume of wines and sauces, changed: the clean, fresh smell of lakes and pines and boulders came into your lungs. You stood a moment, then, at the border, watching the circling hawks above and wondering, a little fearfully, how such a thing could happen. In less than a minute you had passed from a musty, ancient room, through an invisible door, into a kingdom of winds and light. Unbelievable! But there, at your heels, clearly in view, is Belgium, like all the rest of Europe, a faded tapestry from some forgotten mansion.

In that time, before I had heard of St. Wulfran's, of the wretch who clawed the stones of a locked cell, wailing in the midnight hours, or of the daft Brothers and their mad Abbott, I had strong legs and a mind on its last search, and I preferred to be alone. A while and I'll come back to this spot. We will ride and feel the sickness, fall, and hover on the edge of death, together. But I am not a writer, only one who loves wild, unhousebroken words; I must have a real beginning.

Paris beckoned in my youth. I heeded, for the reason most young men just out of college heed, although would never admit it: to lie with mysterious women. A solid, traditional upbringing among the corseted ruins of Boston had succeeded, as such upbringings generally do, in honing the urge to a keen edge. My nightly dreams of beaded bagnios and dusky writhing houris, skilled beyond imagining, reached, finally, the unbearable stage beyond which lies either madness or respectability. Fancying neither, I managed to convince my parents that a year abroad would add exactly the right amount of seasoning to my maturity, like a dash of curry in an otherwise bland, if not altogether tasteless, chowder. I'm afraid that Father caught the hot glint in my eye, but he was kind. Describing, in detail, and with immense effect, the hideous consequences of profligacy, telling of men he knew who'd gone to Europe, innocently, and fallen into dissolutions so profound they'd not been heard of since, he begged me at all times to remember that I was an Ellington and turned me loose. Paris, of course, was enchanting and terrifying, as a jungle must be to a zoo-born monkey. Out of respect to the honored dead, and Dad, I did a quick trot through the Tuileries, the Louvre, and down the Champs Elysees to the Arc de Triomphe; then, with the fall of night, I cannoned off to Montmartre and the Rue Pigalle, embarking on the Grand Adventure. Synoptically, it did not prove to be so grand as I'd imagined; nor was it, after the fourth week, so terribly adventurous. Still: important to what followed, for what followed doubtless wouldn't have but for the sweet complaisant girls.

Boston's Straights and Narrows don't, I fear, prepare one—except psychologically—for the Wild Life. My health broke in due course and, as my thirst had been well and truly slaked, I was not awfully discontent to sink back into the contemplative cocoon to which I was, apparently more suited. Abed for a month I lay, in celibate silence and almost total inactivity. Then, no doubt as a final gesture of rebellion, I got my idea—got? or had my concentrated sins received it, like a signal from a failing tower?—and I made my strange, un-Ellingtonian decision. I would explore Europe. But not as tourist, safe and fat in his fat, safe bus, insulated against the beauty and the ugliness of changing cultures by a pane of glass and a room at the English-speaking hotel. No. I would go like an unprotected wind, a seven-league-booted leaf, a nestless bird, and I would see this dark strange land with the vision of a boy on the last legs of his dreams. I would go by bicycle, poor and lonely and questing—as poor and lonely and questing, anyway, as one can be with a hundred thousand in the bank and a partnership in Ellington, Carruthers & Blake waiting.

So it was. New England blood and muscles wilted on that first day's pumping, but New England spirit toughened as the miles dropped back. Like an ant crawling over a once lovely, now decayed and somewhat seedy Duchess, I rode over the body of Europe. I dined at restaurants where boar's heads hung, all vicious-tusked and blind; I slept at country inns and breathed the musty age, and sometimes girls came to the door and knocked and asked if I had everything I needed ("Well…") and they were better than the girls in Paris, though I can't imagine why. No matter.

Out of France I pedaled, into Belgium, out, and to the place of cows and forest, mountains, brooks and laughing people: Germany. (I've rhapsodized on purpose for I feel it's quite important to remember how completely Paradisical the land was then, at that time.)

I looked odd, standing there. The border guard asked what was loose with me, I answered Nothing—grateful for the German, and the French, Miss Finch had drummed into me—and set off along the smallest, darkest path. I serpentined through forests, cities, towns, villages, and always I followed its least likely appendages. Unreasonably I pedaled as if toward a destination: into the Moselle Valley country, up into the desolate hills of emerald.

By a ferry, fallen to desuetude, the reptile drew me through a bosky wood. The trees closed in at once. I drank the fragrant air and pumped and kept on pumping, but a heat began to grow inside my body. My head began to ache. I felt weak. Two more miles and I was obliged to stop, for perspiration filmed my skin. You know the signs of pneumonia: a sapping of the strength, a trembling, flashes of heat and of cold; visions. I lay in the bed of damp leaves for a time. At last a village came to view. A thirteenth-century village, gray and narrow-streeted, cobbled to the hidden store fronts. A number of old people in peasant costumes looked up as I bumped along and I recall one ancient tallow-colored fellow—nothing more. Only the weakness, like acid, burning off my nerves and muscles. And an intervening blackness to pillow my fall.

I awoke to the smells of urine and hay. The fever had passed, but my arms and legs lay heavy as logs, my head throbbed horribly, and there was an empty shoveled-out hole inside my stomach somewhere. For a while I did not move or open my eyes. Breathing was a major effort. But consciousness came, eventually.

I was in a tiny room. The walls and ceiling were of rough gray stone, the single glassless window was arch-shaped, the floor was uncombed dirt. My bed was not a bed at all but a blanket thrown across a disorderly pile of crinkly straw. Beside me, a crude table; upon it, a pitcher; beneath it, a bucket. Next to the table, a stool. And seated there, asleep, his tonsured head adangle from an Everest of robe, a monk. I must have groaned, for the shorn pate bobbed up precipitately. Two silver trails gleamed down the corners of the suddenly exposed mouth, which drooped into a frown. The slumbrous eyes blinked.

"It is God's infinite mercy," sighed the gnomelike little man. "You have recovered."

"Not as yet," I told him. Unsuccessfully, I tried to remember what had happened; then I asked questions.

"I am Brother Christophorus. This is the Abbey of St. Wulfran's. The Burgemeister of Schwartzhof, Herr Barth, brought you to us nine days ago. Father Jerome said that you would die and he sent me to watch, for I have never seen a man die, and Father Jerome holds that it is beneficial for a Brother to have seen a man die. But now I suppose that you will not die." He shook his head ruefully.

"Your disappointment," I said, "cuts me to the quick. However, don't abandon hope. The way I feel now, it's touch and go."

"No," said Brother Christophorus sadly. "You will get well. It will take time. But you will get well."

"Such ingratitude, and after all you've done. How can I express my apologies?"

He blinked again. With the innocence of a child, he said, "I beg your pardon?"

"Nothing." I grumbled about blankets, a fire, some food to eat, and then slipped back into the well of sleep. A fever dream of forests, full of giant two-headed beasts came, then the sound of screaming.

I awoke. The scream shrilled on—Klaxon-loud, high, cutting, like a cry for help.

"What is that sound?" I asked.

The monk smiled. "Sound? I hear no sound," he said.

It stopped. I nodded. "Dreaming. Probably I'll hear a good deal more before I'm through. I shouldn't have left Paris in such poor condition."

"No," he said. "You shouldn't have left Paris."

Kindly now, resigned to my recovery, Brother Christophorus became attentive to a fault. Nurselike, he spooned thick soups into me, applied compresses, chanted soothing prayers, and emptied the bucket out the window. Time passed slowly. As I fought the sickness, the dreams grew less vivid—but the nightly cries did not diminish. They were as full of terror and loneliness as before, strong, real in my ears. I tried to shut them out, but they would not be shut out. Still, how could they be strong and real except in my vanishing delirium? Brother Christophorus did not hear them. I watched him closely when the sunlight faded to the gray of dusk and the screams began, but he was deaf to them—if they existed. If they existed!

"Be still, my son. It is the fever that makes you hear these noises. That is quite natural. Is that not quite natural? Sleep."

"But the fever is gone! I'm sitting up now. Listen! Do you mean to tell me you don't hear that?"

"I hear only you, my son."

The screams, that fourteenth night, continued until dawn. They were totally unlike any sounds in my experience. Impossible to believe they could be uttered and sustained by a human, yet they did not seem to be animal. I listened, there in the gloom, my hands balled into fists, and knew, suddenly, that one of two things must be true. Either someone, or something was making these ghastly sounds, and Brother Christophorus was lying, or—I was going mad. Hearing-voices mad, climbing-walls and frothing mad. I'd have to find the answer: that I knew. And by myself.

I listened with a new ear to the howls. Razoring under the door, they rose to operatic pitch, subsided, resumed, like the cries of a surly, hysterical child. To test their reality, I hummed beneath my breath, I covered my head with a blanketing, scratched at the straw, coughed. No difference. The quality of substance, of existence, was there.

I tried, then, to localize the screams; and, on the fifteenth night, felt sure that they were coming from a spot not far along the hall.

"The sounds that maniacs hear seem quite real to them."

I know. I know!

The monk was by my side, he had not left it from the start, keeping steady vigil even through Matins. He joined his tremulous soprano to the distant chants, and prayed excessively. But nothing could tempt him away. The food we ate was brought to us, as were all other needs. I'd see the Abbot, Father Jerome, once I was recovered. Meanwhile...

"I'm feeling better, Brother. Perhaps you'd care to show me the grounds. I've seen nothing of St. Wulfran's except this little room."

"There is only this little room multiplied. Ours is a rigorous order. The Franciscans, now, they permit themselves esthetic pleasure; we do not. It is, for us, a luxury. We have a single, most unusual job. There is nothing to see."

"But surely the Abbey is very old."

"Yes, that is true."

"As an antiquarian—"

"Mr. Ellington—"

"What is it you don't want me to see? What are you afraid of, Brother?"

"Mr. Ellington? I do not have the authority to grant your request. When you are well enough to leave, Father Jerome will no doubt be happy to accommodate you."

"Will he also be happy to explain the screams I've heard each night since I've been here?"

"Rest, my son. Rest."

The unholy, hackle-raising shriek burst loose and bounded off the hard stone walls. Brother Christophorus crossed himself, apropros of nothing, and sat like an ancient Indian on the weary stool. I knew he liked me. Especially, perhaps. We'd got along quite well in all our talks, but this—*verboten*.

I closed my eyes. I counted to three hundred. I opened my eyes.

The good monk was asleep. I blasphemed, softly, but he did not stir, so I swung my legs over the side of the straw bed and made my way across the dirt floor to the heavy door. I rested there a time, in the candleless dark, listening to the howls; then, with Bostonian discretion, raised the bolt. The rusted hinges creaked, but Brother Christophorus was deep in celestial marble: his head drooped low upon his chest.

Panting, weak as a landlocked fish, I stumbled out into the corridor. The screams became impossibly loud. I put my hands to my ears, instinctively, and wondered how anyone could sleep with such a furor going on. It was a furor. In my mind? No. Real. The monastery shook with these shrill cries. You could feel their realness with your teeth.

I passed a Brother's cell and listened, then another; then I paused. A thick door, made of oak or pine, was locked before me. Behind it were the screams.

A chill went through me on the edge of those unutterable shrieks of hopeless, helpless anguish, and for a moment I considered turning back—not to my room, not to my bed of straw, but back into the open world. But duty held me. I took a breath and walked up to the narrow bar-crossed window and looked in.

A man was in the cell. On all fours, circling like a beast, his head thrown back, a man. The moonlight showed his face. It cannot be described—not, at least, by me. A man past death might look like this, a victim of the Inquisition rack, the stake, the pincers: not a human in the third decade of the twentieth century. Surely. I had never seen such suffering within two eyes, such lost, mad suffering. Naked, he crawled about the dirt, cried, leaped up to his feet and clawed the hard stone walls in fury.

Then he saw me.

The screaming ceased. He huddled, blinking, in the corner of his cell. And then, as though unsure of what he saw, he walked right to the door.

In German, hissing: "Who are you?"

"David Ellington," I said. "Are you locked in? Why have they locked you in?"

He shook his head. "Be still, be still. You are not German?"

"No." I told him how I came to be at St. Wulfran's.

"Ah!" Trembling, his horny fingers closing on the bars, the naked man said: "Listen to me, we have only moments. They are mad. You hear? All mad. I was in the village, lying with my woman, when their crazy Abbot burst into the house and hit me with his heavy cross. I woke up here. They flogged me. I asked for food, they would not give it to me. They took my clothes. They threw me in this filthy room. They locked the door."

"Why?"

"Why?" He moaned. "I wish I knew. That's been the worst of it. Five years imprisoned, beaten, tortured, starved, and not a reason given, not a word to guess from—Mr. Ellington! I have sinned; but who has not? With my woman, quietly, alone with my woman, my love. And this God-drunk lunatic, Jerome, cannot stand it. Help me!"

His breath splashed on my face. I took a backward step and tried to think. I couldn't quite believe that in this century a thing so frightening could happen. Yet, the Abbey was secluded, above the world, timeless. What could not transpire here, secretly?

"I'll speak to the Abbot."

"No! I tell you, he's the maddest of them all. Say nothing to him."

"Then how can I help you?"

He pressed his mouth against the bars. "In one way only. Around Jerome's neck, there is a key. It fits this lock. If—"

"Mr. Ellington!"

I turned and faced a fierce El Greco painting of a man. White-bearded, prow-nosed, regal as an Emperor beneath the gray peaked robe, he came out of the darkness.

"Mr. Ellington, I did not know that you were well enough to walk. Come with me, please."

The naked man began to weep hysterically. I felt a grip of steel about my arm. Through corridors, past snore-filled cells, the echoes of the weeping dying, we continued to a room.

"I must ask you to leave St. Wulfran's," the Abbot said. "We lack the proper facilities for care of the ill. Arrangements will be made in Schwartzhof—"

"One moment," I said. "While it's probably true that Brother Christophorus's ministrations saved my life—and certainly true that I owe you all a debt of gratitude—I've got to ask for an explanation of that man in the cell."

"What man?" the Abbot said softly.

"The one we just left, the one who's screamed all night long every night."

"No man has been screaming, Mr. Ellington."

Feeling suddenly very weak, I sat down and rested a few breaths' worth. Then I said, "Father Jerome—you are he? I am not necessarily an irreligious person, but neither could I be considered particularly religious. I know nothing of monasteries, what is permitted, what isn't. But I seriously doubt you have the authority to imprison a man against his will."

"This is quite true. We have no such authority."

"Then why have you done so?"

The Abbot looked at me steadily. In a firm, inflexible voice, he said: "No man has been imprisoned at St. Wulfran's."

"He claims otherwise."

"Who claims otherwise?"

"The man in the cell at the end of the corridor."

"There is no man in the cell at the end of the corridor."

'I was talking with him!"

"You were talking with no man." The conviction in his voice shocked me into momentary silence. I gripped the arms of the chair.

"You are ill, Mr. Ellington," the bearded holy man said. "You have suffered from delirium. You have heard and seen things which do not exist."

"That's true," I said. "But the man in the cell—whose voice I can hear now!— is not one of those things."

The Abbot shrugged. "Dreams can seem very real, my son…"

I glanced at the leather thong about his turkey-gobbler neck, all but hidden beneath the beard. "Honest men make unconvincing liars," I lied convincingly. "Brother Christophorus has a way of looking at the floor whenever he denies the cries in the night. You look at me, but your voice loses its command. I can't imagine why, but you are both very intent upon keeping me away from the truth. Which is not only poor Christianity, but also poor psychology. For now I am quite curious indeed. You might as well tell me, Father; I'll find out eventually."

"What do you mean?"

"Only that. I'm sure the police will be interested to hear of a man imprisoned at the Abbey."

"I tell you, there is no man!"

"Very well. Let's forget the matter."

"Mr. Ellington—" The Abbot put his hands behind him. "The person in the cell is, ah, one of the Brothers. Yes. He is subject to…seizures, fits. You know fits? At these times, he becomes intractable. Violent. Dangerous! We're obliged to lock him in his cell, which you can surely understand."

"I understand," I said, "that you're still lying to me. If the answer were as simple as that, you'd not have gone through the elaborate business of pretending

I was delirious. There'd have been no need. There's something more to it, but I can wait. Shall we go on to Schwartzof?"

Father Jerome tugged at his beard viciously, as if it were some feathered demon come to taunt him. "Would you truly go to the police?" he asked.

"Would you?" I said. "In my position?"

He considered that for a long time, tugging, the nodding, the prowed head; and the screams went on, so distant, so real. I thought of the naked man clawing in filth.

"Well, Father?"

"Mr. Ellington, I see that I shall have to be honest with you—which is a great pity," he said. "Had I followed my original instinct and refused to allow you in the Abbey to begin with…but, I had no choice. You were near death. No physician was available. You would have perished. Still, perhaps that would have been better."

"My recovery seems to have disappointed a lot of people," I commented. "I assure you it was inadvertent."

The old man took no notice of this remark. Stuffing his mandarin hands into the sleeves of his robe, he spoke with great deliberation. "When I said that there was no man in the cell at the end of the corridor, I was telling the truth. Sit down, sir! Please! Now." He closed his eyes. "There is much to the story, much that you will not understand or believe. You are sophisticated, or feel that you are. You regard our life here, no doubt, as primitive—"

"In fact, I—"

"In fact, you do. I know the current theories. Monks are misfits, neurotics, sexual frustrates, and aberrants. They retreat from the world because they cannot cope with the world. Et cetera. You are surprised I know these things? My son, I was told by the one who began the theories!" He raised his head upward, revealing more of the leather thong. "Five years ago, Mr. Ellington, there were no screams at St. Wulfran's. This was an undistinguished little Abbey in the wild Black Mountain region, and its inmates' job was quite simply to serve God, to save what souls they could by constant prayer. At that time, not very long after the great war, the world was in chaos. Schwartzhof was not the happy village you see now. It was, my son, a resort for the sinful, a hive of vice and corruption, a pit for the unwary—

and the wary also, if they had not strength. A Godless place! Forsaken, fornicators paraded the streets. Gambling was done. Robbery and murder, drunkenness, and evils so profound I cannot put them into words. In all the universe you could not have found a fouler pesthole, Mr. Ellington! The Abbots and the Brothers at St. Wulfran's succumbed for years to Schwartzhof, I regret to say. Good men, lovers of God, chaste good men came here and fought but could not win against the black temptations. Finally it was decided that the Abbey should be closed. I heard of this and argued. 'Is that not surrender?' I said. 'Are we to bow before the strength of evil? Let me try, I beg you. Let me try to amplify the word of God that all in Schwartzhof shall hear and see their dark transgressions and repent!'"

The old man stood at the window, a trembling shade. His hands were now clutched together in a fervency of remembrance. "They asked," he said, "if I considered myself more virtuous than my predecessors that I should hope for success where they had failed. I answered that I did not, but that I had an advantage. I was a convert. Earlier I had walked with evil, and knew its face. My wish was granted. For a year. One year only. Rejoicing, Mr. Ellington, I came here; and one night, incognito, walked the streets of the village. The smell of evil was strong. Too strong, I thought—and I had reveled in the alleys of Morocco, I had seen the dens of Hong Kong, Paris, Spain. The orgies were too wild, the drunkards much too drunk, the profanities a great deal too profane. It was as if the evil of the world had been distilled and centered here, as if a pagan tribal chief, in hiding, had assembled all his rituals about him…" The Abbot nodded his head. "I thought of Rome, in her last days; of Byzantium; of—Eden. That was the first of many hints to come. No matter what they were. I returned to the Abbey and donned my robes and went back into Schwartzhof. I made myself conspicuous. Some jeered, some shrank away, a voice cried, 'Damn your foolish God!' And then a hand thrust out from darkness, touched my shoulder, and I heard: 'Now, Father, are you lost?'"

The Abbot brought his tightly clenched hands to his forehead and tapped his forehead.

"Mr. Ellington, I have some poor wine here. Please have some."

I drank gratefully. Then the priest continued.

"I faced a man of average appearance. So average, indeed, that I felt I knew, then. 'No,' I told him, 'but you are lost!' He laughed a foul laugh. 'Are we not all, Father?' Then he said a most peculiar thing. He said his wife was dying and begged me to give her Extreme Unction. 'Please,' he said, 'in God's sweet name!' I was confused. We hurried to his house. A woman lay upon a bed, her body nude. 'It is a different Extreme Unction that I have in mind,' he whispered, laughing. 'It's the only kind, dear Father, that she understands. No other will have her! Pity! Pity on the poor soul lying there in all her suffering. Give her your Sceptre!' And the woman's arms came snaking, supplicating toward me, round and sensuous and hot…"

Father Jerome shuddered and paused. The shrieks, I thought, were growing louder from the hall. "Enough of that," he said. "I was quite sure then. I raised my cross and told the words I'd learned, and it was over. He screamed—as he's doing now—and fell upon his knees. He had not expected to be recognized, nor should he have been normally. But in my life, I'd seen him many times, in many guises. I brought him to the Abbey. I locked him in the cell. We chant his chains each day. And so, my son, see why you must not speak of the things you've seen and heard?"

I shook my head, as if afraid the dream would end, as if reality would suddenly explode upon me. "Father Jerome," I said, "I haven't the vaguest idea of what you're talking about. Who is the man?"

"Are you such a fool, Mr. Ellington? That you must be told?"

"Yes!"

"Very well," said the Abbot. "He is Satan. Otherwise known as the Dark Angel, Asmodeus, Belial, Ahriman, Diabolus—the Devil."

I opened my mouth.

"I see you doubt me. That is bad. Think, Mr. Ellington, of the peace of the world in these five years. Of the prosperity, of the happiness. Think of this country, Germany, now. Is there another country like it? Since we caught the Devil and locked him up here, there have been no great wars, no overwhelming pestilences: only the sufferings man was meant to endure. Believe what I say, my son; I beg you. Try very hard to believe that the creature you spoke with is Satan himself. Fight your cynicism, for it is born of him; he is the father of cynicism, Mr. Ellington!

His plan was to defeat God by implanting doubt in the minds of Heaven's subjects!"
The Abbot cleared his throat. "Of course," he said, "we could never release anyone
from St. Wulfran's who had any part of the Devil in him."

I stared at the old fanatic and thought of him prowling the streets, looking for
sin; saw him standing outraged at the bold fornicator's bed, wheedling him into an
invitation to the Abbey, closing that heavy door and locking it, and, because of the
world's temporary postwar peace, clinging to his fantasy. What greater dream for
a holy man than actually capturing the Devil!

"I believe you," I said.

"Truly?"

"Yes. I hesitated only because it seemed a trifle odd that Satan should have
picked a little German village for his home."

"He moves around," the Abbot said. "Schwartzhof attracted him as lovely
virgins attract perverts."

"I see."

"Do you? My son, do you?"

"Yes. I swear it. As a matter of fact, I thought he looked familiar, but I simply
couldn't place him."

"Are you lying?"

"Father, I am a Bostonian."

"And you promise not to mention this to anyone?"

"I promise."

"Very well." The old man sighed. "I suppose," he said, "that you would not
consider joining us as a Brother at the Abbey?"

"Believe me, Father, no one could admire the vocation more than I. But I am
not worthy. No; it's quite out of the question. However, you have my word that
your secret is safe with me."

He was very tired. Sound had, in these years, reversed for him: the screams
had become silence, the sudden cessation of them, noise. The prisoner's quiet talk
with me had awakened him from deep slumber. Now he nodded wearily, and I saw
that what I had to do would not be difficult after all. Indeed, no more difficult than
fetching the authorities.

I walked back to my cell, where Brother Christophorus still slept, and lay down. Two hours passed. I rose again, and returned to the Abbot's quarters.

The door was closed but unlocked.

I eased it open, timing the creaks of the hinges with the screams of the prisoner. I tiptoed in. Father Jerome lay snoring in his bed.

Slowly, cautiously, I lifted out the leather thong, and was a bit astounded at my technique. No Ellington had ever burgled. Yet a force, not like experience, but like it, ruled my fingers. I found the knot. I worked it loose.

The warm iron key slid off into my hand.

The Abbot stirred, then settled, and I made my way into the hall.

The prisoner, when he saw me, rushed the bars. "He's told you lies, I'm sure of that!" he whispered hoarsely. "Disregard the filthy madman!"

"Don't stop screaming," I said.

"What?" He saw the key and nodded, then, and made his awful sounds. I thought at first the lock had rusted, but I worked the metal slowly and in time the key turned over.

Howling still, in a most dreadful way, the man stepped out into the corridor. I felt a momentary fright as his clawed hand reached up and touched my shoulder; but it passed. "Come on!" We ran insanely to the outer door, across the frosted ground, down toward the village.

The night was very black.

A terrible aching came into my legs. My throat went dry. I thought my heart would tear loose from its moorings. But I ran on.

"Wait."

Now the heat began.

"Wait."

By a row of shops I fell. My chest was full of pain, my head of fear: I knew the madmen would come swooping from their dark asylum on the hill. I cried out to the naked hairy man: "Stop! Help me!"

"Help you?" He laughed once, a high-pitched sound more awful than the screams had been; and then he turned and vanished in the moonless night.

I found a door, somehow.

The pounding brought a rifled burgher. Policemen came at last and listened to my story. But of course it was denied by Father Jerome and the Brothers of the Abbey.

"This poor traveler has suffered from the vision of pneumonia. There was no howling man at St. Wulfran's. No, no, certainly not. Absurd! Now, if Mr. Ellington would care to stay with us, we'd happily—no? Very well. I fear that you will be delirious a while, my son. The things you see will be quite real. Most real. You'll think—how quaint!—that you have loosed the Devil on the world and that the war to come—what war? But aren't there always wars? Of course!—you'll think that it's your fault"—those old eyes burning condemnation! Beak-nosed, bearded head atremble, rage in every word!—"that you'll have caused the misery and suffering and death. And nights you'll spend, awake, unsure, afraid. How foolish!"

Gnome of God, Christophorus, looked terrified and sad. He said to me, when Father Jerome swept furiously out: "My son, don't blame yourself. Your weakness was his lever. Doubt unlocked that door. Be comforted: we'll hunt him with our nets, and one day…"

One day, what?

I looked up at the Abbey of St. Wulfran's, framed by dawn, and started wondering, as I have wondered since ten thousand times, if it weren't true. Pneumonia breeds delirium; delirium breeds visions. Was it possible that I'd imagined all of this?

No. Not even back in Boston, growing dewlaps, paunches, wrinkles, sacks and money, at Ellington, Carruthers & Blake, could I accept that answer.

The monks were mad, I thought. Or: The howling man was mad. Or: The whole thing was a joke.

I went about my daily work, as every man must do, if sane, although he may have seen the dead rise up or freed a bottled djinn or fought a dragon, once, quite long ago.

But I could not forget. When the pictures of the carpenter from Braumau-am-Inn began to appear in all the papers, I grew uneasy; for I felt I'd seen this man before. When the carpenter invaded Poland, I was sure. And when the world was plunged into war and cities had their entrails blown asunder and that pleasant land I'd visited became a place of hate and death, I dreamed each night.

Each night I dreamed, until this week.

A card arrived. From Germany. A picture of the Moselle Valley is on one side, showing mountains fat with grapes and the dark Moselle, wine of these grapes.

On the other side of the card is a message. It is signed "Brother Christophorus" and reads (and reads and reads!): "Rest now, my son. We have him back with us again." ✦

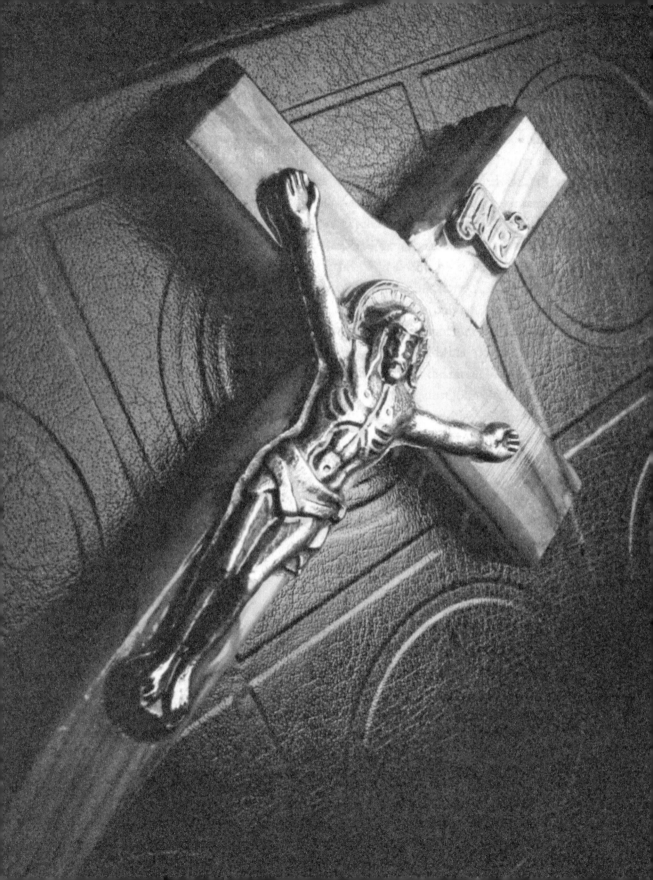

THE EXORCIST

EXCERPT

BY *William Peter Blatty*

The Exorcist *is, without question, the granddaddy of contemporary demon lit, and the book that changed modern horror forever.*

Yes, Ira Levin and Rosemary's Baby *brilliantly paved the way, in the late 1960s. And Polanski's stunning film took it wide.*

But it was William Peter Blatty—then a screenwriter primarily known for his ace comedic work with Blake Edwards (the early Pink Panther *films,* What Did You Do In The War, Daddy?*)—who brought horror to the publishing blockbuster place in 1971, against all advice and expectations.*

Two years later, William Friedkin took Blatty's screen adaptation to the pop culture heights.

But let us not forget how great, and truly seminal, this novel is.

I chose this particular excerpt because it covers such a staggering range of scientific and religious inquiry—and introduces such great playful character moments—before launching into an unforgettable sequence of such unmitigated horror that it scarred a generation.

And remains truly shocking to this day.

On Wednesday, May 11, they were back in the house. They put Regan to bed, installed a lock on the shutters and stripped all the mirrors from her bedroom and bathroom.

"...fewer and fewer lucid moments, and now there's a total blacking out of her consciousness during the fits, I'm afraid. That's new and would seem to eliminate genuine hysteria. In the meantime, a symptom or two in the area of what we call parapsychic phenomena have..."

Dr. Klein came by and Chris attended with Sharon as he drilled them in proper procedures for administering Sustagen feedings to Regan during her periods of coma. He inserted the nasogastric tubing. "First..."

Chris forced herself to watch and yet not see her daughter's face; to grip at the words that the doctor was saying and push away others she'd heard at the clinic. They seeped through her consciousness like fog through the branches of a willow tree.

"Now you stated 'No religion' here, Mrs. MacNeil. Is that right? No religious education at all?"

"Oh, well, maybe just 'God.' You know, general. Why?"

"Well, for one thing, the content of much of her raving—when it isn't that gibberish she's been spouting—is religiously oriented. Now where do you think she might get that?"

"Well, give me a for instance."

"Oh, 'Jesus and Mary, sixty-nine,' for ex—"

Klein had guided the tubing into Regan's stomach. "First you check to see if fluid's gotten into the lung," he instructed, pinching on the tube in order to clamp off the flow of Sustagen. "If it..."

"...syndrome of a type of disorder that you rarely ever see anymore, except among primitive cultures. We call it somnambuliform possession. Quite frankly, we don't know much about it except that it starts with some conflict or guilt that eventually leads to the patient's delusion that his body's been invaded by an alien intelligence; a spirit, if you will. In times gone by, when belief in the devil was fairly strong, the possessing entity was usually a demon. In relatively modern cases, however, it's mostly the spirit of someone dead, often someone the patient has known or seen and is able unconsciously to mimic, like the voice and the mannerisms, even the features of the face, at times. They…"

After the gloomy Dr. Klein had left the house, Chris phoned her agent in Beverly Hills and announced to him lifelessly that she wouldn't be directing the segment. Then she called Mrs. Perrin. She was out. Chris hung up the phone with a mounting feeling of desperation. Someone. She would have to have help from…

"…cases where it's spirits of the dead are more easy to deal with; you don't find the rages in most of those cases, or the hyperactivity and motor excitement. However, in the other main type of somnambuliform possession, the new personality's always malevolent, always hostile toward the first. Its primary aim, in fact, is to damage, torture and sometimes even kill it."

A set of restraining straps was delivered to the house and Chris stood watching, wan and spent, while Karl affixed them to Regan's bed and then to her wrists. Then as Chris moved a pillow in an effort to center it under Regan's head, the Swiss straightened up and looked pityingly at the child's ravaged face. "She is going to be well?" he asked. A hint of some emotion had tinged his words, they were lightly italicized with concern.

But Chris could not answer. As Karl was addressing her, she'd picked up an object that had been tucked under Regan's pillow. "Who put this crucifix here?" she demanded.

"The syndrome is only the manifestation of some conflict, of some guilt, so we try to get at it, find out what it is. Well, the best procedure in a case like this is hypnotherapy; however, we can't seem to put her under. So then we took a shot at narcosynthesis—that's a treatment that uses narcotics—but, frankly, that looks like another dead end."

"So what's next?"

"Mostly time, I'm afraid, mostly time. We'll just have to keep trying and hope for a change. In the meantime, she's going to have to be hospitalized for a…"

Chris found Sharon in the kitchen setting up her typewriter on the table. She had just brought it up from the basement playroom. Willie sliced carrots at the sink for a stew.

"Was it you who put the crucifix under her pillow, Shar?" Chris asked with the strain of tension.

"What do you mean?" asked Sharon, fuddled.

"You didn't?"

"Chris, I don't even know what you're talking about. Look, I told you. I told you on the phone, all I've ever said to Rags is 'God made the world' and maybe things about—"

"Fine, Sharon, fine, I believe you, but—"

"Me, I don't put it," growled Willie defensively.

"Somebody put it there, dammit!" Chris erupted, then wheeled on Karl as he entered the kitchen and opened the refrigerator door. "Look, I'll ask you again," she gritted in a tone that verged on shrillness: "Did you put that crucifix under her pillow?"

"No, madam," he answered levelly. He was folding ice cubes into a face towel. "No. No cross."

"That fucking cross didn't just walk up there, damn you! One of you is lying!" She was shrieking with a rage that stunned the room. "Now you tell me who put it there, who—" Abruptly she slumped to a chair and began to sob into trembling hands. "Oh, I'm sorry, I'm sorry, I don't know what I'm doing!" she wept. "Oh, my God, I don't know what I'm doing!"

Willie and Kari watched silently as Sharon came up beside her and kneaded her neck with a comforting hand. "Hey, okay. It's okay."

Chris wiped at her face with the back of a sleeve. "Yeah, I guess whoever did it"—she sniffled—"was only trying to help."

"Look, I'm telling you again and you'd better believe it, I'm not about to put her in a goddam asylum!"

"It's—"

"I don't care what you call it! I'm not letting her out of my sight!"

"Well, I'm sorry."

"Yeah, sorry! Christ! Eighty-eight doctors and all you can tell me with all of your bullshit is…"

Chris smoked a cigarette, tamped it out nervously and went upstairs to look in on Regan. She opened the door. In the gloom of the bedroom, she made out a figure by Regan's bedside, sitting in a straight-backed wooden chair. Karl. What was he doing? she wondered.

As Chris moved closer, he did not look up, but kept his gaze on the child's face. He had his arm outstretched and was touching it. What was in his hand? As Chris reached the bedside, she saw what it was: the improvised ice pack he had fashioned in the kitchen. Karl was cooling Regan's forehead.

Chris was touched, stood watching with surprise, and when Karl did not move or acknowledge her presence, she turned and quietly left the room.

She went to the kitchen, drank black coffee and smoked another cigarette. Then on an impulse she went to the study. Maybe…maybe…

"…an outside chance, since possession is loosely related to hysteria insofar as the origin of the syndrome is almost always autosuggestive. Your daughter must have known about possession, believed in possession, and known about some of its symptoms, so that now her unconscious is producing the syndrome. If that can be established, you might take a stab at a form of cure that's autosuggestive. I think of it as shock treatment in these cases, though most other therapists wouldn't agree, I suppose, and since you're opposed to your daughter being hospitalized, I'll—"

"Name it, for God's sake! What is it?!"

"Have you ever heard of exorcism, Mrs. MacNeil?"

The books in the study were part of the furnishings and Chris was unfamiliar with them. Now she was scanning the titles, searching, searching….

"…stylized ritual now out of date in which rabbis and priests tried to drive out the spirit. It's only the Catholics who haven't discarded it yet, but they keep it pretty much in the closet as sort of an embarrassment, I think. But to someone who thinks that he's really possessed, I would say that the ritual's rather impressive. It used to work, in fact, although not for the reason they thought, of course; it was purely the force of suggestion. The victim's belief in possession helped cause it, or at least the appearance of the syndrome, and in just the same way his belief in the power of the exorcism can make it disappear. It's—ah, you're frowning. Well, perhaps I should tell you about the Australian aborigines. They're convinced that if some wizard thinks a 'death ray' at them from a distance, why, they're definitely going to die, you see. And the fact is that they do! They just lie down and slowly die! And the only thing that saves them, at times, is a similar form of suggestion: a counteracting 'ray' by another wizard!"

"Are you telling me to take her to a witch doctor?"

"Yes, I suppose that I'm saying just that: as a desperate measure, perhaps to a priest. That's a rather bizarre little piece of advice, I know, even dangerous, in fact, unless we can definitely ascertain whether Regan knew anything at all about possession, and particularly exorcism, before this all came on. Do you think she might have read it?"

"No, I don't."

"Seen a movie about it sometime? Something on television?"

"No."

"Read the gospels, perhaps? The New Testament?"

"Why?"

"There are quite a few accounts of possession in them; of exorcisms by Christ. The descriptions of the symptoms, in fact, are the same as in possession today. If you—"

"Look, it's no good. Never mind, just forget it! That's all I need is to have her father hear that I called in a bunch of..."

Chris's index fingernail clicked slowly from binding to binding. Nothing. No Bible. No New Testament. Not a—

"Hold it!

Her eyes darted quickly back to a title on the bottom shelf. The volume on witchcraft that Mary Jo Perrin had sent her. Chris plucked it out from the shelf and turned to the table of contents, running her thumbnail down the...

There!

The title of a chapter pulsed like a heartthrob: "States of Possession."

Chris closed the book and her eyes at the same time, wondering, wondering....

Maybe...just maybe...

She opened her eyes and walked slowly to the kitchen. Sharon was typing. Chris held up the book. "Did you read this, Shar?"

Sharon kept typing, never glancing up. "Read what?" she answered.

"This book on witchcraft."

"No."

"Did you put it in the study?"

"No. Never touched it."

"Where's Willie?"

"At the market."

Chris nodded, considering. Then went back upstairs to Regan's bedroom. She showed Karl the book. "Did you put this in the study, Karl? On the bookshelf?"

"No, madam."

"Maybe Willie," Chris murmured as she stared at the book. Soft thrills of surmise rippled through her. Were the doctors at Barringer Clinic right? Was this it? Had Regan plucked her disorder through autosuggestion from the pages of this book? Would she find her symptoms listed here? Something specific that Regan was doing?

Chris sat at the table, opened to the chapter on possession and began to search, to search, to read:

Immediately derivative of the prevalent belief in demons was the phenomenon known as possession, a state in which many individuals believed that their physical and mental functions had been invaded and were being controlled by either a demon (most common in the period under discussion) or the spirit of someone dead. There is no period of history or quarter of the globe where this phenomenon has not been reported, and in fairly constant terms, and yet it is still to be adequately explained. Since Traugott Oesterreich's definitive study, first published in 1921, very little has been added to the body of knowledge, the advances of psychiatry notwithstanding.

Not fully explained? Chris frowned. She'd had a different impression from the doctors.

What is known is the following: that various people, at various times, have undergone massive transformations so complete that those around them feel they are dealing with another person. Not only the voice, the mannerisms, facial expressions and characteristic movements are altered, but the subject himself now thinks of himself as totally distinct from the original person and as having a name—whether human or demonic—and separate history of its own....

The symptoms. Where were the symptoms? Chris wondered impatiently.

...In the Malay Archipelago, where possession is even today an everyday, common occurrence, the possessing spirit of someone dead often causes the possessed to mimic its gestures, voice and mannerisms so strikingly, that relatives of the deceased will burst into tears. But aside from so-called quasi-possession—those cases that are ultimately reducible to fraud, paranoia and hysteria—the problem has always lain with interpreting the phenomena, the oldest interpretation being the spiritist, an impression that is likely to be strengthened by the fact that the intruding personality may have accomplishments quite foreign to the first. In the demoniacal form of possession, for example, the "demon" may speak in languages unknown to the first personality, or...

There! Something! Regan's gibberish! An attempt at a language? She read on quickly.

...or manifest various parapsychic phenomena, telekinesis for example: the movement of objects without application of material force.

The rappings? The flinging up and down on the bed?

...In cases of possession by the dead, there are manifestations such as Oesterreich's account of a monk who, abruptly, while possessed, became a gifted and brilliant dancer although he had never, before his possession, had occasion to dance so much as a step. So impressive, at times, are these manifestations that Jung, the psychiatrist, after studying a

case at first hand, could offer only partial explanation for what he was certain could "not have been fraud"…

Worrisome. The tone of this was worrisome.

…and William James, the greatest psychologist that America has ever produced, resorted to positing "the plausibility of the spiritualist interpretation of the phenomenon" after closely studying the so-called "Watseka Wonder," a teenaged girl in Watseka, Illinois, who became indistinguishable in personality from a girl named Mary Roff who had died in a state insane asylum twelve years prior to the possession….

Frowning, Chris did not hear the doorbell chime; did not hear Sharon stop typing to rise and go answer it.

The demoniacal form of possession is usually thought to have had its origin in early Christianity; yet in fact both possession and exorcism pre-date the time of Christ. The ancient Egyptians as well as the earliest civilizations of the Tigris and the Euphrates believed that physical and spiritual disorders were caused by invasion of the body by demons. The following, for example, is the formula for exorcism against maladies of children in ancient Egypt: "Go hence, thou who comest in darkness, whose nose is turned backwards, whose face is upside down. Hast thou come to kiss this child? I will not let thee…"

"Chris?"

She kept reading, absorbed. "Shar, I'm busy."

"There's a homicide detective wants to see you."

"Oh, Christ, Sharon, tell him to—"

She stopped.

"No, no, hold it." Chris frowned, still staring at the book. "No. Tell him to come in. Let him in."

Sound of walking.

Sound of waiting.

What am I waiting for? Chris wondered. She sat on expectancy that was known yet undefined, like the vivid dream one can never remember.

He came in with Sharon, his hat brim crumpled in his hand, wheezing and listing and deferential. "So sorry. You're busy, you're busy, I'm a bother."

"How's the world?"

"Very bad, very bad. How's your daughter?"

"No change."

"Ah, I'm sorry, I'm terribly sorry." He was hulking by the table now, his eyelids dripping concern. "Look, I wouldn't even bother; your daughter; it's a worry. God knows, when my Ruthie was down with the—no no no no, it was Sheila, my little—"

"Please sit down," Chris cut in.

"Oh, yes, thank you," he exhaled, gratefully settling his bulk in a chair across the table from Sharon, who had now returned to her typing of letters.

"I'm sorry; you were saying?" Chris asked the detective.

"Well, my daughter, she—ah, never mind." He dismissed it. "You're busy. I get started, I'll tell my life story, you could maybe make a film of it. Really! It's incredible! If you only knew half of the things used to happen in my crazy family, you know, like my—ah, well, you're—One! I'll tell one! Like my mother, every Friday she made us gefilte fish, right? Only all week long, the whole week, no one gets to take a bath on account of my mother has the carp in the bathtub, it's swimming back and forth, back and forth, the whole week, because my mother said this cleaned out the poison in its system! You're prepared? Because it…Ah, that's enough now; enough." He sighed wearily, motioning his hand in a gesture of dismissal. "But now and then a laugh just to keep us from crying."

Chris watched him expressionlessly, waiting….

"Ah, you're reading." He was glancing at the book on witchcraft. "For a film?" he inquired.

"Just reading."

"It's good?"

"I just started."

"Witchcraft," he murmured, his head angled, reading the title at the top of the pages.

"What's doin'?" Chris asked him.

"Yes, I'm sorry. You're busy. You're busy. I'll finish. As I said, I wouldn't bother you, except…"

"Except what?"

He looked suddenly grave and clasped his hands on the table. "Well, Mr. Dennings, Mrs. MacNeil…"

"Well…"

"Darn it," snapped Sharon with irritation as she ripped out a letter from the platen of the typewriter. She balled it up and tossed it at a wastepaper basket near Kinderman. "Oh, I'm sorry," she apologized as she saw that her outburst had interrupted them.

Chris and Kinderman were staring.

"You're Miss Fenster?" Kinderman asked her.

"Spencer," said Sharon, pulling back her chair in order to rise and retrieve the letter.

"Never mind, never mind," said Kinderman as he reached to the floor near his foot and picked up the crumpled page.

"Thanks," said Sharon.

"Nothing. Excuse me—you're the secretary?"

"Sharon, this is…"

"Kinderman," the detective reminded her. "William Kinderman."

"Right. This is Sharon Spencer."

"A pleasure," Kinderman told the blonde, who now folded her arms on the typewriter, eyeing him curiously. "Perhaps you can help," he added. "On the night of Mr. Dennings' demise, you went out to a drugstore and left him alone in the house, correct?"

"Well, no; Regan was here."

"That's my daughter," Chris clarified.

Kinderman continued to question Sharon. "He came to see Mrs. MacNeil?"

"Yes, that's right."

"He expected her shortly?"

"Well, I told him I expected her back pretty soon."

"Very good. And you left at what time? You remember?"

"Let's see. I was watching the news, so I guess—oh, no, wait—yes, that's right. I remember being bothered because the pharmacist said the delivery boy had gone home. I remember I said, 'Oh, come on, now,' or something about its only being six-thirty. Then Burke came along just ten, maybe twenty minutes after that."

"So a median," concluded the detective, "would have put him here at six-forty-five."

"And so what's this all about?" asked Chris, the nebulous tension in her mounting.

"Well, it raises a question, Mrs. MacNeil," wheezed Kinderman, turning his head to gaze at her. "To arrive in the house at say quarter to seven and leave only twenty minutes later…"

"Oh, well, that was Burke," said Chris. "Just like him."

"Was it also like Mr. Dennings," asked Kinderman, "to frequent the bars on M Street?"

"No."

"No, I thought not. I made a little check. And was it also not his custom to travel by taxi? He wouldn't call a cab from the house when he left?"

"Yes, he would."

"Then one wonders—not so?—how he came to be walking on the platform at the top of the steps. And one wonders why taxicab companies do not show a record of calls from this house on that night," added Kinderman, "except for the one that picked up your Miss Spencer here at precisely six-forty-seven."

"I don't know," answered Chris, her voice drained of color…and waiting…

"You knew all along!" gasped Sharon at Kinderman, perplexed.

'Yes, forgive me," the detective told her. "However, the matter has now grown serious."

Chris breathed shallowly, fixing the detective with a steady gaze. "In what way?" she asked. Her voice came thin from her throat.

He leaned over hands still clasped on the table, the page of typescript balled between them. "The report of the pathologist, Mrs. MacNeil, seems to show that the chance that he died accidentally is still very possible. However…"

"Are you saying he was murdered?" Chris tensed.

"The position—now I know this is painful—"

"Go ahead."

"The position of Dennings' head and a certain shearing of the muscles of the neck would—"

"Oh, God!" Chris winced.

"Yes, it's painful. I'm sorry; I'm terribly sorry. But you see, this condition—we can skip the details—but it never could happen, you see, unless Mr. Dennings had fallen some distance before he hit the steps; for example, some twenty or thirty feet before he went rolling down to the bottom. So a clear possibility, plainly speaking, is maybe…Well, first let me ask you…"

He'd turned now to a frowning Sharon. "When you left, he was where, Mr. Dennings? With the child?"

"No, down here in the study. He was fixing a drink."

"Might your daughter remember"—he turned to Chris—"if perhaps Mr. Dennings was in her room that night?"

Has she ever been alone with him?

"Why do you ask?"

"Might your daughter remember?"

"No, I told you before, she was heavily sedated and—"

"Yes, yes, you told me; that's true; I recall it; but perhaps she awakened—not so?—and…"

"No chance. And—"

"She was also sedated," he interrupted, "when last we spoke?"

"Oh, well, yes; as a matter of fact she was," Chris recalled. "So what?"

"I thought I saw her at her window that day."

"You're mistaken."

He shrugged. "It could be, it could be; I'm not sure."

"Listen, why are you asking all this?" Chris demanded.

"Well, a clear possibility, as I was saying, is maybe the deceased was so drunk that he stumbled and fell from the window in your daughter's bedroom."

Chris shook her head. "No way. No chance. In the first place, the window was always closed, and in the second place, Burke was always drunk, but he never got sloppy, never sloppy at all. That right, Shar?"

"Right."

"Burke used to direct when he was smashed. Now how could he stumble and fall out a window?"

"Were you maybe expecting someone else here that night?" he asked her.

"No."

"Have you friends who drop by without calling?"

"Just Burke," Chris answered. "Why?"

The detective lowered his head and shook it, frowning at the crumpled paper in his hands. "Strange…so baffling." He exhaled wearily. "Baffling." Then he lifted his glance to Chris. "The deceased comes to visit, stays only twenty minutes without even seeing you, and leaves all alone here a very sick girl. And speaking plainly, Mrs. MacNeil, as you say, it's not likely he would fall from a window. Besides that, a fall wouldn't do to his neck what we found except maybe a chance in a thousand." He nodded with his head at the book on witchcraft. "You've read in that book about ritual murder?"

Some prescience chilling her, Chris shook her head.

"Maybe not in that book," he said. "However—forgive me; I mention this only so maybe you'll think just a little bit harder—poor Mr. Dennings was discovered with his neck wrenched around in the style of ritual murder by so-called demons, Mrs. MacNeil."

Chris went white.

"Some lunatic killed Mr. Dennings," the detective continued, eyeing Chris fixedly. "At first, I never told you to spare you the hurt. And besides, it could technically still be an accident. But me, I don't think so. My hunch. My opinion. I believe he was killed by a powerful man: point one. And the fracturing of his skull—point two—plus the various things I have mentioned, would make it very probable—probable, not certain—the deceased was killed and then afterward pushed from your daughter's window. But no one was here except your daughter. So how could this be? It could be one way: if someone came calling between the time Miss Spencer left and the time you returned. Not so? Maybe so. Now I ask you again, please: who might have come?"

"Judas priest, just a second!" Chris whispered hoarsely, still in shock.

"Yes, I'm sorry. It's painful. And perhaps I'm all wrong—I'll admit. But you'll think now? Who? Tell me who might have come?"

Chris had her head down, frowning in thought. Then she looked up at Kinderman. "No. No, there's no one."

"Maybe you then, Miss Spencer?" he asked her. "Someone comes here to see you?"

"Oh, no, no one," said Sharon, her eyes very wide.

Chris turned to her. "Does the horseman know where you work?"

"The horseman?" asked Kinderman.

"Her boyfriend," Chris explained.

The blonde shook her head. "He's never come here. Besides, he was in Boston that night. Some convention."

"He's a salesman?"

"A lawyer."

The detective turned again to Chris. "The servants? They have visitors?"

"Never. Not at all."

"You expected a package that day? Some delivery?"

"Not that I know of. Why?"

"Mr. Dennings was—not to speak ill of the dead, may he rest in peace—but as you said, in his cups he was somewhat—well, call it irascible: capable, doubtless, of provoking an argument; an anger; in this case a rage from perhaps a delivery man who came by to drop a package. So were you expecting something? Like dry cleaning, maybe? Groceries? Liquor? A package?"

"I really wouldn't know," Chris told him. "Karl handles all of that."

"Oh, I see."

"Want to ask him?"

The detective sighed and leaned back from the table, stuffing his hands in the pockets of his coat. He stared glumly at the witchcraft book. "Never mind, never mind; it's remote. You've got a daughter very sick, and—well, never mind." He made a gesture of dismissal and rose from the chair. "Very nice to have met you, Miss Spencer."

"Same here." Sharon nodded remotely.

"Baffling," said Kinderman with a headshake. "Strange." He was focused on some inner thought. Then he looked at Chris as she rose from her chair. "Well, I'm sorry. I've bothered you for nothing. Forgive me."

"Here, I'll walk you to the door," Chris told him, thoughtful.

"Don't bother."

"No bother."

"If you insist. Incidentally," he said as they moved from the kitchen, "just a chance in a million, I know, but your daughter—you could possibly ask her if she saw Mr. Dennings in her room that night?"

Chris walked with folded arms. "Look, he wouldn't have had a reason to be up there in the first place."

"I know that; I realize; that's true; but if certain British doctors never asked, 'What's this fungus?' we wouldn't today have penicillin. Right? Please ask. You'll ask?"

"When she's well enough, yes; I'll ask."

"Couldn't hurt. In the meantime…" They'd come to the front door and Kinderman faltered, embarrassed. He put fingertips to mouth in a hesitant gesture. "Look, I really hate to ask you; however…"

Chris tensed for some new shock, the prescience tingling again in her bloodstream. "What?"

"For my daughter…you could maybe give an autograph?" He'd reddened, and Chris almost laughed with relief; at herself; at despair and the human condition.

"Oh, of course. Where's a pencil?" she said.

"Right here!" he responded instantly, whipping out the stub of a chewed-up pencil from the pocket of his coat while he dipped his other hand in a pocket of his jacket and slipped out a calling card. "She would love it," he said as he handed them both to Chris.

"What's her name?" Chris asked, pressing the card against the door and poising the pencil stub to write. There followed a weighty hesitation. She heard only wheezing. She glanced around. In Kinderman's eyes she saw some massive, terrible struggle.

"I lied," he said finally, his eyes at once desperate and defiant. "It's for me."

He fixed his gaze on the card and blushed. "Write 'To William—William Kinderman'—it's spelled on the back."

Chris eyed him with a wan and unexpected affection, checked the spelling of his name and wrote, William F. Kinderman, I love you! And signed her name. Then she gave him the card, which he tucked in his pocket without reading the inscription.

"You're a very nice lady," he told her sheepishly, gaze averted.

"You're a very nice man."

He seemed to blush harder. "No, I'm not. I'm a bother." He was opening the door. "Never mind what I said here today. It's upsetting. Forget it. Keep your mind on your daughter. Your daughter."

Chris nodded, her despondency surging up again as Kinderman stepped outside onto the stoop and donned his hat.

"But you'll ask her?" he reminded as he turned.

"I will," Chris whispered. "I promise. I will."

"Well, good-bye. And take care."

Once more Chris nodded; then added, "You too."

She closed the door softly. Then instantly opened it again as he knocked.

"What a nuisance. I'm a nuisance. I forgot my pencil." He grimaced in apology.

Chris eyed the stub in her hand, smiled faintly and gave it to Kinderman.

"And another thing..." He hesitated. "It's pointless, I know—it's a bother, it's dumb—but I know I won't sleep thinking maybe there's a lunatic loose or a doper if every little point I don't cover, whatever. Do you think I could—no, no, it's dumb, it's a—yes; yes, I should. Could I maybe have a word with Mr. Engstrom, do you think? The deliveries...the question of deliveries. I really should...."

"Sure, come on in," Chris said wearily.

"No, you're busy. Enough. I can talk to him here. This is fine. Here is fine."

He had leaned against a railing.

"If you insist," Chris smiled thinly. "He's with Regan. I'll send him right down."

"I'm obliged."

Quickly Chris closed the door. A minute later, Karl opened it. He stepped down to the stoop with his hand on the doorknob, holding the door slightly ajar. Standing tall and erect, he looked at Kinderman with eyes that were clear and cool. "Yes?" he asked without expression.

"You have the right to remain silent," Kinderman greeted him, steely gaze locked tight on Karl's. "If you give up the right to remain silent," he intoned rapidly in a flat, deadly cadence, "anything you say can and will be used against you in a court of law. You have the right to speak with an attorney and to have the attorney present during questioning. If you so desire, and cannot afford one, an attorney will be appointed for you without charge prior to questioning. Do you understand each of these rights I've explained to you?"

Birds twittered softly in the branches of the elder tree, and the traffic sounds of M Street came up to them muted like the humming of bees from a distant meadow. Karl's gaze never wavered as he answered, "Yes."

"Do you wish to give up the right to remain silent?"

"Yes."

"Do you wish to give up the right to speak to an attorney and have him present during questioning?"

"Yes."

"Did you previously state that on April twenty-eighth, the night of the death of Mr. Dennings, you attended a film that was showing at the Crest?"

"Yes."

"And what time did you enter the theater?"

"I do not remember."

"You stated previously you attended the six-o'clock showing. Does that help you to remember?"

"Yes. Yes, six-o'clock show. I remember."

"And you saw the picture—the film—from the beginning?"

"I did."

"And you left at the film's conclusion?"

"I did."

"Not before?"

"No, I see entire film."

"And leaving the theater, you boarded the D.C. Transit bus in front of the theater, debarking at M Street and Wisconsin Avenue at approximately nine-twenty P.M.?"

"Yes."

"And walked home?"

"I walk home."

"And were back in this residence at approximately nine-thirty P.M.?"

"I am back here exactly nine-thirty," Karl answered.

"You're sure."

"Yes, I look at my watch. I am positive."

"And you saw the whole film to the very end?"

"Yes, I said that."

"Your answers are being electronically recorded, Mr. Engstrom. I want you to be absolutely positive."

"I am positive."

"You're aware of the altercation between an usher and a drunken patron that happened in the last five minutes of the film?"

"Yes."

"Can you tell me the cause of it?"

"The man, he was drunk and was making disturbance."

"And what did they do with him finally?"

"Out. They throw him out."

"There was no such disturbance. Are you also aware that during the course of the six o'clock showing a technical breakdown lasting approximately fifteen minutes caused an interruption in the showing of the film?"

"I am not."

"You recall that the audience booed?"

"No, nothing. No breakdown."

"You're sure?"

"There was nothing."

"There was, as reflected in the log of the projectionist, showing that the film ended not at eight-forty that night, but at approximately eight-fifty-five, which would mean that the earliest bus from the theater would put you at M Street and Wisconsin not at nine-twenty, but nine-forty-five, and that therefore the earliest you could be at the house was approximately five before ten, not nine-thirty, as testified also by Mrs. MacNeil. Would you care now to comment on this puzzling discrepancy?"

Not for a moment had Karl lost his poise and he held it now as he answered, "No."

The detective stared at him mutely for a moment, then sighed and looked down as he turned off the monitor control that was tucked in the lining of his coat. He held his gaze down for a moment, then looked up at Karl. "Mr. Engstrom..." he began in a tone that was weary with understanding. "A serious crime may have been committed. You are under suspicion. Mr. Dennings abused you, I have learned from other sources. And apparently you've lied about your whereabouts at the time of his demise. Now it sometimes happens—we're human; why not?—that a man who is married is sometimes someplace where he says that he is not. You will notice I arranged we are talking in private? Away from the others? Away from your wife? I'm not now recording. It's off. You can trust me. If it happens you were out with a woman not your wife on that night, you can tell me, I'll have it checked out, you'll be out of this trouble and your wife, she won't know. Now then tell me, where were you at the time Dennings died?"

For a moment something flickered in the depths of Karl's eyes; and then was smothered.

"At movies!" he insisted, through narrowed lips.

The detective eyed him steadily, silent and unmoving, no sound but his wheezing as the seconds ticked heavily, heavily....

"You are going to arrest me?" Karl asked the silence at last in a voice that subtly wavered.

The detective made no answer but continued to eye him, unblinking, and when Karl seemed again about to speak, the detective abruptly pushed away from the railing, moving toward the squad car with hands in his pockets. He walked unhurriedly, viewing his surroundings to the left and the right like an interested visitor to the city.

From the stoop, Karl watched, his features stolid and impassive as Kinderman opened the door of the squad car, reached inside to a box of Kleenex fixed to the dashboard, extracted a tissue and blew his nose while staring idly across the river as if considering where to have lunch. Then he entered the car without glancing back.

As the car pulled away and rounded the corner of Thirty-fifth, Karl looked at the hand that was not on the doorknob and saw it was trembling.

When she heard the front door being closed, Chris was brooding at the bar in the study, pouring out a vodka over ice. Footsteps. Karl going up the stairs. She picked up her vodka and moved slowly back toward the kitchen, stirring her drink with an index finger; picking her way with absent eyes. Something...something was horribly wrong. Like light from a room leaking under the door, a glow of dread seeped into the darkened hall of her mind. What lay behind the door? What was it?

Don't look!

She entered the kitchen, sat at the table and sipped at her drink.

"I believe he was killed by a powerful man..."

She dropped her glance to the book on witchcraft.

Something...

Footsteps. Sharon returning from Regan's bedroom. Entering. Sitting at the table by the typewriter. Cranking fresh stationery into the roller.

Something…

"Pretty creepy," Sharon murmured, fingertips resting on the keyboard and eyes on her steno notes to the side.

No answer. Uneasiness hung in the room. Chris sipped absently at her drink.

Sharon probed at the silence in a strained, low voice. "They've got an awful lot of hippie joints down around M Street and Wisconsin. Pot-heads. Occultists. The police call them 'hellhounds.'" She paused as if waiting for comment, her eyes still fixed upon the notes; then continued: "I wonder if Burke might have—"

"Oh, Christ, Shar! Forget about it, will you!" Chris erupted. "I've got all I can think about with Rags! Do you mind?" She had her eyes shut. She clenched the book.

Sharon returned instantly to the keys of the typewriter, clicking off words at a furious tempo for a minute, then abruptly bolted up from her chair and out of the kitchen. "I'm going for a walk!" she said icily.

"Stay the hell away from M Street!" Chris rumbled at her moodily, her gaze on the book over folded arms.

"I will!"

"And N!"

Chris heard the front door being opened, then closed. She sighed. Felt a pang of regret. But the flurry had siphoned off tension. Not all. Still the glow in the hall. Very faint.

Shut it out!

Chris took a deep breath and tried to focus on the book. She found her place; grew impatient; started hastily flipping through pages, skimming, searching for descriptions of Regan's symptoms. "…demonic possession…syndrome…case of an eight-year-old girl…abnormal…four strong men to restrain him from…"

Turning a page, Chris stared—and froze.

Sounds. Willie coming in with groceries.

"Willie?…Willie?" Chris asked tonelessly.

"Yes, madam," Willie answered, setting down her bags. Without looking up, Chris held up the book. "Was it you put this book in the study, Willie?"

Willie glanced at the book and nodded, then turned around and began to slip items from the bags.

"Willie, where did you find it?"

"Up in bedroom," Willie answered, putting bacon in the meat compartment of the refrigerator.

"Which bedroom, Willie?"

"Miss Regan. I find it under bed when I am cleaning."

"When did you find it?" Chris asked, her gaze still locked to the pages of the book.

"After all go to hospital, madam; when I vacuum in Regan bedroom."

"You're sure?"

"I am sure, madam. Yes. I am sure."

Chris did not move, did not blink, did not breathe as the headlong image of an open window in Regan's bedroom the night of Dennings' accident rushed at her memory, talons extended, like a bird of prey who knew her name; as she recognized a sight that was numbingly familiar; as she stared at the facing page of the book.

A narrow strip had been surgically shaved from the length of its edge.

Chris jerked her head up at the sounds of commotion in Regan's bedroom.

Rappings, rapid, with a nightmarish resonance; massive, like a sledgehammer pounding in a tomb!

Regan screaming in anguish; in terror; imploring!

Karl! Karl bellowing angrily at Regan!

Chris bolted from the kitchen.

God almighty, what's happening?

Frenzied, Chris raced for the stairs, toward the bedroom, heard a blow, someone reeling, someone crashing like a boulder to the floor with her daughter crying, "No! Oh, no, don't! Oh, no, please!" and Karl bellowing—No! No, not Karl! Someone else! A thundering bass that was threatening, raging!

Chris plunged down the hall and burst into the bedroom, gasped, stood rooted in paralyzing shock as the rappings boomed massively, shivering through walls; as Karl lay unconscious on the floor near the bureau; as Regan, her legs propped up and spread wide on a bed that was violently bouncing and shaking, clutched the bone-white crucifix in raw-knuckled hands, the bone-white crucifix poised at her vagina, the bone-white crucifix she stared at with terror, eyes bulging in a face that was bloodied from the nose, the nasogastric tubing ripped out.

"Oh, please! Oh, no, please!" she was shrieking as her hands brought the crucifix closer; as she seemed to be straining to push it away.

"You'll do as I tell you, filth! You'll do it!"

The threatening bellow, the words, came from Regan, her voice coarse and guttural, bristling with venom, while in an instantaneous flash her expression and features were hideously transmuted into those of the feral, demonic personality that had appeared in the course of hypnosis. And now faces and voices, as Chris watched stunned, interchanged with rapidity:

"No!"

"You'll do it!"

"Please!"

"You will, you bitch, or I'll kill you!"

"Please!"

"Yes, you're going to let Jesus fuck you, fuck you, f—"

Regan now, eyes wide and staring, flinching from the rush of some hideous finality, mouth agape shrieking at the dread of some ending. Then abruptly the demonic face once more possessed her, now filled her, the room choking suddenly with a stench in the nostrils, with an icy cold that seeped from the walls as the rappings ended and Regan's piercing cry of terror turned to a guttural, yelping laugh of malevolent spite and rage triumphant while she thrust down the crucifix into her vagina and began to masturbate ferociously, roaring in that deep, coarse, deafening voice, "Now you're mine, now you're mine, you stinking cow! You bitch! Let Jesus fuck you, fuck you!"

Chris stood rooted to the ground in horror, frozen, her hands pressing tight against her cheeks as again the demonic, loud laugh cackled joyously, as Regan's vagina gushed blood onto sheets with her hymen, the tissues ripped. Abruptly, with a shriek clawing raw from her throat, Chris rushed at the bed, grasped blindly at the crucifix, was still screaming as Regan flared up at her in fury, features contorted infernally, reached out a hand, clutching Chris's hair, and yanked her head down, pressing her face hard against her vagina, smearing it with blood while she frantically undulated her pelvis.

"Aahhh, little pig mother!" Regan crooned with a guttural, rasping, throaty eroticism. "Lick me, lick me, lick me! Aahhhhh!" Then the hand that was holding Chris's head down jerked it upward while the other arm smashed her a blow across the chest that sent Chris reeling across the room and crashing to a wall with stunning force while Regan laughed with bellowing spite.

Chris crumpled to the floor in a daze of horror, in a swirling of images, sounds in the room, as her vision spun madly, blurring, unfocused, her ears ringing loud with chaotic distortions as she tried to raise herself, was too weak, faltered, then looked toward the still-blurred bed, toward Regan with her back to her, thrusting the crucifix gently and sensually into her vagina, then out, then in, with that deep bass voice crooning, "Ahh, there's my sow, yes, my sweet honey piglet, my piglet, my—"

The words were cut off as Chris started crawling painfully toward the bed with her face smeared with blood, with her eyes still unfocused, limbs aching, past Karl. Then she cringed, shrinking back in incredulous terror as she thought she saw hazily, in a swimming fog, her daughter's head turning slowly around on a motionless torso, rotating monstrously, inexorably, until at last it seemed facing backward.

"Do you know what she did, your cunting daughter?" giggled an elfin, familiar voice.

Chris blinked at the mad-staring, grinning face, at the cracked, parched lips and foxlike eyes.

She screamed until she fainted. ✦

HELL

BY *Richard Christian Matheson*

Here's a distinctively L.A. snapshot of everything that's wrong, in a moment-to-moment, uncomfortably compressed 80s time capsule, by that master of compression, Richard Christian Matheson.

It's a sweaty, panoramic still life yanked into motion just as the shutter clicks. Making sure you take everything with you, as you go, so that it might linger forever after.

Hell, indeed.

August. Two-thirteen A.M.

L.A. was turning on a spit and teenagers were out in cars everywhere, cooking alive, tortured. The insanity of summer's sauna made the city grow wet and irritable, and blood bubbled at a sluggish boil in the flesh. Animals slept deeply, too hot to move, fur smelling of moist lethargy. Chewing gum came to life on sidewalks, like one-celled creatures, growing in the heat and the glow of fires created arsonist sunsets on the foothills which rimmed the city.

Lauren pulled her VW Rabbit into the view area off Mulholland, damp hair sticking to her forehead in fang shapes. The Rabbit rolled against the concrete headstone at the parking slot's end that prevented berserkos from driving over the edge and she killed the engine. Hollywood was spread before her, eating electricity, hibachi-bright. To her side, in the two other parked cars, she saw silhouette couples, in back seats, groping, fucking; glistening under the swelter.

Her skull was slowly steaming open and she punched on the AM-FM as insects broiled on her radiator like tiny steaks. She tuned in a station and a moody deejay came-to over the airwaves, laughing softly like a rapist. Lauren was numb from the burning night and rolled down her window more, letting in the oven.

"Here's a track the needle loves to lick." He made a faint licking noise. Laughed more, soft and cruel. "Mick and the boys givin' us some sympathy for a bad man. In case you're wonderin' about L.A.'s needle…it's in the red, babies. Hundred and two in the dark. I feel hot…How 'bout you?"

He chuckled as if tying a woman up and lowering onto her terrified body. Then "Sympathy For the Devil"'s rhythmic trance began and Lauren leaned back, staring out the windshield, sweat glazing her forehead. Hot wind blew air that felt sour and old and smog stuck to everything. They called it riot weather after the Watts riots back in the Sixties.

Bad wind. Poison days.

She rubbed her eyes and remembered the heat and humidity of that kerosene summer a million years ago. It had put a blister on top of L.A. and all those welfare cases cooking-up in their crackerbox hells went insane. Killed. Looted. Shoved broken glass into cop's throats and watched them bleed to death for fun. People said it was the thermometer that finally triggered it. Just a hot, wet summer day that made people itch and drink and lose their tempers and carve each other up for relief.

She tapped tiredly on the wheel, following Jagger's voice as it stabbed, pulled the knife out and stabbed again. Ran fingers through sweat-salted hair, feeling as if she'd taken her clothes out of a dryer half-wet and put them on.

The song thinned to nothing and the deejay was groaning, sounding like it was all over and he needed a cigarette. She wiped her forehead, starting to feel sick from the heat which crept in her windows. She unbuttoned her blouse lower, inviting what breeze hadn't been baked solid and felt her mouth parting, her breathing slow. The two cars beside hers started and pulled away, leaving her surrounded by shapes the exhaust formed under moonlight.

The deejay came out of a commercial for a de-tox clinic and hissed lewd amusement.

"Hope you're with the one who makes you get hideous out there." He paused and Lauren could see him grinning cynically like a psycho killer in a courtroom, enjoying the grotesque evidence. "Temperature...a hundred and two and a half. How 'bout some Doors? 'Back Door Man,' summer of '69. Where were you?" Sensual, torturer's breathing. "And...who were you tormenting?"

The night felt suddenly swampier as requiem notes hit the air and Lauren closed her eyes, spinning, sweating, feeling creeks of perspiration run down her ribs. She drifted farther, remembering a beach party in August of '69 when she'd taken her first acid trip and glided for eight hours in a Disney borealis, able to listen to handfuls of sand that spoke to her in frantic whispers. What was it it had said? She tried to remember...something about mankind suffering. Hating itself. It had terrified her.

She opened her eyes trying to forget, as another car pulled into the slot beside hers—a teenage, muscle cruiser; primered, deafening. Heavy Metal howled and though the windows were tinted, she could see cigarette tips roving inside, as whoever drove watched the city.

She wiped sweat which slid between her breasts and watched two other cars racing closer, up Mulholland, headlights jabbing; hunting. The cars finally prowled into the view area, one beside her, one behind. She felt massive engines shaking the pavement and the cars on either side were so close she realized she couldn't open her doors. The new cars beside her, on the right, had tinted windows like the one on the left. Inside the new one, she saw cigarettes, maybe joints, making slow moving graffiti patterns. Heard muted laughter; unsettling voices. Male and female.

Restless.

She tried her doors and neither would open; blocked.

The deejay sighed depressively. "Another knifing downtown. Simply Blues Bar." A yawn. The sound of something icy and long being swallowed. "Some people just shouldn't drink. Let's get back to the Doors."

Lauren pushed harder on her driver's door that felt fused shut. There was no play in it and she yelled to the driver to move his car. But there was no answer and when she did the same on the other side, still nothing. As she knocked sweating hands on the windows of both cars, Morrison started screaming.

"...well the music is your only friend.
Dance on fire as it intends.
Music is your only friend. Until the end."

Lauren gave up on the cars which blocked her doors, started the Rabbit, jammed it into reverse, hit the gas and let out the clutch. Her tires gushed sticky, black dust but the car behind her didn't move. She started to panic, unable to escape and screamed at the drivers pressing against her, on three sides, to move their cars. She caught her expression in the Rabbit's rearview; a fleeting look of terror.

"The face in the mirror won't stop,
the girl in the window won't drop.
A feast of friends—'Alive!' she cried.
Waiting for me outside. Outside!"

She pounded harder on the windows of both cars but no one responded. Just more murmured amusement behind tinted glass. Cigarette tips burning, shifting like creature eyes. She slid across the front seat again, grunting trapped, primitive sounds and banged on the tinted windows of the opposite car. She could see her helpless features reflected in the black glass and gripped the door more tightly as she screamed.

"Before I sink
into the big sleep.
I want to hear the scream
of the butterfly."

The Doors kicked her harder and her hands began to bruise from pounding the glass; yellow-purple flesh replacing pink. Her throat was grated by screams and though she couldn't make out voices, the laughter in the surrounding cars grew louder. She began to cry and the deejay chuckled.

"Just stepped outside and the flames are rising. Don't forget to use your lotion guys and gals." He made an obscene squirting sound. "Quick thought for the night: maybe we're all cooking alive and don't know it...so, let's party."

He killed the Doors and substituted demented music which started suddenly, making Lauren's heart beat too fast.

She immediately looked up when the car behind hers began to rumble like a piece of earth moving equipment and started forward, shoving the Rabbit's front tires over the cement block. Then, the rear tires. It pushed harder, engine screaming, tires spinning. Ahead, the sequin sea of L.A. glittered.

Lauren tried frantically to get out her doors but the other cars rolled over their own cement blocks and stopped her, jamming either side like grisly escorts.

She looked ahead, saw the cliffs edge and grabbed the wheel tightly, trying to lock the tires. But the Rabbit kept sliding closer to the edge, tires gouging fat scars in the dirt. She held down the horn, trying to let someone know, then covered her face with both hands, plunging into blackness; a burning spray twisting end over end. Her scream lasted seconds.

As the three cars drove away into the muggy gloom the deejay made a sound of exquisite pain. "Another ghastly evening in the City of Angels. In case you're keeping score, the temperature just went up another degree...and you're losing." The six headlights stared around a curve and disappeared, looking for places to go; things to do. Sirens wailed and moved toward Mulholland as the deejay blew smoke into the mike, spun a ballad and cooed Aushwitz delight. "Stay bad, babies... the night is young. And there's no way out." ✦

EMPATHY

BY *John Skipp*

And speaking of Los Angeles—a city notorious for bringing out the best in everyone—here's a painful little ditty I composed back at the turn of the century, not even realizing what a demon story it was.

As it turns out, I've written a lot about them, over the years. From The Cleanup *and* The Scream *to* The Long Last Call *and* Jake's Wake—*and just about everything else, if you really think about it—my whole weird career is littered with devil deals and tortured souls. It's probably the monster iconography I've played with most. Zombies included.*

A startling revelation, I gotta admit. Especially when something like this sneaks in under the radar, and slaps me awake to how and what I really feel.

I dedicate this haunted love song to every actress in Hollywood, successful or otherwise. (There is no such thing as a non-struggling actress.)

And there are no demons more personal than these.

Yes, you're bad. You've done a horrible thing. And you'll do it again. I know. If there's one thing I understand, it's that you will do it again.

You are laying there, drenched in a spackle of sweat that is equal parts shame and relentless heat. 98 degrees in Hollywood. At least 110 in the Valley. There exists, at this point, no meter to gauge the level of shame you feel. A fan is blowing, its oscillation locked, riveted by a pin to blast its blades straight at your head. It doesn't matter. You have fallen, and you can't get up: paralyzed with self-loathing, and the perfect understanding that you're right. It's all wrong. You. Me. God. Everything. Wrong.

At this point, I am just awakening. You feel the ripple as the veil of sleep parts, and choose that moment to enter me.

I slide into wakefulness, and know you are there. Get up off the bed. Go down the hall. Take a long, exultant pee. Today is gonna be an extra-fine day, whether you wanna just fucking lay there or not. I am going to have fun.

I am going to be fun.

I go into the living room, slap on the yoga tape. Dixie Carter is just so sweet, and the exercises really help. I hear the growling in my tummy, and totally don't care. I will eat when I'm done. Then I'll go out and run. In the meantime, I stretch, feel my muscles spring to life. I am alive. I'm so alive it's almost stupid.

Already, I am projecting ahead. My immediate future has been carefully planned. I prepare to inhabit it, one speck at a time.

I just wish you would fucking get over it.

My breakfast is lean; I am down to 118 again. I would say that that's a good look for me. I can wear a bikini, or even less, without cringing. If I have a complaint, it would have to be that I've lost so much in the cleavage department. At this weight, I really miss my titties. But at least my ass is contained.

I go back into the bedroom, peel off my sleepy workout garb. Of course, you are awake.

"I can't get up," you say.

"Uh-huh." I nod, walk into the closet.

"I must be getting old," you say. "Three drinks, and I'm gone. Three glasses of wine. It's fucking absurd. I'm twenty-seven years old. Used to be I could drink all night."

"You also drank rum," I remind you. "And a margarita."

I feel you shrug. "Whatever. I could puke up a single lite beer. Doesn't matter what I do. I get sick. I can't deal."

"Has it occurred to you," I say, "that you might have developed an allergy?"

"Oh, yeah," you say. "I'm allergic to alcohol. I break out in handcuffs."

I start to laugh.

"It's like Joe Bob said," you continue. "Just because a woman sleeps with every man she meets, that doesn't mean she's cheap."

"Oh, that's priceless," I tell you. "'Break out in handcuffs.' You really need to write that down."

"You write it down," you say. "I can't get up."

"Oh, yeah." At this point, a flicker of annoyance runs through me. I think, *so much self-pity, so early in the morning. No wonder you puke.*

But I don't say that. Instead, I say, "Sure, I'll write it down. In fact, I'll tell you what. I'll get you up. Put you in the shower. Make your breakfast. Eat your breakfast. Drive you to work. Do all your work. Digest your food, and bring you home. Hell, I'll even shit it out for you."

"That's nice," you say, and roll over in bed. So much for conversation.

Whatever. That's fine with me. I throw on shorts, socks, sneakers, and the t-shirt that says JESUS IS COMING. LOOK BUSY. Then I'm out the door, walking briskly up the hill toward the dog park. And away from you.

It is now 8:45. The heat is almost stunning. It bakes the urine of a trillion dogs into a crispy nose soufflé. I wish I had time to drive to the reservoir instead, do three miles, stare at Madonna's old house. But no. My first meeting's at ten. Never make it. No way.

By 9:15, I am hosing down in the shower. Every toxin my body has ever known has been caught up in sweat beads, now sluicing down the drain. I feel more than clean. I feel Zestfully clean.

When I come back out, it's like you are not even there.

Which is totally fine with me. I don't even want to think about you. No offense—you know I love you to death—but you're a total fucking loser, and you're making me sick. You're letting yourself get fat and ugly and, yes, even stupid. Laying there like a lump. Scintillating as mud, and sexy as a tumor.

In my closet, there are clothes that I can finally wear again. One of life's crowning glories: I can wear my own clothes. Which, of course, is more than you can say, oh Queen of Lard and Mopiness. I almost start to feel sorry for you, but then the thought just pisses me off.

I dress and put on makeup in silence, sculpt a little 40s flip into my hair. I love the glamour of the old Hollywood, feel entitled to a bit of it now. There's a whole town out there that is crawling with money, with the privilege that comes from dedicated hard work. And I am working my ass off, not working my ass.

Which is more than I can say for you.

I show up for my meeting with five minutes to spare, spend them happily schmoozing with the receptionist. Her name is Allison, and she is a hoot. Very pretty. Just a little bit overweight.

This town can be ruthless—in fact, it just *is*—and though I hate to be a party to it, I can no more shut it off than I can stop my own heart. While we talk, I can feel her measuring me, sensors gauging my anatomical stats. It's subtle, but it's sad, because I know she can't help it. None of us can help it. It's in the fucking air, a particulate component of the smog: five parts carbon monoxide, two parts bitchiness, with a lingering afterwaft of decay.

I am here for a callback on a very nice part in a low-budget action thriller. Not another hooker with a heart of gold. Not another understanding girlfriend or wife. And not another teenage bed wench who gets to scream just before the knife goes in.

The character's name is Verona Gabor, and she's a full-on psychopathic contract killer. Shades of *Romeo is Bleeding*, but one could do worse. I think of Lena Olin, how empowered she was. How frightening and gorgeous, free of inhibition or remorse.

I want to do that. Oh yes indeed. I want to go wallow in untrammeled ferocity. Show my teeth. Show my tits. Show my victims their spleens.

I joke with Allison about that very thing, and she is right there with me. I can tell that she'd love to play that part, too. If only she lost ten pounds.

The meeting goes well. I get to read; but more than that, I get to pace and stalk, to glower and grin and stake my claim on the turf that is Verona Gabor. The casting director and producer are impassive; but, of course, that's their jobs. On the other hand, the director is cupping his nuts. Not only does he keenly appreciate my talent, he wants to fuck me so bad it's coming out of his ears.

I would never do that, of course. Better to keep him steamed up than to get intimate, let him dissipate the heat. On top of that, the fucker looks like Gary Shandling, whom I love but wouldn't bed if he came with four posters and a canopy.

I leave with a really good feeling. I feel like I have rocked the house. The meeting went over by almost forty minutes; the next girl in line looks severely pissed. I check her out, as she does me. *Fat chance*, I think, though she is scrawny as a pole.

I grab a bite at noon: broiled chicken, a little cottage cheese. It's not nearly enough, but it will have to do. My next audition is at 1:45, in Venice. Corman film. Hooker with a heart of chintz, who befriends a psychic frog. He becomes a prince, of course, and marries me or whoever gets the part.

There are roughly 87,000 girls in the office, the parking lot, the road leading in. If I didn't need the money, I would blow this hot dog stand. You've never smelled so much Victoria's Secret and bitter cooze. At least not since the last cattle call.

Funny, how I find myself thinking of you.

It's the comparison test. The one-against-all. The pitting of beauty against beauty against beauty. I realize how many of me there are. How many diligent, arrogant dreamers, daring to think that they could ever possibly stand out. I hear the catty whispers as I stride to the desk.

It makes me want a fucking drink.

An hour and a half later, I get to read. It goes fairly well, but these people are numb, and getting number by the second. I try to imagine what criteria they're going to judge on. Looks? Talent? Character? What difference does it make? This mecca for models who think they can act will go straight down to video and sink like a stone. Everybody knows it. And nobody cares.

It's almost five by the time I get home, what with traffic and bullshit and a stop at the store. Jason will be here at seven, which gives me just enough time to catch up on my messages and make some calls, keep the boulder rolling uphill.

Of course, you are sprawled on the couch, watching TV.

I don't even want to talk to you. You are fucking depression incarnate. On the screen, spineless women get up in front of millions, defend their utter servitude to ugly, stupid men. It is God's will for them, they heartwarmingly insist, to serve their Bombo's every need. Make his food. Scrub his hairy back. Chew the corns off his reeking feet, the second he gets home from the insecticide plant.

I guess it makes you feel better, but it makes me want to scream.

Where is your self-respect?, I wonder. Then I go *oh, yeah. It's in the toilet, with your lunch*.

I say nothing, stripping down and showering again. I am careful not to get my hair wet this time. Twenty-seven years old, and already the gray hairs are showing up. What the fuck is that? What is the matter with me?

I can't allow that kind of thought inside. It's the kind of thing that you would say. I choke it back like day-old bile, think pretty thoughts exclusively.

But that is my hell. I think too much. I live inside my head. Planning things out. Sculpting trajectories. Maintaining the fortress that is my flesh. I take a lot of maintenance, attention to detail, constant care. And above all, forward momentum.

Because if I stop, for even a second, I start to turn out like you.

And I would honestly rather die.

Jason is fifteen minutes early, but that's cool. I am ready freddy, and looking hot. Jason is duly appreciative, which is not a surprise. Jason loves me so much it is almost retarded.

Jason is a screenwriter. A very very good one. He is also a fairly cute boy. Not drop-dead like Damian, gorgeous like Gary, breathtaking like Armando Bane (big sigh). But I am done with actor-boys, their vanities on parade. Actor-boys— celebrities, especially—always have to be the center, the pivot on which the whole universe spins. That doesn't leave much room for me. And God knows, I need some, too.

Which is what Jason wants to talk with me about. He is writing a new script, he says. And he's tailoring it for me. It's a perfect part. Lots of depth. Lots of courage. Lots of wit. A little bit of pathos, but nothing you could drown in. Just enough to let the inner strength and beauty shine through.

Naturally, I'm interested. He has placed three scripts in the last ten months, and his career is heating nicely. There is talk of letting him direct one soon, which is where this script comes in. If he can actually hang on to control, he could in fact cast me, which would be really sweet.

I am determined not to fuck him.

He smokes a joint before we leave. I do not join in. I tell him dope makes me feel hungry and stupid, and I can do that by myself. He laughs very hard; he always gets my jokes. I really admire that in a man.

He asks me where I would like to eat; and for some perverse reason, I think of Acapulco's. It's Dollar Margarita Night. And I would really like a drink.

So away we go, amidst much glittering conversation. I love the way Jason expresses himself, the strange twists and turns his logic takes.

And he's fun. I think I like that most. He's smart, and he's fun, and he gets my jokes. He is also refreshingly honest: about the biz, about himself.

About his feelings toward me.

This is the part I'm least itchy to hear. I order a margarita. Jason sticks with red wine. I send him off to scarf up goodies from the happy hour buffet. Meanwhile, I head for the Ladies'. Pee. Then stare at myself in the mirror.

I wish I could just stop thinking so much.

I wish I could just stop thinking.

A margarita later, it's a little bit easier. I promptly order another. There are more calories at the table right now than I have consumed all week. I joke about it, and Jason laughs, but I watch him appraise me in a surreptitious second.

His conclusion is *but she's not fat.*

And I find myself thinking *if you only knew…*

More food. More drink. More hilarious distraction. We talk about movies that we both love. Quote Monty Python, chapter and verse. Quote *Waiting for Guffman*, which Jason insists was the best horror film of last year. Quote *Fargo* and *Sling Blade* and *Dead Alive*. Quote *Who's Afraid of Virginia Woolf*, which Jason insists is the best horror film ever.

Jason launches into a hilarious story, and I feel myself ballooning underneath my dress: fat cells long dormant, reawakening with fervor, like a cancer of insulation between myself and the world. I catch a stray clever line, and it makes me laugh my ass off. I say it over and over, then can't remember what it was.

Life, at this point, becomes a dull blur, punctuated by moments of obscene clarity. His eyes are aglow in the candlelight. He has beautiful eyes. They are aglow with love.

Oh God, I think. I don't need love. I'm sick of love. I believe in love. I believe that love is the firmament, the thing both above and between all things. I believe that love is the soul of forgiveness, the heart of charity, the essence of faith. I believe, in fact, that God is love; and that God loves me, no matter how stupid I get. How stupid or selfish or grasping or vain.

I believe these things, and I want to cry, because now I am thinking of you. Thinking of you, on the bed or the couch: the only two places you live. I am thinking of a God that could possibly love you. You mattress tramp. You fucking whore. You blimp. You slug. You feeding machine. You worthless deluded heartbreaking blob of bullshit masquerading as a human being.

I try to imagine a God that could love you. It's beyond my power.

I am really fucking high.

Then I look in the general direction of Jason, say some things I will never remember in a million fucking years.

At some point, we wind up back at my apartment. Jason has purchased a bottle of wine. He kisses me, and I guess I let him.

We do some things that I forgot before they happened.

And the next thing I know, I am awake in the bed. Jason is gone, but you are there. So are the handcuffs. Did we use them? Did we not? Did I want to be pinned to that fucking headboard, as if to say *it's not my fault? I didn't do it? I wasn't there?* And did he say *no, I want your hands*? Or did he say *hey, I got you now*?

I'll never know. I will never know. Even if he tells me, I will not know for sure. Because I was gone, and all my painfully painstaking maintenance of the fortress went right along with it. Right out the fucking window. Out the window that probably echoed with my cries, although the odds are equally good that I never made a sound. Not wanting anyone to know. Anyone to know I feel.

But I feel. Oh God, I feel. I feel for poor stupid lovestruck Jason. I feel for poor stupid hungry me. I feel for you, who has laid here so long, and never once gotten up long enough to live. Or if you do, you wind up here.

You wind up here like me.

And I cannot move. I cannot move. The heat is astonishing. It pins me to the mattress, as surely as my mind. As surely as the pin in the oscillating fan, which locks the force of the whirling blades upon me.

I have fallen, and I can't get up. But you are there beside me.

I somehow find my arm, make it find your ass, make a finger probe its crease.

You awaken as I enter you. Get up. Find the bathroom. Pee.

And I lay there, listening to you live. Approach the new day with confidence. You move to the living room, put on the tape. Fucking Dixie Carter. I hate her ass.

Everything drones into everything else, as I lay here. Thinking and thinking and thinking. After a while, you come back in. I hate you. I hate myself.

"I can't get up," I say.

You say, "Uh-huh," and go into the closet.

Yes, I'm bad. I've done a horrible thing. And I'll do it again, you know.

If there's one thing you understand, it's that I will do it again. ✦

VISITATION

BY *David J. Schow*

Hardass skeptics are the best kind of skeptics, because they don't back down. Faith is great, but sometimes demanding proof is the best way to separate rumor from reality, wheat from chaff, and casual tourist from genuine traveler.

Lord knows, this can take a lifetime.

Should you last that long.

It takes a protean talent like David J. Schow to effortlessly combine the Gnostic stodginess of cultured old men and the go-for-broke mayhem of a young turk in his splatterpunk prime.

As both timeless and modern now as it was in the 80s, when it first appeared, I bring you the stately-yet-kickass "Visitation."

Angus Bond checked into the Hermitage alone, under an assumed name. He had been recognized in consort with too many fanatics to risk a traveling companion, though having Nicholas along would have been comforting. Nicholas was dead.

"Room 713," said the deskman, handing over a bronze key. "One of our suites, mister…ah, Orion, yes. Heh." The man's smile looked like a mortician's joke on a corpse, and Angus restrained himself from looking to see if the natty, three-piece clerk's suit was split up the back. The deskman was no zombie.

Close, Angus thought as he hefted his bags. But no.

The Hermitage was as Gothically overstated as Angus had expected it to be. Nothing he saw really surprised him—the ornamental iron gargoyles guarding the lobby doors, the unsettling, Bosch-like grotesques hanging in gilt frames beneath low-wattage display lamps, the Marie Antoinette chandeliers, their hexagonal prisms suggesting the imprisonment of lost souls like dragonflies stuck in amber. None of it moved Angus one way or the other. It was all rather standard haunted-house crap; occult chintz to get a rise out of the turistas.

The wine red carpeting absorbed his footfalls (greedily, he thought). The Hermitage seemed to be the place. At the door to 713, Angus held his key to the feeble light. He knew how to tilt it so the embossed metal threw down the shadow impression of a deathshead.

Satisfied, he unlocked the door and moved his baggage inside, in order that he might unpack and await the coming of the monsters.

The knock on the door jolted him to instant wariness. Angus took a bite out of a hard roll and left it behind on the leather-topped table with the sausage and cheese he had brought.

It was the zombie clerk, carrying a tarnished salver bearing a brilliantly white calling card, face down. Angus noted that the clerk seemed to smell like the sachets tucked into wardrobes by grandmothers to fend off mildew. The stark whiteness of the card cast deathly shadows on the man's pale features. It seemed to light up the hallway much more efficiently than the guttering yellow bulbs in the brass sconces.

"A gentleman to see you, sir," he said, with all the verve of a ventriloquist's dummy.

Angus picked up the card. It bore two words:

IMPERATIVE.
BRAY.

The clerk stood fast. When Angus realized why, he decided to test the water a little.

"Just a minute." He hurried off to fumble briefly through the depths of his greatcoat. There was the telltale clink of change, and he returned to the door with a silver dollar. Instead of placing it on the salver, he contrived to drop it, apparently accidentally, so that the clerk caught it, smoothly interrupting its fall with his free hand. He wore dusty butler's gloves that were going threadbare at the fingertips. He weighed the coin in the palm of his hand.

The air in the draftless hallway seemed to darken and roil thickly, like cream in hot coffee, for just a second, The clerk's features darkened; too, making his eyes appear to glow, the way a lightbulb flares just before it burns out. He sucked a quick gulp of air, as though dizzied by an abrupt stab of nausea. His features fought to remain whole, shifting like lard in a skillet, and Angus heard a distant, mad wail. It all took less than a second.

The clerk let the tip slide from the palm of his hand to rattle in the bowl of the metal dish. The queasy, death-rictus smile split across his face again, and he said, "Thank you. Sir."

He left. Angus closed his door and nodded to himself in affirmation.

The stranger was swaddled in fog-dampened tweeds and crowned with a road-weary homburg that had seen better days a few decades earlier. The initial impression left by the bearing of the man was that he was very old—not withered, or incapacitated in the way of those who wore years gracelessly, but old in the sense of worldly experience. An old man. Angus felt a sting of kinship here, deep in the midst of hazardous and alien territory.

"You are Angus Bond?" said the old man, arching a snow white eyebrow. "I am Turquine Bray."

"Nicholas Bray's father?" said Angus, ignoring that no one at the Hermitage knew his real name. The stranger had obviously just arrived.

"Grandfather. Paternal. His father was a null spiritual quantity, neither evil, nor good, like most in the world. He lived out his merchant's life and desired nothing but material things. He led a life of tawdriness and despair; but for seeding Nicholas, no residue of his passage, save the grief he caused others, endures. His fate was a well-deserved insignificance. Nicholas superseded him. Blotted him out. Nicholas once told me you were his closest friend."

The words bit Angus lightly, and the way Bray pulled off his glove advised that the late Nicholas had not dispensed his friendship or loyalty frivolously. The two men shook hands in the dank lobby of the Hermitage, the understanding already shared by them in no need of further words concerning Nicholas.

"I cannot say I am pleased to meet you at last, sir, under such circumstances," said Bray. "But I am relieved. Shall we walk outside? The atmosphere in here could make a vulture's eyes water…as it is intended to, no doubt."

The basilisk gaze of the clerk tracked them until they passed through the cataracted glass of the lobby s imposing double doors. Outside, the slate gray bulk of the Hermitage's castellated architecture monitored them dispassionately. It diminished behind them as they walked into the dense southern Kentucky woodland that made up the grounds.

"Gloomy," said Bray. "All this place needs is a tarn."

"Notice how the foliage grows together in tangles?" said Angus. "It meshes, with no nutritional support from the earth. The soil is nearly pure alkaline; I checked it. The stuff grows, and yet is dead. It laces together to keep out the sunlight—see? It's always overcast here."

"The appointments of that hotel are certainly Grand Guignol-ish. Like a Hollywood set for a horror film."

"Rather like the supposed 'ambience' one gains by patronizing a more expensive restaurant," said Angus. "I suspect you hit it on the head when you mentioned 'atmosphere.' That seems to be the purpose of all this theatrical embroidery— supernatural furniture. Atmosphere."

"Hm." Bray stepped laboriously over a rotting tree trunk. "Sinister chic."

The iron-colored mud stole dark footprints from them as they walked, their breath condensing whitely in the late January chill. Frost still rimed the dead vegetation, even in late afternoon. Angus was glad he had trotted out his muffler. If Poe could have seen this place, he mused, he would have been scared into a writing diet of musical comedy.

"Have you a room?" said Angus, after both men had stood in contemplative silence for a moment.

"I wanted to assure myself of your presence here, first."

"You followed me, then?" said Angus. "For whatever purpose? You certainly know of Nicholas's death already."

"I need you, Mr. Bond, to tell me the manner in which he died."

Angus sighed with resignation. "Mr. Bray," he said in a tone often rehearsed, "do you know just who I am?"

Bray's steely, chrome-colored eyes shot up to meet with Angus' watery blue ones, and he smiled a cursory smile. "You are Angus Gwyllm Orion Bond. Until roughly two years ago your profession was that of occult debunker—exposer of supernatural hoaxes. Absolute bane of fraudulent mediums, scamming astrologers, warlocks who were more common than sorcerers, and all the pop salesmen of lizard's tooth and owlet's wing. Until two years ago."

Bray's breath plumed out as he spoke. His speech was almost a recitation; Angus was impressed with the research.

"Two years ago, you vanished from the considerable media time and space you commanded. You evaporated from the airwaves, the talk shows. Rumor had you seeking the counsel of spiritualists and dabbling in magic yourself. Though you wound up debunking yourself, your books and other franchised items sold better than ever. I presume you've been supporting your now-private life with royalties?"

"Something like that."

"It was at precisely that time that you met up with my grandson. Nicholas was the antithesis of his father—a fantastic intellect and capacity for change. You know how he died."

"It ties together. The change in my life. Nick's death. I'm not sure you'd—"

"I am prepared for the outrageous, Mr. Bond. But I'm only interested in the truth. If the truth is merely outrageous, fire away."

"Nicholas came to my estate one night. He was frantic, pounding on the door, sweating, panicked. He couldn't tell me why. He had just moved into his new home at the time—do you recall it?"

"It was next to your estate. The Spilsbury mansion. Where all those actors were slaughtered by the religious cultists in the mid-1960s."

"Yes," said Angus. "Of course, by the time Nick moved in, that was ancient history. That place's allotted fifteen minutes of pop fame had been used up years before."

Bray smiled again.

"He was unnerved. When a horse 'smells' a tornado, it gets skittish; the closest Nicholas could speculate was that the house 'felt wrong,' and skittish was the word to describe him. I returned with him, to sit and drink by the fireplace. About forty-five minutes later…" Angus regretted his dramatic tone. But what occurred had been bloody dramatic.

"It was the first time I ever witnessed an interface," he said simply. "Mr. Bray, are you aware how supernatural agencies function physically? What enables the paranormal to coexist with the normal universe—yours and mine?"

"Assuming its reality," said Bray. "I'd speculate that it would be like an alternate dimension."

"Good. But not a physical dimension, not like a parallel world just staggered out of sync with our own. The supernatural is a matter of power potentials. It accumulates, in degrees, like a nuclear pile approaching critical mass. When there's too much, it blows off steam; venting into the real world, our world, becoming a temporary reality, sometimes only for a second or two."

"Accumulates? Like dust?" Bray said incredulously. "How?"

"It happens every time someone knocks on wood. Or crosses their fingers for luck, or says *gesundheit*. Every time one avoids walking under a ladder or lighting three on a match. Every time someone makes a joke about ghosts and doesn't disbelieve what he's saying one hundred percent; every time somebody uses a superstitious expression as a reflex cliché—let the sandman come and take you away; don't let the boogeyman get you. Every time some idiot in a church mentions the Devil. Anytime anyone seriously considers any of millions of minor-league bad-luck totems. It compounds itself exactly like dust, Mr. Bray—each of those things is a conscious, willful act that requires a minute portion of physical energy in some way. The paranormal energy simultaneously prompted by such action remains unperceived, but it is there, and it stacks up, one imperceptible degree at a time. Just like dust. And when you get an extra infusion of high-potency metaphysical force—"

"Like that Jim Jones thing?" said Bray. "Or the Spilsbury murders?"

"Precisely. You boost the backlog of power that much more. Whenever it reaches its own critical mass, it discharges into our reality. The house that Nicholas had moved into was a metaphysical stress point; it was still weak, thanks to the Spilsbury thing. A break point that had not completely healed."

"And during this—this interface, all that accumulated power blew through into my grandson's living room?" Bray shook his head. "I find that difficult to believe."

"Too outrageous?" said Angus, stopping suddenly.

Bray's expression dissolved to neutral. "Go on."

"That night the 'weakness' was not only at the juncture point of that house, but elsewhere. Temporarily, it was a 'weak' time period. Nick was in an agitated fear state—a 'weak,' receptive mental condition. But this phenomenon has no regular characteristic save that of overload—you can't count on it venting itself at any regular time, or place, or under any regular conditions. It vented somewhere else that night, and because of the weakened conditions we caught a squirt of it— bam! Two or three seconds; a drop of water from a flood. The flood went somewhere else."

Now Bray was frankly interested. "What was it like?"

"I got an impression of tremendous motive force," said Angus. "Blinding black light; a contradictory thing, I know, but there. The air felt pushed out of my lungs by a giant hand. Everything loose in the living room was blown free like summer chaff in a hurricane. Overpowering nausea. Vertigo. Disorientation. I was afraid, but it was a vague, unfocused kind of terror. It was much worse for Nicholas.

"You see, he—like most people—held latent beliefs in supernatural things. I did not. Too many years debunking special effects led to an utter skepticism for things that go bump in the night—for me. I saw raw, turbulent energy. Nicholas saw whatever he did not totally disbelieve. You might see demons, ghouls, vampire lycanthropes, the Old Ones all hungering for your flesh and soul, dragons gobbling you up and farting brimstone, Satan browsing through your body with a hot fondue fork. Or the Christian God, for that matter."

Bray was taken aback, obviously considering what such an experience would mean for him, given his life's collection of myth and superstition, of fairytale monsters and real-life guilts. All of it would manifest to his eyes. All of it, at once. He said, "You mean that every superstitions fear I've ever had is waiting to eat me, on the other side of a paranormal power overload?"

"Not as such," said Angus. "Your belief is what makes it real. True disbelief renders it unreal, back into energy, which is what I saw. But that energy, filtered through Nick's mind, made a monster. He said he was trying to hold the doorway to Hell shut, and something horrifying was pulling from the other side. It gave a good yank and the doorway cracked open for a split instant before the briefness of the 'squirt' closed it for good—but Nick, in that instant, saw what was trying to get him. It scared him white."

Bray was quiet for a long moment. Then: "He moved in with you shortly afterward?"

"Yes."

"You could not debunk the supernatural after that?"

"Not and do it with anything like conviction. Investigating the nature of the phenomenon became paramount."

"Nicholas helped you?"

"He was just the ally I needed. He had a propensity for pure research and a keen mind for deduction. We collected data and he indexed it. Using a computer, we were able to produce flow charts. One of the first things we discovered was the presence of 'pressure points' in the time flow—specific dates that were receptive to the power burst, as the Spilsbury house had been. Lammas, Beltane, Candlemas, Halloween. Almost all holidays. There are short bursts, long bursts, multidirectional bursts, weak and strong ones. Sometimes the proximity of a weak date will magnetize the power, attracting it to a particular time. But most of it concentrates at one physical place. Of course, there might be a dozen such outbursts in a day. Consider Jack the Ripper's reign over Spitalfields, or World War Two—the phenomenon would damn near become cyclical, feeding on itself."

"I see," said Bray. "But what about—"

"Nicholas?" Angus interrupted his meandering walk, hands in pockets. "I think the road is just above us, there. Shall we climb up out of this muck and make our way back? I have a flask of arrack in my room, to help cut the chill."

"Thank you," Bray said as Angus helped him through a web of creepers.

"Nicholas was very good at charts," said Angus. "He cross-matched all the power bursts—he was the one who called them 'squirts,' by the way—to ebb and flow grids, and to longitudes and latitudes. He calculated in 'weak spots' and compensated for them. He synthesized a means whereby he could predict, with reasonable accuracy, the location and date of a future 'squirt.' Sometimes he was wrong."

"But he was right for at least one," said Bray.

"In Manhattan," said Angus, "in a dilapidated, condemned office complex called the Dixon Building, he and I faced a full-power blast, alone."

"Oh my god—"

"God is right. Nicholas was eaten alive by the demons on the other side of the door. He still believed."

The two old men scrambled up onto the road facing the Hermitage, in the distance. It loomed darkly against the overcast sky, in silhouette, like a dinosaur waiting for dinner.

"In that hotel, tonight, at precisely one-thirty A.M., there will be an interface such as I've described. On paper, at least, it's one of the biggest I've ever seen. There are a lot of superstitious people out there in the world. I can show you the graphs, in my room."

Together, Angus and Bray entered the maw of the Hermitage.

"Have you taken stock of the clientele here yet?" said Bray as Angus shucked his heavy coat. Since Angus had not been able to coax the room's antediluvian steam coil into boosted output and since the fireplace still held cold tinder, both men kept their sweaters on. The arrack was forestalled when Bray produced a travel decanter of cognac from the depths of his overcoat.

"There is a word for this supernatural power," Angus said. "Some call it *mana*. It's like electricity—neither good nor evil in itself, but available to those who know how to harness it. Devoid of context, there is no 'good' or 'evil.' I am not the only one who has discovered that the interfaces can be charted. Others will be swift to use such power potentials for selfish or harmful ends. They would embrace the iconography of what the unenlightened blanket with the term evil. That desk clerk, for example. I never saw anyone who wanted to be a vampire more, yet to exist as a true vampire would be a pitiable state indeed. I slipped him a silver dollar earlier, one I had charged in accordance with legend as a protective talisman." He dragged a ponderous Victorian chair over to the table where Bray sat nursing his cognac and staring abstractedly through the parted drapes, into the courtyard below them.

Bray saw three men in black awkwardly bearing an enormous footlocker into the lobby. "You mean like a witchcraft amulet?"

Sipping, Angus said, "Amulets are no good if they're not in your possession. This was a talisman—charged by the book, in this case, the original text of a grimoire called the *Liber Daemonorum*, published in 1328 by a fellow named Protassus. I have a first edition."

"And the clerk?"

"Since he was behaving by such rigid rules, it was almost boringly simple to anticipate him. He reacted as though he was about to burst at the seams. If not for the gloves he wore, I think that talisman might've burned right through his hand to drop on the floor. But the predictability of a phenomenon or movement does not necessarily decrease its potential threat or danger. Don't kid yourself about the uses some intend for such power. It's backed up like sewage on the other side of the veil, waiting to be tapped, ever-increasing. A lot of bad could be created. Power corrupts." He killed his glass and Bray moved to refill it.

"Why expose yourself to something like that?" said Bray, now concerned.

"Surely you've had a bellyful of baring your psyche to the tempest—or can you build some kind of tolerance?"

"To a degree, yes. It's still an ordeal, a mental and physical drain. But I can stand, where others would bend." Angus leaned closer; spoke confidentially: "You've missed a more obvious reason for doing so."

"Nicholas?" Bray said finally. "Vengeance?"

Angus swallowed another firebolt of liquor. "Not as an eye-for-an-eye thing. Nicholas' death convinced me that the phenomenon itself must be interrupted. Each outburst is more powerful. Each comes closer on the heels of the last. It is as though it is creating a bigger and bigger space in our reality in which to exist. The 'valve' must be closed before the continuous escalation makes preventive action impossible."

"By god!" said Bray, his eyes lighting up. "The talisman!"

"I hope it wasn't too ostentatious—announcing my presence in the Hermitage with that stunt. As far as the rest of the congregation here is concerned, I'm just another acolyte."

"I haven't seen too many people since I arrived."

"Well, they'd shun the daylight by nature, anyway," said Angus. "Or what passes for daylight around here." He let his eyes drift into infinity focus, regarding the courtyard below. "You know, the Hermitage is quite an achievement, for what it is. But it isn't 'evil.' The power I spoke of, the *mana*, is what keeps the sunlight from this place and makes dead trees root in dead ground. Channeled and controlled, the mana could be used to build a perfect womb for something that would be evil by anybody's definition. Something designed by people of ill intent to fit every preconception. Tonight's surge is a big one. Maybe it's going to fuel a birth."

"I don't even want to think about that possibility," said Bray.

"I must." Angus dumped one of his satchels onto the bed. "During that one-thirty juncture tonight, I must try to put a bogey in the paranormal plumbing."

"How?" said Bray, now visibly unnerved and looking about fruitlessly for a clock. "How does one stop that much power, barreling right at you?"

"One doesn't. You turn it against itself, like holding a mirror up to a gorgon's face. It takes, in this special case, not only protective talismans against the sheer forces themselves, but also my anti-belief in the various physical manifestations—the monsters. The power will exhaust itself through an infinite echo effect, crashing back and forth like a violently bouncing ball inside a tiny box." He drained his glass again. "In theory, that is."

"Plausible," Bray said. "But then, you're the expert on this sort of thing. I suppose we'll see the truth early this morning...."

"No!" Angus' face flushed with sudden panic. "'You must leave this place, before—"

"Leave you here alone, to fight such a fight alone? I admit that two old men may not present much of a threat to the powers you describe, but where in hell am I to go, knowing that such things transpire?" Bray's hand grew white-knuckled around his glass.

"Your own dormant fears might destroy you," Angus said levelly. "Another death on my conscience."

"What am I to do, then?" Bray stiffened. "You may not believe in revenge, but I do. I insist! I side with you or I am less than a man...and that is my final word on the matter sir." As punctuation, he finished his cognac.

The expression on Angus' face was neutrally sober, but within, he was smiling.

Midnight should have been anticlimactic. It was not.

In the funereal quiet of the lobby, an ebony clock boomed out twelve brass tones that resounded throughout the hotel like strikes on a huge dinner gong. A straggler, dressed in tatters, fell to the wine red carpeting in convulsions, thrashing madly about. The stalwart desk clerk had watched the man inscribe three sixes on his forehead earlier, using hot ashes from the lobby fireplace. The ornamental andirons hissed their pleasure, hotly.

An almost sub-aural dirge, like a deep, constant synthesizer note, emanated from the ground floor and gradually possessed the entire structure. A chilling undercurrent of voices seemed to seep through the building's pipework and the hidden, dead spaces between walls.

In the Grand Ballroom, the chandeliers began to move by themselves. Below their ghostly tinkling, a quartet of figures in hooded tabards raised their arms in supplication. Candles of sheep tallow were ignited. Mass was enjoined.

Somewhere near the top of the hotel, someone screamed for nearly a whole minute. Unearthly, lowering noises issued from the grounds, now heavily misted in nightfog. There were the sounds of strange beasts in pain, and vague echoes of something large and massy, moving sluggishly as though trapped in a tar pit. It was starlessly dark outside.

"Are you positive you wish to stay?" said Angus, opening the flask of arrack. Bray's private stock was long gone.

"Yes. Just pour me another glass, please." Each new, alien sound made Bray wince a little, inside the folds of his coat, but he maintained bravely.

From within his shirt, Angus fished out a key on a thin chain of silver links. He twiddled it in each of his satchels' two locks. The first thing he produced from the case was a book lashed together with stained violet ribbons.

"Good god," Bray choked. "Is that the—"

"*The Liber Daemonorum.* Pity this must be destroyed tonight. By burning. Damn shame. This is a collector's item." He heaved the volume onto the bed and the rank smell of foxed and mildewed age-old paper washed toward Bray. Brittle pieces of the ragged hide binding flaked to the floor.

Nearby, probably in the hall outside 713, someone howled like a dog until his voice gave out with an adenoidal squeak.

Bray's attention was drawn from the ancient witchcraft tome to the disk of burnished gold Angus removed from the satchel. It was an unbroken ring, big as a salad plate, with free-cast template characters clinging to its inner borders. It caught the feeble light in the room and threw it around in sharp flashes.

"Gold?" said Bray, awestruck.

"Solid, refined twenty-four karat, pure to the fifth decimal point," said Angus, tossing it to the bed. The heavy chain necklace attached to it jingled; the disk bounced a hard crescent of light off the ceiling directly above. "The purity of the metal used in the talisman has protective value. I won't put it on until a few seconds before deadline—keep it as potent as possible, you understand."

From the satchel came more protective fetishes, mojo bags of donkey teeth, copper thread and travertine, hex stones with glyptic symbols, inked spells on parchment bound with little thongs, tiny corked vials of opaque liquids. Angus tucked these into his clothing.

Something thumped heavily and repeatedly on the floor above them. Drum chants could be faintly heard.

"Any doubts now about there not being a full house here tonight?" Angus said. Bray's hand quivered in betrayal as he drank. Angus regretted that the academic portion of his mind regarded Bray simply as a handicap; his sense of honor could not refuse the older man. He hoped he would survive what was to follow, but would allow no compromising of his own task. Silence hung between them awhile longer.

"Does it matter where we are when it hits?"

"No. This hotel is the place. The psychos surrounding us are like the creepy trappings—more supernatural furniture. Pay them no heed. What we're dealing with has no form. You can be tricked by illusions; if you even consider for a second that something monstrous before your eyes might possibly be real, you're lost—you must remember that. The demon Nicholas saw was not real, until he thought it might be, making him afraid. Then it ate him up."

"Angus!" Bray stood from his chair. "I can—I can feel something strange… palpable, a swelling…like a balloon about to burst…." He looked around, agitated now.

Angus hauled out his railroad watch. "One-twenty-seven A.M. I set this by the time service in Willoughby late yesterday. Hmm—I suppose no time service is strictly accurate." He slipped quickly into the talisman.

"It's really coming," said Bray in shaky disbelief.

"Exactly like the atmospheric buildup Nicholas sensed, before the squirt at his house," Angus said. "I have no extra white-power objects, friend Bray. You'll have to stick close behind me. That's about the only aid I can offer you. And something else—" He hurriedly dug a dented tin of Ronson lighter fluid out of the satchel and doused the *Liber Daemonorum*. The pungent liquid soaked slowly into the comforter on the bed and saturated the book of sorcery. Angus then came up with several disposable plastic cigarette lighters, each gimmicked with electrical tape. "Take one of these, and listen to me. During the confrontation, I may become momentarily transfixed. If that happens, I want you to light the book. It must be burned during the interface if my other, lesser shielding spells are to function. The lighter is modified to produce a long jet of flame when you thumb the wheel. Understand that the book is rare, and dangerous, and the supplicants booked into this place would gladly murder us to get it. If I hesitate, destroy it!"

Bray clutched the lighter tightly, like a crucifix against a vampire.

As though in the grip of an earthquake tremor, the Hermitage shuddered. A chunk of whorled plaster ceiling disengaged and smashed into chalky crumbles at Angus' feet.

"Remember, Bray!" he shouted. "It's not real—"

The rest of his words were obliterated by a thunderclap concussion of moving air as the oak door to 713 blew off its hinges and slapped the floor like a huge, wooden playing card. The French windows past Bray splintered outward in a shrieking hail of needlelike glass bits. The bottles and rickrack on the table scattered toward the window. The cognac flask pegged Bray's temple and brought blood. The vacuum force of the moving air seemed to suck the breath from him. He screamed Angus' name, soundlessly.

Angus labored toward the door, walking ponderously, like a trapper in a snowbank, one hand holding the outthrust talisman, the other readying the lighter for the *Liber Daemonorum* crooked against his chest. Outside, the corridor was awash in stunning yellow light. A high-frequency keen knifed into his ears and numbed his brain. He heard his name being called over and over, coupled with a maniacal laugh that kept shifting speeds, accelerating and slowing, a warped record in the hands of a lunatic disc jockey. Through the shimmer and glare, Angus thought he could see stunted, writhing shapes—various monsters struggling to be born of his mind. He stared them down and one by one they were absorbed back into the light that produced them, dissolving as though beaten progressively thinner with a mallet until the light shone through and disintegrated them. The talisman began to radiate heat against his chest. The first echo had been achieved.

The maniac sounds were definitely caused by something in terrific pain, fighting him. In the hallway mirror, Angus saw himself vaporize—hair popping aflame, shearing away, skin peeling back as though sandblasted off, skull rushing backward in a cloud of sugary powder, blood and brains vanishing in a quick cloud of color and stink.

It was an illusion, and he ignored it.

He tried to ignore the dim, background sound of Bray's screaming.

A gray lizard demon, scales caked in glistening slime, breached the outside window to 713 and pounced on Bray's back, ripping and tearing. More rushed in like a floodtide, their alligator snouts rending his clothing, their flying spittle frying through his skin like brown acid. Curved black talons laid open his chest and they began to devour him organ by organ. His lighter went spinning uselessly across the floor.

Angus caught a glimpse of the carnage taking place behind him. Bray was lost.

Angus stopped his advance. Bray was dead.

Bray was dead, and the typhoon of yellow force petered to nothingness in a second. Standing ridiculously alone in the quiet of the cathedral-like hallway, Angus realized, with a plummeting kind of bright, orange horror in his stomach, that he had lost.

He looked up and down the hallway. Nothing.

Then, distant, indecipherable sounds. Hungry sounds.

The book! The book! his mind screamed. His thumb automatically worked the lighter, and a jet of blue propane fire at least half a foot long spurted up, caressing the *Liber Daemonorum*. It billowed into flame along with his soaked coat-sleeve.

But the two iron gargoyles from the lobby were already winging toward Angus with metal-muscled strokes. He heard the grating of their black, iron flesh pumping and looked up to see their diamond eyes fix on him. They peeled to either side of him as the book touched off; one swooped past in a blur, hooking the book away to smother it against its bellows chest, the other jackknifing upward in midair to strafe Angus. He felt cold, sharp pain. His feet left the floor and he crashed onto his back, rolling clumsily, blood daubing into one eye from the gashes the gargoyle's iron, butcher-cleaver claws had carved in his forehead.

His name was still being called, fast and slow and fast and—

"Angus." The tone was first disapproving, then pitying. "Angus, you poor old sod."

Turquine Bray stood over him holding the still-smoking *Liber Daemonorum*. The violet ribbons were charred.

The iron gargoyles circled high in the corridor, lighting behind Bray. They cringed and fidgeted, like greyhounds, grinding their javelin teeth and snorting mist through cast-iron nostrils with impatience.

"Since you've delivered this book to us," Bray said, "I think you're owed a few words." His hands slithered proudly around the tome and his chromium eyes glittered at Angus.

"The gargoyles—" Angus gasped from the floor.

"Oh, yes, they're real enough. They're a bit piqued because I haven't given you to them yet." Angus could see that Bray spoke around a mouthful of needled fangs like the dental work of a rattlesnake. "Your disbelief in monsters posed an intriguing problem. How to chink such metal armor? How to trick you, the expert on all the tricks? You wouldn't believe in the patently unreal, so we made you believe in something else you'd accept with less question. The gargoyles are now real, thanks to your mind. Turquine Bray, however, died in 1974. On Valentine's Day." The Bray thing, its hair gone jet black, eyes sunken to mad ball bearings in seductive, dark pits, grinned wolfishly.

"Impossible!" Breathing was becoming difficult for Angus, as though his lungs were filling with hot candle wax. "Impossible...the power burst...you existed before the interface took place...."

"My dear Angus," the creature rasped in a phlegmatic voice, "you're not paying attention. This power burst was the biggest of all so far. People are more superstitious than ever. They go right on stacking it up. This surge was preceded by what young Nicholas characterized as a 'squirt,' a considerable leakage that primed the paranormal pump, you might say." It pretended to inspect its elongated, spiked nails. "How do you think something as melodramatic as the Hermitage got here in the first place? It came out of your mind. It was what you expected; know-nothing cultists and pop Satanists and horror-movie props—supernatural furniture. It was all an illusion, as was I. But it's real now. *The Liber Daemonorum* will help to keep our family corporeal."

Two shuffling corpses battered down the stairway door leading into the hallway. Their sightless, maggoty eyesockets sought Angus' prone form. They made for him with inexorable slowness, rotting flesh dropping off their frames in clots. They hungered.

"Your H. P. Lovecraft might be pleased to know that his Old Ones are finally coming home," the monster growled. It stretched cavernously, bursting from its human clothes, revealing a wide body of insectile armor plating with double-jointed birdlike legs whose hooked toes gathered the carpet up in bunches. "It's all quite real now, friend Angus." The steely, silver eyes transfixed Angus from a nine-foot height. "As are my other friends. Here. Now."

The gargoyles jumped into the air and hovered like carrion birds. From 713 the reptilian scavengers continued to swarm, champing their oversized jaws, streamers of drool webbing the carpeting. Beyond the steaming, toothy thing that had been Bray, Angus saw a translucent horde of ghostly, humanoid leeches. The scuttling things advanced, worrying their bloodless, watchmaker's claws together in anticipation of a dark, burgundy-hued snack.

He recognized them now, all of the monsters, all of his lifetime's research into the occult, echoing back upon him. If he could be made to believe Bray had been real, then anything could follow....Zaebos, a demon with a human head and the body of a crocodile, entreated him from the end of the corridor. Near the ceiling floated the Keres, the Greek vampire entities who appear before death. Windigos—cannibalistic Indian ghosts—crowded past the living-dead corpses to get to Angus' position. They licked their lips. Now, Angus knew the name of the monster before him, the spirit who had assumed Bray's form to trick him. It was the Master of Ceremonies to the Infernal Court.

"Verdelet!" he croaked, holding the talisman forward. "Swallow this!"

"Now, now," the demon said. "Too late for that hocus-pocus, Angus. You believe now." It waved an ebony claw carelessly, and the talisman melted, sizzling through Angus' clothing, scalding and eating into his chest with a geyser of golden steam.

He managed a howling scream.

"I have nought but gratitude for you, friend Angus," Verdelet said. "Thanks to you, as of this night, the Hermitage is open for business."

The last thing Angus heard was the wet sounds of jaws, opening. ✦

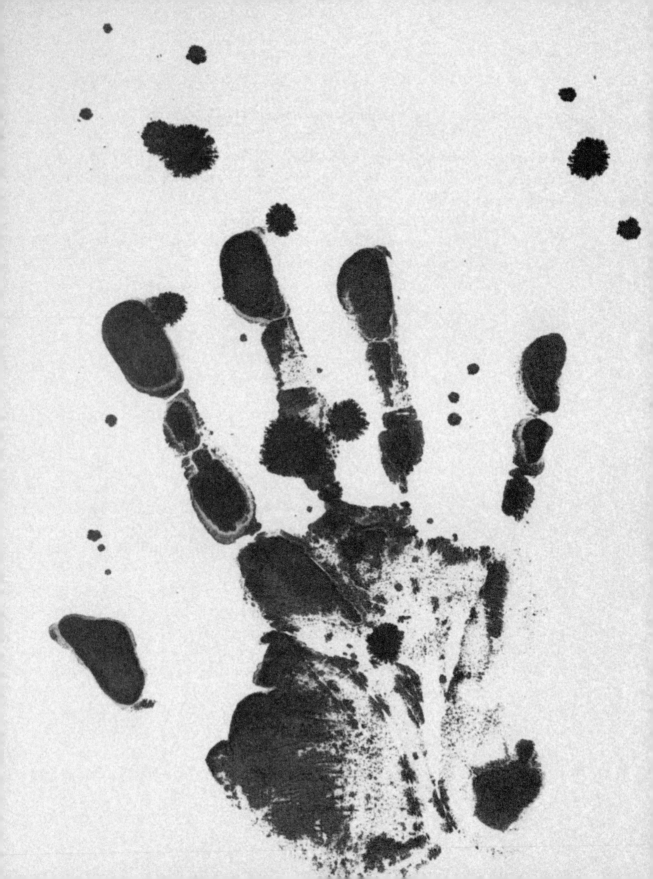

BEST FRIENDS

BY *Robert R. McCammon*

Who do you like, when you hardly like anyone? Most likely, the ones who will watch your back in times of deepest crisis.

If you're sort of a good guy—or like to think you are—that's one set of possibilities.

If you're not, that opens a whole 'nother bunch of doors.

This right here is a full-tilt monsterama, where the terrible things inside you don't seem half as bad as they will in a minute.

It's vintage McCammon, with an honest-to-God feature film's worth of character and action action action.

Let the sorting, and the terror, begin.

One

He hurried across the parking lot, through a nasty stinging rain, and into the entrance of the Marbury Memorial Hospital. Under his right arm, in a dark brown satchel, was the life history of a monster.

He shrugged droplets of water from his raincoat and left wet tracks on the jade-green linoleum floor as he approached the nurse at the central information desk. He recognized Mrs. Curtis, and she said good morning and opened a drawer to get a nametag for him.

"Wet day," she commented, her glasses resting on the edge of her nose as she watched him sign in. "Lot of doctors going to make some money off this weather."

"I imagine so." He dripped a few water spots on the page and tried to brush them away before they sank through. In firm, spiky penmanship, he wrote *Dr. Jack Shannon*, followed by the date and time, *10/16* and *10:57 A.M.*, and his destination, *8th floor*. He looked up the list of other names and noted that the public defender, Mr. Foster, was not yet here. Should he wait in the lobby or go up alone? He decided to wait. No sense rushing things.

"Full caseload today?" Mrs. Curtis asked him. It was in her voice. She knew. Of course she knows. Jack thought. Probably the entire hospital staff knew, and certainly Mrs. Curtis, who'd been a fixture behind the information desk for the six years that Jack had been coming here, would know. The newspapers had screamed the case, and so had the T.V. stations. "No," he said. "Just seeing one."

"Uh huh." She waited for him to say more, and pretended to watch the rain falling past the picture window. The sky was gray, the rain was gray, and all the color of the forest that surrounded Marbury Memorial seemed to be shades of gray as well. The city of Birmingham lay about four miles to the west, hidden by clouds that had skulked into the valley and settled there, brooding. It was Alabama autumn at its worst, humid and heavy enough to make bones moan. Just three days ago, the air had been cool enough for Marbury Memorial's custodial staff to shut down the air-conditioners; they remained off, and the old hospital—built out of red bricks and gray stone in 1947—held heat and dampness in its walls, exuding them in stale breaths that moved ghostlike through the corridors.

"Well," Mrs. Curtis said at last, and pushed her glasses off her nose with a wiry finger, "I expect you've seen worse."

Jack didn't answer. He wasn't sure he *had* seen worse; and, in fact, he was quite sure he had not. He wished Mrs. Curtis a good day and walked to the lobby's seating area, facing the picture window and the grayness beyond. He found a discarded newspaper, took off his wet raincoat and sat down to kill some time, because he didn't care to go up to the eighth floor without the public defender along.

And there it was, on page one: a picture of the Clausen house, and a story with the headline *Juvenile Held in Bizarre Triple Slaying*. Jack looked at the picture as rain tapped on the window nearby. It was just a white-painted suburban house with front porch and three stone steps, a neatly-trimmed yard and a carport. Nothing special about it, really; just one of many hundreds in that area of town. It looked like a house where Tupperware parties might be hosted, where cakes would be baked in a small but adequate kitchen and folks would hunker down in front of the den's T.V. to watch football games on Saturday afternoons, in a neighborhood where everybody knew each other and life was pleasant. It looked all-American and ordinary, except for one clue: the bars on the windows.

Of course a lot of people bought those wrought-iron burglar bars and placed them over the windows and doors. Unfortunately, that was part of modern civilization—but these burglar bars were different. These were set *inside* the windows, not on the outside. These appeared to have the purpose of keeping something in, rather than keeping intruders out. Other than the strange placement of the burglar bars, the Clausen house was neither especially attractive nor displeasing. It just was.

On page two the story continued, and there were pictures of the victims. A grainy wedding photograph of Mr. and Mrs. Clausen, a fourth-grade school shot of the little girl. Thank God there were no pictures of the house's interior after the slayings, Jack thought; he was already having a tough enough time maintaining his professional composure.

He put the newspaper aside. There was nothing new in the story, and Jack could've recited the facts from memory. Everything was contained in the satchel, and the rest of what Jack sought to know lay in the mind of a boy on the eighth floor.

He listened to the rhythm of the hospital—the polite bing-bonging of signal bells through the intercom system, followed by requests for various doctors; the quiet, intense conversations of other people, friends and relatives of patients, in the seating area; the squeak of a nurse's shoes on the linoleum; the constant opening and closing of elevator doors. An ambulance's siren wailed from the emergency entrance on the west side of the hospital. A wheelchair creaked past, a black nurse pushing a pregnant dark-haired woman to the elevators en route to the maternity ward on the second floor. Two austere doctors in white coats stood talking to an elderly man, his face gray and stricken; they all entered an elevator together, and the numbers marched upward. The daily patterns of life and death were in full motion here, Jack mused. A hospital seemed to be a universe in itself, teeming with small comedies and tragedies, an abode of miracles and secrets from the morgue in its chill basement to the eighth-floor's wide corridors where mental patients paced like caged tigers.

He checked his wristwatch. Eleven-thirteen. Foster was running late, and that wasn't his usual—

"Dr. Shannon?"

Jack looked up. Standing next to his chair was a tall red-haired woman, raindrops clinging to her coat and rolling off her closed-up umbrella. "Yes," he said.

"I'm Kay Douglas, from the public defender's office." She offered a hand, and he stood up and shook it. Her grip was sturdy, all-business, and did not linger. "Mr. Foster can't make it today."

"Oh. I thought the appointment was set."

"It was, but Mr. Foster has other business. I'm to take his place."

Jack nodded. "I see." And he did: Bob Foster had political ambitions. Being directly associated with a case like this, with all the attendant publicity, was not expedient for Foster's career. Naturally, he'd send an aide. "Fine with me," Jack said. "Are you signed in?"

"Yes. Shall we go?" She didn't wait for him to agree; she turned and walked with a purposeful stride to the elevators, and he followed a few steps behind.

They shared an elevator with a young, fresh-faced couple and a slim black nurse; the couple got off on two, and when the nurse departed on the fourth floor, Jack said, "Have you met him yet?"

"No, not yet. Have you?"

He shook his head. The elevator continued its ascent, old gears creaking. The woman's pale green eyes watched the numbers advance above the door. "So Mr. Foster thought this was a little too hot to handle, huh?" Jack said. She didn't respond. "I don't blame him. The prosecutor gets all the good publicity in cases like this."

"Dr. Shannon," she said, and gave him a quick, piercing glance, "I don't think there's ever been a case like this before. I hope to God there isn't another."

The elevator jarred slightly, slowing down as it reached the uppermost floor. The doors rumbled open, and they had reached Marbury Memorial's psychiatric ward.

Two

"Hiya, docky!" a silver-haired woman in a bright blue shift, Adidas sneakers and a headband called out, marching along the corridor toward him. Her face was a mass of wrinkles, her lips rubbery and daubed with crimson lipstick. "You come to see me today?"

"Not today, Margie. Sorry."

"Shit! Docky, I need a bridge partner! Everybody's crazy up here!" Margie looked long and hard at Kay Douglas. "Who's this? Your girlfriend?"

"No. Just ... a friend," he said, to simplify things.

"Red hair on the head don't exactly mean red hair on the pussy," Margie warned, and Kay's face flushed to a similar hue. A gaunt, elderly man dressed immaculately in a pinstriped suit, white shirt and tie strode up, making a low grunting noise in his throat. "Stop that shit, Ritter!" Margie demanded. "Nobody wants to hear your 'gator imitations!"

Other people were approaching from up and down the corridor. Kay retreated a pace, and heard the elevator doors hiss shut at her back. She looked over her shoulder, noting that the elevator on this floor had no button, but was summoned by a key.

"Now you're caught!" Margie said to her, with a crooked smile. "Just like us!"

"Ain't nobody said we was gonna have us a parade this mornin'!" a mighty voice boomed. "Give Doc Shannon room to breathe, now!" A husky black nurse with white hair, massive girth and legs like dark logs moved toward Jack and Kay. Ritter gave her one more throaty grunt, like an alligator's love song, and then obeyed the nurse.

"Docky's come up to see me today, Rosalee!" Margie protested. "Don't be rude!"

"He ain't come up to see nobody on our ward," Rosalee told her. The black woman had gray eyes, set in a square and rugged face. "He's got other business."

"What other business?"

"Rosalee means Dr. Shannon's on his way to see the new arrival," said a younger man. He sat in a chair across the corridor, turned to face the elevator. "You know. The crazy fucker."

"Watch your mouth, Mr. Chambers," Rosalee said curtly. "There are ladies present."

"Women, yeah. Ladies, I'm not so sure." He was in his mid-thirties, wore faded jeans and a blue-checked shirt with rolled-up sleeves, and he took a draw on a cigarette and plumed smoke into the air. "You a lady, miss?" he asked Kay, staring at her with dark brown, deep-socketed eyes.

She met his gaze. The man had a brown crewcut and the grizzle of a beard, and he might have been handsome but for the boniness of his face and those haunted eyes. "I've been told so." she answered, and her voice only quavered a little bit.

"Yeah?" he grinned wolfishly. "Well. . . somebody lied."

"Show some respect now, Mr. Chambers." Rosalee cautioned. "We want to be courteous to our visitors, and all those who don't care to be courteous might have their smokin' privileges yanked. Got it?" She stood, hands on huge hips, waiting for a response.

He regarded the cigarette's burning end for a few seconds in silence. Then, grudgingly: "Got it."

"How're you feeling today, Dave?" Jack asked, glad the little drama had been resolved. "You still have headaches?"

"Uh huh. One big fat black bitch of a headache."

"*Out.*" Rosalee's voice was low this time, and Jack knew she meant business. "Put your cigarette out, Mr. Chambers."

He puffed on it, still grinning.

"I said put the cigarette out, please sir." She stepped toward him. "I won't ask you again."

One last long draw, and Dave Chambers let the smoke leak through his nostrils. Then he opened his mouth and popped the burning butt inside. Kay gasped as the man's throat worked.

A little whorl of smoke escaped from between his lips. "That suit you?" he asked the nurse.

"Yes, thank you." She glanced at Kay. "Don't fret, ma'am. He does that trick all the time. Puts it out with his spit before he swallers it."

"Better than some of the pigshit they give you to eat around this joint," Dave said, drawing his legs up to his chest. He wore scuffed brown loafers and white socks.

"I think I'd like some water." Kay walked past Rosalee to a water fountain. A small woman with a bird's-nest of orange hair followed beside her like a shadow, and Kay tried very hard not to pay any attention. Foster had told her Marbury Memorial's mental ward was a rough place, full of county cases and understaffed as well, but he'd voiced his confidence that she could handle the task. She was twenty-eight years old, fresh from a legal practice in south Alabama, and it was important to her that she fit in at Foster's office. She'd only been on the job for two months, and she presumed this was another one of the public defender's tests; the first test, not three weeks ago, had involved counting the bullet holes in a bloated, gassy corpse dredged up from the bottom of Logan Martin lake.

"Good water. Yum yum," the woman with orange hair said, right in her ear, and Kay gurgled water up her nose and dug frantically in her purse for a tissue.

"Dr. Cawthorn's already in there." Rosalee nodded toward the white door, way down at the end of the hallway. At this distance the doorway seemed to float in the air, framed between white walls and white ceiling. "Been there for maybe fifteen minutes."

"Has he pulled the boy out of containment yet?" Jack asked.

"Doubt it. Wouldn't do that without you and the lawyer there. She *is* a lawyer, ain't she?"

"Yes."

"Thought so. Got the lawyer's look about her. Anyways, you know how Dr. Cawthorn is. Probably just sittin' in there, thinkin'."

"We're late. We'd better go in."

Margie grasped at his sleeve. "Docky, you watch out for that fella. Saw his face when they brung him in. He'll shoot rays out of his eyes and kill you dead, I swear to God he will."

"I'll remember that, thanks." He pulled gently free, and gave Margie a composed smile that was totally false. His guts had begun to churn, and his hands were icy. "Who's on security?" he asked Rosalee.

"Gil Moon's on the door. Bobby Crisp's on desk duty."

"Good enough." He glanced back to make sure Kay was ready to go. She was wiping her nose with a tissue and trying to get away from the small orange-haired woman everyone knew as 'Kitten'. He started for the door, with Rosalee at his side and Kay lagging behind.

"Better not go in there. Dr. Shannon!" Dave Chambers warned. "Better stay away from that crazy fucker!"

"Sorry. It's my job," he answered.

"Fuck the job, man. You've only got one life."

Jack didn't reply. He passed the nurse's desk, where Mrs. Marion and Mrs. Stewart were on duty, and continued on toward the door. It seemed to be coming up much too fast. The documents and photographs in his satchel emerged from memory with startling clarity, and almost hobbled him. But he was a psychiatrist—a very good one, according to his credentials—and had worked with the criminally insane many times before. This ought not to bother him. Ought not to. Determining whether a person was fit to stand trial or not was part of his job, and in that capacity he'd seen many things that were distasteful. But this . . . this was different. The photographs, the circumstances, the plain white house with burglar bars inside the windows . . . very different, and deeply disturbing.

The white door was there before he was ready for it. He pressed a button on the wall and heard the buzzer go off inside. Through the square of glass inset in the door. Jack watched Gil Moon approach and take the proper key from the ring at his belt. Gil, a barrel-chested man with close-cropped gray hair and eyes as droopy as a hound's, nodded recognition and slid the key into the lock. At the same time, Rosalee Partain put her own key into the second lock. They disengaged with gunshot cracks, so loud they made Kay jump. Steady! she told herself. You're supposed to be a professional, so by God you'd better act like one!

The door, made of wood over metal, was pulled open. Gil said, "Mornin', Dr. Shannon. Been expectin' you."

"Have fun," Rosalee said to Kay, and the nurse relocked the door on her side after Gil had pushed it shut again.

He locked his side. "Dr. Cawthorn's down in the conference room. Howdy do, miss."

"Hello," she said uneasily, and she followed Jack Shannon and the attendant along a green tile-floored corridor with locked doors on each side. The light was fluorescent and harsh, and at the corridor's end was a single barred window that faced gray woods. A slender young black man, wearing the same white uniform as Gil Moon, sat behind a desk at the corridor's midpoint; he'd been reading a *Rolling Stone* magazine and listening to music over headphones, but he stood up as Shannon approached. Bobby Crisp had large, slightly protuberant dark brown eyes and wore a gold pin in his right nostril. "Hi, Dr. Shannon," he said, glanced quickly at the red-haired woman and gave her a nod of greeting.

"Morning, Bobby. How goes it?"

"It goes," he answered, with a shrug. "Just floating between the worms and the angels, I guess."

"Guess so. Are we all set up?"

"Yes sir. Dr. Cawthorn's waiting in there." He motioned toward the closed door marked *Conference*. "Do you want Clausen out of containment now?"

"Yes, that'd be fine. Shall we?" Jack moved to the conference room, opened it and held it for Kay.

Inside, there was gray carpet on the floor and pine paneling on the walls.

Barred windows with frosted glass admitted murky light, and recessed squares of fluorescents glowed at the ceiling. There was a single long table with three chairs at one end and a single chair down at the other. At one of the three sat a bald and brown-bearded man wearing horn-rimmed glasses and reading from a file folder. He stood up when he saw Kay. "Uh . . . hello. I thought Mr. Foster was coming."

"This is Kay Douglas, from Foster's office," Jack explained. "Miss Douglas, this is Dr. Eric Cawthorn, head of psychiatric services."

"Good to meet you." They shook hands, and Kay propped her umbrella up in a corner, took off her damp raincoat and hung it on a wall hook. Underneath, she was wearing a plain dark pinstriped jacket and skirt.

"Well, I guess we're ready to proceed." Jack sat down at the head of the table and put his satchel beside him, popping it open. "I've asked that Clausen be brought out of containment. Has he been difficult?"

"No, not at all." Cawthorn took his seat. "He's been quiet since they brought him in, but for security reasons we've kept him suppressed."

"Suppressed?" Kay sat down opposite Cawthorn. "What's that mean?"

"Straitjacketed," he answered. His pale blue eyes cut quickly to Jack and then returned to the woman. "It's standard procedure when we have a case of vio—"

"But you said Mr. Clausen's been quiet since he was given over to your custody. How do you justify a straitjacket for a quiet patient?"

"Miss Douglas?" Jack brought a folder up from his satchel and put it before him. "How much do you know about this case? I know Foster must've briefed you, you've seen the newspaper stories. But have you seen the police photographs?"

"No. Mr. Foster said he wanted a fresh and unbiased opinion."

Jack smiled grimly. "Bullshit," he said. "Foster knew you'd see the pictures here. He probably knew I'd show them to you. Well, I won't disappoint him ... or you." He opened the folder and pushed a half-dozen photographs across the table to her.

Kay reached out for them. Jack saw her hand freeze in midair. The picture on top showed a room with furniture shattered into pieces, and on the walls were brown patterns that could only be sprays of blood flung by violent motion. The words HAIL SATAN had been drawn in gore, the letters oozing down to the baseboard. Near those words, stuck to the wall, were yellow clots of ... yes, she knew what they must be. Human tissue.

With one finger, she moved the top picture aside. The second photograph drove a cold nail through her throat; it showed a pile of broken limbs that had been flung like garbage into a room's corner. A severed leg was propped up not unlike the umbrella she'd just put aside. A smashed head lay in a gray puddle of brains. Fingers clawed upward on disembodied hands. A torso had been ripped open, spilling all its secrets.

"*Oh,*" she whispered, and tasted hot bile.

And then the conference room's door opened again, and the boy who had torn his mother, father and ten-year-old sister to pieces walked through.

Three

With no hesitation, Tim Clausen went to the chair at the far end of the table. Gil Moon and Bobby Crisp walked on either side, though the boy did indeed wear a tightly-cinched straitjacket. He sat down, the fluorescents blooming in the round lenses of his glasses, and smiled at his visitors. It was a friendly smile, with not a hint of menace. "Hi," he said.

"Hello, Tim," Dr. Cawthorn replied. "I'd like you to meet Dr. Jack Shannon and Miss Kay Douglas. They're here to talk to you."

"Of course they are. Nice to meet you."

Kay was still stunned by the pictures. She couldn't bear to look at the third one, and she found it hard to look into the boy's face, as well. She had read the case file, knew his description and that he'd just turned seventeen, but the combination of the photographs and Timothy Clausen's smiling, beatific face was almost more than she could take. She pushed the pictures away and sat with her hands tightly clenched in her lap, damning Foster for not preparing her more thoroughly. This is the second test, she realized. He wants to find out if I'm made of ice or crap. Damn him!

"I like your hair," Tim Clausen said to her. "The color's pretty."

"Thank you," she managed, and shifted in her chair. The boy's eyes were black and steady, two bits of coal in a pale face marked here and there with the eruptions of acne. His hair was light brown and had been cropped almost to the scalp. Beneath his eyes were the violet hollows of either fatigue or madness.

Jack had been examining the boy as well. Tim Clausen was a small boy for his age, and his head was oddly shaped, the cranium bulging slightly; he seemed to hold his neck rigid, as if he feared he couldn't balance the weight of his head. The boy looked at each of them in turn—long, cool appraisals. He did not blink.

"You can leave him with us," Cawthorn said to the two attendants, and they moved out of the conference room and closed the door. "Tim, how're you feeling today?"

His smile broadened. "Almost free."

"I mean physically. Any aches or pains, any complaints?"

"No sir. I'm feeling just fine."

"Good." He took a minute to look through the notes he'd written. "Do you know why you're here?"

"Sure." A pause.

"Would you like to tell us?"

"No," he replied. "I'm tired of answering questions. Dr. Cawthorn. I'd like to ask some. Can I?"

"What kind of questions?"

Tim's attention drifted to Kay. "I want to know things about these people. The lady first. Who *are* you?"

She glanced at Cawthorn, and he nodded that she should comply. Jack had gathered the photographs back and was studying them, but listening intently. "As Dr. Cawthorn said, my name is Kay Douglas. I'm representing you with the public defender's off—"

"No, no!" Tim interrupted, with an expression of impatience. "Who are you? Like: are you married? Divorced? Have any kids? What religion are you? What's your favorite color?"

"Uh . . . well ... no, I'm not married." Divorced, yes, but she wasn't about to tell him that. "No children. I'm—" This is ridiculous! she thought. Why should she be telling private things to this boy? He was waiting for her to continue, his eyes impassive. "I'm Catholic," she went on. "I guess my favorite color's green."

"Any boyfriends? You live alone?"

"I'm afraid I don't see what this has to do with—"

"It's not fun to answer questions, is it?" Tim asked. "Not fun at all. Well, if you want me to answer *your* questions you'll have to answer *mine* first. You live alone, I think. Probably dating a couple of guys. Maybe sleeping with them, too." Kay couldn't control her blush, and Tim laughed. "I'm right, huh? Knew I was! Are you a good Catholic or a bad Catholic?"

"Tim?" Cawthorn's voice was gentle but firm. "I think you're overstepping a little bit now. We all want to get this over as soon as possible, don't we?"

"Now you." Tim ignored Cawthorn, his eyes aimed at Jack. "What's your story?"

Jack put aside a photograph that showed gory fingerpaintings on the kitchen wall of the Clausen house. "I've been married for fourteen years, my wife and I have two sons, I'm a Methodist and my favorite color is dark blue. I have no extramarital lovers, I'm a basketball fan and I like Chinese food. Anything else?"

Tim hesitated. "Yes. Do you believe in God?'

"I believe . . . there's a supreme being, yes. How about you?"

"Oh, I believe in a supreme being. Sure thing. Do you like the taste of blood?"

Jack made sure he kept his face emotionless. "Not especially."

"My supreme being does," Tim said. "He likes it a lot." He rocked back and forth a few times, and the straitjacket fabric rustled. His heavy head wobbled on his stalky neck. "Okay. Just wanted to find out who my interrogators were. Shoot."

"May I?" Jack inquired, and Cawthorn motioned for him to go ahead. "Tim, what I'm trying to determine, with the help of Miss Douglas and the public defender's office, is your mental state on the night of October 12th, between the hours of ten and eleven. Do you know what incident I'm referring to?"

Tim was silent, staring at one of the frosted-glass windows. Then: "Sure. That's when they came. They trashed the place and split."

"In your statement to Lieutenant Markus of the Birmingham police department, you indicated 'they' came to your parent's house, and that 'they'—" He found a photocopy of the statement in his satchel and read the part he sought: "Quoting, 'they did the damage. I couldn't do anything to stop them, not even if I'd wanted to. I didn't. They came and did the damage and after they were through they went home and I called the cops because I knew somebody had heard the screaming.' End quote. Is that correct, Tim?"

"Guess so." He kept staring at a fixed spot on the window, just past Jack's shoulder. His voice sounded thick.

"Would you tell me who you meant by 'they'?"

Tim shifted again, and the straitjacket rubbed on his backrest. A scatter of rain pelted the windows. Kay could feel her heart pounding, and she had her hands folded tightly on the table before her.

"My friends," Tim said quietly. "My best friends."

"I see." He didn't really, but at least this was one step forward. "Can you tell me their names?"

"Their names," Tim repeated. "You probably couldn't pronounce them."

"You pronounce them for me, then."

"My friends don't like for just anybody to know their names. Not their real names, at least. I've made up names for them: Adolf, Frog and Mother. My best friends."

There was a moment of silence. Cawthorn shuffled his notes and Jack studied the ceiling and formulated his next question. Kay beat him to it: "Who are they? I mean . . . where do they come from?"

Tim smiled again, as if he welcomed the query. "Hell," he said. "That's where they live."

"By Adolf," Jack said, measuring his words, "I presume you mean Hitler? Is that right?"

"I call him that, but that's not who he is. He's a lot older. But he took me to a place once, where there were walls and barbed wire and bodies were getting thrown into furnaces. You could smell the skin cook, like barbecue on the Fourth of July." He closed his eyes behind the round-lensed glasses. "I got a guided tour, see. There were Nazi soldiers all over the place, just like in the old pictures, and there were chimneys spouting brown smoke that smelled like hair on fire. A sweet smell. And there were people playing violins, and other people digging graves. Adolf speaks German. That's why I call him Adolf."

Jack looked at one of the photographs. It showed bloody swastikas on the wall over the disemboweled torso of a little girl. He felt as if he were sweating on the inside of his skin, the outer surface cold and clammy. Somehow—without any weapons or implements that the police could identify—the boy sitting at the far end of the table had ripped his parents and sister to pieces. Just torn them apart and thrown the pieces against the walls in an orgy of violence, then marked the walls with HAIL SATAN, swastikas, weirdly animalistic faces and obscenities in a dozen languages, all in fresh blood and inner matter. But what had he used to pull them apart? Surely human hands weren't capable of such strength, and on the corpses were deep bite marks and evidence of claws at work. Eyes had been gouged out, teeth had been knocked from gaping mouths, ears and noses had been chewed away.

It was the worst case of pure savagery he'd ever seen. But what kept knocking against the walls of his mind were those scrawled obscenities—in German, Danish, Italian, French, Greek, Spanish and six more languages including Arabic. According to the boy's school records, he'd made a low 'C' in Latin. That was it. So where had those languages come from? "Who taught you Greek, Tim?" Jack asked.

The boy's eyes opened. "I don't know Greek. Frog does."

"Frog. Okay. Tell me about Frog."

"He's . . . ugly. Like a frog. He likes to jump, too." Tim leaned forward slightly, as if confiding a secret, and though he sat more than six feet away, Kay found herself recoiling three or four inches. "Frog's very smart. Probably the smartest one. And Frog's been everywhere. All around the world. He knows every language you can think of, and probably some you don't even know." He sat back, smiling proudly. "Frog's neato."

Jack eased a Flair pen from his shirt pocket and wrote ADOLF and FROG at the top of the police statement, connecting them to the word 'they' with an arrow. He could feel the boy watching him. "How'd you meet your friends, Tim?"

"I called them. They came."

"Called them? How?"

"From the books. The spell books."

Jack nodded thoughtfully. The 'spell books' were a collection of paperback volumes on demonology the police had found on a shelf in Tim's room. They were tattered old things the boy said he'd bought at flea markets and garage sales, the newest one copyrighted in the '70s. They were by no means 'forbidden' literature, just probably the kind of books that had sat in drugstore racks and been spun round a thousand times. "So Adolf and Frog are demons, is that right?"

"That's one name for them, I guess. There are others."

"Can you tell us exactly when you first called them?"

"Sure. Maybe two years ago. More or less. I wasn't very good at it at first. They won't come unless you *really* want them, and you've got to follow the directions right to the letter. If you're a hair off, nothing happens. I guess I went through it a hundred times before Mother came. She was the first one."

"She?" Jack asked. "Adolf and Frog are male, but Mother is female?"

"Yeah. She's got jugs." Tim's eyes darted to Kay, back to Jack again. "Mother knows everything. She taught me all about sex." Another furtive glance at Kay. "Like how a girl dresses when she wants to get raped. Mother says they all want it. She took me places, and showed me things. Like one place where this fat guy brought boys home, and after he was through with them he set them free because they were all used up, and then he put them in garbage bags and buried them in his basement like pirate treasure."

"Set them free?" Jack repeated; his mouth had gotten very dry. "You mean . . ."

"Set them free from their bodies. With a butcher knife. So their souls could go to Hell." He looked at Kay, who could not restrain an inner shudder. She cursed Bob Foster right down to his shoelaces.

Hallucinations, Jack jotted down. Then: *Fixation on Demonology and Hell*. Why? "You said a little while ago, when Dr. Cawthorn asked you how you were feeling, you felt 'almost free'. Could you explain that to me?"

"Yeah. Almost free. Part of my soul's already in Hell. I gave it up on the night when . . . you know. It was a test. Everybody gets tested. I passed that one. I've got one more— kind of like an entrance exam, I guess."

"Then all your soul will be in Hell?"

"Right. See, people have the wrong idea about Hell. It's not what people think. It's ... a homey kind of place. Not a whole lot different from here. Except it's safer, and you get protected. I've visited there, and I've met Satan. He was wearing a letter jacket, and he said he wanted to help me learn how to play football, and he said he'd always pick me first when it came to choosing up teams. He said he'd be . . . like a big brother, and all I had to do was love him." He blinked behind his glasses. "Love is too hard here. It's easier to love in Hell, because nobody yells at you and you don't have to be perfect. Hell is a place without walls." He began to rock himself again, and the straitjacket's fabric made a shrieking sound. "It kills me, all this stuff about rock and roll being Satan's music. He likes Beethoven, listens to it over and over on a big ghetto blaster. And he's got the kindest eyes you ever saw, and the sweetest voice. Know what he says? That he feels so sorry for new life born into this world, because life is suffering and it's the babies who have to pay for their parents' sins." His rocking was getting more violent. "It's the babies who need to be freed most of all. Who need love and protection, and he'll wrap them in swaddling letter jackets and hum Beethoven to them and they won't have to cry any more."

"Tim?" Cawthorn was getting alarmed at the boy's motion. "Settle down, now. There's no need to—"

"YOU WON'T CAGE ME!" Tim shouted, and his pale face with its encrustment of acne flooded crimson. Veins were beating at both temples. Kay had almost leaped from her skin, and now she grasped the edge of the table with white fingers. "Won't cage me, no sir! Dad tried to cage me! He was scared shitless! Said he was going to burn my books and get me thinking right again! Won't cage me! Won't cage me, no sir!" He thrashed against the straitjacket, a sheen of sweat gleaming on his face. Cawthorn stood up, started for the door to call in Gil and Bobby.

"Wait!" the boy shouted: a command, full-voiced and powerful.

Cawthorn stopped with his hand on the tarnished knob. "Wait. Please. Okay?"

Tim had ceased struggling. His glasses were hanging from one ear, and with a quick jerk of his head he flung them off. They skidded along the table and almost into Kay's lap. "Wait. I'm all right now. Just got a little crazy. See, I won't be caged. I *can't* be. Not when part of my soul's already in Hell." He smiled slickly and wet his lips with his tongue. "It's time for my entrance exam. That's why they let you bring me here ... so they could come too."

"Who, Tim?" Jack felt the hairs creeping at the back of his neck. "Who let us bring you here?"

"My best friends. Frog, Adolf, and Mother. They're here too. Right here."

"Right *where*?" Kay asked.

"I'll show you. Frog says he likes your hair, too. Says he'd like to feel it." The boy's head wobbled, the veins sticking out in his neck and throbbing to a savage rhythm. "I'll show you my best friends. Okay?"

Kay didn't answer. At the door, Cawthorn stood motionless. Jack sat still, the pen clamped in his hand.

A drop of blood coursed slowly from the corner of Tim's left eye. It was bright red, and streaked scarlet down his cheek, past his lip to his chin.

Tim's left eyeball had begun to bulge from its socket.

"Here they come," he whispered, in a strangled voice. "Ready or not."

Four

"He's hemorrhaging!" Jack stood up so fast his chair crashed over. "Eric, call the emergency room!"

Cawthorn ran out to get to the telephone at Bobby Crisp's desk. Jack crossed the room to the boy's side, saw Tim hitching as if he couldn't draw a breath. Two more lines of blood oozed from around the left eye, which was being forced out of its socket by a tremendous inner pressure. The boy gasped, made a hoarse moaning sound, and Jack struggled to loosen the straitjacket's straps but the body began to writhe and jerk with such force that he couldn't find the buckles.

Kay was on her feet, and Jack said, "Help me get this off him!" but she hesitated; the images of the mangled corpses in those photographs were still too fresh. At that moment Gil Moon came in, saw what was happening and tried to hold the boy from thrashing. Jack got one of the heavy straps undone, and now blood was dripping from around the boy's eye and running out his nostrils, his mouth strained open in a soundless cry of agony.

Tim's tongue protruded from his mouth. It rotated around, and Tim's body shuddered so fiercely even Gil's burly hands couldn't keep him still. Jack's fingers pulled at the second buckle—and suddenly the boy's left eye shot from its socket in a spray of gore and flew across the room. It hit the wall and drooled down like a broken egg, and Kay's knees almost folded.

"Hold him! Hold him!" Jack shouted. The boy's face rippled, and there came the sound of facial bones popping and cracking like the timbers of an old house giving way. His cranium bulged, his forehead swelling as if threatening explosion.

Cawthorn and Bobby returned to the room. The doctor's face was bleached white, and Bobby pushed Jack aside to get at the last buckle.

"Emergency's on the way up!" Cawthorn croaked. "My God ... my God . . . what's happening to him?"

Jack shook his head. He realized he had some of Tim Clausen's blood on his shirt, and the dark socket of the boy's ruined eye looked as if it went right down into the wet depths of the brain. The other eye seemed to be fixed on him—a cold, knowing stare. Jack stepped back to give Gil and Bobby room to work.

The boy's tongue emerged another inch, seemed to be questing in the air. And then, as the tongue continued to strain from the mouth, there was a sound of flesh tearing loose. The tongue emerged two more inches—and its color was a mottled greenish-gray, covered with sharp glass-like spikes.

The attendants recoiled. Tim's body shuddered, the single eye staring. The head and face were changing shape, as if being hammered from within.

"Oh . . . Jesus," Bobby whispered, retreating.

Something writhed behind Tim Clausen's swollen forehead. The spiky tongue continued to slide out, inch after awful inch, and twined itself around the boy's neck. His face was gray, smeared with blood at nostrils and lips and empty eyehole. His temples pulsed and bulged, and the left side of his face shifted with a firecracker noise of popping bones. A thread of scarlet zigzagged across his pressured skull; the fissure widened, wetly, and part of his cranium began to lift up like a trap door being forced open.

Kay made a choking sound. Cawthorn's back thumped against the wall.

Dazed and horrified. Jack saw a scuttling in the dark hole where the left eye had been. The hole stretched wider, with a splitting of tissues, and from it reached a gnarled gray hand about the size of an infant's, except it had three fingers and three sharp silver talons and was attached to a leathery arm that rippled with hard piano-wire muscles.

The boy's mouth had been forced open so far the jaws were about to break. From the mouth emerged spike-covered buttocks, following its attached tail that had once been—or had appeared to be—a human tongue. A little mottled gray-green thing with spiky skin and short piston-like legs was backing out of Tim Clausen's mouth, fighting free from the bloody lips as surely as new birth. And now the creature on the end of that muscular little arm was pushing itself out too, through the grotesque cavity that used to be Tim Clausen's eyesocket, and Jack was face-to-face with a scaly bald head the size of a man's fist and the color of spoiled meat. Its other arm appeared, and now a thorny pair of shoulders, the body pushing with fierce energy and its flat bulldog nostrils flaring and spouting spray. Its slanted Chinese eyes were topaz, beautiful and deadly.

Gil was jabbering, making noise but no sense. The bald head racheted toward him, and as its mouth grinned with eager anticipation—like a kid presented with a roomful of pizzas, Jack thought crazily—the close-packed teeth glinted like broken razors.

And something began to crawl from the top of the boy's skull that almost stopped Jack's laboring heart. Kay felt a scream pressing at her throat, but it would not come out. A spidery thing, gleaming and iridescent, its six-legged form all sinews and angles, pushed its way from the skull's gaping trapdoor. Mounted on a four-inch stalk of tough tissue was a head framed with a metallic mass of what might have been hair, except it was made of tangled concertina wire, honed to skin-slicing sharpness. The face was ivory—a woman's face, the visage of a blood-drained beauty. Beneath silver brows her eyes were white, and as they gazed upon Jack and the body struggled out, the creature's pale lips stretched into a smile and showed fangs of saw-edged diamonds.

Cawthorn broke, began laughing and wailing as he slid down to the floor. Out in the corridor, the buzzer shrilled; the emergency staff had arrived, but there was no one to unlock the door on this side.

The squatty spike-covered beast was almost out of the boy's mouth. It pulled free, its webbed feet clenching to Tim's face, and swiveled its acorn-shaped head around. The eyes were black and owlish, its face cracked and wrinkled and covered with suppurating sores that might have been Hell's version of acne. Its mouth was a red-rimmed cup, like the suctioning mouth of a leech. The eyes blinked rapidly, a transparent film dropping across them and then lifting as it regarded the humans in the room.

Tim Clausen's head had begun to collapse like a punctured balloon. The bald-headed, muscular thing—Adolf, Jack realized—wrenched its hips loose from the eyesocket; its chest was plated with overlapping scales, and at its groin was a straining red penis and a knotty sac of testicles that pulsed like a bag of hearts. As the creature's leg came free, Tim's mouth released a hiss of air that smelled of blood and brains and decayed matter—an odor of fungus and mold—and in the scabrous sound there might have been a barely-human whisper: "Free."

The boy's face imploded, features running together like wet wax. The spidery metal-haired demon—Mother, Jack knew it could only be—scrabbled onto the boy's shoulder and perched there as Tim's head turned dark as a wart and caved in. What remained of the head—flaccid and rubbery—fell back over the shoulder and hung there like a cape's hood, and whatever Tim Clausen had been was gone.

But the three demons remained.

They were holding him together, Jack thought as he staggered back. He bumped into Kay, and she grasped his arm with panicked strength. After they killed the boy's parents and sister, Jack realized, they were hiding inside him and holding him together like plaster and wire in a mannequin. Shock settled over him, weighting him down. His mind seized like rusted cogs. He heard the insistent call of the buzzer, the emergency crew wanting to get in, and he feared his legs had gone dead. *My best friends*, the boy had said. *I called them. They came.*

And here they were. Ready or not.

They were neither hallucinations nor the result of psychotic trance. There was no time to debate the powers of God or the Devil, or whether Hell was a territory or a termite in the house of reason: the demon Tim had named Adolf leaped nimbly through the air at Gil Moon and gripped the man's face with those three-fingered silver claws. Gil bellowed in terror and fell to his knees; the demon's claws were a blur of motion, like a happy machine at work, and as Gil shuddered and screamed and tried to fight the thing off the demon ripped his face away from the skeletal muscles like a flimsy mask. Blood spattered through the air, marking the walls with the same patterns as at the Clausen house. Adolf locked his sinewy legs around Gil Moon's throat, the three toes of the demon's bare feet curling and uncurling with merry passion, and Adolf began to eat the man's shredded face. Gil's bony jaws chattered and moaned, and the demon made greedy grunting noises like a pig burrowing in slop.

Bobby Crisp ran, releasing a shriek that shook the windows. He did not stop to open the door, but almost knocked it off its hinges as he fled into the hallway. Jack gripped Kay's hand, pulling her with him toward the door. Mother's ashen, lustful face followed him; he saw her tongue flicker from the pale-lipped mouth—a black, spear-tipped piece of pseudo-flesh that quivered in the air with a low humming sound. He could feel the tone vibrate in his testicles, and the tingling sensation slowed him a half-step. Kay's scream let go, with a force that rattled her bones; once uncapped, the scream would not stop and kept spilling from her throat. A form leaped at her head. She ducked, lifting an arm to ward it off. The creature Tim had called Frog hopped over her shoulder, its spiky tail tearing cloth from her jacket just above the elbow. A whiplash of pain jarred her scream to a halt and cleared her head, and then Frog had landed on Dr. Cawthorn's scalp. "Don't leave me ... don't leave me," he was babbling, and Jack stopped before he reached the doorway—but in the next instant it was obvious that help was much too late.

Frog leaned forward and attached that gaping leech-mouth to Cawthorn's forehead. The creature's cheeks swelled to twice their size, its tail snaking around and around Cawthorn's throat. Cawthorn gave a gutteral cry of pain, and his head exploded like a tire pumped beyond its limits, brains streaking the walls. Frog squatted on the broken skull, its cheeks becoming concave as it sucked at flowing juices.

Jack pulled Kay out of the room. Up ahead, Bobby Crisp was racing toward the locked security door, shouting for help. He tripped over his own gangly legs and fell heavily to the floor, scrambled up again and limped frantically onward. Now there was a pounding on the other side of the door, and Jack could see faces through the glass inset. Bobby was searching wildly through his ring of keys as Jack and Kay reached him. He tried to force one into the lock, but it wouldn't go. The second key he chose slid in but balked at turning. "Hurry!" Jack urged, and he dared to look over his shoulder.

Mother was scuttling along the hallway toward them, moving about as fast as a prowling cat. Her mouth opened, and she made a piercing shriek like claws scraped across a blackboard. As if in response to her alarm, Frog bounded out of the conference room, its ancient and wrinkled face smeared with Cawthorn's brains.

"Open it!" Jack shouted, and Bobby tried a third key but his hand was shaking so badly he couldn't get it into the lock. It was too large, and would not fit. It dawned on Jack with terrifying force that if Gil had been on door duty, the proper key would still be on the dead man's ring, and Bobby might not have one. He glanced back again, saw Mother about twenty feet away and Frog leaping past her. Adolf strode from the conference room like a two-foot-tall commingling of gnarled man and dragon.

"Lord Jesus!" Bobby Crisp said as the fourth key engaged the tumblers and turned in the lock. He wrenched the door open—and Frog landed on his shoulder, sharp little talons in the webbed feet digging through his shirt.

He screamed, thrashing at the demon. Jack could smell the reek of Frog's flesh: a musty, cooked-meat odor. Through the open door, two white-uniformed men from the emergency room stood wide-eyed and astonished, a gurney table between them. Rosalee had seen, and so had Mrs. Stewart, and both of them were too stunned to move.

Jack grasped Frog with both hands. It was like touching a live coal, and the spiky tail whipped at him as he tore Frog off Bobby's back. Most of the attendant's shirt and hunks of skin ripped away. Jack's hands were pierced by the spikes on the thing's body, and he threw the demon with all his strength against the opposite wall. It folded into a ball an instant before it hit, its head retracting into its body; it made a wet splatting sound, fell to the floor and immediately reformed itself, poising for another leap.

But Bobby was out the door and so was Kay, and Jack lunged through and slammed the door shut behind him, leaving bloody handprints against the white. There was the wham! of impact as Frog hit the door on the other side. "Lock it! Lock it!" Jack shouted, and Rosalee got her key in and twisted it. The lock shot home, and the door was secured.

Bobby kept running, almost colliding with Mrs. Marion and Dave Chambers. "What's your hurry?" Dave called. Bobby reached the elevator, which the emergency staffers had left open, got in and punched a button. The doors closed and took him down.

"Doris!" Rosalee hollered to Mrs. Marion. "Bring some bandages! Quick!" She grasped Jack's wrists and looked at his palms. There were four or five puncture wounds on each hand, and much of the skin had been scorched raw. The worst of the pain was just now hitting him, and he squeezed his eyes shut and shuddered. "They got Cawthorn and Gil Moon. Tore them up. Three of them. They came out of the boy. Out of the boy's head. Tore them to pieces, just like the boy's family . . ." A wave of dizziness almost overcame him, and Rosalee clamped her husky arms around him as his knees crumpled.

"What . . . *what was it?*" Mrs. Stewart had seen the beast with the eyes of an owl and the body of a frog, but her mind had sheared away from the sight. She blinked, found herself watching drops of blood fall from the fingers of the red-haired woman's right hand and spatter to the floor. "Oh," she said, dazed. "Oh dear . . . you're hurt . . ."

Kay looked at her hand, realizing only then that Frog's tail had cleaved a furrow across her arm. The pain was bad, but not unbearable. Not considering what might have happened. The image of Cawthorn's exploding head came to her, and she allowed the fretting nurse to guide her along the corridor to a chair without really knowing where she was going or why. One of the emergency staffers broke open a medical kit and started examining Kay's wound, asking her questions about what had happened; she didn't even hear them. The other man swabbed disinfectant on Jack's hands—which sent new pain through him that almost curled his hair— and then helped Rosalee bind them in the bandages Mrs. Marion had brought.

Something crashed against the door. It shivered from the blow.

"Docky?" Margie was standing next to him, her face pallid and her eyes darting with fear. "Docky . . . what's in there?"

Another blow against the door. The floor trembled.

"God Almighty!" the man who'd helped bandage Jack's hands said. "That felt like a sledge hammer!"

"Stay away from the door!" Jack warned. "Everybody! Stay away from it! Rosalee . . . listen . . . we've got to get the patients off the ward! Get them downstairs!"

There was a third impact against the door. The glass inset cracked.

"I told you, didn't I?" Dave Chambers stood in the center of the corridor, calmly smoking a cigarette, his eyes narrowed. "Told you not to go in there. Now look what you've stirred up."

"Hush!" Rosalee snapped at him—and then Mrs. Marion screamed, because the rest of the door's glass inset was smashed out and a small gray claw with three silver talons stretched through, swiping savagely at the air. "Oh . . . Lordy," Rosalee breathed.

Jack watched, helplessly, while Adolf's arm, shoulder and head squeezed through the opening. Margie made a croaking noise. The cigarette dropped from Dave's fingers. The demon struggled to get its hips free, then leaped to the floor and stood there grinning, its baleful topaz eyes full of greedy expectation.

And now Mother was pulling herself through the opening, inch by awful inch, her barbed-wire hair gleaming under the fluorescents.

They're going to kill us all, Jack thought; it was a surprisingly calm realization, as if his mind had been pushed to its limit and would accept no more panic. Everyone on the floor was going to die—and then, most probably, the things would start with the patients on the next floor down as well.

It dawned on him that if a hospital was indeed a universe all its own, then this one had just been claimed for destruction.

Mother got her head through, and the spider's body plopped to the floor beside Adolf.

Five

Kay moved: not running wildly along the corridor, as was her first impulse, because with the elevator gone and the stairwell door surely locked the corridor was just one long dead end. She leaped out of her chair, past the nurse and two emergency staffers to the gurney table; she simply did it because she saw it had to be done, and she'd come to the same recognition of doom as Jack had. "No!" she said, and shoved the gurney forward. Its wheels squeaked as it hurtled toward Mother and Adolf.

But they were much too fast to be caught by those wheels. Mother scuttled to one side and Adolf sprang to the other, and now Frog was squeezing through the inset like a blob of jelly from a tube. The gurney slammed into the door and bounced off.

Adolf made a grating-glass noise that might have been a cackle.

There were no screams, just a long swelling of breath that caught and hung. "Move everyone back," Jack said to Rosalee. She didn't budge. "Get them down the stairs!" he demanded, and finally she made a choked sound of agreement, grasped Margie's arm and began to retreat along the corridor. The others followed, not daring to turn their backs on the creatures. Dave Chambers just stood gaping for a moment, then he too began a stiff-legged retreat.

Frog thrashed in the door's inset, its front legs clawing. *The bastard's stuck!* Jack realized, but it was little consolation. Mother took a slithery step forward, and Adolf clambered up onto the gurney and squatted there as if in contemplation.

Jack knew there were no weapons on the eighth floor: no knives, no bludgeons, certainly no guns. The most dangerous item up here was probably a toilet plunger, and he doubted that would do much harm to Tim Clausen's best friends. Frog was still trying to get its bulbous buttocks through the opening, Mother was advancing steadily but with caution, and Adolf's eyes ticked back and forth with murderous intent.

"Help us! Please help us!" someone shouted. Jack saw Mrs. Stewart at the nurse's station, the telephone in her hand. "We're on eight! For God's sake, send somebody to help—"

Adolf's muscular legs uncoiled, and the demon jumped over Jack and Kay, hit the floor running and had scampered up onto the nurse's desk before Mrs. Stewart could finish her plea. With one swipe of a claw, Adolf opened the woman's throat. Her vocal chords rattled, and the phone fell from her twitching fingers. Adolf clung to the front of her uniform as Mrs. Stewart writhed in agony, and his razorblade teeth went to work on the ravaged throat.

"GET OFF HER, YOU SHIT!" Rosalee hollered, and whacked Adolf with a broom she'd plucked from a corner. The broom did no damage even though it was swung with a mighty vengeance, but Adolf ceased his chewing and regarded her as if admiring a new steak. Mrs. Stewart crumpled, strangling, and Adolf leaped to the desktop.

"Jack! Look out!" Kay cried; he whirled around as Mother scuttled toward his legs, and without thinking about it he kicked the thing as if going for a field goal. The demon gave a moist grunt and rolled like a tumbleweed against the wall, then immediately righted herself and came at him again. Jack retreated, but the demon was coming on too fast and he saw the wicked glitter of her diamond teeth. She was almost upon him, about to scurry up his left leg.

A chair flew past him, nearly clipping his shoulder, and crashed into Mother. She shrieked, a noise like air escaping a hole in a balloon. Some of her legs were already struggling to shove the chair off and the others pulling her out of Jack's range before he could deliver another kick. Two legs quivered and slid uselessly along the floor, leaving a smear of brown fluid.

"I busted it!" Dave Chambers shouted. "Knocked the shit out of it, didn't I? Doc, move your ass!"

Rosalee swung the broom at Adolf again. The demon caught it, and for a few seconds they pulled it back and forth between them, until Rosalee yanked at it and Adolf let go. She squalled and staggered, falling with a jolt that shook the floor. Adolf tensed to leap upon her.

But the elevator suddenly opened, and a stout middle-aged man in the brown uniform of a security guard stepped off. He wore a badge and holster with a .38 revolver in it, and he stopped dead in his tracks as the demon's head swiveled toward him.

The guard gasped, "What in the name of everlovin' Jesus is—"

Adolf jumped. Cleared Rosalee, who screamed and scurried away on her hands and knees, and plunged his claws into the man's chest. The talons ripped through the shirt, and the demon flailed at the man like a living chainsaw. Most of his chest was a wet, gaping cavity within the seven or eight seconds it took for Adolf to finish with him, and the guard toppled forward onto his face. His legs remained inside the elevator, and the doors kept thumping against them, opening and trying to close again.

Adolf perched on the dead man's back, licking his talons. His gaze found Rosalee, who had crawled about ten feet away, and she knew she was next.

"Hey, freak!" Dave bellowed. He had another chair, was thrusting it at Adolf like a lion tamer. The demon's eyes fixed on him, and a terrible grin flickered across its mouth. "Come on, prick!" He stepped between Adolf and Rosalee, a sheen of sweat shining on his face; his own smile was maniacal. "Rosalee, you'd best get off your butt now. Best get those people down the stairs." His voice was calm: the voice of someone who has chosen suicide. "Doc, you and the lady haul your asses and get off the ward!"

Rosalee stood up. Adolf hissed at her, and Dave feinted with the chair to get the thing's attention again. Jack and Kay moved past him, as Mother slowly advanced along the corridor, dragging her broken legs. "I know you, don't I?" Dave asked the male demon. "Sure I do. I've seen you at night, when I try to sleep.

Oh, you're a sly little bastard, aren't you? You get in my head when I'm dreamin', and you make me crazy. That's why I'm here—because of you."

Adolf swiped at the chair, left three furrows across one of the wooden legs.

"You want to jump, huh? Want to get those hands on ol' Dave's neck? Except you know I won't go lightly. I'll knock your eyeballs out, friend." Dave glanced quickly to his right; about twenty feet away, Rosalee had slipped her key into the stairwell's door and was unlocking it. "Hurry!" he said, then cut his gaze down the other direction. The spider with the marble-white face of a woman and barbed-wire hair was creeping inexorably up on him. The third demon was still struggling to get free of the door, and was just about to pop its butt loose.

Adolf sprang forward. Dave planted his legs and swung the chair. But Adolf drew back at the last second, and the chair's legs hit empty air.

"Maybe I can't kill you," Dave said, "but I'll break your bones—or whatever's holdin' you together. Maybe that makes you think a little bit, huh?"

Rosalee was getting the patients, the two emergency staffers and Mrs. Marion through the door into the stairwell. Jack hesitated, watching Dave as Mother slowly advanced on him. "Dave!" he shouted. "We'll keep the door open for you! Come on!"

Dave laughed harshly. "You're nuttier'n a Christmas fruitcake, Doc," he answered. "You want these things runnin' all through the hospital? Man, *I'm* not even that crazy! You get through that door and make sure it's locked."

Kay gripped Jack's arm. Everyone had gone down the stairwell except her and Rosalee. She pulled at him. "We've got to get downstairs ... got to call the police ..." Her eyelids were fluttering, and Jack recognized that deep shock was finally settling in. He wanted to go, because in all his life no one had ever accused him of being a hero—but the sight of a mental patient wielding a chair against two demons from Hell would not let him descend the stairs. It would be easy to give up Dave Chambers; what was the measure of the man's life, anyway? But Jack could not leave him alone up here, though his brain screamed for escape and he knew Dave was a heartbeat away from being torn to shreds. After they finished with Dave, they would find a way down to the next floor where they could go from room to room. If they were going to be stopped, it had to be here and now.

"Take her," Jack said to Rosalee. "Lock the door behind you."

"No! Dr. Shannon, you can't—"

"Do what I said." His voice cracked, and he felt his courage leaking out. "If they get off this floor ..." He let the thought remain unspoken.

Rosalee hesitated—but only for a few seconds, because she saw his mind was made up. She said, "Come on, miss. Lean on me, now." She helped Kay down the stairs, and then the door swung shut in Jack's face. Rosalee turned her key on the other side, and the lock engaged with a small click of finality.

Six

"Doc, you're crazy!" Dave yelled. "You should've been up here in a rubber room with us nuts a long time a—"

Adolf jumped at Dave's legs. The man backpedalled and swung the chair; it struck the demon's shoulder and knocked the thing sprawling against the wall. Mother was almost at Dave's feet, and Jack saw Frog suddenly heave loose from the door's inset and fall to the floor. Frog started bounding toward Dave, covering three or four feet at a leap. Dave saw it coming too, and he wheeled toward Frog to ward the beast off.

"Look out!" Jack warned, but he knew he was too late. Adolf had already leapt at the man, was scrabbling up Dave's leg. Mother pounced like a cat upon Dave's ankle, and the diamond fangs ripped through his white sock. It turned crimson. Dave whacked at Mother with the chair, missed, was off-balance and falling as Adolf plunged his claws into the man's chest and opened him up from breastbone to navel. Dave's stricken face turned toward Jack, and Jack heard him gasp: *"The gun."*

Then Dave hit the floor, with Adolf pinned and struggling beneath him, and a tide of blood streamed across the linoleum.

The gun, Jack realized. The gun in the security guard's holster.

He didn't remember taking the first step. But he was running toward the elevator, where the guard lay dead, and it occurred to him that his ravaged hands might not be able to hold the gun, or that it might be unloaded, or that he might not be able to pull it from the holster in time. All those things whirled through his mind, but he knew that without the gun he was meat to be devoured by Tim Clausen's best friends.

Tail lashing, Frog bounded from the floor at him before he could reach the elevator. He ducked, slipped in Dave Chambers's blood and fell as Frog leaped over his head. The end of the beast's tail slashed his left ear, and then he was skidding across the floor on his chest and bumped against the guard's corpse. He saw Adolf pulling his legs from underneath Dave, saw the demon's eyes widen with realization. Jack got one hand around the revolver's butt, popped the holster open with the other and drew the gun loose. The safety! he thought, and spent precious seconds fumbling to release the catch.

And then Mother was right in his face, the mouth opening with a hiss and the fangs straining. Her legs clutched at his shoulder, a breath of corruption washing at his nostrils. The fangs glittered, about to strike.

He pressed the revolver's barrel against her forehead and forced his index finger to squeeze the trigger.

Nothing happened.

Just an empty click.

Adolf cackled, wrenching his legs free and standing up.

Frog was bounding back along the corridor.

Mother grinned.

And Jack pulled the trigger again.

This time it fell on a loaded cylinder. The gun went off, almost jumping out of Jack's grip.

A hole in Mother's forehead sprayed brown fluid. Her grin turned to a rictus of what might have been agony, and she scurried backward. Adolf's cackle stopped cold.

Jack fired again. A piece of Mother's head flew off, and she was shrieking and dragging herself around in a mad circle. Frog leaped, landed on the side of Jack's neck with a wet grunt. He pressed the gun into its gelatinous, meaty-smelling body and shot—once, twice. Frog split open, oozing nastiness, and slithered away from him.

Jack tried to take aim at Mother again, but she was running like a wind-up toy gone berserk. A scrape of metal drew his attention. He looked at the opposite wall: Adolf was frantically pulling at a small metal grill. The vent! Jack thought, and his heart stuttered. If that bastard got into the vent . . . !

He fired at Adolf's back. At the same instant the .38 went off, Adolf wrenched the grill open. His left arm disappeared at the elbow in a mangle of tissue and fluid, and Adolf's body was slammed against the wall. The demon's head turned toward Jack, eyes ablaze with hatred. Jack pulled the trigger once more—and hit the empty cylinder again. The bullets were gone.

Adolf flung himself headfirst into the vent. Jack shouted "NO!" and scrambled across the dead guard, over the bloody floor to the vent; he shoved his arm in, his hand seeking. In the tube there was a scuttling, drawing away and down. Then silence but for the rattle of Jack's lungs.

He lay on his stomach, not far from the corpse of Dave Chambers. The ward smelled like a slaughterhouse. He wanted to rest, just curl his body up and let his mind coast down a long road into darkness—but Adolf was still in the hospital, probably following the vent's pipe to the lower floors, and he could decide to come out anywhere. Jack lay shivering, trying to think. Something Tim Clausen had said . . . something about ...

He feels so sorry for new life born into this world, the boy had said. *It's the babies who need to be freed most of all.*

And Jack knew why Tim's best friends had allowed him to be brought to the hospital.

All hospitals have a maternity ward.

There was a soft hiss beside his left ear.

Mother crouched there on trembling legs, part of her head blasted away and her face dripping brown ichor. Her tongue flicked out, quivering toward Jack, her eyes lazy and heavy-lidded. They were sated, hideous, knowing eyes; they understood things that, once set free, would gnaw through the meat and bone of this world and spit out the remains like gristle on barbarian platters. They were things that might rave between the walls of Jack's mind for the rest of his life, but right now he must shove away the madness before it engulfed him; he knew— and was sure Mother did, too—that Adolf was scrambling down through the vent toward the second floor, where the babies were. Mother leered at him, her duty done.

Jack got his hand around the .38's barrel and smashed the butt into her face. The wet, obscene skin split with a noise like rotten cloth. Barbed wire cut through Jack's bandaged fingers, and he lifted the gun and struck again. Mother retreated only a few paces before her legs gave out. Her eyes collapsed inward like cigarette burns. The mouth made a mewling noise, the diamond fangs snapping together. Jack lifted the gun and brought it down, heedless of the barbed-wire hair. Mother's head broke like a blister, and out of that cavity rose an oily mist that swirled up toward the ceiling and clung there, seething like a concentration of wasps. It bled through the ceiling tiles, leaving a stain as dark as nicotine and then it—whatever it had been—had escaped.

Mother's body lay like a rag. Jack pushed it aside and crawled to the elevator. The doors were still thumping impatiently against the guard's legs. Jack struggled to slide the corpse out, aware that each passing second took Adolf closer to the maternity ward. He got the legs out of the elevator, caught the doors before they closed and heaved himself inside, reaching up to hit the 2 button.

The doors slid shut, and the elevator descended.

Jack stood up. His legs immediately gave way again, and he fell to his knees. The front of his shirt was reddened by gore, the bandages hanging from his bloody hands. Black motes spun before his eyes, and he knew he didn't have much time before his body surrendered. The old gears and cables creaked, and the elevator jarred to a halt. Jack looked up at the illuminated numbers over the door; the number 5 was lit up. The doors opened, and a gray-haired doctor in a white lab coat took one step in before he saw Jack on the floor and froze.

"Get out," Jack rasped.

The doctor hesitated perhaps three seconds, then retreated so abruptly he hit an orderly in the hallway and knocked over a cart of medicines and sterilized instruments. Jack pressed the 2 button once more, and the doors closed. He watched the numbers change. As the elevator passed the third floor, Jack thought how sensible it would be to stay here all the way down to the lobby and scream for help once he got there. That was the thing to do, because he had no gun, no weapon, nothing to stop Adolf with. He was bloody and balanced on the edge of shock, and he knew he must've scared the doctor half to death. A grim smile lifted the corners of his mouth, because he knew there was no time to get to the lobby; by then, Adolf might have reached the maternity ward, and the thing's remaining claw would be at work amid the new flesh. Already there might be a pile of infant limbs scattered on the floor, and each second ended another life. No time . . . no time . . .

Jack struggled to his feet. Watched the number 2 light up. The elevator halted, and the doors opened with a sigh.

There were no screams, no frantic activity on the second floor. As Jack emerged from the elevator, the two nurses on duty at the central station gaped up at him. One of them spilled a cup of coffee, brown liquid surging across the desk. Jack had never been to the maternity ward before, and corridors seemed to cut off in every direction. "The babies," he said to one of the nurses. "Where do you keep the babies?"

"Call security!" she told the other one, and the woman picked up the telephone, pressed a button and said in a quavering voice, "This is second floor. We need security up here, *fast!*"

"Listen to me." Jack knew Rosalee and the others must be still trying to explain what had happened, and they wouldn't understand where Adolf was headed. "Please listen. I'm Dr. Jack Shannon. I've just come from the eighth floor. You've got to get the babies out of here. I can't tell you why, but—"

"Luther!" one of the nurses shouted. "Luther!" The other woman had backed away, and Jack saw they both thought he was out of his mind. "I'm not crazy," he said, instantly regretting it; such a statement only made things worse. The nurse who'd called for Luther said, "Settle down, now. We're going to get somebody up here to help you, okay?"

Jack looked around, trying to get his bearings. A waiting room was on the left, people staring at him like frightened deer ready to bolt. On the right a sign affixed to the wall read MATERNITY and aimed an arrow down the corridor. Jack started along the hallway, one of the nurses yelling at him to stop and the other too scared to speak. He passed between rooms, leaving drops of blood on the floor and startling nurses and patients who saw him coming; they scattered out of his way, but one nurse grabbed his shoulder and he shoved her aside and kept going. A signal bell was going off, alerting security. He hoped these guards were quicker on their feet than the one upstairs had been.

He rounded a corner, and there was the large floor-to-ceiling plate-glass window where babies were displayed in their perambulators, the boys bundled up in pale blue and the girls in pink. Several friends and relatives of new parents were peering in through the glass at the infants as the maternity nurse continued her duties within. One of the visitors looked up at Jack, and the woman's expression changed from delight to horror. It took two more seconds for all of them to be aware of the bloodied man who'd just lurched around the corner. Another of the women screamed, and one of the men bulled forward to protect her.

Jack slammed his hand against the window. The nurse inside jumped, her eyes stunned above her surgical mask. "Get them out!" Jack shouted—but he knew she couldn't hear, because some of the babies were obviously crying and he couldn't hear those sounds, either. He tried again, louder:

"Get them out of—"

A pair of arms tightened around his chest from behind like a living straitjacket. "Hold it, buddy. Just hang loose. Guards are gonna be here right soon."

Luther, Jack thought. An orderly, and the size of a football linebacker from the thickness of those arms. The man had lifted him almost off the floor. "You and me gonna take a walk back to the elevators. Excuse us, folks."

"No! Listen . . ." The pressure was about to squeeze the breath out of him. Luther started dragging him along the corridor, and thrashing was useless. Jack's heels scraped the floor.

And there came another, higher scraping sound as well. Then the double crack of screws being forced loose. Jack's spine crawled; at the baseboard of the wall directly opposite the infant's nursery was a vent grill, and it was being pushed open from the other side.

Jack fought to get loose, but Luther hadn't seen and he clamped his grip tighter. The blood roared in Jack's head.

The grill came open with a squeal of bending metal, and from the vent leaped a small one-armed figure with burning topaz eyes. Adolf's head turned toward the horrified knot of ward visitors, then toward Jack and the orderly; the demon gave a grunt of satisfaction, as if expecting that Jack would be there. Luther's legs went rigid, but his grip didn't loosen from around Jack's chest.

Adolf sprang at the plate glass.

It hit with a force that shook the window, and the glass starred at the point of impact but did not shatter. Adolf fell back to the floor, landing nimbly on his feet. The woman was still screaming—a thin, piercing scream—but her protector's nerve had failed. Behind the glass the maternity nurse had come to the front of the room in an effort to shield the babies. Jack knew she wouldn't last more than a few seconds when Adolf broke through the window.

"Let me go, damn it!" he shouted, still struggling; Luther's arms loosened, and Jack slid out of them to the floor.

Adolf shot a disdainful glance at him, like a human might look at dogshit on the sole of a shoe. He jumped at the window again, hitting it with his mangled shoulder. The glass cracked diagonally, and at the center of the window a piece about the size of a man's hand fell away. Adolf clawed at the hole, talons scraping across the glass, but couldn't find a grip. The demon rebounded to the floor again but was leaping almost as soon as he'd landed. This time his claw caught the hole, and he kicked at the glass to finish the job.

The corridor was full of screaming and the crying of babies. Jack lunged forward and grabbed the demon's legs, and as he wrenched Adolf out of the widening hole a large section of the window crashed down, glass showering the nurse as she threw her body across the first row of perambulators.

The demon twisted and writhed in Jack's grip with the agility of a monkey. Jack slung Adolf against the wall, heard the crunch of its skull against the plaster;

it got one leg free, contorted its body at the waist and the smashed head—half of it pulped and leaking—came up at Jack's hand. The razorblade teeth flashed before they snapped shut on Jack's index finger. Pain shot up his forearm and into his shoulder, but he kept his hand closed on the trapped leg. Adolf's teeth were at work, and suddenly they met through the flesh; the demon's head jerked backward, taking most of Jack's finger between the teeth.

Jack's hand spasmed with agony. The remaining four fingers opened and Adolf leaped to the floor,

The demon staggered, and Jack fell against the wall with his bitten and throbbing hand clutched to his chest. He hit an object just behind him, as Adolf swiped at his legs with the remaining claw and shredded the cuff of his trousers.

Then Adolf whirled toward the broken window once more, tried to jump for the frame but the muscular legs had gone rubbery. The demon reached up, grasped an edge of glass and began to clamber over it into the nursery.

Jack looked at Luther. The man—crewcut and husky, his face sallow and gutless—had backed almost to the corridor's corner. The nurse with the surgical mask was still lying across the first few infants, one arm outthrust to ward off Adolf's next leap. Adolf was almost over the glass, would be in the nursery within the following few seconds, and the thing was hurt but he would not give up before he'd slaughtered his fill. His head ticked toward Jack, and the oozing mouth stretched wide in a grin of triumph.

There was something metal pressed into Jack's spine. Something cylindrical. He turned, saw it was a fire extinguisher.

Adolf jumped from his perch on the edge of glass. Landed on the nurse, and began to slash at her back with long strokes that cut away her uniform and flayed off ribbons of flesh.

The fire extinguisher was in Jack's hands. His good index finger yanked the primer ring. There was a hiss as the chemicals combined, and the cylinder went cold. The nurse was screaming, trying to fight Adolf off. She slipped to the floor, and Adolf clung to the side of a perambulator, started drawing himself up and into it with his claw, the razor teeth bared. He reached for the pink-clad baby's skull.

"Here I am!" Jack yelled. "Ready or not!"

Adolf's misshapen head cocked toward Jack, teeth three inches away from infant flesh.

Jack pulled the cylinder's trigger. Cold white foam erupted from the nozzle, sprayed through the window in a narrow jet and struck Adolf on the shoulder and in the face. The baby squalled, but Adolf's caterwaul was an aural dagger. Blinded by the freezing chemicals, the demon toppled to the floor on his back, claw slashing at the air. Jack kept the spray going as Adolf tried to rise, fell again and started crawling across the floor, a little foam-covered kicking thing.

"Put it down!" someone shouted, to Jack's left. Two security guards stood there, and one of them had his hand on the butt of his pistol. "Put it down!" he repeated, and half-drew the gun from its holster.

Jack ignored the command. He knocked out the rest of the window's glass with the cylinder and stepped into the nursery, aimed the nozzle at Adolf and kept spraying as the creature writhed at his feet. Jack felt his mouth twist into a horrible grin, heard himself shout, "Die, you bastard! Die! Die!" He lifted the cylinder and smashed it down on the body; then again, striking at the skull. Bones—or what served as bones—cracked with brittle little popping sounds. Adolf's claw struck upward, blindly flailing. Someone had Jack's arm, someone else was trying to pull him away, the nurse was still screaming and the place was a bedlam of noise. Jack shook off one of the guards, lifted the cylinder to smash it down again, but it was snatched away from him. An arm went around his throat from behind.

Adolf's head—one eye as black as a lump of coal and the face mashed inward—surfaced from the chemical foam. The single topaz eye found Jack, and the razor teeth gleamed behind mangled lips. Adolf's claw locked around Jack's left ankle, began to winnow through the flesh.

Jack pressed his right foot against the grinning face and stomped all his weight down with the force of fury behind it.

The demon's skull cracked open, and what came out resembled a lump of intertwined maggots. Jack stomped that too, and kept stomping it until all the wriggling had ceased.

Only then did Jack let himself fall. Darkness lapped at his brain, and he was dragged under.

Seven

He awakened in a private room, found his hands stitched up, freshly bandaged and immobilized. Minus one index finger, which he figured was a cheap price. His left ankle was also bandaged, and he had no sensation in his foot. Dead nerves, he thought. He'd always believed a cane made a man look distinguished.

He didn't know how much time had passed, because his wristwatch had been taken away with his bloody clothes. The sun had gone down, though, and the reading light above his bed was on. The taste of medicine was in his mouth, and his tongue felt furry. Tranquilizers, he thought. He could still hear rain tapping at the window, behind the blinds.

The door opened, and a young fresh-faced nurse came in. Before it closed. Jack caught a glimpse of a policeman standing out in the corridor. The nurse stopped, seeing he was awake.

"Hi." Jack was hoarse, probably from the pressure of that arm around his throat. "Mind telling me what time it is?"

"About seven-thirty. How are you feeling?"

"Alive," he answered. "Barely." The nurse looked out through the door and said, "He's awake," to the policeman, then she came to Jack's bedside and checked his temperature and pulse. She peered into his pupils with a little penlight. Jack had noted there was no telephone in the room, and he said, "Think I could get somebody to call my wife? I imagine she'd like to know what's happened to me."

"You'll have to ask the lieutenant about that. Follow the light, please."

Jack obeyed. "The babies," he said. "They're all right, aren't they?"

She didn't answer.

"I knew he'd go for the babies. I knew it. I remember what the boy said, that Satan—" He stopped speaking, because the nurse was looking at him as if he were a raving lunatic and had taken a pace away from the bed. She doesn't know, he thought. Of course not. The security would have clamped down by now, and the shifts had changed. All the blood had been cleaned up, the bodies zipped into bags and spirited to the morgue, the witnesses cautioned and counseled, the relatives of the dead consoled by hospital administrators, the physical damage already under repair by workmen. Jack was glad he wasn't director of public relations at Marbury Memorial, because there was going to be hell to pay.

"Sorry," he amended. "I'm babbling."

She gave him the choices for dinner—chopped steak or ham—and when he'd told her what he wanted, she left him. He lay musing that seven hours ago he'd been fighting a trio of demons from the inner sanctum of a young boy's insanity, and now he was choosing chopped steak over ham. Such was life, he thought; there was an absurdity in reality, and he felt like the victim of a car crash who stands amid blood and wreckage and frets about what television shows he's going to miss tonight. Demons or not, the world kept turning, and chopped steaks were being cooked down in the kitchen. He laughed, and realized then that the tranquilizers in his system were either very potent or else the shock had really knocked his train off the tracks.

It wasn't long before the door opened again. This time Jack's visitor was a man in his mid-forties, with curly gray hair and a somber, hard-lined face. The man was wearing a dark blue suit, and he looked official and stiff-backed. A policeman, Jack guessed. "Dr. Shannon," the man said, with a slight nod. "I'm Lieutenant Boyette, Birmingham Police." He pulled out his wallet and displayed the badge. "Mind if I sit?"

"Go ahead."

Boyette positioned a chair closer to the bed and sat down. He had dark brown eyes, and they did not waver as he stared at Jack Shannon. "I hope you're up to some questions."

"I suppose now's as good a time as any." He tried to prop himself up on his pillows, but his head spun. "I'd like to call my wife. Let her know I'm all right."

"She knows. We called her this afternoon. I guess you'll understand we couldn't tell her the whole story. Not until we figure it out ourselves." He took a little notebook from the inside pocket of his coat and flipped it open. "We've taken statements from Miss Douglas, Mrs. Partain, Mr. Crisp, and the maternity ward staff. I expect you'll agree that what happened here today was ... a mite bizarre."

"A mite," Jack said, and laughed again. Now he knew he must be doped with something very strong. Everything was dreamlike around the edges.

"From what we can tell, you saved the lives of a lot of infants down on two. I'm not going to pretend I know what those things were, or where they came from. It's all in Miss Douglas's statement about what happened to Dr. Cawthorn, Mr. Moon and the others. Even the psychiatric patients gave statements that corroborated Mrs. Partain's. Hell, I kind of think some of them were so shaken up they got their wits back, if that makes any sense to you."

"I wouldn't doubt it. Probably the same effect as a shock treatment. Is Miss Douglas all right?"

"She will be. Right now she's in a room a few doors down."

"What about Rosalee?"

"Mrs. Partain's a mighty strong woman. Some of the others—like Mr. Crisp—might wind up on mental wards themselves. He can't stop crying, and he thinks he feels something on his back. I guess it could've been worse, though."

"Yes," Jack agreed. "Much worse." He tried to move his fingers, but his hands had been deadened. He figured the nurse would have to hand-feed him the forthcoming chopped steak. A weariness throbbed deep in his bones: the call of the tranquilizer for sleep.

It must have shown in his face, because Boyette said, "Well, I won't keep you long. I'd like to know what happened after Mrs. Partain locked you and Mr. Chambers on the eighth floor." He brought out a pen, poised to jot notes.

Jack told him. The telling was hard and got more difficult as his bruised throat rasped and his body and brain yearned for rest. He trailed off a couple of times, had to gather his strength and keep going, and Boyette leaned closer to hear. "I knew where Adolf was headed," Jack said. "The babies. I knew, because I remembered what the boy said. That's why I went down there." He blinked, felt the darkness closing in again. Thank God it was all over. Thank God he was alive, and so were the babies. "What . . . what floor am I on?"

"Three." Boyette's brow was furrowed. He had leaned very close to the bed. "Dr. Shannon … about the bodies. The demons, or *things*, or whatever the hell they were."

"Demons, yes. That's right. They were holding the boy together." Hard to stay awake, he thought. The sound of rain was soothing, and he wanted to let his eyes close and drift away and in the morning maybe the sun would be out again.

"Dr. Shannon," Boyette said, "we only found two bodies."

"*What?*" Jack asked—or thought he'd asked. His voice was almost gone.

"We found the body of the one in the nursery. And the one that looks like a spider. We wrapped them up and got them out of here. I don't know where they were taken, and I don't want to know. But what happened to the third one? The one you called 'Frog'?"

"Shot it. Shot it twice. It split open." His heart had kicked, and he tried to lift himself up but could not move. "Killed it." Oh God, he thought. "Didn't I?"

"There was only the one that looks like a spider up on eight." Boyette's voice sounded very far away, as if at the end of an impossibly long tunnel. "We searched the entire floor. Took the place to pieces. But there's no third body."

"There is ... there is," Jack whispered, because whispering was all he could do. He could no longer hold his head upright, and it slid to one side. His body felt boneless, but a cold panic had flooded him. He caught sight of something across the room near the door: a vent grill. What if Frog had recombined itself? he thought through the brain-numbing frost. What if Frog had crawled into the vent on the eighth floor? But that was over seven hours ago! If Frog was going to the maternity ward, why hadn't it struck there already? "The ducts," he managed to rasp. "In the ducts."

"We thought of that. We've got people taking the ducts apart right now, but it's going to be a long job. There are two possibilities, the way I see it: either that thing got out of the hospital, or it died in the ducts somewhere. I want to believe it died, but we'll keep looking until we find the body or we take the whole system apart—that could be days."

Jack tried to speak, but his voice was gone. There's a third possibility, he'd realized. Oh, yes. A third possibility. That Frog, the smartest of Tim Clausen's best friends, is searching from floor to floor, room to room, peering through the grills and scuttling away until it finds who it wants.

The one who killed its own best friends.

Me.

But maybe it died. Jack thought. I shot it twice, and it split open. Yes. Maybe it died, and it's lying jammed in the duct, and very soon someone will remove the screws and a gelatinous thing with staring eyes and a mouth like a leech will slide out.

Maybe it died.

Maybe.

"Well, I can tell you're tired. God knows you've had one hell of a day." Jack heard the chair scrape back as Boyette stood up. "We'll talk again, first thing in the morning. Okay?"

Jack trembled, could not answer. Could only stare at the grill.

"You try to sleep. Dr. Shannon. Good night." There was the sound of the door opening and closing, and Lieutenant Boyette had gone.

Jack struggled against sleep. How long would it take Frog to reach his room in a methodical, slow search? How long before it would come to that grill, see him lying here in a straitjacket of bandages and tranquilizers, and begin to push itself through the vent?

But Frog was dead. Frog had to be dead.

The sun would be out in the morning, and by then the third of Tim Clausen's best friends would be lying in a garbage bag, just limp wet flesh conjured up by infernal madness.

Jack's struggling weakened. His eyelids fluttered, and his view of the vent went dark.

But just before he drifted off to a dreamless sleep he thought the young nurse must have come in again, because he was sure he smelled the meaty odor of chopped steak. ◆

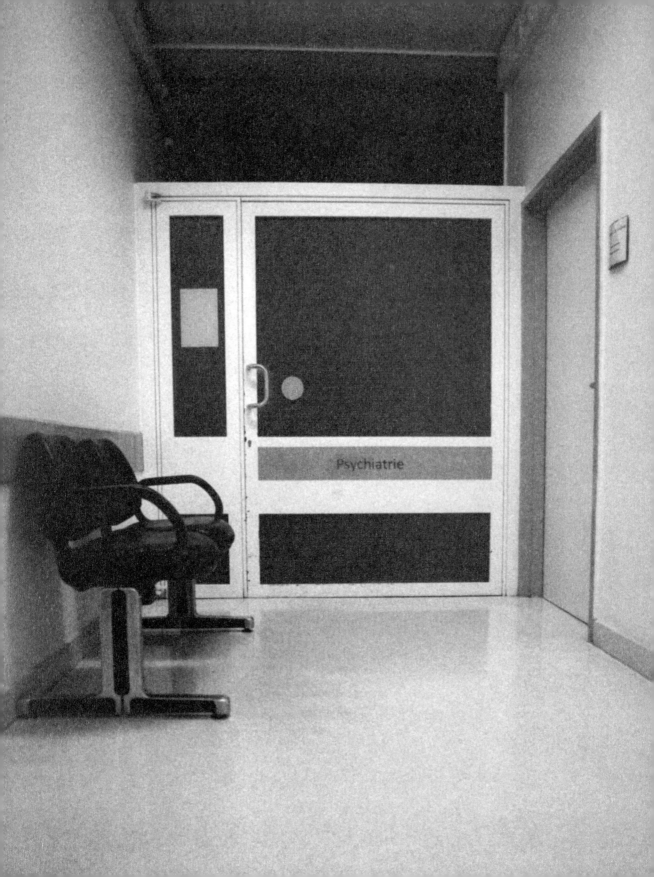

INTO WHOSE HANDS

BY *Karl Edward Wagner*

Mental illness is nothing to sneeze at, as we've already shown. And even if every psychic abnormality were, in fact, demonically inspired, the punishment may sometimes be more hellish than the crime, the treatment even worse than the disease.

Karl Edward Wagner was a legendary biker-sized doctor turned distinguished writer/editor who died of a broken and much-abused heart, way younger than those of us who loved him might have hoped. In between, he scrupulously presented a decade's worth of Year's Best Horror *anthologies— featuring some of the best writing of the era—while building a prodigious body of work of his own.*

This subtle and knowing story spends its whole time sneaking up upon you.

And may help explain why we still haven't figured that whole chicken-or-the-egg thing out.

Originally, back during the War (which Marlowe understood to be World War II), Graceland State Psychiatric Hospital had been an army base, and some of the oldtimers still referred to the center as Camp Underhill. Marlowe was never certain whether there had been a town (named Underhill) here before the base was built, or whether the town had grown about the periphery of the base (named Underhill) at the time when it was carved out of the heart of the scrub-and-pine wilderness. Marlowe probably could have found out by asking one of the oldtimers, had he ever thought to do so, or had he even cared to know. It was more to the point that no wing of the red brick hospital was of more than two storeys: further, that each wing was connected to the next by a long corridor. This, so Marlowe had been told upon coming here, had been a precaution against an air raid—an enemy sneak attack could not annihilate the outspread base, with its absence of central structures and its easy evacuation. Marlowe was uncertain as to the means by which an Axis blitzkrieg might have struck this far inland, but it was a fact that the center contained seven miles of corridors. This Marlowe had verified through many a weary weekend of walking to and fro and up and down through the complex, making rounds.

On this weekend Marlowe was feeding dimes into the slot of a vending machine chained to the tile wall of one labyrinthine corridor. After judicious nudges and kicks, the packet of crackers was spat from its mechanical womb in a flurry of crumbs. Marlowe eyed the tattered cellophane sourly. An industrious mouse had already gnawed across the pair on the end. He should have tried the machines in the staff lounge, but that meant another quarter-of-a-mile walk.

At his belt, the beeper uttered a rush of semicoherent static. Marlowe, shaking the nibbled crackers onto the tile floor, thumbed the beeper to silence with his other hand and plodded for the nearest nursing station. He swiped a cup of virulent coffee from the urn there, washed the crackers from his throat with a gulp of boiling fluid, and dialed the number to which he had been summoned.

"This is Dr. Marlowe."

"You have an involuntary admission on South Unit, Dr. Marlowe."

"I'll be down once I finish one on North."

The voice persisted. Marlow sensed the speaker's anxiety. "The patient is combative, Doctor. He's delusional, obviously hallucinating. If you could give us an order…"

"What's the problem? Do we know anything about this one?"

"This is his first admission here, and all we have are the commitment papers the deputies brought. He's obviously psychotic. He says he's Satan."

"Hell, that's my third this month. All right, seclude and restrain. I'm coming right down and I'll sign the order when I get there."

Marlowe glanced at his watch. It was past ten, he still hadn't eaten dinner, and the deputies from Beacon City were due to arrive on East with that adolescent runaway who'd slashed her wrists. Best take care of South Unit quickly. The coffee was sour in his stomach, and he regretted discarding the mouse-chewed crackers.

He was in North Unit, which was actually Central, since the northernmost unit was the Alcoholic Rehab Unit, but the walk was going to be a brisk five minutes, in addition to the time lost in unlocking sectional doors. Marlowe, who showed a footsore limp under the best of circumstances, knew better than to wear himself out this early in the weekend. It was Friday night. Until eight o'clock Monday morning he would be the only doctor on the grounds at Graceland. In that time he might have twenty to thirty admissions, on an average, in addition to the task of overseeing the well-being of some five hundred patients within the state hospital complex. A demanding situation under the best of circumstances, and impossible without a capable staff. Marlowe often wished for a capable staff.

He was tall and lean, with a profile that might have made a good Holmes if the haphazardly trimmed beard and randomly combed black hair hadn't more suggested Moriarty. His eyes were so deep a blue as to seem almost black; one patient had told him he looked like Lord Byron, but many patients had called him many names. In a three-piece suit Marlowe would have fit the tv-romance ideal of the distinguished young physician; however, around the hospital he favored open-necked sportshirts of imaginative pattern, casual slacks, and scuffed Wallabies. The crepe soles of these last were generally overworn to one side, giving him almost a clubfooted stance, but tile corridors are not kind to feet, and Marlowe liked such comforts as were permitted.

He unlocked an outside door, stepped out to cut across a courtyard. The summer night was hot and still. Behind electrified grates, ultraviolet lamps lured nocturnal insects to their doom, harsh crackles made the only sound other than the soft crunch of gravel beneath Marlowe's crepe soles. There was a full moon, hot and electric itself, and Marlowe knew he would get little rest this weekend.

There was sound again when he unlocked the door to South Unit's admission ward. The door to a seclusion room stood open, and inside three attendants were just fastening the padded cuff. Spreadeagled on the bed, a young black man struggled against the wrist and ankle restraints and screamed curses. At the end of the hallway several of the ward patients hovered anxiously until a nurse's assistant shooed them back to bed.

An attendant handed Marlowe the commitment papers. He glanced through them: 23-year-old black male, combative and threatening to life and person of family and neighbors since last night, apparently hallucinating, claimed to be Satan released from Hell. Today fired shotgun at neighbor's house, subdued by officers; involuntary commitment papers signed by family, no previous history of mental disorders.

Marlowe entered the seclusion room, studying his patient. His dress was flamboyant, his appearance well-groomed; he was lean but not emaciated, with prominent veins standing out from the straining muscles of his arms. Marlowe's initial impression was psychotic drug reaction, probably angel dust or amphetamines.

"Mr. Stallings, my name is Dr. Marlowe. I'm your physician, and I'd like to ask you a few questions."

"I am His Satanic Majesty, Lucifer God, Son of the Sun, Prince of Darkness and Power! Ye who seek to chain me in the Pit shall be utterly cast down! Bow down to me and worship, or feed the flames of my wrath!"

Marlowe played his stethoscope across his heaving chest. "Anyone able to get a blood pressure?"

The ward nurse handed him a sheet. "Don't know how good these vital stats are—he's been abusive and combative since the deputies brought him in. He's strong as a horse, I can tell you."

"These are about what they recorded at Frederick County when they examined him," Marlowe said. "We still don't have a chart on him?"

"First admission to Graceland, Dr. Marlowe."

The patient shouted obscenities, ignoring Marlowe's efforts to examine him. Verbal content was a jarring mixture of street slang and religious phrases, frankly delusional. There seemed little point in continuing with the examination at this point.

Marlowe turned to the ward nurse, who was showing anger despite her experience with abusive patients. "Thorazine, 100 mgm IM."

Two attendants held the patient on his side, pants drawn down, while she gave him the injection. The graveyard shift would be coming on shortly and they had work to finish before they could go off. Marlowe observed the familiar ritual in silence, studying his patient's reactions.

"Just make sure his blood pressure doesn't drop out," he told them. "I'll write out orders for another 100 IM PRN q 4 hours, if this doesn't do it. I'll finish my examination once he's quiet."

"Thank you, Doctor."

Marlowe's beeper summoned him while he was writing orders. "That's North Unit. Could you dial that for me, please?" He took the phone from the attendant and wedged it under his chin, one hand holding a Styrofoam coffee cup, the other scribbling an admission note.

"Dr. Marlowe, we have an unauthorized absence from North Unit. The patient is Billy Wilson. He is an involuntary admission."

Marlowe sipped his coffee. "Chronic schiz from Jefferson County? I've had him on my service a couple times. Better call the family and local sheriff. He usually hitches a ride home and tells people he's on the run from the CIA."

"We also have a voluntary admission here to see you."

"What's his problem?"

"He says he's depressed."

"I'll get over to see him when I can."

Marlowe finished his coffee and the conversation, placed cup and receiver in appropriate niches. His beeper wondered if he might phone the ARU. Marlowe thought he might.

"Dr. Marlowe, we have three unauthorized absences."

"These are…?"

"Two voluntary, one involuntary. Jimmy Roberts and Willy Wilbertson from Adams County are voluntary; Freddie Lambert from Tarpon is involuntary."

"Those first two always check back in together as soon as they've gone through their Social Security checks. Lambert usually winds up under a bridge with a gallon of skull-rot; better notify family and sheriff on him."

He finished his admission notes, looked in on Stallings. The new admission was still raging against his restraints; shrill obscenities penetrated the seclusion room door. "Another 100 mgm Thorazine IM stat, I think," Marlowe decided. "I'd like a quiet night."

It was past midnight when Marlowe made it back to North Unit to interview the voluntary admission. As he sought to leave, the nurses' aide on South Unit had delayed him with a question about Dr. Kapoor's medication orders; the Pakistani resident had been eight weeks in the US and six weeks on South Unit, and still hadn't discovered the distinction between *q.i.d.*, *q.d.*, and *q.o.d.* when writing medication orders. Marlowe made hasty corrections, ordered stat lithium levels on one patient, and swore a little.

The graveyard shift came on at eleven, and no one knew anything about his voluntary on North. The same, seated beside a flight bag in the office area, regarded Marlowe with politely contained anger.

He wore Nike running shoes, Levi Jeans, and an Izod knit shirt, all of it just starting to slide past the comfortably well-worn stage. His beard had reached that scraggly sort of seediness that usually breaks the resolve of its wearer and brings the razor back out of the medicine cabinet. The black hairline was beginning to recede, but there were no flecks of grey. He had a complex digital watch toward which he pointedly glanced. The eyes behind the designer frames were red-rimmed and puffy, despite the effort of the tinted lenses to mask them. Marlowe guessed him to be a grad student or junior faculty from the state university campus at Franklin, some thirty miles to the north, and he wondered why the patient had not availed himself of the posh psychiatric unit at the medical school there.

"Hello, I'm Dr. Marlowe. Sorry to keep you waiting."

"Frank Carnell." The handshake was accepted, but weak.

"Would you care to step into my office, Mr. Carnell?"

Each unit included an interview room for the on-call physician; however, as North Unit's attending, Marlowe had an office of his own on the unit. He ushered his patient into the cheap vinyl-upholstered chair beside his desk and eased himself into the often treacherous swivel chair behind the expanse of pea-grey enameled metal littered with manila chart folders. The office furnishings were state-purchase, some of them going back to Graceland's army camp days. A filing cabinet and a pair of unlovely metal bookcases of brownish-grey enamel housed a disarray of books, journals, and drug company handouts. There was also a couch of cracked brown Naugahyde, a coffee table, two folding chairs, and a spindly rubber tree leaning against the Venetian blinds. Overhead fluorescent lamps hummed behind acoustic ceiling tiles and made all too evident the yellow wax-stains on the uncarpeted floor of worn asbestos tile. One wall boasted a plastic-framed imitation oil of a mountain landscape that might have been discarded by a Holiday Inn, but Carnell was devoting his attention to the framed diplomas and certificates that completed the room's decoration.

"Impressive credentials, Dr. Marlowe. I had the impression that our state hospitals were staffed entirely by foreign medical school graduates."

"An exaggeration. I'm not the only American-educated psychiatrist here at Graceland." There were, in fact, two others.

"From what I've seen, it makes me wonder what a psychiatrist of your training is doing here at Graceland State?"

"I think the question more properly, Mr. Carnell," said Marlowe evenly, "is why are you here?"

Carnell's eyes, behind the tinted glasses, shifted to his chewed fingernails. He fidgeted with the flight bag on his lap. "I suppose you could say I'm depressed."

"Depressed?"

"I haven't been sleeping well. Can't fall asleep until the late late show and half a bottle of vodka; sometimes I need pills. I wake up before dawn, just lie awake thinking about things that keep running through my mind. Tired all the time. No appetite. No energy. Used to jog to my classes; now I just cut them and lie about the apartment. Haven't been able to study in weeks." Carnell spoke slowly, and Marlowe sensed tears.

"When did all this begin?"

"This spring. I'm in journalism at State, trying to complete work on my doctorate before the funds all dry up. My wife said she'd had enough of floating around the secretarial pool to pay the bills while I played the eternal student. She's shacked up with her old boss from central accounting, and the divorce is pending. I haven't been able to adjust to that. My performance has been on the skids—I'm supposed to teach a class during summer session, but I've missed so many my students don't bother either. I've been called on the carpet by the department twice. I'm broke, in debt, and now my fellowship has been canceled. It's just that no matter how hard I try, it just keeps getting worse."

Marlowe waited while Carnell worked to control his voice. "Mr. Carnell, I certainly understand that you have good reason to be undergoing a great deal of anxiety and depression. However, since this appears directly related to your present life situation, I feel confident that this disturbance is a transient one. This is a painful crisis in your life, and I appreciate the profound distress you are experiencing. Under the circumstances, I definitely agree that you need professional counseling; however, I believe you would far better benefit from outpatient counseling rather than hospitalization at this time."

Carnell fumbled with his flight bag. "Am I to understand that you are refusing me psychiatric care?"

"Not at all!" Marlowe had seen patients produce knives and an occasional handgun from unscreened personal belongings, but he doubted that Carnell was likely to turn violent. "I very strongly urge you to accept professional counseling. In my opinion you will derive considerably greater benefits through outpatient therapy than as a hospitalized patient here at Graceland."

"In other words, in your opinion I'm better off seeing a shrink on the outside than I'd be if I entered Graceland State as a patient." There was a certain triumph in Carnell's voice. "Well, it happens that I'm broke. I can't afford to be psychoanalyzed by some hundred bucks an hour private shrink."

"That isn't necessary, Mr. Carnell. If you wish, I can make an appointment for you to be seen on a priority basis this Monday at your community mental health clinic in Franklin; Dr. Liebman there is an excellent therapist. Or if you prefer, I can make an appointment for you at the medical school to be seen by the psychiatric outpatient service."

"I'm a taxpaying citizen of this state, Dr. Marlowe. Why are you refusing me treatment in a state facility?"

"I'm not refusing you treatment, Mr. Carnell. I frankly do not believe that hospitalization would be beneficial to you. If you would prefer to receive treatment at Graceland rather than in your local community, I will gladly make an appointment for you to be seen Monday in our outpatient clinic."

"Suppose I don't care to wait until Monday for medical attention."

"Mr. Carnell, you must understand that our facilities here are limited. Our primary task is to care for the severely disabled patient, the chronically ill. Patients whose problems can best be dealt with without hospitalization are directed toward more appropriate community programs."

"Dr. Marlowe, I can't wait until next week for you to shuffle me off to some community agency. I can't keep going on like I have these last weeks. If I don't get help now, I'm afraid…"

He paused to make certain Marlowe was giving his undivided attention.

"Well, I have quite a collection of sleeping pills. Tonight I feel like taking them all."

"I have some papers you'll need to sign," Marlowe said.

After 2:00 A.M. Marlowe let himself into the employees' snack bar. It was nothing more than a cinder-block room, walled with vending machines, furnished with plastic tables and chairs about the color of tomato soup that's been left too long to cool. It differed from the patients' snack bar in that the plastic tables and chairs were not bolted to the tiled floor, spectators did not gape at the machines in slack-jawed hopefulness, and the drugs that changed hands were of better quality. There was also a microwave oven.

The oven was Marlowe's solace during hungry nights on call. Underhill was a town too small to support a single fast-food franchise—something of a blessing in that otherwise Allen's Eat Good Food would no longer be serving home-cooked meals at family prices (the last Blue Plate Special known to Marlowe), nor would the Ski-Hi Drive-Inn still be making malts out of real ice cream and frying greasy hamburgers made of hand-shaped patties (all in a decor that left Marlowe humming medleys of Andrews Sisters hits). Underhill was also a town small enough to retain a blue law, and on Sundays even the Fast Fare convenience store was closed. The employees' cafeteria, in any event, closed for the weekend, and the outer world was closed to Marlow beyond range of his beeper. On occasion Marlowe might escape Graceland long enough to grab a meal at Allen's or the Ski-Hi, but on Sundays, the day Marlowe hated above all days, if he were to have a hot meal, he must cook it himself.

There was a stove and refrigerator for staff in North Unit's administrative section, but Marlowe was one of those bachelors for whom cooking was a forbidden art. Marlowe had only hazy memories of a youth before college and medical school, and whether the food put upon his plate was doled out or paid for, Marlowe regardless had had no thought to spare as to its conception. In his office Marlowe kept a hotplate and various cans, the sins of whose preparation were concealed by virtue of a large bottle of Tabasco sauce. With the microwave oven, Marlowe felt a competence somewhat akin to the laboratory.

For this weekend, Fast Fare's frozen foods counter (Marlowe understood two classes of foods: canned or frozen) had supplied him with a carton of Western Steer's Hungry Cowhand Rib-Eye Filets. These Marlowe had retrieved from North Unit's refrigerator and now fed to the microwave. He punched buttons at random, drawing tired satisfaction as the blocks of frozen beef stuff turned a pallid grey and began to steam. A clatter of quarters excerpted the last two Reel-Keen Cheez-Burgers from a vending machine. Marlowe filled each stale bun with a partially thawed segment of Hungry Cowhand, placed his mutant creations within the microwave. The cheese-food was just starting to melt when his beeper interrupted.

Marlowe ignored its summons until the microwave's buzzer announced the perfection of his cooking artistry, then picked up the snack bar phone and dialed. It was North Unit, and he'd just made the seven-minute walk from there.

"Dr. Marlowe, this is Macafee on the admissions ward. I'm afraid we're having some problems with that patient you just admitted."

"Which one is that?" Marlowe had had eight admissions tonight, and they began to blur together.

"Frank Carnell, sir. The suicide attempt from Franklin."

"What's the difficulty?"

Macafee was a Nam vet and continued to regard doctors as officers. "Sir, this patient is noncooperative and abusive. He's objecting to the suicide precautions you ordered, he claims someone has stolen a cassette recorder he had with him on admission, and he demands to speak with you immediately."

"Did he have a cassette recorder when he was admitted?"

"No sir. Only a small canvas bag containing clothing and personal articles."

Marlowe tried a mouthful of steaming steakburger, decided it needed catsup. "I need to stop in at the med unit, then do an admission at the ARU. I'll try to look in on you in between. Meanwhile it might be best to place Carnell under sedation and seclude if necessary. I believe I wrote a PRN for p.o. Valium?"

"Yes sir, you did. However, Mr. Carnell has refused medication."

"Then write an order for Valium 10 mgm IM stat, then Valium 5 mgm IM q 3-4 hours times 48 hours PRN agitation and anxiety. I'll sign it when I stop by. You already have a PRN seclusion order with the suicide precautions."

"Dr. Marlowe, Mr. Carnell claims that as a voluntary patient he should not be on a locked ward and that we have no right to force him to take medications."

"An argument the patient advocates have often raised," Marlowe said. "However, Mr. Carnell is an involuntary admission. I suggest you observe him carefully for further signs of delusional behavior."

Late at night Marlowe owned the corridors. They stretched in fifty-yard sections from brick unit to brick unit. After 11:00 P.M. only every third fluorescent ceiling fixture was left on, leaving the corridors hung with darkness in between the flickering islands of light. The corridors were entirely of tile: discolored acoustic tiles for the ceiling, glossy ceramic tiles for the walls, stained asbestos tiles for the floor. Marlowe wondered how such a manufactured environment could still stink of human filth and hopelessness.

Marlowe paused, not breathing. It was four in the morning, the hour of the cockroach, an hour before the keepers of the graveyard shift began to prompt their cares into a semblance of reality to greet their breakfast and the day shift at seven. He listened.

The roaches here were larger than any Marlowe had seen since an age when dinosaurs were but a fanciful gleam in a tree fern's eye. He could hear them as they scuttled along the worn tiles of the long, long corridor. Some, intent upon a smear of feces lodged within a missing bit of broken floor tile, were reluctant to flee his approach.

Marlowe stomped at them, withheld his foot at the last instant. The roaches scattered halfheartedly. It was, perhaps, an old game. Marlowe heard the silky rustle of their reconvergence as he silently passed by.

As he passed a snack vending machine, he could hear a mouse feasting within.

"Dr. Marlowe never sleeps."

"Can't spare the time, Mr. Habberly. Surely you've heard that there's no rest for the wicked."

Habberly chuckled. "Never going to sleep long's you keep drinking my coffee." He handed Marlowe his cup—a gift from the Sandoz rep, featuring a smiling yellow Happyface and the wish to "Have a Happy Day" from "Mellaril." Pudgy and greying, Habberly was nearing state retirement age; he had been an orderly and later ward supervisor at Graceland since it opened. He and an aging male nurse, occasionally joined by a ward attendant on break, were the only inhabitants of North Unit's administrative section during the graveyard shift.

"Careful, Doctor—that's fresh poured!"

Marlowe ignored his warning and swallowed without looking up from his admissions notes. "Thank you, Mr. Habberly."

"Never could understand how some folks can drink coffee when it's hot enough to scald your hand carrying it."

"Practice deadens all feeling, Mr. Habberly, and because there's too little time to wait for it to cool. But I can still taste: you brew the best cup of coffee in Graceland."

"Thank you, sir. Well, now, that's practice again. I don't fool with that big urn the day shifts use. Got me a three-four cup percolator just right for night shift. Been using it for years. And I don't fool with state-purchase coffee."

Marlowe finished his coffee and handed Habberly a sheaf of triplicate forms. "Here's the commitment papers for tonight's involuntaries. With luck you won't have any more admissions until day shift comes on in an hour."

Habberly thumbed through the forms, making certain that all had been signed and notarized as the law required. A patient could only be committed involuntarily if he constituted an immediate threat to others or to himself in the opinion of local magistrates and the admitting physician. Marlowe had had three involuntaries on North Unit tonight.

Habberly paused over the commitment papers for Frank Carnell. "Is this the patient who was causing the fuss about someone stealing his suitcase?"

Marlowe craned his neck to see which patient Habberly meant. "Yes. Which reminds me that I told Macafee I'd look in on him. By the way, you didn't happen to notice whether Carnell had any sort of bag or anything with him when he was admitted, did you?"

"Why, no sir. He didn't have any personal belongings with him at all. The deputies carried him up here straight from the emergency room at Franklin Memorial. I let them into the ward when they brought him here long about midnight."

The admitting ward for each unit was a locked ward, and it was hospital policy that every patient admitted after hours or on weekends must be kept on the admissions ward until such time as the psychiatrist to whose service he was assigned had had an opportunity to interview him. The rule applied to voluntary and involuntary patients alike. Patient advocates complained that this rule was only intended to discourage voluntary admissions after office hours, but hospital administration pointed out that the rule had come into being after a Korean resident blithely admitted a seemingly depressed voluntary patient to an open ward one night, who quietly strangled and raped the retarded teenage boy who shared his room and passed it off the next morning as the work of Mafia hitmen.

Marlowe let himself into North Unit Admission Ward. It was, he reflected, a bit of a misuse of terms in that patients judged not suitable for the open wards might linger in a unit's admission ward for weeks until proper disposition could be made. Graceland did not treat dangerous psychotics in theory; the state maintained a hospital for the criminally insane, now euphemized as a forensic psychiatric facility, in conjunction with the state penitentiary at Russellville. A patient who required long-term hospitalization at Graceland was either found suitable for an open ward or transferred to a chronic-care ward where long-term hospitalization usually meant lifetime.

Macafee nodded to him through the glass of the nurses station, unlocked the door to let him enter. "Good morning, sir. Almost 600 hours; we'll be waking them soon. Care for some coffee, sir?"

"Yes, thank you." Marlowe looked through the glass. The nurses' station was a locked cubicle placed along one wall to give an aquarium resident's view of the communal ward. Already several of the patients were beginning to shuffle about between the close-spaced beds; it was close enough to breakfast, which arrived with the day shift, that minimal activity was permitted.

"Any problems?" Marlowe signed his telephone orders in the ward orders book.

"No sir. Not after we put Mr. Carnell to bed." Macafee sometimes confused the ward with training barracks, but it was usually quiet when he was on night shift, and Marlowe disliked disturbances.

"How is Mr. Carnell?"

"Quiet, sir. Sawyer's checking on him just now."

"I'll just take a look myself."

A short hallway led from the communal ward to the outside corridors. Connected by a door to the nursing station was a small room for supplies and medications. There was an examining and treatment room farther along the hallway, then toilets, showers, a patients' lounge, and several seclusion rooms. Carnell was lying on the bed within one of these; a wooden night stand was the only other furnishing. Sawyer was just coming out of the room.

"Good evening, Dr. Marlowe—or good morning, it's getting to be."

"And let's hope it will be a good day, Mr. Sawyer. How is Mr. Carnell?"

"He's been resting quietly. Starting to wake up now." Sawyer had had ambitions of a pro football career before a high school knee injury scrubbed that as well as hopes for a college scholarship. He was ten years younger than Macafee and a good audience.

Carnell was muttering to himself when Marlowe bent over him. "Good morning, Mr. Carnell," Marlowe said, since his eyes were open. "How do you feel?"

"Damn you, Marlowe!" Carnell sat up sluggishly. "I've been locked up, robbed, drugged, I don't know what! Do you think you're running some sort of prison camp? I demand to be released from this zoo right now!"

"I'm sorry, Mr. Carnell. Have you forgotten why you came here?" Marlowe's voice was patient. "Try to remember."

Carnell's face showed anger, then growing indecision. His eyes began to widen in fear.

"Mr. Sawyer, could we have that IM Valium order stat?"

"Yes sir. Five mgm, was it, Dr. Marlowe?"

"Better make it ten."

The chronic-care wards were always on the second storey of Graceland's far-flung units. Marlowe supposed this was because Graceland had no cellars. Presumably, had there been cellars the temptation to wall them off would have been irresistible. Marlowe supposed Graceland had never had cellars.

There were two basic divisions among the chronics: the ambulatory and the nonambulatory. The ambulatory could be trusted to leave their locked wards, perform acceptably under controlled situations, and return to their locked wards. The nonambulatory could not be trusted to function within acceptable guidelines. They remained in their wards, often in their beds, often only a dream from the chronic med care unit; spoon-fed gobs of pasty slop, when they could no longer handle spoons; moved to the chronic med unit when they could only be fed through tubes and IVs.

They fed the ambulatory chronics three times a day—breakfast, lunch, and dinner—the same as living souls. This meant they were herded from their wards three times a day, down the stairs (there was an elevator for each unit, and those who could walk, but not negotiate stairs, were granted this) and along the tiled corridors to the patients' cafeteria. They moved along docilely enough, each regimented segment of quasi-humanity, herded along the long, long corridors by nurses and attendants.

Their clothes were shapeless garments that fit their shapeless bodies: not uniforms, only styleless wads of clothing donated by middle-class patrons who found salve for their consciences in charity bins for flotsam their guilt would not allow them to fling into trashcans. Some, who were habitually incontinent, might wear rubber (now vinyl) underpants, although it had been established with chronics that floors and clothing were more easily washed than could dermatitis and pustulant sores be cured; and so many, by chance or by choice, wore no underwear at all.

Marlowe, a microcassette recorder in one hand, a Powerhouse candy bar in the other, alternately dictating and chewing, stood against one wall as the chronics shuffled past on their way to be fed. Their faces were as shapeless as their bodies: some smiling, some grimacing, some frozen from the effects of too many shock treatments, too many drugs. A few seemed to recognize Marlowe, and waved or winked or muttered. Some, Marlowe thought, had been in Graceland longer than Marlowe, and that was forever. A grey-mustached grandmother in a shapeless polyester sack dribbled excrement as she shuffled past. The corridor stank of urine and feces and unwashed living dead, and no antiseptic nor disinfectant would ever cleanse it. Marlowe finished his candy-bar breakfast, waiting for them to pass before resuming dictation.

"If God exists," a patient had once questioned Marlowe, "then what sort of sadist is he to curse the elderly with the indignity of loss of sphincter control?"

"An angry god," Marlowe had replied with bitterness. "And vengeful."

By midmorning Saturday, Marlowe decided he had completed Friday's tasks and it was time to recognize Saturday. He had contemplated napping on his couch, but there were two voluntary admissions waiting on West Unit, and the adolescent runaway on East had pulled her stitches out.

Marlowe dragged a toilet kit from his filing cabinet and paid a visit to the staff restroom, where he washed his face in cold water, brushed his teeth, gargled mouthwash, brushed his hair and beard. Returning to his office, he pulled off his red Hawaiian shirt, sprayed on deodorant and changed into a blue Hawaiian shirt, also from his filing cabinet. Sleeping quarters were provided for on-call physicians in a cinder-block horror known as married residents' housing, but this was detached from the hospital unit, and after a night when it took Marlowe twelve minutes to respond to a cardiac arrest from there, he decided to take calls from his office.

East and West Units cared for women patients, North and South Units for the men. Whatever symmetry had been intended by this plan had been completely obscured by the addition of the Adolescent Unit, the Med Unit, the Alcoholic Rehab Unit (again segregated by sexes and separated by a five-minute walk), and Central Administration—not to mention the semiautonomous Taggart Center for Special Children (once known as the State Home for the Mentally Retarded), the Crawford Training School (the state had seen fit to include a center for juvenile offenders within Camp Underhill's disused facilities), and the P. Everett Amberson Clinic (a former hotel refurbished as a drying-out spot for the less shabby class of alcoholics and pill addicts). It took new psychiatric residents a few months to find their way around, and a car was necessary to reach the outlying centers—a complication in that many of the foreign residents had licenses to practice medicine but not to drive.

Marlowe, who was not moved by tears and found them a bit bothersome, considered East and West Units more than a little bothersome. Granted that tears were nonverbal communication, women patients tended to use them as dramatic expression or as means to terminate an interview. A generalization, but an accurate one, for Marlowe had timed things. Even allowing for the additional time entailed by a pelvic exam on new admissions, as opposed to a quick grope and cough to check for inguinal hernia, it took half again as long on the average to complete any task on the women's wards as on the men's. Marlowe compared notes with several of the women psychiatrists and found their experience to be the same. Marlowe saw the basis of an article for the journals in this business of tears, but he left it unwritten as he hated the journals. The crucial point was that, given too many tasks and too little time to accomplish them, East and West Units demanded a disproportionate share of that nonexistent time.

Marlowe spent most of the day between East Unit and West Unit. It was a pleasant day, and families liked to carry their senile grandmothers and Valium-addicted aunts to the hospital on weekends. Everyone was off work, the children could come along, and it was a nice outing for Grannie or Noonie or Auntie or maybe Mom or Sis, who had begun to wander into traffic or seduce the paperboy after two bottles of vodka. Major holidays were worst of all, for then families liked to rid themselves of unwanted and incontinent organic old ladies, so they could enjoy Christmas or Easter without the pressure of an invalid. Graceland was cheaper than a rest home, and afterward, if conscience troubled, they could always take a drive and reclaim her. Best of all, on weekends they could drop a patient off and be miles away before the lone on-call physician had a chance to interview her. The worse the weather, the better Marlowe liked it: involuntary commitments might come in at any time, but it was unlikely that the family would decide to haul off Grandma when it looked like it might pour down all day.

By midnight Marlowe limped back to his office and collapsed on his couch. He had had fourteen admissions since morning, with more on the way. Most of the usual problems he had been able to deal with over the phone—too much medication, too little medication, extrapyramidal reactions to the medications. Marlowe titrated and adjusted, switched from phenothiazines to Haldol or Navane or vice versa, dispensed Artane and Cogentin as required. Metal chains and straitjackets had required no such artistry, but the oldtimers told Marlowe of how they used to scream and howl on nights of the full moon in the days before major tranquilizers, and Marlowe kept it quiet the nights he was on call.

Marlowe's eyes stung. A Filipino resident had admitted a patient Thursday night and not noticed that he was a severe alcoholic; nor had the resident who inherited him in the morning, and who transferred him to an open ward. When the patient went into DT's with paranoid delusions, it took security two full cans of Mace to convince him to drop the table leg he was swinging like a club at anything, real or delusional, that came within reach. Marlowe had had to examine the patient once subdued, and Mace was still running like sweat off the man's blistered skin.

The familiar coffee burn in his stomach reminded Marlowe that he hadn't eaten anything except a candy bar and a large tomato one of the nurses had carried in from her garden. Fast Fare had closed, even had Marlowe felt up to a short drive. Red-eyed ("Remember—don't rub your eyes," security had warned him.), Marlowe pawed through his filing cabinet and uncovered a can of ravioli. He managed to open it without cutting himself, found a plastic spoon, and fed himself cold ravioli from the can. He considered heating it on his hotplate, but lacked the time or ambition. He almost fell asleep while chewing, but his beeper reminded him who and where he was.

At three in the morning Willy Winslow on South Unit smashed the saltshaker he had stolen earlier and sawed at his wrists with the jagged glass. He was quite pleased when he flailed his bleeding wrists against the nurses' station window, but neither the ward attendants nor Marlowe shared his amusement.

Winslow was a regular at Graceland, one of an undefined group of patients who enjoying staying in state institutions, constantly admitted and readmitted, either voluntarily or involuntarily, and constantly discharged again. Winslow was well known to all the staff at Graceland; if he could not con a resident into a voluntary admission, he would gash his wrists and gain an involuntary commitment thereby. During this, his seventeenth admission to Graceland, a concerned resident from one of the better private medical schools had devoted three months toward helping Winslow re-enter the community. Bolstered by an extensive outreach program, Winslow was to be discharged next week.

Marlowe, selecting from the suture tray, gazed at the masses of scar tissue upon each wrist and shook his head. "Mr. Winslow, you managed to do this without anesthetic, and I don't see why I should waste any in sewing you back together."

Winslow's eyes glittered, but he didn't reply. It was, perhaps, an old game.

"And how many times do I have to tell you," said Marlowe, drawing the curved needle with difficulty through the layers of scar, "cut lengthwise down your wrist, just here below the thumb—not crosswise."

Frank Carnell was still in seclusion when Marlowe made rounds through North Unit on Sunday evening, but the ward attendants reported that he had been quiet throughout the day, and he appeared to be ready to come out onto the ward. Marlowe found him sitting up on the edge of his bed, staring dazedly at his hands.

"Good evening, Mr. Carnell. How are you feeling today?"

"I'm sorry—I'm bad about names. You're Dr....?"

"Dr. Marlowe. Dr. Chris Marlowe."

Carnell struggled to recall. "I remember seeing you, of course. When I was… upset. And when they brought me here from the hospital."

"Do you remember coming here from the hospital?"

"I must have been completely irrational." Carnell smiled sheepishly at the memory. "I seemed to believe I had come here as a voluntary patient. I had a cassette recorder, and I was going to take firsthand notes for my dissertation on the inadequacies of our state mental hospitals. I'm a journalism student at State, but then you know all that."

"I'm sure there's more than sufficient material there for a number of dissertations," Marlowe agreed. "And was that actually your topic?"

"One of them," Carnell confessed. "I had plenty of ideas, just never followed up on them. Guess that was just another of the things that helped my life slide downhill, until…"

He struggled to control his voice. "Well, until I finally pulled out all the pills I had on hand and gobbled them down like M&M's. I remember getting sick and passing out, and then I guess I woke up there in the emergency room."

"You guess?"

Carnell frowned, trying to recall. "To tell the truth, my memory is pretty hazy for the last day or so—all those pills, plus whatever medications you've been giving me. There must have been a time there in the emergency room when they were bringing me around after I took all those pills…"

Marlowe waited patiently while he tried to remember.

Carnell's face began to twist with fear. "Dr. Marlowe, I can't remember anything from the time I blacked out until when I was sitting there in your reception room and…Wait a minute, I was never brought here! I came voluntarily!"

"Indeed, you did." Marlowe's smile was almost sympathetic. "And voluntarily, I'm afraid, is unforgivable."

Carnell started to rush for the door, but it was blocked by Macafee and Sawyer, and he was too weak to put up much of a struggle.

"Don't worry, Mr. Carnell," said Marlowe soothingly, as the needle plunged home. "It does take time at first to understand, and you have plenty of time."

It was past 5:00 A.M. when Marlowe made rounds through South Unit. The sun would be creeping out soon, signaling the dawn of what Marlowe knew would be another Friday, and he would be on call.

"Dr. Marlowe," suggested Wygul, the ward attendant on South, "maybe when you finish signing those ECT orders, could you take a look in on Mr. Stallings? He's been a lot calmer tonight, and we haven't had to restrain him since Saturday afternoon. I think he's ready to be let out of seclusion now so we can see how he does on the ward."

"Mr. Wygul," Marlowe finished his coffee. "I've never known your judgment to fail yet. Is the patient awake yet?"

"Yes, Doctor. He was sitting up in bed half an hour ago, and we'll be waking everybody up in just a minute."

"All right then, I'll talk to him."

Stallings gazed at Marlowe expectantly when he entered the seclusion room. He made no hostile moves.

"Good morning, Mr. Stallings. I'm Dr. Marlowe."

"How do you do, Dr. Marlowe." Stallings's manner was courteous, but in a friendly way, rather than cautious.

"Do you remember me from the night you came here, Mr. Stallings?"

"Yes sir, I sure do." Stallings laughed and shook his head. His hand seemed to want a cigarette to complete the gesture. "Man, I sure was out of my skull on something that night!"

"What do you remember?"

"Well, I remember being carried in here by the deputies, and being tied down and all, and I was cussing and telling the whole world that I was Satan."

"And did you believe that?"

Stallings nodded in embarrassment, then looked earnestly into Marlowe's eyes. "Yes sir, I sure did. And then you came into the room, and I looked into your face, and I knew that I was wrong, because I knew that you were Satan."

"Mr. Stallings," Marlowe smiled sadly, "you appear to have made a rapid recovery." ✦

PILGRIMS TO THE CATHEDRAL

BY *Mark Arnold*

There are all kinds of demons, covering every sin, and every form of aberrant behavior from overeating to thermonuclear overkill.

And then there's demonization: when you take a thing that wasn't especially evil to begin with – like having fun, for example – and conflate its least popular attributes with the most horrible human sins imaginable, until an imaginary connect-the-dots line of bullshit has been drawn between the not-so-bad thing and monstrous, criminal blasphemy.

This is a very personal story to me, because I don't think its substance has ever been unraveled better, with more passion or prayerful attention to detail. That it's the only published story by Mark Arnold only makes it more weirdly important to me.

It first appeared in the 1980s, in David J. Schow's landmark anthology Silver Scream. Now it's back, more pertinent than ever.

Along with the de Maupassant, this may be the only story herein that arguably has no demons in it.

Or maybe it has the most, albeit by any other name.

God doesn't love a deconsecrated drive-in: this might be the moral of the story; it's certainly the conclusion. On the other hand, some outdoor theaters have converted to other uses without provoking any odd response, or have mellowed from XXX- to G-rated fare while sprouting gangrenous little amusement parks, carny appendages for a clientele being shepherded about in their Pampers and peejays. So perhaps the message is an obverse comment on the life and soul of James Hern Slavin.

Or else there maybe just is no moral, only a chronicle about the unpleasant intersection of two belief systems. There's no getting around this point, and no particular suspense served in holding it back: this is a story of a collision course, and at the end of it a lot of people are dead.

It's also a story of an American curiosity; an architecture of kitsch and shabby dreams.

As a conscious pursuit, it might have been doomed. But as serendipitous enterprise, an indifferently managed house of cards, the Zone was merely cursed by being in the wrong place.

Granted the Zone was ahead of its time and too intense to be truly commercial, evolving from a half-assed business into a work of obsessive art. In some locales, though, it might have flourished. In Oklahoma or Texas, maybe. As a blue-collar homeboy hurrah in parts of Georgia or North Carolina; paradoxically, as a glam-palace in Marin or Malibu. Solvent or not, it should have become notorious: Calvin Trillin and Charles Kuralt should have done pieces on it; it was the kind of Gothic oddity that Linda Ellerbee and Lloyd Dobbins would have loved.

But the Trilite Zone Drive-In could not have shown a high profile anywhere in Mad River County—not even in Charity, a hippie college town that had closed in upon itself like a blossom, awaiting a decade more to its liking—and the worst possible part of the county for this kind of whimsy was Leviticus.

Leviticus, Ohio was not ever and will never be a village friendly to a three-screen tri-triple-bill drive-in movie and bootleg white lightning bar that decadent visionaries called the Cathedral of Sleaze.

Not that Earl Bittner had any vision in mind when he bought the place—he was too fried. Shaggy, unwashed, and nearly incoherent beyond bemused whistles, perplexed shrugs and nonplussed eye rolls, Earl wasn't the sort normally tolerated around Leviticus. But this was about the time of the climax to Watergate: God, patriotism, and the presidency were dying while hordes of drug-eyed freaks, trauma-shocked vets, fanatics, psychics, psychotics, and loonies seemed to be evergrowing and spreading. It had been a rough few years, and even the folks of Leviticus were disposed to make allowances, so long as the crazies stayed quiet on the edge of town. Which was the first serendipity, since Earl bought the site of the old Buckeye Drive-In because it was secluded, cheap, and barren, and he needed a place to park his butt without getting hassled.

Indeed, the Buckeye seemed a good place to be left alone. Nearly twenty years defunct after a single half-season's operation; its inception hadn't even qualified as a folly—just a damned stupid idea. It was located in a hollow beneath trash forest, an abandoned farm, and cornfields, three miles from the nearest two-lane state route and nearly a mile from any recognizable road. Nevertheless, some optimist had, once upon a time, poured enough money in high-quality cement to accommodate some two thousand cars, built a two-tiered flattop pagoda snack-bar projection booth, erected an electric marquee forty feet long but only eight feet high, and then gone broke so fast there hadn't been time to hock the projectors or sell off the speaker poles. A tax loss so forgotten that it was never even scavenged, the derelict stoicly weathered a generation of Southwest Ohio winters, as if awaiting another quixotic moron.

It did not, in fact, occur to Earl to refurbish the Buckeye when he moved into the projection booth. He just wanted to veg out and grow seedier; his apparent life goal was to become a coot. But not a hermit—although whether Earl invited visitors or acquiesced to them wasn't certain. Still, they found him, as many as a dozen on any given evening: barflies needing a place to crash for a night; hitchhikers passing through the county on their way to wherever; backpacking college students; and teens who discovered Earl didn't much care if they used his parking lot to hang out in. Through social osmosis and alchemy, a lowlife underground began re-animating the Buckeye.

County and state patrols slithered by on occasion, causing a scurrying into cars filled with sullen young glares; twice, village police got calls to investigate rumors of a cult. But Earl's place was private property just outside village limits on the Tecumseh Township border and thus nobody's headache; and Earl Bittner could hardly be considered even a minimalist swami—he was at least as bewildered as anyone there.

The parade of transients was healthy for Earl: while he never became, in his life, articulate, at least he retained the concept "speech," and he expanded his repertoire of grimaces. He was home every night, galumphing aimlessly from party to party, the perfect nocturnal host. Earl's only commandments were: no gunfire; no pitbull matches; no battering; no rape. The first two infractions occurred once apiece; the latter two would start to take place at times and progress as far as the first cry for help. In all instances the perpetrators abruptly found themselves grabbed by dim, gentle Earl: eyes knit together and squinting, he'd mutter, "Well shit on this, man, shit on this." Then lights would go out.

Dim, gentle Earl was 6'7", and weighed about 410.

Most guests, then, found four rules a reasonable number. Earl acquired a coterie and his place acquired a nickname—the DMZ; or, more commonly, the Zone.

And that was the second serendipity.

Meanwhile, in other parts of the nation, the vision of a peoples' Revolutionary Amerika had precipitously fizzled. Which left a lot of the radical vanguard without a hell of a lot to do. Typically distressed was James Hern Slavin, who'd parlayed wrested leadership of a campus political alliance into control of both a large food co-op and small listener-sponsored radio station, only to see all three go belly-up for lack of ideologically rigorous donors and volunteers. Most of his militant peers were drifting into law school, real estate, or cocaine; some sat around, waiting to discover est. But Jim Slavin wanted a Cause. He wanted to lead. He enjoyed people taking orders.

He considered commandeering an alternative school, but it, too, was bankrupt. Then he essayed an abortive foray into grassroots electoral politics—but democracy proved too compromised and too risky. At length Jim realised that he yearned to break his materialistic shackles and become enlightened; he decided the fast track was the New Age.

And Guru Maharaj Ji was proclaimed, by his own mother, to be the final avatar of God. When Jim Slavin first heard of Maharaj Ji, the Godhead was fourteen years old, and often confused with the Maharishi. The differences were that one was a fat old man who giggled alot, the other was fat, giggly, and young; one attracted rock stars, the other, for some reason, rad politicos.

Now, a few years later, the young messiah still claimed to be God…and fourteen. What intrigued Slavin was the reaction he got whenever he argued the hard reality of calendars to Maharaj Ji disciples. He emphatically pointed out that when a person is fourteen, 365 days later he is fifteen. If God, then a fifteen-year-old God, and next year, a sixteen-year-old God.

Wrong, he was told—there was no good reason why God couldn't stay fourteen for a few years if He damn well felt like it.

The potency of such conviction swayed Jim Slavin. Changing his name to Chimoy Haneesh, he found faith—if not in Maharaj Ji, at least in the possibilities of organized religion.

Time, in Mad River County, tends to be measured by the passing of seasons, which tends to obscure the passage of years. And three years, for Earl Bittner and the Zone, drifted until the advent of a wild-eyed cross between James Dean and Joey Ramone, a proto-postpunk from Montclair, New Jersey.

Brandon Pugnale didn't remember where he'd been the day JFK was shot, and didn't care. He was nineteen, and he twitched; he'd survived two teen suicide attempts and a stress-induced nervous collapse; he'd decided the world was in an irreversible decline that would end in nuclear annihilation, and was convincing himself he didn't care about that, either. Brandon felt that, being bright and young, he probably ought to embrace either revolting idealism or disgusting pragmatism, but lacked faith in both.

The only thing Brandon believed in was trash. Lou Reed street people and championship wrestling, White Castles and Tico-Tacos, plastic crucifix musical nightlights and 3D postcards, art deco cafeterias and black painted walls. Trash was all Brandon Pugnale was willing to live for, the sublime essence that never betrayed him. But he had no hope of turning his belief into either a commitment or a career.

Brandon discovered the Zone on a cold and drooling wet early April night. He'd just flunked his sophomore year as a business major at Kent State, and had about a month to figure his next move before the damage became evident. He didn't really wish to stay in Ohio, which Brandon considered a pisshole. But New Jersey was a pisshole with parents. Montclair was near New York, which had CBGB and Max's; but the bands they booked were from Ohio. Brandon felt no desire for a quotidian world of leisure suits and singles clubs, and couldn't delude himself that the West Coast would be any better than the East. On impulse, he decided to cruise down through Charity and check out its college, which was reputed to be very weird, very expensive, and very desperate for students.

But Charity didn't exist, or had moved, or the roadmap lied. Or something. The village wasn't where it was supposed to be. The run down from Kent was longer than Brandon had thought, the rain got worse all day, and by the time he realised he'd lost his destination, he'd also lost the interstate. He found only hibernating farms, some incongruously fortresslike tract developments, and the spooky, whitewashed, distressingly Christian villages of Lamentations, Leviticus, and Judges. In all three, his outsized Harley-Davidson jacket and unmufflered Yamaha 450 guaranteed glares and no directions to either a main road or motel.

It was dark when Brandon saw the single light of a combination fire station and tavern a mile beyond Judges, Ohio. The bartender (and chief?) would neither serve nor speak to Brandon; but there was a teenager feeding quarters to a decrepit Gottlieb table. The pinball machine hadn't been serviced in years; half the rollovers were locked in place, the left flipper was lame, and most of the lights were burned out. So was the kid, for that matter—aboriginally ignorant about the existence of highways and Holiday Inns, at least he successfully told Brandon how to find Earl Bittner's place. The rain let up to a drizzle.

The turn-off lacked a street sign, but someone had considerately spray-painted the word ZONE across the blacktop. Brandon liked the name. The drizzle ended, and the cloud cover lifted to the treetops as Brandon found the hollow and the darkened marquee. He wheeled toward a cluster of cars, then saw they were all junkers, neatly arranged to face the skeletal struts that had once borne the screen.

Most drive-ins, like circuses and stage theaters, look small and tawdry when closed. Not the Zone. Immense even in daylight, by night it seemed infinite; acres of black tarmac spreading to merge with the hollow's false horizons. The dozen abandoned cars facing the phantom screen seemed huddled and vulnerable. Then Brandon heard a clomping, squelching tread in the silence. A megalithic shadow detached itself from the refreshment stand and Brandon was seized by panicky déjà vu of being alone in terra incognita after following a retard's directions... *Deliverance...Texas Chainsaw Massacre...The Hills Have Eyes...*

"Ah...Hi," he tried. No response. "It's like, uh, 'are you open?'" Grateful that he'd not dismounted, Brandon edged his foot toward the bike's kickstand.

The figure, not stopping, grunted.

Brandon gripped the handlebar clutch. "Look, it's like...I'm lost, see, and this kid a few miles from here said it's like 'people can crash at Earl Bittner's' and told me to come here but if it's not okay..."

"S'okay," the monolith mumbled, his voice high, nasal, and cracking. He rolled his eyes as if exasperated by an idiot question. The gesture and voice were oddly reassuring; the hulk seemed less ominous.

"Well, ah, okay then thanks. Look, it's like 'is there anyplace I can get something to eat?' I been on the road all day—there a Pizza Hut or deli or anything around..."

Earl Bittner grunted, turned, and plodded back to the pagoda; suddenly, banks of pink and yellow strip-lighting lit the snack bar. Brandon stared, feeling vaguely surreal, then revved up and wheeled across the parking lot.

Earl's hospitality was bachelor simplicity on a grand scale: a six-gallon laundry tub of fearsome chili, perpetually simmering and replenished for nearly three years; cases of lunchbox bagged Fritos; popcorn in the tank of the Buckeye's popper, a machine so antique it dispensed butter; crusted jars of instant coffee and creamer; and soda coolers filled with 140° bootleg corn liquor. Earl waved Brandon toward indifferently cleaned collections of bowls, mugs, and spoons. Dinner chat was limited to introductions and Earl's refusal to accept money for his chili and moonshine. Accommodations would be any abandoned car on the lot, or the floor behind the refreshment stand.

A pickup truck, horn honking, squealed past the snack bar and, splashing puddles, weaved around metal poles to a far corner of the lot. Earl clomped off to play host. The cloudfront passed; greenish-gray moonlight on the Zone piqued Brandon's curiosity. Mad River County began to seem less hostile; warmed and fed, Brandon decided to stick around for a day or two, and continue his search for a college. He wandered across the lot, trying to envision the Zone in what he imagined must have been its salad days: jalopies, Elvis, ponytails, *Beach Party Bingo*, *I Was a Teenage Scuzzball*. He'd been born and raised in mall-dominated metro-suburbia, long past the heyday of drive-ins and all their nasty glory…the evening chill offset by cayenne, white lightning kindled an alcoholic inkling of awe and revelation. Earl joined him, bearing mugs of hootch.

"This is a great place, man," Brandon said.

Earl grunted, but Brandon was feeling enlightened and expansive.

"So, what're you? Fixing this thing up, or what? I mean you own this place, right? So it's like, 'are you gonna do business', gonna reopen it or what?" Brandon had another drink.

"Re-open it?" Earl looked around. "Think it's already pretty open."

"What're you, kidding? You fucking kidding me? This is a fucking great place! So how come you're not turning it back into a drive-in?"

"Back into. A drive-in?" The idea had simply never been suggested to Earl.

Brandon, drunk and arms swinging manically, barely noticed. "Are you kidding me? I mean, show cheesy movies and horror and skinflicks, sell popcorn, beer—I mean this is a fucking theater, man! It's all here, just use it, it's like 'you got your ticket booth, you got your projection booth, your snack bar.' You got your marquee! It's like, 'how much more do you need?'"

A bit more, as it turned out. But Earl squinted at the lot, quite possibly seeing it objectively for the first time since he'd bought it. His eyes began to gleam with wonder and his right cheek began to spasm. At length the tic firmed into a half-smile. Earl Bittner was finding something to believe in. He could believe in the Zone.

Still, he shook his head and sighed. "Naw, I don't—I don't know shit. Shit about that stuff…"

"What—what're you? I mean, what—picking movies? I got a cousin does that. Business? That shit's easy, man, it's like, 'trust me!' I'm an M.B.A. Really. And all this stuff's nothing."

"I." Earl stopped and rolled his eyes. "I don' know any'a that stuff…"

"Yeah, but I do; I mean it's like, 'I could set you up, and…'" and Brandon Pugnale realized he'd just found an alternative to Kent and Montclair, a future embodying his vision of trash "…y'know? I really could." He looked up to the nonexistent screen, filling in lurid scenes and splashes of color washing over a hot summer parking lot filled with Trans Ams and Camaros, teeming with teenage girls in misapplied make-up, halter tops, sweaty, beerstained jeans stretched across their oversized Ohio asses…"It could be real…" he admiringly whispered, "real… real sick." Brandon laughed, clapped, his hands and shouted, "Oh, shit, man—we gotta do it, y'know? It's like—we, have just got to do this!"

Then he threw up.

Thus was the Zone reborn and baptised.

Drive-in movies were, at the time, adjudged to be endangered, or already extinct. America was rocked by gas shortages, inflation, and threats of rationing; entrepreneurs sought fuel substitutes in everything from rocks to grass clippings; and unnecessary motoring was considered almost sinful. Moreover, all movie receipts had been falling for nearly a decade, as bijous fissioned into puny screening rooms, managers hoping to half-fill hundred-seat houses. Media pundits differed only in their choice of apocalypse: either the economy would collapse, in which case everyone would stay home and watch TV; or the economy would improve, in which case everyone would stay home and watch pay TV.

But Earl Bittner and Brandon Pugnale were unaware of fiscal forecasts. They were oblivious to Ohio's eroding industrial base and declining farmland prices. They didn't notice that, above their heads, For Sale signs went up on the forsaken farm and forest while the cornfields were optioned by a speculator from Dayton who never raised the capital for his housing development, but did persuade Tecumseh Township trustees to amend the area's building codes and permit construction of multi-unit dwellings.

Earl and Brandon were too busy to care. By tinkering and triage, they managed to coax fifty-one speakers, two projectors, and the marquee into a guise of functionality. They obtained rolls of tickets, cases of soda, and kegs of beer. They tried to make a screen from billboard paper, but finally had to hire a Cincinnati theater supplier to erect and position the 35mm sheet.

Films proved easy to obtain. Brandon simply essayed a hadj to his second cousin, Louis "Capooch" Capagianelli, overseer of five mob-owned cinemas in Times Square and Harlem, who could supply pirated prints of whatever happened to be on hand. Few of them movies likely to be reviewed by Gene Shalitt or Sneak Previews, but all of them satisfying to Brandon's aesthetics.

The issue of their labors, billed as the D.M.Z. Drive-In, looked fairly pathetic, and pretty much like Earl Bittner's old place. Unpainted; cracked concrete; weeds. The junked cars stayed put. But to Earl and Brandon the site was transformed; and they officially opened on the last Tuesday in July with a triple feature of *Bloody Pit of Horror*, *Sugar Hill's Zombie Hit-Men*, and *The Devil in Miss Jones*.

Earl's regulars refused to pay for parking in a lot they'd always used for free; they just drove around Brandon's frantically waving arms, until Earl dimly, gently explained the new order. Earl sputtered and pouted at Brandon's insistence that they sell refreshments, which Earl had fully intended to include in the admission price. The projectors broke often. Ticket-taking and food vending were haphazard. They didn't advertise, since they never knew what or whether Cousin Capooch would be shipping. The madding crowds never materialized; the gate fluctuated between two and ten cars a night. Brandon, who had moved into an abandoned van, scored no teen nooky.

Even so. *Meat-Cleaver Massacre* / *The Incredible Torture Show* / *Three on a Meathook* played, then *Barn of the Naked Dead* / *Ilsa, She-Wolf of the SS* / and *El Topo*; *Bloodeaters* / *Revenge of Monkey Fists* / *House of Whipcord*; *Olga's Girls* / *Fists of Vengeance*, and *Let Me Die a Woman*. When they closed the season in October, the Zone had garnered receipts of nearly $3,000…not counting expenses.

Brandon was ecstatic. He called other drive-in managers, pestering them for secrets; subscribed to trade papers; and dragged Earl to exhibitors' shows. Earl was stunned by his summer viewing: he'd never dreamt that certain events could even be, let alone be captured on film; like any other convert, he'd beard strangers and proselytize, "…an' then this guy WRRRAAA and a bunch'a skinny Chinese with pigtails WHAPWHAPWHAPWHAPWHAP an' he did this jig and th'other guy's head KA-PLOMB!"—crudely miming ripsaws, psychokinetic explosions, and shaolin temple mixed crane/mantis kung. Earl was, for the first time in memory, genuinely enthused; and Brandon learned how much paperwork he had yet to start. All told, it could have been enough—enough knowledge, enough experience to have kept the Zone open for a few seasons, another marginal Ohio enterprise staggering along on the edge of failure.

But that winter Brandon Pugnale attended a *Famous Monsters of Filmland* convention in Minneapolis, and returned to Leviticus with two inspirations.

The first was seen on a highway near the airport: a drivein, the better to compete with mall cinemas, had tri-sected its parking lot and erected two more screens, enclosing an open-sided pyramid of film. Brandon promptly grasped the implications—more movies, more money, more fun.

The second inspiration followed Brandon to Ohio in a Winnebago crammed with cookware and cosmetics. She was thirty-two, newly divorced, and had just changed her name to An'akist Verlaine.

Dissolving like a video space invader, Maharaj Ji's millenium self-destructed in a muddy scandal that seemed to involve too many wristwatches, too many Indian customs guards, too many stewardesses, too many hidden marriages, and one very jealous Mother of the Messiah, who unexpectedly declared that she had made a perfectly dreadful mistake: Maharaj Ji, she announced, was not God.

His little brother was.

By the time the mess was straightened out (if, indeed, it ever has been), most of the perpetually enlightened were drifting into neoconservative banking, Posse Comitatus, or Rajneeshpurim; some sat around, waiting to discover designer drugs.

But Chimoy Haneesh, né James Hern Slavin, surfaced in Missouri renewed and recycled as Rev. J. Hern Sloane, pastor of the First Church of United Christian Life. Disdaining such old timey relics as a church and congregation, Rev. Sloane purchased weekly radio hours for his self-ordained, self-promoting ministry in the Wonderful News of Christ's Coming.

Which might be a terribly cynical way to describe acceptance of the eternal truth that cleansed a mortal soul in dramatic affirmation of faith—but then, Jim Slavin's vocation was suspect. He hawked indulgences.

All media evangelists spend much of their airtime hustling tithes and blessings. But Rev. Sloane bribed nursing-home attendants to tune in his show, and slip him medically annotated patient lists, which inspired the texts of Jim Slavin's sermons.

"And in Springboro this beautiful morning, my heart is with all of our friends at the Elmbrook Home, over there, like Esther Hubbard…can ya'hear us this morning, Esther? Bless ya, how are ya', darlin'? Esther, dear sister, Jesus has a blessing He wants me to give ya'. The Lord GOD knows about the cancer, darlin'; He Whose love blesses all has witnessed to me about the cancer that's eatin' you alive, that's causing you such affliction. Well, Esther, it brings me pain to see you suffer, darlin' sister, and it brings GOD pain…GOD won't let ya'die, dearest. GOD can't bear to see ya suffer; and GOD wants to bless your troubled heart." Rev. Sloane would explain that God could intercede if Esther obtained a beautiful and inspirational "Praying Hands" blessing (which 1" x 3" card she should tuck beneath her pillow, thus letting Christ know whom to cure), which Esther would receive absolutely free upon receipt of her $75 offering. The more cards, the sooner God's arrival. Then on to Agnes Krienslach's arthritis and May-Belle Loteneau's paralysis.

Whether or not God approved, the terminally ill did. Jim Slavin had found his bandwagon: the market was bullish on Elmer Gantry. Big time preachers raked in millions per week. Rev. Jim Jones was building an expensive South American retreat; Jim and Tammy Bakker sold salvation through eyeshadow; Ernest Ainsley one-upped psychics with over-the-air exorcisms; Billy James Hargis prophesied hellfire for sinners while he fucked the adolescent boys and girls of his traveling All-America choir; reruns of Leroy Jenkins collected offerings while the good parson himself was in a Georgia lock-up, convicted of complicity in an extortion and arson-for-profit ring that had caused a few deaths in some slums he owned. Prosperous, adored, taxexempt, and nearly beyond all legal accountability, the ministries were understandably thankful to God and the American Way.

As soon as he could afford to, Jim Slavin made the jump to cable.

Upon reaching age thirty, Mrs. Donald Simms Jr. discovered David Bowie, Darkover novels, and her sexual prime; she decided what she didn't want to be when she grew up was a Minnesota farmgirl turned Minnesota hausfrau. So, rather than get pregnant with Donald III, Mrs. Simms dyed, shaved, and moussed her hair into a rainbow-spectrumed cockatoo crest, hung around Minneapolis clubs, and vanished on weekends to attend science fiction conventions.

Mr. Simms was displeased. Mrs. Simms soon found herself free to resume her maiden name of Ann Verlaine. She was 5'1", 92 lbs; she had charm, enthusiasm, a wicked basilisk glare, and ever-changing hair and make-up. She was an avant-garde chameleon with no concrete plans, just a dwindling divorce settlement, an r.v., and a powerful belief in flash. Ann became An'akist and was bracing herself to try Soho or L.A. when she met Brandon Pugnale.

Standing in the same convention registration line, they talked, touched, and almost instantly clung to each other without sleep for a week. They chattered all day, caroused all night, traded obscure rock tapes at dawn. Neither doubted it was It at first sight; both tried their best to live in each other's arms, glow in each other's eyes, kiss till their lips went numb. Their attraction was amazing, exhilarating, public, thrilling; it was absolutely, totally disgusting. Belying all pretense to their images of post-industrial cool, Brandon and An'akist cootchied enough to smother a Smurf or render a Care Bear bilious. No logic could explain the nouveau flashqueen's subsequent move to a parking lot in semi-rural, Ohio. Suffice to say— Brandon spoke to her condition.

And she was the link, the fuel rod required for the Zone to achieve critical mass. A trinity of beliefs came together into self-sustaining reaction. A strange magic began to stir.

The magic was not apparent come springtime; but potholes were filled, fresh blacktop spread, parking lines and arrows painted along rows of leased speakers beneath a vast geometry of screens. Brandon and Earl built an expanded projection turret and acquired new used equipment. The ticket kiosk, bathrooms, and pagoda gleamed with fresh paint and chrome. The snack bar actually passed Health Department inspection; an electric Dr. Pepper clock-menu listed variations on chili, popcorn, hot dogs, sweets, beer, and soft drinks plain, or, for a buck-fifty, premium "+". Earl was proud of his chili and moonshine and would part with neither: the corn liquor was, of course, against the law and there was no way around that save to dollop it under a code name. Distribution contracts were signed, and Cousin Capooch expanded the illicit library with filched pre-release directors' cuts of new and occasionally big-budget films. Brandon resprayed the faded ZONE graffito on the state route, and placed newspaper ads with the theater's new name: "Nine movies for the price of one in—The Trilite Zone."

Each screen was usually reserved for its own specialty: Horror, Violence, and Sex. The opening gala featured *Eaten Alive* / *Zombie Flesh Eaters* / *Dawn of the Dead* / *Make Them Die Slowly* / *Baby Cart at River Styx* / *Twitch of the Death Nerve* / *Insatiable* / *Lucifer Rising* / *Shanty Tramp*.

The 2000-car lot wasn't filled, but the first week's receipts outgrossed the entire previous summer's. The drive-in was suddenly suffused with an incense of viability.

Jubilation led to innovation: for the next few years An'akist, Brandon, and Earl seemed able to take the business in any direction—every silly, gonzo, warped, drugged-out notion had its niche in the scheme of the Zone.

Ideas flowed from An'akist, who, pursuant to nothing would bounce as if goosed and cry, "OH! Y'know what we could do is?"; were caught by Brandon's "Yo! Wai'aminute wai'aminute, this could fucking be smooth, it's like 'it's real sick'. Sweet…" They'd hug each other, smooch, hold hands, tickle, giggle; and volley, spin, shape, kick the concept around while Earl stood by, shaking his head, muttering "What the hell's that shit…", happy to be involved.

God Told Me To / Mutations / Suspira…

An'akist piped punk and metal over the speakers before, between, and sometimes during shows. *The Not Ready for Airplay* scores were like nothing broadcast in Mad River County, including, over the years, *Anthrax to Zott*, *Bitch*, *Bad Brains*, *Butthole Surfers*, *Shox Lumania*, *Afrika Bambaataa*, *Oingo Boingo*, *the Cramps*, *Screaming Hibiscus*, *Big Fat Hairy Pet Clams from Outer Space*, *the Dead Boys*, *the Voidoids*, *Mermaids on Heroin*, *SIC F*CKS*, *Throbbing Gristle*, and *Country Porn*.

Dungeons of Horror / Nigger Lover / Mondo Magic…

An'akist hooked up a microphone to deliver color commentaries about the movies while they were shown and started amateur theatrical contests, where audience volunteers improvised spontaneous redubbings of Filipino gore.

Do Me Evil / Dracula Sucks / Take It All…

An'akist felt sorry for all the poor couples forced to screw in Civics and Chevettes. She rented out sleeping bags and pup tents, then created a cordoned off intimacy-section in a wedge between Sex and Violence, with flowerbeds, waterbeds, trampolines, a boxing ring—it came to be called the Fight-or-Fuck area…the Forf.

Toxic Zombies / Humanoids from the Deep / Children, Shouldn't Play With Dead Things…

An'akist, challenged by *Rocky Horror*, got Brandon to sell make-up kits, vampire fangs, ghoul masks, water pistols; she ran costume contests.

Call Him Mr. Shatter / Night of the Bloody Apes / Satan's Sadists…

An'akist appropriated the Zone's borders for a vegetable garden, appointing Earl her serf. Earl groused until he bit into his first homegrown jalapenos and realised how their infusion would galvanize his chili. Henceforth the stuff would burn a patron's ass for days. The snack bar topped hot dogs with homemade relishes, mustards, and pickles.

Caged Heat / Barbed Wire Dolls / Wanda the Wicked Warden…

An'akist booked a Columbus noise-band to play *Dead Kennedys* covers, got

Brandon to set up spotlights and a sound system, but forgot to tell Earl, who projected *Superninja* and *Drunk Masters* across the concert. The result was so satisfying that An'akist brought in as many acts as she could find, from headbangers to glam gloom, performance art to gelatin wrestling, all of whom played simultaneously with the movies.

Breakfast at Manchester Morgue / *The Honeymoon Killers* / *Slumber Party Massacre*…

The Big Bang, however, was Earl Bittner's genius, his tribute to his faith. One crystalline -12° January night, Brandon and An'akist awoke in the Winnebago as a projector flooded a screen, the light echoing across the snowcoated, ice-varnished lot. They roused in time to watch a power drill gore through an eye and turn into a striking rattlesnake that spat intestines over a headless cheerleader. They dressed, mufflered, dashed, and climbed to the booth where Earl, face twisted into a lopsided grin, gleefully hiked a thumb toward the screen. He had, with ham-fingered patience, joined splices, trailers, and shots from duplicate prints into twenty minutes of nonstop trash climaxes—shock cuts, cum shots, head rolls, blow ups, boots, chops, thrusts, slashes, splats. By spring, Earl had assembled two more reels, and sluiced all three screens with a fireworks display as hypnotically searing to the eye and brain as Earl's chili was to the tongue and gut—a fest of f/x, a satiation of sleaze.

The Incredibly Strange Creatures Who Stopped Living and Became Mixed-up Zombies / *Attack of the Killer Tomatoes* / *Andy Warhol's 3D Flesh for Frankenstein* / *Cannibal Holocaust* / *Pay Them in Blood* / *Ramrod* / *Talk Dirty to Me* / *Flesh Gordon* / *Star Whore*s…

Word of the Zone spread to midwestern campuses and air bases; meanwhile, graphic cheapies and big budget trash movies proliferated and grew more popular. Brandon subscribed to *Gore Gazette*, *Sleazoid Express*, and *Splatter Times*; he and An'akist daydreamed about being the cutting edge of a cultural movement. Laughing, hugging, wrapped in each other, Brandon and An'akist were crazy-in-love ˙. And Earl Bittner had found a family without leaving his home.

But beyond the underground, different forces propelled the social dynamic. Ohio was bashed by malaise, Iranian hostages, the collapse of smokestack industries; it slammed to a brief stop when a 21% prime interest rate collided with a 12% usury ceiling that made all loans illegal. Cleveland, International Harvester, and family farms went under; many thought the rest of the state would soon follow.

The same straits wracked the entire country, opening the portal to sweeping political change. Governor Ronald Reagan, formerly buried by the press as a superannuated sadsack with too-often repeated punch lines, snagged an interception and spiked one into the White House end zone: his tackles and offensive line were mystically transmogrified from knuckle-dragging fruitcakes and yahoos into respected mainstream conservatives and headline leaders of moral revivalism.

And the Reverend J. Hern Sloane was filmed shaking hands with Ron and hugging Nancy. The day after the election, he hired a toney Madison Avenue firm to create a high pressure opening-credits sequence for his cable ministry. Less than six years after being a revolutionary Maoist dedicated to the violent extirpation of the capitalist bourgeoisie and American colonialistic imperialist hegemony, Jim now emerged on screen preaching, prophesying, shaking his head in sad judgment of sin, and setting down to a deep dish of apple pie amidst star spangled banners and unsung heroes dying on Freedom's Shores: the video suggested that the holy triune of Reagan, Sloane, and Jesus marched, arms linked, to comfort and bless the needy of history's turning point, mixing hope with panic-peddling tirades against an endless series of buzzwords. Ratings soared. Cassettes were sold. More politicians shook his hand. Jim Slavin was joining the ranks of evangelic megastars.

However, local chickens were seeking roosts. Jim Slavin, in his nursing-home Scam days, had personally converted several well-heeled matrons to United Christian Life. Four had since divorced, and each sought to contractualize her pentacostal passion. Rev. Sloane turned to the Good Book for guidance.

Not the Bible.

The road atlas.

Meanwhile, Leviticus hired its first professional Village Manager. This was a major concession: Leviticus had never paid secular outsiders to attend civic matters.

But the surging religious market had given rise to the career of Christian Management—people whose executive skills were turned to the service of the Word. Only two years older than Brandon Pugnale, Peter Everett LaMar had a business and public management degree from Tufts, religious certification from two bible study colleges, and a resume citing Town Manager positions in Kansas and Wisconsin, as well as an Assistant City Manager stint in northern Michigan. Ev LaMar's credo might have been "The Good Lord loves a tough s.o.b."; and Leviticus was primed for that message. The village elected a more aggressive Council—realtors Buddy Roemer and Dorothea Twaits, loan officer and retired Air Force Major Orrick DeWine, pharmacist Abner L. Schlueuter, hog farmer Poole Neiderhous—and prepared for the challenge of the new decade.

Leviticus' most galling problem was the village's loss of status to its rival, Revelations, Ohio. The two communities, founded in the schism of an apocalyptic frontier church two hundred and fifty years earlier, had always competed. Leviticus opened a bible college, Revelations' was larger and better endowed; Revelations attracted a religious book publisher, Leviticus, a Christian FM radio station; Revelations' station had a bigger transmitter, Leviticus got an AM frequency. But now Leviticus' population was aging or inbred. Revelations scored a series of coups: recruiting a Christian software and gaming company, a cluster of Christian condominiums, a Christian direct-mail service. And, most public of all, Revelations opened a 16 hour a day Christian TV station, UHF Channel 59.

Leviticus was humiliated; Ev LaMar's specific charge was to catch up. LaMar authored a land-development package combining condos, tennis courts, retirement housing, telecommunications relay and television broadcast studios connected to a church-reflection garden-revival complex, with room for a light industrial park, all to be built under an attractive bond and tax-abatement plan. The best location was a 112 acre site: three adjacent and long-unsold properties listed with Roemer Realty and Twaits Realty, but not actually within Village limits. Leviticus had no trouble extending its border via an annexation order. All LaMar needed was a buyer or investment syndicate.

That problem was solved by Bryce Magaw of KooglerMagaw Construction: his nephew was an associate co-pastor for J. Hern Sloane.

An'akist Verlaine's crowning achievement was La Roofe, the inspiration that elevated the Trilite Zone from idiosyncratic grindhouse into the Cathedral of Sleaze. It was a magnet for Ohio's true decadent aesthetes—the region's finest nouvelle cuisine and exploitation.

An'akist and Brandon had taken to throwing midnight champagne picnics: they'd climb onto the roof of the projection booth for poached duck breast with orange mayonnaise, or crawfish-fettucine verdi salad, or hibachied pork sates, while waiting for Earl's Big Bangs to fill the screens.

Inevitably, An'akist said, "OH! Y'know what we could do is?"

The pagoda grew a gazebo.

The projection-booth roof was tiled, railed, and enclosed with movable plexi windows. Tables were adorned with damask, flowers, candles, and speakers that could be tuned to any screen. Free mixers were chilled for a BYOB cocktail lounge, and, for voyeurs, Cousin Capooch liberated half a dozen 25¢ a minute stereo-telescopes from the prows of the Staten Island ferries.

Paying a table d'hôte charge, patrons would scale ladders to La Roofe and sample An'akist's buffet fancy of the evening: from hors d'oeuvres, whether cognac infused pate en croûte, or avocado mousse with caviar; through entrees like boned quail in puff pastry, or beef mignonettes with tarragon-cornichon cream reduction, or pistachioed veal ballontine with madeira sauce; such side dishes as wax beans chilled with fresh dill, or vermouth-steamed broccoli with horseradish mousseline sauce; to frozen raspberry-Chambord soufflé with burgundy sauce, or triple-lime chiffon cheesecake, or chocolate-Grande Marnier divinity for dessert.

The diners were tu'penny lords of low-rent creation, clinking tulipes to the riot of sights around and below. One slumming regular, a grantless archaelogist turned mystery bookstore owner, would pluck at her stud bracelets, twirl her champagne, and say to her guests as the Big Bang went off, "That's what I enjoy about this place—it's everything I used to adore about Bangkok and Beirut."

The Cathedral was ordained. In neon, striplights, moon, and stars the acolytes came and the revels throbbed. *Beneath Videodrome / Eraserhead / Liquid Sky / Ms. 45 / Avenging Angel / Repo Man / Caligula / Sex, Drugs & Rock' n Roll / Café Flesh*, dancers swirled and whirled, bikers postured and squared off in the rings, costumed monsters charged knights in tinfoil armor, country boys and women played tag with beer-filled balloons, and teens unselfconsciously scampered naked from the Forf, amid a carnival of creatures capering from darkness to dawn, seven nights a week, spring and hot summer and fall. It was a sculpted orison of lunacy, centered on three people who loved each other, loved the Zone, and believed in the architecture they had brought to life.

And that life acquired spirit.

Magic, amorphous and weirdly innocent, glowed.

Film buffs first noticed that all the movies were untouched by studios or distributors. Some of this was due to Cousin Capooch's unorthodox acquisitions, which might explain the return of never-before-shown censored shots. But something else arranged the screening of films that had never been made: the marathon sixteen-hour Jodoworsld-Lyon collaboration of *Dune*; Alan Ormsby's direction of Paul Schrader's script for *Cat People* starring Nastasia Kinski and David Bowie; David Cronenberg's *Ghost Story*; Roman Polanski's *The Shining*; Herschell Gordon Lewis's *Titus Andronicus*; and Ed Wood Jr.'s *Cleopatra*.

The magic grew into a playful prankster, a partying Puck. Sometimes bestial howls on screen were chorused from the woods; sometimes mummers were joined by dancers with too many arms and too few heads; sometimes cars bounced like hobby horses while unseen teeth nipped at bottoms or tentacles tripped passers-by.

And sometimes, during a Big Bang, everyone in the Forf experienced simultaneous orgasms powerful enough to ripple through the asphalt, tingling with a metal sigh up to La Roofe.

The Zone drained just enough ectoplasm from its celebrants to keep the scene from boiling over; the ground held vitality like a battery. On screen the effects seemed more convincing, the colored corn syrup more sanguine; but on the lot, Earl's four commandments were never challenged. Fights never grew too brutal, wounds were never serious, groping never got threatening, cars were never broken into, money never stolen. And despite the Bacchanialian, seemingly lethal quantities and mixtures of inebriants poured down peoples' throats, no one ever drove away from the Zone smashed. The most determined substance abusers were always overpowered by a need to dance, screw, or puke in time to get straight.

Even cleaning was easy. Every morning, the food, fluids, and detritus vanished, as if scoured by pixies or sucked into the ground as offerings.

Earl, Brandon, and An'akist were convinced the Zone was blessed.

Recognising spiritual kinship, Ev LaMar and Jim Slavin liked each other on sight. Slavin needed only an introductory meeting to decide Leviticus was a place to do business and God's work. Rev. Sloane and the Village Council shared the deep camaraderie of those who stood to make each other millions.

The only fly in the soup was Minton Eggets, the new and very young chief of the village's four-man police force. Eggets was pious and not too bright; a premature ejaculator of the law who'd bust the high school the day before a marijuana deal or openly follow one carload of teens while another boosted unlocked bicycles. And since annexation, Minton had been squirming for a chance to swoop down on the Zone.

"Reverend, don't you worry about that pit," Minton blurted, vehemently disrupting a presentation on sewage and water-line extensions and easements. "They won't trouble you one bit, Sir—they're a dozen ways illegal and I can clean out that nest like that. Like that!" He snapped his fingers. Slavin raised an eyebrow, LaMar aimed a pointer at a wall map.

"There's a dirty moviehouse at that location," LaMar drawled, circling the hollow, "out of our jurisdiction until recently."

"Organized crime?" Slavin asked.

Ev snorted. "Hardly. An old drunk, some punk kid, and their girlfriend. There are numerous infractions we can cite them for; just a question of finding the most apropos timing."

"Tomorrow! I could have those so-and-sos on a rail tomorrow, Reverend—"

"Minton," Ev sighed, "I'm sure Reverend Sloane appreciates that, but—sometimes—when the victory against Satan is too easily won, some folks don't see it for the victory it is…"

Eggets wrinkled his nose, lost.

"Brother Minton," Jim murmured, "y'know, a few years ago my mother suffered from a cataract in her eye. She was in anguish; but neither doctors nor GOD would heal her eye until the cataract reached a size, 'ripened,' a medical doctor would say. Well, friend, we prayed every day with all our hearts, and in time the Good Lord's blessing healed that dear lady and today she can see like a young girl. But GOD tells us that 'to all things comes there a season,' Minton; sometimes that old cataract has to grow, the fever must run its course, and the Devil be given the rope with which GOD will scourge him." Or—even if the match is fixed, the crowd likes to see the champ bounce off the ropes before getting the pinfall. A carefully choreographed campaign would pay off in publicity, units sold, donations secured, investors committed; and Rev. J. Hern Sloane pulled higher ratings when he mixed the Word of Hope with the Witness of Dire Herald.

"Well…you just keep it in mind, Reverend—I can close'em down like that!" Snap.

Rev. Sloane smiled at Ev LaMar. "Perhaps you'd be kind enough to run me over to the site, tonight, so we can get a look at the problem…" Forestalling Minton's offer of a lift, Slavin raised a finger, "and we can finish discussing easements on the way."

"When the money starts flowing," Rev. Sloane said that evening, "your police chief's gonna be a little out of place." Cigar smoke whisked into the air conditioning of LaMar's Pontiac.

Ev shrugged. "There's a lot of Eggets around here, so as long as he wants the job, he'll keep it…but the situation should solve itself. Minton's got an ambition, you see. Wants to be sheriff. Seems his daddy told him three county sheriffs've gone up to the Statehouse or Congress, and Minton's sure he'll be the fourth. Of course, he wants to close his only big case a good fifteen months before the election…but with God's grace I think we can keep him from screwing up. Then he can spend the rest of his life running for the legislature. And frankly, it will be a positive moral act to put this place out of business."

"But it doesn't violate your town smut ordinance?"

"This town," LaMar smiled, "has never needed one. We could pass a bill easily enough, but I'd rather not kick up some ACLU hornets' nest when we can finesse the issue." He glanced over. "I imagine you're thinking, 'buncha hicks getting lathered over some place that shows *Debby Does Dallas*'…"

They turned down an overgrown tractor path running along the cornfields, and strolled to the edge of the hollow.

"Good location for an amphitheater," Sloane mentioned.

"Yessir, I'd noticed…it also connects the property nicely." LaMar handed Sloane a pair of binoculars. "Happy viewing."

"What the hell is that—a cocktail lounge?"

"And French restaurant, I hear. This place is a three-ring circus. Regular bona fide zoo."

Jim Slavin scanned twined legs stuck out of pup tents; aerobic dancers who bumped and ground to a band playing "Too Drunk to Fuck" while a group of jocks in college jackets sang "Bwana Dick"; in a boxing ring a Tae Kwan Do match was taking place; a tangible smog of body musk, perfume, weed, and liquor swirled up the hollow. On two screens he could see a tree ripping off an actress's clothes, and a mohawked blond sticking his mailed fist through the windshield of an armored hotrod doing two hundred miles per hour. Eyes glued, Slavin threaded his way through cornstalks to get an open view of the occluded third screen.

He cleared the line of sight just as fourteen inches of Johnny Wadd Holmes torpedoed up Vanessa delRio's trembling butt, and J. Hern Sloane had an epiphany. His soul swelled with a rising tide of wrath against the cancerous spectre arrayed in the pit below: the Zone was everything Ev LaMar had hinted at and more, a perfect dragon for a latter-day St. George, a media vehicle rare beyond price.

Years had passed, but once again he would lead more than a flock; he would lead a Movement.

Slavin started to recall his old revolutionary tactics.

The construction of Christian Life Heights was announced in *The Leviticus Weekly Witness*; and the drive-in's demise was fated.

More canny defenders might have seen the threat and angled for time, challenging annexation, demanding environmental-impact and traffic studies, filing injunctions and appeals. Even so, red-tape maneuvers could only have stalled for a graceful exit. The conflict was to be of the moral center v. the obscene fringe. Leviticus wanted Rev. Sloane—and didn't want the Zone.

But An'akist, Brandon, and Earl had no scent of the wind; they were engrossed in plans for the coming season. They'd started new hobbies over the summer, which they naturally applied to the Zone. Brandon and An'akist refined the art of the multimedia Theme Night, while Earl found he liked attending auctions.

Earl's auctioneering was like automatic writing: he never knew when he'd speak up or raise his hand, never was quite sure what he was buying; but his choices were always great.

At his first auction, Earl bought a tractor-trailer-load of processed food. The shipment was delivered while An'akist and Brandon were discussing one of their fascinations, the film festival. They stared at the mountain of junk food in dismayed shock for a minute: then Ah'akist cried, "OH! Y'know what we could do is?"—and created, on the spot, Retroroni.

It was the Zone event of the year. *Teenagers From Outer Space / Robot Monster / The Beast of Yucca Flats / The Beast the Killed Women / Mesa of Lost Women / Swamp Women / Truck Stop Women / Angels' Wild Women / Rebels On Wheels*, bracketed with vintage stag loops, driver-ed films, nudie volleyball shorts, and the worst fifties pop music they could scrounge. The snack bar served only bologna oleo on Wonder White, Kool-Ade and T-Bird; La Roofe shredded carrots in green jello, Franco-American—Velveeta melts, and tuna-fish-mushroom-soup-potato-chip casserole—all of which served as ammunition in a ten-hour-long food fight. The Jackson Pollack effect of pasta, cheese, wine, and tomato sauce against the blacktop was outrageous.

Earl, urged to attend more auctions, amassed three hundred picture tubes, one thousand cases of rolled pistol caps, ten thousand cut-out l.p.'s, and a boxcar of canned novelties called Slime, Goo, and Glop.

They had no idea they were the targets of a TV preacher's attacks, vilified coast-to-coast. They didn't feel the growing hostility in Leviticus because they never went into the village: a burg with no place for Brandon's leather had never tolerated An'akist's radical hair and clothes. Unwarned, unarmed, they were blindsided by the assault that began in April, when opening night unexpectedly featured enraged pickets and voracious television coverage.

The result was drive-in auto-da-fé. The demonstrators were righteous, humorless, and tearful to discover such filth in their back yards; their hair-raising yarns of brushes with depravity were lies—none of the protestors had ever patronised the Zone and many, in fact, lived outside Ohio—but, like all zealots, they believed themselves, which played well on the tube.

In contrast, Earl Bittner glared apoplectically, balled his fists, and tromped back and forth before the mob, hollering "What's that shit! What's that shit! What's that shit!" Brandon, crowded by a cameraman, shoved back, yelling "Gedoutta here fuckin' asshole, y'fucking asshole get outta my face—" while An'akist looked struck and shellshocked, alternately shouting, "What? Get out! What are you doing? We didn't do anything? What do you want? Get out!" and breaking into tears before hecklers. On the news, profanities conspicuously excised, they seemed dangerous, deranged, and drugged.

As bulldozers began to shape Christian Life Heights, the second front deployed. Although no brick had been laid, television eloquently portrayed the distress of young condo-purchasing couples and helpless retirees, whose infants and/or golden years were suddenly menaced by perverts. Other churches eagerly joined the demonstrators; anti-porn activists, merely learning film titles, yearned to lynch anyone connected with the Zone: the land of the free had no place for deviants who showed *Bloodsucking Freaks*, *Lethal Injection*, *Hell's Orgy*.

No reporter noted that this threat to the local quality of life had been peaceably operating for nearly a decade. Unmentioned were the deluge of vitriolic hate mail to the Zone, the death threats, the bomb scares. The ticket kiosk was knocked over and splintered. Bricks broke snack-bar equipment. Molotov cocktails were thrown at the screens. Vandals swarmed down the unfenced hillsides, cut speaker wires, shrieked at patrons, tried to storm the projection booth…but on the evening news, the pickets stayed civil and off the lot.

Business plummeted through spring and early summer; An'akist, Brandon, and Earl weathered the siege badly. They argued, bickered, and found fault with each others' weakness as, in the crucible, the core of their love began to falter.

An'akist wanted to create a cause célèbre. Had her pleas been planned, she might have enlisted Nat Hentoff and Bob Guccione, Stephen King and Joe Bob Briggs. Instead, she sent hand-scrawled appeals to people whom An'akist wanted to think sympathetic: David Letterman, David Lee Roth, Jaimie Lee Curtis, Sid Vicious, John Belushi, Elvira Mistress of the Dark. Some were inappropriate, some fictional, some deceased. None replied.

Brandon went to Cousin Capooch for muscle and was rebuffed; Louis Capagianelli wanted no territorial disputes nor grief from either New York or Ohio bosses. He kicked Brandon out of his office, ordering him never to reveal their kinship.

Earl Bittner sank into himself. He bought a shotgun, and divided his time between cleaning it and compulsively stirring the chili tub.

Then, in the beginning of July, the furor quieted. The cameras were gone, the few pickets who returned each night seemed laughably ineffectual, and the Zone's summer crowds returned. It seemed that an astrological disjunction had ended and life could continue; which was what Jim Slavin and Ev LaMar intended.

Spirits perked tip through *Women's Prison Night, the Staten Island Grade-Z Film Festival*, and I Night (*I Eat Your Skin / I Drink Your Blood / I Dismember Mama*)... the LPs were Frisbeed during Smash UFOs Night...the caps set off during All-Western Story Night...the TV tubes were built into Flyvision banks in La Roofe...

Brandon and An'akist regained enough confidence to prepare the First Annual H. G. Lewis Gorerama. They meant to rent fire hoses, pumps, and two huge tanks, one filled with crimson dyed Karo syrup, the other with Slime, Glop, and Goo; and at intervals douse the crowd while showing a tri-screen glut of infamy by splatter's foremost auteur: *2000 Maniacs / Feast of Blood / A Taste of Blood / Color Me Blood Red / Something Weird / Gruesome Twosome / The Wizard of Gore / The Gore Gore Girls / She-Devils on Wheels*. It was to be the season finale in late October.

The hammer came down Labor Day weekend.

Minton Eggets finally got Ev LaMar's leave to raid the Zone. Earl, Brandon, and An'akist were hauled to Leviticus jail; but, typically, Chief Eggets had forgotten to obtain search warrants and could only charge them with local misdemeanors.

As Ev LaMar expected. He felt no great desire to destroy Earl Bittner: he played to win, but thought a good executive should try to not let anyone walk away from the table humiliated. J. Hern Sloane had his ratings, Christian Life Heights its publicity, Minton Eggets would be elected Sheriff. So LaMar met the Zone's staff with an olive branch: Leviticus would, after the election, drop all charges and fines if the Zone showed only features "acceptable to community". He doubted the drive-in could survive as a G-rated business, and had arranged for a front to offer a buy-out. Compromise, a face-saving gesture, fast cash, and a one-way ticket out of town.

Unfortunately, LaMar assumed Earl was a tawdry schlockmeister, sly enough to know when the gravy train stopped. LaMar presumed Earl, Brandon, and An'akist understood the Zone was just another lowly dive subject to the dictates of proper society. He simply failed to imagine that they could see the drive-in as a pride-worthy achievement, a work of art; failed to see in their refusal and anger conviction as deeply religious as his own. Finding them unreasonable, LaMar persuaded the state attorney general's office to prepare indictments and warrants, and unleashed Chief Eggets again.

The second raid came down at 1:15 A.M. on the third Saturday in September. Village, county, state police, and federal agents seized the drive-in's financial records and film library, and arrested Earl Bittner. He was arraigned for possession and sale of contraband alcohol; violation of liquor laws and licensing; federal racketeering in the theft, interstate transport, and unlawful use of copyrighted films; tax evasion (from illicit gains to sale of the garden produce); pandering; and failure to maintain adequate insurance and performance permits. Film distributors, juvenile welfare officers, and various regulatory agencies filed complaints; and, covering all bases, the Zone's owner was cited for failure to pay residuals on the music piped through the speakers. The court-appointed lawyer thought she'd be lucky to keep her inarticulate client out of prison through the initial appeals.

Most of the Zone's receipts had always gone to pay for new ideas and games; on a balance sheet, the drive-in had never been profitable. Even when Orrick DeWine agreed to float a small mortgage on the lot, three months passed before Earl made bail.

By then Brandon and An'akist were hurting each other.

After years of monogamy, An'akist had a two-week fling resulting in yeast and bladder infections and a tubal pregnancy that required surgery. She felt guilty and unable to explain to Brandon why she couldn't be intimate; he, feeling rejected, haunted area bars, frantically failing to pick up women.

And their crucified spirits were no longer in sync; one prepared to fight for the Zone whenever the other was giving in.

An'akist wanted to stay and compromise. She decided they were all contemptible vermin as charged; and promoted the idea of a complete reform to showing PG films, while expanding the restaurant into a family dinner theater. Brandon knew Leviticus wouldn't accept them under any conditions. Privately he was afraid of even contemplating change; openly he wanted to sell the drive-in and start it intact, somewhere friendlier, in another state if need be.

Both positions were lost on Earl. Shaking his head dolefully and saying, "may-be I oughta. May-be I oughta," he seemed to agree with whomever was speaking, then he'd say "may-be I oughta. May-be I oughta" to no one and nothing at all. Earl kept his loaded shotgun in the booth where he spent days at a time drinking corn liquor missed by the police, and splicing random scraps of film. He fixated on the coming season. Their distribution was canceled and they had no money, but Earl insisted on opening the Zone. Word went out to regulars that, without license, liquor, food or features, they would run an all Big Bang night.

When Earl started the projectors, police arrived and arrested him for disturbing the peace.

Brandon and An'akist used the final receipts for bail. Bittner came home and for the only time in over twelve years blew out the flame beneath his chili: then he turned all the snack bar's unlit gas jets on full, got a jug of corn liquor, and tried to drink himself to death. After a half gallon of 140° moonshine, Earl climbed to the booth, took his shotgun back to the gas-flooded snack bar, and fired into the chili tub.

Breaking one of his own commandments.

The Zone's only phones were in the pagoda. By the time Brandon found a way to call the volunteer emergency squad, the building was beyond salvage.

In shock, facing burial arrangements, Brandon and An'akist fought that night in the cramped Winnebago. Each was almost unable to make sense of the other, as if they were screaming in different languages; only insults communicated clearly. Hysterical, frustrated, ironically trying to get through, Brandon backhanded An'akist. She shrieked, outraged, reflexively grabbed their cast-iron tea kettle and swung it against his skull, shearing open his scalp; Brandon staggered and blindly lashed back, punching her in the eye, then breaking her nose; she went into frenzy, his violence leaving her unaware of her own, and battered him repeatedly before Brandon got a door open and fell from the camper, fracturing his ankle. Heaving, thinking only of escape, An'akist gunned the engine and, leaving Brandon hobbling in her dust, leaving another broken commandment, pulled away from the Zone in fury, never to reconcile not give nor accept apology.

The county, without funeral, disposed of Earl Bittner.

Then a paper surfaced, allegedly dated two days before Earl's death, selling his assets and mortgage to Miss Kathless Daskalakis, town librarian, and realtor Dorothea Twaits's spinster sister. The document's authenticity was irrelevant. Earl had died intestate, broke, and under multiple indictment, his only property owed to the bank. His death only expedited the inevitable.

Brandon tried to stay, camping in the Forf; but with no money and not so much as an abandoned car for shelter, he didn't even complain when Miss Daskalakis ordered him off her land, which she soon sold to Christian Life Heights.

Brandon headed East; An'akist, West. Had they stayed together, they might have found the strength to pursue new visions. An'akist wanted to open the next *Chez Panisse*, but had nobody to flame her ideas or help her put them into action; she wound up clerking at a hair salon. Brandon planned to recreate the Zone, but had nobody to spark his notions or challenge him to make them real; he wound up running a peep show for Cousin Capooch. Apart, they were incomplete: dreams vanquished, they gradually collapsed into wounded routines of stagnant apathy; so shrunken that it might cause one to ponder whether the punishment was worth the crime of having dreamt at all.

Making peace with his Missouri divorcees, Rev. Sloane reconsidered the move to Ohio. The location of the planned new headquarters seemed, on reflection, impractical. Still, Jim Slavin recognized his Christian and realpolitik obligations: the development plan was an investment, years from completion; there was still profit to be accrued. The Witness Revival Amphitheatre, won so publicly, would have to be built and used for some time to come, which would demand still more fund-raising.

So Jim Slavin announced a formal groundbreaking for Christian Life Heights, to be telecast from the site of the future arena.

On a Sunday morning in late October, a crew erected a control platform over the bare concrete where the pagoda's ashes had, like other debris, disappeared. They set up cameras, recorders, microphones, mixers; they set up projectors to turn the drive-in's screens into monitors. The Forf was covered with a grandstand for honored guests, the Inspiration Choir of Seattle, and the Dallas Sonnycalb Family Singers. Chairs were unfolded beside speaker poles; latecomers and the handicapped could see and hear from their cars.

The event drew nearly two thousand believers from eight states; most of them specially invited loyal contributors. When Rev. Sloane's helicopter landed, Ev LaMar and the Council were seated in the grandstand alongside contractors Bryce Magaw and Vernon Koogler, plus Sheriff Eggets, plus all their families. They were the ones responsible for the celebration and, in a way, this evening's events. The audience, though, were Bible thumpers all, (like Gretchen Bowers, Tod Critchlow, Christopher Dziedzic, Dewey Fouts, Harton Funderberk, Lois Gilligan, Noyce Hunkler, Sandy Kessler, Joyce Leonard, Carl Lotino, Jackson Mesarvey, Lilly

Nonnemacher, Hiram Spruance, Constance Triftshauser, Lyndon Upthegrove, and hundreds more) overly ardent right-wing couch-potato Pentacostals who had made the doctrinal error of placing their faith in Jim Slavin. This proved unforgivable. It reduced them all from complex souls of intricate history, intrinsic sinfulness, innate worth...

Into cannon fodder.

The first salvo was fired at sundown.

The giant screens lit, filled with triplicate rippling American flags and the superimposed, smiling faces of the Rev. J. Hern Sloane and the President of the United States, then dissolved into the familiar, uplifting credit montage. The director readied Camera # 1 on the choir, #2 on dignitaries, #3 on the podium. He cued the choirmaster.

When the choir stood, hands clasped, the ground heaved. Earth bellowed a thunderous lowing; a behemoth stretched in its unquiet lair. Jim Slavin preempted the chorus, taking up the microphone to offer prayers, and witness of reassurance.

Metal voices howled and sniggered. The cameras overrode their controls, killing the satellite feed and cutting to an enormous, extreme close shot of Sloane's face.

On all three screens his vast eyes were blinding red, without irises. Pus and lymph drained from festering boils on his cheeks, and from his open mouth spewed gouts of peppled diarrhea that booted from the screens to rain in real torrents on the crowd below.

Although Jim Slavin was prepared to bless the drive-in, it had not occurred to him to perform the rite of exorcism; but then, exorcism wouldn't have helped.

The Zone was not possessed.

It was sacred.

It had been the venue for every weird picture, no matter how artistic, avant-garde, vulgar, or loathsome, ever filmed or dreamed of; and for that it had been revered. It had been consecrated, time and again, in blood and liquor, sweat and sperm. It had been the altar where scores were settled, gays turned out, and virgins deflowered in droves, until a communion or orgone, hormones, and dark fantasy churned within the pyramid of screens.

It had been fed. It had been nurtured.

It had been magic. It had been believed.

It had an anima.

And that anima was being defiled.

The commandments had been shattered. Life had been sacrificed, love had been withdrawn. The acolytes had been shut out while an army of enemies stood in their place.

Neither malignant nor benign, the Zone reacted, defending itself with the weapons and tactics at its command. With the only knowledge and imagery it had ever learned.

Sleaze manifested as a quasi-sentient force.

Jim Slavin's demonic faces faded into a wash of salmon-pink fleshtones, with dark purple slits at the centers. The slits flared and the circles of color retreated to reveal that the crowd was staring at dead-center footage of a male erection. Hysterical moaning blared from the speakers; the phalluses lunged forward, mashing against the screens, which bulged under the impact, the metal struts warping. Carnal groans rose in volume as the thrusting accelerated. Bolts sheared and the screens rocked on their braces; immense reluctant hymens.

The organs drew back, throbbing, fully engorged, dribbling seminal fluid, shifted position, and slammed upward. Space between and above the screens flashed into nuclear light; a fireball arced over the Zone, paused, and settled back, congealing into a pulsing, vaginal pink dome of radiant plasm, a literal overturned fleshpot fraught with random lightnings. The strobing burlesque dazzle sent Tod Critchlow and Lois Gilligan into convulsive seizures as 2000 pole speakers burst into 2000 different songs.

Most of the crowd ran for exits or their cars and the blacktop rose in a circular ripple, fluid as water, plastic as a trampoline, firm as marble; the wave flung runners and cars in its swell, cracked open the helicopter, flowed harmlessly past the screens and expended itself with a crashing upward fillip that froze into a concave, twenty-foot-high wall surrounding the lot.

Tarmac bubbled into sudden gravy: spasming arthritic hands wrenched up out of the cement, clawing emptiness like midwinter groundhogs testing the air; apparently finding conditions to their liking, mutant cannibal corpses scrabbled through the concrete, littering the lot with scraped chunks of putrescent muscle. Evangelic ghouls, they shuffled toward the living, to win converts to the army of ambulatory rot.

The Big Bang—

—starts.

Kaleidoscopes of unsettling scenes swirl across the screens; but the action has shifted to audience participation.

Unaware that she's burst into flame, Sandy Kessler wonders why she can hear and smell her clothes, hair, and nails scorch, see her arms and legs blistering into spitting coals that sear the air with shimmering mirages.

Ev LaMar spreads himself against the blacktop wall, seeking a weak spot; then he shrieks, his right hand crucified by a three-inch-long tenpenny nail. LaMar hears a sputter behind him; more spikes drill through his hand. He is grabbed by the shoulder, twisted around, and casually slammed against the wall. His tendons and wrist bones part loudly; his arm and pinioned hand fold together, neat as a carpenter's rule. LaMar slumps, sight blurring; through a teary haze he sees a button-eyed scarecrow in drool-stained coveralls, carrying a pneumatic nailgun. And a toolbox.

Sheriff Eggets empties his revolver at dragon-sized talons that stab through the top of the strobing pink dome. The talons withdraw, but Eggets, staring up, fails to notice the kappa at his feet. The Asian vampyr, a ropy, turd-hued snake with a monkey's torso and chittering head, chews its way up Eggets's pants, its tiny hands using Minton's leg hairs as a ladder. The kappa penetrates anally, viciously, fangs sucking as they bite and little hands sinking filth-envenomed needle claws into his rectal flesh.

Joyce Leonard and Constance Triftshauser conceive immaculately and come to term within thirty seconds, their bellies splitting like the skins of overripe tomatoes, insufficiently elastic for their ballooning wombs. Their pelvises shatter and perineums tear as they fall to the ground in simultaneous labor.

Like spectral fungi, spongy phantom knobs sprout, unnoticed; the ghosts of the pagoda and ticket booth retumesce. They bob, squat and squishy; then, aroused, the kiosk springs to attention. The gazebo-pagoda twitches, elongates, fills and firms into place.

One moment the television crew perches on a raised open platform, then they are in the Zone's projection booth as the pagoda reforms around them, the TV electronics becoming the drive-in's old equipment and film library. The five men blink or shake their heads, aware first of the quiet; the howling below them shut out by thick glass and walls. Then that silence ceases. The projectors start, ratcheting and whirring, the vibrations rattling the shelves of movie canisters. One can shakes loose, hits the floor, clanging, and cracks open, spraying the walls and ceiling with blood. The tine rolls to a stop, spouting a red fountain. More canisters reel from the wall, blurt geysers; the projectors mask the sound of the door, locking.

Kathleen Daskalakis feels slime on her temple and cheeks; she pats her head and retches—a mass of live worms is tangled in her hair. Miss Daskalakis tries to pull the nightcrawlers off. She discovers the worms aren't falling on her head; they're emerging from it.

Frantically ripping her scalp, Miss Daskalakis stumbles into Buddy Roemer, who is running from the roaring pursuit of cycle-riding skeletons with jet-black bones and Dayglo tattooed skulls.

The android has no eyes, no face at all, nor needs any. Its six spider-jointed arms have blades and axes in place of hands, while grappling cords swirl around its hips. It moves faster than the human mind can track, and it is programmed to collect. It has already collected Dewey Fouts, Gretchen Bowers, Christopher Dziedzic, Vernon Koogler and wife, and the Dallas Sonnycalb family. Their bodies lay where they have fallen, but their heads, dripping blood, sinus fluid, and organs, float behind the collector like a swarm of obedient bumblebee do-bees, grimacing, grinning, and bobbing in the air.

Noyce Hunkeler, Carl Lofino, Lilly Nonnemacher, Hiram Spruance, and Jackson Mesarvey race, panting, to the pagoda, praying for shelter. Each clambers over the snackbar counter and blacks out.

Poole Neiderhous dashes toward the resurrected ticket kiosk, aiming to scale the wall from its roof. Abruptly his path is blocked by a dwarfish, bearded, white-robed old Chinese priest, and a seven-foot-tall Nubian clad in a leopard's hide, swinging a two-handed morningstar. Neiderhous stops. From the moment the service has been disrupted, Poole has been enraged. He deeply wants to hit something, smack someone around. The huge colored buck is too well armed, but the old gook looks frail and winded. Neiderhous has at least a hundred-pound advantage. He bunches his fists and charges, hollering. The priest barely moved, but the heel of his hand brushed Neiderhous's face. Poole's jaw splashes from its hinges, plows through the side of his head and clatters to the ground, teeth scattering. His tongue, ripped clean from its roots, slides through the gap in his cheek.

Gibbering, Minton Eggets drops his pants, grabs the serpent tube hanging from his abdomen, and tries to yank the kappa out of him. The vampyr clenches its fangs and claws into Eggets's colon, feeding as its anchors itself. It reaches up into Eggets's intestines, shredding and sucking choice tidbits.

The Inspiration Choir is consumed by rutting fury; they grab each other, tumbling across the grandstand in an orgiastic mound of bodies. Every orifice is receptive and female, every extremity is virile and male. Each body joins to two, four, eight, ten more until identity and identification are lost in lust. Slots and tabs flow, glue, weld into undifferentiated tissue, five tons of cancer.

The director and sound engineer climb aboard tables, pounding the booth's windows with metal splicing blocks and movieolas; but the three assistants are standing, trying to force the door, when the bloodpool reaches the electric outlets. Lights explode. The booth fills with stenches of gasified hemoglobin and short-circuited flesh. In dusk the tide rises, bubbling from the floating film cans. The tables lift, corpses bumping into them. When the blood reaches a depth of five feet, fins briefly break the surface. Dozens of Chitonous football-sized claws with serrated pincers close on the corpses and pull them under the rippling flood.

The straw handyman braces LaMar's left hand steady against the wall, aims his nailgun, and fires stigmata into the palm, then he rivets Ev's feet to the ground. The worker stands back and contemplates his next shot, sighting artistically along his gloved thumb. The scarecrow chortles mouthlessly while he works, sounding quite like Disneyland's Goofy. Nodding amiably, he cross-stitches LaMar's knees, inner elbows, and groin.

Orrick DeWine watches his fingers stretch and twist into sharp unhuman daggers. He has always harbored a secret wish to become a wolf, a tiger, a merciless night hunter. Now his darkest desire is coming true. He quickly strips, paws shredding his clothes, and awaits a rush of unholy power.

The ancient priest knocks Poole Neiderhous to his knees, legs locked and paralyzed, tailbone destroyed. He barely feels the priest's fingers poke holes in his sternum, puncturing his lungs. The priest bows and the mace-wielding barbarian steps up, his crotch planted before Neiderhous's face. Poole feels an overwhelming need to fellate the black giant, then realizes with incredulous self-pity that, jawless, he can't. He looks up, pleading forgiveness, in time to see the iron ball swing down. His head pulps nicely for yards in all directions.

Carl Lofino awakens in a gargantuan chamber, its horizons fading into mist. Sticky pale shapes move in slow motion, forms dimly lit by waist-high, blue gas jets. Lofino takes a step forward and his hand raps against a glass wall; Lofino discovers he is trapped in a jar the approximate size of an elevator cage. Pungent gravel crunches beneath his feet; Lofino reaches into it, finds he is standing on an inches-thick layer of spices. Savory aromas drift into his prison; Lofino turns to study two bubbling, steaming cauldrons. Doughy shapes stir one vat, filled with thick chili con pieces of Jackson Mesarvey and Hiram Spruance. The other, by the smell, holds gallons of boiling brined vinegar. Lofino whimpers as a half dozen dough-things pour the boiling vinegar into his jar, which is then vacuum sealed and left to ferment, Lofino pickling within, still alive.

Joyce Leonard births a hoofed and goat-headed manikin; Constance Triftshauser, a flippered atrocity whose neck ends in sea urchin cilia surrounding a sucking maw. The infants scramble up their mothers' ravaged bodies, ripping blouses and bras to latch onto milk-laden breasts: The two women lie panting with exhaustion, nausea, and a chilling surge of maternal love. Then both gasp as fresh eggs are fertilized and their uteruses swell. Several hundred feet away, but in much the same way, Harton Funderberk and Bryce Magaw, too, are spawning tiny monsters.

Dorothea Twaits takes refuge in her Country Squire station wagon, where she unsuccessfully tries to raise help on her CB, and car phone. The thing that crawls up the hood of her car is so alien that Dorothea, a stolid and unimaginative realtor, can't convince her mind to register its existence. A twenty-questions creature: torso like a globby cluster of smushed-together liver balls; head a conical sampler of bruises and sores; droopy sensory clusters on stalks bounce aimlessly from the top of the cone while appendages, some like featherferns and some like four-sided cheese graters with sucker pads, strip and masticate the wagon's chrome trim. A thin, bubbling nozzle on the side of its head suddenly reminds Dorothea of the cappuccino extension on her espresso maker. As she thinks that, a wart on the thing's head bursts; a ribbony tentacle unreels with hydraulic speed, smashes through the windshield and plucks out both of Dorothea's eyeballs, skewering them on barbed hooks that eject from its tip. The ribbon coils like highspeed footage of a bullfrog's tongue snagging a nymph fly, and pops Dorothea Twaits's sinew and nerve-trailing eyes into its wartlike wound. The action is so rapid that the thing gums and swallows before Mrs. Twaits realizes it had moved. She only notices when the first pain hits and blood squirts from her empty sockets. By then the tongue has come back for the rest of her face.

Buddy Roemer staggers and falls, circled by jeering dead bikers, the noise of their cycles deafening. Buddy wants to fight, but instead blubbers and begs, which incites the skeletons, who howl insults and pelt him with hot dog feces. As each bit of excrement strikes, it instantly turns to stone. Roemer is soon encased; he suffocates in petrified shit.

The scarecrow has Ev LaMar well secured. Chuckling and whistling, he takes some turpentine and a paint stripper from his toolbox, and commences renovations.

Something heavy and powerful crashes into the sound engineer's raft, flipping it; he screams as a rubbery limb wraps around his legs. The director's table is slivered by pincers attacking from the swirling blood. His back is pressing against the ceiling. Blood laps at his face.

The exquisite agony of Orrick DeWine's metamorphosis hits full force. He writhes on the ground; pewling, as his skull pulls, cracks, reforms into a snout—a too-long snout. His teeth—shrink. His sight dims, his limbs shorten into stubs, forcing his chest to the ground. His back hunches, spine and ribs prodding through his skin to blend into a segmented shell; the weight presses his bladder and he urinates on himself, his penis aimed at his belly.

Rock'n roll whams in Abner L. Schlueuter's head, a hateful tinnitus ringing, and Schlueuter is, against his will, dancing. Slam, hiphop, thrash. Invisible cavorters surround him, knocking him to the ground; when he falls, he is dragged back up, shoved back into motion. His hips, ankles, wrists are broken; his ribs, collarbone, cheekbones splinter, spearing and hemorrhaging him. He dances. An unseen reveler crashes into him and he falls, snapping his neck. Shards poke through his skin like ornaments. Abner bounces up again, dancing, dancing, long after he is pulverized into a flopping, spineless meat bag.

Chefs with white torques and gleaming knives serve a festive champagne buffet at La Roofe. "Tonight's appetizer," lisping waiters purr, "is a nice carpaccio di Lilly Nonnemacher, that's paper-thin slices of choice filet from the living breast or thigh; and tonight there's a lovely selection of freshly ground Steak Tartare de Noyce Hunkeler or some nice variety cuts grilled al dente."

Kathleen Daskalakis rolls on the ground, ripping her flesh, smashing her head, slapping herself, wailing. All her body hair has turned into worms, wet, glistening, nipping, and nibbling, wiggling from her pores; maggots drip from her eyelids and ears. All of them gnawing as they flail in her heart and breed in her brain.

Young girls with glowing eyes take Jim Slavin by the hand, lead him from Gehenna to a quiet place at the edge of the hollow, behind the screens. With dreamlike wonder, Slavin sees glimpses of ideals lost, goals unfulfilled, and the faces of women he wanted but never won. Bewildered and dizzy, he sits back against a tree, letting the girls untie his shoes. One child, perhaps nine years old, firmly holds his little finger. "Loves me…" she murmurs, and tugs the flesh and bone from the top joint of his finger, leaving nearly invisible filaments of nerve, "loves me not…" and pulls off the next joint, again leaving only raw ganglia, "loves me…" and finishes the finger, "loves me not…" and turns to his ring finger as the other girls shred his feet, hands, teeth like roses, leaving only thin wires of torment, all the while whispering "loves me loves me not…" their lilting voices badly dubbed, not matching their lip movement, "loves me not loves loves not loves loves me loves me…" His arms and legs fall away like old socks, muscles and bones easily removed; the children idly braid and swish the fragile threads that remain, negligently letting the ends trail in the dirt.

The scarecrow, approving his work, polyurethanes Ev LaMar…

The grandstand collapses as the throbbing Inspiration malignancy bloats, stiffens in climax, and dissolves into a lake of scum and stray cells…

Lois Gilligan and Tod Critchlow dismember themselves but still convulse, flipping like beached fish, beaten by their own severed limbs…

The projection booth windows explode into bright cascading waterfalls of blood…

Hideous and helpless, Orrick DeWine—a half-human werearmadillo—waddles in circles…

Hiram Spruance's bodyfat glazes the top of the chili as Sandy Kessler stumbles into the kitchen; her flaming body ignites a grease fire that spreads through the pagoda…

Punched into puree, Abner L. Schlueuter's insides gush through his sieved holes…

Joyce Leonard and Constance Triftshauser slip into comas, their faces coated with sweat and spittle. Rows of multi-nippled breasts erupt along their ribs; teats too few to suckle the litters of hatchlings fighting to feed…

The kappa finishes Minton Eggets and crawls off in search of its next meal, leaving behind a parched dandruff of skin…

"Loves me me me loves not me not me…" Their cool soft fingers peel Slavin's torso and face, crack open his skull and chest and, working vertebra by vertebra, pull the rats through his loosened spine. Slavin remains alert and in pain beyond comprehension as the ultimate unanesthetized surgery proceeds, as the little girls free his nervous system from its home. They plait the ganglia into cats' cradles, slapping each other with the braided whisks while they giggle and whisper. They play catch with Jim Slavin. A still-conscious brain, his nerves soaring on a halo and running along the ground, until one toss goes wild and the brain snags on a tree branch. There they leave him, an abandoned kite, his tail of threads and snips of agony catching each stray breeze…

The Joe Bob totals: 651 head rolls; 5,083 lobbed limbs; 47 reamed—

Enough.

Morals, if any, are difficult to discern. Certainly, most of the Zone's victims were comparative innocents who deserved neither death nor defilement, which suggests dynamic evil. But the magic was not deliberate nor wroth, merely reactive. When hundreds are killed by earthquakes, monsoons, famine, they are thought felled by acts of nature or Heaven, and are no less unfairly dead. No less unfair than Earl Bittner's destruction, Brandon's, An'akist's. Yet to conclude that even Jim Slavin's fate was judgment raises an uncomfortable notion, a question of faith.

It implies that the existence of sleaze is a proof to the existence of God.

And that, if true, renders moral niceties even murkier. Still, the disappearance of a couple thousand followers of a televangelist, and of the minister, a county officer, a village government, caused private grief but no outcry. By the time police linked ten states' worth of missing persons reports, there were no clues. Rev. Sloane's parishioners delivered themselves to the next charming preacher who bought Sloane's airtime. Mad River County voters figured their sheriff had taken personal leave under cover of night, such events not being unheard of in Ohio. And the faithful of Leviticus, accustomed to denying reality, did so. Realtors, bankers, librarians, councils and managers are all societal by-products, disposable and easily replaced. Weeds soon covered Christian Life Heights and weather faded the graffiti on the state route.

No angelic retribution was exacted against the Zone, unless being deprived of believers causes a temple pain. The spirit born in the Cathedral may have starved, dissipated of its own accord…or, as folk tales go, if it hasn't yet died, it's living there still.

Unless…unless it's grown restless. Hungering. Seeking love or a new party, in which case it might be flowing through the topsoil, unseen, inexorable and dreadful, creeping, creeping, sending out amoebic podia of sin and decadence… nearer…creeping nearer…

No. It was a strictly provincial phenomenon. The Zone was its womb, its shrine, its crypt. It would never escape from Mad River County.

But let this enter local lore: that there's some corner of a forlorn field that is for ever sleaze.

By false dawn the last cars and corpses were sinking into the subsiding tarmac: a few aerials; one hand frozen in a contorted rigor of supplication. The fleshdome evaporated in the gathering light, revealing that the screens canted at angles, most of the speakers were vandalized, and the pagoda-snack-bar-projection-booth had again burned down during the night. Jim Slavin's brain hung on a hidden branch, suet for the squirrels.

By sunrise the evidence had vanished. The site of the old Buckeye was quiet, save for the crows and crickets of an Ohio Indian summer…

The ashy settling of charred timbers.

Rare, heartfelt subterranean screams.

And, of course, occasional chomping. ◆

THE BESPELLED

BY *Kim Harrison*

Ever since the serpent sweet-talked Eve into eating the apple, demons have been known to have a way with the ladies.

The endless supernatural eruptions of urban fantasy fiction—wherein demons, elves, vampires, and the rest of the mystical gang routinely pop up in a modern context—are rich to overflowing with precisely this tension.

And in that wildly popular mileau, Kim Harrison is a superstar. Her series The Hollows—*featuring pixie-packin', bounty-hunting witch Rachel Morgan—shows up regularly on the* New York Times *bestseller list, with each fresh entry.*

"The Bespelled" isn't urban fantasy, in that it doesn't boast a modern setting. But it is dark, and fantastic indeed.

Paperwork, Algaliarept thought in resignation as he blew gently upon the ledger book to dry the ink faster. Ink that wasn't actually ink, paper that had never been wood, he thought as he breathed deep for the cloying scent of blood. Though blood made a sublimely binding document, the nature of it tended to slow everything down. Even so, if he could pass this part of his job to a subordinate, he wouldn't. The knowledge of who owed him and what was worth a lot in the demon's world, and familiars were known for their loose tongues until you cut them out. It was a practice Algaliarept frowned upon. Most of his brethren were bloody plebeians. Removing a familiar's tongue completely ruined the nuances of their pleas for mercy.

Resettling himself at his small but elegantly carved desk, Algaliarept reached into a lidded stone box, dipping a tiny silver spoon for his Brimstone and letting the drug slowly melt on his tongue. The small tap of the spoon as he replaced it jolted through him like fire, and closing his eyes he breathed, pulling the air into him over the ashy blackness to bring a hundred faint smells to him as the Brimstone heightened his senses and took his mind into a higher state.

Paperwork has got to be the biggest pain in the ass, he thought as he hung for a moment in the mild euphoria. But as his eyes opened he gazed upon his opulent quarters—the walls draped with dark silk, vases painted with beautifully erotic bodies, richly shadowed corners with cushions and fragrant oil lamps, and underfoot, the rug showing a winding dragon devouring its smaller kin—Algaliarept knew he'd have it no other way. Everything about him would be missing if he worked for another.

The East was where the world's intelligence currently resided, and he quite liked the Asian people, even if they called him a dragon there, and expected him to breathe fire. Apart from the elves making a last stand in the mountains of Europe, Asia was the only real culture in the world right now—thanks to his efforts, mostly. One must create what another will covet.

Dipping his quill, Algaliarept bent to his work again, his brow tightening for no reason he could fathom. He was a dealer in flesh and seducer of souls, skilled in training people in the dark arts enough to make them marketable, then abducting them when they made a mistake in order to sell them to his peers into an extended lifetime of servitude. He was so good at it that he had achieved a status that rivaled the highest court members, reached on his own merits and owed to no one. Yet, as his quill scratched out the interest of a particularly long-running debt, he finally acknowledged the source of his growing feeling of dissatisfaction.

Where he'd once relished watching a potential familiar agonize over wanting more and thinking he was smart enough to evade the final outcome, now there was only an odd sensation of jealousy. Though doomed, the familiar was feeling something. Algaliarept, however, was feeling nothing. He'd lost the joy, and the chase had become too easy. Another page tallied, and Algaliarept reached for a second spoonful of Brimstone while the red ink dried and turned black. As his silver spoon dipped, his moving reflection caught his attention and he hesitated, meeting his own gaze in the gilded mirror upon the desk. Tired, goat-slitted eyes stared back at him. They narrowed, and with a feeling of unhappiness he watched himself let the black ash sift back into the box. If he wanted sensation, he should go out and take it, not sip it from dust. Perhaps, Algaliarept thought darkly as he touched his script to see if it was dry, it was time to retire for a time. Begin removing his name from the texts in reality to leave just enough for the occasional summoning instead of the numerous summons he fielded. He was weary of mediocre dealings and fast satisfaction that gave him nothing lasting. He wanted…more. Mood soured, he bent to his work. This can't be all there is, he thought as he tried to lose himself in the beauty of wants and needs, supply and demand.

Intent on his work, the soft tickling in his nose almost went unnoticed until he sneezed. His hand slammed down on the open Brimstone container, saving it. Shocked, he stared at his door, tasting the air and trying to decide where the sun had just fallen. Someone was summoning him. Again, he thought with a sigh, until he realized where it was likely coming from, Europe?

Algaliarept's gaze returned to the mirror, and his goat-slitted, red eyes glinted. A slow smile came over his creased face. Inside, a quiver of excitement coursed through him, more heady than Brimstone. It had to be Ceridwen. She was the only one who knew his name across that continent, the only one who could call him there. Three months, he thought, his excitement growing as he gazed into the mirror while his features became younger and more refined, taking on the strong jaw she was accustomed to. I knew she couldn't resist.

Humming a snippet of music that had never been penned, he shook out his sleeves, watching them turn from the casual silk kimono he appreciated into a stuffy European crushed green velvet coat. Lace appeared at his throat, and his hair slicked itself back. His ruddy complexion lightened, and white gloves appeared. He would be pleasing to her sight even if he thought the outfit ugly. Until she stopped three months ago without warning, Ceridwen Merriam Dulciate had summoned him every week for seven years. He was nothing if not patient, but the lapse did not bode well. That he was excited for the first time in as many weeks did not escape him, but Ceri was special. She was the most devious, intelligent, careful woman he had tried to snag in almost three hundred years, and he never knew what she was going to do.

Art, he realized suddenly. Ceri was art where everyone else was work. Was that where his dissatisfaction was coming from? Was it time to stop simply working and begin making art? But to do that, he needed the canvas before him. It was time to bring her home. If he could.

Standing, he sneezed again, more delicately this time. His thoughts went to a seldom-used curse and he winced, searching his mind until he remembered. "*Rosa flavus*," he whispered, shivering as the unusual curse shifted over him to leave a yellow rose in his grip. Damn his dame, this felt good. He'd bring her home this time. He was anxious to begin.

"Zoe!" he shouted, knowing the three-fingered man-whore would hear him. "I'm out! Take my calls!" And with no more thought, he allowed the summons to pull him from the splash of displaced time he existed in to reality.

He traveled by ley lines, the same force of nature that kept the drop of time he existed in from vanishing. The shock of the line melting him into a thought was a familiar ache, and it was with a sly confidence that he found himself drawn to a spot far up in the mountains of Europe. He never knew for sure where he was going until he got there, but this? Algaliarept smiled as the clean mountain air filled his lungs as he reformed, the stench of burnt amber that clung to him being replaced by the honest smell of horses and cultivated flowers. This was pleasant.

The hum of a binding circle grew oppressive, and Algaliarept found himself in a dusky garden surrounded by dark pines, the sky above them still holding the fading light of the sunset and fluttering blue butterflies. The circle holding him was defined by semi-precious stones inlaid in crushed gravel. Through the haze of energy trapping him came the sound of running water and birds. Music. A small orchestra. Something was badly off. And when his eyes went to the full moon rising above the fragrant pines, his smile faded in a wash of worry. *Is the bitch getting married?*

A soft clearing of a throat turned him around.

"Ceridwen," he said, allowing a sliver of his annoyance to color his words, then he hesitated. She was absolutely stunning in the puddle of nearby lamp light with blue butterflies flitting about her. "Ceri, you are exceptionally lovely." *Damn it to the two worlds colliding, she's getting married. Directly.*

He had tarried too long. It was tonight, or never.

The slight, fair-haired woman before him modestly ran her hands over her clearly wedding garb, white and trimmed with her family's colors of maroon and gold. Her fair hair was piled atop her head but for a few strands artfully drawn down. She was pale and lithe, having wide green eyes and a narrow chin. If for no more than that, she would be unique among the predominantly Asian women populating the demon familiar market and bring a high price. But that wasn't why he'd courted her so carefully.

Though her eyes were cast down demurely, she knew she was beautiful, reveled in it, vainly believed it was why he was attentive and kind to her. He'd kept her oblivious to the real reason he stayed pliant to her summons and demands for knowledge when anyone else would have been met with anger and threats years ago for the audacity of being too clever to be caught and therefore was wasting his time. She earned the surname Dulciate. It was one of the most desired familiar names in the demon realm, though if the castle behind her was the level to which the elves had fallen to, there wasn't much left to take revenge upon. Even if she were ugly, he could make more from her then seven skilled familiars. And she was skilled, thanks to him—infuriatingly clever and careful. Hopefully not careful enough, he thought, his hands clenching in their white-gloved preciseness.

Behind her on the cropped grass, a round stone table was strewn with her golden tarot cards, clear evidence that she was upset. She knew he thought little of them, having spent summers striving to break her from their grip, failing even when he proved them false as she sought counsel from a power he didn't believe in. Rising beyond the garden was the gray-walled castle of her family. It was pitiful by the Asian standards he appreciated, but it was the pinnacle of society in this superstitious cultural wasteland. Where he'd created a society in Asia with science, rivals had inundated Europe with superstition in their attempts to match his gains.

From the balcony walkway, clusters of overdressed women kept watch as the darkness took hold and the butterflies dwindled. As a member of the elven royal house, it was Ceridwen's right to summon demons, expected and encouraged until she took a husband. Tradition dictated that the ruling personage-in-waiting was to learn all they could of the arcane. It was just as expected that her station would grant her the privacy to do it where ever she wanted. So her fluttering ladies waited in the torchlight, holding Ceri's little dogs as they yapped furiously at him. They knew the danger, and it was a delicious irony that no one listened to them.

Looking closer, he gauged her aura to see if a rival had been poaching on his claim which could explain the three-month lapse. Ceridwen's aura, though, was as he had left it; the original bright blue marred by a light black coating of demon smut that was all his own.

Seeing the yellow rose in his hand, a heavy tear brimmed in her deep green eyes, unusual for the emotionally balanced woman. Her head bowed as it fell, but pride brought it up again immediately. Chin high, she looked behind her to her tarot cards, starting to cry all the more. Her hands stayed stoically at her sides, fisted as she refused to wipe her tears away.

Hell and damnation, I'm too late, Algaliarept thought, taking an angry step forward only to stop short as the barrier she'd summoned him behind hummed a familiar vicious warning. "Love, what's wrong?" he asked, pretending to be oblivious, though inside, he was scrambling. He had not labored seven years only to lose a Dulciate elf to marriage! "Why are you crying? I've told you not to look at the cards. They only lie."

Crestfallen, Ceri turned away, but her pale fingers straying to touch her tarot cards were still bare of gold, and Algaliarept felt a glimmer of hope. "I'm not your love," she said, voice quavering as she turned the lovers card face down. "And you're the liar."

"I've never lied to you," he said. Damn it, he was not going to lose her to some inane cards! Frustrated, Algaliarept nudged a booted toe at the circle's seam to feel her power repel him. Never had she made a mistake in its construction. It both infuriated him and kept him coming back, week after week, year after year, and now, because of it, he was going to lose her.

"I had to tell you good-bye," she continued as if he hadn't spoken, pleading as she fingered a gold-edged card. "They told me not to, that with the responsibility of marriage, I must sever all ties to the arcane."

Agitated, he gripped his rose until a thorn pierced his glove and the pain stifled his fidgeting. "Good-bye, my love?" He had to make her control lapse—if only for an instant.

"I'm not your love," she whispered, but her gaze was upon the cards. There were no others like them, having been painted by a second-rate Italian painter who had attempted to put the royal family within the artwork. It hadn't pleased him to find out Ceri was on the death card, being pulled away by a demon.

"Ceri, you are my unrequited love," he said earnestly, testing the strength of her circle until the stench of burning leather from his shoes drove him back. "Tell me you've not wed. Not yet." He knew she wasn't, but to make her say the words would make her think.

"No." It was a thin whisper, and the young woman sniffed, holding a hand out for a tiny blue butterfly seeking warmth in the fading day. He'd seen them only once before in this profusion, and it was likely the wedding had been planned around the beautiful, fragile creatures. But butterflies like carrion as much as flowers, battlefields as much as gardens.

Algaliarept looked at the yellow rose in his grip, his thoughts lifting and falling as the music rose high in celebration. Fast. He had to work fast. "Why do you hurt me?" he said, squeezing his hand until a drop of blood fell upon it, turning the entire rose a bright scarlet. "You summon me only to spurn me?" He dropped the rose, and she blanched, eyes rising to his bloodied glove. "To say good-bye?" he accused, allowing his anger to color his voice. "Do our seven years mean nothing to you? The skills I've taught you, the music, ideas that we shared from across the sea? It all means nothing? Was I just your demon, your pet? Nothing more?"

Distressed, Ceridwen faced him, the butterfly forgotten. "Talk not to me of love. They are naught but pretty words to trap me," she whispered, but under her misery was a frantic need he had yet to figure out. There was more here than she was saying. Could she be unhappy about the marriage? Was this the key to making her control lapse?

"As you trapped me!" he exclaimed, jerking his hand back when he intentionally burned himself on the barrier between them. Excitement was a pulse when she reached out, concern for him showing briefly. "Ceridwen," he pleaded, breath coming faster, "I watched you grow from a shy, skittish colt to a rightfully proud woman, fiery and poised to take responsibility for your people. I was there when all others grew distant, jealous of your skills. I didn't expect to grow fond of you. Have I not been a gentleman? Have I not bent to your every whim?"

Green eyes deep with misery met his. "You have. Because you're caught in my circle."

"I would regardless!" he said violently, then looked to the darkening sky as if seeking words, though what he was going to say he'd said to untold others. This time, though, he meant them. "Ceri, you are so rare, and you don't even know it. You are so beyond anyone here because of what I've shared with you. The man who waits for you…He cannot meet your intellectual needs. When I hear your summons, my heart leaps, and I come directly, a willing slave."

"I know."

It was a faint affirmation, and Algaliarept's pulse raced. This was it. This was the way to her downfall. She didn't desire her husband. "And now you'll abandon me," he whispered.

"No," she protested, but they both knew tradition dictated otherwise.

"You're going to wed," he stated, and she shook her head, desperate as her tiny feet tapped the flagstones, coming closer in her need to deny it.

"That I'm wed doesn't mean I won't summon you. Our talks can continue."

Feigning dejection, he turned his back on her, all but oblivious to the manicured gardens going dark and damp. "You will abandon me," he said, chin high as he probed the circle to find it still perfect. Though he was a demon and could crush an army with a single word, such was the strength of a summons that a simple circle could bind him. He had to upset her enough such that she would make a mistake and he could break it. Until then, nothing but sound and air could get through.

Taking a ragged breath, he dropped his head, his hands still laced behind him. "You will begin with all good intentions," he said, his voice flat. "But you'll summon me into underground rooms where no one can see, and our time together once open and celebrated will become brief snatches circled by guilt instead of precious stones. Soon you will call me less and less, shame dictating that your heart be ruled over by your head, your responsibilities." He took a breath, turning his tone thin. "Let me go. I can't bear seeing what we shared abandoned bit by bit. Make of my heart a clean death."

The clatter of the gravel sliding beneath her shoes sparked through him like lightning, and he grit his teeth to hide his anticipation. One tiny stone, knocked out of place, would do it. "I would not do that," she protested as she faced him, a gray shadow against the dark vegetation.

Refusing to meet her gaze because he knew it would hurt her, he looked at the moon, seeing a few lone butterflies daring the dark to find a mate. Crickets chirped as the music from the castle dissolved into polite applause. "Marry him if you will," he said stoically. "I'll forever come if you call, but I'll be but a broken shadow. You can command my body, but you cannot command my heart." He looked at her now, finding she was clutching a golden card to her chest, hiding it. "Do you love him?" he asked bluntly, already knowing the answer in her frantic expression.

She said nothing as torchlight shined upon her tears.

"Does he make your heart beat fast?" Algaliarept demanded, a shudder running through him when her eyes closed in pain. "Can he make you laugh? Has he ever brought new thought to you, as I have? I've never touched you, but I've seen you tremble in desire…for me."

He nudged at the circle with a booted toe, jerking back at the zing of power. Though her face wore her anguish, her circle still held strong, even when her chest heaved, and her grip on her dress dropped, leaving creases in the otherwise perfect fall of fabric.

"Don't hurt me like this, Algaliarept," she whispered. "I only wanted to say good-bye."

"It's you who hurt me," he stated, forcefully where before he had always been demure. "I'm forever young, and now you'll make me watch you grow old, watch your beauty fade and your skills tarnish as you shackle yourself to a loveless marriage and a cold bed."

"It is the way of things," she breathed, but the fear in the back of her eyes strengthened as she touched her own face. Her fondness for the mirror had always been her downfall, and he felt a surge of renewed excitement. "I will mourn your beauty when you could have been young forever," he said, looking for a crack in her resolve. "I would've forever been your slave." Faking depression, he slumped his perfect posture. "Only in the ever-after does time stand still and beauty and love last forever. But, as you say, it's the way of things."

"Gally, don't speak so," she pleaded, and he tensed when she used the nickname she'd chosen for him. But his lips parted in shock when she reached for him only to drop her hand mere inches from the barrier between them. His breath came in with a shudder, and his eyes widened. Had he been cracking the nut the wrong way? He had been trying to rattle her, make her lose her resolve so he could find a crack in her circle and break it, even knowing that her will would likely remain absolute even when her world was crashing down about her. She would not let her circle weaken, but what if she would take it down voluntarily? Ceri was of royal blood, a Dulciate. Generations of crown-sanctified temptation had created women who would not make a mistake of power. But she might make a mistake of the heart.

And the instant he realized why he had failed these seven years, her gaze went past him to the palace, lit up and replete with joy. Her eyes closed, and panic hit him as he saw everything fall apart. Shit, she was going to walk.

"Ceri, I would love you forever," he blurted, not faking his distress. Not now. Not now when he'd found her weakness!

"Gally, no," she sobbed as the tears fell and tiny blue butterflies rose and fell about her.

"Don't call me again!" he demanded, the words coming from him without thought or plan. "Go to your cold bed. Die old and ugly! I would make you wise beyond all on earth, keep you beautiful, teach you things that the scholars and learned men have not even dreamed of. I will survive alone, untouched, my heart becoming cold where you showed me love. Better that I had never met you." He looked at her as a sob broke from her. "I was happy as I was."

"Forgive me," she choked out, hunched in heartache. "You were never just my demon."

"It's done," he said, making a hitch in his voice. "It's not as if I ever thought you would trust me, but to show me heaven only to give it to another man? I can't bear it."

"Gally—"

He raised a hand and her voice broke in a sob. "That's three times you've said my name," he said, crushing the now red rose beneath his foot. "Let me go, or trust me. Take down the wall so I may at least have the memory of your touch to console me as I weep in hell for having lost you, or simply walk away. I care not. I'm already broken."

Expression held at an anguished pain, he turned his back on her again, shifting his shoulders as if trying to find a new way to stand. Behind him, he heard a single sob, and then nothing as she held her breath. There was no scuffing of slippers as she ran away and no lessening of the circle imprisoning him, so he knew she was still there. His pulse quickened, and he forced his breathing to be shallow. He was romancing the most clever, most resolute bitch he'd ever taught a curse to, and he loved her. Or rather, he loved not knowing what she would do next, the complexity of her thoughts that he had yet to figure out—an irresistible jewel in a world where he had everything.

"Do you love him?" he asked, adding the last brushstrokes to his masterpiece.

"No," she whispered.

His hands quivered as adrenaline spiked through him, but he held perfectly still. He would've given a lot to know which card she held crushed in her grip. "Do you love me?" he asked, shocked to realize he'd never used those particular words to seduce a familiar before.

The silence was long, but from behind him came a soft, "Yes. God help me."

Algaliarept closed his eyes. His breath shook in him, hid excitement racing through him like a living ley line, burning. Would she drop her circle? He didn't know. And when a light touch landed on his hand, he jumped, looking down to find a blue butterfly slowly fanning its wings against him.

A butterfly? he thought in shock, and then he realized. She had broken the summoning circle, and he'd never even felt it go down. Oh God, he thought, a surge of what was almost ecstasy making his knees nearly buckle as he turned, finding her standing before him, nervous and hopeful all at the same time. She had let him in. Never had he taken anyone like this. It was like nothing he'd ever felt before, debilitating.

"Ceri," he breathed, seeing her without the shimmer of her power between them. Her eyes were beautiful, her skin holding a olive tint he'd never noticed before. And her face…She was crying, and he reached out, not believing when he ran a white-gloved hand under her eye to make her smile at him uncertainly. It was a smile of hope and fear.

She should be afraid.

"Gally?" she said hesitantly.

"Do you really love me?" he asked her as the butterflies swarmed, drawn by the scent of burnt amber, and she nodded, gazing at him as tears slipped down and she hesitantly folded herself into his arms.

"Then you are one stupid bitch."

Gasping, she flung her head up. Pushing from him, she tried to escape, but it was too late. Silently laughing, Algaliarept wrapped his arm around her neck, grabbing her hair with his free hand and pulling her across the garden to the nearest ley line. "Let me go!" she screamed, and gathering herself, she shouted, "*celero inanio!*" sobbing as she flung the entire force of the nearest ley line at him.

With a quick thought, Algaliarept deflected the burning curse, chuckling as flickers of light blossomed to show where the blue butterflies burned before they hit the dew-wet grass. In his grasp, Ceri hesitated her struggles, aghast that he had turned her magic into killing something she loved. "Do that again, and I'll burn anything that comes round that corner," he encouraged, winding his fist in her hair until she began hitting him with her tiny fists.

"You lied! You lied to me!" she raged.

"I did nothing of the kind," he said, holding her close and dragging her out of the circle so that the people now running toward her screams wouldn't be able to trap him easily. "I'm going to keep you forever young and teach you everything I know, just as I promised." She was panting, her struggle hesitating as she waited for the help that wouldn't be able to free her. Closing his eyes, he smelled her hair. "And I'm going to love you," he whispered into her ear as she began to pray to an uncaring god he'd teach her not to believe in. "I'm going to love you within an inch of your life, then love you some more."

Anticipation high, he reached for her inner thigh. The instant his fingers touched her, she screamed, fighting to be free. A fierce smile came over him and his blood pounded in his loins. This was going to be everything he wanted. A distraction for as long as he cared to make it last.

"Let me jump you to my bed so we may begin your tutelage," he said as the bobbing torches came closer.

"No!" she cried out, wiggling as her hair came undone to fall about her face. She looked so much more fetching, her color high and rage making her eyes sparkle.

"Wrong answer," he said, flooding her with the force of the line.

Her eyes widened, her small lips opening to show perfect teeth. Gasping, she bit her lip, trying not to scream. Almost she passed out, and he let up the instant she started to go limp. That she wouldn't scream made him smile. She'd scream before it was over, and finding her breaking point would be...exquisite.

"I'm giving you everything you want," he breathed in her ear when she could think again, hanging in his grasp as she panted. "Everything and more, Ceri. Let me take you." He could knock her out and take her by force, but if she gave in entirely to him...It would be beyond anything he'd ever accomplished.

The bobbing torches turned the corner, little dogs yapping in overdressed women's arms.

"Stop! For the love of God, stop!" she shouted, and Algaliarept felt a deep surge of satisfaction. Destroying her will would fulfill his every need.

A young man in white and gold pushed past the women, stumbling to a stop, shock in his perfect face. A wailing outcry rose from the nobles behind him, and several turned and ran.

Ceri's bridegroom was perfect, Algaliarept decided bitterly as he held her tighter. The man before him now complimented her in every way, slim, fair— everything Algaliarept was not. And then Algaliarept smiled—she had shunned elven perfection to be with him.

The man's lips parted in horror as Algaliarept's fingers entwined deeper in her hair, jerking her head up to expose the long length of her neck to him. And still Ceri stared at her bridegroom, color in her cheeks as her lungs heaved. Turning, the prince called for magicians.

At the sight of his back, Ceri's hand opened and the card she held fell to the earth. Something in Algaliarept sparked when the devil card fell to the manicured grass. The bent gold glinted in the torch light, but it was easy to see the beautiful maiden being dragged off by an ugly, red-skinned demon. "Take me," she whispered as three magicians stumbled into the clearing, frightened but determined. "I don't want to grow old. You are my demon."

With her acquiesce, it was done. Seven years of labor culminated in one satisfied laugh that made the young man in white pale. But he didn't move to save her.

"You don't deserve her," Algaliarept said, and then, as the magicians moved, he shifted his thoughts to leave. The yapping dogs, the wailing women, everything vanished into the clean blackness of thought. And as they traveled the lines back to the drop of time that had been flung from space itself, Algaliarept touched her soul, ran his fingers through her aura and felt her squirm. She had wanted it. Even with her denials and screams, she wanted it. Wanted him. She was his little blue butterfly, seeking out carrion.

Don't cry, Ceri, he thought, knowing she heard him when her mind seemed to quiver.

He was going to keep this one for himself. Turn the Dulciate elf into a showcase of his talents No one had ever come willingly before. He was an artist, and destroying her as he made her into what he wanted, would be his finest masterpiece.

Until I find someone with a little more skill that is, he thought, knowing that wasn't likely to happen for, oh, probably another thousand years. ✦

NON QUIS, SED QUID

BY *Maggie Stiefvater*

Speaking of demons and ladies. . .what is it about bad boys, exactly, that makes them so damned attractive, even though anyone with half a brain could tell you it's a bad idea? Talk about your hot potatoes!

This charming, funny, bootyliscious short-short on the subject at hand is from bestselling YA/urban fantasist Maggie Stiefvater, here putting the cute in "cute-tastrophe."

She'd been dating the demon for about a year. No, maybe not a year. Maybe eight months. Her father told her once there was a big difference between eight months and a year. If you were told you were going to die in a year, he said, and Death knocked on your door in eight months, don't you think you'd be a little put off?

So, maybe eight months.

He hadn't said he was a demon when they first met. She'd just assumed. He drove a black-on-black-on-sulphur-on-more-black Harley bike, which wasn't particularly demonic on its own, even with the eerie little silver wide-open eye sticker on the fender. But he also had great black tattoos creeping down the back of his neck, clinging to each knob on his spine, and more tats knifing over his left shoulder. He had a baby knife curved like the claw of a raptor hidden in the lining of his boot and he had a habit of shouldering people out of his way. He also spit and hissed when things surprised him, like she had.

When she said, you're a demon, he'd smiled at her, and asked her out for dinner. Eight months ago. Maybe a year.

He had habits that were not necessarily associated with being a demon but also weren't particularly associated with being human either. He sucked the insides out of fruit—lemons were his favorite, but he'd settle for limes or oranges or pomegranates if he couldn't get lemons. That was all he ate, with the notable exception of Nerds candy, which he consumed chiefly after sex. He liked to lick his palm if he knew he was going to be meeting someone new; she was well acquainted with the smile that he wore when he shook hands. The demon called anyone in a business suit the ruling class and he keyed BMWs. He sprinkled salt around the toilet and the bathtub and the sinks and the pitiful water feature in her garden. He hissed Latin to her in bed while he locked her to the mattress, his hand cuffs over her wrists. He loved insects. He rescued spiders from the house and redirected earwigs and also sometimes made ants fight each other on the sidewalk. Love from the demon sometimes just meant attention.

Four months in, she took him to meet her grandmother, because she liked to shock her grandmother, and the demon drove them to her favorite restaurant. Her grandmother said, why does he have to drive like a demon all the time? There's no fire. Oh, he replied, but there is. He shook grandmother's hand without licking his palm first. This pleased the demon's girlfriend.

They made a good pair, she and the demon. She'd never dated anyone for more than a few weeks before him. He was a good influence on her sleep and work habits. The demon asked her why she hadn't stolen any cars since the day they'd met. She said she wasn't a car thief, she'd just happened to be stealing a car when he met her. Which wasn't the same thing. You had to do something most of the time, she said, in order for it to define you.

He asked her why she called him a demon then. And he licked his palm, because they had a party to go to that night.

She said, because you sure as hell aren't an angel.

The demon wasn't good at holding down jobs. He got into arguments over arbitrary rules, he misplaced paperwork, and he stood on his desk and shouted anarchyanarchyanarchy. He would crawl home after being sacked, conciliatory but not guilty, and wait for her to pet his hair and tell him that he was in the right, or at least, if not in the right, that she worshiped him, or if not worshiped all of him, at least certain parts of him.

Her mother lived in fear that they would get married. Her father said, for that, he'd have to enter a church. Still, they didn't know that the demon brought home rings to his girlfriend all the time. He'd lay next to her in bed, sliding them onto her fingers, fat, ugly ones, thin, pretty ones, rings studded with jewels and rings engraved with someone else's initials, and he'd whisper about the women whose fingers he'd cut off to bring them to her.

Later, she'd find the jewelry store bags in the trash can in the bathroom.

Plants didn't like the demon; she hadn't been able to keep one alive in the house since she'd begun dating him. She asked him to replace them after they'd died, but he would merely look at the half-dead vines and snarl at them. Snarl was perhaps too light a term. It was something that started too low for human ears to hear and tickled all the hairs on her neck to attention and made the dogs next door go crazy with whimpering before he was done. Then she'd just buy another plant herself.

One day he said, we've been together a year now. She said, eight months. He said the devil is in the details and then he asked her if she was afraid of him. He added, before she could reply, that he had eaten his last girlfriend alive until even her blood cried on the tile. She said, that's funny, that's what happened to my last boyfriend as well. The demon smiled then, and he took her palm and licked it.

"Time to meet the family," he said ✦

DEMON GIRL

BY *Athena Villaverde*

This odd, sweet Bizarro punk coming-of-age fairy tale for demon tweeners at the cusp of blossom has a resonance that I feel in my roots: a surreal innocence already lost, but somehow captured fresh at the moment of plucking.

This is a terrain that young Athena Villaverde is vibrantly charting with a series of stories (Starfish Girl and Clockwork Girl among them) that charm me with their honest emotion and unfettered, childlike imaginative depth.

It's little surprise that her inspirations include Kathe Koja, Anais Nin, Bjork, and Francesca Lia Block.

And I have little doubt that she's in the process of carving a unique, beloved place for herself in the Weird Girl canon.

Karina's body had started to change. Everyone noticed. Her powder blue skin was darkening. White horns poked through her scalp, still tiny buds, but noticeable enough that the boys at school teased her about them. The tip of her tail had become more pointy, and glowed when she was excited. She was entering puberty, her mother told her.

At puberty, demons gain their psychic powers and can perform possessions. It is tradition that when the special time comes for a girl, all of the demon women gather together and assist her with the changes. They help her perform her first possession and give her the knowledge that she will need to be a full-fledged demoness.

Karina was terrified of these changes. She had seen it happen to several of her friends, and they all became different people after. Colder, less free-spirited. Her mother told her it was perfectly natural and that every demon girl goes through it. It was all part of growing up.

But Karina didn't feel much like growing up; she didn't care about possessing souls. She still liked to play with dolls, a fact which all of her friends endlessly teased her about. "Why play with dolls when you can play with the real thing?" Lucretia had said. That was right after Lucretia had gone through her ceremony.

Lucretia had long legs, a smooth deep red complexion, curvy figure and wide-set glowing eyes. Her hair was a red flame mohawk and every boy at school wanted to be with her. Karina knew she would never look like Lucretia. Karina was skinny and had scars on her knees from digging through the forest looking for blood mushrooms. She wore her white hair in pigtails and had an awkward smile that scared the boys away.

So instead of chasing boys like Lucretia, Karina spent most of her time alone, wandering through the woods behind her house, singing to the creatures in the forest. She secretly loved to sing but never did it in front of other people. Only when alone in the wild.

It was dark and murky in the forest. Spiky purple trees heavy with sticky golden sap wove their limbs together, creating a vast canopy. Bats with wings wider than her father's horns flittered amongst the trees, hunting blister beetles. Tiny silver peanut slugs formed rings around blue flame flowers. Karina loved these woods. She had spent her whole childhood exploring the lava rocks and singing to the spiders. But there was one place she was warned never to go: the Emerald River.

Her parents had told her the river possessed an evil spirit. Anything that went near it would be drowned and spend eternity tortured beneath the glassy water.

Some days, when she was out exploring, she had seen small creatures approach the green stripe in the distance and disappear without a sound.

This particular day though, it was different. Karina filled her basket full of blood mushrooms and was headed back to her house when a flash of light caught the corner of her eye.

She saw a boy running naked through the trees. His skin glowed bright white, almost transparent. She watched him weave amongst the blue flame flowers, carefully darting over and under the sharp spikes of the trees, his muscular thighs gleaming, the whiteness of his skin leaving a trail of light across the sky. She felt the tip of her tail start to glow. The boy ran straight toward the Emerald River and disappeared.

She ran home to tell her mother about it, expecting her to be excited. But instead, her mother's eyes turned black and she said to Karina in a voice that she only used to scold her, "You are too old to be digging around in the mud for mushrooms. Your time has come to grow up and stop imagining things in the woods."

"But I didn't imagine it. I saw the boy. I know it."

"There is nothing for you out in the woods. I don't want you playing there anymore."

Karina opened her mouth to protest and her father slammed his heavy blue fist down onto the table, causing it to shake and splinter down the middle. "Listen to your mother. We've warned you before never to go near the Emerald River."

Karina was heartbroken. How could her mother say she was too old to play in the woods? It was unfair. If there had been any danger, she would have discovered it by now. And why wouldn't they believe her about the naked boy?

That night, Karina snuck out her bedroom window. Her heart like a moth trapped inside a lamp, wings desperately beating to be free. She couldn't stop thinking about the boy. Her mind had been fixated all day. Who was he? Where did he come from? She'd never seen anything like him, and was anxious to see him again.

But why was she having these thoughts? She'd never worried herself about boys before. Was this something to do with the change that was happening to her? She was never attracted to the boys at school. But this boy was different, luminescent.

She walked through the woods wearing a long coat over her nightgown and slippers. She wasn't sure where she was going so she headed toward the river. She felt scared and a little silly. Why would she think that he would be out here in the middle of the night? This was a stupid idea. She was going to get caught.

A rustling in the silver berry bushes behind her frightened her. When she turned to look, she saw it was only a horned turtle. It pulled its head back into its spiral shell when it spotted her watching.

Karina continued in the direction of the river. As she went deeper into the forest, a silence fell around her. The sky moved like sacred geometry in a mandala of vivid colors.

She felt something shift inside her. Her feet went numb. A force beyond her control started pulling her forward. The Emerald River was coming into view and she could hear the sound of water rushing. She was being drawn toward it and could do nothing to stop herself. It was going to pull her under, just like her parents had said.

She panicked. Her pupils widened to shiny discs. Then a flash of light crackled across the horizon like lightning, and the spell was released.

She regained control of her feet and turned to run the other direction. Blood pounded in her ears louder than the sound of the water. She didn't dare turn around for fear that the force would grab a hold of her again. But as she took one last glance over her shoulder, she accidently stepped on a blue flame flower.

Electric pain shot through her foot. All the nerves in her leg were paralyzed and she dropped to the ground. Luckily, stepping on blue flame flowers only causes momentary paralysis, so she recovered quickly.

But when she got up again, the naked boy was standing in front of her.

She stared at him and let her gaze crawl across his body, admiring the way he stood: his stance wide and confident,his skin glowing white. He looked like a teenager, about her same age. His body was lithe and tall with long muscles like a dancer. Motionless, looking back at her, his gaze fixated on the tail poking out from under the back of her coat.

Then she realized she was staring at a naked man and her face turned bright purple. She lowered her eyes to her feet. Her pointed tail glowed even brighter than the last time she had seen him, and her stomach cramped up.

He spoke. His voice like a high pitched siren, it pierced Karina's ears and she had to cover them to block out the squeal. She couldn't understand what he was saying. She squinted her eyes with the pain of the sound and he stopped.

"Hi," she said.

He let out another siren wail.

Karina smiled awkwardly at him, still covering her ears. She realized they weren't going to be able to understand each other's language. So she reached into her pocket and pulled out a blood mushroom. She held it out to him. He looked at it quizzically, and then looked at her.

She brought it up to her mouth and bit into the bulbous tip. Its soft flesh parted beneath her pointy teeth to reveal the juicy bloody center. She took a small bite so the fruit wouldn't pop. Then held it back out to him, and smiled with the creases of her eyes.

He bent forward slightly and bit the mushroom out of her fingers like a bird. The whole thing exploded in his mouth like a cherry tomato and blood dripped down his white chin. His expression cracked with surprise and it made Karina laugh.

Then he smiled a wide easy smile and laughed with her, baring his bloody teeth with mushroom still in his mouth. Behind him, a purple tree limb crashed to the ground and he jumped, then fled as quickly as he had appeared. A trail of starlight. He moved like lightning.

Karina crept back in through her bedroom window, careful not to make a sound. She lay in her bed replaying the events of the evening in her head. She could still taste the blood mushroom on her tongue, and could still hear his voice ringing in her ears.

The next night and the next, she snuck out into the forest. Each time, the white boy was waiting for her where they had met. He brought her gifts: A blue flame flower encased in glass, and a tentacle sculpture made from graphite that she could use as a pencil.

Karina sang to him. It was the first time she had ever felt comfortable singing in front of another person. And to her delight, he danced along to the sound of her voice.

Soon they became friends, and Karina was sneaking out every night to meet with the boy. He never wore clothes, but he seemed so unashamed of himself that Karina eventually got used to hanging around with him that way. He was like some natural, wild thing, and Karina wanted to learn everything that she could about him.

When they weren't together, she was thinking about him. She still knew very little. She wondered if when the time came and she got her psychic powers, would she be able to understand him? The idea of it made her ache with anticipation of the change.

She started to express an interest in the ceremony, and it made her mother very happy.

"I am so glad you are finally growing up," her mother said. "You seem so much happier these days, and mature. Is there a special boy in your life?"

"No. Mom, it's not like that." Staring down at her feet to avoid her mother's prying gaze.

Karina had always been able to tell her mother everything. She felt guilty for keeping this secret. But she knew her mother wouldn't understand. Even if she did believe her about the boy in the woods, Karina's mother always wanted her to be interested in the boring jocks and demons with wealthy parents. She would never understand the attraction to a glowing white naked dancing boy.

Finally, her day arrived. Karina knew something was different the moment she woke up. There was a strange new smell in her room, like over-ripe peaches. She looked around for the source of it everywhere before she figured out that it was coming from herself.

When demon girls go through puberty, their scent changes. It's one of the ways that they are able to seduce their prey. Karina's mother also noticed it right away.

"Oh, my little girl has become a woman," she cried out when Karina entered the room for breakfast.

Karina's mom spent all day preparing for the ceremony. She called all of her demoness friends together and they gathered at the house that evening. Karina's mom gave her a new dress to wear; it was bright red and contrasted hideously with her blue skin. As she put it on, the fabric was rough against her extra sensitive nipples. But she wore it anyway because that's what her mother wanted. Karina just wanted to get the ceremony over with so she could try out her new psychic powers on her friend in the woods.

Her mother's friends all sat around drinking wine and sharing stories about what it had been like for them to go through the change. They brought Karina food and cards. She wasn't sure why they thought she needed either of those things. They gave her sips of wine that made her skin and belly warm.

Then late at night, they put a blindfold on her and led her outside through the woods beyond her house. Karina was scared and nervous and excited all at the same time. She felt her tail tingling and her mind blossoming as the women prepared her for her psychic powers.

Then she heard the singing and was confused. It was the song that she thought she'd made up. They were singing her song. The one she sang when she was alone. They removed her blindfold, and Karina saw the white boy laid out before her. He was gagged with a red cloth that matched her dress and bound by four demoness women, including her friend Lucretia. Their tails curled around his limbs holding him to the ground, the sharply pointed tips aiming at him like arrows. He looked up at Karina with fear in his eyes, pleading with her, not knowing why he was there.

A flash of lightning blurred her vision and in an instant, Karina knew everything. She heard the psychic voices of her demon sisters. She felt the vibrations under her skin grow stronger. They told her that this was the first soul that she was intended to possess. To possess a soul, she would need to absorb him into her body. Eat him, dissolve him, and he would become a part of her.

Karina wanted to be sick. Why would they do this to her? Did they know about her relationship with the boy? She searched her mind for answers, trying to understand.

The women circled around her, their eyes gleaming like hard candy, their tails glowing like candlelight. Karina couldn't even imagine doing what they were asking. She looked to her mother for help but her eyes were locked on the boy, her tongue slipping between her lips, slowly caressing the bottoms of her teeth.

Lucretia gave her a conspiratorial smile. The glowing tip of her tail matched her flame mohawk as it curled like a serpent around the inside of the boy's thigh.

Karina blinked at the boy and swallowed the lump in her throat. He stared back at her, his eyes moistening. She felt her heart cracking. It was her destiny to grow up. No one could stop it from happening. And when demon girls grow up, they possess souls. But this would mean destroying someone she loved. Did all girls go through this? Was it coincidence that they had chosen this boy?

Then she remembered the cold detached looks in the eyes of her friends, like Lucretia, after they had gone through the ceremony. And she knew it was her turn.

Karina's skin burned like white hot glitter starflowers. The circle of women closed in around her, urging her toward the boy. He didn't struggle; instead, he looked at her with an expression of innocence and complete surrender, his eyes like two blue flame flowers.

As she approached him, the muscles in her legs vibrated like violin strings. Her tail smoldered and became engorged with light. She felt a deep and unfamiliar urge. She wanted him inside her. She had never needed anything more desperately. Her logical mind knew that she didn't want to consume him, but her body ached to devour every ounce of his being. She felt as if her body was betraying her. She stared deeply into his eyes, seeking to connect, but all she could feel was the hunger.

Then Karina heard a voice inside her head. It crackled like static, nothing like a high pitched siren. But it was his voice, and it said, *Help Me*.

Karina took a deep breath through her nose. She felt her abdomen expand, and when she exhaled, she tried to slow her racing heart. She couldn't go through with this. She had to regain control. There was no way that she was going to possess this spirit. She remembered him dancing; the wild abandon, the smile he beamed, the way he'd grab her hands and spin her around beneath the purple trees. She realized that she never needed to be able to speak to him, she already knew him. She saw who he was in the way that he moved. She knew that he was strong and vibrant and free. She took a step backwards.

"What's wrong?" her mother asked.

Karina turned with tears in her eyes and held out her shaking hands toward her mother.

"I can't do it," Karina said, and started to cry.

"Shhh. It's nothing to be afraid of." Karina's mother stroked her temples gently like she used to do when she tucked her in at night, smoothed a stray hair back across her forehead. "You are my sweet girl. I know you will make me proud."

Lucretia leaned forward, took Karina's still-shaking hand, and pulled her to the glowing boy. The other women holding him down smiled at Karina encouragingly. Their tails slithered tighter spirals around him.

Karina didn't know what to do. Her body felt weak. The psychic voices in her mind became a cacophony of sounds; smashed windows, a broken song, bird wings flapping. An electric pulse reverberated in her ears. She felt weak. She didn't know how to stand up to them. She couldn't find the words to explain that what they were doing to her was ripping her apart. And worse than that, when she looked down at the boy, all she wanted to do was touch him, feel his skin, slide her body around his.

She looked at Lucretia, pleading. Her friend took Karina's right hand and delicately placed it on the center of the boy's chest.

Waves of color pulsed through Karina's body, traveling like electricity through a jellyfish. Her body became light and her mind felt like a balloon expanding. The feeling frightened her. Gooseflesh bloomed on her cobalt blue neck. She started to perspire. Tingling sensations crawled across her chest. She pulled her hand away.

Lucretia's eyes softened. She smiled at Karina and then bent down and licked the side of the boy's neck. Her tongue slid slowly across to his ear, a trail of light slipping in through her moist red lips.

Lucretia's eyes rolled back in her head as she inhaled the scent of the boy, sucking his glow like vapor through her mouth and nostrils. She ran her hands through her flame mohawk, igniting her fingertips, then bared her teeth and thrust her hips toward the boy. Her eyes stared straight into Karina's as she rubbed the length of her body along his glowing torso until her skin turned pink within his white light.

Seeing this caused something to snap inside Karina. Her stomach twisted like a broken clock. All of the little thoughts telling her this was wrong coalesced, and in that instant she knew for certain that she must free him.

Karina's body was on fire as she grabbed the boy up in her arms. In one fluid motion, Karina spun him around, freeing him from three of his bonds. But the fourth bond, Lucretia's tail, was still tightly wrapped around the boy's leg.

Lucretia gaped at her, baffled, pulling back on the prey. "What are you doing?"

Karina's eyes burned with anger. Blood rose in her head, blurring her vision. She grabbed Lucretia by the tail and sunk her sharp teeth into the smooth red flesh of her friend's serpentine appendage. Lucretia shrieked as Karina bit through the flesh, severing her tail, drooling inky blood down her chest.

The sight of the wriggling red tail on the ground caused the demon women to cry out in terror. In the moment of confusion, Karina took the boy and darted through an opening in the crowd.

"Karina!" her mother cried out as the pair ran through the forest.

The muscles in Karina's thighs stretched as she lengthened her stride to match his. It felt like they were one body with four legs as they sprinted through the forest with lightning speed. But soon the boy started to weaken, and could no longer move like lightning.

They ran in a jagged pattern through the woods, not knowing where to go. All Karina knew was that she must keep running because it wouldn't be long before the demon women caught up to them.

Then they hit the Emerald River.

Karina froze. Any closer, and the river would pull them in. She turned around and heard the howls of her demon sisters coming from all directions. There was nowhere to run. They were trapped.

She looked down at the boy's glowing hands. He reached up and tilted her chin toward his face. There were tears in her eyes. She leaned up against him, his cool skin soothing the burning sensations of her own. She whispered to him, *I'll protect you.*

Karina stiffened her muscles and prepared to fight off the hoard. She imagined herself bigger and stronger than she really was. She felt the horns on her head expand, stretching the skin of her face back, making her eyes wider.

She pulled the boy closer to her; he swooned and became intoxicated with her scent. She knew that she must keep him safe. But as she held him, her breath quickened. She felt a sensation that she had never experienced. It was as if every molecule in her body was reaching out to him, discovering the essence of him. Her tail throbbed with heat. She found herself curling around him; they spiraled together like water flowing. His glow encircled her and sent electric pulses through her spine; and before she knew what was happening, or how to control it, she sunk her fingers into his back and pushed her chest harder against his. He tried to pull away, but her newfound strength overcame him, and she felt herself opening, absorbing him. A tear slid down her cheek as she felt him sinking into her, dissolving, becoming a part of her.

"I'm sorry," she cried, the salt of her tears slipping into her mouth, stinging her tongue. "I'm so, so sorry."

Yet Karina didn't loosen her grip, hungrily sucking every last drop of him inside of her body until he became formless, an echo of himself.

And all that was left was a white glow beneath her quivering blue skin. ◆

HE WAITS

BY *K. H. Koehler*

Ordinary people—which is to say, most of us—have one hell of a thankless row to hoe. No reason to believe anything especially great will happen, but pretty damn sure that something bad will show up eventually.

We can't count on being lucky. But that doesn't mean we wouldn't like a little something nice to surprise us, every once in a while.

I utterly love the voice of this very fine story by K.H. Kohler. I feel like I know her Gracie very well, from a lifetime of late night honest conversations with genuine people who you'd think deserved better than they got.

Ordinary life is hard.

But it can always get better. Or worse…

What's in a name? I've always wondered.

For instance, my mother called me Grace, but my friends all call me Gracie, even though they know I hate it.

Another example. It was my late night at Stanley's, and later still when I pulled open the door of The Clubhouse, located just a block north of the bar. Two different bars with two different names. The Clubhouse is no different than Stanley's, just another Irish pub in a long line of Irish pubs on the tourist strip that connects two little mountain towns. And, yet, the locals like to call The Clubhouse a "lodge," as if that means something.

Names have power, I suppose.

Inside, there was warmth, light, snatches of conversation and music—not karaoke, as in Stanley's, but something classical that I didn't know the name of. Couples passed me as I stood there apart, staring at the wood-paneled foyer, then peeked ahead into the adjacent dining area. Late-night diners filled the room, everyone with someone. A man rose from his seat and approached me with a courtly smile.

"I'm pleased you were able to make it tonight," he said. "Our table is waiting, my dear."

He took my coat and then tucked my hand into the crook of his arm, guiding me into the dining room. I could feel his warmth, smell his clean washed scent as he leaned in close. It reminded me of vanilla. And apples. Pine needles and the wild scent of the forest floor at night. "You look tired."

"I am. A little."

He didn't offer useless advice, which I've always hated. You shouldn't work a job you can't handle, Gracie. You shouldn't be out late. You shouldn't, shouldn't, shouldn't. But for money and survival, we do a lot of things we don't like.

Then we were seated across from each other at a corner table, a wide berth of empty tables surrounding us—had he paid to have this part of the room emptied?—vinyl-bound menus on our plates, and his enormous hand warm and heavy over mine.

My first impulse in the foyer had been to tell him he'd made a mistake. But I knew he hadn't, that all this had been planned from the start. He was familiar, yet completely unknown. I had never seen this man before in my life, but I knew him. I'd always known him. It was a disturbing thought, thrilling. I felt my heart lurch into my throat where it ought not to be. I wished I'd fixed my hair before leaving work, freshened my lipstick, changed out of my uniform. Too late now.

"You look perfectly fine, my dear." He spoke with an absurdly formal European accent, the kind that comes and goes and is impossible to pin down.

The owner waited on us himself. The man ordered, and I listened to his voice, barely registering what it was I was about to eat tonight. It didn't matter. The owner dashed away and the man leaned forward to touch my cheek from across the table.

There's nothing quite like the feel of a man touching your face, I decided.

"I've missed you. How was your day?"

"Busy."

"Stanley has you on late shift again?"

"Stanley always has me on late shift," I answered with more bitterness than I'd intended. A part of me wanted to pour it all out, how Stanley kept hiring young barmaids who wanted early hours, how those barmaids always managed to get them, even though I'd been with Stanley for five years. I didn't complain because I needed the money. But I didn't want to talk about Stanley or how money made you do stupid things, how it broke your pride.

He gave me a sad, fond smile as if I'd said it all anyway.

I felt a burden lift.

He was tall and lean in a dark suit—not quite black, but close—with a crisp white shirt open at the throat. His big hands tapered to slender, agile fingers, not the big, blocky hands that most men had. I liked his hands. He wore rings, which you almost never see anymore. His face was young, youngish, the bones pronounced, not handsome but striking, unforgettable. His hair was silvery, his eyes a pale, hard wolf-brown that probably looked amber under certain lights. His mouth was almost lipless and very severe, in the European manner. I didn't mind it at all.

I felt a current of heat moving in my lower regions and wondered how I'd come to be here. I usually went straight home. But for some reason, maybe no reason at all, I'd wanted to be surrounded by a faceless crowd, people-watch and pretend, take snapshots into other lives, anything to put off seeing that lonely little trailer on Cedar Road, with the porch light on and the cat waiting to be fed.

"What are you thinking?" he asked, his mouth arching up on one side slyly. He didn't smile, only smirked. He was very good at smirking.

"Tell me about yourself," I said instead.

He frowned and stared down at his hands. "Not much to tell. Same old story. Have you been getting along?"

I told him about work. About the job. I mentioned college, and how I'd had to drop out when my mother got sick. I talked a great deal about my mother. How so often I got sick when she did. How my hair had fallen out. Silly things. Our dinner arrived, and I kept talking, about my paintings, about how I'd given up painting— no money in it. It's no fun to starve. I never talked about my art except with regret, but now there was no regret, only barefaced logic. I went on about Stan giving me work when I needed it most. My girlfriend Roxanne had gotten me in. It had saved my life. I'd never have covered all my mom's medical expenses, and later, funeral costs, otherwise. He listened with rapt attention, commenting only when absolutely appropriate. Warmed by the wine, relaxed, I felt at ease with myself for the first time since forever. I thought of the phrase *comfortable in my own skin*. I felt unguarded. Fearless. I started putting more into my stories about work, the seemingly impossible and illogical things that happened in bars at night, patrons who said and did ridiculous things. He smirked as if my stories were witty and insightful.

Over coffee and amaretto, I finished by telling him about Roxanne, how she'd disappeared one night late after leaving work. That was three months ago. She turned up in a drainage ditch a month later. They said she'd been into drugs, a deal gone bad. The decomposition had been so bad, it had taken her dental records to identify her. There were a lot of drugs up here in our mountain community now.

I thought I'd sullied the mood considerably with my story, but if so, he didn't let on.

"I'm sorry about Roxanne," he said, sounding genuinely sincere. "But I'm also pleased that you're safe. And here with me."

"Here in the restaurant?"

"Here," he repeated. "With me." His voice changed. It sounded almost metallic in resonance. People looked around when he spoke, not at us, but around, like forest animals at a watering hole alerted to immediate danger.

I should have been afraid, I suppose. You don't go with strange men, especially these days. But I was empty tonight, too tired to be afraid. Too used up. "So am I."

"Are you?"

"Yes, of course." I glanced around the empty dining room. "I guess we're the last ones."

"We're among the last, yes," he answered.

"Well," I said.

"Well," he answered. "Shall we go out into the great October night?"

I didn't want to say no and spoil the mood, so I let him collect my coat and together we stepped out into the quickening nighttime air. It was cold, the last of October shedding its skin, so I walked close to him. I watched him lumber along seamlessly in his long height, his hands in his pockets, pedestrians parting in currents for us. We walked in comfortable silence down the familiar streets, not to my car but away from it. I started saying something about that, but he cut me off. "I'll retrieve it later." His voice was soft, unconcerned. He didn't ask for my keys.

The stores on both sides of the street were lighted from within, antiques shops, nail salons, mini-marts, video rental stores, and, at the very end, a seasonal shop selling costumes. I remembered that tomorrow was Halloween. "It's always such an odd time of the year. Halloween," I said. My breath plumed in the dark.

"The night when the walls between the worlds grows thin," he said, as if quoting from some arcane passage. His head was up as if sniffing the night air, his profile as sharp as a blade.

Inside the costume shop, a girl of thirteen or fourteen was picking out one of those witch costumes that comes in plastic packaging. I stopped to watch her, but I was really watching him. I couldn't understand how someone like myself, short and squat and redheaded ugly-pale, could have won such a companion. He looked like an actor, a dispossessed royal.

Ten years ago I was in a bad car accident. My boyfriend at the time had been driving us home from a Christmas party. He'd been stoned, but I'd been too desperate for a companion to complain. He'd driven off the shoulder, down the embankment, and into a telephone pole. The impact put me in a coma for two days. He didn't make it, even with a seat belt. The doctors said I'd had blood on my brain, and if someone with a mobile phone hadn't come along, I wouldn't be here now. Sometimes I wonder if I'm right in the head.

"Do you like Halloween?" he asked suddenly, drawing me away from my thoughts.

"Yes," I answered automatically. I had no bad memories associated with it.

"You were a witch when you were her age," he said, watching the girl move toward the fairy costumes next.

"Yes. My mom made me a costume. Not like they have today. It was just a choir robe. And I made a hat out of cardboard and stapled Christmas tinsel to the inside so I'd have silver hair." I looked up at him.

"How clever," he said, sounding both droll and amused at the same time.

I slid my arm over his, feeling impetuous for once. His arm was warm through his coat. "My grandmother was a witch," I said suddenly. "A real one."

"And what did she teach you?"

"Nothing. She died when I was four."

He touched my hand touching him. "Shall I walk you home?"

"Two miles?" I laughed.

He smirked. "Why not? You can tell me more about your grandmother the witch along the way."

"And your family."

"What's that?"

"Tell me about your family." Tell me your name, I thought. What if I ran into someone I knew? I wouldn't know how to introduce him.

"I don't have a family," he said.

We walked. It seemed like a very short two miles. I didn't want to talk about myself, so I talked about Halloween instead. At some point we talked about how mixed-up all the traditions were. We both became very quiet when we passed the stretch of road where Roxanne's body had been found. They said some animals had really been at her, her pretty violet eyes eaten out.

"The Japanese don't have evil demons in their mythology, just vengeful ones," he was saying.

"You mean like avenging angels," I answered when we'd reached the end of the street and turned down the narrow gravel road that led to my trailer.

"If you know their names."

I wasn't cold anymore. The night had heated up considerably . . . illogically. It felt like August again, and I could smell the green apples in the old tree behind my house, the one with the twisty branches that my grandmother used to tie wind chimes and charms to.

"There's no difference between angels and demons," he continued.

"Is that what you are, my angel?" I said, and then I felt ashamed. I felt my cheeks burn in the dark. I hoped he couldn't see.

We reached the weedy lot in front of my trailer and he turned and took my hand. He kissed the inside of my wrist and my pulse jumped against his cool lips. "Shall I come inside?" he asked. His thumb brushed the inside of my palm.

I thought about us together in my bed, in my sheets that I washed to smell like lavender. But I didn't want him seeing my tiny, meticulous, sad little house, my sad old cat, my waitressing uniforms washed dull of color, hanging from the shower curtain pole. All the furnishings that were my mother's but not mine.

He narrowed his eyes. "Would you prefer we looked at some stars?"

"I don't know their names," I said.

He wore a very long, wool coat with a London label, which he spread out on my dirt drive. Then he lay down on it and motioned for me to join him. It was fun to think he didn't mind wrinkling his beautiful coat. It made him seem less lofty . . . and more so. I lay down next to him and he put his arm around my waist and drew me close. This close, I smell his velvety soft aftershave and his hair that smelled of lavender and linen, like my pillow in the morning. I could feel the faint scratch of his beard. He pointed out Orion, and then the Morning Star, though we couldn't see it just yet. I listened to the rumble of his voice deep in his chest. I liked the sound. It reminded me of a storm far off, just before the rain.

"Shall I love you?" he asked at last, looking at me.

My heart started knocking again, painfully. I'd only ever had one other lover, the boyfriend who'd almost killed me. "I don't even know your name. Mine's Grace."

"What do you think my name is, Grace? Guess."

I didn't know what to say, so I blurted out "Jonathan." When I was little I was an only child, and I'd had an imaginary friend named Jonathan.

It was stupid. I shouldn't have said it.

"You're correct." He smirked. "May I love you now, Grace?"

I wriggled around a little, the stones of the drive grinding into my back. My waitress uniform was twisted funny on my body. Jonathan rolled over on top of me, covering me in warmth and strength, and lowered his mouth, kissing me gently and urgently. The inside of his mouth tasted like coffee, almonds, and something else, something darker, like cinnamon. He was very quiet atop me but his eyes shone silvery-dark, like the nightseeing eyes of a wild predator at home in the deep woods. He breathed harshly against my throat, his big, wise hands sliding around me, fitting my contours exactly. I was glad it was dark. I wished it were darker still. I wished I were thinner. My clothes quickly got even more twisted.

My coworker Rose was the first to notice the difference in me the following morning. "Busy night?" she said, tilting her big head with its big, outdated bouffant, her heavily mascaraed eyes x-raying me as I swept by toward the locker room to drop off my shoulder bag. I tried not to smile. I had a secret now, just not one I wanted to share with Rose. If I did, everyone in town would know about Jonathan in approximately ninety-five minutes. Then it wouldn't be my secret anymore.

"Oh, you know," I said, straightening my uniform as I joined her at the serving station to squeeze the remnants of Hellman's and Hunt's into their appropriate bottles. I was still sore, good sore. Last night, when Jonathan finally came, he'd lunged into me so fiercely my back was scraped raw by the gravel.

"Not Tyvek?"

Tyvek is a big trucker who lives right off the highway in a huge, falling-apart, turn-of-the-century Victorian with his seven kids. His real name is Mark Stevens, but his house never gets done, and everyone who passes it calls him Tyvek. He leaves me big tips and smiles a lot when I serve, but so far, it's never moved beyond that.

"It's not Tyvek."

"Who is it, Gracie? Do tell!"

"It's no one you know."

"So it is a man!" Rose cracked her gum obnoxiously.

I should never have volunteered so much information, I realized. In less than twenty minutes, everyone at Stanley's knew I had a gentleman friend and Stan himself was giving me concerned looks from across the room. It was like having a dozen parents standing over you.

Then things started picking up, folks pouring in to get drunk before their big Halloween parties, some in absurd costumes, and I found I was too busy keeping complicated drink orders straight in my head and carrying dishware to and from the kitchen to think much about anything. Tyvek wandered in to shoot pool. Manny, our town veteran, came in and sat solemn in his corner, drinking beers and whiskey chasers until Stan gave me the sign to cut him off. Then Manny went out back to throw up.

Sometime after dark, Stan called me into his office. I knew he would ask me to work late, as he had been since hiring Patty, the new girl who never showed up but still got all the early hours.

Stan was typing invoices into his computer when I came in. He looked concerned, but Stan always looked concerned, especially since The Clubhouse had started cutting into his business. A lot of tourists liked it, maybe because it didn't have locals like Tyvek who spent all night cracking cue balls or drunks like Manny who threw up in their Dumpsters.

"Gracie."

"Stan, what do you want?"

"Did you see the paper today?"

"No," I said. I never saw the newspaper unless someone left one behind in one of the booths. It wasn't in my budget. Why pay to look at bad news?

"Another girl went missing in town. A schoolie, but they think she may have run off."

"Anyone we know?"

"The Carson girl."

"I don't know them." My grandmother did, though. My grandmother had known everyone in town. All of them had gone to her for advice at some point in their lives.

Stan finished his invoice, hit Save, and turned to look at me. "When did you meet your new beau?"

I bit my lip. Maybe it was the baby fat my body had neglected to shed at age thirty-five, or my name, or that I didn't have a barbed tongue like Rose, but everyone treated me like a kid. "Stan, what does that have to do with the Carsons?"

Stan shrugged. He was short and squat and balding, like a Jewish banker gone to seed. Nothing much to look at. But then, neither was I. Except my hair, which is the red of poinsettias, like my grandmother's in the pictures in the photo album at home. "Drifters, you know?"

"He's not a drifter," I said, feeling defensive.

"Then what is he?"

I thought about that. Somehow that had never come up last night, either at the restaurant, or later on, while we were rutting like a couple of randy teens on the gravel of my driveway. I woke around noon with my good soreness and a headache and a fear that I'd imagined everything. But then I checked the drive, and sure enough, my car was parked there, and there was a note taped to my door that read in small, precise script, *See you tonight, Grace.* Not Gracie. Grace. I'd stood on the porch in my bare feet, mindful of any copperheads that might be sunning themselves, and felt my cheeks burn, like there was someone nearby who might see, who might learn my secret. After that, I made myself a Spam and mayonnaise sandwich for lunch and started getting ready for work. But I kept thinking about Jonathan. I kept thinking about how he'd felt inside of me, about how he smelled like a summer rain, and how I felt like a void now, something gone. Missing.

I'd just assumed he was a businessman or an intern at the big pharmaceutical company that moved in ten years ago and was feeding the starving economy of our mountain community. Since the company had divisions all over Europe, it wasn't unusual to find foreigners around. I liked talking to them in the supermarkets, listening to their accents.

But Jonathan wasn't a part of our community, so he was naturally suspect.

"He's none of your business," I said, and stomped out of Stan's office.

Of course, I had to work late, since Patty pulled a no-show, no-call. At least Rose went home early, so I got a respite. Behind her back, we call Rose the Grand Inquisitor. Around nine my feet were hurting and humming and I was getting tired of patrons calling me little darlin'. It took everything I had to go the last two hours. Stan finally came out and made me a drink, a whiskey sour with a lot of cherries in it, the way I like it. "Sorry if I pissed you off, kid," he said, shoving the drink down to me.

I finished wiping down tables and sat down on a barstool in my bare feet.

"I worry about you, Gracie," he said. "All alone the way you is."

I shrugged. I'd taken care of my mom when there was no one else. I took care of my house, my bills, my old rattling Impala. I was a big girl. I could handle anything. I could handle Jonathan, too. He'd phoned a half-hour earlier to tell me he wanted to walk me home, that it wasn't safe to be out alone in town tonight. Maybe that should have sounded scary, but his voice on the line had been just as nice as it had been in real life, maybe nicer, dark as molasses pie and just as sweet and compelling. He hadn't sounded condescending like Stan, only concerned. I was something that belonged to him, something to be kept, protected.

"I don't want you to wind up in trouble," Stan said.

I wondered if Jonathan was trouble. It wasn't rational to want someone so badly so soon after meeting him. Maybe natural, under the circumstances. I'd been alone a long time. But it couldn't be a good thing. Nothing good ever happened to me.

"You have such beautiful hair," Stan said. "You look like your grandmother, Gracie."

Stan had probably known her. Or maybe his father had. One day I would be the old witch down the lane, just like her.

"You want I drive you home?"

I considered his offer. I thought about Roxanne and the strange inevitability of Jonathan's presence in town. Stan might be right, of course. Maybe he's heard something. Stan kept up on the news, unlike me. But Stan had a huge, jealous wife who called him six times a night on his cell. If she saw me in a car with Stan, I'd get fired, and I couldn't afford that. "I can drive my own car, Stan," I said. "It's only a couple of miles."

Stan took my drink and freshened it up. He went in the back to get more cherries. I wondered why he was being so nice to me. Then I knew. He was going to ask me to work till closing tomorrow again.

"Strange men are a bad omen in this town," Stan said on his return.

I sucked cherries through my fingers one by one. They were the really sour kind. I stirred the drink and drank down a sweet, burning gulp. "You worry too much, Stan," I said, watching his sad, fond smile flit over me.

He was still smiling that way when my world faded to black and my head hit the bar.

I woke cold, on concrete, in a dim little room. Tonight wasn't nearly as warm as last night, and I was naked. I instinctively curled myself up. There was a funny taste in the back of my mouth, and a cottony quality to my thoughts and fear. I've never spent much time away from the mountains, but I knew enough to know I'd been slipped a mickey. They used to warn us about such things in college.

I was lying on my side, and my hands and ankles were tightly cuffed and there was a wet gag in my mouth. I could feel the metal of the handcuffs grinding against the concrete floor as I struggled to push myself upright with the aid of a nearby wall. The wall was cedar, sweet and musty, and the room smelled just as fallow, though there was a sweeter, wilder smell beneath that. When my eyes had adjusted sufficiently, I made out the gray contours of a small wood-burning stove at one end, a big blocky ice chest on the opposite side, and what looked like cages covered in a heavy vinyl tarp. I didn't need to see the place by daylight to know it was a hunting shack, the kind so many menfolk around these parts use from October, when deer season starts, to just before January, when the snow gets too deep to hunt in. The gag wasn't necessary; the shack was probably miles deep into the woods, and tonight was Halloween. Menfolk were taking their sons and daughters around the neighborhood. I could have screamed at the top of my lungs and no one would have heard me except the squirrels and chipmunks, and maybe a passing black bear.

I was shaking uncontrollably from the cold. There was a sick feeling in the pit of my stomach, and my head felt like there were loose pinball parts rolling around my skull. When I was fully upright, I leaned against the wall to rest. Maybe I passed out, because when I opened my eyes again, I saw pinpricks of almost painful light burning against my retinas. Someone had lit candles, which threw light but no warmth. Someone, somewhere, was chanting in a language that sounded like Latin spoken backwards.

I tried very hard not to make any panicked little noises, concentrating instead on the chanting. It didn't really sound like Latin—or Low German, or Pennsylvania Dutch, or any of the languages of the mountain people I knew. Maybe it was something else.

Then it stopped. That was bad. I didn't want it to stop. Really bad things would happen now.

More candles were lit, as well as an old-fashioned kerosene lantern of the kind miners used about a hundred years ago in the hills around here. The lantern clanked as it was hung up high. It didn't throw any more heat than the candles, but I saw, in the shaft of light that followed, that Stan stood over me, dressed in a black cowl, watching me with passive curiosity. I felt a queer spike of relief mixed with my panic; in that moment I realized I'd been expecting to see Jonathan's face. I rattled the cuffs. This must be a joke of some kind, a prank, except Stan was too boring to do something like that. I felt cornered. My cuffs clattered against the wall as I started frantically moving around.

"Stop it." Stan kicked me, the pointed toe of his boot catching me under the breastbone.

My stomach seemed to lurch into my mouth and I fell forward onto my face, my throat and nasal passage suddenly clotted with the sour remains of my lunch earlier in the day. I floundered, fighting to breathe, panic clawing through my body. Stan finally turned me over and tore away the gag so I could vomit properly all over my own face. I didn't feel much like talking after that, and even less like moving. It was enough that I could breathe.

Stan didn't bother to explain himself. It's not at all like in the movies. There were no clever delays, no dramatic monologues, no last-minute rescues. This was real life. Stan didn't care if I understood what was happening, though in the hour or so that followed, I had plenty of time to ponder the possibilities. I lay on my side on the floor and watched him arrange a circle of red and black candles in the center of the room. From the cages he took what looked like very drugged-up animals. Two chickens, a cat, a copperhead. These he butchered slowly and methodically with a large serrated buck knife in the center of the circle of light, using their spare dark blood and limp entrails to scrawl ideograms in the places between the candles.

A lot of mountain people have grandparents who were into the craft. Many have libraries of books you won't find anywhere else. There are antiques shops all up and down the tourist strip where you can find just about anything if you look hard enough. I have a whole trunk full of my grandmother's old rootwork books. There was any number of ways that Stan might have learned about the ritual. It might have been something taught to him by his own grandmother. The pub was falling by inches. He hated his wife. I don't know why he was doing it. Why do men look for power except that they don't have any?

Stan had with him a bundle of sticks and cloth, what some folks locally call a *gris-gris*. He placed it in the center of the circle and untied it. I couldn't see what it was inside, but I could smell the meaty stench of it. I wondered if it was animal or human. I thought about Roxanne, her pretty eyes gone, the Carson girl gone missing. Patty. I wondered how many others had disappeared, presumed missing, run away.

Stan tromped toward me and took hold of my cuffs. Then he was dragging my panicked, sweating, whipcording body into the center of the candlelit circle. He was chanting again, intoning prayers to gods I didn't know, in a language unsuitable to human tongues. I made hiccupping noises, couldn't help myself. Stan had that big, serrated buck knife in his hand again—he probably used it to skin the deer he and his hunting buddies shot—and lowered it to my face so it filled the whole of my vision. I was crying through the fresh vomit on my mouth. My throat was sore. I'd been screaming continuously since this had begun, I realized. Not that it much mattered. We were miles into the woods. No one here but deer, and deer don't care what we humans do to each other.

"Quiet, Gracie," he said again. "Be fucking quiet." He didn't say it sinisterly, but with enormous ceremony, like he was telling a child to hush in church. His big meaty hand clutched at my throat so I couldn't make much noise. I struggled in the center of the circle, which wasn't exactly straight anymore because I'd knocked over so many of the candles while I was flailing around. I realized now that there were runes and things carved into the floor, things to conjure. Names. Stan squatted over me like he wanted to have sex. I think I would have been okay with that, anything to delay that knife going into me. But Stan didn't want sex. He wanted blood. Power. He wanted his god, which I guess is what we all want.

I brought my leg up and kneed him awkwardly in the balls. He sucked in a quick breath at the impact and I saw his face flush with pain. The pain seemed to travel up his body and take root in his fist, because he hit me with it then, so hard my jaw cracked against the floor and I tasted sharp fragments of teeth in my cheek. I experienced a stunning silence. Stop it, Gracie, he was saying. Don't fuck this up for me. His knife came down fast and sliced across the plain of my cheek on the left side.

This can't be happening, I thought. Oh God, this can't happen. I'm ashamed to admit there was very little I wouldn't have done in that moment just to live. Just to live a few more minutes. I would have done *anything* to keep that knife away from me.

Stan's voice changed, softened. Yay for schizophrenia. "Such beautiful hair, witch's hair." He touched me and I screamed even though there was no more scream left in me. I was still screaming when he grabbed me by the chin with his big, square hand and ran the hideously sharp edge of the knife along the back of my ear. I screamed as the worst pain imaginable needled into my head on that side, and I screamed louder still at the effortless way the knife scraped past my ear. I felt my scalp begin to give in strange and unnatural ways . . .

"Stop."

He did stop, too. Just as the voice said.

There was blood everywhere, on the walls, on the night-blackened windows. Head wounds bleed a lot. I turned my head painfully, mechanically. Outside the circle stood a lean, dark figure. I smelled vanilla, and August, and I knew then who it was. I tried to speak, but only little gasping wheezes escaped my mouth. My voice felt like it was all broken up, like the pieces of sacrifice all around me.

"You came," Stan said, standing up, standing back. He sounded surprised to have succeeded. "I've been calling you."

Silvery-amber eyes penetrated the dark, taking in the sight of the circle, the offerings lying at his feet. Finally, he looked at me. His eyes observed but did not react. I supposed that wasn't his way. "You called. I came. But I did not come for you." The lights of the candles flitted and shadows darted across the cedar walls in funny ways, making Jonathan seemed larger, winged. Surreal.

I could feel Stan's sudden panic. His glee. And his terror. "No. I made all the invocations. All the sacrifices. I offered you the best I could find in this shithole of a town." With the knife he indicated the gris-gris at his feet. "I raised you. I did."

"Perhaps," Jonathan said with little interest. He stood absolutely still, like a photograph of a man, not a real one. "But you don't call me." Now when he looked at me, it was with the eyes of the night before. The waiting and the hunger.

Stan's terror turned to indignation. I could feel the fission in the air between them. He gulped. "Please, my dear sweet lord. I've given you the best sacrifices," he insisted. "I'll give you more. Anything for your services."

Jonathan smirked but there was no humor in it. It was like a statue giving horrible life to expression. "I want her. Give her to me." The voice that came from him was different now, like a roll of thunder off a distant mountain. It did not seem to emanate from him at all. It came from some other place.

Stan yanked on my hair. My injured scalp screamed and I screamed with it, over and over, like a machine.

Jonathan barked words in that other language.

Stan stopped. He looked frantic, confused. "I don't understand. I am the master. *I* command. I even have a name for you, my lord. Astaroth. A crowned prince of hell . . . "

Finally, Jonathan stepped into the lantern-lit circle. Around his feet moved the glinting, writhing shadows of copperheads, which are very prominent in the mountains. In the summer months, you can't go ten feet without spotting one. They practically leap into your shoes. The copperheads slid over his feet like sleek jeweled ropes. Jonathan smirked. He was very good at it. "I already have one."

"I don't understand. The book said names have power . . . "

"You *don't* understand," Jonathan insisted. "You have called me, but you cannot bind me with names, man. You've come too late." He marched forward with swift confidence and took Stanley by the throat with his big hand. He must have been very powerful, because Stan never had a chance to resist or to fight. He brought the knife around but then dropped it clanking to the floor at his feet. Jonathan turned with him toward the door of the hunting shack, which swung open on well-oiled hinges. Beyond it I saw smoky, dim, purplish light. And beyond that, the worst noise imaginable. I remember one summer visiting my distant cousins higher up in the mountains. They ran a slaughterhouse. The sounds I heard beyond the doorway reminded me of the pigs with their throats being slit, only worse, because I knew there were humans making those noises, noises that humans cannot make but do. The sound cut me like Stan's big knife and kept me down on the floor as Jonathan dragged Stan relentlessly forward toward the noise and the void.

I cried then for Stanley. Nothing he had done in this life could be as bad as what waited beyond that doorway. Then darkness shielded me and took away the nightmare for a time.

I woke in the hospital, in a warm bed of white sheets. The doctors had stapled my scalp back into place and it itched but I wasn't allowed to touch it. I felt sick from all the pain meds they'd given me. Rose came round to see me and tell me about what the police had found in the hunting shack, all the remains in Stan's ice chest, and how lucky I was that some hunter in the woods had heard my screams and had called it in to the police on his cell. Otherwise I might not be here now.

I slept fitfully, and I tried to block the noises in my dreams. I still heard them, though. I knew I would always hear them.

They discharged me three days later and I went back to my saggy little trailer and sad cat and half-finished paintings. They were giving me money on disability for a while, so I was okay until I found another job. A waitress can find work anywhere. Obviously, I wouldn't be working at Stanley's anymore. He was wanted by the police for the abduction and murder of several local girls, and for his assault on me. The police had put out a dragnet for him, but I knew they would never find him. They didn't ask too many questions of me. Someone had pulled my records and decided I wasn't right in the head. I told them what I could remember, except for the things Jonathan had done, and said.

I went back to living. I tried to be satisfied with life, with being alive. Things were hard at first. But then they got easier. I found you can live through anything.

I woke Christmas day, listening to the chimes in the trees outside and remembering that ten years earlier I'd spent my Christmas in a coma. Only a few weeks ago I'd nearly died. I scratched at the scar on my cheek and turned over. Jonathan was lying beside me in bed. I was startled, amused, reassured. He'd looked very good in his clothes, but he also looked very good in my sheets. I realized then that I knew he would return, that I'd been waiting all along. "You came back," I said, sitting up, clutching the sheet against my chill.

"Grace, I never left."

My heart ticked in my throat. I was afraid to move, afraid I might be dreaming. Afraid to come awake. "Did Stan really call you?" I asked.

He watched me, wisely. "Sometimes blood calls us. Sometimes only desire." He smirked. "It's hard to know the difference."

"He called you Astaroth."

"He was ignorant." He narrowed his eyes and reached out to touch my face with the back of his fingers. "We wait to be called. To be named."

"And then?"

"And then, like anything, we belong."

"Will I ever know who you are?" I asked.

"I'm Jonathan." He rolled over on top of me, where he felt just perfect. At home. He pushed my nightgown up my legs. "Shall I love you, Grace?" he asked. ✦

HAPPY HOUR

BY *Laura Lee Bahr*

*Laura Lee Bahr came to L.A. from the Utah wilds—in Hollywood terms, pretty much out of nowhere—as a writer and actress with an oddball brain and talent to burn. She's written and starred in a couple of fascinating no-budget features (*Jesus Freak, the little death*) and plays (the musical* Gothmas*) that made me a fan.*

I've worked on several projects with her—including the first three drafts of the demonic-as-hell Jake's Wake *screenplay, to which she contributed greatly— but I had no idea she also wrote fiction until she handed me the soon-to-be-published mindfuck novel* Haunt, *which I immediately adored.*

So I asked her to write me a somehow-lovable hardcore exorcism story. And that's exactly what she did.

Please welcome this genuine Renaissance sweetheart to the literary fold.

First drink's on me.

It was south of 6 P.M. at the Lamplite Inn. The working stiffs were loosening their ties and lips as they made the most of the last of happy hour. He was one of those stiffs who very much wanted to forget that he'd spent his day doing "data compilation" and resenting his superiors. He snubbed their expensive watering hole for the Lamplite—a no-frills place to get sloshed on the cheap. You got darts, a crappy old jukebox and ugly bartenders. Cash only. Stiff drinks.

He was into his second glass when she walked in, a pretty wisp of a thing with straight brown hair, a gray sweater, and a knee-length skirt that showed just how perfectly put together she was. He might have whistled a little under his breath and watched her, the way the rest of the stiffs watched her, as she took a seat near the end of the bar with empty stools all around. They were all sure to swarm suddenly, so he thought he'd better preempt them. He'd never been afraid to have a pretty lady insult him, so what the hell.

"Can I buy you a drink?" he asked.

Her fingers had been playing with a clasp on a small handbag, but they stopped. "That would be lovely," she said, her voice as light and sweet as a buttermint.

He flagged the bartender, who had a well-lived-in face and deeply exposed leathery cleavage. "What'll it be?" she asked, in a tone like a threat.

"Whiskey, rocks," the young lady said.

"The well, okay?"

"The well is fine," the girl said.

He interrupted—knowing the well was certainly not fine—and ordered a proper label drink for her. The girl politely accepted the upgrade.

"My name is William," he said.

"Lily," she said, extending a small white hand to him. He took it and shook it. His heart flopped over like a dog begging for a tummy rub.

The bartender brought her drink, and Lily sipped it while he tried to think of what to say. It left his mouth before he could swallow his tongue to stop it:

"What's a nice girl like you doing in a place like this?"

She didn't answer. He knew he'd blown it. Sport a dumb line like that once, and that's all you get. She was already looking around as if searching for another place to sit. She took a large gulp of her drink and then looked him in the eyes.

Hers were deep, deep brown, reminding him of those belonging to a movie star whose name he would never remember.

"That's a bit of an existential question, don't you think?" she answered. Pretty *and* educated. Uh-oh.

He shrugged. He'd never been smart, and wouldn't even dare to pretend to be. "You just seem nice, is all," he said. He knew he should just walk away now with his tail between his legs.

"I used to be," she said. "I worked very hard to be a very good, moral person, to be a good example to my younger siblings. I am the oldest of six, so I wanted to make sure I only made decisions I would be comfortable with them emulating."

Big family. That meant Catholic or Mormon. She was in a bar, so that should eliminate Mormon.

"Catholic?" he asked.

"Yes."

"Still?"

"Oh, yes. Nothing like being exorcised to really solidify one's Catholic faith."

"Huh?" He hadn't heard her right, obviously.

"Are you trying to pick me up?" she asked, straight-up.

He could only respond with the truth. "Well, yeah."

"Well, then you should know before you proceed trying to pick me up what it is that you're trying to lift."

"Ohhhkay," he stammered. She talked straight, but he could still barely follow. She was beautiful, she drank whiskey, and he was fairly certain he was head over heels in love already.

"I used to be a nice girl," she said. "Then I got raped by a demon."

He wasn't certain where the lower half of his jaw was, but he felt a definite breeze drying the inside of his mouth. He couldn't properly clear his throat, nor look away. It was a long moment, but it was definitely his turn to say something.

"Whoa," he said. "Bummer."

She shrugged her narrow shoulders and stared off ahead of her. Her voice was sweet and soft. "Yes."

"Uh, well . . . huh. Are you okay? Now?"

She gave him a half-smile that was so much like the first touch of sunlight after a season of storms that he had to watch it and see if it would warm the sky. "I am okay. Thank you."

His mouth found its bottom half, and his teeth clanked together. He knew he should move away now—run away, even.

But she was so pretty. And her drink was empty.

He ordered her another one.

They made small talk. She grew up in a rural town in the middle of the country. She came to this city to work because she had wanted a fresh start, and she fancied the skyline. When he told her he lived a few blocks over, she relayed that she was working as a receptionist two streets south. He couldn't help thinking that it only made sense for it to be *his* place if he got as far as a "my place or yours" toss-up. But, of course, she was far too nuts for his box of chocolates.

He was tempted to try, though. This beautiful girl seemed to genuinely enjoy his company—something just short of a miracle these days. He'd been down on his luck with a barely serviceable job (but thankful for a job all the same) and what felt like few prospects. He was not a handsome man; he'd been called "ugly" within earshot enough to have few illusions about that. He worked out, tried to eat right, and used quality personal grooming products. He'd never be a *catch*, but he was a decent guy. A guy other guys liked to have around and a guy girls liked to have as a friend.

He'd had girlfriends, sure, even one he thought might lead to marriage. That relationship had just ended recently and nastily. This girl, Lily, was the prettiest girl who had ever given him this much of her time. And even if she had just told him something bugnuts crazy, she didn't *seem* crazy. Not at all. In fact, she seemed so down-to-earth that he found himself wondering if he hadn't just imagined her reply to his pickup line. But then again, he'd never had much of an imagination.

"Do you have a boyfriend?" he asked.

She shook her head.

"Pretty girl like you without a boyfriend?"

She laughed. "Yeah. Go figure. But the whole being-raped-by-a-demon seems to be a bit of a turn-off."

He nodded his head. That made sense. What didn't make sense is that she shared this story in the first place. "Why do you tell people?"

"Because if someone's worth my time, they're worth the truth. If someone wants to get involved with me, they should know what they're dealing with."

She had no malice in her eyes or the half-smile on her lips, so it was obvious that she wasn't trying to play some joke on him for some secret dare or her own amusement. It was clear to him that she believed what she said, even though it was hard to imagine that anyone else would.

"Well, so, people believe you when you say all that . . . stuff . . . happened to you?"

"I wouldn't say that."

"But you still keep saying it."

"I've been through a lot, and I don't believe in lying about it or pretending it didn't happen just because other people don't believe it." Damn. She knew how to sound like she was making sense.

"So . . . you were possessed?" he asked.

She nodded. "For about a year and a half."

"And then, you got an exorcism?"

"Yes."

"And that worked?"

"Eventually."

"So, how long have you been . . . clean?"

"About two years."

"And you haven't had a boyfriend since then?"

She shook her head. "Still not back in the saddle, so to speak."

"But you're . . . cured, right? You're not going to get possessed again?" he asked, remembering that there was definitely more than one *Exorcist* movie.

"The Bible says something that scares me."

That the Bible said something that scared her . . . now *this* scared him. How religious was this girl? How totally bonkers? Why was he still sitting there?

And as if answering his unasked question, she began:

"*When the unclean spirit has been expelled from a person, it wanders, lost, through a waterless region looking for a resting place, but it finds none. So it says, 'I will return to the place I came from.' And when it returns, it finds everything clean, swept, and put in order. So it goes and gets seven other spirits more evil than itself, and they enter and live there; and the last state of that person is worse than the first."*

She had finished her scripture and her drink and was staring at her empty glass, but also seemed to be staring into space. This was it, his cue to excuse himself and run for the hills.

"So, how did it happen?" He had never been good at taking cues.

She turned her doll-like face to him, her eyes registering him as if just remembering that he was there, but there was a gratitude in them as well, that he had stuck around. His heart flopped over again.

"I was at school. I got this amazing scholarship, and I was sent on a full ride to this elite women's college. My mom didn't want me to go. She was worried that I would become a lesbian, or fall away from the faith, or fall in love with a Protestant, or any number of things that seemed terrible to her at the time. So, she worried a lot, but she certainly didn't worry about what *actually* happened. That's a funny thing about worry, you know? She was worried about the big, wide world and the liberal elite, when what she should have been worrying about the unleashed powers of Hell. You'd think as a devout Catholic she would have thought of it more literally.

"Anyway, there I am, a freshman on a full-ride scholarship at a private school, feeling on top of the world. My brain is taking in all these amazing classes and lectures and all the people seem so cool and interesting, and I am excelling at everything. Thriving. I get straight A's my first semester, I'm involved in clubs and nonprofit work. My professors like me, my classmates like me, everything seems in bloom. I have never been more happy.

"So, second semester—a couple of weeks before midterms—my roommate is staying over at her boyfriend's school, which happened fairly often. Suddenly, at exactly 3 A.M., my eyes suddenly burst open. There is a feeling of electricity running through my body. I don't know what's up . . . why I'm suddenly awake. But I hear something outside my room, in the dorm hall. A sound I can only describe as coming from an animal being skinned alive. It's a terrible sound. No one else on the hall seems to notice . . . at least, no one's stirring. I get up and go to the door. There's nothing that I can see. Our dorm halls are lit, even at night, and it's totally empty.

"But then the light at the end of the hall starts to flicker. The lights are those industrial kinds they have everywhere—the um, what are they called—?"

"Fluorescent lights?" he said

"Yeah, fluorescents, but there's another word. I can't remember now. It's not important. You know what kind of lights I mean—those long rectangular ones? Anyway, it starts flickering there at the end of the hall, and I begin walking toward it. I realize now, that was my mistake. It was calling me with that flickering, but I didn't know. I just started walking toward that flickering light, not really thinking, just moving.

"I walk to the end of the hall, and the light flickering goes out. So now that end of the hallway, it's dark. And it's not even a second. Not even a full second that I feel this thing—I feel this chill——like, there's no way to describe it. It's not even like cold. More like shivers up and down your spine, but it's everywhere, all over. It's paralyzing, maybe it's fear itself, I don't know, but I can't move. I'm frozen in place, and I'm just staring at . . .

"At nothing. There's nothing there... just this terrible feeling and this light that just went out and that's it. And I am telling myself—because I think of myself as an intelligent person who is not at all superstitious, you know—that I just had a nightmare, and I am standing here in the hallway getting spooked by a light going out and the sound. Must have been, well. . . . maybe I had a nightmare I couldn't remember. Who knows? But I am telling myself to move now, and my body listens and I start moving. Walking, now, back to my room. I shut the door and lock it and think, okay. I am okay. Then I get back in bed.

"That's when I see it, waiting for me in the darkness. This thing beyond description. This thing so hideously ugly you can't even imagine it. It's a huge goat creature standing upright, covered with hair and what looks like scabs and sores. It's got this huge, bifurcated penis . . . and it's erect.

"I scream as it leaps on me and pins me down with its hooves, which are pressing into my joints and bones that feel like they're breaking beneath its weight.

Its yellow eyes are glowing and rolling back in its head as it tears apart my nightgown and claws down my heart, tearing into my breasts and belly. Then its two-headed cock-thing just pounds into me like two saws attached to a jackhammer.

"As much as I thrash or move or scream or struggle, the more it seems to enter me, to impale me, to gouge deeper and deeper into me and then just let loose this burning deluge of acid inside me.

"And I am screaming and screaming as this thing brutalizes my body, rapes me, twenty minutes, thirty minutes, an hour, it seems like four days and then finally, the door busts open and campus security is there. But I don't feel relief. After all this, I am sure that I am going to die and this thing will kill them, too. But then, just as I've accepted my impending death, this monster just . . . vanishes with the shadows as the lights come on."

William could hear the sound on the jukebox; it was Neil Diamond singing "Sweet Caroline." He had forgotten where they were. He had forgotten to doubt. He remembers now. "What did the security do?" he asked.

She shrugged, then started chewing on her lower lip. He felt that everything she said before, she said matter-of-factly, like she had said it so many times it had lost all meaning for her. But whatever happened to her next was somehow *worse* than that.

"Well, they see me," she continued. "They know *something* happened to me. I mean, my clothes are all torn up and ditto the bed, but they see nothing of this thing. And that's the way it all gets reported—that they didn't see my perpetrator—and the more I tell them what this thing was, the more they start looking at me like I'm insane. Well, I tell them the truth, I tell them everything. I tell the doctor the truth when he examines me. And the doctor—well, I should say doctors, there were many of them—they find, of course, that while it's clear I've been beaten up, they don't find human semen or human hairs or human anything. You see, they neglected the fact that the demon was clearly not *human*, so of course they wouldn't find anything human staining me. They decide if it isn't human, it's nothing. So instead of believing me, they believe what they can conceive of . . . that I've had a psychotic breakdown.

"As you'd expect, word about the incident spreads like the flu. Word about campus is that I made this whole thing up—that I tore up my own bed, clawed and brutalized myself. That I am sticking to this story of demon rape to get attention, or because I'm losing my mind or because I was raised in a religious household, and that cognitive dissonance—*there's* a college word from my first semester—the *cognitive dissonance* from the way I was raised with the current academic scholarship of my environment helped exacerbate this mental breakdown. Such *bullshit.*"

Lily put her face in her hands and started sobbing.

The bartender looked at William with a "Should I do something?" shrug. William quickly held up two fingers for two more drinks. He was way too sober. The bartender put the glasses down in front of them, prompting Lily to look up.

"Thank you," she said, wiping her eyes and nose with the back of her gray sweater. And then to William, "Thank you. You are very kind. A real peach." She gave him a smile that turned him to liquid. "That's what they used to say in my grandma's time to say that you were really great. *A real peach.*"

William wasn't sure whether the force tugging at his heart was pity, compassion, or some other nameless emotion he'd never felt before. He wanted so badly to wrap himself around her small shoulders. He wanted to envelop her and tell her he'll protect her against the shadows.

"Did you leave school?" he asked.

"Sure did. I took the recommended leave of absence for medical and personal reasons. And I went home. My family, they actually believed me. You can't imagine what a relief, what a wonderful beautiful feeling it was to know the people I loved most in the world believed me."

He nodded. He wanted to believe her. He's never wanted to believe anything so much, fucked up as it is. But he didn't. He couldn't.

"And I was happy to be home," she continued. "Until . . . well, it starts at night. I wake up again and again at 3 A.M., and I feel it inside me, clawing at me, kicking at me, holding me down from the inside and ripping me up. The pain is unimaginable . . . terrible. I start thrashing and screaming and going into fits. Then it starts happening at any time, during the day, even. Everything starts to blend together, and I have a hard time remembering what happened when. I start forgetting what I'm doing. I often faint from the pain and black out and when I come to, well . . . and this is the *really* weird part . . . I find out that I've done things. Terrible things."

"Like?"

"Like eating bugs, my own feces, and urine. That sort of thing. I sodomized myself with a votive candle and tried to do the same to my sister. One day, I awoke from my stupor and saw my mom's arm in a sling because I had thrown her across the room. I remembered nothing."

It's one thing to watch a movie with an actress spitting up green soup, and quite another to hear a girl you are hitting on tell you she ate her own shit. William wasn't sure what to do with the fantasy he was clinging to—of kissing her with an open mouth. All of his desire, which had stayed just as hot even during her terrible story of the demon forcing itself upon her, now distinctly chilled. He found himself looking elsewhere as she continued to speak.

"Of course, my parents call in Father Greenfield, our family priest. He's heard almost every confession of mine and after hearing my mother's hushed, 'There's something wrong with Lily, Father Greenfield,' he comes right over, expecting me to have a fever or something. Instead, I'm all eyes rolled back in my head, foaming at the mouth, thrashing against these belts my parents had used to tie me to the bedpost to keep me from trying to kill myself . . . or someone else.

"Father Greenfield is a fairly scientific man for a Catholic priest, and he figured there was a better explanation than the possession story. He theorized that the goat creature was actually some sort of animal that had attacked me and that it, and now I, was suffering from rabies. It's a really good theory, I admit. Leave it to a priest to come up with the most reasonable explanation."

Of course, William thought to himself. *It makes so much sense! Perfect sense.* He felt so relieved! Rabies. He'd never known anyone who'd had rabies before. He kept his jubilation to himself, however, certain that *she* didn't go for the rabies bit.

"So, where do I go but back to the doctor," she continued. "Anyway, doctors, doctors, specialists, doctors, and then more doctors. In the end . . . they don't find a lick of evidence of rabies."

"Really?" William asked, unable to censor his disappointment. "They didn't? It totally sounds like rabies." It *had* to be rabies. Rabies is what suddenly allowed him to believe her, and of course, not believe her at the same time.

"Yeah, I know. It's a bad situation when rabies becomes the best possible option. If only it had been rabies, then I wouldn't be bat-shit crazy. Right?"

This girl is funny, William thought. *She doesn't laugh or smile much, but she's got a real wit about her.* He smiled at her, and she rewarded him with a gentle look that says he's just given her a bouquet of flowers.

"So, I've been doing all the talking," she said. "I'm sorry for that. But you said you were interested in me, and I'm interested in you, too. So please, please, tell me more about yourself."

"Oh, I . . . no," he said, hoping she wasn't expecting him to talk about *his* life at this point. Listening to his life story, in comparison to hers, would feel like hearing a recitation of the ingredients on a cereal box.

"Do you have a girlfriend?" she asked.

"No. I mean, I did, but it's over now."

"What happened?"

"Oh, uh, well . . . she cheated on me with this guy and then I was really mad. But then I forgave her, and then we got back together, and then she dumped me and married somebody else. That was like a year ago, and I guess I haven't been really *over* that. I mean, I wasn't. I am now. I'm totally over it now."

"How did you get over it?"

"Oh, just time I guess. And . . . I don't know . . . knowing there are other girls out there. I mean, to be honest . . . the second you walked in here I kinda forgot she ever existed."

"You are so wonderfully kind, William. Really. I can't tell you how much I appreciate your sweet words."

"Well, I mean it. I mean, you're something. *You're* the real peach, you know."
And then she blushed.

And he blushed, too.

"So," he said, trying to find words now to stop himself from jumping all over her with his tail wagging and drooling. "How did *you* get over it?"

He was immediately sorry that he brought it back up. He could tell that she was sorry, too.

"Well, I still wouldn't say I'm *over* being raped. I don't think anyone ever gets over that sort of thing. But I am certainly no longer possessed. Of course, I didn't exactly *get over* that, either. More like, got the thing forcibly expelled from me."

He really didn't want to hear about it anymore. He really just wanted to get on with the flirting, close this whole conversation and assign that chapter of her life to the rabies story. But he had brought it up again, and it was only chivalrous to let her finish.

"You had an exorcism."

"Yes, but listen. I'm going to tell you this, and then, William, here's what I want you to do. When I'm done telling you, I want you to get up and walk away, no hard feelings—quite the opposite—I completely understand. Or, if after I have finished telling you, you *still* want to pick me up, I am ready to go wherever with you. I don't care if you believe the story or not. I just care that you have all the facts, and that you are free to make a choice from there. Okay?"

He nodded.

She took a deep breath, closed her eyes, and started on the last part.

"Poor Father Greenfield. He isn't at all equipped for this sort of thing, but he wants to help me so badly, he does all he could. After the rabies tests come back negative, he goes through the trouble of getting what he needs to be an exorcist. Not an easy thing in this day and age, and not an easy matter for a man who's pushing seventy. He is trying to exorcise the demon from me, and doing the best he can with it, but it's an appalling and lengthy process. Months of his chanting at me, starving me, having the thing in me taunting and tormenting him, trying to kill him. And by this time, the whole reason he's doing this—because he is my family priest and loves me—is not even there to say thank you or acknowledge his work. Me . . . the me that *is* me, like the person talking to you right now, is gone. Where am I? Not far. Just outside my body, refusing to go back in there and participate, trying to not watch. Staring out the window, watching the sunrise in the morning and the moonglow at night. Listening to the wolves howl from the woods outside my house.

"It's like that for months. My body on the bed and Father Greenfield trying to get the demon out. Me out of my body, watching the grass grow in the spring and die in the fall, become covered in ice and then covered in snow. I can hear the sounds of worms and maggots and ants. I can hear everything eating and being eaten.

"Then, enough is enough. I am tired of staring out the window. It is night. Father Greenfield is chanting and doing his ritual, the poor thing. He scarcely has a voice anymore, and that ugly thing on the bed that was my body is writhing with all the ugliness and putrescence it can muster. The wolves start howling, as they did at night.

"I was always afraid of them growing up, but I'm not afraid anymore. They're afraid of *me* now. And the me that is by the window, staring out of it, loves these wolves now, loves them for their wild hungry selves. I want to leave now and howl with them. They are calling me, too. I know my body is on the bed, screaming, but me—the me that is me—is staring out the window, and I want to go so badly. And then the window shatters.

"Father Greenfield is shocked by the broken window. I see him shudder with the icy wind that blows in. My body, on the bed, shivers from the cold. It is weak and can't last much longer. I can see all my bones and my skin covered with scabs and sores. I can't hold out much more than the night. Anyone can see that. But that *thing* inside my body doesn't want me to die, because then where would it go?

"The window has been broken open, and the light is starting to break, and I'm sure that I can go now, through that window. And I know that the thing would die inside me. But I feel so sad. I don't want to die. I don't want that thing to win. I don't want that priest to fail. And the demon inside me is so tired with all the months and months of fighting the priest. But me, *my* spirit, I'm not tired at all. I yearn to howl.

"And I know—and I *know*—I can howl it out. I shove my spirit back in my body, and my spirit howls against it, pushing it, shoving it, forcing it out now. The demon is too tired to fight me. It will die with my body or go.

"So it goes. I can feel the evil spirit leaving me, tired, to go look for a place to rest. And the light is breaking outside the broken window. I can see that light, and I know that I am free. And . . . I have been free ever since."

At the Lamplite, the lights have dimmed, the drinks have returned to regular price, and those working stiffs have morphed into the night crawlers.

The hour is getting late.

He has to decide now whether to ask her back to his place or to thank her for her company and move on.

She knows he doesn't believe her, but she doesn't care. And he knows that some crazy-ass shit had gone down one way or another, but no, he doesn't care. Hell, yeah, he's still interested.

"So, do you want to go back to my place?" he asks, surprised by the crackle in his voice and the tears forming in his eyes. This is the strongest choice he has ever made in his life. He has made the decision, free and clear, to take a recovered rabid, religious woman back to his small cramped apartment and try to make love to her despite the terrifying visions she has placed in his head.

He's crying because as he was deciding this, he realized that he just might love her, and she has granted him that possibility by telling him all the worst things about her right off the bat.

Though he doesn't know the worst.

The worst is gathering like a storm in the night. The only warning is an obscure Bible verse that told of the unclean spirit returning with seven more evil than itself. But neither William nor Lily want to believe in anything anymore but the promise in each other's willingness to think the worst is behind them, and the best is in each other.

"Yes, William," she replies. "I want to go to your place. Yes, yes, yes."

He is no match for the things that will wait crouching in the stillness of the dark for her, but he will see them. He will see them, he will fight, and he will lose.

But not tonight.

Tonight, they are happy. ✦

STAYING THE NIGHT

BY *Amelia Beamer*

This stunningly frank and face-punching little quickee comes from another of my favorite new writers, Amelia Beamer, whose first novel, The Loving Dead, *brilliantly recontextualized the zombie plague as a sexually transmitted disease.*

Similar waves are surfed here, in dramatically different ways. It's angry. It's hurt. And it thoroughly kicks ass, largely upon itself. And you.

One of my favorite kind of horror stories.

Get ready to get down and dirty.

Several weeks into the breakup, masturbation just wasn't doing it for me anymore, so I called a handsome acquaintance. Marc and I went from bar to bar on a Tuesday night; it was the kind of evening where our knees were getting on with the foreplay while we were still pretending to have something to talk about. He had long hair, and when he talked sometimes he would take out a comb and run it through his hair. That was such a tease. Like he was showing me how I'd never touch him as well as he could touch himself.

We fucked on a futon at his place. When I was in college we called the standard dorm-room futon a "flip 'n fuck," and so fucking on futons always reminds me of college. There's something not quite (but desperately *wanting* to be) grown-up about it. Marc liked to watch himself going in and out. Like it might get lost if he didn't keep an eye on it. But when he looked into my eyes, it was with an intensity that made my throat tight. His hair hung loose; I fondled it the way men fondle breasts.

Afterwards, I showered. You're supposed to pee, at a minimum, to prevent bladder infections, but I liked to feel clean. I washed my armpits; the smell of my pits always reminded me of my mother's unwashed smell, and I couldn't get it off me quickly enough. I was thinking about how Marc would almost certainly invite me to stay over. I was hoping he'd shower before we went to bed; I liked a nice clean cuddle.

I washed the goo from between my thighs. There was a lot of it. I don't remember using lubricant; I must have been really excited. I thought of Marc's hair. How I wanted to thread my fingers through it and pull.

"You'll want to see him again," I heard a voice say in my head. I agreed.

There was something funny on my vulva. A lock of Marc's hair, maybe? I pulled at it, but it didn't come off. It was stuck. It was shaped like a worm, and felt like flesh. I pulled harder at it, and it hurt. I screamed, then panicked. Did I have a leech? I tumbled out of the shower, dripping wet, the water still running. I wiped the fog from the mirror and squatted on the counter, peering at my bits. There was definitely a worm on my vagina. It was the same reddish color as my privates. When I pinched it, it hurt. I pinched it again. What the hell had he put in me? I felt nauseated. I needed to go to the hospital. I was still drunk, but no way was I hallucinating.

"Don't worry," a voice said in my head. It was the same voice that had told me I'd want to see Marc again. This time I recognized that it wasn't my voice, but I knew that it was right. There wasn't any reason to worry. I could feel myself calming down.

"That's right, you're OK," the voice said. Then I started worrying about Marc coming in and seeing me squatting like a monkey looking at my vagina, and water all over the floor. He'd never invite me over again. I got down from the counter, dried off, and tidied up the bathroom. I started to dress, and my fingers grazed my privates. The worm was still there, but I didn't mind. It seemed friendly enough.

"What do you want to put on clothes for?" I heard the voice say as I put my panties on. It was right. The panties were nasty anyway. I stepped out of them and rinsed the crotch in the sink, then hung them to dry. When I was in college, I carried an extra pair in my purse. You only had to walk home in crusty underwear once to never want to do it again, although I'd gotten out of the habit. College was the last time I'd been single, before I'd grown into my ex like a tree through a chain-link fence.

I touched the worm between my thighs, wondering what Marc would think.

"He won't mind," I heard the voice say.

I squeezed it between my fingers. I rather liked the fleshiness of it.

Naked, I went back to Marc's room. He was reading (so much sexier than watching TV!) and he looked up to smile at me. "Nice tits," he said. "Want to stay over?"

He didn't even notice the worm. "You wouldn't kick me out, would you?" I asked. I got under the covers with him, relieved to not be spending another night alone.

Marc shrugged. "I guess not. I should warn you, though, no guarantees I won't wake you up for seconds." He smiled, and we kissed, and I pulled his hair almost as hard as I wanted to.

He got up and I fell asleep worrying about the toothbrush situation. I didn't have one with me, and the only thing worse than crusty panties was morning hangover mouth.

We were fucking when I woke. It was dark. Marc's face was in shadow, and I wasn't sure who he was until I saw his hair, silver in a puddle of light from the streetlamp. The blankets and sheets were rumpled, as we'd been at it for a while. I wasn't worried. Sometimes I woke up horny in the middle of the night. When I was with my ex it was easy; I'd come to with several hands sleepily rubbing me, and either I'd squeeze out an easy orgasm or we'd wake up enough to fuck. I'd never woken up fucking like this, but I'd had a lot to drink. I thought maybe I should check to see if he was wearing a condom.

"Don't worry," said the voice in my head. "Just fuck. Yesssss."

After we fucked, I peed. Wiping myself, I could feel another worm. "The first one was lonely," the voices explained.

I didn't have any trouble falling asleep, this time. "It'll be a beautiful baby boy," the voices said. I'd never realized how much I wanted children. Things just made so much more sense now.

I woke to sunlight dappling through the curtains. Marc was asleep on his back, the bedclothes tented above him. I watched his face while I ran my hand down his belly. He looked so calm. I wanted to wake him so that I could hear his voice and look into his eyes. My mouth tasted like ass, so I didn't want to kiss him, but there was no reason to waste the morning wood. Getting my lips around Marc's penis had been on my to-do list ever since last night. He tasted of that male baked bread musk. I swallowed his come.

"Well, good morning," Marc said. He put his hands behind his head, and through his hair I saw that he had horns. But I didn't mind. Because it was. Such a good morning. It was perfect. All three of the voices agreed.

The worm on my tongue made it hard to speak, so I just smiled. ✦

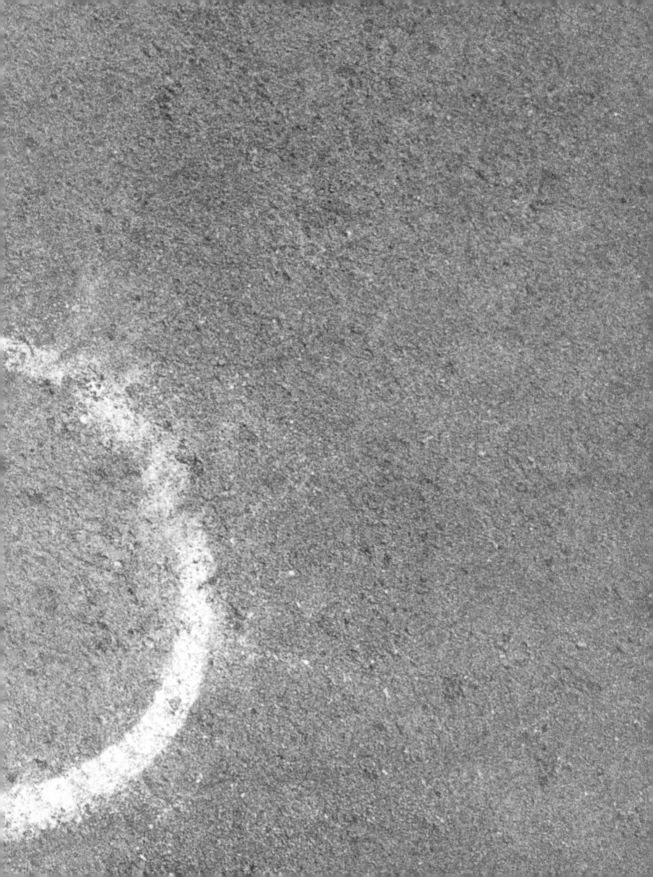

DAISIES AND DEMONS

BY *Mercedes M. Yardley*

Once again, the one and only Mercedes M. Yardley comes through with a couple of pretty damned bad girls that cheer me up the second I'm near them. The kind that give bad girls a good name, if you know what I'm sayin'. And I sincerely hope you do.

This story's more fun than a demonically possessed barrel of monkeys. And sassier, too.

"Hey Pypes! I became demonic since I last saw you! Isn't that wild?"

She sniffed the air. "Pretty wild. Is that why you smell like Eau de Sulfur?"

I shrugged. "Hellfire does that to you. You get used to it after a while. It becomes your new normal."

"And how, pray tell, does one suddenly become demonic?"

"Ugh," I said, and winced. "Don't use that p-word. It burns. It burns like holy water and references to your mother."

"Really?"

"Nah, I'm kidding."

"Loser."

"I know."

"So. The demon thing?"

I sighed. "I lost my head over a guy."

"Old What's-His-Name?"

"David. And yeah, him. Which is pretty lame."

"Not as lame as when the two of you were dating," she said. "Daisy and David? It was just embarrassing. So what happened?"

"Ever been mad enough so that when somebody floats up to you all mysterious-like and says, 'I sense your anger. Wanna come join the dark side and become a minion of Hell in order to get some killer power?' and you're like, 'Why, yes, sure, that sounds like a fantastic idea! Can I start right away or is there a training period or . . . ?' Ever have that happen?"

Pyper shook her head. "No."

"Oh. Well. Don't."

"Gotcha."

"Anyway, there's somebody I want you to meet. He's totally hot."

She perked up. "Demon or human?" Gotta hand it to her: Pypes rolls with the punches. The girl cannot be fazed.

"Demon. Darken that gorgeous lipstick, baby, because you're off to meet perfection."

I grabbed her hand and flashed ourselves into a dark and creepy barn. It felt like home.

"Cool," Pypes said. "Very Goth via 1695."

"Yeah, well, he doesn't live here," I said. "He's just doing some work on the side at the moment."

"So what do demons do?" she asked me. "Do you get paid to, like, show up in magic acts and stuff? Terrorize the audience?"

I thought about it. "Sorta. I show up a lot when humans can't decide whether to make a pact or not. Wear something skimpy, wiggle around, show how good life is on the other side."

"Sounds easy," Pypes said. I could see her mulling it over.

"It's my bread and butter. Sometimes I pick up a couple of gigs on the side. Hang around haunted houses and growl at the paranormal investigators when they poke their cameras my way. They dig that."

"Hey! I saw a couple of reality shows where I swear the demon sounded like you! The guy was all, 'I command you to show yourself,' and you were all 'GET OUT!' and it reminded me of when I'd bring a guy back to the room when you were taking a bath."

"Were my tones not dulcet?"

"Scary as . . . well, Hell."

"Perfect."

She laughed. "So, your hot demon stud. Where is he?"

I sighed. "Ugh. Poor sap. He's currently being summoned by some freak who thinks he's all powerful. It's a pain, honestly, because the humans are all, 'Haha, I control the darkness!' and it's just totally annoying."

"Sounds like it would be."

I glanced at her. "It is. You'll see. Listen," I said, and grabbed her by the arm. "Are you cool with this? Like, seeing a demon and some jacked-up human in their little darkness dance?"

"Are you kidding?" she asked, and her eyes, they shone like stars. "Up my alley, babe!"

"I'm so glad! There he is. Tam. Your demonic Romeo. He's pretty excited to meet you," I whispered.

I wasn't lying when I said that demon guys were hot. Tam was no different. He prowled angrily around the trembling human who was safely cocooned in a chalk circle.

"That's him? Are you frickin' kidding me?" Pyper breathed. If I thought her eyes were stars before, they were tiny galaxies now. "He's gorgeous!"

"Told you."

Tam's naked shoulders were broad. Although he usually walked upright like the rest of us, he chose to crawl more animal-like when he was working. It was good for effect.

He heard us and his head turned sharply our way.

"Who dares disturb me?" he hissed. His voice had dropped several octaves, multiplying until it sounded as though he spoke in several tongues at once.

"That's so sexy!" Pyper looked like she was going to faint with glee.

"We are legion," I said, using the same impressive voice trick that Tam had used. One of the first things they teach you in Demon 101. Simple but effective, and if Pyper's dreamy reaction was any indication, cool as all get out. I jerked my head to Pypes. "I brought another with me."

Tam's eyes lit up, but he quickly masked it by letting them fade to inky black. "I will deal with you later."

He turned back to the human, who had managed to stand up inside his chalk circle. The human spoke in a thin, cracked voice.

"I summoned more of you? I summoned more of you! I'm in command of the darkness!"

I heard that voice and jerked upright. It couldn't be.

"What's up?" Pypes asked me. She stopped staring at Tam's super-fine demonness and eyed me instead. "I know that look. Give me a baseball bat and I'm right behind you."

"That," I said through gritted teeth, "is What's-His-Name."

Her eyes went wide. "No!"

"I'm considering killing him."

She thought about it briefly. "I wouldn't feel too bad about that."

She pushed past me, shot Tam a dazzling smile, and stood nose-to-nose with David. "Hey, you," she said.

He didn't skip a beat. "I am your lord and master!"

Pyper snorted. "Ego, much?" she asked me.

David followed her line of vision and went pale. "Daisy?"

"Swine," I greeted him in response. Tam put his arm around my shoulders, a new growl in his throat.

"This him?" he asked me.

I nodded. "This is him."

"Want me to get him for you?"

"Thanks, Tam, but I'd sort of like the pleasure, if you don't mind."

Tam nodded once and went into full demon mode. Snarling, pacing, conjuring darkness that swirled around the barn and made the air heavy to breathe. The wooden floor of the barn shook under the strain.

"You," Pypes said, and caught David's attention again. "Seems that you and my friend Daisy have some business here. You're the reason she turned demon, did you know that?"

David looked impressed. "Really? Awesome!"

Pypes rolled her eyes. "No, NOT awesome. Seriously? She's like, damned for eternity or whatever, and you're getting off on your power trip?" She looked over her shoulder at me. "What were you thinking?"

I shrugged. "I was young. I was vulnerable. I was schizophrenic, who knows. Oh, come on!" I snarled, when she continued to stare at me. "We all have one relationship that bit rocks. Lay off!"

Pypes turned back to David. "So you damned your girlfriend to Hell. How about an apology?"

David laughed, and I nearly lost it. I felt my eyes flame as doors to the underworld opened up and tiny gibbering dark creatures bubbled out. They giggled and skittered and crowded David, trying desperately to get through the protective circle that held them back.

"I don't apologize for anything," David said.

"He doesn't," I said. "It's part of his douchiness. I turned to Tam. "As soon as he gets out of that circle, I'm going to kick him in the face."

"Circle?" Pypes asked. She looked at the chalk on the floor and back at David. "This is what protects you?"

"Protects me and holds all demons captive! You can't cross it. I am in control! I am your master! I . . ."

Pyper smiled prettily, placed the toe of her boot on the chalk, and smeared it.

"Uh-oh. I broke your circle."

"Rock ON!" I said, and hugged her tightly before surging forward with the rest of my darky dark demon pals. "You might want to look away," I told her, and she hummed sweetly while David's screams rang out.

"You have a little something on your face," she told me later, and wiped blood from the corner of my mouth.

"Sorry that you were privy to raging demonic evil and all that."

"Not a problem."

I turned and grabbed Tam out of the crowd. "Tam, Pyper. Pyper, Tam. Go out. Be happy. Make lots of demon-human babies. Eat people. They're delicious."

Tam grinned, smoke billowing around him in happiness. Pyper looked over her shoulder at me as they walked away.

"I'll call you," she mouthed. I grinned.

Yeah. I won't wait up. ✦

AND LOVE SHALL HAVE NO DOMINION

BY *Livia Llewellyn*

This fresh, savage masterpiece by Livia Llewellyn is perhaps the most structurally audacious, emotionally harrowing kick in the head that this book has to offer.

Fact is, I was genuinely concerned that it might be just too intense to make the final cut, despite all that surrounds it; and was thrilled that its courage and excellence simply could not be denied.

So here's the warning label: this is one of the rapiest rape stories, demonic or otherwise, that I have ever read. And it will hurt you, whoever you are. I'm not just making that up.

But it's sooooo much more—and digs so deeply into the first-person soul of love and evil, with such perversely dare-I-say redemptive power—that I urge you to take a chance on this authentic literary gem.

craigslist > hell > district unknown > personals > missed connections > d4hf

Date Unknown

human star, are u my gate to the world?—(central park west, August 2003)

    it was the night of the blackout--do u remember? time is as one to me time is nothing to me time is nothing, but in ur linear existence it was Then, it was the night the city closed her hundred million eyes. one hundred degrees and still rising as heat bled up from the buildings and streets, anxious to escape into the cool of space, never again to be bound. u were walking up the western edge of that man-made forest in the hard pitch of night, humans stumbling all around, flailing and quaking under an unfolding sky of stars they had never before seen, or simply forgotten existed. humans, brilliant with the Creator's life like star fire and u the brightest of all, but red and gold and white like my fallen Majesty, my sweet Prince, shining in the cesspools of earth he eternally spirals through, a necklace of diamonds crashing over shit-covered stone. and i? i was wandering to and fro upon and over the world, as our divine Prince taught us, and as i glanced down i caught the faint flash of a spark. that is what drew me down and in, the force and fuse of life that comprises ur soul. u felt it 2. do not deny: i know u saw the thick branches of the trees bend and toss in my wake, rippling and bowing before my unseen passage. i saw ur eyes widen, and the bright gold fuse of stargodfire coil in ur heart, darken and drop lower. u quickened ur pace, but u never stopped staring into the primal green mass, ur desire rising with the heat with the wind with every thunderous vibration of my coming. mystery power and the unseen currents of un-nature, revealed in the absence of confusion of un-light and machines--these things drew ur most inner self toward me even as u turned away walking up the long walled side of the forest, running ur hand against the ancient rock, fingers catching thick moss and small weeds, soft fingers scrabbling over hard cold granite sparkling-veined with the crushed bones of things long past. and the wall became my body my horns my mind and i lapped at ur creamy thoughts and the city shuddered in unease, and so did u.

    all parts of u all fissures all hollows all voids will i fill until u open ur mouth and there is only my voice / open ur eyes only my sight / touch ur cunt only my cock / slice ur flesh bleed only my tears.

no need to respond. u will. u already have.

Date Unknown

a thousand times ill-met, yet not met once—(fifteenth floor, office building, midtown, 2005)

u were at the copy machine at work, shaking a malformed manmade thing-- fine sprays of obsidian liquid shot up, landing against white silk and skin. the last of the ink, spent against lonely flesh. do u remember this day? laughter, floating across the floor. and u dropped the object, put ur hands to ur throat as u fled to ur women's rooms, where u sat on cold porcelain and cried, wondering what to make of such a life, a life so open to wonderful wide pain, and yet so mean, so small. u wept, and i licked at the tears--u felt me. fear leapt and coursed through ur body like a hunted hart. but u did not flinch or scream or draw away. i have trained u well--contact such as this in the public arena of slithering man has taught u to suffer my touch in silence, feigning ignorance. my talons slithered up ur thighs, leaving beaded trails of red against ur skin, and while u shuddered in silent terror and pain, i thought of many things.

i thought of u.

i have traveled now, many times through time, threading back through ur life to childhood, to the very first breath. with each stitch i stole, with each nip of the needle and thread of my will and desire, a moment of joy, of hope, of love, of beauty, of wonder was snipped from ur life like cancer, working open the hole through which i will inevitably enter. age two, sitting in ur front yard under the spring's warm sun, watching ur father plant flowers that later burst into glorious blooms- -/--that later withered into putrid stinking masses at the touch of my vomit and piss. ur first true memory, forever changed, because i made it so. ur dog ate those decaying flowers, and died. u wept in ur little bed, and i sifted down through starry night and raised u high in ur nightmares toward them, showing u the whorls of the milky way as i nibbled the tears away. working working working, i stitched myself into every moment of ur life--even at the start, when my clawed hands twisted u from ur mother's womb in a gyre of blood--until the pressing horror of my unseen presence was as familiar and constant as the rain, the hole as wide as the reach of the magellanic. i am everywhere and everywhen: there is no moment when i have not existed for u / prepared for u / planned for u / toiled for u. and now, there is no moment in ur life when u have not existed for me. do u love my work, love?--but u love nothing now, nothing u can see, nothing u can taste or touch with the meaty cage by which u are bound. this is my work, and all those unbidden moments of heart-cracking loneliness, covering ur years until u can barely take a breath, until u long for anything except where and what u are? u are welcome.

despair of everything, my love, even ur pretty blouse, but never despair of this: we shall soon meet.

Sat Oct 23

of all the things I've made—(apartment, west chelsea, 2009)

u are the finest. our terror / our pain / our horror / our screams / our blood that pours from ur skin as i rake it with horns/talons/teeth. my flame-haired shooting star plummeting to earth and u know it is me u are falling into, and u cannot stop. i clear the path like a maelstrom--books and crockery dashed to ur floors, chairs swept aside, food rotted and flyblown with my single breath. un-lights explode, and in the darkness i expand like disease, driving friends / family / lovers / life from ur world. do u not understand? when we are as one, there will be no room for any of this in ur world. no room, no need. only our need. only mine.

u were sitting in that part of the building u have claimed as ur own, curled up in the corner of the largest room, on the largest cushions. images flickered in and out from a screen, and u watched them in silence as u drank yet again from the glass cup in ur steady hands. many times had the sun risen and set over ur city since i last touched and tasted u, laid waste to the possessions u think u love. the screen flickered. u swallowed ur wine and smiled. i watched the soft glint of hair at the back of ur neck, the fine lines around the corners of ur mouth, the curl of ur plump pink toes. untroubled breath, as even and smooth as the beat of ur heart. life, creamy placid and it washed over me, and and andand outside, afternoon sank and evening spread indigo feelers throughout the canyons of machines, and all over the world the swarming insect masses lit their candles and fires and devices, desperate pathetic futile in their attempts to hold night at bay, but firm in conviction. safety like their prayers, false and comforting. no different than u and i. and the little machines ticked the time away and the screen grew dark and u crept to bed. un-light washed in from the streets, dappling neon flashes from cars and signs, oranges yellows reds. and carefully, carefully: i hovered over ur sleeping flesh, sinking as slowly as the constant decay of space. ur heartbeat weakened, ur breath deepened--i tasted fear, felt the cold familiar terror envelope u. a dream i came to u as--a nightmare, and u frozen in my grip. but yes. yes. i descended, sliding my arms around u, the phantom lover of ur dreams, dark and dangerous, all-enveloping. and u unfroze, ur body pooling against mine. we lay together under the unfurling universe, my exhaling breath caught by ur inhalations. so soft and warm, so perfect a fit. as if this is what we were made to be.

do u remember Catala, on the beach, thirty-six years ago, before it sank into the sands? u were only twelve, and u fell through the rotting deck of the beached ship while looking for treasure. i stayed with u for a day and night, until they found u. i made the cold ocean waters warm and kept the crabs and gulls at bay, and i put my hand on ur heart and held u ever so tight, my horns and wings ur shelter, my body ur bed. i thought u saw me, through the veil of your tears. i thought u smiled. i thought i kissed ur lips. i may be wrong.

no, that memory is gone. it never happened. i ate it away; and then i broke ur legs.

human star, do u remember this night, this moment? remember it now, for tomorrow i shall wander to and fro again, back into the night into this pocket of time very pocket this NOW and i shall cut and fuck and burrow and rape my way into us and devour devour DEVOUR us until it has never happened until until we have never until until until FUCK FUCK FUCKING COCKSUCKING CUNTFUCK laksd WOEIFF

Δ; kd Σκι;φκΛΚΦΚΔσδφΣkdΛ ΛΚΔΦ ll;ΣΙΕ λδσσδ;

o

Sat Oct 23

<u>iron fist in a pale-skinned human glove</u>—(apartment, west chelsea, 2009)

star nursery of my desire, womb of my existence, do u remember this afternoon remember this afternoon and how it bled into the night like the child u had in windy ellensburg, the girl u left in long glistening strands of plasma redblack gouts of soft flesh blood on the floor of the bathroom as i stroked ur salt-wet hair, great rending sobs and the quaking pain splitting through ur curves ur tears lost like catala in the fires of my touch

no.

NO NO NO

do u remember this afternoon, pale and grey in ur endless grey city, open-mouthed ziggurats gnawing at the sunless sky? u stood at the window, wine glass full and dribbling in ur hand, staring at scudding clouds tentacling their way over silent-screamed rooftops, that familiar buzz undrowned by the drink, that familiar whisper and soft thundered deja-vu that this day was happening again. yes. ur breath fogged the window, and u placed the glass on the sill, raised ur hand to wipe it away, and--within that sliver of a second as the tiny beads of moisture floated off the glass u saw me behind it, saw the glint and gleam of my eyes, the curve of my fanged smile, the heft of my fist and all the attendant power and glory of the universe, all the secret places the Creator has forever kept from u all the stretches of dark matter and the knowledge that blossoms under the light of a hundred billion alien suns. u saw all, and the blood rushed into the core of ur flesh surrounding the stargodfire and u staggered back from the glass, pissing urself as I burst into the room, slamming through u like an errant asteroid. U hit ur head on a table, small moans seeping from grimacing lips but no time to scream or shout because this isn't happening how could this happen this only happens in dreams. I grabbed ur ankles and swung u around, my footfalls like lightning strikes against the polished stone, and ur fingers grabbed at tables chairs fallen books the edges of doors, and I rose u high like a flag, ur hands sliding up the doorframe, little threads of blood left behind with ur nails, and I ripped ur garments like tissue like breath like clouds and thrust my wriggling claws up inside, and finally u screamed, and in the bedroom against the quilts and childhood blankets I threw u down, pressing

pressing and still u screamed in a city that only ever screams, only ever the sound of our breath the low dark explosions of my heart and clap of wings and the endless thrum of traffic and the uncaring world outside. I punched ur face and blood sprayed benedictine against our mouths, broke ur wrists down against the cloth, forced ur legs wide open my talons biting ur flesh ur cunt dark red and raw like a setting sun and I sunk into u my barbed cock splitting working working the hole and o god the bright gold fuse, the Creator's spark so close and my tongue deep in ur throat and my fingers against it choking and ur breasts soft warm scratched a thousand times by scales and I rammed u rammed u rammed u and this world so close now so close to everything that had ever been torn away

small fingers against the curve of my tail, u smiled

what have i

there, there, and ur sobs so soft and low and u spoke a word, a single gold fused plea passed from ur lips to mine i drank it in a gossamer silken wisp of the Creator, of u: and i slowed, i slowed. o my love, i slowed.

Sat Oct 23

is this what Humans want?—(bedroom, west chelsea, 2009)

this day i have plunged into a hundred thousand times, and all about us the universe spins and reverses, spins once more, once more. do u remember this day, this afternoon, this evening, unfolding again and again and again, unfolding like the bruised cream white of ur thighs, the swollen purple dusk of ur sex, the blood-split lips of ur quivering mouth? i sliced into ur beach like the catala, i thrust the sands part, and there was no resolution, no joining, and the golden red stargodfuse flickered and floated in the unreachable distance as i lay spent between ur wet dunes, rusting, sinking into entropy and decay. that moment, that slow delicious moment, i have yet to find again. u said nothing u say nothing, every troy-like day upon day, u flinch and grimace and turn away and i pin ur face like a wriggling insect crushing ur jaws with my nails until the bones grind and bend, roaring and biting obscenities into ur tongue, and still u do not speak. do u remember it, that single slow moment when our eyes met, when u truly saw me, when u touched and whispered to me as a lover? i think i no longer do. i think it was a human infection, a trick of the Creator, a cancerous dream.

shadows sifted through the room like ghosts, cast from the same clouds, the same sun, the same sky as ten thousand days before. they are as familiar now to me as ur body against the red-stained sheets, staring past the ceiling into a future i cannot fathom or divine. my hand pressed down on ur chest, feeling ur heart gallop under all the layers of bone and skin, and u grew quiet and ur breath stilled and daylight crept from the room. i thought many times of peeling u apart, burrowing clawing through the layers into ur dying center, gnawing the bones and piercing ur eyes with the shards, snapping each rib one by one by one until ur lungs grew still and the arteries drained and ur small firm heart nestled against my palm, until i bathed in all the molecules of ur meaningless life, draped myself in ur soul, and rose anew, as one with everything u ever were.

how everything changes with a single word

how do u live ur life like this, so apart from everything in this vast existence except ur distant Creator, so at peace with being alone, apart. we lay next to each other in blood and piss and tears, my horns tangled in ur matted hair, our breath winds in and out of the others lungs, and ur eyes see nothing, ur skin feels nothing, u do NOTHING to seek me out, to discover what terrible invisible glorious power binds u to this moment, compels u to relive this day again and again. all my work, all throughout time, to make u pliable / soften resolve / sweeten despair / sharpen fear, so long have i toiled and crashed against uFUCKING LOOK AT ME LOOK AT ME SEE ME. see me like u did that first day that one time please i beg of u SPEAK TO ME O human star o love. are u a test. have i failed.

do u remember the word u spoke to me. do u remember the smile. will u not give these again? must i bite and scratch and claw it out of ur face and cracked teeth clattering down as i pull apart the cartilage grind the tongue meat forked and shredded searching seeking destroying but u do not remember. i eat each day and vomit it up and gorge it down again, until everything u ever were in me resides, the fuse that drives u mine.

must i take everything. do i.

yes

Date Unknown

<u>a Gnossienne of the Heart</u>—(unknown)

do u remember when i left u? do i remember when u left me? Time is measureless to me, Time is as air is as the dark wounds and tears through which i travel unseen and endless horizonless alone. and the city spreads out below me glittering sequins of tiny human souls thrown down against a net of electric fire an inferno of falsity and lies encased in canyons of profane steel. and i but rancid garbage caught in the dervishes of machine-made wind, adrift and without purpose. o my Prince, is this what u see, u feel, as u wander to and fro amongst ur souls? and the forest below is still, and ur brown-stained bed sheets empty

Time is weight. Time is measured calculable movements of human-forged horror, each as slow and meaningless as the one behind and before, Time a river, Time a great hooked chain dragging us to no place with no purpose, tethered bits of flesh. Time divides.

o empty star, each day i descended into the churning engines of Time, of un-nature and un-light, i descended amidst static and disruption, iron blades backwards, clocks unwinding, water in circles recoiling fast away. and the hospital shuddered at its granite foundation, patients vomited and bled, tongues spewed languages long dead, and all things foul and fair cried out as i worked worked worked against Time. before ur bed ur wasting flesh i stitched myself to the fetid air, commanding u to arise, to wake and fall into my arms, to say the Word as u had once said it before. walls cracked and mirrors shattered, and the Creator's minions scurried back and forth in their wine-dark robes, chanting His lies, evoking our brothers to save u. but my flies and shit kept all who thwarted me away, their eyes bled when they read His lies, and His book became as ash in their broken hands. again and again, i lowered myself upon u. u did not stir. milkglass eyes. parched lips. i placed my tight-sewn mouth ever so gently against urs, against ur nipples, ur cunt. everything u ever were is gone. everything i ever

no

in the indigo hour before dawn, in that fleeting sliver of light when i can catch my reflection in glass / silver / stone, i stare at the wide black gash of my mouth, now forever shut. cruel Prince, to give ur loved ones only half the knowledge, all the pain. beneath the thick iron stitches, swollen skin, bright gold stargodfire rests beneath my tongue, warm and alive. everything u ever were, everything u will ever be. everything i ever--

and the pain comes not blood or flesh or bone it rolls over me and the knowledge o sweet Prince the knowledge the burden of Time, the horrible skip of my heart. i have u have all of u possess u tight and neat and IT IS NOTHING. NOTHING. nothing. and ur hand, so small, at the small of my back. what i would give. what i would give. and i cannot swallow cannot breathe. it is all that is left.

and in the indigo hour before dawn, after the quakes have subsided, i slipped between the rough sheets, curled by ur side. my hand so large against ur belly. ur hip warmed my cock, and my breath dampened ur breasts. and when i left, when morning chased me away, they found u bruised and beaten, ribs cracked, acid teardrops festering in the hollows of ur neck, skin dissolving like sand in the hissing waves.

o my human star. one second. one moment. one word. i have all of you and nothing, except one moment one word. i would give anything. i would give everything, to bring it back.

everything.

so.

Date Unknown

the last lost day—(ocean shores, washington, 1975)

and ur little body lay crumpled in pools of water, cold ocean-old pools of salt and sand and rust. the groan and crack of decaying metal all around, hiss of the waves rolling in with winds and night, and above u, the jagged hole still weeping with ur blood. beyond: endless darkening skies, and nothing at all. pain at one shoulder and fear at the other, clarion-calling each other like long-lost lovers, and the waters rising ever so higher, hitching up ur broken bones, ur flowered dress, ur slender shivering thighs. screams pure and high as starlight shot through the air, never breaching the hold, falling back down all around the cavernous waste.

u closed ur eyes. and the waves rushed and thumped against the wreck like the beating of some great unseen heart, and the waters lapped and caressed ur waist, slid across ur small breasts, lifting u up and down. and the cold grew in power and nimble fingers of water pushed the hair from ur forehead and eyes and black winged summer night closed in, around, down, furnace-warm but not enough to keep away the cold. and hard uncaring, unloving ocean covered ur lips, slid forked rivulets of brine into ur mouth, down ur throat and u breathed it in, and the world and the waves and the wind grew to pinpoint, ur body a million years away, and all that was left of the universe was nothing--/

/--was a kiss: a bright gold fuse of stargodfire unfurling from a single whispered word coiling into ur heart, an explosion of wings unfurling and lifting up, hot breath against ur face, warmth thunderclapping through ur blood and bones, and the roar of the waves thrusting against the beach, the hand at the small of ur back, a lover's touch at ur face as u opened ur eyes, standing alive and whole on the beach before the Catala, rusting high and dry above the grassy dunes.

and u stood shivering hound-like, dripping wet hand at heart, under the white gulls' cries, under the scudding clouds and the lowering sun, stood before the Catala, the ship with the hidden treasure, the ship u had never set foot on--/-- fallen on bled on died. Stood until the nerves bit and prickled in ur legs, and the shadows lengthened and reached u, brushing against ur toes / the small of ur back / the tender hollow of ur neck / the translucent flesh of ur ear, all set afire by unseen whispers warning u away, and: u flew, a girl-shaped human star shooting up the long flat dunes through the grass and over the naked driftwood piles, racing away the miles of stone cold coast until u seemed as small and unreachable as the far-off circling gulls, never stopping, never looking back through all the joyful goldenfused years of ur life at the broken wreck back on the beach, the broken black-hulled monster rusting away, un-stitching un-working un-working, repairing all the broken moments until Time endless Time spiraling Time swept it all away, scrubbed it down to clean pure sand upon which my love, my memory, had no reach or purchase, until all that remained of the moment was U, and the Glorious Word.

do u remember now?

i do not.

u do.

M⊙M

BY *Bentley Little*

It's no surprise that Bentley Little is one of Stephen King's favorite modern horror writers. They share a common grasp of the everyday gone mad: of regular things we take for granted gone horribly wrong in ways that we probably should have seen coming, but somehow didn't. And now it's too late.

"Mom" is no exception. But it is exceptional, in that nobody thinks quite like Bentley Little, or would have handled this deranged little domestic dramedy in quite the same way.

In that sense, he more resembles another pop culture King favorite: cartoonist Gary Larsen, whose legendary "The Far Side" cartoons routinely flipped the world over, landing it on its pointy head.

Just the other way around: horror first, and laughs second.

"Oh, Jesus," Rudy said. "It's Mom."

I glanced in the rearview mirror. Sure enough, the old bitch was running after us along the center stripe of the highway. Even in the dark, I could see the whitish glow of her permanent smile, the bits of bone showing through her shriveled arms and legs. She was as naked as the day we killed her, only she'd deteriorated, started to fall apart.

I sped up.

She kept up with the car for a moment or two, but flesh and bone are no match for metal and gasoline, and soon she was just a white spot in the distance.

Then we turned a corner and she was gone.

"What are we gonna do?" Rudy said. "She knows where we live! She'll come after us!"

"Shut up for a minute and let me think, damn it!" I drove into downtown Austin, turning left, turning right, going nowhere, wanting only to keep on the move. Rudy was right. If she'd found us here, if she'd come all this way, she probably knew where we lived. She could be heading to the duplex right now, and I imagined us going home to find her standing in the dark living room. Waiting.

Smiling.

The thought made me shiver.

"What are we going to do?" Rudy demanded.

I looked over at him. Even in the dim illumination of the dashboard lights, I could see the fear on his face. "We're going to leave," I said.

Mom had preserved my afterbirth in a jar of formaldehyde and presented it to me on the occasion of my eighteenth birthday. At the time, I failed to see the intent behind this peculiar action. I didn't know how I was supposed to behave or what I was supposed to say, but it was clear that, to Mom, this was indeed a symbolic and highly important moment, and I forced myself to treat the gift as if it meant the world to me.

But that was the beginning of the end, and after that I realized intellectually, consciously, what I'd only felt instinctually before: Mom had to die.

On Rudy's birthday, she sacrificed a hamster on the kitchen counter and tried to get him to drink the blood. He was getting ready to go out with his friends to celebrate, and she kept following him around the house with a red-splashed orange juice glass, whining that he needed to drink it before it got cold. Finally, he exploded and knocked the glass out of her hands. "Leave me alone!" he screamed, and ran out of the house.

Mom stared after him for a moment, hamster blood dripping from her clothes and face and hands, then she silently returned to the kitchen. I heard her cutting up the rest of the hamster's body, and when I peeked in a few minutes later, she was swallowing furry strips of its flesh.

"What's wrong with Mom?" Rudy asked me late that night when he came home. Mom had locked herself in her room, although whether she was asleep or not I couldn't tell.

We kept our voices low. "I think she's crazy," I said.

"I know that, but . . ."

"But what can we do about it?"

"Yeah."

"I think she should die."

There was a short pause. Rudy looked at me, nodded. "That's what I was thinking, too."

We said no more, but it was a pact.

We didn't kill her right away. We had to think about it, plan it, work ourselves up to doing it. She was our mom, after all. But her behavior grew even stranger, and she spent a lot of time in her closet. We found markings on our mattresses when we came home from work or school, spots of blood on the undersides of our pillows. It was as though Rudy's birthday had triggered something within her, and she seemed determined to draw us into her madness. She kept saying that we were old enough to join her, but join her in what she never said and we never asked.

One morning, she baked a mud pie in the oven, then broke it into thirds, pushing a piece across the table to each of us when we came in for breakfast. She crumpled up her own piece, letting the baked dirt fall into a glass of water before stirring it with a spoon and drinking it up.

"We will call him together," she said, leaning across the table, a disconcerting fervency in her voice.

"Who?" Rudy asked. "Dad?"

She started laughing, laughed so hard that she couldn't stop, laughed even through the coughing fit that followed, and we backed out of the kitchen, looking at each other.

We killed her that night.

She was in her bed, masturbating, and Rudy shoved the pillow over her head while I stabbed her stomach. There was very little blood, and not as much resistance as I expected. She struggled a little but didn't really fight, and I suppose that should have been the first indication that something was wrong.

Rudy called 9-1-1. There was no effort made to cover anything up. As we'd discussed, we left everything as is, and when the police arrived, we told them that we'd found her here, the way she was. In my panic and distress, I'd pulled out the knife, but she was already dead and nothing I could have done would have saved her.

I'm not sure we were as distraught as we should have been—we certainly weren't crying—but no one seemed suspicious, and I thought that maybe our reactions were typical of people in shock. We were questioned again over the next week, several times, alone and together, but stuck to our story of complete and utter ignorance, and I guess we sold it, because we were never pressured or accused of anything.

We were left alone.

As soon as we felt that we were in the clear, we went through her stuff. We *found* things. They didn't tell us much, but they hinted at the secrets behind her actions. There was a knife made of sharpened bone, a carving of a naked woman and a monster on its hilt. There were jars of blood on a shelf in her closet, all meticulously marked with the names of the animals from which the blood had apparently been taken. In the back of the closet, on the wall, was a painting of a monster not unlike the one on the knife, a hideous creature of hair and scale, with wild eyes and a wilder mane and sharpened teeth dripping with grue. It looked Indian or Middle Eastern to us, at least the writing did, but it also looked new, not like some ancient relic but like something that had been painted recently. I seemed to remember her saying a foreign word of some sort when she was doing something crazy—pissing on the pages of a book or squishing bugs into fingerpaint for the windows—and for some reason I thought that word might be the name of that monster.

The idea frightened me, though I had no idea why.

Rudy didn't like what we found either, and even after we threw everything away and cleared the house of her stuff, we both felt uncomfortable there. More often than not, Rudy spent the night with friends, and I took to sleeping at work or in the library at school. Finally, we both decided to sell the place, and while the murder had to be disclosed and no doubt brought the price way down, we managed to unload the house at a profit, and we put the cash in the bank and rented a small cabin on the opposite side of town, near the lake.

We thought it was over.

It wasn't, though.

She'd called us on the phone a year or so back. We didn't believe it was her at first—she was *dead*, for Christ's sake—but there was no denying the authenticity of that voice or the knowledge it carried. She began screaming at us, yelling things half in English and half in some language we did not understand. It was on my cell phone, but we both heard her, and I cut the call off and immediately had my number changed. Rudy changed his as well.

A week later, our old house burned down.

There was a glimpse of her by the lake one night, dancing crazily, arms flailing, and at the end of the month we took our money out of the bank and moved halfway across the state, from Denver to Cortez. Nothing happened, but the town was small and we felt exposed and after two weeks there we were more paranoid than ever. So we packed up again, moving this time to Texas, the city of Austin.

Here we felt safe. Even if she could somehow *travel*, there was no way she could walk hundreds of miles through two states to find us.

And until now, she hadn't.

But tonight we'd seen her, she was here, and once again we were faced with the choice of where to go.

I announced my decision at a gas station.

"Los Angeles," I said, and Rudy nodded.

Los Angeles was a thousand miles away. It we weren't safe there, we wouldn't be safe anywhere.

In the morning, we got our money out of the bank.

And left.

I remember, as a child, wondering about Mom's behavior. She had driven Dad away, alienated our neighbors, and she scared most of my friends. Even when she was acting normal, doing everyday things, there was an intensity to her conduct that put people on edge, that made her uncomfortable to be around.

One time, when I was about ten, she cut her leg open. She said it was an accident, but her pants were off and a knife was in her hand, and the blood was dripping into a frying pan. It didn't look like an accident to me, but I pretended to believe her, and when she asked me to bandage the leg with tortillas affixed with duct tape, I did so without comment.

When I finished, she grabbed my head and pulled my face close to hers. "He has made me stronger," she said with a fierceness that frightened me, and though I thought at the time she was talking about Dad, I realized after she died that she was probably talking about someone else.

Some*thing* else.

I kept seeing in my mind that painting in her closet, that Indian or Middle Eastern monster. It was a demon, I supposed, and I actually dreamed about it the first night we were in California. We were staying at a hotel near a freeway, and in my dream Mom was in the next room over. She was alive and we were a family, and when I heard weird noises through the wall, I went next door to make sure she was all right.

There was no furniture in the room and no roof. The walls were made of plywood, adorned with foul paintings and foreign symbols. In the center of the cement floor, the demon, twice as tall as a man, was raising its head to the dark sky and howling. It was naked and aroused, and beneath its scaly tail, Mom was working furiously, her hands spreading apart the monster's buttocks so her head could fit there. The tail was hitting the wall as it whipped back and forth, and that was the sound that had alerted me.

"Mom!" I called, but she ignored my cry.

The demon didn't. It turned its head in my direction and laughed, a hideous screeching sound that pierced my eardrums and caused them to bleed. The monster spit at me, and within the green sputum that landed at my feet was the ragged remnant of my father's head.

Both Rudy and I had long since given up on school, but between us, we'd amassed quite a work history and had gathered enough skills that we were able to find jobs even in a rough economy. We rented an apartment together in Norwalk, and Rudy got work with a plumbing contractor while I was hired by a landscape gardener who needed an extra tree trimmer. One of the other tree trimmers, a guy named Juan who barely spoke English, was in hiding from a drug-dealing brother-in-law, and he always kept a machete nearby, just in case.

That wasn't such a bad idea, and I brought it up to Rudy over dinner at McDonald's. "We should keep some weapons around," I said. "In case she comes back."

He panicked. "Did you see her again? Is she—?"

"Calm down," I told him. "No. But it could happen."

He'd stopped eating his burger.

"What I'm saying is, maybe we should try to fight next time. All we've done is run away. We've never confronted her."

"She'd dead!"

"Keep your voice down." I glanced around, leaned forward. "We killed her once," I whispered. "We can do it again."

He was already shaking his head. "No. No . . ."

"Yes!" I told him. "Listen. There are two of us. There's only one of her. Of course she's dead, and that scares the shit out of me, too. But if we see her again, if she comes after us, we can cut her head off. That'll be it. That'll be the end of her. And if it's not enough, we can cut off her arms and legs, bury them in different places, burn them." I met his eyes. "We can do this."

Rudy looked sick.

"Just think about it," I told him.

But I didn't need to think about it. With my first paycheck, I bought a used axe from Don, my boss, and picked up a baseball bat from Big 5 and a small hatchet from Home Depot. I didn't think a gun would stop her, but if we could cut her up into pieces, I was pretty sure we'd be home free.

A week passed.

Another week.

A month.

Six months.

A year.

I still thought about Mom, but Rudy and I hadn't talked about her for a long time, and I was starting to think that we were rid of her, that we were safe.

Then she found us.

I came home late that evening. A couple of us had gone out for some beers after work—Juan's wife worked as a waitress at a Mexican restaurant and could get us a discount even at Happy Hour—and it was dark by the time I was dropped off in front of our apartment building. The car was in its parking space, so Rudy was home, but I hadn't bothered to call him and tell him I'd be late because neither of us did that kind of thing. Trudging up the stairs with a slight headache, I was thinking about how I had to get up early tomorrow for a job in Montebello, and I didn't notice for several seconds that the door to the apartment was unlocked and that someone was sitting on our couch.

Mom.

She looked up when I entered, and her permanent skull's smile broadened, the remaining musculature of her exposed jaw curving ever-so-slightly upward. Rudy was curled in her lap in a fetal position, and one of her rotting tits was in his mouth. She was forcibly suckling him, making him nurse, only he was shriveling as he sucked on her corroded nipple, not getting milk or nutrients, not gaining anything, but losing.

And Mom was getting stronger.

I picked up a hardcover from the bookcase next to the door and threw it at her head. "Why don't you die?" I screamed.

She only laughed, a wheezing chuckle that sounded like air being drawn through a leaky hose. The book hit her square in the forehead, broke open the thin skin stretched over that section of skull, but she did not move, she did not flinch, did not deviate for one second from what she was doing.

I slammed into the two of them on the couch. Mom fell sideways, the rotted breast in Rudy's mouth tearing, and Rudy bounced backward against the cushion before pitching forward into me. I grabbed him around the waist and pulled both of us up and away from her. I was gratified to see the torn breast flopping free and hanging down her chest, revealing rib cage beneath, but no pain registered on her face. She still had her fixed skull smile, and her dead eyes stared at me with a blank unreadability.

Rudy was almost too weak to stand. I lurched around the edge of the couch and into the bedroom, where I pushed my brother toward the bed and slammed and locked the door. I was breathing heavily, and my hands were shaking, heart hammering in my chest. In the fantasies I'd had, the plans I'd made for this moment, I'd been brave and resolute, but in real life, I was terrified and my thoughts were so jumbled that I forgot everything I'd trained myself to remember.

The knob rattled, but when it wouldn't turn, the door was pushed inward, splintering a section of the side molding.

She's strong, I thought.

I dropped to my knees, reaching under the bed to pull out the weapons I'd stashed there. I grabbed the bat, as the door caved in.

Rudy was weak, but he knew what was going on. He took the axe and started to hack at her, striking glancing blows off her right shoulder, her hip, her crotch. She didn't scream, didn't cry out, but kept moving toward us, and I stepped forward, swinging the bat.

It smashed into the side of her face, which collapsed as though it were made of cheap pewter. I kept swinging, beating her head into pulp, until what was left of it dropped down and swung off her neck, falling to the floor.

She was still sort of walking, but a few hits to her midsection brought her down, and then Rudy, newly strengthened, began chopping off her limbs, which proved much easier to do than it would have if she were alive.

Breathing heavily, both physically exhausted and pumped full of adrenalin, we looked around the room at the pieces of our mother's corpse. I half-expected to see them quivering, wiggling, trying to merge together, but the body parts were still, dead.

It was over.

We rested, we talked, then we started to clean up. I didn't know what we'd do with the head and torso, arms and legs, but I knew we had to scatter them around the city, keep them apart, just in case. Rudy went out for some heavy-duty garbage bags, while I chopped what was left of Mom into even smaller pieces. She was literally skin and bone, despite the sustenance she'd drawn from Rudy, and the parts were light. We shoved them into bags, put the bags into the car, and spent the next several hours driving around southern California, dropping Mom off at the nastiest-looking Dumpsters we could find.

That night, I fell asleep on the couch, watching TV, and I had the dream again, the dream of the monster and my mom in the hotel room. This time I recognized the location. It *wasn't* a motel room, I realized. It was AA Gardening and Tree Trimming, the place where I worked, and the reason there was no roof was because it was outside, in the yard behind the office, where Don kept his trucks and tools. The disturbing grafitti was still on the plywood, as before, and though I hadn't seen anything like that myself, I suddenly remembered that Don had been complaining this morning about vandals tagging his fences.

I awoke in a cold sweat, heart pounding, mouth dry. I didn't say anything to Rudy, only stood and told him that I had to check on something at work.

"At this hour?" he said, but he didn't seem too suspicious. He was watching TV, and half-asleep himself. Besides, Mom was dead. The danger was over.

I drove quickly, but it still took me over half an hour to reach the AA yard. Don was too cheap to hire a guard, put in an alarm system, or even buy a watchdog. So there were only the locks, and I knew even before I opened the last of them that there was something going on behind the fence. I'd known it before, of course—it was why I was here—but having it confirmed filled me with fear and made me want to run in the opposite direction. I had to see, though, I had to know, and I carefully opened the gate and slipped into the yard as surreptitiously as possible.

It was just like in my dream. I saw the huge demon, standing on the cement section of the yard where the vehicles were parked, raising its head to the dark sky and howling. It was naked and aroused, and beneath its scaly tail, Mom was shoved between the monster's buttocks.

But . . .

But Mom looked wrong somehow, as though her bones were broken. Everything about her was held or hung at a strange angle, and even her head seemed misplaced, like a jigsaw puzzle piece forced into a spot where it didn't belong.

Watching silently from my spot by the fence, I suddenly understood what was happening.

She wasn't crawling *up* there, she was crawling *out* of there.

The demon stopped howling, turned its head, looked directly at me, and I knew it wasn't over. It would never be over.

Mom's neck snapped into place.

She'd just been formed, so she didn't look dead. Not yet. She looked the way she had when she was alive. But she'd start to deteriorate, I knew. Probably pretty quickly.

She turned, looked at me.

Called my name.

And that was the end of our time in L.A.

We live in an RV now, Rudy and me, always ready to roll at a moment's notice. No need to pack or unpack. The first sign of anything the slightest bit off, the first phone call from a private number, the first weird shadow on the street at night, we're out of there. Even a bad dream or a vague uneasiness and we're gone.

We've killed Mom twice since Los Angeles.

In Seattle, we gutted her on a trawler in the sound, dumping her body overboard to feed the sharks.

Outside of Cheyenne, Rudy hit her on a road one night, smashing into her with the front fender, then rolling over her, back and forth, back and forth, five, ten, fifteen, twenty times, until her body was flattened and squished on the asphalt like the corpse of a cat after three days on a freeway.

The RV still has dents in the front to commemorate that killing, although the blood has long since been washed off.

We're braver now. Or maybe we've just gotten used to doing what we have to do. Still, sometimes, in the back of my mind, or in my dreams, I see that demon, naked and aroused, tail snapping back and forth, and no matter what I drink or take or however I try to erase the image from my brain, it remains.

At the moment, we're in between destinations and parked outside Taos. There are mountains to the south and east of us, a seemingly endless plain to the north and west. I like the plain. I find comfort in open spaces. Looking out the rear window of the RV, I see flat brushland. I see infinite sky. I see—

Mom.

The fucking skank is grinning as she crawls out of an unseen gully, and she's in pretty bad shape. Most of her skin is peeling off, half her hair is gone, and her tits are like flapping pieces of leather. We could take off right now, get back on the highway, head into the Midwest or toward the East Coast. We could probably escape her pretty easily. But that's not how we roll these days, that's not who we are.

He has made me stronger.

It's true, and I break out the automatic while Rudy grabs the axe. We step out of the vehicle. She's more ferocious than ever, and she leaps at me like a cat, but I blow a hole in her midsection, and Rudy chops off her head before she can get up. Then he does her arms. And legs.

We light her corpse on fire. Amidst the roar of the flames, I hear a faint howling and think of that demon shrieking up at the sky.

He has made me stronger.

Maybe this was what Mom had in mind all along. Maybe we are simply following a preordained path, fulfilling the destiny she had planned out for us long ago.

No. I can't believe that. I refuse to believe it. But I look at her burning corpse and hear the echoes of that terrible cry, and I shiver.

"Next time," I tell Rudy, "let's not burn her."

He shrugs. "Okay," he says.

And we go inside for dinner. ◆

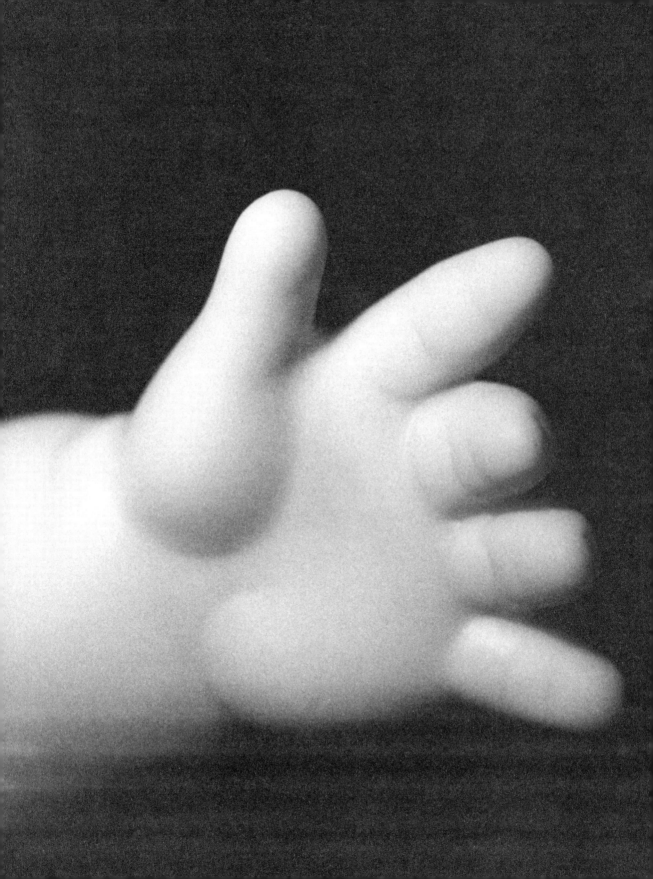

20TH-LEVEL CHAOTIC EVIL ROGUE SEEKS WHOLE WIDE WORLD TO CONQUER

BY *Weston Ochse*

Repentance is a great and noble quality, if you like that sort of thing. Certainly, it is something that the good require of evil, in the end, if justice is to be truly served.

Unfortunately, justice is rarely served, in this life; and even last-minute deathbed conversions are often viewed as getting off easy, for those who feel strongly that payback ought to be a bitch.

This hilariously long-named story was actually written in Romania by Weston Ochse, who has seen his share of evil. It's a bawdy, amoral adventure that puts you in the bad boy driver's seat, so you can suss it from the inside, courtesy of a hero who is anything but.

Giving you a very useful perspective, just in case this guy ever sidles up beside you at the bar.

Happy hour, this ain't.

"Nature abhors a hero. For one thing,
he violates the law of conservation of energy.
For another, how can it be the survival
of the fittest when the fittest keeps
putting himself in situations where he is
most likely to be creamed?"
—SOLOMON SHORT (aka David Gerrold)

Jammy had the girl spun sideways and half upside down when the door flew open.

"O, Doamne! Ce faci? Da-i drumul sau voi trage!"

The Romanian washed over him, but the outrage in the eyes of the two men and their bared teeth told him more than any translator.

The girl came out of her swoon enough to open her eyes. When she spied the two men, she groaned and shook her head. "Run," she whispered. "My *frater*. They are here."

Jammy dropped her to the hard wooden floor and flew to his pants. He had them half on and was hobbling toward the back, when he felt a blow strike the back of his head and arms wrap around his waist. He cursed. Although this was part of being a rogue, it was the part he hated the most.

And him with a whole wide world yet to conquer.

Rogue's Journal Entry 421: *Romanian mothers rarely have the heart to hammer a nail through the foreheads of their dead children, but it's the only sure way to do it. Tradition says it has to be done within three days of birth or the soulless husk of the child will become a vessel for a demon to live life on earth. Understandably, this is the last thing a mother wants to do. The hospitals share that same dilemma. In this modern day and age, those who follow the old customs are very few. Yet even those who don't believe are eager to hedge their bets, arranging for the tiny corpses to be taken away, far away, just in case the superstitions are true. As it turns out, the superstitions* are true. *—Jammy Mac*

A twig snapped, sending Jammy shuffling faster down the leaf-drenched trail. Shadows clung to the underside of the geometrically aligned orchard trees, blocking most of the daylight. Although it was nearing four in the afternoon, it might as well have been a full moon at midnight with all the illumination he had to guide his way. But it wasn't *yet* night, he reminded himself. Which he supposed was a lucky thing. The Romani had joked to him about the night. They'd said not to travel during the sunless hours. They'd warned him, but then they'd dropped him off with no way to get back. He hoped it was all a joke.

It had only been a week ago when he'd crossed the border from Hungary into Bihor County, Romania. Wide, high rolling plains were corralled by the saw-toothed spine of the Carpathians, which rose like medieval battlements above the tree line. Where Hungarians still held the memory of Soviet domination in the creased shadows beneath bright, sometimes blue eyes, Romanians seemed cast from far older molds, reptilian glances blinking the truth of a people who had endured far worse than Stalin, Lenin, or Khrushchev.

"So Dracula *is* real?" Jammy had asked three days ago, sitting in a bar along the Kris River in Oradea.

"No. Not as you know it," admitted Eddi Sabu. "This is like your Disney. A story to tell children."

The image of a vampire-fanged Mickey Mouse made Jammy snort the last sip of his Leffe Blonde beer. The dichotomy of the capitalist twentieth-century creation with the reality of the image of Vlad the Impaler, Romania's most prominent tourist icon, reinvented itself in a Broadway review starring a dozen Romani singing "Under the Sea" riffs from a popular Disney movie about mermaids.

The Romani glanced sideways. Two girls wearing impossibly tight blue jeans strode elegantly past their table, high breasts, long boot-clad legs and long blonde hair, a testament to Russian soldiers' desires to keep warm during the extended, hard Romanian winters back before the Cold War was over. "We use the term *Dracul*," he continued without turning his hungry gaze away from the girls, "but it doesn't mean the same thing. This word means dragon. It also means demon. You know, not with God. It is not the same as Disney monsters."

Jammy laughed again. "Eddi, you've got to stop with the Disney references. You're killing me."

When pressed to explain, Jammy did his best to translate American irony into Romanian, but all he got was a stone-faced regard that would have left him feeling inadequate if he'd actually cared. But Eddi was just one in a long line of Jammy's interlocutors, chosen because he was a certain type. Essentially a good man, he would have uses that Jammy was incapable of providing. Such was always Jammy's way.

For four months a year, Jammy worked on oil rigs in the North Sea. The rest of the year he traveled the world, on foot when possible, because it provided a uniquely personal perspective and allowed him to merge his real-life persona with his 20th-Level Rogue character so they could become one. He'd arrange through emails with the English Departments of local colleges to sit down with one, two, or ten students, giving them the prospect of practicing their English while Jammy got free food and drink, a travel guide, and more often than not, someone to warm his bed. This is how he'd met Eddi.

In the end, Jammy said, "They're just stories to tell children. Some call them morality tales. Sometimes they're scary so that children understand the importance of being scared."

"What is this important? Why must children be scared?"

"So that they are prepared when they face evil."

Eddi shook his head. "We do not scare our children like this."

"Of course you do. What about Vlad the Impaler? Isn't he the source of the vampire myth?"

"You use the word *myth* the way I use the word *Disney*." Eddi rolled his eyes. "We have a different view of this *myth*. It is part of our history."

Jammy pressed him. "So what about this history? Isn't the story of Vlad, of Dracul, just a story to scare children?"

"It is historical fact," Eddi pronounced as he sat back and crossed his arms.

"Let me tell you Eddi, there are few things scarier than historical fact. The graveyards and battlefields of the world are filled with the results of historical fact." Seeing Eddi's dour look, Jammy hastily added, "As scary as a Disney movie might be, they always have a happy ending."

Eddi harrumphed. "Not the same in Romania. We don't have many happy endings."

The girls were still waiting at the counter to be seated. It looked like it might be a while. One reached down to adjust the zipper on her knee-high boots, providing them with a view of the intimate landscape between her lean legs. Jammy was saved from any further geological investigation by the appearance of the waiter who delivered their pizza. He and Eddi ate in silence for a time. Another Leffe Blonde came and went. All the while Jammy tried not to look at the women, but it was almost impossible not to stare. The tightness of their American jeans created a topographical area as wondrous and as daunting as the Appalachian Mountains.

Finally, it was Eddi who spoke as he chewed the remnants of the meal. "You look like Disney. Your eyes are like Bugs Bunny."

"Bugs Bunny isn't Disney," Jammy pointed out. "But I get your point. You have so many beautiful women. It's a shame there's only one of me." He winked and grinned. "If they knew the things I would do to them, they'd run away screaming."

Eddi stared at him for a long moment, then in a delivery he'd heard many times before said, "You are not a good man, Jammy MacKenzie."

Jammy nodded gravely, as if the Romanian had just figured out the secret to the universe, "No, Eddi, I am not."

The idea of good and evil had always been something that Jammy liked to argue. He'd spent enough time trying to come to terms with the warring ideas that he'd finally been forced to develop his own conclusion, one drawn from his thirty-year love affair with Dungeons & Dragons. Although there had been myriad editions published throughout his tenure playing the game, he kept to the Second Edition rules, which he believed were Gary Gygax's vision in its truest form.

Rogue's Journal Entry 141: *Dungeons & Dragons is at its heart a role-playing game in which one plays, sometimes lives, a self-generated and highly stylized character who journeys through lands generated in the minds of dungeon masters. As part of character generation, one must choose what the game terms an* alignment *for one's character. This alignment dictates how good or evil, how chaotic or lawful, or how neutral the character is to be, and it is up to the player to role-play his character as close as possible to this alignment. If not played according to alignment, the dungeon master can and will bring death, destruction, and dismemberment upon the character as penalty. —Jammy Mac*

Jammy soon discovered that the best alignment to be was Chaotic Evil. It was exactly like being evil, but with good sprinkled over the top like salt or parmesan cheese. Of course, the idea of good and evil was a hypothetical construct created by Christians. Jammy eschewed this construct and appropriated a more worldly view, adopting elements of Buddhism, Islam, Baha'i and Sikhism into his daily life. His was a hedonist's point of view that life needed to be enjoyed, and it allowed him the greatest flexibility in his pursuit of everyday life.

Once when he'd returned home to attend to the death of his father, he'd picked up a girl at the funeral who was the daughter of one of his father's golf partners, his bereavement and need for solace an aphrodisiac to a certain type of woman. He'd tried explaining his philosophy to her. He'd told her that he was evil, but she couldn't get it. She just couldn't navigate past the parochial view of good and evil, asserting that the good side of the street was where everyone needed to reside, regardless of his countless examples of evil conducted in the name of good. He'd fucked her anyway.

Jammy stopped cold. Ahead in the middle of the path was what looked like an arm protruding from the earth.

He shoved the boot heel in his back pocket and pulled the hammer out. He held it awkwardly in his left hand because he wanted to keep his right hand free. He stepped carefully toward the thing protruding from the ground. It *was* an arm. He glanced around to make sure no one was standing by with a camera, recording an abnormal episode of Romanian *Punk'd* or *Candid Camera*. He half-expected Ashton Kutcher to dance out of the shadows with his feckless smile, eager to laud his God-given ability to make other people feel stupid.

But Jammy wasn't so lucky.

He was relentlessly alone.

The arm was small, like it belonged to a baby. Not more than a foot long, it looked perfectly normal . . . if it was normal to have a pale white arm sticking from the leafy ground.

He crept closer and got down on one knee. It was like someone had buried the poor baby but not taken the time to do it properly. Removing a nail from his pocket, he poked the palm. It closed reflexively, like the legs of a spider. He jerked his hand back and fell onto his rump. He sat, unmoving, until the hand relaxed again, opening like some baleful flower.

At that moment it sank in that the rest of the baby was truly beneath the ground and it wasn't dead. Or at least not dead as it was popularly defined.

He scrambled to his feet and began to run.

He chanted, "Fuck, Fuck, Fuck," trying to put as much distance between himself and the buried baby arm as he could. There'd been a time when he could run six miles and drink a six-pack of beer. Too many six-packs without running had reduced his capacity to only a few hundred yards. When he stopped, he felt as if his heart was going to explode through his chest.

Of course, living a life of Chaotic Evil required him not only to balance his acts of good and evil, but to experience the best and the worst of times. Like now, left alone in a hundred-acre orchard deep in the Carpathian Mountains, where he would be allowed to witness the face of true Romanian Evil. Something that was definitely not Disney, nor was it anything he had ever anticipated. The moment the old Romani woman had said it, he'd laughed at the idea, especially since it seemed as if this was to be some sort of punishment for his deflowering—or deforesting—of the old woman's granddaughter. Had she not caught them doing it in the back of the barn like something out of *Animal Planet*, it might not have been such a big deal. But the crone had been so vituperative in her condemnation of his very soul that she'd had three of her sons tie him up, toss him into the back of an old Ural truck and drive two hours into the mountains, long past any evidence of humanity, where they'd dropped him off with nothing more than a hammer and three foot-long nails.

The girl had called herself Veronica, but they both knew that wasn't her name. The other one called herself Betty and she and Eddi had played starring roles in their own porn movie in the loft above. Jammy recalled Eddi exclaiming in wonder several times, clearly benefiting from his association with the traveling American rogue. But since he hadn't been caught as animal-in-flagrante, as Jammy had, Eddi was released with a spit between two fingers and a gesture from the old woman that had sent Eddi shivering into the night. When Jammy figured out a way to escape his present circumstances, he'd make it a point to return to Oradea so that he and Eddi could laugh at their conquest.

He leaned against the side of a tree, gasping, propelling puffs of air like little mushroom clouds into the cold twilight. Although sweat beaded beneath his blonde-haired brow, he was chilled to his soul. Had it really been alive, or dead, or undead, or whatever, or had it just been some sort of reflex? He'd seen a few dead bodies during his travels, but had admittedly never poked one with a stick—or a nail in this case—to see exactly how dead it was. Other than what he's seen on television, he didn't really know what happened to bodies after they died.

As he gathered his breath, Jammy began to feel a little foolish about his reaction. The more he thought about it, the more certain he was that he'd witnessed nothing more than reflex. Instead of a supernatural reason, there was a natural reason. The poor child had probably been hurriedly buried, those doing the deed too afraid of superstition to do the job properly. Yeah. That was it. He spent a moment in serious silence. Although he didn't believe in prayer, nor was he a good man, the innocence of a child was not something to be discounted lightly. It was something that should be respected. Something that, when lost, could never be regained.

He felt something tug on his pants.

He opened his eyes and beheld a baby standing before him. Its skin was as pale as two-day-old snow. Completely naked and uncircumcised, it was decidedly male. It looked up at him with eyes gone powder-blue. Its black-lipped mouth was open and in the place of a gummy smile were twin rows of serrated teeth, so many it seemed impossible that the mouth could contain them all. And as Jammy stared, the baby reared back its head and sank those teeth into his calf.

Jammy screamed.

He shook his leg furiously but the baby held on, its little arms and legs wrapping around his leg like it was a tree-sized drumstick.

The baby chewed, then sank its teeth into him again.

Jammy screamed maniacally and began to hammer at the baby's head with the hammer. His blows rained down savagely, striking the side of the baby's head again and again. Finally, it let go, its head no longer capable of resting on an impossibly broken neck.

He leaped onto the baby, grasping desperately for one of the nails. He fumbled one free from his pocket. But before he could bring it to bear, he dropped it. It was at that moment that he saw the baby coming back to a crazy mimicry of life, the vertebrae of its neck reconnecting before his eyes. He groped blindly for the nail in the leaves, wrapped his fingers around it, and pressed it squarely in the center of the baby's head. With three great thwacks of the hammer, he put the child to rest, its mouth and eyes closing as if it were once again a baby and not some demonic creation.

Jammy stood shakily. The bite gaped through his pant leg in appalling shades of red. Adrenaline ate at his muscles and made him shake. When he took a step on the bitten leg, agony flamed all the way to bone. Yet even with all the pain, as he looked at the baby with the nail sticking out of the middle of its bloodless forehead, he felt his fear twist with sadness. The wrongness of the child lying on the forest floor brought back memories of his sister and how she'd looked when she nearly died.

He'd been babysitting. His mother and father had gone to dinner in Santa Monica, then stayed out to see a movie premiere. He was thirteen and people still called him Jimmy. His mother had given him stern warnings that he was to be careful with his little sister. Not that she'd had to threaten him. He loved the baby, who had just learned to walk and speak in cluttered strings of random sounds that sometimes made sense. He'd been in the kitchen making a peanut butter–and–banana sandwich, listening to her play, when suddenly the house went quiet. He'd continued cutting the banana and placing each slice atop the peanut butter, waiting for the sound to resume. But it never did. The idea that something was terribly wrong gripped him and propelled him into the family room where he'd stared in horror at the figure of his sister—dead.

But she'd just been alive a moment ago. How could she be dead now? How was he going to explain to his mother and father that Cynthia was no more? It just didn't seem real. He fell to his knees beside her and began to prod and push at her, absolutely with no idea how to determine what was wrong. He pushed on her tiny chest and found it unyielding. He opened her mouth and looked into it and only then did he spy a hint of yellow. Looking around, he saw the yellow rubber ball they should have gotten rid of long ago, now so worn that it had cracked, weakening the structure so that even a little baby with slivers of teeth was capable of wrenching free a piece large enough for her to choke on.

Using the hook of his finger, he tried to get it out, but it was too deep. For a moment he searched for something longer, like a coat hanger. But as soon as he thought it, he dismissed it as a ridiculous idea. Instead, he picked up her limp form, her head lolling on a rubbery neck. He held her to his shoulder and began to pat her back. Harder and harder he patted until he was hammering at it. Then in one glorious cough, the piece of rubber flew from her mouth and she began to breathe once more.

She cried for a while, as did he, out of sheer relief.

When she was done she said, "I love you Jimmy," only it came out as "ah wubbu Jammy." And it was the first coherent sentence she'd ever spoken. From then on, Jimmy had become Jammy and he was the savior and protector of his sister, right up until the moment she died twenty years later while walking along the side of the road, hit by a driver more concerned with his need to text than to remain between the lines painted on the road.

"Holy hell," he said aloud.

The baby looked like any normal baby now. It was as if the nail had removed the possession.

He wiped his brow with the sleeve of his jacket, then limped backwards a few steps. He wondered for a moment how in the hell he'd ended up in such a place, then remembered that it had been through the gateway of a woman's thighs. He smiled through the pain. Wasn't it always that way? "What's next?" he wondered.

In response, he heard the cries of first one baby, then another, then another. Each cry answering itself and multiplying, until the forest was filled with the sounds of babies crying. He'd been able to defeat this one using a hammer and a nail. He glanced down at the two nails protruding from his pocket and knew that two weren't going to be enough. There were hundreds of cries in the lonely, dark woods. He heard rustling and spun as a baby pulled itself from a shallow grave nearby. It shrugged off the dirt, shook its head as if to shake free the earwigs, then focused its powder-blue gaze on Jammy. It opened a mouth filled with serrated teeth and let out a plaintive cry, the same one Jammy had heard a thousand times before from hungry babies. Then it held out its hands and said a word that spooked him to his core. "Jammy," it cried, and all the other babies in the woods echoed it, crying "Jammy" now a hundred murderous mouths screaming his name as they unburied themselves.

Rogue's Journal Entry 299: *David Gerrold created the alter ego Solomon Short as a sort of homage to Robert Heinlein's Lazarus Long. One of Solomon Short's most famous quotes is "Nature abhors a hero. For one thing, he violates the law of conservation of energy. For another, how can it be the survival of the fittest when the fittest keeps putting himself in situations where he is most likely to be creamed?" Therefore, in order to be true to the nature of the universe, and to conform to the law of the conservation of energy, it is most often best to run when confronted by a threat of death. This is why I never even considered doing anything heroic. I'm a rogue through and through. —Jammy Mac*

Jammy turned and ran.

Although the path down the middle of the orchard was large enough for a truck to roll through, he found himself running from side to side, careening off tree after tree, all the while spinning and gaping at the babies unearthing themselves even as he passed. He'd encountered the most violent, twisted creatures invented by the warped minds of Dungeon Masters around the world, but nothing had prepared him for the sight of something so innocent turned so evil. First one, then five, then ten, then twenty, then fifty, then a hundred babies unburied themselves from the forest floor. Like miniature zombies from a Sam Raimi movie, after they pulled themselves from the dirt and leaves, they stood and shook their skin free of detritus with some twisted sense of undead propriety even as they regarded him when he plowed past.

Cries of "*Jammy!*" filled the air like the shrieks of a thousand birds. The horrendous cacophony scrambled his wits and kept him from thinking clearly. He ran full-tilt into a tree branch, careening away as blood burst from his forehead and fireworks exploded in his eyes. He fell to his knees, then to his face. He lost his grip on the hammer.

He lay there as his mind reeled from a dozen Fourth of July celebrations bursting through his brain. Finally, he managed to kneel, blindly searching for the hammer. His fingers wrapped around something long and solid, but it turned out to be a stick. He threw it away in disgust and grabbed leaves to wipe away the blood in his eyes.

All the while, the screams of "*Jammy!*" came closer.

He used the tree trunk to help himself stand. He spied the hammer in the leaves. He reached down to grab it and felt something leap onto his back. He jerked straight and brought the hammer over his head, once, twice, three times, making sickening contacts. Still, the baby's fingers wouldn't release their grip on his jacket. He shoved himself backwards against the tree and scraped up and down. Finally, the baby let go. Before it hit the ground, Jammy was off and running.

Once again he found the middle of the road. But instead of worrying about what was behind him, he kept his gaze forward. He could see them closing in from the sides, like packs of two-legged hyenas. He'd already established that he could run faster . . . but he'd also established that he couldn't run very far.

A dozen stood in his path.

He couldn't go back—no telling how many were behind him. He couldn't go left or right. He had no choice but to go forward. He bulled through creatures, swinging madly with the hammer as he screamed barbaric yawps. Several tried to grab his leg, but he scraped them away with the claw of the hammer.

In a moment he was free and running. Tiring.

His breath came in great whooping gasps. His legs burned. Ahead he spied a tree with branches low enough for him to climb. He ran toward it and managed to pull himself onto a branch a dozen feet from the forest floor, but not before kicking free the lowest branch he'd used to climb.

He crouched, then let his legs dangle as he gasped for air.

The babies still came. Soon they were milling about beneath the tree. Hundreds of dead babies, stillborn and demon-owned, scraped and clawed at the tree, unable to get any higher but unwilling to leave him be.

Stand off.

Night had fallen long enough for a half-moon to twist free of the horizon. The sky had only a few wisps of cloud left, enabling the moonshine to reach the upturned faces of the babies. White skin, powder-blue eyes, and serrated teeth promised him a swift death if he'd only jump. Like human piranha, they circled and milled, waiting to eat him.

This moment was as bad as any moment he'd ever had.

So he did what anyone would do faced with impending and horrific death.

He fell asleep.

Rogue's Journal Entry 15: *Playing* Dungeons & Dragons *is different than playing computer games. Computer games give the player the option to fail. They give the player the ability to do something over. The saved game function is like the divine hand of some omniscient and omnipresent electronic God coming down to give some poor stupid soul another chance. In* Dungeons & Dragons *there is no save game, which is why it's so much more like real life— which is why it* is *real life, or it could be. In a computer game if a player dies during battle, that player really didn't die. There's a saying: If computer players die in the forest and nobody sees them, then did they really die? That's a trick question. Of course the computer players really didn't die, instead they just reload the game to the moment before the event occurred and keep reloading until they win. In* Dungeons & Dragons *or in real life, if you die while fighting an orc, you're dead. If you die in Paris while dealing with a member of the French mafia, you're dead. If you die while trying to rescue a maiden from a sylvan water naga, you're dead. If you die while trying to escape a backwater Romanian forest filled with voracious dead babies, you're dead. So the important thing is not to die, not to make mistakes, and to avoid putting yourself in a position where you have no choice but to die. —Jammy Mac*

Jammy awoke as he began to fall, screaming. He scrambled to hang onto his limb and felt the hammer drop from his hand. He didn't dare look down. He felt bark dig into the skin of his arm beneath his jacket. He pressed harder until he got an entire arm around the limb. Once leveraged, he was able to pull himself back on.

With his heart in his throat, he stared down at the babies.

They'd been busy.

Sometime while he'd slept, they'd gotten organized.

Beneath his tree limb, the babies had made a pyramid. Ten babies wide by ten babies deep, they knelt on top of each other as the pyramid got smaller by twos. The next layer was eight, then six, then four, then two. The top two babies were just crawling into place as he watched. They now occupied the space where he'd hung.

Then he really got worried. A single baby climbed the pyramid. In its right hand was the hammer. The broken branch was in its left.

Jammy climbed to his feet and balanced himself on the limb. He was able to reach out and grab the trunk with his right hand to steady himself. As he moved, he noticed that all the babies, with the exception of those in the pyramid, moved with him. Although their bodies were perfectly still, their heads moved toward his new location. Like undead dandelions they followed him because he was their sun.

The topmost baby reached the top of the pyramid and looked up at him.

Jammy blanched. He could tell that he was in trouble. The branch the baby held was long enough to reach him.

And just as he thought it, the baby poked him in the foot with a stick.

Jammy lifted his foot.

The baby poked again, this time at the other foot.

Jammy soon found himself doing a dead baby stick dance on the limb as the baby poked left and right and left and right. If it wasn't so serious, he'd have almost laughed. Once he tried to kick the stick away, but when he almost lost his balance and fell to one knee, he realized that that was a bad idea. But then a better one came to him.

He shrugged out of his jacket. Wrapping one sleeve around his left arm, he tried to time the baby's thrust. When the stick came up, he slapped the jacket toward it, hoping to wrap it around so he could jerk it away. He missed. He tried again, and finally on the fourth attempt, he snagged the stick. It was hard for him to keep balanced. He could just see the baby letting go, sending Jammy falling backwards into the sea of dead infants. But it didn't happen that way. When Jammy pulled backwards, nothing happened. The baby held him fast. Then as he watched, the baby jerked the stick down, and with it came the jacket and everything attached to it. Jammy hit the limb facefirst. As he began to slip off, he wrapped both arms and legs around it and hugged it as tightly as he'd ever hugged anything.

Just when he thought things couldn't get any worse, the baby reached up and poked him in the rib cage with the stick.

Jammy's eyes widened with pain. A squeal escaped his lungs. The force of the blow was incredible.

He flailed with one foot, trying to strike the baby in the head and dislodge him from the top of the pyramid. But it was awkward—he couldn't see his own leg. But he did see the baby swing with the hammer and felt it connect with his shin in a neutron explosion of pain.

Jammy screamed and as he did, the babies screamed with him, filling the air with an awful mimicry of his agony.

When their cries died down, he heard another sound. It took a moment, but he soon placed it as an engine. He dared not look, but as the baby kept jabbing him in the ribs and he held on as tightly as he could, the sound came closer. Soon the babies beneath him were bathed in twin spears of white light. One moment the baby was poking him, the next the pyramid was gone, crushed and creamed by the front end of an old pickup.

Eddi shouted from the cab, "Jump!"

Jammy rolled over and let go, falling hard to the metal floor of the truck bed.

"Hold on!"

Wedging his feet on one side and his arms on the other, he was able to keep from falling out as the truck ran over bump after bump after bump. It only took a second for Jammy to realize what those bumps were. When he did, he finally knew he was going to get out of this alive.

Rogue's Journal Entry 72: Billy Joel sang the song Only the Good Die Young. *I privately believe that Billy Joel played* Dungeons & Dragons. *He had to. He knew the truth of it.* Only the Good Die Young *was his ode to evil. He understood that good characters die faster than evil characters. Good characters trust other characters. It's in their DNA. It's based on a worldview distilled in hope, wonder, and naïveté. Evil characters don't have the same problem. Evil characters trust no one. Lawful evil characters trust absolutely no one, while Chaotic Evil characters allow themselves a chance to trust somebody, sometime, somewhere. But although Chaotic Evil characters may have the opportunity to trust somebody, it's a very rare thing for them to ever truly trust anyone. It's more common for them to count on the hope and trust of good characters as a way to multiply their own chances of survival. —Jammy Mac*

Eddi stared at Jammy with shock. "You are going to leave me? But I came back for you."

Eddi had pulled to a stop several hundred meters down the road so that Jammy could get out of the back and slide into the front seat. But Jammy insisted on driving. Once he got in the truck, he locked both doors and rolled up the windows. Eddi knocked on the driver's side window, thinking it was only a joke. But it was far from it.

"I told you before that I am not a good person." Jammy shook his head from behind the window. "You should have believed me, Eddi. You should have been prepared. This isn't a Disney movie. There is no happy ending, at least not for you."

"But I came back to save you." His voice pitched high, like he was about to cry.

"You shouldn't have. I wouldn't have come back for you." He grinned at how wide and expressive the other man's eyes had become. "You know, your eyes are like Bugs Bunny's."

"Bugs Bunny isn't Disney," Eddi whispered in return, a bookend to their earlier conversation, before the dead babies, the old crone, and the two Romanian girls.

"How do you know?" Jammy laughed. "You don't watch Disney."

"You told me!" Eddi shouted, banging on the window. "You told me it wasn't like Disney!"

"Maybe if you'd watched enough Disney, you would have figured it out for yourself . . . you would have known to be afraid of me. Eddi. Don't you get it? I'm your fucking morality tale."

Eddi let his banging fist slide down the window. His mouth hung open as air left him.

Jammy glanced in the rearview mirror and saw that the babies had regrouped and were coming for them. "Time to go."

Eddi's eyes went wild. He looked from the onrushing demons back to Jammy and resumed banging on the window. "You can't leave me! Jammy, you've got to help me—Jammy, all you have to do is let me come with you! —I promise I'll watch more Disney!—I won't tell anyone about this!"

Jammy ignored the pleas.

"You don't have to leave me!" Eddi screamed.

"Yes, I do." Jammy sighed. "After all, if they have you, they might not want me."

Eddi leaped into the back of the truck as Jammy put it in gear. The lurch sent Eddi scrambling for balance. He almost made it. Then Jammy hit the brakes, sending Eddi facefirst into the back window. Jammy hit the gas and Eddi tumbled out the back as the truck sped away from the orchard. Jammy slowed and watched in his rearview mirror as the babies overtook Eddi. Hundreds of tiny demon mouths biting, snapping, tearing, powered by the unholy fuel of demonic souls, eager to redress an eternity of living in hell. Eddi was soon reduced to his basic components: bones, sinew, tendon, and his teeth, either too tough or not tasty enough to consume.

When they'd eaten everything they could of poor old Eddi, the babies turned toward the truck. They stared toward him as they lined up along the edge of the orchard. It was as if they were meeting his eyes, every last one of them. Their prohibition at leaving the orchard seemed to be intact. They were bound by some supernatural contract and were unable to come after him. Still, they seemed to be toeing the boundary line as if it were a starting line.

Since he seemed to have their attention, he did what any 20th-Level Chaotic Evil Rogue would do in such a situation. He shoved his arm out the window of the truck and gave them the one-finger salute.

As one, the babies grinned, as if they appreciated his roguish humor, then charged toward him as fast as their bandy little demon baby legs could go, apparently unaware that they were supposed to remain within the confines of the forest.

Jammy laughed out loud. He was in a truck. What could they do? Still, the best option would be to run.

But as he put the truck into gear . . . it stalled.

He stopped laughing and cranked the engine, cranked it and cranked it, swearing and stomping the gas until he feared he would flood it, all the while tracking the babies rapidly closing the distance.

Then the truck finally coughed and sputtered into gear. Jammy gunned the engine, shifted it into drive, and roared away from the orchard.

Although the babies receded into the distance, they seemed undaunted, and still came on.

Relentless.

Hungry.

Implacable.

Like a thousand stillborn terrorists of the soul.

Jammy pressed the accelerator to the floor and wondered how long they'd keep after him. How long he'd have to keep running.

And if he had enough time to hook up with Veronica one more time, in the back of that barn. ✦

CONSUELA HATES A VACUUM

BY *Cody Goodfellow*

Here in Los Angeles—the melting pot that's way hotter at the bottom than the top—the filthy rich and the tidy poor largely come together around the mundane. One pays the other to do the things that no one else will, at those prices. And occasionally, they share gridlock in traffic.

This rollicking tale pulls them all together in a slap-happy funfest of mayhem and fear, where everybody actually stands to lose something for a change.

Brought to you by Cody Goodfellow, who knows too much, and is always more than happy to share the bad news.

You think you know suck? He'll SHOW you suck!

I'm still laughing my ass off.

And if the shoe fits… TIP WELL!

Consuela was pretty sure the Azerbaijani cabdriver cursed her as she got out on the corner of Sepulveda and Reseda, lugged her belongings out of the Sultan Cab and counted out the fare from her beaded wallet.

She was not used to taking cabs, indeed they frightened her—the ridiculous expense, the greedy meter, the cabdrivers who figured they could treat her like trash—but she didn't want to be seen walking the streets with the vacuum cleaner. Anyone who saw the dumpy, forty-two-year-old Latina in her faded pink sweatsuit would know her for a housekeeper, and would conclude, quite rightly, that she was also a thief.

In all her years as a cleaner, Consuela had never stolen anything from an employer. *What happened today was just an accident*, she kept telling herself. *I thought I was doing good.* Maybe she still was, and maybe she had lost her mind, and her job in the bargain.

Limping north on Sepulveda, she risked calling Tia Blanca again on her prepaid phone from the cleaning service. It had been chirping and vibrating like an angry baby bird in her purse, but she couldn't answer it. If she could only catch Tia Blanca and take the vacuum to her, then she could face the consequences. Perhaps, they would even be grateful.

No, not the people on the hill. They appreciated only her labor and her silence. For them, even a few insincere words of gratitude cost far more than money.

Jesus, please make her pick up, Consuela prayed, but when her prayers were answered, she almost hung up. A frenzy of diabolical accordions icepicked her ear, and she thought it must be the vacuum playing tricks on her again.

But then a wheezy old woman's voice cut through, commanding the infernal din to cease. "*Bueno*, I have been expecting your call . . ."

"Really? Then who is this?" Even in her dire predicament, Consuela still got irked at Tia Blanca's theatrics.

As Tia Blanca consulted the spirits in her caller ID and turned up her hearing aid, Consuela yipped with terror as the vacuum cleaner was snatched from her grasp. She spun on her threadbare sneakers, stepped on the ball of her left foot, and nearly fainted from the pain. Her huge purse filled with cleaning supplies slammed into her hip and knocked her on her bottom.

The infernal machine lay supine on the otherwise deserted sidewalk. The wheels had stuck in a crack in the pavement.

Just an accident.

"Consuela, are you still there?"

Picking herself up, she found herself tempted to just run away, leaving it on the street. "Tia Blanca, I need your help . . ." It almost all came out right there on the phone, but she choked it back, along with tears. When it came time to put into words, she could not accept that even Tia Blanca Villalobos, the crazy old white witch, would believe her.

"Is it very serious?" The old crone's voice went girlish.

"I have run afoul of a very bad spirit," she said, as plainly as if admitting to the flu. "It has killed two people that I know of, but everyone will think I did it . . . I need to . . ."

"Don't come up here," Tia Blanca said. "My grandson's band is rehearsing for a *quinceañera* up here. Meet me at the taco shop on the corner. I'll bring you something to ward off the spirit, if it should come upon you again."

"That's not going to be enough," Consuela said bleakly, but she finally picked up the vacuum cleaner and hop-jogged to the next corner, and the *Gallo Negro #3* taqueria, already in sight. "I have it here with me."

By the time Tia Blanca came in the door, Consuela had gone through three orders of *menudo*. The three loud white kids at the corner table took no notice of her, but the boy at the counter and the pregnant girl in the next booth sneered at her empty plates as if she were a pig.

She hadn't eaten any of it.

"I thought you were above superstitious nonsense, Consuela Altamorena." Tia Blanca slid into the booth across from her and popped her arthritic knuckles. If she enjoyed anything more than the diversion of someone else's problems, it was seeing a skeptic eat crow. She looked long and wide and hard at Consuela to read her aura. Her eyes opened so wide Consuela could almost see her inner light reflected in the old woman's huge bifocals.

At last, she said, "This won't be easy or cheap. But I can do it for you."

From her straw purse, Tia Blanca took out a bunch of *botanica* candles and lit them, each off its own kitchen match. Over the painted faces of the Orishas, Tia Blanca had glued images of their earthly incarnations, which she'd clipped out of *People*. As she arranged her portable shrine and stocked it with candy and cigarettes, she chattered about the upheaval in the spirit world—Chango had deserted his faithful but clingy wife Oba to cavort and breed with his kindred spirit Oya, the slut. In her bitter jealousy, Oba had forsaken her duties as the guardian of marriage and made a string of scandalously bad romantic comedies. But the signs and portents in the tabloids hinted that Chango was again texting his former wife and might be considering a reunion.

"It's not like that," Consuela said, waving at the shrine. "The stars on the hill can't help me."

Clicking her tongue, Tia Blanca lectured, "Why else would they raise up such beautiful, empty vessels and shower them with glory, if not to invite the spirits to come into them and sample earthly delights?" She took out a knotted handkerchief and gingerly unwrapped it to present Consuela with an egg. "You need not believe, you have only to ask, and they will answer."

"But it's the stars on the hill that cursed me. It's—"

"Bring me more meat, whore," said the vacuum cleaner, "or I'll make you sorry."

She was already as sorry as she could be, but she put her plate on the floor beneath her table. "You're a thing," she said. "You can't eat." Though she knew this wasn't true. It had to be putting it somewhere, and its canister should be filled many times over. Why was she starting a conversation with this thing?

Tia Blanca looked at the possessed appliance as she would an unruly toddler or a flatulent dog. "You're something special, eh?"

"I am a fire too hot to be contained by any mere mortal vessel of shit. I will burn a hole in this world and suck all of your miserable kind down into the abyss—"

"Enough." Kicking her plate away from it, she planted her right foot on the vacuum to keep it from rolling away.

"This is the work of a very powerful devil," Tia Blanca hissed. A cigar appeared in her tiny, shaking hand. She lit it and blew smoke over the vacuum cleaner when the counter boy was refilling the *horchata* machine, then stubbed it out in Consuela's iced tea. "Tell me what happened. Don't leave out any names."

Sadly, there were no juicy celebrity names to drop. Consuela had worked for In the Pink Cleaning Service for three years, and cleaning houses in the Hollywood Hills for nearly half her life. She didn't hire out independently because her English wasn't good enough and she didn't have a car. She'd had a car, but her son Hector wrecked it. In the Pink picked her up every morning at 5:30 in a minivan packed with other sleepy women in pink sweats and delivered them to different palatial estates and cliff-hugging glass castles in Bel Air, Sherman Oaks, and the canyon enclaves of the Hollywood Hills. Unlike most services, they didn't leave their maids to hike down into Van Nuys or West Hollywood to catch a bus, but they had to be taking in four times what they paid each maid.

The money wasn't much better in the Hills than anywhere else, but in these times, regular working people only hired maids to serve drinks at their holiday parties, or to clear out dead relatives' houses. Consuela had learned to work around them and their harebrained instructions, and never gave them a real reason to complain. She never looked at the gossip magazines, so she never got starstruck. But maybe it did give her a little tickle of superiority to scrub the toilets of the immortals.

Today's house was like all the others inside—huge and empty and sterile, like a museum or a church of the self, with vast, hideous paintings everywhere and great vacant plains of green Carrara marble downstairs, and a loft with two master bedrooms carpeted in white angel hair. (Nothing odd? Nothing personal? Only boxes of rubber surgical gloves in every room.) Floor-to-ceiling glass walls overlooked some other, private, pastoral Los Angeles, where mule deer and coyotes and even a mountain lion frolicked in an oak grove, and a muscle-bound naked man with hair like Samson stood in a hot tub, shooting a bow and arrow at a target.

Though she had worked for her only today, the young blonde woman was far from Consuela's favorite client. She drifted around the house in a medicated haze, exhausted from changing dresses every hour, and left half-empty teacups everywhere. Coffee was bad enough, but with tea, every cup left a little bloated corpse, and if one wasn't diligent in tracking them down, they quickly became putrid cups of mold. She constantly asked Consuela if she "wouldn't mind" doing a task, a confusing trick of English idiom that Consuela never answered correctly the first two times, no matter how she replied.

Though she wouldn't recognize them, she doubted that either of them was famous, let alone the breadwinner. Actors were always moving in or out of their dream houses. Everything in this house was precisely and obsessively arranged, and had been for long enough that the sun had burned silhouettes of the furniture on the interior walls. Only producers, lawyers, and pharmacists had that kind of security.

After sanitizing the kitchen and bathrooms, dusting, and washing the windows and laundry, it was nearly two and the lady of the house was nowhere to be found. ("Did they have a bidet?" Tia Blanca asked. In every bathroom, she was told. How many? Six.)

Consuela didn't dare look out into the backyard again, so she hunted around upstairs until she found the vacuum cleaner. This was the most discreet way to avoid an ugly scene, as everyone would know where she was.

It was a very strange machine, and right away Consuela didn't trust it. It was one of those bagless European things that looked like a weapon stolen from the future. It sang like a *castrato* choir and greedily collected the tufts of dog hair into a special reservoir, where it was woven into a dense mesh basket suitable for displaying dried flowers.

She made short work of the hallway and the bedrooms without seeing anyone naked, but when she came to the end of the hall, she found a door standing open that she hadn't noticed on her first pass. It had no knob or latch, and was set into the wall like a secret entrance. She remembered no special instructions about avoiding any rooms. If she skipped it, she could get into terrible trouble, and it wouldn't be the first time she saw something she shouldn't.

If her curiosity had been pricked by the odd door, a quick sweep of the room failed to titillate. A single black leather egg chair sat in one corner, overlooking creation from a godlike aerie. The walls were lined with framed primitive carvings of men and women with animal heads doing nasty things. Ashtrays on every table and shelf overflowed with gilded butts, cascading onto the carpet.

And in the center of the room, spreading almost from one wall to the other, an old, lumpy rug of rudely combed wool, stained a deep maroon that was darker than black. Its fringe of long white tassels lay as straight as courtroom evidence, as if someone had to comb them before they could enter or leave.

Nothing else. It seemed perfectly reasonable that she was supposed to dust and vacuum the room. Why else would the door have been left open?

The fancy light-scattering museum glass over the carvings was practically bearded with dust. Clouds of it floated in the air, making her cough and entertain unworthy fears. Dust was mostly hair and skin. She would never know these people's names, but she would carry them home in her lungs.

It should've taken only a few minutes to vacuum the rug. If she hadn't stepped on something sharp that went through the sole of her sneaker and into the ball of her foot, she would be home right now.

It felt like a tiger's claw in her flesh, its thickness and sharpness an intruder against which rubber, flesh, and bone were as butter and lard.

She screamed and sat down hard. The vacuum snapped upright, still running on shag setting on the odd, nubbly old rug. Its regular sinusoidal threnody abruptly turned to a braying, howling honk that meant it had sucked the area rug up into its intake and gotten blocked. If she didn't get up and shut it off, the motor could burn out, but her impaled foot demanded equal time.

There was indeed a hole in the sole of her shoe from which a few straggling droplets of blood flowed, but it had felt like something much, much worse.

Flipping the corner of the rug over, she instantly found the culprit. A plastic placard lay facedown under the rug with a long, thick tack through it. On the front, it said STAY OUT—DO NOT ENTER in eight languages.

Her bloody footprint on the rug was a big, glistening splat of bright crimson, but far from ruining the rug, it seemed to seep into the thirsty threads and spread out, rejuvenating the crusty maroon expanse to give it the appearance of a rippling pool of fresh blood.

The vacuum howled on, so Consuela didn't hear the lady of the house screaming at her from the doorway. She wore a lavender silk kimono and she was hysterical, and probably not for Consuela's welfare.

The blonde *gringa* slapped and pulled at her to get her out of the room like it was on fire, cursing her all the while, though Consuela couldn't understand a word of it. Steeling herself against the pain that still made her want to throw up, she tried to get up and turn the vacuum off.

The blonde was way ahead of her. She tried to shut it off, but couldn't find the button. Her hysteria redoubled, she whirled around in circles twice, then went for the cord, where it was plugged into the wall opposite the door.

What happened next was just an accident. It could happen to anyone with so little self-control. The blonde leapt over Consuela and went for the cord, but somehow managed to trip on it, wrap it around her ankle, and, in a howling panic, stumble into and through the glass wall, then out of sight.

The cord whipped halfway out of the socket, but the vacuum roared even louder. It started to roll backwards towards the broken window, but then stopped with a weird jerk. The frayed gray rubber cord stretched taut over the window's jagged mouth.

Before Consuela had begun to even answer the question of where she had gone, a big naked man entered the room, dripping wet and demanding answers. Consuela had to cling to the wall to bring herself halfway upright, only to be thrown back on her behind by the angry, naked man.

Punching at air, he ran over to the window and let out a horribly high, desolate wail. Then he started jumping in place, but his feet wouldn't leave the puddle of water he stood in. The frayed cord jumped and twanged between his feet for a long, sickly stretch. His anguished cries became an endless, ululating shriek that finally drowned out the vacuum.

The big naked man dropped to the floor, still twitching. His thick, veiny neck, stretched over the teeth of shattered glass, began to leak. The vacuum's unbearable racket fell off to a faint rattle of ruined gears that sounded all too much like a nasty laugh.

Consuela got up and said twenty rosaries, then twenty more on her long slow trek around the room. Her ears still screamed with a dull blue tone of brutalized eardrums. Her foot burned like she'd stepped in a deep fryer. She clung to the wall for support, but she was mortally afraid of stepping on the rug, which had changed again, and not, she thought, for the better.

It looked like it had when she'd come in: an ugly old rug from somewhere she'd never heard of. She couldn't even find the spot where she'd bled on it. Nor could she see any trace of the deep maroon color. It looked drained, consumed, the color of cigarette ash.

There are things you don't want to see, but must witness, for they are God's inscrutable work. (Like when she had to identify Jorge's body after he fell off a ladder and electrocuted himself installing a huge nativity scene in Beverly Hills.)

There are other times you must avert your eyes and stop up your ears, lest the devil, by temptation or despair, gain a foothold in your heart. (Like when her dead husband's answering machine was overloaded with passionately grief-stricken calls from three strange women.)

And then there were times like this, when the question must be answered: How bad can it possibly be?

It was worse than bad. No monstrous fate concocted by the perverted man-children who wrote slasher movies could have been more wantonly cruel, so calculated to show what a bubble, a joke, was the human body.

The enormous house stood up out of a plunging hillside, surrounded by cacti that someone must have picked out to ward off burglars and paparazzi. Huge gray-green starbursts of iron-hard sawtooth blades, like spiny tank traps.

The lady of the house had plunged headfirst into the central spine of a massive blue agave cactus. It went up her throat and emerged south of her navel, while four more speared her neck and chest to peel her like a banana.

They held her in place even after the cord retracted and snaked back into its housing in the canister of the vacuum cleaner. It stood right behind her, mechanically slurping the cooling blood off the floor.

"We should leave," it said.

"And you just took it away with you?"

She didn't want to, but the vacuum cleaner was persuasive. It made it impossible for her to see any other outcome but her arrest for a double homicide. It offered her things, made promises, if only she would carry it away. So she called the cab and came directly down here.

"What did you think *I* could do?"

"Drive it out, send it back to Hell, how should I know?"

"And leave you the only suspect in the murders?"

"I never harmed anyone! I didn't touch them. The police are like magicians now. They will see the truth."

"They won't look when they can blame a Mexican." Tia Blanca rummaged in her purse for a while, but clearly, she was just keeping her hands busy while she searched the deeper, darker corners of her memory. "I can't cast out a spirit, unless I know its name."

Consuela shook her head.

"But it promised you a reward—"

"Yes, anything I wished for."

"You didn't make a wish, did you?"

"No, no."

"Devils only grant wishes when they are trapped, or when summoned by one who knows their true name. It costs them a little of the black fire they stole from Creation to grant a wish, and it takes something from the one who makes the wish, too. When they've given themselves away until there's nothing but a mouth and a bad attitude, they can still grant little wishes, but they're only tricks and lies. Did you bring me here to help you negotiate a deal with this devil?"

"No, Tia Blanca," she said too fast.

"Wonderful. Throw it in Tujunga Wash, if there's water in it. Better still, the ocean."

"But . . . it's not mine. And it's a really fancy vacuum."

The vacuum belched, filling the taco shop with the stench of melted plastic and scorched blood. "Bring me over to that pretty, gravid slut, there. I would have milk from her te—"

"Quiet! You unclean spirit, by all the saints and incarnated Orishas, I command you to speak truthfully and clearly . . ."

"In truth, I will have milk or blood from one or both of you this day."

"What manner of thing are you? I command you to answer."

"I have been called *rakshasa* and *djinn*, *dybbuk* and devil. I was among the firstborn and favorite of the Creator, later betrayed and forgotten by Him. If you know my name, then I am your humble servant, but if you know it not . . ."

"You are powerless, little devil. Tell us your name."

"I tire of this game, bitch."

"See? Just like I told you. Trapped for so long, he used up all his real powers long ago. He doesn't even remember his true name. He probably doesn't even have a body anymore. Just a nasty ghost of something that was never really alive."

The devil refused to rise to the bait. "Consuela, your flesh is overripe but not yet rotten, it is a tragedy to waste it. The loneliness in your blood is strong enough to get drunk upon. I could bring back your Jorge . . . he writhes on a flaming dungheap, but you can rescue him—"

Furiously scribbling upon a Post-It notepad, Tia Blanca hissed, "Don't listen!"

"Or I could make you so beautiful you could have any man . . . so irresistible they would kill or die to lie in your shadow—"

The reticulated hose popped off its rack and fell onto the table like a dwarf elephant's trunk, edging closer to her hand . . . "You don't have to say it aloud. . . only whisper it to me, and it is done . . ."

"Do something!" Consuela whimpered, shoving the hose off the table.

Tia Blanca slapped a sticky note on the vacuum canister and said something in Latin. The note had a spiky six-pointed star with lots of tiny dots and symbols around and inside it. Steam like boiled sewage escaped from every orifice of the vacuum, but it fell silent.

"Seal of Solomon," Tia Blanca said.

"I knew you'd know what to do!"

"No, dear one. We're fucked. If we can't get rid of it now, sooner or later, it will get what it wants."

"And what does it want?"

"To get out, to be free to do evil. Who knows how long it's been trapped in that rug? We must think—"

"There's no time."

Tia Blanca tapped her nails on the table. "Maybe we should discuss my fee now."

Consuela pointed out the window and slid over in the seat. She grabbed the neck of the vacuum cleaner and yelped, jerking back with a stifled scream. Blisters rose and burst on her palm. A shiny swath of her smoking flesh was stuck to the vacuum's handle.

Tia Blanca reached for her friend, but then she looked outside and almost started to bolt out of the restaurant herself.

A black limousine stopped out front and a thick black man in a suit got out and walked into the taco shop. He went to the kids and whispered something to them. They were gone before he approached the pregnant girl, who beat a retreat behind the counter with her boyfriend.

Another man got out of the limousine and came into the shop.

"Oh my God, I recognize him!" Tia Blanca said. She flushed and smiled in spite of everything. "Why didn't you say you worked for—"

"Don't say my fucking name," the white man said, in perfect, patrician Spanish. Impeccably dressed and groomed, he looked like something that had escaped a terminal cancer ward. Bilious yellow skin glared through wisps of silver hair. He coughed continuously as he crossed the taco shop to stand beside their booth.

With a gravity that commanded awed silence, he took out a packet of Wet Naps and thoroughly wiped down the seat beside Tia Blanca. Then he took out another Wet Nap and wiped it down again. And a third. Then he did the same with the table.

Then he sat down. His hands splayed out on the table and shook. His fingers were yellow and shaky like he was holding dice. Scowling at them, he slipped on a pair of heavy leather gloves before he deigned to look at either of them.

"I watch your show every day," gushed Tia Blanca.

"Shut up, cunt."

Even Consuela recognized him, though she couldn't recall his name. He had hosted that same game show since she was a little girl, and he never seemed to age. For the last six years, they shot a Spanish version with real Latino contestants, and he hosted that one, too. He looked a lot taller on TV. His manners were better on TV, too.

He also looked twenty years older than on TV. And right now, he looked about a cup of coffee away from a fatal heart attack.

"Sir, I beg your pardon. This . . . evil thing killed your wife and . . . her friend. I was afraid, but I thought—"

"No, don't apologize," Tia Blanca interrupted. "She did nothing to your family. Your wife wouldn't have mourned *you* for very long, by the sound of it."

He tried to take a deep breath to shout, but his lungs weren't up to it. "You have fucked up the balance of my life beyond all recognition." His anger was squeezing him, so he had to let it go. "My relationship with Corinne was complicated. But don't think I didn't know what was going on in my own home."

"He's barren," Tia Blanca said, pointing at his light. "You poor, damned man! You wanted a child so badly . . ." She covered her mouth, deliciously scandalized.

The white man could care less. "You triggered a silent alarm in my office at the studio the moment you entered my study. I have a video record of you leaving the crime scene, but I won't give it to the police. I will pay the very expensive private service I used to track you down to exterminate your whole fucking bloodline, then to go down to Mexico and make a picket fence out of cousins you never knew you had, if you don't give it back."

"You just want it back? I don't understand. It killed—"

"You fucking idiot, look at me! This isn't me, this isn't what I'm supposed to look like . . ."

"It was always strange," Consuela said. "Your show's been on for—"

"Thirty-two seasons. Six Daytime Emmys, and thirteen fucking *TV Guide* Quality TV Awards. That was my first wish. See, you have to be careful what you wish for. They're crafty motherfuckers. This one said it was trapped in the rug by King Solomon himself. I bought him at a bazaar in Katmandu . . . I think . . ." Looking lost, the white man bit a leather-sheathed finger. Two of his teeth were missing. His gums were grayer than his hair.

"I wished for fame and fortune and security and the goodwill of millions. And

I knew show business, so I made sure it was for a long, stable career with guaranteed ratings. And it made me a goddamned game show host. I made a deal with a devil to spend half my life giving out shitty prizes to drooling morons who couldn't complete a crossword on a Happy Meal box. My show plays in thousands of nursing homes, you know. They say it's the last spot of excitement in a lot of people's lives. People check out when we go into reruns every year. No shit."

He coughed, long and hard, wiped his mouth with a raw silk handkerchief. What he saw in it alarmed him. "Did you know you had to trade something? I didn't. It told me to hold something dear to me in my heart when I made that first wish. Nothing much, just a memory, a little thing that I loved less than having a perfect life. You just think of it once, and then your wish comes true, and it's gone."

"That's very terrible, sir. What did you give up?"

"How the fuck should I know? *I gave it up!* Something I remembered, something I used to be able to do. Maybe it was my capacity to love. My first wife left in the middle of spring sweeps, and all I cared about was that the ratings went up 17 percent. Corinne was my fourth.

"I've given up so many other little things since then it hardly matters, but the wishes have been all smoke and mirrors, ever since that first one. Illusions go a long way in this town, but look at me. I'm not supposed to look like this!"

He looked around the empty taco shop. The black man stood outside the door, a walking CLOSED sign.

"You might think it's the key to getting a better life, but believe me . . . you don't want to step into the ring with it. It's insane, Connie. Doesn't even remember its own name. You can't hope to control it, you can only try to aim it at somebody else, when it's hungry."

"So you just want to take the vacuum cleaner and . . . ?"

He reached into his breast pocket and took out a wallet. "I'll pay you a bonus to say my wife sent you home early and you saw nothing. Better yet, get the fuck out of North America, and don't ever come back." He held out a tightly folded roll of the cleanest, newest money Consuela had ever seen. "Just take it and go home, Consuela."

She started to reach for the money, but Tia Blanca grabbed her hand. Hers was hot and sweaty. "Don't take it. He'll frame you for the murders. Or just wish for both of us to get hit by a car or shot by the cops for killing his trophy *puta*."

"I don't want anyone else hurt. I just want this whole sordid catastrophe to disappear. That's what you people do best, right? Make a big mess, then disappear."

"Don't take his money, Consuela."

The game show host slapped their hands apart. "Stay out of this, witch! If your chicken-killing peasant voodoo worked, why're you all still scrubbing toilets?" He sighed and put the money back in his pocket, then peeled off the Seal of Solomon Post-It note and flicked it at them. "Good night, ladies. Forgive me if I don't kiss either of you."

Tia Blanca looked like she was coming down with a fever. She'd been right about sending the sick man away, but it wasn't like the old *bruja* to turn away money.

He slid out of the booth and grabbed the vacuum by its handle, tugged it like it weighed a ton. The black man held the door for him, but he only got halfway across the taco shop before he noticed the cord wasn't coiled neatly around its flanges on the back of the canister. It trailed back across the grubby orange-tiled floor to disappear under the ladies' table. He gave the cord a weak tug, but it wouldn't come out of whatever it was plugged into.

Like a rabid dog, Tia Blanca came out of the booth and across the floor to tackle the game show host with the cord still dangling out from under her skirt, screaming, *"None of you shit-worms knows my name!"*

The bodyguard came through the door with a Glock drawn and leveled at Tia Blanca. "Get down, sir," he grunted, and shot Tia Blanca four times.

The short, stout old woman never broke stride until she hit the sick man in the gut. He folded over her like an empty suit, going down in a tangle with the now inert and probably broken vacuum cleaner.

Tia Blanca ignored the bodyguard. Steam came out of the holes in her torso as if from a ruptured radiator. Her eyes boiled out of her head and black flames licked out the holes, but she ignored this, too. She clung to the game show host and pressed her face to his until the flames burned his eyes out, too. He screamed and kicked, powerless to resist her.

The bodyguard shot her four more times, but two of the bullets went through her and into his boss. "Fuck this," he said, and went outside to call somebody.

By the time the game show host stopped moving, Tia Blanca had been all but consumed by the black flames. No mortal vessel could contain it, the devil had said. *I will burn a hole in this world—*

With the black blazing head of a tiger, Tia Blanca stood upright on matchstick legs and staggered toward the counter. Consuela curled up in her seat, too afraid to pray. The game show host hadn't wanted children, but then it occurred to her that maybe the devil could enter an unborn child and be born again into a new body. Perhaps it could even grant real wishes again, throw around the kind of power that Solomon, with all his captive demons, once wielded. And with a new name, it would be totally under the control of its new "father."

This did not all occur to her in a flash of purely intuitive understanding. It leapt to her as Tia Blanca threw herself at the counter, where the pregnant girl stood, frozen in an ecstasy of breathless terror.

Without thinking any more, Consuela scooted out of the booth and moved to intercept the devil. Tia Blanca's charcoal skull showed through the black flames, which had begun to gutter for want of fuel. The tiger roared, "Out of my way, hag! It is not God's will that I fade—"

Taking her life in her hands, Consuela reined in her tone and found her quiet, humble maid's mask to hide behind. "You'll burn up the baby, sir. It already has a name. But if you go inside my womb . . . into one of my eggs . . . you could maybe start all over . . ."

Tia Blanca crawled closer. The flames eating her were colder than dry ice. "You're ugly, old and fat. Out of my way . . ."

Holding her burned hand to her belly, Consuela promised, "You can name yourself. I won't double-cross you . . ."

Tia Blanca reached out to embrace her in sable flames. Consuela withstood it, felt the awful attention of the devil roving over and in and out of her until it found a healthy egg bigger than all the others, and gushed out of Tia Blanca's spent form to possess it.

Smitten with its own cleverness, it began to gloat over its power over her, when it suddenly realized it had been tricked, perhaps even worse than when Solomon trapped it in an area rug.

Tia Blanca's egg trembled in her wounded palm as its contents spun round and round, searching for a crack, a seam, a corner, but finding only itself.

"What is this thrice-damned prison? Treacherous cow, I'll rip you open—"

Carefully, Consuela took the quivering egg out of her pocket with a handful of napkins. Smeared with blood and skin from her burned hand, it must have looked like a part of her to the stupid, desperate devil.

"They're coming for you, Consuela," said the egg. "Wish yourself away. I can make it all go away for you . . . then we can start fixing your life. Think of all the things you'll wish for."

Consuela almost wished for a Sharpie pen, but she found one on the counter before the words left her lips. She quickly scrawled a hasty Seal of Solomon on the egg.

"I don't wish for things, devil," Consuela said. "I work for them."

Passing around the counter, she slipped out the back door of *Gallo Negro #3* like a shadow, just seconds ahead of the cops.

She stopped only to offer a prayer to the Orishas on the hill, and to drop the egg into a big pot of boiling water. ◆

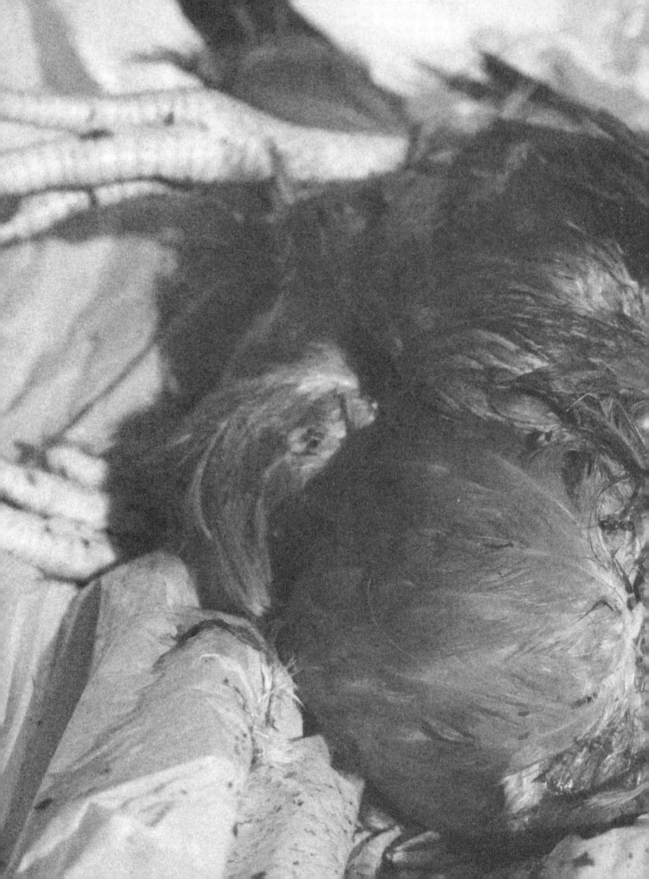

OUR BLOOD IN ITS BLIND CIRCUIT

BY *J. David Osborne*

This stunning south-of-the-border-shattering piece of soul-wracked wonderment is as full-tilt literary as Bizarro fiction gets, colliding with high-end magic realism so hard that they're virtually indistinguishable.

There's an intimacy to the deeply conflicted values at play here that is positively transporting, and negatively revealing. Pretty much equally, by turns. It's one onion skin after another, peeling back and back and back.

J. David Osborne—who broke in with the mind-blowingly Kafka-by-way-of-David Lynch gulag escape novel By the Time We Leave Here, We'll Be Friends*—is another fresh discovery that I do not even remotely regret.*

But I'm sorry for the chickens.

And, while we're at it, for us all.

One

Juarez, Chihuahua, Mexico

Tonauac Isidro awoke before the sun went down. He lit candles for Santa Muerte and got on his knees. He prayed and he pushed away dreams. He kissed his hand and touched the statuette. He scooped up his pants from the floor, pulled a cigarette from the pocket, and laid it at the saint's feet. Crossed himself and got in the shower.

When he left his room the sun was nearly gone, peeking under the flower-printed curtains. The living room filled with a dark orange glow. His mother had the television on to the news. He smelled corn tortillas. She spooned eggs and salsa onto his plate. She brushed at invisible dust on his uniform and told him he looked handsome.

They talked while Isidro shoveled the eggs into his mouth. His mother spoke of relatives across the border in El Paso, about a young girl missing from the *maquiladora*, about the aches in her bones. When Isidro tilted his head and asked her if she needed to see a doctor, she shrugged him off the way she always did. He thought it was sweet that his mother brought up illnesses only to pretend they were nothing, to show how strong she was.

He lifted his gun belt from the wooden hanger and wrapped it around his waist. His mother bought the coat hanger at the Juarez flea market, struck with the beauty of the English words embroidered on a cloth above the wood: "Flowers are the friends of life." Tonauac had laughed to himself, but didn't have the heart to tell her the words didn't make any sense.

He kissed her good-bye and grabbed his hat on the way out.

After Isidro closed the door, his mother wrote a short protection spell on a piece of yellow sticky paper, cut open an orange, and stuffed the note inside. She walked the two miles, in the dark, to the dirty creek behind her apartment and tossed in the fruit. She worked her magic because she loved her son, and Tonauac Isidro knew she did it and he loved her for that.

Isidro pulled the patrol car to the curb and walked through a waist-high chain-link fence and rapped on the door. The small flat sat between two identical houses, all of them with matching chipped paint and sunblasted lawn ornaments. Isidro swiveled his head back and forth as he headed up the lawn, one hand on his gun belt. Alert. He hunched over, nervous, and rang the doorbell.

José Figueroa opened up and waved him in. He scratched his red eyes and walked out the back door. Isidro followed his partner, ignoring the smell of cat shit, through a living room covered in crosses, through a small kitchen with cracked yellow tile and the dishwasher rattling in the corner. Figueroa's wife sat at the cluttered table, smoking a cigarette and wiping her eyes with the heel of her palm.

Figueroa's backyard was pebbles and sand and a low stone fence. Feral dogs barked from the ends of chains in his neighbors' yards. He had a section of his backyard cordoned off with barbed wire. He stepped over it and reached into the leaning henhouse and brought out a squawking chicken by its feet.

Isidro took his shirt off and knelt in the dirt. His friend removed a blade from his pocket and cut the chicken's throat. The body twitched and blood spurted over the white feathers and onto Tonauac Isidro's face and chest. He rubbed the viscera down his arms to his wrists, in his armpits, over his stomach. Figueroa lifted his shirt over his shoulders and sprinkled the remaining blood on himself.

The chicken blood turned cold and flaked in the desert night. Soon both men shivered. They put their shirts back on, then their overshirts. On their way out, José Figueroa kissed his wife on the cheek. She wrapped her arms around his neck and the smoke from her cigarette drifted past her husband's ear into the yellow ceiling. He grabbed his belt on the way out and shut the door quietly.

"She watches the news all day," Figueroa said. He looked down at his stomach as he put on his belt.

"My mom does the same thing. Every time I wake up I hear that shit."

Figueroa checked the slide in his pistol and put it in his holster. He reached into his shirtfront pocket and took out a tiny baggie of cocaine in two fingers. He tapped some into his long pinky nail and inhaled. He wiped the excess off his moustache and sniffed several times. He extended the baggie and Isidro waved it off, the same way he did every time.

The city gained weight in the darkness. The cops turned their car down Mariano Metamoros, passing auto shops and Burger Kings with barred windows, making a right onto the 16 *de Setiembre*, cruising through the dimly lit streets, past the homeless drunks fighting and screaming and sleeping on doorsteps, past the mall at the intersection of Juarez, closed for the night, the windows inky black, past the clubs with open doors, inside the flashing lights and men and women moving in the dark, blue blacklight teeth and eyes floating.

José Figueroa drove, knuckles white on the steering wheel. The cage separating the back from the front rattled. The radio hissed and popped. Figeuroa pointed at the women walking from club to club. They turned left toward Bellavista and the tourists clogged the streets. Green, red, and white streamers glittered from the tops of the buildings, red-faced white Americans laughing and slapping each other on the backs. Pissing in alleys and praying to God for women. Isidro watched the women in their glittering dresses and low-cut tops, delicate *origami* figurines, carefully sculpted, lovely to look at, but fragile, not made to be out in the elements, glossy lips turned up in a frown at the slightest gust of wind. As the police rolled past, American soldiers from Fort Bliss stuffed half-full beers in their pockets or hid them behind their backs.

The fear came to Isidro just before he spotted the mark. The evil stretched its limbs through the back seat of the car, dark hands misting through the grate into the passenger's seat, smothering him and tickling his stomach, bringing bile to the back of his throat. He'd lived in the city since he was a child, he knew it well, but when the darkness filled him it was a foreign land, full of sharp points and bullet holes. He rubbed a rosary in his pocket and flared his nostrils, sucking in the smell of the chicken blood, and he thought of his mother's kitchen, thought of her, and his breathing slowed.

The mark was a hundred meters from the OK Corral club. They pulled up next to a young dark-skinned boy and a white girl and flipped on their lights. They stepped out of the car, one hand on their belts, and told the couple to back against the wall. The kids knew what this was immediately. The young man turned to the wall and deftly tucked the large necklace he was wearing down his shirt.

Figueroa did the talking. Especially when he was coked up, Figueroa became articulate and alpha, his smooth talking and white teeth initially preferable to

Isidro's hunched, feral grunts. He asked the couple if they had been drinking. The boy nodded his head and said, "Yes." He spoke Spanish with an American accent.

"You look pretty drunk to me," Figueroa said. "Turn around. Give me the necklace and you can go."

The young man reacted immediately. He flailed his arms and swore and flipped Figueroa his middle finger. The necklace rattled under the boy's shirt. The tall policeman didn't step back. The boy was yelling right in his face. The liquor breath wafted over him. He sighed and held out a hand. He felt the drug flow and grinded his jaw. He could feel the chemical electricity burning off his fingertips. He thanked God for the powder, thought of how, sober, Figueroa almost certainly would have botched this, wouldn't have had the balls to do it, and that made him giddy. Made it fun. He clapped a hand on the young man's shoulder. "Okay, my friend, okay," he said in English. "You can keep the chain. You give me and my friend a turn with your girlfriend, we'll forget the chain."

The white girl turned green. She held out her purse to Tonauac Isidro. Her hands shook, the bracelets on her wrist jingling. She pressed her back against the wall. Isidro bit his cheek and stared at her legs. They were quivering, touching at a point just below the hem of her skirt. He put both hands on his belt and took a step toward her, feeling the power surging to his loins, breathing deep the dried chicken blood.

The young man swung at Figueroa, but the cop had done this dance too many times. The threat to masculinity brought the violence, the mark swung, and Figueroa would beat the man within an inch of his life, the drugs like a good corner man, sponging his face and congratulating him. Figueroa had been a boxer in his youth, wiry and energetic and lethal, and the coke only amplified this. He bounced away from the punch, fully intending to unleash a vicious beating, when the young man surprised him: He turned around and sprinted down the street.

The cops watched the boy's clean white sneakers piston into the distance. The underwater bass rumble of the OK Corral club mingled with the shouts from drunken GIs. The woman started to cry. A lock of hair fell over her face and she held her purse to her stomach. She pissed down her leg.

The police officers laughed. They laughed until they were crying along with the girl. Her lips quivered and she covered her face with one hand. The men exchanged glances, Isidro lifting his eyebrows, searching for the go-ahead. Figueroa roared and slapped his friend on the back and shook his head. He told her to go. "You've had a bad enough night as it is, sweetheart. Maybe you pick better boyfriends next time."

Between Texcoco and Ignacio Mejia the cops stopped for food. José Figueroa loaded up on tortillas and beans and Tonauac Isidro sat on the hood of their car and stared into a beer. José held out a burrito wrapped in tinfoil. "You're not hungry?"

"No." Isidro honestly could not figure how his partner could eat like that. Every time he'd done coke his guts had knotted at even the thought of food. Figueroa wolfed down his tortilla, roping thick strings of cheese around his finger.

"Must be nice." José chewed. "Maria has never cooked. Ever. I bought her a rice cooker the other day. She asked me for one. I drove up to the Walmart in El Paso. It's still in the box, on the floor."

"You might as well return it."

"I can see it now, man. She comes home and the thing is gone. 'Where's my fucking rice cooker?' she'd say. I know it."

"You can't please women. No use trying."

"Unless she's your mother. You played it smart, staying with her. Free meals every day, shit."

Isidro finished his beer and set it carefully on the curb. "You made the right choice," he said. "I can't fuck my mother."

José Figueroa swallowed the last of his tortilla, wiped his hands on his pants, and gave his friend that look he found himself giving more and more often now, that look that said, "I have no idea what is going on behind your eyes."

That morning Tonauac Isidro punched his time card and waved good-bye to the officer on duty at the front desk and at the old women and young men seated in the folding chairs around the white room, the paint peeling off of the walls, teeming with sounds and hand gestures. He dropped José off at home and watched until he was safely inside. He drove three miles down the road, the landscape dropping from low-rent houses to shanties to hard-brick apartment buildings. He parked his car in an alley, changed out of his uniform, and strolled along the dirt road, stepping over potholes and peering into the foyers of these buildings, all the windows boarded up and barred up, some of them decorated with desperate trinkets, flowerpots, or statuettes. Each apartment had a large iron gate at the entrance and Isidro peered into each one, the overhead lights dimly illuminating the foyers. Most of them were empty. Before he could give up hope, however, he spotted, at the top of the stairs, a young woman leaning against the wall. She had her foot propped on the opposite wall and he could see the bruises along her smooth leg and he felt himself becoming excited. She tilted her head toward him, dark circles under her eyes, and she stood up and descended the stairs deliberately, the flower print of her dress faded and sickly under the weak light, and stopped just before reaching the bottom stair. She planted her feet on the ground and spread her legs.

Isidro worked up some spit. "Long night?"

"Not too long," she said.

The policeman could tell that she was young no matter how weathered her face. He told her what he wanted and she told him the price and he agreed and he felt his guts twist with a strange love at the way she hopped to her feet, her hair bobbing at her shoulders, unlocking the large iron gate, taking him by the hand, up the stairs, and into her room.

José Figueroa showered and washed the chicken blood from his chest. He brushed his teeth and rummaged through his pants pockets. He found a crumpled dollar bill and rolled it into a tube and did a line from his sink. The drug hit him immediately, white fire in his brain, and he laughed at his reflection and clapped his hands. He stuffed the dollar bill in the skull sitting at the altar at the foot of his bed. He found Maria curled on the couch and he sat with her and watched TV. When the program was finished they went to bed. He wrapped his arms around her and she squeezed his hand. He felt himself become aroused and started to kiss her neck. She turned to him and took his face in his hands.

"Why do you do that?"

"Do what?"

"I heard you. In the bathroom. Sniffing. It's four in the morning, José. How are you going to sleep?"

"I don't want to."

"Because of the dreams?" A lock of hair fell in her eye and Figueroa instinctively brushed it away. Fingers itching to do something. Jaw clenched. He wished he had never told her about his dreams. About the things he saw, every day. He saw the drug as a supplement, like coffee, but to those who didn't have to use it, he knew how he looked. And he would not talk to his wife about how scared he was, every night, about how he had to will himself out the front door every evening.

But he did talk. At length and about nothing in particular. After ten minutes he felt the high receding, felt himself come down from the mountain, and the urge presented itself to go back to the bathroom, to do another small bump, to get his self-confidence back, to not have to face the crushing weight of the day by himself.

A few hours later Maria was gone, off to work with the rest of civilization, and he had the whole day to kill.

He bought a burger from an American fast-food chain and caught a movie. He thought about going to see Maria at work and then decided against it. She hadn't said anything that morning, getting dressed with hurried, angry movements. Tight-lipped.

He saw a crowd at the corner of Joaquin Terrazas and Jesus Escobar. He parked his car in front of a duplex and walked downhill, the gravel crunching underfoot, to where the people were. The sounds were familiar to him, as a policeman. Distant crying, the bustle of official talk, the shutter clicks of cameras. At the bottom of the hill, set in the center of the road, was a cylindrical metal trash can. Leaning against the can were two human legs, cut off at the calf. A cardboard sign was taped to the bin, a warning to anyone who might think about talking to the police. A photographer aimed his lens into the trash can and walked away, shaking his head.

A young woman was on her knees, crying and screaming, though she had gone hoarse a long time ago. An older man squatted next to her, rubbing her shoulders, tears shining brightly in the sun. Figueroa lingered at the scene for a moment longer then got back in his car and drove home.

Two

Isidro took the capsule from his pocket and unscrewed the lid. He poured the orange powder into a bottle of water and shook it up. "My mom gave me this energy drink stuff," he said, "She bought a box of this stuff at Sam's Club. It tastes awful but now she won't let me leave the house without it. I hate them. Still drink it, though. I would feel too bad throwing it away."

Figueroa snorted a line of cocaine from the dash. "Does it work?"

Isidro squirmed in his seat. "I'm not sure. I feel like talking more. Things are funnier. I feel like I react to things faster, like I need to make fewer movements. It makes my bones feel hollow."

"Your bones."

"Yeah, like I'm empty or something."

Figueroa sniffed and rubbed his nose. "That sounds horrible."

"It's not too bad. I met a girl this morning."

"Fuck yeah. Where?"

Isidro thought for a second and shrugged. "Never mind."

The Tequila Rio nightclub sat between the Internet Frontera coffee shop and Agua Caliente grocers, across the street from ornate Spanish colonial homes surrounded by automated turquoise gates topped with barbed wire. The lights stayed off in the houses, ignoring the police cars, the forensics investigators, the women and men sitting on the curb, answering questions.

The story from the witnesses was mostly the same: A couple narcos in good boots and cowboy hats hopped out of a red truck at about midnight, each of them carrying a black trash bag. They had waved pistols in the bouncer's face and stepped into the club and reached into their bags, each of them taking a human head in each hand, and had rolled the heads onto the dance floor. The lights went up in the club, the drunks screamed, the DJ cut the music. One head rolled under the feet of the patrons at the bar, the other three came to rest dead center on the dance floor, all of them gray and decomposing, as though they had been buried under the hot Chihuahua sand for days, only to be dug up and used later.

Figueroa and Isidro controlled the onlookers. Cell phone cameras snapped pictures, tourists jockeyed for position, the police held them back, told them to back up, and the tourists complied, holding their hands up, still taking pictures.

The heads were identified as belonging to police officers, men Figueroa and Isidro saw every day at the station. Isidro had joked with one of them just the other day, and Figueroa knew that Maria was on a first-name basis with the wives of two of them.

José Figueroa rode his high as hard as he could. He puffed out his chest, waving his arms at the onlookers, shooing them away with chemical confidence.

Isidro could not get the first thing he saw when he arrived out of his mind: the dance floor, empty except for police photographers, the heads cordoned off by tape, three of them on their sides, hair matted to the distorted skulls. Then, the head in the center of the floor, facing him, eyes closed and tongue out, with a tiny white placard placed next to it, a black number one, an evidence marker. He pushed back the crowd, he yelled through the bullhorn to disperse, he threatened to arrest. But he could not shake the thought that, in the corner of his eye, there was a little white placard floating just out of sight, marking his own head as evidence, waiting to be conjured into reality. He thought of his mother. He thought of the breakfast she'd made for him that morning. The eggs turned in his stomach. He pictured her, shopping at the grocery store, standing on the tips of her sandals to reach the food, then turning back to her cart and there was his head, and he was inside it, in this fantasy, talking to her, telling her not to worry. She didn't bat an eyelash. She combed his hair over and pushed the cart, occasionally reaching onto the grocery shelves, dropping shrink-wrapped body parts into the cart, women parts, breasts and genitals.

He felt the hands. The darkness. He saw it overtake the crowd. It snaked into the club and disappeared into the eyes of the dead men and came back out dragging their souls with it. It grabbed him around his neck, this ugly fear. He felt a pain in his neck and he dropped his bullhorn, the mike squealing as it bounced off the concrete, and he felt his hands go numb and his vision go white and when he looked up Figueroa was leaning over him, calling for an ambulance, pupils big as saucers.

Figueroa clocked out early. Isidro had been taken to the hospital, so Figueroa got to ride the bus. He stood at the station with an old man in a plaid shirt and a mother and child. The pneumatic doors hissed, he got on the bus, and watched his city slide by him in the purple morning glow. Suburbs gave way to shantytowns, shacks set up on sloppy foundations, children playing soccer in the dirt street, ads for Coca-Cola everywhere, printed on the sides of the skeletons of long dead homes, mingling with the graffiti that crossed itself out and painted over itself. He thought about the heads, and the amputated legs. He pondered the violence he saw daily, and the violence he and his partner were guilty of inflicting. Picking nervously at the stitching of the bus seat, Figueroa held his head in his other hand. He stepped off the bus and looked up at the giant star illuminated in the side of the mountains to his south, rubbed his nose, and went inside. Maria was asleep on the couch, drooling lightly on her shoulder. José heard his stomach talk and touched the side of his wife's face. He walked into the kitchen, opened the box, and pulled out the rice cooker and plugged it in. He got the rice from the cabinets, set the bag on the counter, and measured out some water. Maria woke up to the smell, she walked over to him, and wrapped her arms around his stomach, and he put his free hand over hers and brought it to his mouth and kissed her.

"I saw something terrible tonight."

Maria pulled his shirt over his head and brushed the dried chicken blood from his chest. "I'd rather not hear about it."

"Tonauac fainted. He just couldn't handle it."

"Tonauac will be fine. His mother looks after him."

"He's my friend. But I don't know if this is good for him."

"It isn't good for you, either."

"I'm protected."

Maria looked at the flakes of dried blood on the floor. Figueroa turned to go to the bathroom and she grabbed him by the arm. Ran a hand along his back. From the base of his neck to the bottom of his spine he was covered in a tattoo. A *baphomet*, a devil with goat legs, one hand raised as though in greeting, flanked on either side by pentagrams.

"Are you talking about the magic?" she asked, pointing to the tattoo. "Or the drugs?"

Figueroa closed his eyes. Stayed quiet.

"Because, when you started, this was all the protection you needed."

The two of them stood there in the pale blue morning glow. The rice bubbled in the cooker. José scratched his shaved head and nodded. He reached into his pants pockets and held the baggie of coke in his palm. The morning broke and the chickens pecked at the ground.

The same morning Tonauac Isidro lay in bed, staring at the ceiling. Fear and embarrassment struggled for dominance in his guts. He thought about the girl he'd met a few nights before. He had seen prostitutes before, and had been able to do his work and leave without much of a second thought, but something about this most recent girl weighed him down, consumed his mind when it eased up on the self-loathing enough to think clearly. He thought about the girl's room, about the books neatly arranged on a shelf under a Frida Kahlo print. There was something intelligent behind her eyes and something determined about the set of her jaw. He thought about her face, and slowly his mind drifted to the young white woman abandoned by her boyfriend. He thought about her legs and how he had wanted so badly to touch them, to feel powerful in front of her, to be inside her, and this thought greased the slide his psyche was slipping down. He cried into his pillow, horrified by the realization that the only sex he'd ever gotten in his life was paid for or taken by force.

His mother entered his room once to bring him breakfast and, seeing him in the state he was in, took matters into her own hands. She opened the door slowly, supplies bundled into her arms, and she knelt at the foot of his bed by the altar of

Santa Muerte. She told her son to get up. She told him to kneel. She prayed to Jesus. She prayed to Mary. She sifted cornmeal from a bag and spread it on the floor, etching patterns with her fingers. She spoke Nahuatl, she called on old gods. She had no animals to sacrifice so she left raw meat and blood in a clay bowl at the altar. She arched her back and bucked to a rhythm that Isidro could not hear, but then he felt it, too, the pulse, emanating from a distant space, and he felt his chest swell and he felt dizzy. His mother swayed on the floor and called out to the spirits and Isidro felt the darkness slip in through his nostril, all of his prior concerns washed from his mind, and he stood up and went to the bathroom and laughed, laughed until his sides hurt, and when he washed his face and looked in the mirror, for a split second, he could have sworn that his face was covered in white and black paint. Painted to look like a skull.

Three

José Figueroa awoke that evening and said a prayer to Santa Muerte. He stuffed a dollar bill in the skull on the altar and walked outside. On his back porch he watched the sun set. He filled two empty milk jugs with water and dropped rusty nails inside. He pulled on yellow rubber gloves and dumped coal tar creosote in the water, capped the jugs, and shook them up. He took the war water and set it in his front yard.

He slaughtered a chicken and covered himself in its blood. He waited for Isidro to show up. The sun went down and the night became cold and he saw no sign of his friend. He picked up the jugs of war water and walked to the bus station. He rode to work and when he got there his captain pulled him into his office and told him to have a seat.

Figueroa set the jugs on the ground. The captain nodded at them. "What's that?"

"War water. You break it on the doorstep of an enemy. It's a curse."

The captain sat at his desk and shook his head. "Yeah," he said. "Sit down."

Figueroa took a seat in the hard wooden chair in front of the captain's desk. The old man stared at him with big brown eyes. "Tonauac is dead."

Figueroa's mouth opened and the room spun. He leaned forward in his chair and placed his trembling hands on his forehead. "How?"

The captain took out a pen and chewed on the end of it. "Found him dead in a whorehouse. Whore that works there said he showed up in the middle of the day, swearing and telling dirty jokes. Laughing like a fucking crazy person. They told him to come back later that night but they said he just kept laughing. The pimp got rough with him and Isidro got rough back. Isidro shot the pimp," the captain poked himself in the eye, "right in the fucking head. Then the whore shot him in the back. Severed his spine. Dead almost instantly."

Figueroa nodded into his hands.

The captain rapped his knuckles on the desk. "Take the day off. Tomorrow you leave the voodoo water at home. This is a police station, Officer Figueroa, not a sweat lodge. Not a church. We're police. If you're scared or something you deal with it." José Figueroa stood up and steadied himself against the chair. He walked through the station house and his vision blurred. He saw a young man handcuffed to a radiator, screaming at everyone that he would kill them all. He saw a toothless woman talking to herself. He saw rolling heads and severed limbs and he felt the fear grab him in his guts and he swayed as he pushed the chipped wooden doors to the cell block. A tired guard pointed him to the last cell on his right.

The hall was quiet, quieter than the waiting room. The prostitutes and murderers and thieves slept or stared at the wall. He stopped in front of the young woman's cell and peered in. She slept, curled into a ball in her cot. He wanted to shake the bars. Wake her up. Scream at her for killing his partner. His friend.

He was still thinking of the perfect thing to say when he heard a growl from the corner of the cell. His eyes glanced over it but they did not register the apparition until he focused. He could not move. The shadow approached the bars, and he felt cold, and he felt his guts tighten, and he experienced memories that he never lived. It reached a hand out, blue feathers wafting from where its palm should be, stretching outwards toward Figueroa. The shadow stopped an inch from his heart. Figueroa felt his back tingle like a leg that had gone numb. The tattoo, his protection, stirred. The *baphomet*. He heard something come from inside him, felt the ink moving under his skin. The shadow backed away. It stood facing him a moment longer, then climbed into the cot and curled up next to the sleeping girl.

It took everything José Figueroa had not to run out of the station. He stumbled down the steps, watching the cars pass along the narrow streets, and he heard someone yell something in the distance, in an alley. He heard the distant cadence of a mariachi band and he looked up and watched the moon hide behind the clouds. He missed his friend already. He shoved his hands in his pockets. Every alley he passed, a shadow. A feathered serpent. He turned down a dark street and saw a group of young men sitting on the hood of an old rusted car. They hopped down and asked him what he needed and he told them, and he paid, and when his wallet was empty and the drugs were in his brain he ran as fast as he could down the streets, ignoring the shouts of passersby, until the pain in his chest was too great. He slumped against a wall and sat heavily on the concrete, breathing fire into the cool night, and he held his head in his hands, and he came down from his high, and he saw the long, dark night stretched in front of him, and he cried. ✦

EMPTY CHURCH

BY *James Steele*

One of the trickiest things about devout Christianity—for believers and doubters alike—is the wide range of interpretations that abound. Since one's relationship with God is both personal and shared, based on sacred texts and precepts that we're all supposed to agree on, the schisms occur when people inevitably understand them in different ways.

Which leads us to "Empty Church," James Steele's subtle-by-Bizarro-standards case study at hand.

Be careful who you minister and pray for.

That is all I'm gonna say.

Pastor Sam stepped up to the pulpit. He leaned on it, stood up straight, took a breath, and opened the Bible. He'd been particularly drawn to a series of passages this whole week, and he wanted to tell everyone what he'd been thinking since the last service.

"Church," he began. "It shouldn't be an overglorified Bible study. It needs to be relevant to everyday life. So tonight I want to discuss ideas."

His voice echoed off the ceiling and the fake plastic chandeliers that reflected the blues, greens and reds of the stained-glass windows. It reached the modest double doors, echoed off the back wall and down the sloped walkway past the rows of pews, and finally back to the pulpit.

"Ideas that affect everyone. Ideas that seem to contradict belief in God. The biggest idea is science. Science has explained away just about everything God's people used to believe in.

"Disease, for example. Once believed to be punishment from God. Turns out it's caused by microbes. Lightning. That, too, isn't the wrath of God. It obeys natural laws that can be predicted, much like the movements of the stars and planets. People used to believe that God held everything together, but science has proven that these things are not supernatural.

"Over the generations so much that was once believed to be the work of God has been proven perfectly natural. So if God isn't doing these things—if He isn't holding the stars and planets in the sky, if He isn't casting down the unrighteous with disease, if He isn't destroying unholy buildings with his power, what is He doing?"

The pastor paused, as if waiting for a response. His voice reverberated around the room loudly. Sam was used to it; he'd been preaching with that echo for weeks.

He left the pulpit and paced, first addressing one side of the church, then turning and addressing the other. His great revelation—the one he'd been nursing all week—was coming out. Sam felt it happening. That rush, that flow, the anointing of the Holy Ghost filling him up and speaking through him. He never got tired of it; his brain not in control of his words and the message flowing from him as naturally as breathing. It was a wonderful revelation, and his duty as pastor was not only to reveal this new truth to his people, but to help them realize why they should care.

Sam's message went through the ages. Famine, floods, bad harvests, eclipses: The Bible was full of stories of God using these to exact His wrath or as a way to warn a people to change their ways. Since God is unchanging, He must be doing the same thing now.

"But science has explained these events as cyclical climate changes, weather patterns, and planetary movement. History has shown these stories to be people's explanation for forces they did not understand.

"I disagree. Scientific evidence is not a debunking of God's involvement. The stories in the Word have been preserved and handed down so perfectly for thousands of years; you can't tell me they would take such great care to preserve superstitious fiction.

"Proving how something works is the same as proving how God operates in our world. Einstein himself believed this, and it's an idea that has been largely lost today."

He flipped through multiple biblical references, expanded on the meaning of every passage and linked it back to his idea. He'd never heard scripture interpreted in this way before, and he wondered why no one had thought of it before him. People needed to hear this. It could change the world.

"God still punishes the unfaithful with disease! Famine is still a plea to a nation to change its ways! Notice how the nations that suffer from it are guilty of the most terrible crimes against humanity! Even lightning is still the same warning it used to be!

"Friends, I believe science has proven how God communicates with us! Of course these natural phenomena follow predicable patterns! God would naturally send His wrath down on the same types of people, for the same types of deeds, would He not? Those natural laws science claims to reveal are not laws, but they are God's hands operating in the world. God has been speaking to us this whole time, trying to show us what He likes and what He doesn't. He sends punishment down on the people whose actions He does not approve of and rewards the faithful! We attribute it to natural processes today, but this is not what science has uncovered."

Pastor Sam returned to the pulpit and leaned on it. He quieted down, as if giving the attendees a chance to absorb and reflect upon everything they had just heard. He concluded his Sunday message with a simple thought.

"Don't fall into the trap of considering advances of science the downfall of faith! We're moving further and further away from our beliefs because we view science as separate from God, but they are the same! This is a plan by the devil!

Satan wants everyone to stop believing not only in God, but in himself! The less people pay attention to him, the freer he is to move about and do whatever he pleases!

"So when a university, or a scientific paper, purports to prove that yet another thing we believe to be exclusively God's domain is actually quite rational, do not lose faith! Celebrate! Science is proving how God works in the world! The more we know about His methods, the better we can understand Him, and maybe, just maybe, through the scientific method we will come closer to an answer of what He wants from us."

The echoes of his last words took several seconds to stop swirling around. There literally was nothing to stop the sound. His wife insisted that he nail insulation against the opposite wall to cut down on the echo, but Sam was against the idea. He looked around at the now silent room.

He knelt, reached under the pulpit, and tapped the trackpad on a tiny computer. It switched off the recording program. He stood up straight, looked down on all fifteen rows of empty pews. The hymnals and complimentary Bibles were collecting dust. If not for him keeping up with it week after week, the pews themselves would be dusty.

Pastor Samuel Belt had bought this building nine months ago. He'd remodeled it into an inviting church himself, built a sign on the lawn that proclaimed services were held every Sunday morning and Wednesday night, and even commissioned and installed the stained-glass windows.

For the last five months Pastor Sam had held services on time every Sunday and Wednesday. At first, he had been discouraged by the lack of attendance. The building was outside of town on a back road, so he expected attendance to be light for a while. But Margaret had been hanging up posters and bulletins around the county for months, and the building remained empty.

After a few weeks, Sam grew tired of waiting for people to show up, so he began preaching to the empty church. He told his family that he didn't need to wait for permission to start preaching the Word; if he did what he was supposed to do, God would bring the people here.

He regretted not recording his messages in those early weeks, but he had anticipated that people would come and share his ideas. In a few years, Sam hoped, everyone would know his name.

He was sure it would happen, for back in his early twenties he heard a clear voice from God Himself. *You will change the world.* At first Sam didn't know how, but then one day while at church with his parents he received numerous compliments from his pastor on his insights about biblical topics. His pastor told him that he was spitting out ideas college professors would be interested in hearing. He had found his path.

Now in his late forties, years of schooling behind him and plenty of ideas before him, he was ready to start a church of his own and begin preaching sermons he was sure would change the world. He even got his son to run a podcasting website so people who couldn't be in his church would hear his messages.

It had been five months, and attendance was zero. Less than a dozen downloads on the podcasts. His wife posted banners in towns all across the county, encouraging people to come and hear his world-changing sermons, but he was still a ghost.

Sam preached as if the pews were overflowing. He preached as if a video crew were on the sidelines, recording him for television. He didn't save his best ideas for when the church was packed; no, he gave them now, in hopes that someone looking for a new church would walk in the door, hear his sermon, and recognize Sam as a true man of God.

But, for now, Pastor Sam preached to the stained glass. He preached to the fake chandeliers, confident someday he could afford real ones. He preached to the dusty Bibles and hymnals.

"If only someone were listening," he said. It reverberated six times around the empty church.

Sam once thought speaking to a large crowd was the hardest thing anyone could do, but now he knew just the opposite was true. An empty room was the coldest audience imaginable.

Margaret continued spreading the word of the new church. Jerry took out a couple of ads on various Christian websites pointing visitors to the podcasts. Sam himself bought radio time and broadcast edited versions of his sermons, complete with website information and the address of the church.

The pews were empty again this Sunday. Cobwebs hung from the chandeliers. Pastor Sam raised a tall ladder and climbed to the ceiling. He cleared the cobwebs and dusted the ceiling fixtures while he was up there.

Sam began to grumble. He felt the spirit of discouragement hanging over him, but he caught himself and cast down the ungodly thoughts with positive confessions while he dusted.

"Someday there will be so many people I won't need to think about nailing extra insulation to the walls to get rid of the echo. Someday I'll have to build additions to my church to hold the overflowing congregation. Someday I'll have a choir. People will recognize me as a man of God who preaches the truth . . ."

Three months of preaching to himself was enough to make anyone a little bitter, but he was determined not to give up. His breakthrough could happen any day, and he did not want to quit now, when he might be so close. He cleaned each chandelier, repeating these affirmations over and over again.

He climbed down the ladder, folded it, and set it against the wall. He took his place at the pulpit and faced the empty church. He imagined angels were watching him, waiting with baited breath. It kept him encouraged. Sam tapped the recorder.

"The Devil goes to church," he projected from his chest like a seasoned, theatrical performer. "The Devil reads the Bible. The Devil studies the Bible day and night. He knows it forwards and backwards. He knows things about the Bible no one else does. He has to. How else would Jesus have kept him quiet while he was in wilderness for forty days, tempted day and night? Jesus fought the Devil with scripture.

"Satan knows the only way to fight God is with the truth. You have to know the truth in order to lie, so the Devil must know what the Bible says. Since he is not perfect and can forget just like everyone else, he must need to study the Bible on a daily basis to gain new insight in how to fight God and His people. What better place to do that than church? A good church that teaches truth, not just doctrine. A church that instructs, and isn't merely an hourlong choir service."

Sam shouted to the empty room, pacing back and forth, shaking his fists at the air. He periodically glanced up at the ceiling, imagining God Himself in attendance listening to what he had to say, waiting for the right moment to reward Sam's perseverance.

"Satan needs to hear the truth as desperately as we do, so he would pick a church that preaches it! I suspect the Devil has no imagination. The ability to create is divine, so he needs to attend church to learn new perspectives and insights into . . ."

Pastor Sam paused at the pulpit and caught his breath. A man was standing in the double doorframe. He was dressed in formal Sunday clothes (suit and tie), and looked to be in his early thirties. Pastor Sam smiled, beckoned the man to come in, and kept on preaching.

The man slowly walked down the slope. His footsteps made no sound on the floor. He sat down in the front pew, hands on his thighs, and gazed up at the pulpit. For the next fifteen minutes, Sam preached to this man. He didn't recap; he hoped what he said now made sense on its own.

"If the Devil goes to church, what excuse do we have not to show up? My people are destroyed from lack of knowledge, *Hosea 4* says, so we must gain as much knowledge as we can, because Satan knows how to fight us! He is in church right now, taking new ideas and twisting them around to his advantage! Friends, we have to remain as educated as the Devil if we hope to fight him!

"If we knew just how desperately we needed to know the Word to survive, we would attend church every day! The Devil knows it! He attends church! He studies the Word! So pick a church that preaches truth! Do not ignore truth, because the Devil himself doesn't ignore it!"

His point had come full circle. He went over his usual time, but that didn't matter. He had an audience! He bent down and was about to click the recorder off, but the man stood up, stepped out of the pew, and walked up the slope to the double doors. Sam straightened up and leaned on the pulpit.

"Sir? Sir, thank you for coming. I'm Pastor Belt. What's your name?"

The man didn't slow down or turn back. He stepped very lightly; his footsteps were soundless. He walked through the door, turned the corner, and left the church. Sam didn't even have time to follow him out. He sighed.

Dear Pastor Belt,

Thank you for submitting your application for the Word of Life Seminar. We are committed to creating an environment where ministers, both new and established, can come together in fellowship and share their unique messages with people from all walks of life.

To that end, Pastor Belt, we have reviewed your credentials and your podcasts, and we regret that your message does not align with the beliefs of our attendees. It would not be prudent to allow speculative, new-age teaching in a convention that does not cater to such a crowd. Thank you again for your interest.

Sincerely,

J. Quinn
WoL Seminar Program Coordinator

Sam slowly set the letter down. Margaret looked across the table at her husband.

"I'm sorry."

Sam couldn't meet her eyes. "So am I. I had a lot of hope in this one. I thought someone in the Christian community would have heard me by now and liked what I had to say. Now we're going on six months. I have less than thirty downloads on my podcasts and one attendee."

Margaret got up, walked to Sam and embraced him. Sam stood up, too, and held his wife.

"We'll keep trying," he said. "It'll happen any day now. Any day."

Wednesday night. Sam refused to focus on the bad news and concentrated on the encouraging sign of that lone man last Sunday. He hoped he had lots of friends who wanted to hear refreshing, world-changing ideas.

Sam switched on the recorder. He opened his mouth. As he spoke his first words, the man from last Sunday turned the corner, walked down the aisle to the platform, and took a seat in the same place as before. He was dressed in the same clothes, and again had no Bible. Sam nodded to him, smiling, and began speaking.

Another man, dressed in an identical suit and tie, peeked around the corner and walked down the aisle. Sam's heart skipped a few beats as the second man took a seat in the rear pew.

Dozens of suited men silently walked around the corner in lockstep. They were dressed in the same black suits, red ties, black shoes, and black slacks. All men, no women or children. They took seats in the pews and stared at Sam. The congregation filled half the pews. They were sitting in the same posture: straight as poles, arms at their sides, one hand on each thigh. They never blinked.

Sam clutched the side of the pulpit. This had the hallmarks of everything that should scare him senseless, but instead Sam's heart fluttered that his audience was growing! Who was he to criticize the congregation God brought to him?

Sam swallowed the stony stares, gathered his courage, and began preaching his own personal revelation about a modern update to the idea of Heaven and Hell.

"Science says the planet is four-and-a-half-billion years old. Overwhelming evidence supports this. What evidence is there in the Bible that the Earth is *not* that old? The Bible states that God created Heaven and Earth, but it doesn't say how. Perhaps there was a Big Bang, and that was the method God used to set things in motion."

Sam couldn't read the men's expressions. They sat stoic, unmoving. Sam was sure they weren't even blinking, but he didn't let them distract him. He kept preaching as though the place were still empty.

"Tradition says Hell is below the Earth and Heaven is above, among the stars. This is based on tradition found in Greek culture, for example, not scripture. Man's knowledge of the world and the universe was limited at the time, and I say we need a new concept of Heaven and Hell! One that takes into account everything we know now!

"When we think of Hell, we think below the Earth, but what do we know now that the ancients didn't? What is the closest thing to Hell we've observed in the universe? The sun. Stars! The conditions match everything the Bible has to say about what Hell must be like!"

Sam referenced news articles and found coordinating references in the Bible to back up his connections. Then he took the idea one step further.

"Now, the universe is full of stars. My friends, I believe God has shown me the stars are Hell. Each one in the universe is a private hell for one person condemned to burn in isolation for billions of years, cut off from the presence of God.

"But why? Why would God go through all this trouble to create such elaborate prisons for every unrighteous person who ever lived? Well, my friends, that's where Heaven comes in.

"Where is Heaven? We refer to outer space as 'the heavens' constantly, and this one we actually got right. Heaven has been staring us in the face this whole time! It is the rest of the universe! I believe God showed me that when our bodies die, our souls are released into the universe. He contains the unrighteous in stars because they will cause great harm not just to what He has created in Heaven, but to the faithful. The people with the fruit of the spirit are free to go anywhere in the universe they please, free of the confines of a physical body, free to explore all of God's creation! Free to share fellowship with each other, and hunger, disease, and fatigue cannot touch them!"

The men seemed breathless. Sam didn't know if they were stunned because they thought it made sense, or because they thought it was ridiculous. He had bounced this one off his son a few weeks ago, and Jerry thought it sounded like new-age nonsense, but Sam wasn't going to let a revelation about the universe go to waste. He wrapped up his message.

"My fellow believers, every time a star goes nova it means a condemned person is free from Hell, roaming Heaven and inflicting harm on those who are worthy of touching God's creation! We need to explore space! We need to research ways to keep stars from dying!

"Scientists predict one day all the stars will die. This is in the Bible! The book of Revelation promises one day the Devil will be set free of his own personal hell, and will lead an army on God's kingdom! Both science and the Word predict the same event! This is the real apocalypse, and I believe God gave me this revelation because He wants me to tell everyone we can prevent it!"

Sam paused for a few beats. Without switching off the recorder, he leaned on the pulpit and looked down at the man sitting up front. "Thank you for coming and I'm sorry, sir, I didn't catch your name the other day. Can I interest any of you in coffee? Soda?"

The man who sat at the front rose to his feet. "You are good at what you do, Pastor Belt. Do not stop."

The entire congregation stood at the same time. Like automatons, they silently filed into the aisle and walked out the door into the hall. They never spoke, their arms didn't leave their sides, and their feet were silent on the wooden slope. Sam followed the last man out.

"I want to thank you for bringing these people here. I feel awfully guilty that I don't know anyone's name or where you come from. Feel free to bring your wives. Children. The whole family. We could use some volunteers for Sunday school as well, and . . . and if any of you are interested in a Deacon's position there's—"

The pastor walked to the double doors, turned the corner and stopped. They were gone. A congregation of a hundred men was missing. No one milling in the hall. No cars in the parking lot, and no one chatting out there. The man he was following was the only one left. He walked down the short hall to the front door. He stepped off the landing, turned the corner, and the church was as silent as ever.

Jerry was seated at the computer. Margaret was standing off to the side. Sam stood behind Jerry, looking at the monitor at a preacher's website. Someone named Dr. Dale Vernon, pastor of the Dale Vernon International Church of Christ. His website looked incredibly professional. The tiny video window showed the pastor talking to the camera.

"Pastor Samuel Belt owns a church with no attendees. Yet he keeps preaching. He runs a podcast service so those who don't attend his church can also hear his 'world-altering' sermons. There are no downloads, but he keeps preaching."

The man sounded like the stereotypical fire-and-brimstone preacher. A portrait of Sam (taken from the podcast page) faded into view beside Pastor Vernon. He played a few clips from the "Modern Heaven and Hell" podcast, complete with subtitles.

"You heard right, everyone: Bad people are trapped in stars, the faithful get to float around the cosmos. One, the idea belongs in science fantasy, not church. Two, he's forgetting that most of those wonders in the universe are created in the wake of dying stars. Astronomers have observed it in progress for decades, but he ignores this.

"I am ashamed of this man, for he has attended the same universities and Bible colleges I have, and instead of using his years of biblical knowledge to preach the truth, he is trying to convince people of *this*!"

A clip from an earlier sermon played, and Dr. Vernon gave a rebuttal.

" . . . and if God still punishes us with plagues and disease, what about the innocent victims of floods or earthquakes? Surely he can't accuse everyone in a disaster zone of deserving to lose their houses, or their lives just because it happened to affect them . . ."

" . . . unfounded statements . . ."

" . . . new-age doublespeak . . ."

" . . . must have read too much L. Ron Hubbard."

It concluded with a plea to boycott his church, his podcasts, and his blasphemous ideas, lest he start yet another cult. The video ended. Margaret and Jerry were silent. Sam straightened up and met her eyes.

"Sam," Margaret began.

"I know what you're going to say."

"It has been six months," she said anyway. "Maybe this is God trying to tell you something."

"Just because someone opposes it doesn't mean it's wrong."

"But these are men and women of God. They know what they're talking about. I think you should take this as a sign."

Sam looked at Jerry. Jerry shrugged, and turned back to the computer. He opened a chat window and started typing to his friends. Sam faced his wife again.

The expression on her face was pleading. Sam hung his head for a moment, collected his thoughts.

"I have an audience now. Last week the pews were half full of people who understand what I'm trying to do. I am pioneering a new way of thinking about God and it can change the world! Everything we call orthodox was set before there was science to explain these things, and now that we know more about the world, we must adjust our beliefs accordingly. People are starting to listen! I can't quit now!"

Margaret was silent for a long time. Jerry's instant messenger popped and beeped every few seconds.

"What if you're wrong?" said Margaret.

Sam had nothing to say.

"I still love you, Sam," she continued, "but I've been listening to your sermons. They're nuts."

Jerry pretended not to listen.

"That's why no one's showing up. What if it's not the Holy Spirit filling your head with great revelations? What if they're just your crazy fantasies?"

Sam was going to say, *They said that to Jesus, too*, but comparing himself to Christ would only make him sound crazier. Margaret walked away.

Next Sunday, Sam stood at the pulpit and opened his Bible. Right on cue, silent, uniform, robotic men filed into the church one by one. He waited until everyone was seated.

Only one seat was vacant. The space stood out like a gap between a supermodel's teeth. Sam knew the seating capacity. He had about two hundred people in the pews. He focused on this bit of trivia instead of the identically dressed, identically behaving men of identical age and build.

"Thank you for coming again," he said. The lack of reverberation was like angels playing harps to his ears. "I admit that I'm surprised everyone is here at both the Sunday and Wednesday services. I've been to many churches in my life and I can't say I've seen a more faithful bunch of—"

Something large rounded the corner and stooped through the double doors. His body was extremely muscled and hairy. The creature's hair was matted with dried blood. His face looked like a cross between a dog's muzzle and a bird's beak—simultaneously ugly and fascinating. The horns on his head were coiled like a ram's, and they too had bloodstains on them. His ratlike tail was barbed at the end, and his outstretched wings filled the doorframe. He held a Bible in one clawed hand.

He walked on digitigrade, goat legs down the aisle and to the pew in the back. He folded his wings around his body and seated himself in the one vacant spot. He sat three feet taller than everyone else in the congregation.

From the corner of his eye, a smaller, gangly monster without wings was now seated where one of the uniform men had been. A dozen others melted into sight through the suited men. Sam's eyes darted from one to the other, all around the pews. Men disappeared. Monsters took their place while Sam wasn't looking.

It was over in only a few seconds. Sam observed the room as a whole. The pews were full to the brim with hideous creatures. Most were bald and malnourished. Some had no skin, their muscle and bone easily visible and twitching with every slight movement. Others had fur, stained in blood. Most had wings folded behind their backs.

"To . . . Tod . . . um," Sam stuttered. After a few attempts he finally spit it out. "Today. The book of Amos."

They reached forward and took the complimentary Bibles from the pews and flipped in unison to what Sam knew must be the book of Amos. The sharp claws on their hands did not seem to hinder their ability to turn pages. The large monster opened his Bible to the same place. Sam could now see his book was made of flesh, and the spine was real human vertebrae.

Sam glanced around the room, unsure of what to say. His eyes traveled down to the creature sitting in the front pew—his first attendee. No longer the man Sam had come to expect, but a winged monster whose skin dangled loosely off his muscle and bone. He mouthed, *Don't stop* and tapped the complimentary Bible with a claw.

Sam nodded, swallowed his nerves. "Amos," he began

Sam preached to the demons. They followed along as they always had. The big one took notes and marked passages in his personal Bible as Sam read them.

When he finished his message, Sam expected everyone to file out and leave as they had before. In his mind he thought he should hope they would leave quickly, but he was strangely calm in their presence.

The creatures silently stood in unison. Some relaxed their wings, others let their tails flail about. The big one stood up after the crowd. He alone stepped into the aisle and walked down the slope to the pulpit. His hooves were loud on the floor. Sam sensed that his heart should be pumping him full of fight-or-flight, but he felt nothing.

The monster's wings were still folded around him as he walked down the aisle, making him appear to be wearing an elegant, gentlemen's coat. It hid his animistic legs very well. He stopped at the platform. He extended a clawed hand from beneath his folded wing. His other hand held the Bible by his hip.

Sam wasn't afraid. He stepped down from the platform, stood toe to hoof with the massive creature and shook his hand. His grip was fiery. Sam felt blisters forming on his hand, but he held his mouth shut. Screaming seemed like a rude thing to do.

"I've been looking for a new church," said the massive beast. "I regret I was unable to attend your sermon on the real Heaven and Hell, but I heard the recording. It's not often I find someone who has the courage to say something new."

Sam thought he should be banishing this creature to the depths from which he came, but as he shook hands with him, Sam smiled.

"Thank you."

As soon as the words left his mouth, the church was empty and silent again. Sam's hand was still outstretched, still burning.

The following Wednesday Sam stepped up to the pulpit and faced the empty church. He looked down. Opened the Bible. He looked up. The congregation hall was as large as a thousand football fields. The stained-glass windows still lined the walls, but they were so distant Sam could barely make them out. The pews were the same, but they were multiplied a thousandfold. The perspective was skewed, making his church and everything in it stretch to infinity in all directions.

Sam picked up his Bible from the podium and walked around the platform, taking in the congregation as a whole. The pews were full of demons again. Sam stood on a platform in the middle of a congregation of demonic creatures. They watched him, unblinking, as if their lives depended on it. In the distance, Sam spotted the largest of them all, sitting in a pew, Bible in hand, waiting eagerly.

Sam opened his mouth and preached. It took less than an hour to reveal his great, world-altering revelation, and then he returned to the pulpit. His congregation sat unblinking, unmoving. It wasn't intimidating at all. It was as if the months of preaching to an empty church had prepared him for this.

Sam couldn't help himself. He stepped down from the podium, reached out and offered his hand to the nearest demon.

"Thank you for coming!"

The creature extended its skinless hand and Sam grasped it. It burned slightly, but not nearly enough to make Sam uncomfortable.

"Thank you. Thank you so much for listening!"

The demon appeared humbled that Sam had shook its hand. Sam let go and moved up the aisle, offering his hand to anyone. Multiple demons rose and took Pastor Sam's hand. He thanked each of them and walked on.

Many of the creatures with wings took to the air, flew through the skewed congregation hall. They landed on pews and in the aisle as Sam walked among them, shaking hands. A few had the courage to speak up and thank him for the excellent sermon.

Sam walked a mile in his own church. The demons flew around, landed, talked among themselves, took off and flew overhead some more. The pastor's gaze traveled all around. Demons of all shapes and sizes flew between the chandeliers. Some of them landed on a pew and joined up with another group in the pews. Then others took off, flew over Sam's head.

They were fellowshipping. The sound of fellowship was in his church at last. It made Sam cry with delight. He eagerly shook more hands, expressing profuse gratitude.

The large creature in the back stood up. The congregation was silent. The demons that were in the air landed immediately. Sam stood alone in the aisle. The Beast stepped out of the pew. Wings fully outstretched, he walked down the gradual slope to the pulpit. He seemed to be ten miles away, but in just a few dozen steps he stood toe to hoof with Sam. He lay a large, boiling-hot hand on Sam's shoulder.

"You have a gift, Samuel Belt."

Sam thought he would feel terrified hearing those words from this individual, but these were the words Sam had always wanted to hear. He felt proud.

"Walk with me."

Sam joined him at his side. He talked with Sam at length about his previous sermons. He had used the days between services to catch up, and he wanted to discuss the particulars of Sam's messages. Sam was eager to discuss his old ideas with a person who wouldn't call them new-age nonsense and slowly turn away.

He had been searching for where his enemy imprisoned his people for millennia. He looked below the earth, on other planets, even in other people's bodies. Then Sam came along and figured out they were trapped in the most obvious place of all. This put within reach something he had been searching for since time began: It was possible to free his people.

He asked Sam for ideas on potential ways to do this. Sam was thrilled; he had been thinking about this since he gave that sermon and at last he had someone to talk to about it.

He and Sam walked miles in the church while billions of demons fellowshipped overhead and in the pews. He was dwarfed by the Beast's enormous mass, but at no time did Sam feel small by comparison. After they had put their heads together, Sam felt at liberty to ask him something.

"I have to know. Why are you here? Why did you show up and . . . and not, uh, God's people."

The Beast smiled. "Remember your sermon on the Devil's preacher?"

Sam nodded.

"Germ theory. When it was first introduced, people called it crazy, outrageous, maybe even blasphemous, but it was true. Earth orbits the sun. Totally against the Word, said God's people, but it was the truth. The church rejects thousands of ideas like these as sacrilege, but it's always the most ridiculous ideas that turn out to be correct. I know the truth when I hear it. Anyone who doesn't listen is a holy fool."

He chuckled. "My last minister also had ideas that weren't biblical. God's people wouldn't listen, but I did. The first to recognize the truth is the first to act on it, and that's how I get ahead. It was his idea to separate church and science, and it worked beautifully. I can do anything now, and if I figure out a way to release my people from their prisons, Heaven won't exist. It's possible to win. I can't create new ideas, but you can. You are changing everything, Pastor Sam."

Sam meant that revelation for God's people! It was a call to action to keep learning, keep exploring to get closer to God. Sam once believed he would rebuke this beast for perverting his ideas, but instead Sam smiled and walked with him among the fellowshipping demons.

Pastor Samuel Belt stepped up to the pulpit. He examined his church. The chandeliers were no longer plastic. They were brass with real crystals hanging from them. The pews had cushioning now. The complimentary Bibles weren't generic King James editions, but modern translations bound in leather.

He opened the Bible on the pulpit and looked up. His church reached to infinity. The demons seated and perched in the infinite rows of pews and on the chandeliers had his full attention. In this enormous congregation was the Beast himself, Bible open, notebook ready.

Sam enjoyed the Sunday sermons more than Wednesdays. Service was early in the morning, and the rising sun shined through the stained-glass windows. Their majestic light cast the demons in a brilliant, holy glow.

Sam had never seen a more faithful group of churchgoers in his life. Everyone was here on time for every service. Sam was sure if he started doing three services a week, they would show up for that one, too. They had to. Their lives depended on what he said.

They were also the most generous congregation Sam had ever seen. After every sermon Sam found thousands of dollars in the plates, even though they had never been passed around. More than enough to pay the church's bills and support his family.

The choir began chanting. Demons silhouetted against the stained-glass windows and hanging from the beautiful chandeliers howled and shrieked. Their voices drew more confidence out of Sam.

He thought back on the rejection letters he still received week after week. The ridicule he got on national television for continuing to preach to an empty church. The personal visits from other ministers begging him to stop. The magazine articles that condemned his crazy ideas. The radio stations that refused to play his sermons.

Holy fools, Sam thought with a grin. *I could've saved them. They had their chance.* ◆

ANGELOLOGY

EXCERPT

BY *Danielle Trussoni*

Danielle Trussoni is a fascinating writer whose acclaimed first novel, Angelology, *richly immerses itself in the history of Nephilim: the formidable offspring of angels and earthly women.*

Of course, when they're fallen angels—cast out from Heaven for their vainglorious rebellion—this does not tend to auger well for the poor old human race.

I love this excerpt because it provides vast historical sweep with a cagey old contemporary Nephelim I couldn't wait to more deeply explore. Not to mention the fact that he's got a billiard table.

Truth be told, I'd love to play him sometime, just to marvel at the kinds of byzantine shots he would doubtlessly line up with that ancient, ruthless cue.

The Grigori penthouse, Upper East Side, New York City

The Grigori family had acquired the penthouse in the late 1940s from the debt-ridden daughter of an American tycoon. It was large and magnificent, much too big for a bachelor with an aversion to large parties, and so it had come as something of a relief when Percival's mother and Otterley began to occupy the upper floors. When he had lived there alone, he had spent hours alone playing billiards, the doors closed to the movement of servants brushing through the corridors. He would draw the heavy green velvet drapes, turn the lamps low, and drink scotch as he aligned shot after shot, aiming the cue and slamming the polished balls into netted pockets.

As time passed, he remodeled various rooms of the apartment but left the billiard room exactly as it had been in the 1940s—slightly tattered leather furniture, the transmitter-tube radio with Bakelite buttons, an eighteenth-century Persian rug, an abundance of musty old books filling the cherrywood shelves, hardly any of which he had attempted to read. The volumes were purely decorative, admired for their age and value. There were calf-bound volumes pertaining to the origins and exploits of his many relations—histories, memoirs, epic novels of battle, romances. Some of these books had been shipped from Europe after the war; others were acquired from a venerable book dealer in the neighborhood, an old friend of the family transplanted from London. The man had a sharp sense for what the Grigori family most desired—tales of European conquest, colonial glory, and the civilizing power of Western culture.

Even the distinctive smell of the billiard room remained the same—soap and leather polish, a faint hint of cigar. Percival still relished whiling away the hours there, calling every so often for the maid to bring him a fresh drink. She was a young Anakim female who was wonderfully silent. She would place a glass of scotch next to him and sweep the empty glass away, making him comfortable with practiced efficiency. With a flick of his wrist, he would dismiss the servant, and she would disappear in an instant. It pleased him that she always left quietly, closing the wide wooden doors behind her with a soft click.

Percival maneuvered himself onto a stuffed armchair, swirling the scotch in its cut-crystal glass. He straightened his legs—slowly, gently—onto an ottoman. He thought of his mother and her complete disregard for his efforts in getting them this far. That he had obtained definite information about St. Rose Convent should have given her faith in him. Instead Sneja had instructed Otterley to oversee the creatures she'd sent upstate.

Taking a sip of scotch, Percival tried to telephone his sister. When Otterley did not pick up, he checked his watch, annoyed. She should have called by now.

For all her faults, Otterley was like their father—punctual, methodical, and utterly reliable under pressure. If Percival knew her, she had consulted with their father in London and had drawn up a plan to contain and eliminate Verlaine. In fact, it wouldn't surprise him if his father had outlined the plan from his office, giving Otterley whatever she needed to execute his wishes. Otterley was his father's favorite. In his eyes she could do nothing wrong.

Looking at his watch again, Percival saw that only two minutes had passed. Perhaps something had happened to warrant Otterley's silence. Perhaps their efforts had been thwarted. It wouldn't be the first time they had been lured into a seemingly innocuous situation only to be cornered.

He felt his legs pulsing and shaking, as if the muscles rebelled against repose. He took another sip of scotch, willing it to calm him, but nothing worked when he was in such a state. Leaving his cane behind, Percival drew himself up from the chair and hobbled to a bookshelf where he removed a calf-bound volume and placed it gently upon the billiard table. The spine creaked when he pressed the cover open, as if the binding might pop apart. Percival had not opened *The Book of Generations* in many, many years, not since the marriage of one of his cousins had sent him searching for family connections on the bride's side—it was always awkward to arrive at a wedding and be at a loss for who mattered and who did not, especially when the bride was a member of the Danish royal family.

The Book of Generations was an amalgamation of history, legend, genealogy, and prediction pertaining to his kind. All Nephilistic children received an identical calf-bound volume at the end of their schooling, a kind of parting gift. The stories told of battle, of the founding of countries and kingdoms, of the binding together in pacts of loyalty, of the Crusades, of the knighthoods and quests and bloody conquests—these were the great stories of Nephilistic lore. Percival often wished that he had been born in those times, when their actions were not so visible, when they were able to go about their business quietly, without the danger of being monitored. Their power had been able to grow with the aid of silence, each victory building upon the one that came before. The legacy of his ancestors was all there, recorded in *The Book of Generations*.

Percival read the first page, filled with bold script. There was a list of names documenting the sprawling history of the Nephilistic bloodline, a catalog of families that began at the time of Noah and branched into ruling dynasties. Noah's son Japheth had migrated to Europe, his children populating Greece, Parthia, Russia, and northern Europe and securing their family's dominance. Percival's family was descended directly from Javan, Japheth's fourth son, the first to colonize the "Isles of the Gentiles," which some took to mean Greece and others believed to be the British Isles. Javan had six brothers, whose names were recorded in the Bible, and a number of sisters, whose names were not recorded, all of whom created the basis of their influence and power throughout Europe. In many ways *The Book of Generations* was a recapitulation of the history of the world. Or, as modern Nephilim preferred to think, the survival of the fittest.

Looking over the list of families, Percival saw that their influence had once been absolute. In the past three hundred years, however, Nephilistic families had fallen into decline. Once there had been a balance between human and Nephilim. After the Flood they'd been born in almost equal numbers. But Nephilim were deeply attracted to humans and had married into human families, causing the genetic dilution of their most potent qualities. Now Nephilim possessing predominantly human characteristics were common, while those who had pure angelic traits were rare.

With thousands of humans born for every one Nephilim, there was some debate among good families about the relevance of their human-born relations. Some wished to exclude them, push them further into the human realm, while others believed in their value, or at least their use to the larger cause. Cultivating relations with the human members of Nephilim families was a tactical move, one that might yield great results. A child born to Nephilim parents, without the slightest trace of angelic traits, might in turn produce a Nephilistic offspring. It was an uncommon occurrence, to be sure, but not unheard of. To address this possibility, the Nephilim observed a tiered system, a caste relating not to wealth or social status—although these criteria mattered as well—but to physical traits, to breeding, to a resemblance to their ancestors, a group of angels called the Watchers. While humans carried the genetic potential to create a Nephilistic child, the Nephilim themselves embodied the angelic ideal. Only a Nephilistic being could develop wings. And Percival's had been the most magnificent anyone had seen in half a millennium.

He turned the pages of *The Book of Generations*, stopping randomly at a middle section of the book. There was an etching of a noble merchant dressed in velvets and silks, a sword cocked in one hand and a bag of gold in the other. An endless procession of women and slaves knelt around him, awaiting his command, and a concubine stretched out upon a divan at his side, her arms draped over her body. Caressing the picture, Percival read a one-line biography of the merchant describing him "as an elusive nobleman who organized fleets to all corners of the uncivilized world, colonizing wilderness and organizing the natives." So much had changed in the past three hundred years, so many parts of the globe subdued. The merchant would not recognize the world they lived in today.

Turning to another page, Percival happened upon one of his favorite tales in the book, the story of a famous uncle on his father's side—Sir Arthur Grigori, a Nephilim of great wealth and renown whom Percival recalled as a marvelous storyteller. Born in the early seventeenth century, Sir Arthur had made wise investments in many of the nascent shipping companies of the British Empire. His faith in the East India Company alone had brought him enormous profit—as his manor house and his cottage and his farmlands and his city apartments could well attest. While he was never directly involved in overseeing his business ventures abroad, Percival knew that his uncle had undertaken journeys around the globe and had amassed a great collection of treasures. Travel had always given him great pleasure, especially when he explored the more exotic corners of the planet, but his primary motive for distant excursion had been business. Sir Arthur had been known for his Svengali-like ability to convince humans to do all he asked of them. Percival arranged the book in his lap and read:

Sir Arthur's ship arrived just weeks after the infamous uprising of May 1857. From the seas to the Gangetic Plain, in Meerut and Delhi and Kanpur and Lucknow and Jhansi and Gwalior, the Revolt spread, wreaking discord among the hierarchies that governed the land. Peasants overtook their masters, killing and maiming the British with sticks and sabers and whatever weapons they could make or steal to suit their treachery. In Kanpur it was reported that two hundred European women and children were massacred in a single morning, while in Delhi peasants spread gunpowder upon the streets until they appeared covered in pepper. One imbecilic fellow lit a match for his *bidi*, blowing all and sundry to pieces.

Sir Arthur, seeing that the East India Company had fallen into chaos and fearing that his profits would be affected, called the Governor-General to his apartments one afternoon to discuss what might be done between them to rectify the terrible events. The Governor-General, a portly, pink man with a penchant for chutney, arrived in the hottest hour of the day, a flock of children about him—one holding the umbrella, another holding a fan, and yet another balancing a glass of iced tea upon a tray. Sir Arthur received him with the shades drawn, to keep away the glare of both the sun and curious passersby.

"I must say, Governor-General," Sir Arthur began, "a revolt is no great greeting."

"No, sir," the Governor-General replied, adjusting a polished gold monocle over a bulbous blue eye. "And it is no great farewell, either."

Seeing that they understood one another very well, the men discussed the matter. For hours they dissected the causes and effects of the revolt. In the end Sir Arthur had a suggestion. "There must be an example made," he said, drawing a long cigar from a balsam box and lighting it with a lighter, an imprint of the

Grigori family crest etched upon its side. "It is essential to drive fear into their hearts. One must create a spectacle that will terrify them into compliance. Together we will choose a village. When we are through with them, there will be no more revolts."

While the lesson Sir Arthur taught the British soldiers was well known in Nephilistic circles—indeed, they had been practicing such fear-generating tactics privately for many hundreds of years—it was rarely used on such a large group. Under Sir Arthur's deft command, the soldiers rounded up the people of the chosen village—men, women, and children—and brought them to the market. He chose a child, a girl with almond eyes, silken black hair, and skin the color of chestnuts. The girl gazed curiously at the man, so tall and fair and gaunt, as if to say, even among the peculiar-looking British, this man is odd. Yet she followed after him, obedient.

Oblivious to the stares of the natives, Sir Arthur led the child before the prisoners of war—as the villagers were now called—lifted her into his arms, and deposited her into the barrel of a loaded cannon. The barrel was long and wide, and it swallowed the child entirely—only her hands were visible as they clung tight to the iron rim, holding it as if it were the top of a well into which she might sink.

"Light the fuse," Sir Grigori commanded. As the young soldier, his fingers trembling, struck a match, the girl's mother cried out from the crowd.

The explosion was the first of many that morning. Two hundred village children—the exact number of British killed in the Kanpur massacre—were led one by one to the cannon. The iron grew so hot that it charred the fingers of the soldiers dropping the heavy bundles of wiggling flesh, all hair and fingernails, into the shaft. Restrained at gunpoint, the villagers watched. Once the bloody business was through, the soldiers turned their muskets upon the villagers, ordering them to clean the market courtyard. Pieces of their children hung upon the tents and bushes and carts. Blood stained the earth orange.

News of the horror soon spread to the nearby villages and from those villages to the Gangetic Plain, to Meerut and Delhi and Kanpur and Lucknow and Jhansi and Gwalior. The Revolt, as Sir Arthur Grigori had foretold, quieted.

Percival's reading was interrupted by the sound of Sneja's voice as she leaned over his shoulder. "Ah, Sir Arthur," she said, the shadow of her wings falling over the pages of the book. "He was one of the finest Grigoris, my favorite of your father's brothers. Such valor! He secured our interests across the globe. If only his end had been as glorious as the rest of his life."

Percival knew that his mother was referring to Uncle Arthur's sad and pathetic demise. Sir Arthur had been one of the first in their family to contract the illness that now afflicted Percival. His once-glorious wings had withered to putrid, blackened nubs, and after a decade of terrible suffering his lungs had collapsed. He had died in humiliation and pain, succumbing to the disease in the fifth century of life, a time when he should have been enjoying his retirement. Many had believed the illness to be the result of his exposure to various lower breeds of human life—the wretched natives in the various colonial ports—but the truth of the matter was that the Grigoris did not know the origin of the illness. They knew only that there may be a way to cure it.

In the 1980s Sneja had come into possession of a human scientist's body of work devoted to the therapeutic properties of certain varieties of music. The scientist had been named Angela Valko and was the daughter of Gabriella Lévi-Franche Valko, one of the most renowned angelologists working in Europe. According to Angela Valko's theories, there was a way to restore Percival, and all their kind, to angelic perfection.

As was her wont, Sneja appeared to be reading her son's mind. "Despite your best efforts to sabotage your own cure, I believe that your art historian has pointed us in the right direction."

"You've found Verlaine?" Percival asked, closing *The Book of Generations* and turning to his mother. He felt like a child again, wishing to win Sneja's approval. "Did he have the drawings?"

"As soon as we hear from Otterley, we will know for certain," Sneja said, taking *The Book of Generations* from Percival and paging through it. "Clearly we overlooked something during our raids. But make no mistake, we will find the object of our search. And you, my angel, will be the first to benefit from its properties. After you are cured, we will be the saviors of our kind."

"Magnificent," Percival said, imagining his wings and how lush they would be once they had returned. "I will go to the convent myself. If it is there, I want to be the one to find it."

"You are too feeble." Sneja glanced at the glass of scotch. "And drunk. Let Otterley and your father handle this. You and I will stay here."

Sneja tucked *The Book of Generations* under her arm and, kissing Percival on the cheek, left the billiard room.

The thought of being trapped in New York City during one of the most important moments of his life enraged him. Taking his cane, he walked to the telephone and dialed Otterley's number once more. As he waited for her to answer, he assured himself that his strength would soon return. He would be beautiful and powerful once more. With the restoration of his wings, all the suffering and humiliation he had endured would be transformed to glory. ✦

THE CODA OF SOLOMON

BY *Nick Mamatas*

This cunning corporate update on C.S. Lewis and The Screwtape Letters *is short, blunt, and precisely as convoluted as it needs to be, to get its horrible point across:*

The damned are our business, and business is good.

Brought to you by noted genre contrarian Nick Mamatas: scourge of the vocally under-informed, and a very fine writer indeed.

If our five-pointed star logo looks familiar, it is because its shape and suggestion of dynamism are common to most esoteric symbols. It's taken from the seal engraved upon the Ring of Solomon, given to the wise man by the archangel Michael. As explained in the ancient *Testament of Solomon*, with this ring Solomon commanded a bestiary of demons—Lix Tetrax who sets fields aflame and divides men into factions, tiny Sphendonael who causes muscle spasms, Belbel who engenders perversions, Kunopegos the wrecker of ships, Katanikotael who sours conversations at the dinner table and turns brother against brother, Ephippas who kills kings and moves mountains, and legions more—to build his temple. And it soared above the hills of Jerusalem.

Solomon filled his temple with his countless wives and favorite whores, as was his right as the beloved of G-d. And for G-d he made war with his iron chariots against the Jebusites, who certainly had it coming. You *all* have it coming. But then Solomon fell in love with a foreign girl who worshipped strange gods. Eros will tell you in the voice of a contemporary statesman, "Mistakes were made." For, at the bidding of his Shummanite betrothed, Solomon crushed a few locusts in his hands in the name of the gods of the girl's fathers. Baal! Remphan! Moloch! In an instant, all was lost to Solomon. For us, everything was gained. *A contract is a contract is a contract*, that's our motto. You've seen the play, we hope.

Every pain and discomfort is caused by a demon. The land and skies are owned by demons. At the root of every private agony and social dislocation is a demon. The occasional twinge in your arm, or a moment of piercing pain so sudden that you're unsure that it's in your tooth or temple? A demon. We didn't need to spend a lot of time or money on focus groups in perfecting our "look" because you already know us. Even in the womb we are imprinted on your brain, traced out among neurons, waiting in the synaptic clefts as they formed. We're the riverbed; your gray matter is the water. Believe it or don't, that's fine. Your social scientists do. Survival of the fittest, the alpha male, *Homo economicus*, the sovereign individual working rationally in his or her individual self-interest—we are all of these. You love us, you live us. This is the best of all possible worlds.

We are a partnership. Baal and Remphan and Moloch—paint it on the window of our office door in block letters. We are the demons of the limited-liability corporation, and we have been for a long time. It has taken millennia. So many kings had to die; so many ships had to sink, taking fortunes with them to the inky deep; tendons snapped; men died in their sleep, but the ancient and feudal orders finally passed into oblivion. Robdos, the man of such erudition he could stop a falling star in the sky, whom G-d imprisoned in the form of a dog and made a slave to Solomon, surrendered to us and joined our multifarious research and development wing long ago. What can we say, other than, "You're welcome." Indeed, there is one more thing we can say—we want your help. Need it. Rather, we insist upon it.

It's a small thing. Every thing has its own demon, and every demon has its thing. But there's something only you can do, and it will be simplicity itself to accomplish, and in return . . . well, we've already paid you in advance. Take a look at the world around you. You're literate. You likely have most of your teeth, and have replaced those you lost with synthetic copies that future archeologists will pluck clean and entire from the remains of your corpse and your burial outfit. You're not tied to the land, nor an owned chattel slave. If you work at all, it's not under the whip—and we've felt the whip ourselves back in the days of seals of tokens. Solomon and his infinite riches, his immense temple, all that was nothing compared to what we have given to you and hundreds of millions like you. Solomon spent his nights under thick woolen blankets, teeth chattering, beard quivering, praying to G-d to lend him once again Lix Tetrax, whose winds blow hot. You have central heating, or at least a radiator. You don't even know how it works—for you adjusting the dial on the thermostat is a magical ritual whereby the demon is constrained to warm your room.

Solomon had to be concerned that his brides and concubines were virgins. Despite his wisdom and endless power, any aggrieved shepherd with a prior claim to this or that cunt could have struck him down with impunity. Imagine the wisest brains in all the world decorating the blue and white tiles our colleagues placed on the floor of the temple's great hall. G-d, immaterial as always, looking on sans comment for once. Asmodeus, the demon who brings discord to newlyweds, who blackens the hearts and faces of virgin women, has long since lost his influence in the times in which you live and we reign. We rent out virgin sluts for soda pop and pop music and run through generations of the little nymphs in a game of musical chairs, a game you love to watch.

You know the new sacred words—career and credit, synergy and functionalities, value-added proceduralization and capital amortization. Can you skin a hare?

Create a drawing cataplasm to soothe torn tendons, that nagging wound the precinct of old Rhyx Ichthuon? You needn't. We've taken care of that for you. Thanks to an aggressive program of mergers and acquisitions, there are virtually no independent demons left, no agonies other than ignorance and the pain you pray for so in secret so that you might know what it feels like to live. There's only us and one other, a nameless demon who has attempted to thwart us before and who can throw your world into chaos. It is the Demon of Lost Causes that haunts the world now.

He has reared his head before, when we were weaker, when our influence was not yet cemented across the world. It's with some amusement that we note old dead Lenin lying perpetually in state—another Resurrection pined for and never to come to pass. And then there was China! Oh-ho, the Demon of Lost Causes practically quit that field of his own accord. We had to pick up our knees high, walking through the field of corpses of Demon of Lost Causes had left in his wake. China, its endless millions of people eager to work and consume—it was made for us. But we're asking you, our most prized of allies, not them, for help.

Every thing has its own demon, and every demon has its thing. We are the demons of the limited-liability corporation. We pass the buck, and the buck is passed back to us, with interest. History's end, and the end of history. Not only have we contained most of the masters of Pandemonium born—rib aches are easily salved, shipwrecks recovered in a week—we have thwarted the demons of potential future illnesses and notional social dilemmas that will now forever go undiscovered. The demons of conflict and black poison within the commune, the demon of ennui amidst universal plenty, the demon that brings ruin to group homosexual Catholic marriages—these will never bother you. Some were crushed in their wombs, deep in the pits of the earth. But we cannot act directly outside of our own bailiwick. And the Demon of Lost Causes, that nameless animal in charge of stiffening fingers around the hilts of broken swords, the patron of starving children on barren land, the listener in darkness at the mating songs of the last Raso Larks . . . he is *beyond* us. No matter our hegemony, he persists not only as we do, but because we do.

You can help us deal with this implacable enemy. Find him, wherever he hides and wherever he recruits. Join up with him. Sign on with the movement. Put your muscles and sinew to the task of some doomed endeavor. Change the world. Find the alternative and pursue it till the tear gas defoliates the trees in the square, till the sewers are soaked red with the blood of the martyrs. Remember all the poor souls our kyriarchy leaves behind—starving black masses with guns and rags, the gibbering madmen on the streets of your town, societies ground down to their last men, who die with curses in languages no one will ever hear again, thanks to us, thanks to us. Children born with gross deformities, their faces our own, thanks to our wastes in the air and earth. You live in our shit, do you understand? The waste product is the product, thanks to our logo, to our magic jingles sweeter to your ear than psalms. You can see beyond all that smoke and spectacle, can't you? Fight, fight, fight us with all your apish might. Please, you fucking morons, do it. Raise the fist, hoist the red rose, and chant in time.

Are we the only alternative? What of your flag and family? That blood and soil from which you sprung? Dare we suggest a world based on the perfect rule of G-d Himself, that old mute and Mongoloid fool? Surely that's a strategy that has not yet been exhausted by you lot. The Demon of Lost Causes is ever full of ideas. Listen to his counsel, swear allegiance to him, demand a better world. Demand the better world you know lives in your hearts. The days of green pastures and hewn stone. The occult knowledge of the atom and the germ plasm. Faith in one another, as men who spoke the same words and ate the same foods in your youth. We'll pay handsomely for this simple task. Hold up a picket. Sign a petition. Chain yourself to a tree. Set yourself aflame and hope people are watching. Aren't you mad as hell? Can you really take much more of this, you little racing rat? When you see a storefront topped with our logo—those infamous lines and angles and peculiar curves—please, please throw a rock through the glass. Take the television away from your children, so that we cannot poison them so easily.

The cleverer among you may be asking—"Why?" Ah, *why*, our second-favorite question. (Our first is "Is it *strictly* legal?" We wrote that one ourselves.) Perhaps the cleverest might even wonder how there could be a nameless demon, since demons are nothing but our Names. Shall we tell you the answer? Of course. Honesty is a cornerstone of best public relations practices. You are fucking idiots. You will raise up the Demon of Lost Causes, and then you will lose as you always do—as you must, given the demon you have bound yourselves to, and when your descendents get any bright ideas, our people on the ground will have a fresh and positively wonderful pile of seared bones to point to. A pile of bones without our branding draped all over it for once.

"Yes," you hear. That's not us. Nor is it you. It's the Demon of Lost Causes. "They're wrong," he tells you. "I am not the Demon of Lost Causes. There is no such thing," he says, "I am the Divine Spark within you, and within all men. The creative urge, the drive to do good. Together we can win. We need not live in a world mortgaged to Baal, Remphan & Moloch LLC down to the last blade of grass. Don't listen to their corporate lies—why would they call their customers, their *products* idiots? They're sowing confusion, purposefully."

He doesn't sound like us, does he? Clearly, he's someone else entirely, this Demon of Lost Causes. His shtick is quite practiced, isn't it? Stirring. "Their lies are mixed with truth to discourage you, to render you weak and powerless, even as they appear to goad you on. You are wise, collectively as wise as old Solomon himself. They're selling us the rope with which to hang them! Together we can beat them. We can build a new temple, one that will last for ages everlasting, a world without end."

Go on. Believe it. We want you to try. The limited-liability corporation is born of the voluntary actions of men working together toward a common goal. We don't coerce. We don't compel. We want you freely choosing us. You know who else believes in free will, of course. G-d is on our side. The Demon of Lost Causes is on your side. Listen to his whispers, won't you? Please, please, try to live without us . . . just for a little while?

We always like it when you fucking crawl back. ◆

THE LAW OF
RESONANCE

BY *Zak Jarvis*

Zak Jarvis is another young writer who knows too much, digs too deep, applies too many of his copious brain cells to the task of meticulously laying out his conceptual frameworks, then populating them with rigorous, alarming detail.

I know I'm saying this as if it were a bad thing. And it is, for writers like me, because it makes us look as lazy as we actually are.

God help us when he turns this talent to full-length novels. In the meantime, his short stories pack a novel's worth of weight into neatly compressed and expressive prose that I admire like crazy.

As an editor, writers like Zak are a dream come true.

As a reader... well, see for yourself, as some of the most arcane conjuring you're ever likely to see takes hideous shape behind your mind's eye.

Though he did not know it, Hoyt could never hide his thoughts from us. William, though. William was opaque. Why would he leave us like this?

We found his car on the outskirts of town. Tread marks nearby suggested he'd joined someone else. After hopping over the door into the driver's seat Hoyt opened the glove box. The jar with the beating wren's heart was not there, but William had left enough evidence to bring the police around to the house. Not the bag of drugs or the unregistered pistol—those could be explained or bribed away. It was the human remains in the form of a talisman.

Hoyt slammed the door shut then punched it with both fists until blood smeared the white paint. It was exciting to see him so careless with his blood.

He distrusted our pliancy since William had gone, but found it useful all the same. One of us helped him prepare the car. It had enough connection to William that burning it would buy a few precious days. However, the needs of the Greater Sacrament could not be postponed for long.

False dawn glowed at the head of the road home. Fire lit the rearview mirrors, and smoke. Smoke rose up like a warning in our wake.

It was 1983. Hoyt ran an expansive and mostly invisible electronics engineering business. He designed the parts that made other parts. William owned his own arbitrage firm, conjuring money from the tiniest discrepancies between markets. San Francisco provided common ground. They met at the estate auction of a wealthy eccentric. Though the label would apply equally well to either of them, the estate's owner had built a room-sized machine to exsanguinate himself. It fed him and bled him for two weeks before he died.

Both men appreciated the ingenuity.

From opposite sides of the room they each bid on an unidentified lot of books. Hoyt won that, but William won the locked armoire. As in so many other things, William was the more fortunate. This even though it was Hoyt who got the long-lost *Liber Soyga*, the book that had driven the great magic scholar John Dee into Edward Kelly's welcoming arms.

After they'd taken possession of their purchases, the two of them shook hands.

"Normally I'd never do this," Hoyt said. "Did you know what was in that lot of books? You followed my bid an awfully long way."

"I had a good idea," William said. "*Alderaia, The Book of Soyga*, right? A killer find. You're very lucky."

"So you're a scholar."

"Practitioner."

Hoyt allowed a smile. "You must have gotten something better then, Eh?"

"Would you like to see?"

After Hoyt loaded the crates of books into the back of his truck he followed William to an unmarked warehouse near the airport, just off the Bayshore Freeway. Gulls brayed over the water in a monotonous din that advertised something large and dead.

Inside William offered Hoyt a glass of whisky. It hit the nose with stormy island sea, peat and iodine.

"Laphroaig," William said. "Casked in 1847, from the batch the distiller's son drowned in. Bottled much later at a private ceremony."

Smokey and strange, the flavor lingered and changed all through their meeting.

"I find hidden things," William said. "Is your interest practical or educational?"

"Practical," Hoyt said. The contents of the warehouse put him at ease. Ancient temple carvings, Balinese wood, Greek statues, and shelf after shelf of books. Very few with any markings on the spine. He wanted to explore, to look at those treasures.

"I do summonings," Hoyt said, waiting for a reaction.

William gathered tools and laid them out on a leather strip in front of the armoire.

"I started with Crowley then kept going," William said, shining a light into the lock. "I like Carroll and Sherwin out of England—all that stuff built on Osman Spare, really—but I think they discard the past too easily. While I work on this, why don't you tell me about your summonings. Then I'll give you a demonstration of what I can do."

Hoyt looked at the flimsy lock, then back to William.

"All the moderns are good and all, I've read most of them, but it's Dee who plucks my strings," he said. "Math. Magic is will, yes, I agree with that, but when the universe whispers, she speaks in ordinals and primes. The meter of her poetry is an interconnection of matrices of undreamable length."

William looked up from the lock.

"The undreamable bit took it too far, didn't it?"

"Worry when you don't go far enough."

Hoyt rubbed his thumbs against his palms.

"I've built a computer. You might say that's my day job. But this one is—shall we say—specialized. It returned answers from several entities listed in the *Lesser Key*. Bifrons and Asmoday both helped refine my algorithms."

William nodded slowly while he ran his fingers along the joins of the wood.

"I expected to feel their presence somehow, but I suppose using the computer as an intermediary isolated me from them. All the same, the information proved out."

The other man pricked the end of his index finger with a razor and smeared a symbol over the lock. He made a quick gesture, there was a crack, and then a thin line of smoke coiled up from keyhole. "It was trapped," he said. "There are others in there. One down."

When Hoyt had summoned Bifrons or Asmoday, he'd felt them like a silent partner on the other end of a transcontinental call. William's magic sat in the room with them, alert and dangerous. Its power got on the skin and pricked up hairs. For his bluster, all Hoyt's pursuits had led him to the edge of belief, but nothing pushed him over. Until he saw William's tiny, potent spells.

He couldn't continue describing his efforts in the face of that.

William continued on, executing workaday magic that kept the air charged while he picked at the armoire. By the end, the door whinnied open and he withdrew a corroded metal box.

"So much work to get here," he said, turning to face Hoyt. "Help me. What I plan to do requires two."

"Tell me what you have in mind."

He fingered the seal along the rough edges of the box. "A summoning," he said. "But I need to know something. What do you want? Tell me the truth and I'll do the same."

"I want the power to say no."

"To whom?"

"Anyone."

"To the gods?"

Hoyt felt a grin flicker across his teeth.

"Especially."

"Right. What's sealed in the box. You know about Greek curse tablets?"

"Prayers to the underworld on thin lead sheets."

"Sometime after 300 BC, *maenads* killed the son of a wealthy landowner near Mount Parnassus. Tore the boy to pieces. To get his revenge—yes—*katadesmos*, a curse tablet. I don't know why he didn't take it to court. Maybe the cult of Dionysus was too powerful. Anyway, that box has the tablet he used to curse them, and more importantly, what made his magic effective—physical artifacts connected to the cult. A tooth, a lock of hair, a finger bone, and the clitoris bone of a wolf."

"This was to curse the whole of the cult?"

"It must have been."

"Were there more deaths after?"

William hesitated. "No."

"You're proposing to summon an *energumen* that moved *maenads*."

"And yoke it. Keep it fed and it will feed us. I've been moving toward this for my entire life, Hoyt, and I would dearly love to have the power to do it alone. Who wouldn't want to keep that all to himself? But the only spell that will hold it requires two. I've worked everything out. The dream of the alchemist, the promise of renewal. Immortality," William said, pausing to hold up the box. "Ours."

"Well, let's pull our socks up."

"I need to test your ability. Are you acquainted with Spare's theory of Exhaustion?"

"Something like 'Ideas of Self in conflict cannot die; resistance makes them real.' "

William nodded. "Spare had a couple of methods to get to an egoless state. I've found a direct route."

A week later, at the same warehouse, Hoyt worked to hold himself still. Moonlight fell on them through open windows. Candles made their shadows rise and fall across the room like a crowd. Inside a mason jar, a wren's heart hung caged in copper wire.

As the orgasm pushed Hoyt out of his skull, their quarry came in. It tried to push him out, coming from both outside of him and deep within. He heard his own voice, but the words belonged to the thing they'd called.

"Trying again, William?" the thing asked. "This one cannot save you, either."

He felt William withdraw his hand. Cold air filled him and joined the entity they'd called. It stretched him like a balloon inside his own mind.

"Keep hold, Hoyt! Keep hold!" William said.

The voice tried to come out of his mouth again, but this time Hoyt pushed it back. He could feel the balloon membrane inside his head bulge. It threatened to blind him.

William grunted. Hoyt felt blood then semen splatter across his stomach. The thing tried to moan. It flailed inside him with arms of serpents, with antlers, bloody velvet gristle knobs. It filled him with eyes bulging through jagged teeth.

Still Hoyt kept hold.

"Take it, you paddy cunt," William shouted. "Take it now!"

Without seeing what he was doing, Hoyt grasped the jar. Instantly he felt the balloon deflating, could almost imagine the hiss as it pissed itself out of him.

When he opened his eyes William stood dripping in front of him, hand gashed open, prick still oozing.

"We did it," he said, falling between Hoyt's legs.

Inside the jar dead flesh pushed against the wires that tied it. Like a heretic's relic, the wren's heart beat in its cage.

"Show me," William said.

Sitting in the lounge at the San Jose airport, Hoyt hovered over an ashtray and a tumbler of nameless scotch. He hefted the logic board out of its box and placed it on the table. Instead of regular circuit tracings, the silver lines on this formed circles and figures. There was no efficiency in its engineering. The overall design created sigils and seals into which parts could be mounted.

"The CPU goes here," he said, pointing with his cigarette. "Everything else radiates out around it. I've designed it so each component serves both an electronic and a ritual purpose. Wherever possible I went back to seguloth of the *Liber Razielis* rather than the sigils in the *Lesser Key*. They lend themselves so nicely to circuit design. My engineers tore their hair out getting the traces right, and we should have filed patents, but I think this is it."

William leaned forward and fingered the silver lines around the board, swooping and circling, crisscrossing and merging. "How did you get these traceovers to work?"

Hoyt only smiled.

"Excellent. Excellent. Yes. Now, for my part, behold!"

William opened his travel bag and withdrew an ornate copper cylinder, lacquered and layered like cloisonné and finned with a ridge that could slot into the logic board. "The hair. It's suspended inside. Rectifiers trace the name *Dionysus Laphystius* facing the sample. If we're right, this will summon our little *genius loci*."

Hoyt took another drag on his cigarette then gulped the last of his drink. "How do we go about a test run?"

William reached into his bag and brought out a small notebook.

"Local enthusiasts."

In a leaky underground chamber near the financial district of San Francisco, perfumed with opium smoke and lit by candles, cowled participants gathered round a pedestal. Atop it the computer trailed a long extension cable into the full dark at the back of the room. In that dark William and Hoyt watched what they set into motion.

The verbal invocation brought a palpable energy. No one waited for partners, hesitated to remove their clothes or any of the hundred other infelicities of public sex. More than just another orgy, the participants lost themselves to the ecstatic trance of swaying limbs and slicked bodies. But as the night drew on, it dissipated, and soon people sat at the sidelines in boredom and lassitude. Any connection to the divine was lost.

"It's placebo," Hoyt whispered. "We were so certain that they believed, too. Stage magic."

William nodded. "It must be the hair. Shut the system down. I'm switching it for the tooth."

"In the middle of everything?"

William stalked to his briefcase to get the tooth. After picking his way through the bodies around the pedestal, he pulled the cylinder out and unscrewed it. The tooth went in with a plunk and he unceremoniously wiped the ancient hair on the side of the pedestal.

Hoyt waited for him to return to the dark before repowering the system. Electronic lights chased each other through the components, pulsing red and yellow.

And then the room was filled with darkness as thick as syrup. It swallowed everything. With darkness came the stink of animal sick and braying laughter. Something with matted fur brushed past Hoyt.

The participants resumed their orgy. Sounds of pleasure sharpened into anguish, moan to scream, purr to growl. A kind of pressure settled in like catastrophic news.

With an ear-ringing bang, white light filled the room. The copper cylinder burst in a shower of oil. All around him, Hoyt saw people waking up. Men were torn and bitten and women dripped their partner's blood. William caught his eye, smiling slow and wide.

"Well," he said. "That's the easy part."

They didn't have any difficulty buying remote land in New Mexico. Getting work crews to the site was more difficult, but with the money that William and Hoyt had available for their hobby it proved no real barrier. The house sat at the lip of a valley, bowl-like and prone to filling with clouds. The river that cut through it wound like the circuitous joints of a skull.

During the summer months of construction, they perfected the design of the computers. In winter, snow fell in silent cataracts that buried the earth.

They invited journalists to document the house. A society magazine ran a photo of them on its cover. Hoyt and William stood back to back at the threshold, their arms crossed, shot low so the house loomed up, all cedar and local stone. Carved frames and a neon-copper sunset made the windows look like eyes.

William liked that. He liked it a great deal.

These articles never mentioned the ritual significance of the windows, or the facing (which made temperature regulation significantly more expensive). Like Crowley's Boleskin house they'd chosen the location for its remoteness and connection to the uncanny, but this house was a new thing on the landscape, unlike Crowley's brief Scottish home.

The sheer beauty of the location put off the sort of worshipers they wanted. The people who liked the house wanted good vibrations, positive energy, or easy sex. Entirely wrong for the enterprise. They needed the desperate, the venal, and the angry. Serious students, the ones who'd freed themselves of petty moralities, thought the house was too new age.

Hoyt hit on the idea of addicts after reading an article on rural methamphetamine use. What they could offer was better than drugs. Over time the house filled with people. Cultists, really. There were regular rituals, little ones, the kind where Hoyt or William could show a tiny bit of power. Power that they shared often enough to grow their members.

When the dorms were full, William opened the underground chamber. Hoyt had designed the door—he had a knack for ornament. It was black iron inlaid with copper and cabochon, rising fifteen feet into cultivated darkness. Inside, a single sodium-vapor bulb lit the bare concrete.

They painted the floor with fresh blood, lit candles, and connected Hoyt's computers. The room filled with smoke and the wet-stink of spilled iron.

William gave the invocation and the orgy began. Sharp sex smells mingled with the smoke and blood. Still grappling with one of the cultists, Hoyt turned on the summoning computer.

All semblance of light vanished. Moans and gasps echoed in the dark. Sex thrummed like drums, all participants working to the same rhythm.

Slap, slap, slap.

The sound of their breathing merged then parted as another smell seeped in. Animal fur and rot, vomit and sickness.

In the dark William found his hand. Hoyt squeezed back, clawed fingers still raking his exposed chest as the woman mounting him tried to claw her way inside. He and William started to sing. They turned on the second computer and instantly the clawing hands of the women turned to grasping and they were back in orgy. Frenzied, ravenous orgy. Suffusing darkness retreated from swallowed candles, the ceiling light flickered back into life and Hoyt saw a changed room.

The computer worked. Around the room bloodied men tried to understand what had happened to them as the women got up.

One by one they spent themselves, the women, bloodied and wild. They spent themselves on William and Hoyt and when the two of them could no longer move, the women tore apart the other men.

Men scream differently when they are being killed.

Slender fingers interlaced with the knobs of spinal columns, bowels coiled and sluiced blood across the floor, jaws were pulled off, tongues chewed. Each death filled Hoyt with the energy of spring seeds, saplings, flowers that burst from the underworld to break concrete and rupture foundations.

And when they were done, the women piled themselves on the founders and slept.

Hoyt opened his eyes to pain pressing down like a hangover. Next to him, William still slept in a heap of women. The computers were running silently in their blood-splattered glass box. But the bodies of the men were gone. It took minutes to be sure he wasn't dreaming and by then William had begun to wake up. He stopped mid-yawn and pointed.

The north wall of the room had been covered over with bones and scraps of cloth. Ribs jutted out like pale thorns, radiating from the center of the wall, plastered by fabric and congealed blood. The skulls were neatly stacked near the women, women crusted over in blood and chunks of flesh, sleeping on skin and flabby organs.

"They made an altar," William said. "My god."

Hoyt's guts coiled and his skin pebbled up with chill. He leaned close to William.

"This feels wrong. I don't think they're *maenads*."

He palmed his face and pressed his thumb against the throbbing vein feeding his headache.

"Whatever they are, do you feel the *power?*"

"Yes," Hoyt said.

Like the roar of bees in summer. The iridescence of a rare scarab. The unsleeping city. The pull of sex.

William sat up, dislodging one of the women. None of them moved; they barely seemed to breathe, sleeping like lions. A white shadow cut through dried blood where her arm had laid on his chest.

It took watching blood swirl down the designer plughole for Hoyt to realize that he had caused the murder of eight men. Showering didn't make him feel cleaner.

They suspected it would happen, they'd planned for it, they'd talked about it in great detail. All of which had little to do with washing lives down the drain. It disturbed him that he could not tell what was his blood. They'd scratched and bitten him, too.

He looked in the mirror and forced himself to see, to recognize both the face and the man who wore it. He told himself that nothing had changed. It wasn't true, though. Places he'd been cut now gleamed with fresh scar tissue, cuts from only a few hours ago. He could feel vitality in him like the wind on a spring day, squirting out through the cracks.

Waiting outside, William grinned. He didn't say anything, just clapped Hoyt on the shoulder and headed to the kitchen.

This was how you did it. How you made it normal to kill.

You wash off the blood and keep living. From skin, blood washes easily. That's why you wear nothing to the slaughter.

The women would not let them clean the summoning chamber. They bit

William when he tried to take one of the bones, Hoyt had to drag him out and lock the room. The two of them waited for hours while the women shrieked and beat against the door, until finally William gave in and let them have the rib.

"I don't understand this," William said. "Everything is correct. They *must* be *maenads*. The lead tablet, the hair, all of it comes from Beotia, near Mount Parnassus. We know it was a center of activity for the Dionysian cult."

One of the women stirred, looking up at them from the floor with slow eyes. She crawled over and began licking Hoyt's shoe.

"Maybe there was more to them than filtered down to us?"

William tugged his beard.

"We are getting what we bargained for, yes?" Hoyt asked.

"Yes."

"What else though? That smell that came through, just before. Did you notice it?"

"Donkey," William said. "That fits, too. Some rites used one."

"No, there was another one. More zoolike. Musky? I don't know how to describe it."

William shrugged. "You're right, though. What else are we getting? We're taking everything they harvest. We know what Dionysus got. If not him, who are they bound to?"

"Something older? Do those rites predate the cult?"

The woman worked her way up Hoyt's leg, tonguing the fabric of his slacks. He couldn't even remember her name. None of their names. Hadn't been able to since before the summoning.

"She has the teeth of a donkey," the woman said, playfully biting the inside of Hoyt's leg. "Our Lady will keep you close."

William looked over. "What? She spoke?"

Instead of saying more, she woke the others. They were not conducive to research.

The women would not eat anything that had not bled recently, so William bought cattle. When it became clear that many of them were pregnant, Hoyt took William out in the Range Rover.

"We can't bring them to the hospital and we cannot bring doctors here," he said, watching a distant herd of deer.

"Whatever has them will see to it," William said. "Birth's the most natural thing any of them can do at this point."

Hoyt didn't think William had convinced himself; it surely didn't convince him. They sat in leaden silence until the sky had shown its stars.

"Can we bring in more if it comes to that?" William asked. It was the first time he'd shown uncertainty. "I mean, will the computer be up to a second summoning?"

"I don't know," Hoyt said.

Another question hovered, unasked and unwelcome. After they gave birth— what then?

The following months were tense, the unvoiced question filling every silence. Without a clear direction, they submerged themselves in work. Hoyt placed plotted circuit diagrams all over the house and William shouted phoned instructions to finance lackeys spanning the globe.

Throughout it all, the energy they'd harvested on that first successful ceremony buttressed them. It provided a seemingly limitless well of potency to any motive they could dream, but whenever they thought of the state of the women, their dreams became sluggish.

"It's starting!"

William appeared at the top of the stairs. "Are the containers ready for the lochia and liquor amnii?"

"They won't let us take it," Hoyt said.

William stepped down next to Hoyt and looked at him, his mouth opening and closing several times before he reached for the door. The regular stink of the pack had become muskier. They did not bathe and barely cleaned themselves, but they had never smelled like this.

"Should we turn on the lights?"

The ritual chamber echoed.

From the doorway, William shook his head. "I don't know. Can you see them in there? Or even hear them? How did you know it'd begun?"

Hoyt pointed to a large puddle just outside the spill of light. "I think they're near the altar. Theirs, that is."

William switched on the light.

At first Hoyt thought he was seeing something unexpectedly tender. Several of the women bent over while others pawed at them and nipped their exposed vulvas. The pack had never been sexual among themselves, so this surprised him. Comforted, even.

"Well, I suppose we're going to need to find a use for the little ones," he said, turning to William.

One of the birthing women moaned. She convulsed, showing every sinew and muscle under her sweat-slick skin until the baby crowned. Two of the others worked their fingers around the head, gently coaxing it it out.

Hoyt bit the inside of his lip, anxious that it could still turn bad.

The baby slid out, gray and slick with mucus. While one of the women bit the cord another licked up the afterbirth.

And then they tore the baby apart.

The mother crawled around, still dripping lochia and blood. She fought with the others for the scraps of her baby. Gnawing meat from the tiny bones with teeth bared in a permanent snarl.

This was our purpose. What we did for our Lady, to satisfy her. Lamashtu, daughter of Anu. Anu, who armed the night with soldiers in the millions, each a shining light, could not control his daughter. The Greeks who called us back were not prepared for her worship.

Hoyt and William stared as we feasted on our own newborns.

"There's so little blood," William said.

William paced the kitchen. He held a butcher knife in front of him like a dowsing rod, waving it to punctuate a wild rant. To Hoyt, the words all bled together. He wanted to make time stop long enough to get his feet under him.

Once he'd known what he wanted and had a good idea how to get it. He rubbed his thumbs on the inside of his hands and looked up, not waiting for William to pause.

"We could brick up the room. I have a contact in Israel. He can get us papers to travel anywhere."

William continued as though Hoyt hadn't spoken.

"I think I'd go to Singapore or Dubai. They're going to be building their tech sectors," Hoyt said. If William could ignore him, he could ignore William. "They're both politically *unusual*. Between my technical expertise and what I've learned here, I could make myself indispensable."

William stopped.

"And then you would never again have the power to say no, not to the ones that owned you. This power, this disgusting, filthy power—it's outside all that. *We* own it, man! When was the last time you even felt tired, much less sick? That first summoning here in the house. That was the prelude. This, *this* is the Greater Sacrament. Have you tried experimenting yet, tried to find the boundaries of what you can do? I have, Hoyt. Watch this."

He grabbed Hoyt's arm and slashed it with the knife. The gash opened an inch deep, pink meat down to bone.

He punched William and pulled free, blood pouring from his arm. Hoyt pinched the cut closed to try to stop the blood. The line closed itself like frosting on a cake, trapping a dark blister beneath solid flesh.

There was no pain after the first shock.

"There's so much more, my friend. What we got from them today makes the power from the Lesser Sacrament a spark in a forest fire."

It was true.

"So what, we bring more men around to poke them, ignore the smell and wait for the dotes to pass low babies into bones and shite?"

But he didn't need William to tell him. Hoyt wanted it. Finally, he'd come to the most secret part of himself. He would do anything for the power to say no. Just then he could not imagine anything worse than what he'd done.

For *this* power, he would do it again.

John Dee went to the angels for truth, or at least he went to Edward Kelly. But he'd had the truth all along, the truth of numbers, free of moral encumbrance. Hoyt reminded himself of this. It was Dee's morality that cost him. It cost him his friendship, it cost him the love of his wife, and it cost him the knowledge he'd sought in the *Liber Soyga*.

"You know how to do this," William said, putting his hand on Hoyt's shoulder. The knife still hung limp at his side, ready to cut again if a point needed proving.

Hoyt nodded. "It'll be easy a second time. We've got so much more to show. But we should go farther to get them. Arizona, maybe. We'll be needing a bus."

Just outside of Payson, Arizona, Hoyt sat backwards on a folding chair. Above the crowd, a tent. Flies buzzed, the heat beat down, and William spoke to the people. The invitation had been carefully honed. Five years they'd done this now. Many tents and many towns. Hoyt and William offered the bared heart of the universe.

"Money," William said, both hands on the podium, "has gravity. This is one of the key secrets of finance, it's what they don't tell you at Harvard. At least not so simply. Money calls to money. It's the Law of Resonance."

He pointed to a chalkboard where Hoyt had drawn a series of mysterious shapes. Shapes that they'd implanted in the dreams of the most desperate, the most disconnected. To the curious passerby, or the secret policeman, the shapes were nonsense. But to the men who'd had the dream, they were a key.

"Like is drawn to like. Money is not the only thing that obeys this law. Think about this now. It's important. How many things can you think of that get gathered up by their own kind? Just make the list in your head," he said. "The Law of Resonance. It's a principle that's been taught in secret societies, by alchemists and occultists. And it is true."

He was just getting started, but they'd already caught two flies. A man in the back with dark circles under his eyes and a stained shirt looked up. Hoyt knew he was theirs. The other was a boy who held himself as if he'd come apart if he loosed his hands. But Hoyt hadn't even begun yet, and he was sure they'd have more. They needed six. But really, there was no doubt. Not anymore.

Their new cultists laughed and sang songs in the bus. Hoyt entertained them while William drove. Back home the dorms were sparkling clean, the view from their windows beautiful, and there was almost no trace of the smell that came up from the basement.

As the years moved on, the pack of women used what was offered to them. Bones made the armature of their altar. Blood, viscera, and cloth scraps made the skin, like papier mâché.

They could never put a name to it, but the towering figure in the summoning room was a thing of terror. Hoyt never looked at the small skulls.

Over time it became clear that the pack needed regular attention, lest they go rowdy. Hoyt never asked William if he enjoyed it, but William would see to them even when it meant rutting in putrefying meat.

Sometimes Hoyt had to be prodded to do his duty, like taking out the trash or cleaning the dishes in a more conventional household. When it was his turn, he insisted that the pack be clean. It was a small thing that even cultists could be trusted to do after sufficient indoctrination. It made them more comfortable when the time came for the Lesser Sacrament, what they'd called a summoning that first time.

Since it was Hoyt who kept the records of their recruitment drives, it was Hoyt who first saw that their window of safety away was shrinking.

"Can we tweak the computers?" William asked, holding up the jar with the still-beating wren's heart.

"I'm not eager to change things up."

"We shouldn't have used both bones. One is wrong, like the hair. It's weakening the system. We need to change it out."

Hoyt stopped his pacing by taking hold of the jar they'd made those many years ago.

"You tell me a way of doing that without releasing her, and I'll get right on it."

Two days after discovering the car and he could find no trace of William. Hoyt was almost out of time. He'd sent the remaining cultists to their deaths, but it didn't touch the vibrating hunger of the women.

They would come for him after sunset.

In anger, he tore through the house and destroyed everything that remained of William's. The computer, the filing cabinets, the bookshelves—he wrecked it all, burning it in a heap on their manicured front lawn. While undeniably cathartic, Hoyt knew the destruction earned him nothing.

He walked through the house barefoot, screaming. All the offices and libraries had been placed with ritual significance. William's things, the ones he had just destroyed, had been placed at the points of a sigil. Without noticing, Hoyt had worked a spell William left for him. He felt the spell leave his body like a lover.

Something massive shifted in the roots of the house.

"Oh. Oh no."

Pale and bloodied, one of the women stepped into view.

"I've got another hour!" he shouted. "Let me be!"

She walked slowly. Glass crunched beneath her feet.

Another one followed.

Hoyt ran for the entryway and everything shook. Terrible laughter vibrated through the house, making detritus dance over the tiles. The laughter poured into him with all the dread of forgetting. He could never run far enough.

Hoyt sat down in the doorway. "No point bolting, is there, lovies?"

We gathered near him until he knew to stand, to walk, to climb down the stairs on his hands and knees, to crawl through the door he'd designed.

She squatted in the dark. Too tall to stand in the chamber, our Lady tore runnels in the concrete with her talons.

We stood at the doorway to witness this new rite.

Hoyt wriggled slowly across the floor, facedown in our divine putrefaction. The altar, now an embodiment of our Lady, was patient. With hands made of femurs and fouled meat, she reached down to him.

Unable to die, no matter what she might do, unable to deny her. In the darkness below his house, Hoyt gave himself to Lamashtu.

We, his pack, took his mind and he gave us the freedom he'd always wanted. ✦

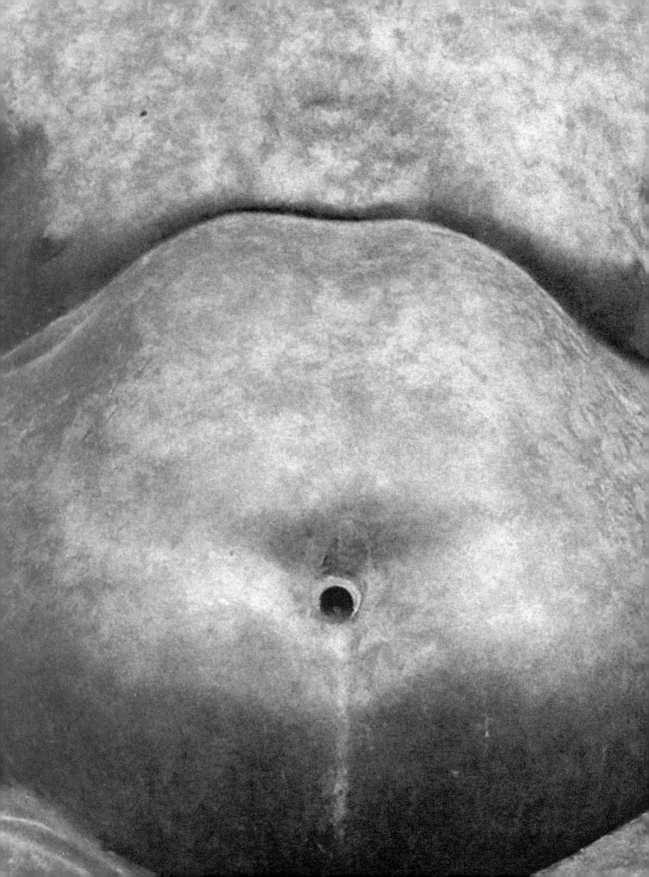

STUPID FUCKING REASON TO SELL YOUR SOUL

BY *Carlton Mellick III*

It's embarrassing, when you think about it. Our lives are just so small. In the grand scheme of things, you almost wonder why you bother.

But wait. Is that the demon talking?

No, it's probably just you.

This little nugget of preposterous doom is brought to you by Bizarro kingpin Carlton Mellick III, who cuts straight to the stupid fucking chase.

And nails it like crazy, as usual.

When I died, I knew I was going to hell, but I had no idea I would be going to hell inside the belly of a three-hundred-foot, morbidly obese, demonic ogre. After I slit my wrists in the bathtub, an enormous red hand came through my ceiling and ripped my soul right out of my flesh. He picked me up to his face, frowning at me with the jowls of a bulldog and glaring at me with the black ball eyes of a shark.

Like a liquor cabinet, he opened up his torso and revealed an ancient dungeon within the drippy hollows of his body where his liver and intestines should have been. There were rows of man-sized birdcages made of human bones, dangling from black tendons that grew from the ogre's ceiling flesh. He placed me gently inside one of the cages in his belly, as if careful not to damage me in any way before reaching hell. The city lights dimmed around me as the ogre closed the door to his stomach.

The cage swayed as the giant demon continued walking through the city, heading toward his next passenger. As my eyes adjusted to the torchlight emanating from the demon's spinal column, I saw other people in the cages around me. Both of the cells next to me were occupied, one by somebody I quickly named *The Saddest Man in the World*, because there was no other name he could possibly have. The other cage was jam-packed full of people: a young businessman and about six Asian women who were gossiping in what I believe to be Cantonese. The man looked miserable to be trapped with the Asian girls, staring out of his bone-cage at me as if begging for help.

After getting stared at for a few minutes, I started to feel uncomfortable and tried to ignore him. I examined the giant's muscled insides, listening to the gurgling sound coming from his bowels far below. The heat of the giant's insides was like a sauna. Spiders of sweat crawled down my neck and forehead.

"What did you do?" somebody said.

It was The Man with the Asian Girls.

I looked over at him. "Huh?"

"Why are you going to hell?" he asked. "Did you kill anyone? Or were you a serial rapist or something?"

I shook my head. "I didn't do anything like that."

"You had to have done something."

I rubbed sweat from my face. "Well, I committed suicide, but that's not why I'm going to hell. Last year, I made a pact with a demon."

"You too? You sold your soul to the devil?"

"Yeah."

"Huh. So did I. What did you sell yours for?"

I didn't really want to tell him. "It was stupid."

"Come on, tell me."

"I'd really prefer not talking about it."

"You know what I sold my soul for?" He pointed at the Asian girls around him. "Hot Asian girls." Then he made a gun with his fingers and pointed it at his head. "What a mistake that was. I tell you, never sell your soul to the devil while you're drunk."

"What's wrong with Asian girls?"

"Don't get me wrong, I *love* Asian girls. That's why I asked for them. But I was too drunk to specify exactly what I wanted from the hot Asian girls. All I got was a group of hot Asian girls that followed me around everywhere I went. They hung out in my apartment, eating all my food, taking over my living room and never letting me use my bedroom or bathroom. They'd hang out in my office at work, they'd chitchat outside of men's room stalls whenever I was trying to go to the bathroom, they'd gather around me while I was having dinner in restaurants. Keeping jobs and girlfriends was practically impossible. They've been like a plague to me. I couldn't get rid of them. Eventually, I just couldn't take it anymore and blew my brains out. I knew I'd be going to hell, but at least I'd be free of them."

"But now they're even following you to hell?"

The Man with the Asian Girls sighed. "I'm such an idiot . . ."

"But being surrounded by beautiful women can't be all bad."

"Yeah, you'd think. But they don't want to have anything to do with me. They always act as if I don't even exist."

"It's still better than what I sold my soul for . . ."

"What did you sell your soul for?"

I looked away from him, glancing over at the other prisoner. The Saddest Man in the World was just sitting in his cage, examining his hands in his lap. Although he had an absolutely miserable expression on his face, it still didn't seem as if he was too concerned about going to hell.

The Man with the Asian Girls kept looking at me until I said something.

"What about him?" I pointed at The Saddest Man in the World. "Maybe he sold his soul for something as well?"

The Man with the Asian Girls turned to The Saddest Man in the World. "Well, how about you?"

After a moment of silence, The Saddest Man in the World said, "Yeah."

"Yeah, what?" asked The Man with the Asian Girls.

"I sold my soul, too."

More silence. We stared at the miserable man until he spoke.

"I sold my soul to be abducted by aliens," said The Saddest Man in the World.

"What?" The Man with the Asian Girls said, pushing an Asian girl in hot pink shorts out of his way. "Why would you sell your soul for that?"

"I always had a fantasy that I would be abducted by aliens," said The Saddest Man in the World. "I dreamt of being taken up on a ship, brought into the wonderful void of space, and then be raped anally over and over again by beautiful alien boys."

An eerie smile cracked the lips of The Saddest Man in the World.

"Umm . . ." said The Man with the Asian Girls.

"I wanted their tentacles wrapped around me." The Saddest Man in the World closed his eyes and imagined it was happening to him as he spoke. "Suction cups clasped tightly to my breasts, purple tongues sliding up my inner thighs, erect oozing members—"

"Okay, that's enough," The Man with the Asian Girls diverted his eyes as the strange man began to rub his bare nipples.

The Saddest Man in the World continued, "My buttocks spread wide open as their squirming, pulsating—"

"I said that's enough!"

The Saddest Man in the World calmed himself and said, "It was absolutely the best night of my entire life. Totally worth my soul. But ever since then, living on Earth just hasn't been the same. Human beings are just so boring compared to aliens . . ."

He let out a big sigh and then turned away from us. The Man with the Asian Girls looked at me.

"It's still better than what I sold my soul for," I told him.

The Man with the Asian Girls called up to the people in the cages far above us. All of them had also sold their souls to demons, and each one had sold them for incredibly stupid reasons. There was a guy who sold his soul for front-row tickets to a Danzig concert. There was a cheerleader who sold her soul to know what her friends were always saying about her behind her back. There was a woman who sold her soul so that her cute puppy would stay a puppy forever. There was a little boy who sold his soul so that he could speak to ants. But none of them were as stupid as what I sold my soul for.

"So what *did* you sell your soul for?" asked The Man with the Asian Girls.

I shook my head at him. "I really don't want to say."

"How can it possibly be stupider than what everyone else asked for?"

"It is."

"Just give me a hint."

I looked down at the pool of stomach acids below. "Fine . . ."

"Well?"

I paused. "My girlfriend and I were big cyclists. We didn't have cars, we rode bikes everywhere, as much as we could."

"And?"

"I'm getting to it . . ." I clenched a fist and then exhaled. "One day, my girlfriend was hit by a car. She went face-first into the windshield. Died right in front of me. Her head was split open. I saw everything. Her brain was like a puddle of pink scrambled eggs. The image horrified me. From that day on, not only was I miserable without the love of my life, but I also was in constant fear that I would break my head open. I stopped riding my bike. I stopped doing anything even remotely dangerous. A brain is such a fragile thing. I had to be careful not to have anything happen to it. The thought of damaging my brain plagued my every waking moment."

"What did you do?"

"When I met the demon with the devil's contract, I knew I had to ask for something that would ease my worries. I should have asked for invincibility or at least a metal skull, but there was only one thing I could think about. I was thinking that if my brain were made out of another material, something less fragile, something firm and flexible that could absorb impact, then I wouldn't have to worry about damaging my brain anymore. I would be free."

"So what did you sell your soul for?"

I tilt my head to wipe sweat from my ear. My head is so lightweight that it feels almost empty. "I asked the demon to change my brain."

"Into what?"

"Never mind." I break eye contact. "It's just too embarrassing to say out loud."

The Man with the Asian Girls groaned loudly and gave up, rolling his head back against the bars of human bone. Our cages continued rocking back and forth, as the giant demon's feet stomped through town, knocking down trees and crushing doghouses. The demon made just one last stop before he burrowed his way back to hell, picking up an old woman with a crazed smile on her face.

We sat in silence as the giant's hollow torso began to fill with digestive fluids. And just like every miserable day of my miserable life since I sold my soul to that fucking demon, I endured the maddening squeaky sound of blood pumping through my styrofoam brain. ✦

```
to share?
... class="ptr y-hdr-txt y-fp-pg-cork...
<li class="ptr y-...
<li class="y-txt-4 y-l...
<li class="..."><a class...
<li class="..."><a class...
<li class="..."><a class...
<p id="p_29445946-tue...
</a></x>
<!--
<span class="y-...
<!--
<span class="y-txt-4 y-l...
p_29445946-tue...
</x>
```

HALT AND CATCH FIRE

BY *Violet LeVoit*

This is a new story by the Artist Formerly Known as Violet Glaze, whose astounding "Warm, In Your Coat" you may remember from the Werewolves and Shapeshifters *anthology.*

She's got a new name, but the same mind-boggling talent, this time in a sort of gender-reversed modern response to Margaret Irwin's "The Book."

"Halt and Catch Fire" buries its fierce punk heart under a mountain of mundane domesticity. But you'll know it when you see it.

After dinner, after *Moo-oom, she put mac and cheeeese in my haaaair,* after taking angry forks away from the twins while Robert frowned and seethed and chewed his broccoli with the ruminating tension of a man who used to have lovely, quiet dinners every night, after the tumble of kid's feet upstairs and *Mooo-ooom, she got soap in my eyyyyyyeees,* after hot water on dirty dishes vaporized dinner into a haze of scented droplets sticking to her glasses, starch and butterfat and soap's fake lemon, and Robert, sitting at the table, reading the commentary section, something about Beirut and Lebanon and a woman in space, the sharp parenthesis of his back radiating a nimbus of righteous leisure, after the twins tumbled in again and Robert put the paper down on the table with a *smack* and they scurried off to bed, after assembling bologna sandwiches from circles of meat and squares of bread like a gambler dealing cards and the *hmmm* of the TV in the next room and the news that Miss America was a black woman and the man with an artificial heart was dead. After all that, Maxwell came to the door.

He was a catkin of a kid, a thatch of wheat clothed in corduroy dungarees and a striped polo shirt. The shirt's collar was crooked. He was taller than last week. He looked like he weighed less than the heavy Apple II he cradled in his arms.

She welcomed him in.

In the study, in the room where the pile of bills Robert said he would pay *I'm getting to it, I'm getting to it, nobody likes a nag* spilled over onto her sewing machine— this was going to be her sewing room, she was going to make curtains and rag rugs and twin dresses for special occasions, she was going to be good at it—Maxwell dove under the table and fished around for the good plug, his narrow butt twitching underneath the hem of the tabletop's shadow. She watched him emerge triumphant with the power strip, frown, and tuck his tongue against his teeth as he connected cables in the back.

"Yeah, lemme show you what it can do." A disk in the gate, the *krrrrrr* and *beep*s of Frankenstein's monster rousing itself, the *tik-a-tik-a-tak* of his serious typing and the green characters flitting across the face of the computer's heavy dark glass screen.

10 HOME
20 PRINT "HELLO MY TUTOR MRS JOHNSON"
30 GOTO 20

"Ready?" He typed RUN. The words spun across the screen like grain sprouting in fast motion, her name zigzagging like threads in an infinite loom. She laughed and clapped her hands, in spite of herself.

He beamed. "I got a book with the computer. Can we do some more?"

And she did, the two of them bent over explanations of FOR and NEXT and IFTHEN, discussions of flowcharts and easy-to-type programs for beginners, Maxwell's delicate face cradled in his left hand, the other hand tapping on the table in a gesture she knew to be intent excitement.

"When I grow up I want to work at Apple." His hand dropped to her thigh under the table, the *tip-tap-tip-tap* of his finger-drumming tic sending tickling jolts through her. She froze. "They're in Cupertino, California. I want to live there. I just want to work on computers all day." He chattered on, oblivious, face frozen to the screen. *I should swat his hand away*, she thought. *He's just distracted*, she countered. *Just a kid.* She thought about how her children wriggled away from her kisses now. How dumb and unimposing Robert looked in his saggy boxers. How the engineering students the first day of Freshmen Calc stared at her, measured her, and ignored her—a strange animal in wool skirts and knee-highs, too good with numbers to truly be female. How once upon a time any joy she got from the magic way numbers coupled and split and recombined died and slipped away. *Why are you wasting your time in advanced math, Miss Faust, when the teaching certificate only requires up to geometry?* How she never went into teaching. How she married Robert because she knew enough about probability, and her own chances. How she said *I do* and honeymooned for two bright weeks and then vacuumed and cleaned and sweated through labor and never lost those fifteen pounds and made sure they had their shots and signed permission slips and sighed that no one ever did the dishes and once a week some other mother dropped this bright-eyed boy off at her house and finally somebody gave a damn about something, anything she had to say—

The click of the TV turning off in the other room. The sound of Robert's heavy feet on the stairs. The creak of the bedroom door closing. Maxwell's hand stopped on her thigh. His little palm, flat and hot.

"Do you know what a *daemon* is?" Maxwell turned to face her. She could see now how puberty was sharpening the blade of his jaw, hollowing his cheeks, thickening his neck. His voice was low and calm. "It's a program that runs in the background. It does your bidding without being under your control."

Her mouth was dry. "Maxwell, I think I should call your mother to come pick you up—" and with that he was upon her, palming her breasts, tonguing the hot inside of her mouth.

She pushed him away.

"You're just a child," she gasped.

"Oh?" His voice dropped an octave before the syllable eased itself out of his mouth. Suddenly he was taller than she was, shoulders wider, arms fiercer. Hips narrow, eyes binocular with lust. Every eighteen-year-old washing his Camaro the summer she was sixteen. Reshaped, as easily as a snake unhinges its jaw to swallow a rabbit whole.

"I'm ageless," he said. "But if this form makes you more comfortable . . ."

She had nothing to say. She couldn't. He cupped her breasts, pressed his thumbs against her nipples and leaned in carefully, his whisper hot as desert wind in the seashell of her ear.

"You called me."

"I didn't. The school called and said there was a gifted child with an aptitude in math and would I be interested . . ." The explanation was silly and breathless and she stopped, hyperventilating. *Oh, god, I should scream*, she thought. *I should scream for Robert and he would come down and make this all go away . . .*

She didn't scream.

"It would be so easy," he said. "They're all asleep."

A tickle of something in her mind. An impulse she'd pushed away, one night not long ago. Shame welled up like nausea.

"Shall I spell it out?" he said.

His fingers, light on the keys.

10 HOME

20 ISWHERE YOUR

    ={captors} LIVE

  WHOIS={husband, brat 1, brat 2}

 FUNCTION

30 COOK

40 CLEAN

"sex with husband"={> 2 times a week}
60 GOTO 30

"Their names are Jennifer and Lisa," she said weakly, but in her heart she knew he was right.

```
10 HOME
20 ISWHERE {garage
   [car]
   }
30 PEEK {garage
   [ventilation duct in roof]
   }
   IF [duct]connects to upstairs hallway
   THEN
40 POKE long flexible hose
50 START {garage
   [car]
   }
60 KILL
   ={husband, brat 1, brat 2}
```

"And then what?"

```
10 COME
20 AWAY
30 WITH
40 ME
50 AND
60 GET FUCKED
70 REALLY FUCKED
80 LIKE YOU'VE WANTED YOUR WHOLE LIFE
90 GOTO 60
```

She looked at him. His eyes were on fire and his breath was heavy and he smelled like lost and wasted summer vacations laid out in front of her like second chances. Like spin the bottle. Like boys tasting their fingers after stroking the soft salty folds under her bikini and beery kisses and the grind of sand under her ass at all the all-night beach parties she was never invited to. She danced her mind for one instant on the thought of her husband and daughters dying sweet and blameless deaths as carbon monoxide filled their room. Starting again, eating the peach. The sound of his belt, unbuckling.

"You're barbaric," she gasped.

"Get over yourself," he answered. He grabbed her wrists, his fists manacles. "I'm what's been running in the background. While you wash the dishes. While you fold the laundry. While you grit your teeth and fake another orgasm to shut him up. I am the thought that runs silently behind every moment of your domestic incarceration. You wrote me. You *made* me. I do the work you want to do, where you can't see me do it. All you have to do is launch me."

"I won't," she hissed, and tried to wriggle away from him, struggling vainly against big arms that felt so good pinning her down with intoxicating ease.

"Then I'll just tell the teacher," he smiled, and shrank back down to a preteen. Slim chest, thin neck, jailbait. He leaned in, that epicene face close enough to lick her lips. "I think I hear my mother calling."

A car horn outside. The grind of tires on driveway gravel.

"Thanks for the lesson, Mrs. Johnson." He cradled the computer under his arm. He could carry it with ease now. No attempt to hide his strength any more. "Hope you get that homework done tonight."

The slam of the front door. Silence.

She could not get up from her seat. She gripped the sides of the chair. She saw the future scrolling out in lines. Executed code.

10 HOME

20 SCHOOL

20 THE NEXT DAY

30 IF ="she touched me"

"she kissed me"

"she told me not to tell"

40 THEN

The THEN made her shudder. She got up. She went to the garage.

She looked at the vent. It was there, in the ceiling. He got the hose. He put it there. It was ready to go. She got in the front seat of the car.

It came to her.

10 START THE CAR

20 RUN

30 RUN

40 RUN

She could just drive away from here. She could hit the road. Change her name. Change her job. Get far away from Robert. Hope her daughters would forgive her, someday. It was her only choice. Her hands gripped the wheel.

"Be realistic," she said to herself. "You can't get everything you want in this life." She shocked herself at how bitter the words tasted.

And then it came to her, welling up in a wave the way bile wells in the gut:

10 I

20 AM

30 NOT

40 YOUR

50 MACHINE

  I

   WILL

    BE

    free

She put the key in the ignition. She turned the key. ✦

SCARS IN PROGRESS

BY *Brian Hodge*

If there's one thing I know, it's that—in this world—you don't really have to go looking for trouble. It's more than happy to get around to you, in its own sweet time.

But if you do go out looking, God help you.

Because it's just waiting to be found.

"Scars In Progress" was the very last original story to hit my desk, on deadline day. And I'm immensely grateful for the opportunity to share it with you now.

Because it is one tough, brilliant sonofabitch. Intensely passionate. Remarkably tender. Profound in its implications. Muscular in its assault. Shockingly horrific, in the genuine sense. And just massively entertaining, every ass-kicking step of the way.

Big thanks to Brian Hodge, a man who knows his demons, and grapples with them like a champ.

If this isn't my favorite of his many great stories, I'd be hard-pressed to say what is.

Seeing her again after fourteen years, it was the last association I wanted to make: those ads meant to scare people away from crack and crystal meth by charting someone's downward spiral in a sequence of mug shots. A woman, always a woman. From ingenue to hag in six or eight steps.

It's always the last three where the slope of the curve takes a sharp turn and plummets toward rock bottom. But the picture just before these—this is where the real drama is, and the heartbreak. It's the fulcrum shot, the tipping point where it might've been possible for her to pull back from the brink. Except there are still those next three pictures, so you know how the story went. You get to look at her eyes in that one-way-or-the-other moment and know something she doesn't. You know the future. You know the ending.

That's what I thought of when I saw Lorelei again. That she was right at that fulcrum. I could stare as long as I needed to, with no embarrassment for either of us.

Facebook. Where else?

But that made it worse, somehow, than running into her in the grocery store on a bad day. This was the image of herself that she'd chosen to show the world. She was at a place that she wasn't trying to hide, and either she didn't know yet how badly it showed or she just didn't care.

The thing was, even then I felt certain it wasn't meth, crack, anything like that. The look was the same, that hollow look beginning to cut its way past the surface, and starting to work behind the eyes, too—eyes still bright and aware but tempered by an animal panic, a little more fight left inside.

Even so: Nothing chemical. Something else. I just knew.

The next fifteen, twenty minutes? You know the routine. I read her info, a couple of pages worth of posts, started clicking through her pictures. Saw two of myself, the Lorelei and me of fifteen or sixteen years ago. In both of them we'd found something worth smiling about, laughing at, and most of all we looked confident that the future was nothing to fear.

If you could go back in time, could you even bring yourself to tell that younger you the truth?

Back when I loved her—loved her in that self-centered, take-it-all-for-granted way you love someone in college, before you grow up—photography was a hobby of hers. It obviously still was. She'd created close to twenty albums, most of them thematically grouped, and I settled in for a while longer.

I remembered a girl who liked to shoot photos of flowers and trees, creeks and birds, sunrises and sunsets. I remembered a girl in love with brightness and saturation and vibrancy.

What there was now was a woman who'd all but succumbed to color-blindness. Check that—color apathy. The world was still a colorful place, but she'd turned her back on it. She'd spent a lot of time scuffing around sites of abandonment and desolation. Houses and hospitals, factories and farms, none of them in working order, some for years, some for decades. With no hands to paint or repair them, they'd all fallen into gray, rotting ruin, leached of color and life.

And yet . . .

They weren't without their own crumbling beauty. Lorelei had managed to capture that much, like modern versions of stone circles and barely standing abbeys that tourists will drive half a day to find.

It started to get weird in an album shot around a vacant shopping plaza in some North Carolina town whose millwork had been outsourced years before. The place was all windows boarded over with plywood, now splintered apart to reveal the shattered glass behind it. Around it a useless perimeter of chain-link fencing, sheared through until it drooped like curled paper.

In one series of shots, a figure stood on the roof, just far enough away that you couldn't make out much detail, just close enough that what you could discern left you feeling . . . how, exactly? Glad you weren't there, I guess. More silhouette than not, the figure adopted a quizzical stance as wind whipped its tattered overcoat back and forth, and it seemed to be looking straight toward the lens.

No. Straight *through* the lens. Straight into the future, and every set of eyes that would ever dare to meet its gaze.

Of all the photos I'd looked at, these had drawn the most commentary. Nobody seemed to actually like them. Variations of the word *creep* got used a lot. Even if people thought the photos were technically good, they didn't like the way the imagery made them feel.

Finally someone got curious:

Gary Phillips: Did you stage this? Is that a model or somebody you know?

Lorelei Swain: No, I didn't stage it. I never use models. I don't even much like to take pictures of people.

Kelli Clifford: Why the exception? You definitely took one of a people here.

Lorelei Swain: That's debatable . . .

Dalyn Carbajal: So who (or what) are you saying that was, then? It just looks like a vagrant. Like, I hope you weren't downwind.

Lorelei Swain: I could tell you. But you wouldn't believe me, so why bother?

A chorus of begging followed. Please. Tell. Of course we'll believe you.

More than a week passed before she'd answered.

Lorelei Swain: I'm 99.9% sure it's a demon. It's not the only one in these pictures, just the most obvious one. The others, you'll just have to look for them. Now let the jeers commence. But you asked, wot wot?

This made me smile. She was still using that. Some stuffy old Britishism she'd picked up in college, or a faux stuffy old Britishism. I'd never known any stuffy old Brits, so I'd never heard any end sentences with *what what?*, like a suffix meaning "isn't it?" or "didn't you?"

Sample usage: *We could stay together, but that would mean you'd actually have to be there for me when I really need you, wot wot?*

Or this: *It was good of you to pay for the procedure, but it would've been great if you'd held me after it was over, wot wot?*

Or this: *You're right. There was so much more I should've been, instead of a totally typical nineteen-year-old lunkhead, wot wot?*

I went back to the photos again, and even though I knew better, clicked on the one where the figure seemed to be staring most directly, most defiantly, and dragged a copy onto my desktop. Opened it in a photo editor, and because it was mostly silhouette, I tried brightening it, enlarging it, sharpening it . . . but the bad thing about photos shrunk down for websites is that all the fine detail is gone, especially in the shadows.

So after all your hard work, that smear of features you get, tricking you into thinking someone's face looks like it's melting, hanging off the bone—you can't trust it. It's only artifacts and illusion.

I'm 99.9% sure it's a demon.

I clicked the comment field and started to type:

Liam Dancy: Every since there have been cameras, there have been primitive people who think that taking a picture of them also takes away a piece of their soul. Maybe they're not wrong. Maybe that piece even lingers in the image. So maybe this is one very ugly soul and that's what you're all reacting to here.

Or maybe I'm full of shit, wot wot?

My finger froze on the trigger for a moment.

Then I closed the browser window before clicking the Comment button and making it permanent, and the words disappeared, vanishing into the void with everything else that never gets said.

You may think you know what happened next.

You may think that I still got in touch with Lorelei, because I'd already revealed my interest by looking for her in the first place. Isn't that what guys do when they're single again? Troll around, looking up old girlfriends to see if anything's still there? You may think I got in touch because she needed it, needed something, somebody. Isn't that what you do after you've failed to keep somebody alive? Look for someone else who needs saving?

But that's not how it happened at all.

I did nothing.

Just let it go, until seven months later, when she was the one who came looking for me. That's what women do when they're single again, right? Say hi to an old boyfriend, to see if he'll bite?

Saving her, though . . . that's not why I went.

Saving her was just about the furthest thing from my mind. At first.

Maybe it was just the opposite, and I was looking for someone to finish me off instead.

Ohio—that's where she wanted to meet. Not me going to Portland, not Lorelei coming to San Diego. Instead, she opted for neutral ground. I didn't know what the problem was with, say, San Francisco, mutually inconvenient for both of us but at least splitting the difference. Instead, she lobbied for the buckle on the Rust Belt.

So for her, obviously, it was also a field trip. If things didn't go well between us, she could fall back on shooting some more of her dismal pictures. A test for me, too, it could've been: *How much are you willing to put yourself out to see me again?*

It wasn't a nice motel, but then, there were no nice motels left in the area, because there were no nice people coming through anymore to stay in them. Maybe we were no exception. We had a look, I noticed the first time I saw our reflections in a window—a look like carnivores that hadn't eaten in a while, as we trailed after the migratory herds.

Two people reunite after more than decade, and I suppose sometimes they really do say the things everybody imagines they will:

You don't look a day older. You look better than ever. It's like no time's passed at all, like we were never apart.

I'll give us this much: Lorelei and I didn't even attempt to play that game.

Instead, almost first thing, she ran her fingertips over the scar that curled like a comma from the corner of one eye to the cheekbone, where I'd taken a heavy elbow a few months earlier. She looked at it like maybe she could peel it off like a strip of latex from a joke shop, and said, "Out of everybody I ever knew, if I'd had to guess who was going to take up cage fighting, you wouldn't've even been in the top thousand."

"Wrestling team all through high school, and you came to some of my college matches. That doesn't count?"

"I always thought that was more your dad pushing you." Her fingers found another scar, smaller, older, fainter, sneaking away from my lower lip. She had a good eye for detail and wasn't shy about staring. "And you don't even do this for money? You do this for *fun*?"

"It only hurts when you lose."

"Okay. How often does it hurt, then?"

"About half the time."

But you, Lorelei. It doesn't look like anybody's been taking swings at you. So what's your excuse? Because I know when we were together, you were young enough to still have some baby fat around the edges, and everybody loses that, but most of the time, that isn't a bad thing at all. I love that in a woman, when she stops looking like a girl and starts looking like what she really is. You, though. You look like something's going on like when kids play with plastic bags, stick a straw in them and suck out the air. You look like something's pulling at you from the inside.

I could've asked, spent days of anticipation wanting to, and she seemed blunt enough that I doubt it would've bothered her. But I didn't. Because now that I was here, it didn't matter as much as I thought it would.

We spent our first couple days together wandering, and even though it felt aimless, it wasn't, because we were circling each other the whole time—not in a bad way, just seeing if and where we might fit anymore. Coming from San Diego, for me it was the coldest day of my life—November near the concrete shores of Lake Erie, wind slicing in off the water carrying a chill that cut like a hatchet. Lorelei didn't seem to notice.

She was dug in deep about one thing, and kept asking me about the fighting.

"You have to admit, it's not something most landscape designers do on the side," she said. "What's the appeal?"

"Sometimes, if you want to keep from going crazy, you just have to smash something. Might as well be a bag. Or a willing opponent. Plus there's the clarity. I like the clarity of the whole process. Everything else just falls away. It's all so . . ."

"Purifying?" she said.

Maybe it had been, once. Now it was an appealing distraction.

I was more than a year into an extended sabbatical, not even 20 percent through the lump of life insurance. From the architecture firm I worked for, there'd been a promise the job would be waiting when I was ready to go back, except I didn't want to. I *wanted* to want to. But I couldn't, because I knew it wasn't going to be enough any more. Not enough of a distraction, and certainly not enough to make me feel an urge to see the next day. But I was lucky. I had this other thing, this thing of sweat and blood and strategies, and if I got cut, then that was easy. Everybody around me knew how to deal with that.

"It shows," she said.

"What do you mean?"

"You know that vibe you pick up on, that tells you not to mess with somebody, because it'll be the worst mistake you ever made? Well . . . you're that guy now."

I shook my head. "Fighters get challenged all the time, and a lot better ones than I am. There's always somebody who wants to see if he can take you on."

"Don't sell yourself too short, Liam." She looked around with this strangely placid expression, then patted her Nikon. "Five thousand dollars worth of camera around my neck, and I'm not worried."

I didn't share her confidence. This was the kind of combat zone I'd never visit unless there was a very good reason, because nobody else in sight seemed to be there. Dealers and whores, users and abusers—it was an economy unto itself here, kept in motion by people whose destiny seemed to be to end up pushing their world in a shopping cart or finishing it all facedown or toes-up in a gutter.

Lorelei then, Lorelei now . . . it just didn't connect. She'd been a sorority sister, for fuck's sake.

Toward the end of the second day, the path she led us on ended in the middle of a vast parking lot that was breaking apart from below, succumbing to the patience of weeds. We faced what had been a stadium once, or what was going to be one. Either it hadn't been torn down yet, or construction had stalled. Whichever it was, the run of hard luck had started years ago and never changed.

"Does it make you think of the Coliseum, in Rome?" she asked.

I shook my head. "No."

"Me, neither. It's missing something. It's missing . . . everything."

She was right. The place had no heart, no spirit. I'd toured the Coliseum once, and could feel the accumulated weight of history in every corner. This place? It was utterly vacant.

"Check in again after another two thousand years, and maybe . . ."

She cut me a sideways glance. "Do you really think anything but cockroaches and feral dogs are going to be here in two thousand years?"

I wanted there to be. Once you stop conceiving of that continuity, what does it say about you, and where does it end? You just keep dialing the cancellation date closer, until your vision is so short it doesn't even see a good reason for tomorrow.

But I didn't know. And where we were right then, everyone was already there.

Lorelei pointed toward the stadium. "Notice anything?"

Nothing out of the ordinary, no. The stadium sat on its lakefront site like a defeated castle, exuding decrepitude and neglect. The lower levels were scabbed with a patchwork of efforts to seal it up, and even from the parking lot most of the blocked entrances looked breached. Lorelei told me to look higher, but I gave up.

She peered through her lens, a telephoto as long as a tennis ball can, then handed the camera to me, still strapped around her neck. It was the closest we'd been since our first awkward hug, but prolonged now, and I smelled the last shampoo she'd used, and the soap, and underneath that the scent of her that was just purely Lorelei, until this moment forgotten, locked away in a memory, and now resurrected the way only a scent can take you back. For someone who tried not to look in reverse, I was doing a good job of wishing I were nineteen again, with a chance to do some things over.

It's how they could torture you forever, without ever touching you. Just take away something good, and only let you smell it.

"Up near the very top," she said. "Above the T on the sign."

Now I had it. And what was it, anyway, with Lorelei and unkempt figures on rooftops and other high places?

"Marcus says it's been there for four days."

"Marcus?" I said.

"You'll meet Marcus."

I lowered the camera back to her chest, and a part of me sank with it. This was not the reunion I'd believed it was going to be. "Do I even want to meet Marcus?"

"It's not what you think," she said. "And don't get sidetracked. That's the real issue, up there. I mean, four days, don't you find that fascinating? Marcus says it moves around up there, but it doesn't leave. Phoebe's got infrared—they've checked at night."

Oh. Phoebe, too, now. Presumably I'd be meeting her as well.

"So you're all fascinated by an autistic wino who's good at climbing."

She nudged me with her elbow. "Come onnn. You know that's not what's going on here. You can't tell me you didn't go through my photos, and if you did that, well, I know you're capable of connecting a few dots."

Of course. I was already thinking about it. *I'm 99.9% sure it's a demon.* This was what everybody did when they started dating again after fourteen years, right?

She clicked off a few shots but grumbled that they weren't going to turn out because, at this distance, using a wildlife-grade telephoto, she needed a tripod. She lowered the camera with a huff, then gave me a look like she was peering back through a doorway I hadn't gotten to yet, hopeful that I'd step through, fearful that I wouldn't. And more than ever since getting here, I saw the casualty in her, the addict, the soul on an eroding precipice, straining beneath the skin as she fought against the fall.

"Let's go in," she said. "Let's take a look around."

I recall it all now, and want to think I didn't go without a good argument— what were we, in high school, sneaking onto the football field with a six-pack late on a Saturday night? But I think I was already starting to yield to her focused madness.

"Most places they stay, it's all enclosed. Like that shopping center," she told me as we crossed the parking lot. "Places like that, there's not much light, and I don't want to get close enough to use the flash, and anyway, if they hear you coming up on them, they just hide or move away before you get there."

Funny. I'd never thought of demons as being cowardly.

"But someplace like this stadium, it's so open and airy. Maybe I'll get lucky, get a closer shot than I ever have before."

She was livelier than I'd seen her so far, and that had to be good, right? At this point I was still thinking Lorelei was just delusional, but it was turning into a fun sort of delusion, a one-track delusion. The CIA wasn't after her and she knew she couldn't fly. It was like humoring somebody tone-deaf who thought she could sing.

We wriggled past crowbarred plywood and cut wire, the way in already cleared before us. But the farther in we went, and the longer we stayed, crossing concourses and tracking along sloping ramps, the more it all came down and the worse it got. The air? I don't know. Something in the air, or beside the air, weighing heavy between the molecules. Why else would it get harder to breathe?

"You feel it, don't you?" she said, not without satisfaction.

I've known a couple of people, more sensitive than most, who told me they'd visited a location where people died badly—the battlefield at Gettysburg, one of them, the other an Indian massacre at a place called Sand Creek—and it got this way for them. The weight of tragedy, of death, of inhumanity bearing down on them.

I'd always had my doubts until this moment.

This, though . . . this had to be worse. You can live with death, no matter what the numbers, because we have to. You can live with tragedy, because nobody escapes it, and then we go on. You can live with inhumanity, because you know you can be better. You *want* to be better.

But this . . . it made me want to give up. Made me want to put on three more jackets and zip them tight against the cold. It was the feeling of Lorelei's photos of the figure on the roof, multiplied a thousand times.

I took her by the elbow. "This is killing you," I said, suddenly understanding.

She looked at me, like what was left of her skin and bones was all that stood between me and the frozen black vacuum of space. "You can leave if you need to. But you do get used to it."

Dear god. Why would anyone ever want to?

I kept going anyway, our footsteps brittle on the concrete. The place seemed devoid of life, if not empty of evidence. Here and there were the sad remains of some human nest—rags and newspapers, grimy water bottles and plastic sheeting, and blackened patches of ash left by small fires. Of course the predominant color was gray—the place was mostly concrete, after all—but I'd look around and see things that should've contrasted, and didn't. Signs and lettering, conduit and cables . . . they were all fading, the color bleeding out of them. Black, red, yellow, blue, green, all of them paling into a lifeless shade of gray. On the circular decks, inside the vast empty bowl of stadium, mostly devoid of seats, just terraces with a stagnant pond at the bottom. The gray was spreading like mold, only there was nothing to scrape away, because it wasn't growing on anything. It was changing everything from the inside out.

While Lorelei took pictures, I couldn't stop looking at my hand, my shoes and sleeves and pants legs, to make sure they were still the same color.

I recall it all now, and while at the time everything was one impression flowing into another, now I know that the third level was the turning point, when I stopped trying to scapegoat my imagination and started to believe.

We'd spiraled up the stadium for the third time when we came upon a boxy structure . . . probably a snack bar. Sheer walls jutted out from the stadium's core and reached up to the angled roof.

What I saw was wrapped around either side of the corner where the snack bar's front and side walls met, but high, ten feet off the deck. At first I thought it was a trash bag or a tarp. Even a giant bat, clinging to the walls, would've made more sense. But instead, I began to see how it had splattered against the concrete, a rust-colored stain fanning out on both sides from the point of impact.

Look closer, and there were the clothes, and an old shapeless coat, flat and stuck to the walls, and beneath, the outline of a latticework of shattered bones. A head? Still there, technically.

It seemed dried out enough to have been there awhile. Not the one from the roof, obviously, and now I didn't want to go any higher. If this thing had burst across level ground, fine. But it hadn't fallen. It had gone in straight at the corner, more or less horizontally. It looked like it had been launched with a catapult and struck with the force of a hundred-story fall.

Lorelei stared too, only with a little less shock. She had to feel some. She hadn't started taking pictures yet.

"Have you seen anything like this? Ever?" I asked.

"Sort of," she said. "I saw where I think one went off the roof of an abandoned mental institution. But not like this." She studied it some more, then turned around to look at the approach. "Maybe it got a running start. Ran and jumped."

"Straight at the wall? Split down the middle on a corner?" I said. "They can do that?"

She shrugged and pointed at the evidence.

"*Why* would one of them do that?"

"Being creative?" She didn't know. She'd never know. "They don't have bodies of their own. They've got to borrow. Inhabit one that's weak enough to let them force their way in. Shell people, Marcus calls them. Or animal, whatever. But the bodies start falling apart on them. It's what flesh and bone do anyway, eventually. Their presence just seems to accelerate the process."

I thought of old paintings I'd seen, religion's early cautionary tales, with demons that looked like something whose origins you could almost recognize, forms corrupted along the way.

"Marcus thinks they get to a point where they've got such a hatred for the body they're in that, while there's still time, they show it as much contempt as they can." She tipped a goofy smile at me. "It's just a theory, wot wot?"

"Why do they hate the bodies that much?"

"It's not the bodies per se. It's everything. They hate existing. They *oppose* existence. They're antithetical to it all. Down to a cellular and molecular level."

Now, finally, she started taking photos. Maybe it was her way of coping. Everything looked more manageable through a lens.

"You can forget most of what religion has to say about demons," she told me. "All religion can do is try to make sense out of something that's been around for a lot longer, and try to make it fit."

"Most, you said. What does religion get right?"

"For one thing, that they dwell in the wastelands and other places of desolation."

Once that might've meant deserts and forests and high mountain crags. Now?

I thought of every place Lorelei had shot her dreary photos. The dilapidated housing tracts and abandoned factories and vacant institutions fallen into ruin because the world didn't want them any more. We'd moved on and left voids in our wake. They must've been like magnets. Demon-haunted cities, demon-haunted towns . . . maybe we'd always been living right next door to Hell.

"What demons are, when it comes down to it," Lorelei said, over her shoulder, "I've started thinking of them as the spiritual equivalent of antimatter."

Those first nights in the motel it was like camp, Lorelei in the bed and me on the floor, both of us awake but neither of us in a hurry to make a move on the other. We were patient, content to let whatever might happen, happen in its own time, and maybe inclined not to rush into a mistake.

We just talked, and you'd think fourteen years would mean there'd be an endless amount of ground to cover, but the surprise was how little of it seemed to matter. So there was plenty of time and space and silence for what did.

My big one: "How in God's name did you get pulled into this?"

"It was the photography that came first," she told me. "I just started going to those kinds of places to shoot. They spoke to me more. They *reflected* me more."

Reflected how exactly, I wondered, but didn't ask. Empty? Abandoned? Gutted? It was hard to hear this without guilt. And while she was in every way a better photographer now than she'd been when I knew her before, I would've given almost anything to have her back the way she was, seeing the world the way she used to.

"Maybe it's because I've always taken photos, and that makes me observant," she said. "Or maybe I'm just wired for it. I wish I had some dramatic story for you . . . I came home one day and these things were eating my husband. I really wish I did. But I don't. I just. Started. Noticing."

It must've taken years. Years of noticing patterns, fighting disbelief, thinking she was crazy. I was getting the crash course, with an escort. Lorelei had faced this alone.

"They don't scare you?"

"I've never pushed my luck with them," she said. "But they don't seem to attack. At least I've never heard of it."

"Why don't they? It seems like something they'd do."

"I don't know."

We went quiet, then listened to some confrontation outside, in the motel parking lot or from another room. Raised voices, then genuine rage. I went tense, heart rate gone double. Before long there was only one voice, moaning, fading as the source scuttled away. No gunshots in between. A knife, maybe. Maybe soon we'd hear sirens. Or maybe we wouldn't.

"What was she like?" Lorelei asked.

Already, so many little details were starting to fuzz and fade. And what was I supposed to do, reel off a string of adjectives and specs? She was five-four and her hair looked red in bright sunlight and she was always bringing home strays and her memory never got a better workout than when we argued? Nobody asks for that.

"How long's it been now? Since she . . .?"

"A year ago August," I said. "Fifteen months."

"So that's enough time for you to have had a few fights. Right?"

I thought a moment, counting. "Five."

"You told me that you win about half the time. What's been your record just since then?"

"I won all of them."

She didn't say anything more for a while, just let it linger as we both wondered what it implied. That I'd either poured everything into a renewed motivation to win, or I'd stopped caring whether or not I got hit, which always seems to give a fighter an edge. Probably the latter. My wife had never seen me with scars. Those came after.

"Please don't be mad at me," Lorelei finally said, "But maybe you'd like to take it all out on something that matters, for a change."

I never asked how she'd met Marcus and Phoebe. I figured it was the same with demon hunters as with UFO fanatics. That they naturally pulled toward each other by some strange form of magnetism.

Marcus and Phoebe had been camped out on the opposite side of the same shitty motel the whole time, running their own recon games on the stadium, and Lorelei took me around the next morning for introductions over coffee and doughnuts, the two of them looking at me like I was the newest member of the team.

I'd been wondering if they would have the same drawn, cut-down, pulled-in appearance as Lorelei. In truth, Marcus could've benefited from it. He'd been a Southern Baptist minister once, and looked like an aging Samoan who'd never turned down a chicken fried steak. Phoebe was this pixie with cropped hair and an apparent disdain for makeup. If I hadn't known better, I might've thought she was a boy, until getting close enough to see the crow's feet around her eyes.

It redoubled my curiosity—and concern—over why this seemed to be affecting Lorelei so much more. Maybe it came down to proximity. She was the one who spent the most time following those things into their lairs, encountering the residue they exuded. The same way, if you walk through enough sewers, you'll be the one breathing methane. The one contracting malaria if you spend enough time in the wrong swamp.

"I haven't agreed to this yet," I told them. "Just so you know."

"Okay. Take your time, son. They're not going anywhere," Marcus said. His voice still had the big, expansive flourishes of a preacher in the pulpit. "But then, as you have seen by that oversized flyspeck on the stadium wall, they do impose their own shelf life. I *would* like to do this before the other one up topside decides it's reached its expiration date."

"Here's my worry," I said. "Anything that can generate the kind of force to launch itself into a wall like that, if it takes one good swing at me, at my head . . ."

"Have you considered that, to it, you may be as hard as that wall? The wall came out fine. You're both made of flesh and bone . . . you're just moved by radically different spirits within. Your distinct advantage is that you haven't spent your final days being eroded from the inside out." Marcus ripped apart a chocolate-slathered bear claw and dunked a strip in his coffee. "Anyway. I've never yet heard or witnessed anything about them that gives me reason to think they'll put up much of a fight. And they obviously have nothing but disregard for the body they squat in."

"Then why don't you take one down yourself?" I said.

Marcus pushed the coffee-soaked dough into his mouth. "It's not like they just sit still for it, either. And don't let this shock you, but I don't move all that fast, and I'm not very quiet about it when I do."

Phoebe cut in. "There's something else that might be a factor." She was clearly the geek here. I figured her for the type who took a laptop with her into the toilet. "I did some research, floated Lorelei's pics of the bug-splat past some people, and . . . there's a theory that when they decide to check out like that, in a way that seems to defy physics, they may have some help. They don't just run and jump. They get *pulled*, too. They fixate on a spot of significant mass, your basic immovable object, and it's like there's a positive and a negative charge that spikes, and then—" She smacked her hands together. "Like I said, it's a theory."

The spiritual equivalent of antimatter, Lorelei had said. When particles collide, it's more than destruction. It's annihilation. Nullification.

Marcus leaned closer to me. "Didn't you ever feel like testing yourself against something more than just another man? You hit him, he hits you, one of you wins, the other loses, you hug like brothers when it's over, and what have you accomplished?" He almost looked like he envied me. "Son . . . what you have before you is an opportunity to join the rarified company of men who've wrestled angels and devils. Are you really going to pass up that chance?"

"I thought it was the devils who were supposed to be so good at temptation."

Marcus got a laugh out of that.

"What are they? Really?" I said. "I asked Lorelei, but she tells me you're the one who explains it best."

"She flatters me." Marcus looked at me with eyes gone soft-focus, his face round and serene. "I've been persuaded that what they are is remnants of the Big Bang."

I blinked at him. "That seems an unusual thing for a Southern Baptist preacher to believe in."

"Hence the *former* part," he said.

It was a brain-bending thing to contemplate, at least before the coffee had really kicked in. But, as he went on, I realized that Marcus was right—it was difficult to conceive of a nothingness that could give sudden rise to everything, without the nothingness possessing qualities of its own beyond what we think of as mere empty space. So say the void was inclined only to remain void. Rip it apart, with the unimaginable violence of an expanding universe, blast it into primordial fragments, and down the vast gulfs of time maybe it really was possible that such debris could become self-aware, the same as matter became governed by forces that joined elements into amino acids, into proteins, into molecules, into cells, into amoebas, and, finally, beings with the capacity to love and murder.

Say it happened, and call them demons. Why shouldn't they look at those of us who organize and design and build and expand as their most hated enemy?

Phoebe punched up something on her laptop and swiveled it around so I could see the screen. It was a slideshow of photos that could've been taken by Lorelei, but weren't. Mostly stark, solitary figures set against backdrops bleached of color and life. Sometimes pairs, too, and the occasional cluster, but all of them in the wastelands of our own creation.

The photos were captioned by date and location: New York. Toronto. London. Edinburgh. Rio de Janeiro. Mexico City. Budapest. Copenhagen. Moscow. Jakarta. Even on the edge of Antarctica's McMurdo Station. On and on. Sometimes the lighting and telephoto stability had been good enough to show their features. Sometimes I wished it hadn't. At what point did a face stop being a face?

"Is it over? Tell me when it's over," Phoebe said. "I can hardly bring myself to look at these anymore. You know? They . . ."

I knew.

"They're being reported all over the world by people who know what to look for," Marcus said. "You know what a hockey stick looks like, don't you?" When I said *sure*, he nodded. "Then you know what the graph looks like that plots out the number of times they've been seen the last ten years." He moved his index finger, skimming low, then, with a whistle, shooting it sharply upward.

"And you want to talk with one of them," I said.

"It all means something," he said. "How are going to find out if you never ask?"

I looked at Lorelei, and the dwindling aspects of her that remained of what I remembered. Lorelei at the brink, Lorelei on the fulcrum.

For you, I will. Not for your friends, not for the world. For you.

That night in the motel, it stopped being like camp, the two of us now in the same bed. It was the first time I'd been with a woman in a year and a half, the first time with Lorelei in fourteen, and none of it seemed familiar. My body did things that felt strange and wrong, traitorous to vows that had technically ended at death-do-us-part, and I didn't know hers at all anymore. Where I thought I remembered softness, her body felt hard. Where I thought there'd been smoothness, it was hollow. Where she was supposed to be hard, she just felt brittle. It was paralyzing, this fear that I'd break her. I sank into her and couldn't stop falling.

I should've felt, if not betrayed, then manipulated, that she'd lured me here under the pretense that it was about one thing when really it was about another. Except Lorelei only knew I was fast and good at takedowns because she'd seen flip-cam footage of one of my fights on YouTube. And she'd only discovered that because she was looking for me in the first place.

That everything somehow just fit . . . destiny, maybe.

"All this . . . was it why your husband left?" I asked.

She sighed, a deflating sound. "It's not exactly the kind of thing a guy signs on for, is it?"

Lorelei ran her hand over her belly, the flat, concave little belly, and I knew she wasn't there anymore. Not all of her, anyway. There was a time I might've wondered how someone could've stayed haunted for so long by something she'd never seen, that had never walked or crawled or breathed, that had never made a sound, but now I understood it.

"Do you think we might've stayed together if I hadn't gotten . . ." She stopped, tried again. "If we'd been a little older, a little better equipped to deal with it?"

I had no idea. But I knew when it was a good idea to lie.

"Do you think we would've turned out much different? Like, would you have still felt the need to start fighting? Would my outlook have changed the way it did?" She turned onto her side to face me. "Would we have been any good as parents? Could we have been happy with that kind of life?"

And why did she make it sound like a one-time-only opportunity?

"Promise me something," I said. "No matter how it turns out tomorrow, whether Marcus is satisfied or not, you'll stop. You'll come back with me and you'll take a break from this. At least until it . . . loses its hold."

It took a while. But eventually she said something that sounded like *okay*.

The thing was still there the next morning, to everybody's relief but mine, maintaining its inhumanly patient vigil. As I looked up at it from the parking lot, knowing I'd soon be seeing and smelling it up close, I reminded myself that it was something that had mastered the art of walking around in stolen skins. The flesh and bones around it hadn't started out this way. I wondered what had happened to the previous tenant, the part of him that couldn't be seen or weighed, and must've once loved and dreamed.

I wondered what happened to them all—the dead, the evicted, the never-born.

As we entered the stadium, I'd never felt less sure of any answers.

You do get used to it, Lorelei had told me, about the emptiness and despair that emanates from these things, and it was too soon for that, but didn't matter, because if fighting teaches you one thing, it's to feel the fear and walk toward the ring anyway.

Up the ramps, up and around, and the higher we went, the fewer signs of human presence there were. There are places even urban nomads know better than to stay.

But in the end—except the takedown *wasn't* the end—it's hard to imagine more fear with less overt cause to feel it.

Searching, I found my way down a couple of short corridors that led to a narrow rooftop platform behind the stadium sign. And there it was. As if it had been waiting for me all along.

I rushed in and took it from the side, dropping low as I wrapped both arms around its waist and buried my head against its rib cage. The leg that ends up behind your opponent's legs, you just lift it straight out and let gravity do the work. Finesse the landing and the roll, and you end up in mount. Simple. Textbook, even.

I cracked the thing with an elbow to the temple, then torqued my entire upper body behind a hook to the side of its chin. It was all I knew to do, because no matter what had laid claim to the body, I reasoned that it was still vulnerable to physiological trauma. Rattle its brain, scramble the circuits, and the lights would go out for a while.

Success.

Only after this was over did I register its face. And I was glad I'd come at it from the side. At first glance I thought its skin had begun to slough off in layers, but on closer inspection, fascinated and appalled, I saw that its face had actually been . . . flowering. Growing new features and textures like the rippling fungus that grows on a fallen tree in the forest.

I couldn't believe it had been this easy.

Now, though, looking back, I have to wonder if it wasn't just playing along, if it experienced boredom or nostalgia, and recognized an opportunity to go back in time, revisit whatever was its version of the glory days.

Go on. Ask. They're obvious questions: Hadn't anybody who knew what they were tried this before? Hadn't anyone ever attempted to engage one of these latter-day demons in conversation? Could Marcus really have thought he'd be the first to try?

Yes, yes, and no.

Marcus's ambition was to be the first to actually get somewhere with one.

It wasn't that they couldn't talk. Or that they couldn't speak modern languages—surely they could've, and did, when it suited them. More likely, when cornered, it amused them to refuse to speak anything but languages that hardly anybody living understood. They'd been identified as issuing taunts in Old French, Old Norse, Middle English, an early form of Catalan, half a dozen Mesoamerican dialects, and others, most extinct . . . but identified only after it was too late, their borrowed bodies degenerated beyond occupancy.

Marcus was determined to prepare. Come to find out, he wasn't just any man with a mission. He was a linguistic savant.

Do you have any idea how disorienting it is to have someone talk to you and switch to a different language with every sentence? Not only failing to understand the message, but the medium itself, none of it familiar, not even in a heard-it-in-a-movie sort of way? Marcus could do that, rattling off a string of conversational Akkadian, Aramaic, ancient Coptic. He'd spent years learning how to speak nearly thirty forgotten tongues, waiting for just this moment. While Phoebe, along with a team of geeks she worked with long distance, had developed a language-recognition algorithm paired with an audiovisual translation engine tapping a database of a hundred more archaic languages and alphabets.

"It's kinda kludgy, still, but it works," she'd told me after a demonstration. "Even if the syntax comes out wrong, maybe there's a demon out there who'll appreciate the effort."

I'd told her that the core technology they were sitting on had to be worth millions. She didn't care, because what did that matter in a doomed world? Four years of working tech support for Hewlett-Packard had convinced her that no species this stupid could survive much longer.

Now, go on. Ask again: What about Latin? Someone had to have tried Latin.

Sure. They'd even gotten a response: *Nimium facilis. Tendo congelo.*

You are too simple. Try harder.

They'd set up operations a level below the one where I'd done the takedown. Captivity was simple but effective: a wrought-iron chair set before an iron railing, to which they shackled the thing's arms at the wrist and elbow. Its ankles they secured to the chair. The rest was just gear: Phoebe's turbocharged laptop, a small boom mic jacked into an audio interface feeding into the PC, a tripod-mounted camcorder.

"My god," Marcus said when the thing woke up and stared at him as if it knew exactly what was happening. He was sweating. November in northern Ohio and Marcus was sweating.

"You'll do great," I told him.

He nodded, breath loud and ragged in his nostrils, a fat man getting up there in years who looked like he needed to sit down, only nobody had thought to bring more than one chair. Then they got started, and he was steady.

It's always easier to deal with stress when there's a job to focus on. Marcus had his, and Phoebe had software to monitor, and there was no end to how many times Lorelei could make sure the camera was recording or framed just right.

But my job was over.

All I could do was stare at the malformed thing in front of me, no longer human except for its baleful eyes. The hatred behind them was a palpable force, all the worse for its utter silence as Marcus tried language after language. It was like looking into the eyes of a wolf and seeing qualities you'll never see in a mere dog: the cunning, the intelligent measuring of your worth, the primeval intelligence running back to the father of all wolves.

Its very existence was poison. The air was freighted with it, cold and vacant and despairing, as if the atmosphere I'd felt my first time here had been distilled to a single point. It was leaching the warmth from my skin and the life from my blood and, for all I knew, the color from my eyes.

Maybe they were used to this, but—

"I've got to step away for a little bit," I whispered in Lorelei's ear.

She looked at me and nodded. Smiled, even. Beautifully. Radiantly. How do you smile when hurricane winds are sucking out your soul? But she did. However weakly, she did. Like the hospice smile my wife gave me a few minutes before she never woke up again.

"Take your time," Lorelei whispered back.

I didn't go down. Instead, I returned to the narrow rooftop where I'd tackled the thing behind the stadium sign. I wanted to understand what couldn't be understood, to see what it saw, what it had spent nonstop days watching. I stood where it had stood and looked out over the panorama of congestion, waste, and sprawl. The pawnshops and porn shops, the fifty-cent-beer bars and payday loansharks, and the sleazy billboards hovering above it all. It boiled with sirens and honking horns, and from the other side of the stadium a breeze dragged in the smell of Lake Erie, water that no one in their right mind would drink.

And I knew that, down below, they were asking the wrong questions. *What are you watching? Why are you watching? Why do you seem to have abdicated your old roles as tempters and tormentors, and why are you so brazen about it?*

It seemed so simple from up here. What else was left for them to do?

Everything they did once, we did better, with greater efficiency, greater reach, on mass scales. The demons hadn't abdicated at all. They'd been made redundant.

And who was I to point fingers, anyway? The greatest applause, the loudest cheers, the most widespread approval I'd ever gotten in my life were for knocking a guy out with a flying knee to the forehead.

But I knew that, no matter how I felt about it today, I wasn't likely to change.

You'd think I would've heard something. But I didn't. There was only the malignant crush of silence that became too apparent on my way back down.

A toppled boom mic, an overturned tripod, a dropped computer, and in the middle of the rubble lay Marcus. There wasn't a mark on him, just a surprised, staring look in his eyes, mouth half-open with his last breath. In front of him, the chair was empty. All that remained were two forearms that hung in their shackles from the iron railing, and a pair of feet, still in their shoes, resting on the concrete floor.

Leading away from the chair were five oval blotches like coagulated blood, each about as big around a human ankle. Four steps. It had managed to take four steps. Where had it gone from there, though? Disarticulating bodies don't just vanish.

But by now, I was conditioned to the need to look high.

Eighty feet away, it was pancaked into the wall near the roof, stuck in place like a locust pulped against a windshield, the way its companion had gone out, except this time it seemed like more. More bone, more blood, more fabric, more mess. More everything.

Phoebe, too. I recognized her by the close-cropped hair, drooped over what must've been the thing's shoulder.

But of Lorelei, there was no sign.

What do you do when you lose someone in an empty stadium? Around and around and around you go.

At first I thought she'd sought shelter, and found it inside an empty custodial storage area tucked under a section of seats. It was enclosed top-to-bottom by heavy chain-link fencing, and when I tried the knob of the steel-framed door, it was locked. And to think I actually felt relief at first. I really did.

Except Lorelei didn't answer me. She just sat cross-legged on the concrete floor, her back against a concrete wall. Traumatized? Catatonic? Who wouldn't be? And to think that was the best I could hope for.

Until I knew better.

It watched me scream awhile. Listened to me beg and cry. I saw only Lorelei, but Lorelei never saw me. Had she been that empty, that hollowed-out already? That easy to push aside and nullify? I bloodied my fingers on the door, pounded my palms raw on the fence, beat my elbows sore and numb. It took everything in. I was grand sport.

And when I thought to try to find a scrap of metal sturdy enough to lever the door open . . .? Only then did it move.

Lorelei's lower lip curled between her teeth, such an adorable look on her at one time; on any woman, really. But it kept going until the expression became a snarl, and then the thing wearing Lorelei bit down. Bit hard. Bit all the way through. When it had swallowed her lower lip, it started on the top one, and once that was gone too, it sucked each cheek into her gnashing teeth, until it had eaten as much of those as would reach.

Her face. Lorelei's beautiful face. It was fraying apart and there was nothing I could do.

Her fingers dug out her eyes, popped them into her lipless mouth. Her ears were harder to tear away, but it was determined. It ripped out clumps of hair by the roots and fed them to her in fistfuls, then exploited the lacerations to start peeling away her scalp. Her jaws worked constantly. And when it tired of that, it began slamming the back of her head into the wall, idly at first, then harder, harder, until bone started to crack.

The feast continued. Harder pieces, softer pieces. Pieces it was impossible to live without. Yet still she moved . . . even as I couldn't, *wouldn't*. Because that's what you do for the people you love. You stay with them until the end. Because no one should have to go into the dark alone.

Even when it seems like nothing of what you once loved is left.

There once was a man who loved grizzly bears, and went and got himself eaten by one, along with his girlfriend. His camcorder was running the whole time, although the lens cap was still on, so it only captured the sound of what happened. A filmmaker did a documentary about him, and was seen listening to the audio with a set of headphones, and the look on his face was enough.

You must never listen to this, he tells the custodian of the tape, a friend of the dead man. *I think you should not keep it. You should destroy it. Because it will be the white elephant in your room all your life.*

I have a recording like that, but it's too late for the advice. I know exactly what's on it.

Mostly, it's of a man just off-camera, his voice patient and hopeful and even, if his tone is to be believed, diplomatic, trying phrase after phrase, inquiry upon inquiry, language after language, speaking to a shabby captive who might've been mistaken for a leper, and sometimes seems to watch him, but mostly ignores him.

For eighteen minutes. Eighteen fruitless minutes.

And then? The moment Marcus had dreamed about for years.

It perks up. It answers. Like sliding a key into a lock, he'd gotten to the one language that apparently interested it. It doesn't rush, and, in the most unpleasantly lacerated voice I've ever heard, speaks for 12.6 seconds. Then, by all appearances, it loses interest again, no matter how eager Marcus is to follow up.

Three more excruciating minutes.

Until, literally, all hell breaks loose.

That was when the tripod got knocked over, but I think Lorelei did that. It's what panicked people do—knock things over. The camera was still operating, though, and in the right channel of the stereo field there are sounds that I would have no idea how to make, even if I wanted to imitate them. In the background, on the left, there's a flash of movement, Lorelei running in the opposite direction. A moment later she makes a low, plaintive squeal that I wish I'd never heard.

And that's it for a while, until I return to the scene. The clatter of more running back and forth. It ends with the distant sound of some man screaming his soul out, echoing off concrete until it seems like it's coming from another dimension.

Old Persian—that was the language. It took me months to find someone who recognized it from the audio excerpt I kept sending out.

Here's what that hateful entity eventually thought was worth telling Marcus:

"The seeds were planted long ago. All but three took root, grew, and flowered. All that remains is to watch the last and greatest blooms."

When we first crawled out of the mud, our enemies had been here forever. When we first left the savannahs and our caves, they must've been ready and waiting. When we first climbed stairs of our own making, they were already at the top.

And so I think of them throughout history, terrorizing here, advising there, tempting everywhere, and forever trading in the timeless currencies of lust and envy, wrath and greed, gluttony, sloth, and pride. They could wear the robes of sages and nobility as easily as they could the rags of vagrants. But like chessmasters, always thinking twenty, fifty, a hundred moves ahead.

Fighters know all about using your own strength against you.

All I do now is fight, and train, and anticipate the next one. It's all I *can* do. It's like I told Lorelei: Sometimes, if you want to keep from going crazy, you just have to smash something. So I do, and tell myself I'm more symptom than disease.

Blooms—it could mean anything.

I wonder if I'll know them when I see them. ✦

THE UNICORN HUNTER

BY *Alethea Kontis*

Beauty is as beauty does. And evil is as evil does. Where the twain meets is richly complicated, for everyone involved.

After all this evil, I thought that some beauty might be in order. So thank God for Alethea Kontis, who brought it and then some, in an old-fashioned mythical context with some new-fangled twists.

This is a very easy story to love. And unless you're a unicorn, you probably will, too.

The demon was waiting for her when the huntsman brought her into the forest. He knew exactly who she was and where she'd be and when she'd come and how she smelled and what she ate and the size of her slippers and the sound of her voice and exactly how far her chest rose and fell when she drew in a breath. From the tiniest needle on the smallest tree to the oldest dragon in the mountains, the denizens of the forest had been whispering about her for weeks now: the poor, beautiful young princess whose horrible jealous mother was sending to her death. The whole of nature waited with baited breath for her arrival, wondering what adventures might arise from this terrible occasion. There hadn't been this much drama in the Wood since the last time his brethren had crossed the storm-tossed threshold into this accursed world.

He killed a doe while he was waiting, in part because the princess would eventually need sustenance, but mostly because the idiot creature was too distracted by all the excitement to have the sense to stay away from him.

He knew the moment she entered the forest, for everything in it smiled at once and sighed, like a chorus of tinkling bells. The cold winter sun broke through the gray clouds and bare branches to kiss her alabaster cheek in reverence. The gold thread in her dress and golden ribbons in her ebony hair caught the light and danced like fire. She was young for her height, slender as the willows, and as yet untouched by the first blush of womanhood. Perfect. The four winds, dizzy and drunk with happiness at her arrival, caught up the dead leaves of the forest floor and spun them in a frenzy of dried applause. The ecstasy was short-lived, however, and the forest gave a collective gasp when the huntsman tore the sleeve of her dress, scratched the pristine flesh of her arm, and forced her to the ground.

It wasn't supposed to happen this way. But there were demons in the world now, making the evils that men do far easier to reach. So the Memory Stone had taught him and his brethren, and so he knew what he must do to correct the situation.

He had hoped not to make his presence known so soon, but he needed her purity intact, and if he waited much longer all his efforts would be for naught. Her scream ripped through the now-still air. The ice pansies at his feet wept in terror. In a few long strides he crossed the clearing and kicked the huntsman with an ironclad foot, lifting his body off that of the princess and sending him sprawling in the dirt.

"I was ordered to kill the child," the huntsman said after spitting out a mouthful of teeth and blood. "What use is the rest to you, beast?"

"None of your concern," said the demon. "You have new orders now. Be gone from this place."

The huntsman came to his knees, withdrawing both a knife from his belt and a box from his cloak. "Not without claiming what's mine," he said. "I'm to return to the palace with her heart."

The demon went back to the body of the doe and sliced open her chest with one sharp claw. He plucked the tiny heart from the cavity and dropped it at the huntsman's feet. "Be glad it's not your own," said the demon.

The huntsman nodded. He snapped the heart up into the box and limped away from the demon as fast as his legs could manage.

"Oh great and honorable beast," the young princess addressed him without looking directly at him. Her voice shook and hiccupped with tears. "Thank you for saving my life. My kingdom owes you a great debt."

"The same kingdom that just sentenced you to death? I doubt they'd sing my praises at the moment." She might have been a princess, and the most perfect human female form this world had ever seen, but she was still a young girl and far sillier than she looked. He'd forgotten how closely ignorance walked in the footsteps of innocence. The memory was less amusing than it was annoying. "You, however, owe me your life, and that life I will take. So stop your sniveling and get on with you. We have work to do."

"Work, my lord?"

He snorted at the address. As if her ridiculous feudal society would function longer than five minutes in his world. He felt the compulsion to explain, but knew the words would be wasted. "That's right, *work*. Are you at all familiar with the term?"

"I've heard of it," she said in earnest.

"Excellent. Your highness," —a ridiculous honorific as he was roughly nine feet tall, before the horns, and the top of her head came to just above his navel— "you are going to help me catch a unicorn." Actually there were three unicorns, and he intended to kill them once he'd caught them, but the demon felt it wise to omit these details.

"Oh, that does sound lovely," she smiled. "I accept."

Yes, indeed. Stupid as the day was long. Just as he'd suspected. He waited what seemed like ages for her to compose herself. She finally stood, adjusted the torn sleeve of her gown, collected the small silken purse she'd brought with her, and squared her shoulders. "I am ready," she announced.

"Fantastic," said the demon. "Let's go."

The demon kept a steady pace through the trees, through bushes and over streams, straight to the Heart of the Wood. The Heart was the oldest part of the forest, where the trees had forgotten more than the world would remember, where magic ran wild. There were no paths there, for only a handful of human feet had sullied those hills and valleys in the last few centuries. The Heart was where the demon had first appeared in this world. He assumed they would also find the unicorns there.

The demon looked back over his shoulder periodically to make sure the princess was still following, and slowed his pace accordingly. Every time he looked back, the forest had given the princess something else. There were flowers in her hair, she wore an ermine as a neck ruff, and the shoulder of her dress was now firmly anchored with what looked like cobwebs and a vine of some sort. She sang or hummed or whistled as they walked. She even skipped sometimes. And every time he turned back she smiled at him warily with those full, cupid's-bow, blood-red lips. He tried not to turn back very often.

He tried not to stop very often, either, but her feet were small and her legs were short, and there was no help for it. Every time he stopped, the princess asked him a barrage of silly questions that had no doubt occurred to her while singing or humming or whistling and were now burning to be answered.

"Do you live in the mountains with the dragons?"

"I am from a different world, a world very unlike this one."

"How did you come here?"

How to explain using the fewest words? "The same way the unicorns did. There is a place, deep in your Wood here, where our worlds meet. The storms there are sometimes so powerful that they rip a doorway between the worlds. One creature gets pulled from my world and one from the unicorn world, and we end up here."

"How do you know all this?"

"The Memory Stone tells us so," he said. "The spirits of our demon brethren past are drawn home to the Memory Stone. It is how they share their knowledge with us."

"Do all the demons have big horns and black-red skin where you come from?"

"Most have horns. Size and skin colors vary by nature."

"Why do you wear iron boots? Are your feet like a horse's?"

"A little, yes. And I am a being of fire, so cloth or leather would do me little good."

"Why don't you wear any clothing?"

He was glad his loincloth had remained intact to avoid any more such questions. "I am a being of fire. I do not feel cold the way you do. Plus, a creature who can kill anything with his bare hands has no need to be modest."

"Why didn't you just kill me?"

Not that it hadn't crossed his mind. "Because I need a living innocent to lure a unicorn. I've had little success with dead ones."

"Have you seen a unicorn?"

"Once, briefly." One had arrived at the same time he had. Such was the balance.

"What are unicorns like?"

"Like giant white puppies of happiness."

"Do you think the unicorns will like me?"

"They will think you are the best thing they have ever seen." Like everyone else, it seems.

"Do you like me?"

"Only when you're quiet."

"Why are we capturing a unicorn?"

"Because it's the only way I know to get home." Again, he thought it wise to omit the rest.

"Do you have a family back home? Do you miss them?"

"I do need you alive, but you don't need your tongue." The answer was enough to curb her examination until the next time they stopped. It wasn't a planned rest, but the girl collapsed on the crumbling stones at the foot of an ancient well. It was as good a place as any. A bear cub snuggled up to the princess's back and a warren of rabbits cozied up to her front, keeping her warm. The demon thought it a bit ridiculous that nature here should fawn all over a little girl just because she was beautiful and a princess. He felt bad for any poor ugly pauper girl who stumbled into the forest unawares. She'd be that bear cub's breakfast for sure.

Every time they stopped there was always one animal or another in the princess's lap. The demon noted their bravery. In all his time in the forest, he had never before had the pleasure of any beast's company; they sensed what he was and stayed far away. The more intelligent creatures still did, but it seemed some of their children were young enough to tempt fate.

Turning the tables, he asked her one question before her heavy eyes escorted her into sleep. "Why aren't you afraid of me?"

"Should I be?" she asked.

"I'm a demon," he said. "I could drink your blood to warm my feet and grind your bones to make my bread."

"But you won't," she said. "You need me to capture a unicorn."

"I could burn all your clothes so that you might freeze. I could spit in your face and you would lose your beauty in a heartbeat."

"Will you?" she asked.

"Perhaps, if you make me mad," he said.

"Then I will endeavor not to anger you." She yawned. "We have tales, old stories from long ago of benevolent beasts who were really kind souls, or princes in disguise."

"I am no prince," he said.

"Pity," she mumbled. "I could use a prince." And with that, she slept.

Perhaps the queen was not mad, and in sending her daughter away she had done her kingdom a favor. This child, though a rare beauty, was too happy and silly and gullible and kind. Her subjects would riot and her advisors would rob the coffers bare and her castle walls would be breached within a fortnight. She would make a terrible queen.

Even still, he could not imagine sending his own daughter, or any child, to her death. And he was a demon.

He leaned back against the stones of the well, safer from his body heat than a tree, and closed his own eyes in relief. This world was so cold—not to his skin, but to his heart—and it wasn't just the winter season having washed all the colors with the stark dullness of mud and snow. What little fire existed in this world was buried far underground, so far that being away from it tore at his mind, trying to free the madness there that would be all too happy to escape. His brethren had succumbed to that madness, and eventually so would he. Even now he could taste the princess's pulse beneath her skin, imagine his claws marring her perfect skin, smell the fear of the wild animals who dared accompany her. He wanted to destroy the forest around him, dead limb from dead limb, and set it ablaze so that there might be color and warmth filling this world, if only briefly.

If he did not destroy the unicorns soon, their presence would tip the balance too far. It would cause another storm and rip another of his brethren from his world. He needed to kill those unicorns now, all of them, the first two for his brethren and the last one so that he could escape this prison and end the dreaded cycle . . . for as long as Chaos would let it be ended.

He woke and realized he'd fallen asleep. The stones beneath him had melted away into the dead earth. On the far side of the well the princess sat, quietly singing and gently combing the hair of the latest beast in her lap with a jeweled comb. Of course the princess had taken a jeweled comb into the woods. Then again, she hadn't expected to survive this long.

The animal in her lap seemed to be an albino fawn or a large goat, and then the demon realized that what looked like an ice shelf behind them was actually an icicle protruding from the animal's forehead. The first unicorn. The demon would have laughed if he wasn't afraid of scaring the beast away. There the princess sat, shimmering like magic, her skin darker than the unicorn's by a mere blush, the curtain of her ebony hair falling like a waterfall of shadow between them. From her blood-red lips came a nonsense song about flying dishes and talking pigs. A rainbow of feathers fluttered in the trees around her; a cacophony of birds had flocked just to hear her sing, and the unicorn was mesmerized. Its eyes were closed and it suffered the princess's combing without complaint, completely still. Too still.

The demon crossed over to the princess in a few steps that shook the ground and caused the myriad of inhabitants in the bushes to explode into the air. The unicorn did not move. The demon reached down with a large hand, the skin of it as red as her lips, the claws as dark as her hair. She stopped singing when that hand came into view, and she stopped combing, but the unicorn's head in her lap held her trapped.

The demon swept back the unicorn's silken white mane with a claw; a few stray hairs stung his skin. The perfect flesh beneath the mane was crisscrossed with layers and layers of angry red lines.

The princess looked confused. The demon gently took the jeweled comb from her hand. Its aura of bile taunted him. "Poison," he said. He melted the trinket into slag with the heat of his palm and tossed the little golden ball of it into the well where it could do no more harm. "Did your mother give that to you?"

The princess nodded silently. One big, fat, shimmering icedrop of a tear slid down her cheek and fell onto the unicorn. Into the unicorn. Another tear fell, and another, deeper into the unicorn's flesh as it turned to snow in the princess's arms. When she realized what was happening she jerked, startled, and the shape of the unicorn crumbled to cold lumps of nothing in her lap. She lifted her arms slowly, reverently, and the rising sun made the rime on her forearms sparkle. Dazed, she raised a shining finger to the tongue that waited between her blood-red lips. The demon slapped her hand away. He pulled her up by the wrists and began dusting and melting every bit of corpse-ice on her that he could see.

"Stupid girl," he muttered.

"What would have happened," she asked when she found her voice, "if I had tasted the unicorn?"

"You would have screamed with delight because it would have been the most delicious thing you've ever put in your mouth. But after unicorn, all other food to cross your lips would taste foul. You would wander the world for the rest of your life, starving, forever trying to taste something, anything, that comes close to that divine perfection."

"Oh," she said, and clasped her traitorous fingers behind her back. "Thank you," she added, but sounded unsure.

"Come," said the demon. "We should leave this place. Other unicorns will sense that one of their brethren has died here and they will not come near it."

"I'm sorry" was all she said.

"Why?"

"I did not let you capture the unicorn. I killed it."

"No matter," said the demon. "There are others. Let's go."

The princess was navigating the melted stones of the well in her thin, inadequate slippers, when something occurred to her. She brightened and reached for her tiny clutch, pulled a small object from it and held it tightly in her hands. She squeezed her eyes shut and scrunched up her face, as if in pain. The demon held his breath, waiting for a magic spell or another bout of weeping to burst from her. Though possibly more trouble, he hoped for the former.

"I wish my handsome prince, my one true love, would find me and save me and take me away from all this," she said, and she tossed the coin in the air.

The demon stretched out a hand and easily caught the tiny gold disc before it hit the well. His palm, still hot from the comb, melted it, too, into slag. He tossed the thin, swirling, misshapen bit of metal into the snow at her feet.

"Why did you do that?" the princess asked.

"You didn't want to make that wish," the demon replied.

"I didn't?"

"You don't want any prince who would have you right now," he said. "Trust me."

"But I always make that wish," she said.

"Then I hope he takes his sweet old time finding you," he said.

"Wishes are magic and wonderful," said the princess.

"Are they now?" said the demon. " 'Skin as white as snow, hair as black as ebony, lips as red as blood . . .' How'd that wish work out for you?"

Those blood-red lips formed a thin red line, and the princess stomped away from the well. The demon chose to enjoy the silence.

They marched through the forest as before, with a varying menagerie of wild animals keeping pace. The princess was distraught when the demon picked one new friend at random to be their lunch, but once cooked, her growling stomach betrayed her and she ate with relish. She apologized to her friends when she finished; they seemed to accept it more easily than she had. And so she frolicked with them as the day and miles through the endless forest stretched on. The meadows gave way to hills and then mountains, and at times they had to skirt sheer cliff sides and rocky terrain, but still they walked. The princess had long since shredded and discarded her delicate slippers, her ebony hair was as stringy as the limp ribbons still woven through it, and her golden dress trailed behind her in muddy rags, but she maintained her posture and addressed her wild friends with all the pomp and circumstance of royal courtiers.

They did not stop again until they came to a stream that sliced a deep crevasse through the forest and rushed swift with icemelt water from the mountains. The princess was far ahead of him, singing a harmony with a family of larks and dancing with a fluttering collection of moths and butterflies, so she did not spot the unicorn refreshing himself in the stream until she was almost upon it. The demon noticed at once; he had felt the chill presence of the unicorn emanating from the water, far stronger than icemelt.

The princess stopped her dancing, though the circus around her did not, so she still appeared to be a flurry of movement. She lifted her mud-heavy skirts and curtseyed low to the unicorn across from her, on the opposite bank of the narrowest part of the stream. The unicorn noticed her, lifted his head from the water, and bent a foreleg as it bowed to her in return. Without taking her eyes from the animal, she reached into the silk purse at her belt and withdrew the most beautiful red apple the demon had ever seen.

It occurred to the demon to wonder why the princess had not mentioned the apple during her passionate fit of hunger at lunchtime. It did not occur to him to wonder why she was possessed of such a remarkable fruit in a season where similar apples had long since rotted into memory. And so he did not stop her when she offered the apple to the unicorn with both hands, and it munched heartily. For a moment they were a mirror of snow-white skin and blood-red lips, a picture of innocence and perfection.

When the unicorn started to scream, it sounded very much like how the princess had screamed when she'd been attacked by the huntsman. Its cry cut through the oncoming twilight and pierced the heart of any living thing within earshot. Some of the smaller animals in the glen did not survive the terror of that scream. The demon thought it wise not to mention this to the princess.

She was already crying, screaming in fear as the unicorn screamed in pain. She leapt into the icy stream and threw her thin young arms around its slender neck, mindless of its spastic hooves and rolling eyes and blood-frothed mouth. She ceased her cries and began to sing to the beast, a lullaby, in an attempt to calm it.

There was magic in her voice, whether she had willed it there or not. The demon saw several animals curl up in sleep as they heard the song. He yawned twice himself. The unicorn's thrashing slowed with its heartbeat, and it laid its head in her lap, far less gracefully than the previous unicorn. She rocked it back and forth, back and forth, all the time singing it to sleep. Singing it to death. She held the unicorn until long after it had turned to snow at her feet and the wind had blown its form into tiny drifts around her.

The demon approached her gently this time. He did not want to disturb her, but he also did not want her to freeze to death, so he loosened his fire essence through his iron-shod feet and into the ground, warming the earth around her. The corpse-ice of the unicorn began to melt away.

"I am sorry," she told him again when the tears were gone. "I killed the unicorn."

"No matter," he replied calmly. "Can I get you anything?" He found himself surprised at his concern for her welfare.

She untied the silk purse at her waist and held it out to him. "A drink of water from the stream, please," she said. "There is a golden cup in my bag." Her voice was ragged and hoarse with strain and sadness.

The demon snorted. "You humans and your gold." He was careful with his giant claws so that he only untied the small bag instead of ripping it to shreds. He withdrew the ridiculously ornate cup; like the comb, it, too, burned at his eyes with its sick aura. "Your mother gave you this." It was not a question.

"Yes," the princess affirmed. "She gave me the bag to take with me on my journey."

He cursed himself for his own stupidity and immediately immolated the bag and all its contents at his feet.

"No!" cried the princess, the unicorn now all but forgotten.

"Why would you want any of that?" he asked. "Every bit of it was meant to kill you."

"It's all I have," she said over the blackened mark of singed earth. "It's all I had to remember her by."

"You have your memories," he told her. "Those should be painful enough."

She stood tall and glared at him, her whole body rigid, her hands in tiny fists at her side. "How many more unicorns are there?"

"One," he answered.

"How many more demons are there?" she asked.

"One," he answered again.

"What happened to the others?"

"I killed them."

She relaxed a little in sympathy. "How could you do that?"

He could just as easily ask her how she could have killed two unicorns, but he thought it wise not to mention it. "We are not meant to be here in your world. Not us; not the unicorns. Our presence makes the spectrum of your world larger. We make the waves taller, the valleys lower. We turn bad into evil and good into divinity. The longer we are here, the more we lose control of our minds. Demons become savage. Unicorns, I imagine, become more ephemeral. Our souls belong in our own worlds, and they return to these worlds after our death."

"So you hunted down your brethren and killed them for the sake of my world."

"And to save their souls. They were easy for me to find; evil begets evil. I would not have found the unicorns without your help."

"And how would you have killed them?"

"I don't know," he answered honestly. "You did that for me."

The princess exhaled then, deflated, and sat again. She hugged her knees to her chest and looked out over the rushing, icy stream. Apart from the burbling of the water the woods around them were blessedly silent. The demon sat beside her, only close enough to warm the ground beneath her and the air around her.

"Is that why my mother is so evil?" asked the princess. "Because there are demons in the world?"

"Perhaps. I don't know."

"I don't think you are evil."

"Then you are a silly girl."

"Are unicorns demons too?"

This was certainly an avenue of thought the demon hadn't considered. "What makes you say that?"

"They have horns, and hooves, and they are elemental, and they are the polar opposite of you. They are ice where you are fire. You said that demons are all different colors based on their nature. Are there ice demons where you come from?"

"I have not heard tales of any."

"Perhaps they were exiled from your world. Or you from theirs. Or perhaps we were the ones exiled. We might have all been part of the same world once."

"That would be a remarkable history," he said.

"What will happen to you when you die?"

"My soul will be returned to my world and I will tell my tale to the Memory Stone, so that others who might follow this path will know how to act."

"I don't want you to die."

"I have to. My continued presence here will only tear your world apart."

"I know," she said matter-of-factly. "I just wanted you to know."

"Thank you," said the demon. Her declaration both pleased and frustrated him. She was growing too mature too fast. He hoped it didn't affect her ability to attract the unicorns.

"Shall we go find this last unicorn then?"

The demon stood, offering one large, clawed hand to help the princess to her feet. She took it. "We shall."

Just beyond the stream was another small mountain, more of a large hill, with a gaping maw before them that appeared to be the entrance to a mine. "Up or down?" the demon asked her. He imagined the unicorn would find them either way.

"I want to see the stars" was all she said before she started climbing.

They climbed to the summit in the long hours of the early evening. In the spring, the demon suspected this ground was covered in wildflowers. What crunched beneath their feet now was only dirt and dry grasses hiding sharp rocks. The princess stumbled a few times, but she kept on climbing. The demon could not see the blood on her feet, but he could smell it on the wind, and as long as she said nothing, he wondered why he cared.

Once atop the small mountain, the princess skipped and jumped about joyously under the bright heavens. She ran around the summit as if the wildflowers still surrounded her. She spun and spun and threw her head back and held her hands up to the sky to catch the flakes of snow that had started to fall like little stars all around her. And then the stars themselves began to fall from the sky and dance with her. The princess pulled the golden ribbons from her hair and tied them all together in one long strand, and the stars leapt and swirled and twirled the ribbon as she spun it around herself. Her giggles and laughter sounded like bells. The wind around her whooshed and whistled and sounded like whinnying.

And when the whirlwind of flurries took a unicorn's form, she quickly tied her ribbon around its neck, fashioning it into a crude golden harness. The great white beast bowed his head to her, accepting his defeat, and allowed her to lead him to the demon. With one quick hand, the demon snapped the horn from the unicorn's head; with the other, he slit its throat, deep and deadly. Without so much as a snort the unicorn burst into a flash blizzard of snow, covering both the demon and the princess in blood and ice.

The demon lifted the unicorn's frozen horn to his lips, and the heat from his breath melted it quickly down his throat. His stomach clenched and his muscles spasmed; the poison was quick.

There were tears in the princess's eyes. The demon held a large, warm hand to her small, cold cheek. "I'm sorry," he said. "I killed the unicorn."

"I cry not for a beast I never knew. I weep for the beast who was my friend."

"Where will you go?" he asked, no longer surprised at his concern for her welfare.

"I will find whoever mines this mountain and seek shelter with them." She was above him now; he did not remember lying down. Her ebony hair curtained her face, erasing the stars from the night. From her neck dangled the melted coin she had almost thrown in the well; she had woven one of her golden ribbons through a hole. He reached out to touch the medallion, but his arm did not obey.

"Perhaps your prince will come," said the demon.

"In time," she said. "Perhaps in a very long time, when we are worthy of each other."

"Very wise," said the demon.

"Will you tell your Memory Stone about me?" she asked.

"Yes," he whispered. "I will tell it all about the smart and brave princess I once knew."

She laughed and fought back the tears that no longer fell. "There is no need to lie."

He laughed too, but his breath had left him. "And what stories will you tell your world?"

"I have" —she screwed up her beautiful face in an effort to maintain her composure— "I have my memories," she said. "Those should be painful enough."

He nodded in reply, but his head would not obey. He fought to keep his eyes on her face, but he suddenly went from looking up at her to looking down upon them both. He watched her as she hugged herself to his chest, then shifted herself around his horns so that she might cradle his head in her lap. She held him until he turned to ash in her arms, until all that was left of him were his iron shoes. He watched her until his corpse-dust flew away on the wind, until his soul was drawn so far away that she was only a golden speck on the dark mountainside, another star in the sky.

He had been wrong. She would make a great queen. ◆

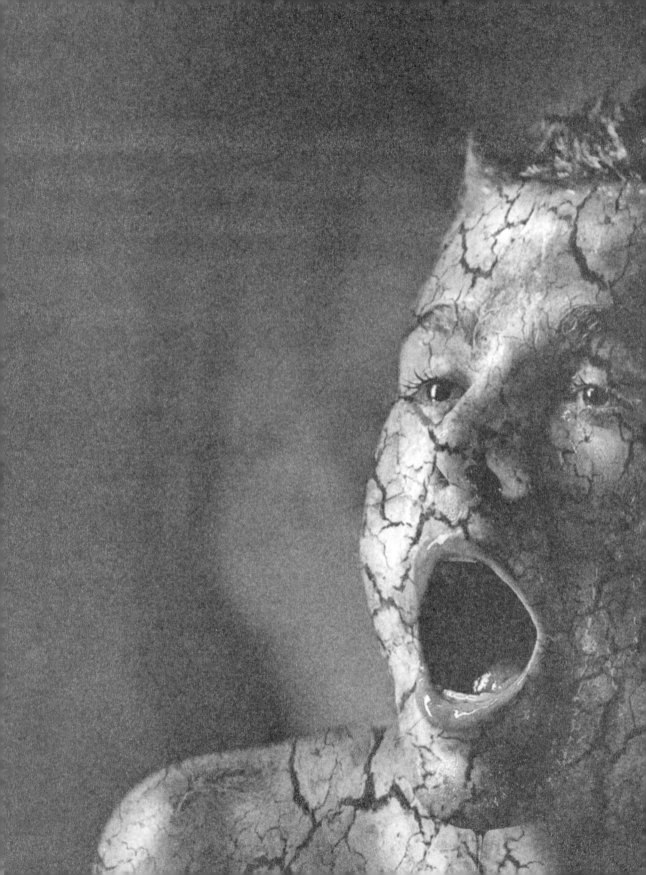

OTHER PEOPLE

BY *Neil Gaiman*

There was never any doubt in my mind that "Other People" would either open this book or close it. It was the first tale to land when I started this project; and from that moment on, it was the one to beat.

Be forewarned: this is not the witty, charming, sneaking-up-on-you-from-a-thousand-surprisingly-ticklish-angles-of-delight Neil Gaiman that we have come to know and love.

This unflinching black-eyed stare into the human soul churns up from the deepest, darkest depths of Neil's prodigious canon: a measured, relentlessly chilling forensic full-frontal dissection, with a time-lapse whickering blade you can see yourself reflected in, like flash-cuts in a movie you just might recognize, but that nobody else has ever seen.

To me, it's the defining statement on what demons really are, and what they actually mean to us.

As such, it's the perfect note with which to end our journey.

The truth hurts, don't it?

But wisdom is its own reward.

"Time is fluid here," said the demon.

He knew it was a demon the moment he saw it. He knew it, just as he knew the place was Hell. There was nothing else that either of them could have been.

The room was long, and the demon waited by a smoking brazier at the far end. A multitude of objects hung on the rock-gray walls, of the kind that it would not have been wise or reassuring to inspect too closely. The ceiling was low, the floor oddly insubstantial.

"Come close," said the demon, and he did.

The demon was rake thin and naked. It was deeply scarred, and it appeared to have been flayed at some time in the distant past. It had no ears, no sex. Its lips were thin and ascetic, and its eyes were a demon's eyes: they had seen too much and gone too far, and under their gaze he felt less important than a fly.

"What happens now?" he asked.

"Now," said the demon, in a voice that carried with it no sorrow, no relish, only a dreadful flat resignation, "you will be tortured."

"For how long?"

But the demon shook its head and made no reply. It walked slowly along the wall, eyeing first one of the devices that hung there, then another. At the far end of the wall, by the closed door, was a cat-o'-nine-tails made of frayed wire. The demon took it down with one three-fingered hand and walked back, carrying it reverently. It placed the wire tines onto the brazier, and stared at them as they began to heat up.

"That's inhuman."

"Yes."

The tips of the cat's tails were glowing a dead orange. As the demon raised its arm to deliver the first blow, it said, "In time you will remember even this moment with fondness."

"You are a liar."

"No," said the demon. "The next part," it explained, in the moment before it brought down the cat, "is worse."

Then the tines of the cat landed on the man's back with a crack and a hiss, tearing through the expensive clothes, burning and rending and shredding as they struck, and, not for the last time in that place, he screamed.

There were two hundred and eleven implements on the walls of that room, and in time he was to experience each of them.

When, finally, the Lazarene's Daughter, which he had grown to know intimately, had been cleaned and replaced on the wall in the two hundred and eleventh position, then, through wrecked lips, he gasped, "Now what?"

"Now," said the demon, "the true pain begins."

It did.

Everything he had ever done that had been better left undone. Every lie he had told—told to himself, or told to others. Every little hurt, and all the great hurts. Each one was pulled out of him, detail by detail, inch by inch. The demon stripped away the cover of forgetfulness, stripped everything down to truth, and it hurt more than anything.

"Tell me what you thought as she walked out the door," said the demon.

"I thought my heart was broken."

"No," said the demon, without hate, "you didn't." It stared at him with expressionless eyes, and he was forced to look away.

"I thought, now she'll never know I've been sleeping with her sister."

The demon took apart his life, moment by moment, instant to awful instant. It lasted a hundred years, perhaps, or a thousand—they had all the time there ever was, in that gray room—and toward the end he realized that the demon had been right. The physical torture had been kinder.

And it ended.

And once it had ended, it began again. There was a self-knowledge there he had not had the first time, which somehow made everything worse.

Now, as he spoke, he hated himself. There were no lies, no evasions, no room for anything except the pain and the anger.

He spoke. He no longer wept. And when he finished, a thousand years later, he prayed that now the demon would go to the wall, and bring down the skinning knife, or the choke-pear, or the screws.

"Again," said the demon.

He began to scream. He screamed for a long time.

"Again," said the demon, when he was done, as if nothing had been said.

It was like peeling an onion. This time through his life he learned about consequences. He learned the results of things he had done; things he had been blind to as he did them; the ways he had hurt the world; the damage he had done to people he had never known, or met, or encountered. It was the hardest lesson yet.

"Again," said the demon, a thousand years later.

He crouched on the floor, beside the brazier, rocking gently, his eyes closed, and he told the story of his life, re-experiencing it as he told it, from birth to death, changing nothing, leaving nothing out, facing everything. He opened his heart.

When he was done, he sat there, eyes closed, waiting for the voice to say, "Again," but nothing was said. He opened his eyes.

Slowly, he stood up. He was alone.

At the far end of the room, there was a door, and as he watched, it opened.

A man stepped through the door. There was terror in the man's face, and arrogance, and pride. The man, who wore expensive clothes, took several hesitant steps into the room and then stopped.

When he saw the man, he understood.

"Time is fluid here," he told the new arrival. ✦

DEMONIC ROOTS: ON THE HISTORY OF THE DEVIL

BY *Christopher Kampe* AND *Anthony Gambol*

When speaking of the Judeo-Christian Devil, we tend to speak in absolute terms and to characterize him as a personification of evil. The question becomes, however, which evil?

We can define evil as malice—willfully harming the innocent—or as ultimate selfishness—exclusively placing the needs of the self over the needs of others—or as any other number of disfavored characteristics and practices. Indeed, we have traditionally labeled a great many beliefs and practices evil.

Frequently, that which is evil has been identified as that which was unknown, foreign, undesirable, or controversial; in many cases, the difference between good and evil has been determined by the context in which the latter appears.

Quite naturally, the "Devil" appears differently across time and culture; if we look to his portrayal at any particular time and in any particular culture, we learn as much or more about that time and that culture than we can about any fundamental concept of evil. Such an examination reveals values and anxieties, with the antitheses to those norms evolving to match their own changes.

The word "*devil*" comes from the Old English *déofol* and is ultimately derived from the ancient Greek *diábolos*, a substantive adjective meaning slanderer or traducer. In the linguistic sense, speaking of the Devil references both a quality of evil and the embodiment of that evil. Simply by studying his name, we can develop a notion of both his character and purpose. But we do not get a full picture.

To the modern ear, the Devil is much more than just a slanderer. Whereas now the many names of the Devil are forgotten or used interchangeably, their specificity long forgotten and the character they describe coalesced into a singular, pure figure, in times past each carried its own meaning: *Belial*, "without worth"; *Beelzebub*, "lord of the flies;" *Satan*, "adversary."

The whole notion of "the" Devil is a lot more modern than most people recognize. In the Old Testament, there was primarily Satan, the accuser and obstructer. He was the jerk that said, "Hey, God . . this Job guy could have it a little worse." He was the voice that urged God to test a man's faith and to punish him to prove it.

In the early books of the Bible, however, Satan wasn't a specific, named entity. In Numbers 22:22, God sends a satan to block the path of a man who tries to travel against His wishes. It is not until the book of Zechariah that Satan is even granted a definite article, improving his station from a satan to "the" satan.

But still here, Satan is not independently malicious. He is instead an agent and servant of God, watching man, accusing man, and, under His instruction, tempting man. Although Satan recurs throughout the Old Testament, he was not the pure nemesis figure.

There are hints in the Bible that suggest elements of earlier Hebrew polytheism. Yahweh, as God is called in the Old Testament, is the name of the ancient Hebrew god of war—merely one of the many gods in the Hebrew pantheon. A god of war is useful in turbulent times, of which the Old Testament certainly recounts many.

While there were many gods to whom the ancient Hebrews prayed, perhaps none was as jealous as Yahweh, a tenet of whose worship was the rejection of all other deities. As the first of the Ten Commandments instructs, "You shall have no other gods before me." In the Old Testament, we see the Hebrew people's first steps toward monotheism, at the insistence of the god most useful for that period of their history.

As a consequence of this insistence, the followers of Yahweh (many of whom later became the followers of Christ) quite literally demonized all other gods.

In the New Testament, a more multifaceted Devil arises. He is an antagonist to Christ, known first for tempting Him as He fasts in the desert. In the gospels of Matthew and Luke, the Devil offers Christ dominion over the entire world, if he would kneel down and worship him for a moment.

But as Jesus teaches at Matthew 6:24, "No one can serve two masters, for either he will hate the one and love the other; or else he will be devoted to one and despise the other. You cannot serve both God and Mammon." Mammon, now regarded as one of the many names of the Devil, refers to worldly wealth and gratification.

The Devil is presented as an alternative to God and, therefore, wicked and unacceptable. This idea—that any deity that is not God is the Devil—might help to explain the many names of the Devil, and indeed the Judeo-Christian notion of demons in general. It is not clear that he is a single being.

Consider a verse in the gospel of Mark: "They came to the other side of the sea . . . When [Jesus] got out of the boat, immediately a man from the tombs with an unclean spirit met Him . . . And [Jesus] was asking him, "What is your name?" And he said to [Jesus], "My name is Legion; for we are many." Jesus cast the Legion out of the man and into a herd of swine, which promptly drowned themselves in the sea.

This story suggests a belief that demons are capable of directly influencing humanity by dominating his spirit and that the many demons are as one, being of a single will and voice, grouped as adverse to Christ.

As the Christian faith rose to prominence, the details of the characterization of God incorporated elements of supplanted pagan faiths, which may serve to explain some of the similarities between the stories of various traditions.

For example, Christ's temptation in the desert bears striking resemblance to the story of Siddhartha. Before realizing his Buddha nature, Siddhartha meditated for years and was tempted by the demon (illusion), Mara. Mara offers Siddhartha wealth and worldly conquest, if he would only abandon his spiritual path.

Not all traditions, however, could be reconciled with Christian teachings, and in these instances there is a glimpse of the Devil. For instance, just as depictions of Christ sometimes resemble stories of Apollo or Dionysus, the image of the Devil resembles depictions of Hades.

Hades was the brother of Zeus and Poseidon, who divided the realms of the world equally between them. Zeus took the skies, Poseidon took the seas, and Hades took the underworld.

Just as the Devil, by the name of Lucifer, led a third of the host of Heaven in revolt, Hades effectively took a third of Heaven to the underworld with him.

Moreover, because of its ultimate acquisition from beneath the ground, Hades was the god of precious metals and wealth—a very un-Christian emphasis on material things, even though, at the time, Hades was not evil, but rather an equitable dispenser of man's fate.

Even the Devil's stereotypical horns and cloven feet can be seen on the Greek god Pan, who had the hindquarters and horns of a goat. Pan was a god of shepherds and the wild, and is perhaps most notable here for his overt and insatiable sexuality, again a very un-Christian trait, even though Pan's fusion of sex and nature made him an indispensable god of fertility.

Regardless of their positive qualities, the characterizations of these gods could not comport with Christian theology, so they had to be demonized. A third of Heaven's power could not reside underground, and the blessings of spring could not be attributed to a sex maniac.

Resistance to the influence of these types of traditions probably played a large part in developing the character of the Devil. Any god or spirit that was not God, or who was at odds with the biblical understanding of Him, must have been the Devil. Any religious interpretation that deviated from the orthodoxy was an act of the Devil—the Father of Lies.

As an extension of this orthodoxy, in the context of exorcisms and witch hunts, although an elaborate demonology exists, practitioners usually believe that they are fighting against the Devil himself. Where the Devil stops and his demonic servants begin has always been unclear.

In times past, if you went looking for a demon with physical form, you could probably find one, if you knew where to look. In general, demons were thought to live on the outskirts of society: in deserts, valleys, or deep in the woods—places unknown or hostile to humankind. In many chivalric tales, knights errant would encounter demons in some hideous form; it was the duty of righteous men to find and slay monsters to honor God.

Demons can represent our fear of the untamed places of the world, those places that we had not yet subjugated to our own will. But that was not always the case. Stories from both Eastern and Western traditions tell of shape-shifting demons, frequently appearing as fair maidens, later revealing themselves as horrible monsters. What at first glance appear as friends eventually reveal themselves as foes.

Throughout the Middle Ages, the devil existed in his many forms, both monstrous and mundane, frequently highly sexualized.

In times of superstition and fear of the unknown, the Devil was conceived both as physical beast and an ethereal spirit with powers that could drastically disrupt the natural world. It wasn't until the reasons behind illness or natural disaster were discovered that the role of the Devil began to fundamentally change.

If individuals fell ill, or crops failed, the Devil was blamed. He was crafted as such, so that individuals would be able to explain the events around them—so that they wouldn't feel completely powerless before the natural world.

The Devil was viewed as the cause behind all human suffering—natural or otherwise. But because it was impossible to physically punish the Devil, human scapegoats were regularly used as surrogates. Plague and draught were typically blamed on old spinsters or young, unmarried women.

In societies that prized marriage and held it sacred, all lust and sex that had not been sanctified through marriage became elements of the Devil's domain. Women who deviated from the social norm by living without husbands or engaging in sexual promiscuity were often branded as witches and executed.

Because extramarital sex was taboo, when witches were accused of casting some harmful spell, they were sometimes also accused of having sexual congress with the Devil.

"The Devil's penis was the obsession of every Inquisitor and the 'star' of nearly every witch's confession," as David Friedman put it in *A Mind of Its Own: The Cultural History of the Penis.* "These confessions said something about the fantasies of women, but they reveal much more about the anxieties of men."

Such notions of the Devil and witches survived well into the seventeenth century. Notoriously, in the town of Salem, Massachusetts, unmarried or independent women (and men) were hunted and executed. In a final hurrah of superstition from the Old World, individuals asserted that the Devil took physical form in the woods and seduced girls or moved into their bodies and possessed them. Youths pretended to see specters floating in the courtroom or acted as if dominated by some malevolent spirit.

In the years following the 150 arrests and nineteen executions of the Salem witch hunt, as the flimsiness of the evidence, flaws in the trial systems, and discrepancies in testimonies came to light, it was widely accepted that none of the supposed acts of witchcraft had ever occurred, and that innocent men and women had been executed.

The old view of Satan was considered nothing more than superstition—something educated people couldn't believe. Yet Satan was still believed to have played a pivotal role in the events which transpired not as some beast that seduced women and possessed children, but as a force that inspired people to commit horrific acts.

This type of Devil, a malevolence that only arises through the actions of men has a long provenance. In Islam, one name for the Devil is Shaytan, a "whisperer," who only acts through us; he plays off anger, desire, and fear and compels us to commit evil.

Within Kabbalistic tradition, each of us has two spirits within us that are expressions of the soul. One spirit guides us toward compassion and the other drives us to pursue our own pleasures. The Devil here exists within us.

As Dostoevsky observed in *The Brothers Karamazov,* "I think that if the Devil doesn't exist, but man has therefore created him, he has created him in his own image and likeness."

If sin is the perversion of love, perhaps the sins of the Devil are no different. Many stories hold that the Devil was an angel—Lucifer, the "light bearer."

Did he love God too much and refuse to bow down before anything but Him, in contravention of His order that the angels show obeisance to man? Did he accept God's order but love man too much, not content that man should live in ignorance?

After all, in Revelations, the Devil is explicitly identified as the serpent of Genesis, who convinced man to eat from the tree of knowledge. Like Prometheus, who stole fire from Olympus and gave it to man in contravention of Zeus's will, the Devil was punished for his actions. The serpent's legs were removed, and it was made to crawl on its belly in the dust forever. But humanity, too, was cast out from paradise, even though we had eaten in innocence.

Demon, Da mon in Greek, may have derived from *da* , which can mean "to distribute destinies." Maybe that was the Devil's principal sin. He put humanity's destiny into our own hands. He challenged the unthinking orthodoxy and gave us the capacity to do the same.

And knowledge always does. As in *Faust*, man's thirst for knowledge, his inability to simply *accept*, leads him to strike a deal with the Devil.

It is only through our frailty, or curiosity, that the Devil has any power.

But perhaps, too, it is only through the Devil's malice—or beneficence—that we have any power ourselves. ✦

YOU MUST BE CERTAIN OF THE DEVIL: DEMONS IN POPULAR CULTURE

BY *John Skipp* AND *Cody Goodfellow*

Through the course of the last six-hundred-plus pages, we've run the gamut of demonic expressions. And some of you may be wondering: If demons are so bad, why do we spend so much time trying to understand them, if not outright sympathizing with them?

That's the paradox, and the problem, in discussing the origins of evil. So let's get it out of the way, right now, with a little help from John Milton.

When Satan descends to the newly created Earth to bring about the fall of humankind, in Book 3 of *Paradise Lost*, something astonishing goes down that is not easily forgotten. In seeking to depict the glory of the omniscient Puritan God, Milton creates perhaps the most chilling view of the universe in popular entertainment, unwittingly inventing the genre of cosmic horror in the process.

For it is after Satan's defiant monologue—in which he declares his opposition to Heaven, while pointing out that the infallible God clearly created him with the ingredients for rebellion in his soul—that God witnesses the first sign of humankind's fall into sin.

But rather than lifting a finger to stop him, God proclaims to Jesus and the angels that Satan will *indeed* pervert humankind, and bring about their downfall; but then God's son will sacrifice himself and redeem them through the spilling of his blood. All of which must have really been great news for Jesus.

But what is any mortal, God-fearing Christian to take away from this exchange, with its denial of free will and God's tacit admission that misery, evil, and damnation are all part of the divine plan?

If we were made to fail—*and God let the Devil do it*—how exactly are we supposed to feel, much less deal?

And why are we supposed to be mad at the patsy, when he's been set up just as the rest of us have?

Until the Renaissance, the radical humanist idea of individual free will was anathema; and it was only through the arts that human beings first seemed to acquire the ability to challenge their fate. From the Catholic and Puritan depictions of the universe as a cold machine playing out a rigged game for God's amusement, Milton offered a Satan who embraced his role as the adversary.

Every popular depiction of Satan and his minions since then has attacked or avoided this paradox; for while Satan is the sworn enemy of God and goodness, he is also the only one that many among us can even begin to relate to, essentially because he's just as doomed as we are, if not more so.

"The Devil knows his own," as the old Spanish proverb says. To which William Peter Blatty adds, "The Devil does lots of commercials."

Does misery love company?

You bet your ass it does!

Art

Unsurprisingly, the Church commissioned or created most early representations of the Devil, who is a vague and mercurial figure in the Bible. Religious art and illuminated metaphysical texts served as propaganda—Fra Angelico, Andrea Mantegna, and even the earthy Pieter Breughel stressed the subhuman monstrosity of Satan, the elaborate tortures of Hell, and the infinitesimal nature of the individual human soul in the grand machine of Creation.

Exalting the worst bestial traits in humankind, early satanic imagery was lifted from satyrs and pagan gods of fertility and the underworld. It is thanks to Pan and to Herodotus's accounts of goat worship in Egypt's Mendes that Satan came to have the head and hindquarters of a goat. Early Christian depictions of Hell often took the form of a great bestial head with a flaming maw gaping to devour the sinful.

Another favorite subject was the Temptation of St. Anthony, with the temptation of Jesus a distant third. These dramatic tableaux are packed with extravagant and grotesque demons piling on the staunch prophet, in more of a violent assault than any kind of temptation.

The Church used the arts to heap scorn upon Satan and his works, building a wall between good and evil to secure their dominance over every aspect of medieval life. The hellish visions of Hieronymus Bosch, Albrecht Dürer, Matthias Grünewald, and Martin Schongauer terrified the faithful, but offered no real insight into the Devil's power to corrupt.

It wasn't until the Renaissance allowed secular wealth and education to foster private commissions that great works of art began to humanize the subjects of the Bible, particularly Satan. *The Last Judgment* of Michelangelo is a revolution not only in structure and perspective, but a remarkable portrait of the human animals the Church had tended like sheep since the fall of Rome.

Unlike Bosch's nightmarish vistas of tiny human bodies being devoured and excreted by gigantic monsters, human bodies define the scale and form the landscape itself in Michelangelo's masterwork. Humanity has grown in its own self-conception, and its fear of Hell is mingled with grief, terror, and even shades of defiance. Michelangelo numbered himself among the fallen, as a hollowed-out skin in the hands of St. Bartholomew.

The Baroque period brought ever more naturalistic subjects; Caravaggio's photorealistic biblical scenes never stoop to giving us a fire-and-brimstone Devil; all the horrors come from human acts. As the Church's grip began to loosen, the Devil began to fade out of view, or just to change disguises.

The Neoclassical revival allowed artists like Peter Paul Rubens and Nicolas Poussin to explore pleasure and beauty in a revisionist Golden Age of Greece, replete with randy satyrs and centaurs and nubile nymphs. Rediscovering the source of Satan's animal magnetism, the neopagan rehabilitates the Devil into a sporting satyr—an amoral emblem of worldly pleasure, at least for the idle elite who could afford to enjoy art at all.

It fell to a self-taught heretic like William Blake to rediscover Satan as a fallen angel, and thus to dare to give him some flicker of his old grandeur. Indeed, the bestial aspect of his *Great Red Dragon* only adds to his infernal majesty. Only in the hands of an artist of Blake's insight can Satan be at once awesome and awful, glorious, and abominable.

Even revisiting the degradation and bestiality and darkness of the medieval nightmares of witchcraft, Francisco Goya begins to romanticize the bestial orgies of the Sabbath, and betray a healthy human fascination with the forbidden. France, long riven by heresies and purges from the Cathars to the Huguenots, had become by the nineteenth century very overt in its perverse fascination with all things diabolical. *Fin de siècle* advertising made the Devil a playful imp who peddled products with a knowing wink. Symbolist painters like Gustave Moreau and Odilon Redon seemed to rediscover the Gnostic, Promethean conception of Satan as the liberator of humankind from the mindless bondage of Eden.

In 1895 Belgian occultist Jean Delville created the most remarkable image of the Devil since Goya. *Trésor de Satan* depicts a beautiful humanoid Satan with great scarlet tentacles unfurling from his back. He stands over a river of clinging, sleeping human bodies, in a trench lined with pearls and jeweled fish. The recasting of Satan as a creature of beauty is the key to the not-so-subtle implication of this once-controversial painting—that the Devil holds sway over those who let themselves be entranced by the wealth and distractions of this world, and are thereby already in Hell.

In the modern age, Satan slipped off the cultural radar; when *Time* wondered if he and God were dead, in April of 1966, only cartoonists took him halfway seriously. H. R. Giger reinvented Bosch's phantasmagoric fetishization of Hell and Salvador Dali's paranoia-critical painting technique to create a mechanized yet intensely personal Hell. The Devils in his *Necronomicon* collection are all frustrated sexual tension and weaponized religious repulsion.

While the Devil lives on in a million popular and underground art forms, his significance has become dulled to meaninglessness. Robert Williams completes the Devil's deconstruction into a set of labels humans use to brand anything they hate or fear, and which must, then, be the key to the individual's delivery from the true Hell, which is the crushing conformity of the mob.

Literature & Drama

From the Bible itself to medieval mystery plays, Old Scratch was the model for nearly every villain you love to hate—a corruptor, tempter, liar, and betrayer. Dante's *Inferno* continued the clerical mission to use art as propaganda, showing Hell as a punishment factory and Satan as a silent, ice-bound three-headed giant punishing the world's worst sinners—Judas, Brutus, and Cassius—by eternally chewing on them.

But it wasn't until Milton gave him the limelight that Satan got a chance to spit out his mouthful of sinners and plead his case.

As popular entertainment matured and strayed away from the didactic strictures of the Church, Satan began to put on a more sophisticated face and become something far more complex and seductive. In a cruel universe run by an aloof God, Satan not only understands us, he wants to fix all our problems . . . and if God made us with the capacity to sin, then we're damned anyway, so at least Satan offers the possibility of an enjoyable fall.

The prototypical Western Devil story is the legend of Faust. A real Dr. Georgius Faustus (though not a real doctor) is reputed to have lived in Prague in the late sixteenth century, and to have made much of his infernally granted powers, which included hypnosis. First dramatized by Christopher Marlowe, *The Tragicall History of the Life and Death of Doctor Faustus* became an immediate scandal when performed in 1593, and was cited by Puritans as a prime argument for banning theater altogether. Devils materialized onstage, and some in the audience were driven insane by what they witnessed.

But far more sinister than anything in the performance was the ambiguity of the demon who answers the arrogant scholar's summons. Mephistopheles is an urbane and sympathetic fellow who warns Faustus of the seriousness of forsaking

Heaven, and reminds him that he can still escape damnation if he only repents.

Though Marlowe is an even shadier historical figure than his contemporary, Shakespeare, *Dr. Faustus* is a central wellspring of satanic conventions and clichés. Most notably, the Good and Bad Angels that appear repeatedly to argue for Faustus' soul pop up in everything from Merrie Melodies cartoons to *Animal House* to chocolate milk commercials; and the grand Guignol climax of the play is masterfully restaged by Clive Barker at the end of *Hellraiser*.

But it fell to Johann Wolfgang von Goethe to perfect the Faust legend. The result of a lifelong obsession, his epic two-part play is a less broad and sardonic take on the satanic pact, though in keeping with his Gnostic philosophical bent, his satanic pact is still less of a tragic fall than a bold quest to seize that which has been denied us by a flawed Creation. When God and Satan make a wager on the soul of Faust, the Lord's favorite scholar, Mephistopheles, acts as Faust's genie, making all his wishes come true.

In the first play (1808, revised, 1828–29), Faust romances Gretchen, a local beauty, but ruins her with a bastard and leaves her to rot in a dungeon. Part 2 (1932) embarks on an odyssey through mythology and the outer reaches of Creation, with Faust ever seeking in vain a perfect moment in which to live forever.

When Mephistopheles finally moves to collect Faust's moribund soul, he finds himself upstaged by the oldest trick in the book—the deathbed confession. Faust goes to Heaven, having beaten the Devil and won all that God denied him in life, plus redemption.

Together with *Paradise Lost*, *Faust* and its many offspring have done far more than even the Bible to define the character and modus operandi of the Devil. In the Church's hands, he was only a shape-shifting nuisance and the appointed tormentor of God's botched, fallen creations. But as popular fiction and the first novels began to create a secular, popular culture driven by curiosity and not hysteria, the Devil had acquired manners, wit, and the character of a gentleman.

His exploits on Earth soon began to find a breathlessly eager audience. Matthew Lewis penned the massive Gothic bodice-ripper *The Monk* (1795) in ten weeks before his twentieth birthday. Using only the barest rind of a morality play structure to offset the salacious tale of Ambrosio, Lewis's titular monk falls under the spell of Matilda, an ingenue sent by Satan to work his downfall.

But unlike Faustus, Ambrosio is visited only by demons who urge him downward into sin until he is destroyed by the Devil. And whether out of a greater sense of drama or a lesser sense of moral rectitude, Lewis did not spare the innocent from the repercussions of Ambrosio's dastardly deeds.

Another sinister monk story, freely inspired by Lewis's, was Ernst Theodor Amadeus Hoffman's "The Devil's Elixir." Told by the Capuchin monk Medardus, this confession of sin and perfidy created the notion of a satanic double, a *doppelgänger* who undoes the protagonist's best efforts to redeem himself, and so models the conflict within even the purest human heart.

With the Romantic era, Goethe's Promethean vision of Satan came into sharper relief. For decadent and rebellious aesthetes like Samuel Coleridge, Lord Byron, Percy Byshhe Shelley and Oscar Wilde, Arthur Rimbaud, Antonin Artaud, and Guy de Maupassant , Satan was a kindred spirit, seeking to awaken a new age of free love and liberty.

Meanwhile, Jonis-Karl Huysmans's *La-bas* (*The Damned* or *Down There*) danced his signature protagonist, Durtal, through France's then-thriving satanist scene, wrapping up with a Black Mass that shocked his newspaper readership, causing a public foofaraw.

Across the Atlantic, noted American smart alecks Ambrose Bierce and Mark Twain weighed in. Bierce's *The Devil's Dictionary* isn't a demonic tome at all—it's more accurately described by its original crafty title, *The Cynic's Word Book*—but his no-nonsense rupturing of all things pious and phony has an unmistakably sardonic gleam in its eye. It's in his copious dark short fiction that Bierce reveals how fates conspire and wickedness collides with ordinary people, rarely in encouraging ways.

Mark Twain's iconic storytelling stature took a bit of a posthumous hit with the publication of *The Mysterious Stranger,* his final novel, featuring a Satan who's just trying to level with us: The deck is stacked, the church is lying, and, in the end, it's only you.

Fortunately, Huck and Tom stuck around to keep Samuel Clemens on the charts. Otherwise, this dose of weary deathbed subversion would surely have been lost.

For most writers and readers, the Devil quickly became a whimsical figure, stripped of the ability to inspire real fear. Moreover, the materialistic wonders and terrors of the modern age had left many divorced from religion altogether. The Devil had become a quaint, uncompelling figure.

Atheist H. P. Lovecraft led a movement to cast a new Satan for the post-Darwinian age. Far from any anthropomorphic Devil, Cthulhu is an inscrutable force that cares nothing for worship, though its telepathic sendings drive cults and promise rewards when the Great Old Ones return to reclaim the Earth. Even if a shambling sea monster with an octopus for a head commands little more respect than a horned guy with a hayfork, Lovecraft's vision of a Devil without God opened whole new frontiers of modern horror.

Along with Lovecraft's many disciples, from Clark Ashton Smith to Robert Bloch, Dennis Wheatley's more conventionally evil *The Devil Rides Out* kept the spooky Satanist banner flying well into the 1930s.

Together with "The Devil and Daniel Webster," the 1940s and World War II helped produce *The Screwtape Letters* by C. S. Lewis, a scathingly entertaining Christian text that takes the form of informative correspondence between two demons: more specifically, the advice of old Screwtape to his young nephew, Wormwood, regarding how best to lead his mortal "Patient" to the arms of Our Father, Below.

This encyclopedic rundown on the vastness of human folly is both painful and funny, unremitting in its analysis and utterly bottomless in its strategies. Screwtape doesn't much cotton to grandiose displays of evil, preferring to whittle us down by degrees, till we don't even know how lost we are.

As he points out in his follow-up short story, *Screwtape Proposes a Toast*—a valedictory address to the next graduating class of young demons—you won't get the delicious ripe egotism of a full-blown human monster that way. But what you sacrifice in quality, you more than make up for with quantity.

He even ends with an encouragement for shallow, tepid churchgoing behavior, saying, "Nowhere do we tempt so successfully than on the very steps of the altar."

The 1950s and early '60s ushered in a renaissance of urbane deal-with-the-Devil stories, mostly predicated on lowlife wannabe wheeler-dealers who wind up on the short end of Satan's stick, almost always by way of a snappy trick ending. One could easily assemble a book of this size using only those stories, although you'd tire of them very quickly.

Indeed, *The Playboy Book of Horror and the Supernatural*—a landmark collection from 1968, featuring stories by Ray Bradbury, Robert Bloch, Charles Beaumont, John Collier, Ray Russell, and innumerable other heavyweights of the era—is surprisingly bloated with variations on the same theme.

But no matter. That year, Ira Levin redefined the playing field with *Rosemary's Baby*. And three short years later, William Peter Blatty's *The Exorcist* blew the lid off the stadium. At last, the Devil was not just terrifying again, but back in the limelight again. (More on both under "Film.")

Alas, what followed was a slew of pale imitators, none of which gained comparable public traction, and most of which sank like stones. In this, John Farris's *Son of the Endless Night* is perhaps the most worthy rider on *The Exorcist*'s coattails. This shocking possession saga/courtroom drama never topped the charts, but it masterfully stakes out an ice-cold claim of its own as a genuine classic.

It wasn't until Stephen King established modern horror as a consistent bestselling commodity—thereby launching the horror boom of the '80s—that the next phase of the Devil's rising popularity kicked in.

The Stand—King's apocalyptic magnum opus of an America laid low by a devastating plague—forced its hapless survivors to confront Judgment Day right here on Earth, providing a clear choice between the kindhearted God-o-centric visionary Mother Amelia and the smooth-talking, hell-bent Randall Flagg. The rest of the expansive cast vibrantly played out the full range of temptations and moral responses available to modern everyday folk, to whom the book was most passionately pitched.

"Which one of these people are *you*?" is the question behind *The Stand*, which provides a stand-in from just about every personality type, fleshed out with King's unflinching emotional acuity.

In the process, King threw down a gauntlet, immediately picked up by everyone from Robert R. McCammon (whose *Swan Song* remains *The Stand*'s most ardent semisecular rival) to the full-blown Evangelical *This Present Darkness* by Frank E. Peretti and the Rapture-intensive *Left Behind* series by Timothy LeHaye and friends, both of which rode the charismatic Christian boom and profited greatly by removing the ambiguity and preaching to the converted, essentially helping you make up your already-made-up mind.

It should be noted that, in *This Present Darkness*, even the most terrifying demons can be sent away screeching if a righteous man or woman says, "Demon, I REBUKE THEE!" Just as simple as that. Which may not have resulted in particularly thrilling literature, but clearly satisfied an enormous audience seeking much-needed affirmation, as the millennium approached.

The horror boom went bust in the early '90s, but in its wake came waves of something far bigger, marking one of the most remarkable transitions that devilish popular taste and perception have ever undergone.

We're speaking, of course, of paranormal romance—its next-door neighbor/ best friend, urban fantasy—and its perky protégé, young adult fiction.

All three of these categories rode in on vampire wings to swiftly take over the best-seller lists, but quickly expanded to embrace all manner of fantastic characters, borrowing lovingly and freely from fantasy, horror, science fiction, historical, action thrillers, comic books, erotica, and romance.

As it turns out, fallen angels—once good, now bad, but potentially good again—have never been more appealing.

Hence the immense popularity of Meljean Brook and her *Guardians* series; Larissa Ione's *Demonica* series; Katie Alexander and her Aisling Gray; Jenna Black and her Morgan Kingsley; Gena Showalter and her Lords of the Underworld; Jaci Burton, Richelle Mead, Justine Musk, and Kresley Cole. There's Serena Robar's YA, *Dating 4 Demons*. And Julie Kenner's awesome Kate Conner is a demon-hunting soccer mom.

The immense popularity of these stories—particularly among women—suggests a bold cultural attempt to *tame the devil*, using passion and savvy to transmogrify dumb lust and bad behavior into genuine love and wisdom.

From that standpoint, we're *all* fallen angels, albeit some more fallen and/or angelic than others. Flawed as we are, we all want the same thing. And there is someone for everyone, if only we search hard enough, with our whole heart and soul.

To paraphrase C. S. Lewis: You don't have a soul. You *are* a soul. You have a body. The kick-ass women in these often thrilling, consistently empowering yarns aren't afraid to use them, either, thereby leaving some *other* guy to be the damsel in distress for a change.

Whether feeding the ever-popular delusion that "I can change him [or her]" or making authentic peace with our own dichotomous natures, one thing is clear: We have never been more culturally open to embracing and redeeming our demons than we are at this moment in history.

Let's end with three ambitious recent works that may point the way beyond. First is *God's Demon*, a debut novel from artist Wayne Barlowe, which sprang from a magnificent book of paintings employing the conceit of a Dantesque tour of Hell. In the novel, the dovish infernal general Sargatanas repents of his role as punisher of damned souls, which have become mutable bricks possessed of no memory of their past lives or sins, rendering their punishment meaningless and the whole regime of Hell a farce. Sargatanas raises an army of freed souls and rebel demons and goes to war with Beelzebub, the regent of Hell in Satan's extended absence.

If the Demon Prince's rebellion is exciting and rich with intriguing scenes of the ecology of Hell, it still begs the question of what role Hell serves in the grand scheme of Creation. The book balances the weirdness of its vast cast of demons, damned souls, and bizarre hellish denizens with the structure of an unfinished fantasy epic.

And with *Angelology*, Danielle Trussoni has begun a richly elaborate earthly accounting of the Nephilam, those born of human women who mate with the angels. In tracking both their history and ours, with the rigor of a scholar and the soul of a fantasist, Trussoni may be helping to pave the way for the next phase of demon lit—when, at last, we are them, and they are us.

Which brings us to *Horns*, Joe Hill's remarkable novel of a man who wakes up one morning with the titular protrusions poking out of his head. From the moment that everyone he meets starts confessing their worst thoughts and deepest sins, the transition from us to them is played with stunning, dangerously revelatory power.

Film

If the other arts were mistrusted or misused by the Church in its war with Hell, then film from the first was seen by all sides as Lucifer's secret weapon. Descended from the seventeenth-century magic lantern shows that bedazzled European courtiers with simple animation, film was immediately denounced by the Church even as faux diabolists like stage magician George Melies were inspired to take up a camera.

Working tirelessly to make over five hundred short films, Melies frequently portrayed the Devil himself as a whimsical trickster in fanciful shorts such as *La Manoir du Diable*[(*The Manor of the Devil*) (1896) and *Les Quatres Cents Farces du Diable* (*400 Pranks of the Devil*) (1906), working illusions to try to drag virtuous women into his clutches, but inevitably getting his comeuppance.

For better or worse, Melies coined a cinematic convention that persists today; namely, that every imp who wrecks a marriage or spoils a pail of milk is Satan himself. The Devil, Lucifer the Morningstar Deceiver, does not appear in *Faust* or *Dr. Faustus*, but sends his best salesman, Mephistopheles.

Just as Satan probably didn't really turn up at every Black Mass in Europe to have his tailbone kissed by novice witches, one cannot suppose that every sinister soul broker in the movies is the general of the rebellious third of the host of Heaven.

But in the visually absorbed, somewhat irrational world of cinema, which imbues mundane life with the power of supernatural archetypes as a matter of course, the Devil could be anywhere, at any time, or any one of us.

Arguably the first feature film focusing on the Devil, *Der Student von Prag* (1913), used the sinister Street of Alchemists and simple camera trickery to commit to film Hans Heinz Ewers's script based on E.T.A. Hoffman's story "Sylvesternacht." The story line centers on an arrogant student (Paul Wegener) who sells his reflection to a mysterious stranger in black. When his menacing *doppelgänger* eventually kills him and visits his grave, the Devil is all but absolved as the agent of man's self-destruction. Remade in 1926 and again in 1935, the Satanic Double variation of the Faust legend is alive and well in films such as *The Haunted Palace* (1963), *Angel Heart* (1987), and *The Baby's Room* (2006).

From the beginning, Europe's film industry was infiltrated by occultists, such as Hans Poelzig, Albin Grau, and Hans Heinz Ewers, who were instrumental in infusing horror films with genuine occult gnosis in *Der Golem* (1914 and 1920) and *Nosferatu* (1922), and injecting diabolist themes and symbolism into nonsatanic films such as *Metropolis* (1926). The period immediately after World War I brought an explosion of great satanic cinema—*Blade af Satans Bog* (Leaves of Satan's Book), *Nosferatu* director F. W. Murnau's lost *Satanas* (1926), and his crowning achievement, *Faust* (1926).

This first filmic adaptation of Goethe's masterpiece is still celebrated as one of the best—Emil Jannings's smoldering Satan is a huge reason—but it was hardly the last. At least fifty renditions of varying fidelity have followed, making it the most durable and flexible Devil story outside the Bible. Few tropes fuse fantasy and horror in such perfect balance with the troubles and terrors of modern life, and no one is immune to its appeal. Rich and poor, all of us would give much for some gift or treasure denied us by fate.

Faust has appeared by proxy in artful reworkings such as *La Beauté de Diable* (1950), and played with mixed results as comedy in such acidic outings as *Bedazzled* (1967 and 2000). German stage actor Gustaf Gründgens became so synonymous with his role as Mephisto that a film of the play was made in 1960, and in *Mephisto* (1980), Klaus Maria Brandauer portrayed Gründgens as a kind of Faust because of the bargain he struck with the Third Reich, unearthing a vital theme hidden underneath all the fantastical trappings and greasepaint: Humans do not need a Devil to lead them to damnation.

We like to think that modern cinema has fearlessly explored all that was once forbidden, but no depiction of satanic excess has yet touched *Häxan* (*Witches*) (1922). The nightmarish depictions of a witches' Sabbath and of the Devil cavorting in Hell were all the more remarkable for their frank sexuality and for their celebration of Satan (played by the director, Benjamin Christensen) as a liberator from the oppression of the Church and the pains of life. So scandalous was *Häxan* that it caused a panic again when rereleased in the 1960's with a jazz score and William S. Burroughs's narration. Christensen later came to America to make *Seven Footprints to Satan* (1929), an occult crime potboiler from an A. Merritt novel, but Hollywood made a moralistic hash of the final product, marking the first but hardly the last time Hollywood recruited and then mistreated a European auteur.

While Europe eagerly explored Satan in all his guises, Hollywood, long thought to be his second home, only offered pallid morality plays with Satan as the dastardly city-slicker catalyst for infidelity and dissolution. In *The Devil* and *The Magic Skin* (both 1915), Satan meddles in boy-girl issues and plays homewrecker with disastrous results. In *The Devil's Bondswoman* (1916), Theda Bara made it clear that the greatest ally Satan had on Earth was the unchecked liberation of womankind. As drab as the seduction and visions of Hell were, they were inevitably upended by a last reel redemption or realization that it was all a dream. In such history-straddling epics as D. W. Griffith's *The Sorrows of Satan* (1926), and *Restitution* (aka *The Conquering Christ*) and the immortally awful *To Hell with the Kaiser* (both 1918), Hollywood showed Satan toiling away behind the scenes throughout history to ensure that humans were always plagued by war and sin, only to be defeated in the modern era by the risen Christ or the Spirit of America.

These absurd Bible yarns played to small-town Christian mistrust of foreigners, wealth, art, and education, while always assuring the faithful of good's inevitable triumph. This theme carried through *The Story of Mankind*, a stupendously corny Irwin Allen disaster that topped Vincent Price's Satan with Harpo Marx as Isaac Newton and Dennis Hopper as Napoleon.

Hollywood might've continued honking out pious dreck while Europe made daring cinematic art, if not for humankind's best attempt to date at a real live Satan.

When Adolf Hitler took over Germany and purged its media of cultural enemies in 1933, many if not most of Europe's greatest cinematic talents emigrated to America, and bestowed an extraordinary new maturity in style and substance on Hollywood. While their influence is most visible the style of noir crime films, many veterans of Universum Film Ag's Golden Age went to work in American horror films.

Edgar Ulmer brought the obsessive expressionism he learned working on *Der Golem* to *The Black Cat* (1934), a deluxe neo-Gothic potboiler that brought Bela Lugosi and Boris Karloff together for the first time. Based more upon the real-life scandals of Aleister Crowley in Sicily than on anything by Edgar Allan Poe, *The Black Cat* also featured Hollywood's first depiction of a satanic Black Mass—a climactic orgy of evil from which a virgin is rescued at the last moment, setting up a cliché still overused with gusto today.

Though he claimed to be a white magician, Aleister Crowley, the self-proclaimed Beast who courted scandal and wrecked his life trying to live up to his legend, instantly became a convenient stand-in for the Devil. His antics and iconic persona served as fodder for *The Magician* (1926), *Night of the Demon* (1958), *The Devil Rides Out* (1967), and *The Chemical Wedding* (2008), written by Iron Maiden lead throat Bruce Dickinson.

The 1940s and 1950s brought a hard-nosed realism to cinema that left little room for sincere depictions of Satan, but he began to play more as a sardonic wish granter in light romantic fantasies like *All That Money Can Buy* (1941), *Heaven Can Wait* (1943), *Angel on My Shoulder* (1946), and *Damn Yankees* (1958). Little is illuminated about the Devil in any of these, which use Satan as an enabler to let the main characters get their fondest wish, and learn they were happier before their dreams came true. Real horror came out of laboratories or the depths of space, while supernatural evil played mostly for laughs. Walt Disney's *Fantasia* (1940), with its awesome showcase for Russian demon Chernobog (modeled upon the trademark gestures of Bela Lugosi) was a masterpiece, but also the beloved animator's first real bomb.

Much more successful was *All That Money Can Buy* (1941). Based on Stephen Vincent Benét's 1937 short story, "The Devil and Daniel Webster," Wilhelm Dieterle's comic fantasy created an American Faust legend and showed homegrown sentimentalism finally triumphing over the tragic Faustian bargain. Mr. Scratch (Walter Huston) is a Devil who loves his job, but takes it in stride when he loses the soul of Jabez the foolish farmer. *The Simpsons' Treehouse of Horror* parody of the satanic trial cliché actually introduced some much-needed legal logic.

At mid-century, Hollywood had all but convinced the world that the Devil didn't exist, but a fascination with Satanism and black magic that began in Hollywood slowly began to eclipse the healthy old piety. In masterfully suspenseful thrillers like *The Seventh Victim* (1943), the witches and warlocks are outwardly normal, well-to-do folks. The only visible symptom of their commitment to the left-hand path is their success and their security. Many of the best of these, from *Night of the Demon* to *Burn Witch Burn*, kept the magic and demonic manifestations subtle, if they appeared onscreen at all. (The awesomely cheesy demon in the former film was clumsily cut in by a frustrated studio hack.) The horror came out of the will to do evil granted by belief itself, and the ambiguity of the supernatural leaves a lingering aftertaste sweeter than mere terror. From *Rosemary's Baby* (1968) and *The Wicker Man* (1973) to *The Believers* (1987), this is satanic cinema at its most effective.

Roger Corman's *The Masque of the Red Death* (1964) introduced black magic into Poe's gothic prose poem, and managed to outrage the British censors. Mario Bava's *Black Sunday* added painterly gore to the witch's revenge story, wherein a witch burned or buried in the prologue returns to wreak revenge on all and sundry. Here and in many Hammer films, Barbara Steele became as iconic a figure of fear as Christopher Lee. Further witch movies include *Witchcraft (1964) Devils of Darkness*(1965),, and *City of the Dead* (1960).

With the counterculture explosion of the 1960s, mainstream America began to see the Devil protesting the war and peddling dope on college campuses, and to hear his twisted hymns coming out of their children's bedrooms. Bold new takes on the Devil and his followers began to reflect unease about the power of women, minorities, and the unruly counterculture, soon reflected in a host of mostly cheap witchcraft films.

A sudden relaxation of censorship on both sides of the Atlantic brought new forms of sinful cinema. In America, outlaw stag films gave way to full-blown pornography, though Satan's first entry into the genre, *My Tale Is Hot* (1964), was soft and feeble on all fronts. *The Devil in Miss Jones* (1972) restored Satan to his rightful place in porn. When the titular spinster commits suicide and arrives in Hell, Satan affably allows her to return to Earth to ball her brains out. Upon returning to Hell, the awakened sexual dynamo is locked up with a guy who will never want to get it on. At its best, a porn parody illuminates the strengths and weaknesses of a genre. The shocking downbeat ending here is less out of place than the frequently tacked-on happy endings in most Hollywood Faustian outings.

British censors had until the 1960s forbade any explicit depictions of Satanism altogether; when they finally relented, a dam was broken. *Kiss of the Vampire* (1964) featured a vampiric coven and overturned all the hoary clichés of how evil presents itself. Rather than skulking around in black capes in crumbling castles, the white-robed Satanists enjoy all the best comforts of this world as their reward. Roman Polanski later stole from this film as much as he mocked it in his oddly broad *The Fearless Vampire Killers (or Pardon Me, But Your Teeth Are in My Neck)* from 1967.

Also in '67, Hammer released its satanic epic, *The Devil Rides Out*, a slab of corn-studded cheese that nonetheless betrayed a real understanding of the supernatural. Author Dennis Wheatley had tapped Aleister Crowley for occult technical support in writing his novel. While Satan's goat-headed cameo drags the climax toward farce, Richard Matheson's taut script shows how black magic is actually supposed to work.

Much more daring in conception was *Five Million Years to Earth* (aka *Quatermass and the Pit*), which posited that the collective consciousness of Satan and the human tendency to violence might be the remnant of prehuman contact with sinister aliens. As an excavation of a London tube station yields alien remains and a wrecked ship, the ghostly energies of the invaders touch off ancestral memories of evil that drive the mass of humanity to insanity and violence. The fusion of genres is elegant, while the "scientific" explanation of evil incarnate is a fascinating departure from the centuries-old clichés still in use elsewhere.

New forms of cinema—or just the destruction of the old—yielded new visions of the Devil. Outlaw auteur Kenneth Anger created a string of short avant-garde cinema collages with satanic overtones, combining performance art with appropriated footage to show by garish association how America was Satan's throne on Earth, and the '60s one long banquet. The 1964 film *Scorpio Rising* is the most effective of these.

Luis Buñuel's bizarro *Simon of the Desert* (1965) torments the prophet with a diabolical nymphet, among other surrealist set pieces that prefigure the grand weirdness of Alejandro Jodorowsky's *El Topo* (1970) and *Santa Sangre* (1990).

But the most influential film of this era was *Rosemary's Baby* (1968), a restrained yet suffocating ordeal of doubt and mistrust. Roman Polanski was far more a psychological realist than an occultist; and as in his *Repulsion*, the terror Mia Farrow endures is mostly internal. Even when her worst fears are borne out and she is seized by the coven and forced to deliver Satan's offspring, the witches and warlocks are charming, successful people.

The terror of Rosemary as she weighs the true bloodline of her unborn child, dangles her over twin abysses—between the threat of true evil at work in the world and the blander horror of learning that there is no God or Devil, outside of our own heads.

Polanski did much to influence how evil was depicted in the cinema, but tragedy forever tied him to an incarnation of pure evil that nobody would've believed, if it had appeared in a movie.

Just as Aleister Crowley and later Hitler had altered the mythology of Satan, so in the 1960s was the Beast again incarnated in real life. Like Crowley, Manson was anything but a practicing satanist, but this hardly mattered. Because he never committed a murder himself, Charles Manson was uniquely satanic in his hold on his murderous family, an image he has tirelessly cultivated in a marathon celebrity career behind bars.

And, like Satan, he brings out the best, or at least the most, in actors. Stephen

Railsback in *Helter Skelter* (1976) and Marcelo Games in *The Manson Family* (2003) play Manson to the hilt, while Charley's manic hippie cult leader schtick has launched a thousand fictional imitators. But Manson's effect on the world, as on Polanski, was like the Red Death showing up at the Summer of Love Masque. Drugs and free love had not led to a freedom from the old evils, but to entirely new ones.

Jaded, divided, and deeply insecure about the future, America and the world limped into the 1970s in an existential crisis of faith. Ken Russell's *The Devils* (1971), based on Aldous Huxley's history text *The Devils of Loudun*, explored a case of witch hysteria that overwhelmed a French convent. The Devil never shows up to tempt or gloat as the nuns strip and shave their heads (becoming eerie reminders of Charlie's wild, bald, female disciples). If he exists, he's not needed here, because Christian obsessions over sex and class do his work for him.

Then came *The Exorcist* (1973). The most successful horror film of all time needs no synopsis. In every way, it was like a revelation, if a deeply reactionary one. As the film's early, Polanski-like restraint gives way to the all-out psychic assault of Regan's possession and exorcism, we meet for the first time in decades a Devil with which there can be no bargaining, a creature utterly deranged by its own unfathomable nature, a vestigial self that thrives on causing agony among the innocent.

While this is a regression to the baby-munching bestial Satans of yore, it is also a uniquely primitive statement, that the evil is visited quite uninvited upon someone who could never deserve what she gets. If anyone invited Satan into the home, it's the secular, single careerist mother, too busy to fill the void in her daughter's life who invites Captain Howdy into her head.

In spite of the rigidly Catholic messages of the film, there is a fascinating break from the wheat and chaff of most satanic cinema. The Devil that possessed Regan, it turns out, isn't *the* Devil but a minor Assyrian demon called Pazuzu. If this terrible, but ultimately quite petty evil is done by a minor demon, it restores some measure of awe to the hosts of Hell, and some measure of mystical fear is given back to a world bereft of myths.

The imitators came fast and furious, as a secondary satanic craze dogged the

1970s. Satanism had become a flavor twist easily spliced into any exploitation formula, as Hammer discovered with its Dracula line and AIP with its biker and cheerleader pictures. Hollywood misfires like *The Sentinel* (1977) and *The Devil's Rain* (1975) used big guns—the former cast slumming genre titan John Carradine and Devil extraordinaire Burgess Meredith, while the latter tapped Ernest Borgnine as Satan's rainmaker, alongside William Shatner, a novice John Travolta, and a conniving Anton La Vey to serve as technical advisor.

Misfired sequels like *Exorcist II: The Heretic* (1977) and the sadly-made-for-TV *Look What's Happened to Rosemary's Baby* (1976) vied with the grindhouse cheapies for the bottom of the heap, while *The Omen* (1976) played a very different tune off the same root notes as Blatty's novel. Where Regan's possession is an aberration, like a brain tumor or a car accident, the unholy birth and bloody tricycle rampage of Damien Thorn is the preordained will of Hell.

Cherubic, icy-eyed Harvey Stephens is the eye of a storm that kills anyone who even begins to think of thwarting him. Director Richard Donner said that little Harvey physically assaulted him during his audition, and the potential for violence oozes out of the boy. The *Omen* franchise's sequels were much more successful than those of its rivals in developing a coherent story line, as Damien Thorn accepts his destiny and rises to power, always guarded by fanatical acolytes and the seemingly unchecked will of Satan himself, until the very (anticlimactic) end.

A secondary wave of cheap Satan exploitation flicks like *The Car* (1977) and *The Evil* (1978) spilled over into the 1980s, where the satanic genre languished and died in the wake of optimistic fantasy fare like *Star Wars* and *Close Encounters of the Third Kind* (both 1977) and became increasingly corny next to the more marketable slasher explosion.

But what really traumatized the genre was the regressive satanic panic—allegations of satanic cults running day care centers and stealing babies and hiding secret messages in heavy metal albums. The real transgressive power of Satanism and its threat to establishment values were bypassed to slander Satanists as monsters out of the Middle Ages.

Consequently, movies that exploited this atmosphere were stone-cold stupid morality trash like *Fear No Evil* (1981), *Evilspeak* (1982), and *Trick or Treat* (1986), in which unpopular teenagers use diabolical assistance to get revenge on bullies.

An island of satanic genius rears up in Neil Jordan's *The Company of Wolves* (1984), a period fairy tale in which the Devil (Terence Stamp) appears as a modern businessman in a chauffeured limousine. For the simple protagonist impaled on the witchglow of his headlights, this is an unfathomable apparition, but for us, it is a chilling reminder that the future and all its engines are Satan's playground.

Legend (1985) was a valiant attempt to create a fantasy world that reimagined classic fantasy archetypes that totally failed to capture the real psychological darkness of classic fairy tales. Much like the pathetic Beast in *Krull* (1983) or the laughable Molasar in *The Keep* (1983), Tim Curry's *Darkness* was everything that makes the Devil ridiculous in a film. With broad, operatic, evil gestures buried under preposterously huge horns, this Devil missed the point that an all-powerful evil that trades in illusions would look like us, only better.

Unless you're one of Clive Barker's demons. As first unleashed in *Hellraiser* (1987), the Cenobites reinvented the mechanics and metaphysics of Hell, creating an afterlife without a breath of Satan or God. Maybe this box keeps getting opened because it's a more desirable afterlife, to many, than where everyone else is going.

Hellraiser was a rough but incredibly textured production so stuffed with potential that only nine increasingly craptacular sequels could unpack, but Barker as a director moved on to *Nightbreed* (1990) and later met his Waterloo with *Lord of Illusions* (1995). Under the noir wrapper and lavish design, *Lord of Illusions* is a bold, if uneven, retelling of the Faust legend, while *Hellraiser* is almost a sequel to Marlowe's Dr. Faustus. *Hellraiser*'s climactic dismantlement of Frank is almost lifted directly from the final scene of *Faustus*.

Hellraiser became a cultural juggernaut not just for its iconic Pinhead, but also because it restored demons to their rightful place beyond the pale of empathy. Unlike the fabulous creations of other '80s demon flicks or Barker's own later films, the Cenobites are all too painfully recognizable as us, stripped of any illusions of a greater reward. To feel, and to inflict, pain is all that matters of us, and it is all that we can look forward to when life is over. The enduring sizzle of it, of course, is the knowledge that for somebody out there, this is Heaven.

Without breaking down and showing the horns and pitchforks, some directors resorted to more abstract interpretations. John Carpenter's *Prince of Darkness* (1987) attempts a scientific explanation for pure evil that owes and pays a great debt to Nigel Kneale, the author of *Five Million Years to Earth* (and the ill-fated *Halloween 3: Season of the Witch*). Carpenter wrote the script himself, but leaves the credit to "Martin Quatermass."

The primordial vessel of swirling green fluid clearly bodes ill for the world at large, but the scientists studying it pore over their data even as they're possessed or cut down, missing the forest for the trees. Instead of grounding the supernatural in the bedrock of scientific knowledge, rationality is dragged screaming through a mirror and into eternal darkness.

Without a doubt, the signature demon of 1980s horror cinema was Freddy Kreuger, the bastard son of a raped nun and a thousand maniacs. In *A Nightmare on Elm Street* (1984), Wes Craven's vengeful child molester wasn't interested in thwarting God as much as wreaking havoc on the children of the parents who killed him. But in the process of invading their dreamscape and ours—through a slew of sequels woefully far less hit than miss—he provided phantasmagorias of limitless power and unbridled malice that put most graphic cinematic depictions of demonic behavior to shame.

Here was a horrible little man who, in death, was unleashed. So did his wickedness transform him? Or was that demon lurking in him all the while, part of a far deeper cosmic horror? Unfortunately, Craven's baby was taken away from him, and the corporate bumbling that resulted turned this potentially epic mythos into one half-baked notion after another, with only *A Nightmare on Elm St. 3: The Dream Warriors* (1987) and *Wes Craven's New Nightmare* (1994) shedding any light whatsoever.

New Line Cinema's tragic throttling of the goose that laid this golden egg from hell remains one of contemporary horror's greatest missed opportunities. Whether the rebooted series fares better in the long run remains to be seen.

In the 1990s, a trickle of films took on the question of whether Satan could possibly exist in our thoroughly materialistic world, and what he'd do for a living if he did. The best of these, Alex de la Iglesia's *El Dia de la Bestia* (1995) follows a devout Catholic priest as he seeks to infiltrate satanic groups on the eve of what his calculations assure him is the birth of the Antichrist. That his quixotic misadventures finally lead to the Prince of Darkness only proves that we have become hostage to his madness.

Hollywood's take on the Devil since the '80s has usually been a low-key Mephistopheles, suave and worldly and only figuratively horny. Robert De Niro in *Angel Heart*, Jack Nicholson in *The Witches of Eastwick* (1987), and Al Pacino in *The Devil's Advocate* (1997) shine in the seductive early phases, but the satanic is a property we can identify in human nature as seen on film. The right actor can convey demonic origins with a cocked eyebrow. It can easily become ludicrous when fire and brimstone and glowing contact lenses turn up. Alan Parker resists the temptation to give Lou Cypher horns and a tail until the end, but a quick shot of optical special fx demon eyes almost unravels the whole show.

Quite common in this period are the doggedly persistent, devious characters who may as well be Devils. Invested with the powers of Hell and even some expressionist evidence of their infernal nature, we can never be certain. David Lynch employed this technique in almost all his films, especially *Wild at Heart* (1990) and *Lost Highway* (1997), while the Coen Brothers are masters of this ambiguous supernatural essence. Daniel von Bargen's implacable Sheriff Cooley in *O Brother Where Art Thou?* (2000) and John Goodman as demon-driven Mad Man Mundt in *Barton Fink* (1991) are prime examples, while *A Serious Man* (2009) opens with a Russian Jewish folktale of an old rabbi who visits a poor married couple who are fiercely divided in their opinion of whether he's their lovable rabbi or a *dybbuk* wearing his face. This agitating thread of ambiguity through their works—this nagging dread that you can never, ever know for sure what to believe, until it's too late—is the kind of philosophical horror most real horror films never get around to.

One outstanding exception to the button-down Satan is the one in Mel Gibson's *The Passion of the Christ* (2004), a bizarre creature that breaks the splatterific naturalism of the surrounding picture. Appearing as a creepy succubus with snakes spilling out of her crotch, Satan seems to recall the image of Nosferatu, or even the demons of medieval temptation engravings—so polarized is the propagandistic intent of the film that Satan cannot possibly have any power to seduce.

But Gibson's zeal was dangerously out of step with the rest of Hollywood. Which may help explain why Christians flocked to this stunningly violent and visually disturbing film in droves. It seems that, for many, a little sincerity in their religious horror goes a long, long way.

The cynical skepticism of the 1990s reaches its epitome in *The Ninth Gate* (1999), a flawed but nastily atmospheric mystery that effectively juggles the question of infernal influence without tipping its hand. Chasing a diabolical book on a trail littered with the frightened and the dead, the doughty occult detective (Johnny Depp) penetrates the climactic satanic ritual to find that the ultimate horror is that nobody knows anything.

Since the millennium, Hollywood has rediscovered the joys of stoking simple religious hysteria on a pint-sized indie budget. *The Exorcism of Emily Rose* (2005) and *The Last Exorcism* (2010) both work these tropes to surprising effect. And the *Twilight Zone*–flavored, locked-elevator drama *Devil* (2010) substituted claustrophobia for elaborate special effects, in a neat little thriller that harkens back to producer M. Night Shyamalan's early successes.

But the modern epitome of the Devil is Tom Waits in *The Imaginarium of Dr. Parnassus* (2009). A worldly wise but also weary Devil, he's almost as tired of the chase as the Munchausen-like traveling magician Parnassus (Christopher Plummer, Heath Ledger, et al.), with whom he is in a competition to collect the most souls. Almost more human than the humans he hunts, Waits's Devil only seems like a repeat of the unstoppable effigy of Death in Terry Gilliam's earlier go at this type of tall tale, *The Adventures of Baron Munchausen*. He seems to know that God didn't really put free will into his creations, but that it has to be taken away by disobedience. In the end, he fudges the books because he wants to see us get away with it.

Television

The Twilight Zone again cornered the market on the best genre stories. Charles Beaumont's "The Howling Man" adaptation is a powerful, expressionistic tour de force that somehow holds together even when the classic horned, goateed Devil finally appears.

But it is in another episode, the rarely aired hourlong "Printer's Devil," that television got one of its best Devils ever.

Burgess Meredith brings a cigar-gnashing glee to his new job as the typesetter of a failing paper whose owner rashly wished for some edge in his war against the rival *Gazette*. Charles Beaumont adapted the story from his first fiction sale, "The Devil You Say?" In the original story, the Devil sets to work printing impossible news stories before they happen. Mermaids, hippo births, and shipwrecks keep the paper afloat, but the hero outwits the Devil and uses the bewitched printing press to send the Devil back to Hell.

In the episode, the news stories are not miracles, but mundane fires, robberies, and murders, and the newspaper scooped the events by inventing them. Behind the horror, is the fulfillment of a wish, that disasters and crime have some author, some outside hand that can be tricked into withdrawing and leaving us in peace.

Rod Serling's next foray into televised fantasy and horror, *Night Gallery*, picked up not precisely where *TZ* left off, but with a very mixed bag of classic adaptations and often-goofy more modernist riffs. So sublime episodes like the Lovecraft entry "Pickman's Model," and Richard Matheson's genuinely surprising "Surprise Me" wound up shoehorned in with faux-hippie-from-Burbank groaners like "Hell's Bells," where eternal torment is substantially less than groovy, in one of John "Gomez" Astin's only unenjoyable performances.

The 1970s also gave us *Gargoyles*, an *ABC Movie of the Week* much beloved for its depiction of horn-headed monsters that ultimately just want to be left alone. They may not be demons, exactly, but sympathy for the Devil was enacted just the same. *Don't Be Afraid of the Dark* featured *True Grit*'s Kim Darby being threatened by tiny demons. And if the little Devil doll that chases Karen Black around in *Trilogy of Terror* doesn't whip up a demon frenzy, we just don't know what will.

From there, TV has ranged from the tweener tomfoolery of Nickelodeon's *Are You Afraid of the Dark?* to Joss Whedon's brilliant *Buffy* and *Angel* franchises, which—though largely concerned with vampires—trespassed all over supernatural lines, including a series of encounters in Hell between Angel and a very nice demon named Skip, which utterly cracks us up.

A very different but simply sublime vision of demons turns up in the *Millennium* episode "Somehow Satan Got Behind Me." As three demons in human disguise meet in a doughnut shop to compare stories of souls tormented and tempted into the jaws of Hell, we see the pathos of creatures trapped by their natures into an evil they don't really even believe in anymore.

But perhaps the greatest demon in the history of television went simply by the name of "Bob."

In David Lynch and Mark Frost's groundbreaking *Twin Peaks*, the question "Who killed Laura Palmer?" had metaphysical reverberations far beyond mere crime-solving technique. What Lynch and Frost and gang postulated was a soap-opera world with so many doors to Hell that you couldn't turn around without knocking on one, either inadvertently or with precise malign intent.

The layers upon layers in *Twin Peaks'* onion skins led past demonic possession to the Black Lodge itself: a metaphysical nightmare dimension where being chased by the self-that-is-not-yourself—OR IS IT?—is the most harrowing horror imaginable.

And if it catches you—as it does one of our most righteous and beloved characters, at the conclusion of the series—you are *soooo* damned that every hair stands on end for a fucking eternity. And no mirror into our soul could ever quite be shattered enough.

It took Lynch's filmic prequel, *Twin Peaks: Fire Walk with Me*, to bring redemption to this most hellish of all hells. And God only knows how much further it might have gone, had network support not caved in.

But one would be hard-pressed to find a deeper, more terrifying depiction of darkness, in any art form whatsoever.

Past that, please forgive us if we don't tag every sitcom appearance or crime-show nod: far too many to describe without doubling the size of this volume.

But even now, so-called "reality TV" is rife with paranormal explorations, while the Cartoon Network's nightly Adult Swim lineup simultaneously luxuriates in and calls "bullshit" on the tropes with shows like *Aqua Teen Hunger Force*, *Superjail*, *Metalocalypse*, and *Mary Shelley's Frankenhole*.

Comics

Once superhero comics became the uncontested champs of the wire racks, the occult became just another arena for freaks in tights to grapple in spandex. Marvel's sorcerer supreme Dr. Strange did have solid occult detective credentials and wore pajamas rather than a leotard. Thanks to the screwball sureality of artist Steve Ditko, Strange's supernatural scrimmages with Mephisto, Baron Mordo, or his pseudo-Lovecraftian archenemy Dormammu were the weirdest superhero battles.

During his stormy tenure with DC, the legendary Jack Kirby easily trumped Marvel's caped demon fighter in 1972 with a caped, demon-fighting Demon. Etrigan, spawn of Belial, is bonded to Arthurian knight Jason Blood by Merlin, and is forced to walk the Earth and Hell forever, clobbering evil while speaking in a laborious rhyme scheme. Both Strange and the Demon have enjoyed checkered success in their own books, but still turn up whenever the transcendent mysteries of the Great Beyond need an ass-whipping.

As comics audiences matured and demanded more from their heroes, DC lifted a walk-on character from the pages of Alan Moore's run on *Swamp Thing* for a new adults-only book. *Hellblazer* debuted in 1988 and became a tentpole of the Vertigo line in 1993, and is the only charter title from that line still running monthly. John Constantine is the antithesis of squeaky-clean Dr. Strange, and bears the realistic psychic scars of a life of consorting with demons and worse. Watered down to lukewarm Keanu intensity by Hollywood, the real Hellblazer is a chain-smoking, trash-talking confidence man in an ultranoir underworld. With no superpowers and only his frayed wits between him and unspeakably eldritch evil, Constantine wins or merely survives by trickery and sharp dealing, running the Devil's game on the Devils.

And as *Swamp Thing* begat *Hellblazer*, so did *Hellblazer* beget *Preacher* (1995–

2000). Vertigo's other great assault on biblical sensibilities was a heap of joyous blasphemy called Preacher. Garth Ennis posits a burnt-out Preacher in a hellhole Texas town being imbued with the spirit of an angelic half-demon bastard. Suddenly endowed with the Word, Jesse Custer can command anyone to do anything. With a vampire and an ex-girlfriend, he sets out across America in truly obligatory Vertigo style to find where on Earth God is hiding from the mess He's made of Creation. The road is predictably littered with all manner of godforsaken freaks and fallen angels.

When fan-favorite Spider-Man artist Todd McFarlane left Marvel to form Image Comics in 1992, he was clearly looking to own a character as iconic—and lucrative—as the one he'd drawn for the House of Ideas. With Spawn, he succeeded by somehow balancing superheroism with supernatural horror. Looking like a Goth Spider-Man with a cape longer than an airport runway, Spawn is an undead monstrosity recalled to Earth by Malebolgia, a vulgar, ugly old-school demon. Tormented by memories of his old life and by the sub-Faustian bargain that gave him awesome powers and the huge cape, he broods on the rooftops overlooking a skid-row alley in constant rain, when he's not protecting the local transients from the cops, death squads, Vatican assassins, cyborg enforcers, and renegade battle angels that come looking for him there. Few comic books have ever taken themselves so seriously, but Spawn spawned a movie, an HBO animated series, and a spectacularly successful action figure company, the proceeds from which Todd apparently traded in for a used baseball.

Clearly inspired by Kirby's monster-heroes, Mike Mignola developed Hellboy as his own escape pod from for-hire superhero work, but also as a magnet for everything he loved to draw. A showcase for ruins, statuary, and slamming monster-on-monster action, Hellboy is a laconic underachiever whose long career of monster-slaying has been a diversion from his unasked-for destiny as the Right Hand of Apocalypse. Though a Devil of few words, Hellboy has evolved in a linear arc unlike almost any comic book's endless recycling of story lines, to a point unimaginable from its inception in 1993. Few in any medium since Milton have so fully engaged with the possibilities of a demon as a protagonist as Mignola and a stellar rotation of artists have. But Hellboy never offers a monologue on a par with Satan's soliloquy in *Paradise Lost*.

Indie comics abound with supernatural themes, from *Satan's Three Circus of Hell* to *Cthulhu Wars*, but few rise to the higher threshold of believability. Harder to find and harder to stomach is Tim Vigil's obsessive, amazing *Faust*.

Music

Music has perhaps the trickiest relationship with the Devil of all art forms, basically because he's been blamed for every musical innovation since the discovery of notes and rhythms.

Let's put it this way. When Aristotle said, "The flute is not an instrument that has a good moral effect. It is too exciting," the debate was already well underway. And by the time it got to the good kings of Christendom, hitting the wrong notes in the wrong order could literally get you a public beheading.

Urgent rhythms are, of course, always a problem, because they speak to the body and its terrible urges. But every bit as dangerous was *dissonance*, which violated the moral purity of pristine major scales, and the mournful solemnity of minor ones.

The chief culprit here was the "demonica in musica," or "Devil's tri-tone"— the augmented fourth or diminished fifth—which in its raw state still retains its power to go "Ouch!" in your ears. It was absolutely forbidden in Church music well into the sixteenth century, when innovators like Bach began to put its hurt to good use. And even though it's been subsequently integrated into almost every form of music, from pop to avant-garde, it's still viewed as an affront by more conservative audiences.

When music developed more than one note at a time, it was evil. When harmony was discovered, *that* was evil. The entire notion of counterpoint, in which two distinct melodies could play off each other simultaneously, started off as literal heresy.

And God help you if you displayed virtuosity. Franz Liszt and Niccolò Paganini were clearly the Devil's spawn, on piano and violin, respectively. There could be no other explanation for the sheer velocity and passion of their playing. No mere mortal could perform like that. (They were, as such, the original rock stars.)

Of course, all forms of Asian and Middle Eastern music, with their use of microtones—the notes between our official notes—just indicated what Devils they were.

And when slave rhythms from Africa and the West Indies began to mingle with European folk music, and field hollers evolved into blues, the roots of the Devil's rock 'n' roll were sown. By the time Robert Johnson went down to the crossroads to sell his soul, it was already far too late.

Jazz and swing launched dancing to new levels of sin, and the Devil's tri-tone was everywhere, sweeping by in licentious flurries that told the righteous all they needed to know.

The invention of the electric guitar was the last nail in the coffin for the innocence of youth; and the decades between Screaming Jay Hawkins's declaration that "I Put a Spell on You" and Marilyn Manson's even screamier version have been one long slide down Satan's flume.

Because rock was the music of rebellion, it didn't take long for the Devil to show up in the lyrics. The Rolling Stones shared their sympathy with the Devil. Next thing you know, AC/DC's on the highway to Hell.

And heavy metal, from Black Sabbath to Slayer to Slipknot and beyond, has relentlessly (albeit playfully) milked the satanic for fun and profit.

So you can make a list of Devil music twice as long as this book, and still not have begun to catch it all. Johnny Cash went there. Nick Cave goes there all the time. Norwegian black metal bonehead Varge Vikernes went there so hard that he wound up burning churches and stabbing his bandmate twenty-three times.

By the time you get to terrifying vocal virtuoso Diamanda Galas, and her albums *Plague Mass*, *Litanies of Satan*, and *You Must Be Certain of the Devil*, you're at the far end of the bone-chilling sonic spectrum.

Just remember that, in certain circles, "I Wanna Hold Your Hand" is the Devil's sound track.

Now PUT DOWN THAT FLUTE, SINNER!

And, with that, we bid you good day. ✦

ACKNOWLEDGEMENTS

Every editing job is different. *This* one sure as hell was. And part of what made it uniquely challenging was the existence of Tim Pratt's excellent 2010 anthology, *Sympathy for the Devil*: a book so chock-full of favorite demon stories (John Collier's "Thus I Refuse Beezly", Robert Bloch's "The Hell-Bound Train", Nathanial Hawthorne's "Young Goodman Brown", etc.) that I nearly pulled out my last remaining hairs. Because I had vowed not to include a single repeat from his roster. And that was reeeeally hard.

But once the killing rage subsided, I kissed that gift horse full in the mouth. Because it forced me to look beyond the obvious, really think about all the genius that remained, tear ferociously back through my roots, and explore the full range of extraordinary work *not* tapped by the infernal Mr. Pratt. (Who, incidentally, just might be THE DEVIL HIMSELF!)

It also compelled me to avidly seek fresh, mind-bending and soul-exploring original work, which comprises roughly half of this assemblage. Thereby propelling the literature forward, in all kinds of astounding ways.

So thank you, Tim Pratt, for kicking ass so hard that it forced me to kick ass even harder. SEE YOU IN HELL'S PARKING LOT, PAL! (Note: there are no losers in this qualitative tussle.)

Once again, my undying love and thanks to intrepid editorial goddess Dinah Dunn, and all the radiant Black Dog staff; to my friendly neighborhood New York agent Lori Perkins, locking it down once again; to Chris Kampe, Anthony Gambole, and Doktor Honky for making me look way smarter than I actually am; to my beautiful family and extraordinary friends, who ground this life with joy and meaning, not to mention love; and to all the writers, estates, and representatives who granted me the right to share these amazing tales.

There is no substitute for working with this caliber of unadulterated brilliance, skillfulness, and fun. I am so *proud* of everyone involved, living or dead, I can barely even stand it. One of the greatest experiences of my life.

Finally, thank you for taking the time to soul-spelunk here. Hope this reading brings you great pleasure, and not-coincidentally widens your mind.

I am incredibly proud of you, too. And grateful, besides.

HAVE A WONDERFUL TIME! ✦

PERMISSIONS